M B Ager

Coffee, Cats & Conmen

www.mbager.com • @mbagerauthor

First published in 2017
ISBN-13: 9781976020988
ISBN-10: 1976020980

ABOUT THE AUTHOR

M B Ager wanted to write a novel from a young age but lack of time and confidence always defeated the dream until August 2017. Taking advantage of an extended break, *Coffee, Cats & Conmen* was born and published within a month.

Moving from Milton Keynes to North Essex in the late nineties, M is luxuriating in an awesome marriage and bursting with love for Kate, Emily and Jack.

For V. SLU x

PROLOGUE

I don't have a solicitor with me because I'm only "helping police with their enquiries...for now" as the cocky sergeant put it. He knows I'm involved, he's just hoping I can spare him the work and confess. *Not a chance.*

He gets up from his chair, walks out of Interview Room 1 and closes the door, leaving me on my own. No doubt this is a tried and tested method to allow criminals to ponder their futures.

I'm cold. I've got *the* shortest skirt on, the room is freezing and I'm sat on a cheap metal chair. Any colder and I swear my legs are going to feel like a tongue licking an ice cube. It's like one of those chairs that gets put outside of a cheap restaurant for smokers to take the weight off their artery-clogged legs. You would have thought that, considering this is the last seat many have before getting banged up, the Old Bill might have allowed a tender moment between backside and chair before the backside ends up in prison and becomes tender for more than a moment. Saying that, if I had just become the victim of a heinous crime, I can't imagine I'd be thinking "I do hope the suspect is having a comfy seat in the cop shop."

I hear footsteps in the corridor outside, getting louder as they approach Interview Room 1. *They've got nothing on me, so they'll have to release me.* Sergeant Cocky comes back in, holding a clear bag. After closing the door, he walks up and drops the bag on the table I'm sat behind. He doesn't sit down himself. I look down at the bag; it has EVIDENCE emblazoned across the top in thick red print.

Leaning over the table with both hands either side of the bag, he looks at me with piercing eyes. "Would you mind explaining this, Miss?"

My heart sinks as I make out the outline of what's inside.

CHAPTER ONE

You must be Gemma. The sound of his voice is almost as beautiful as his body. As he gets closer, I can feel my knees start to buckle. *Gemma.* He repeats my name, as if to confirm that it suits me. He says it abruptly, but I quite like it; As long as he stays that close to me, he can say it how he likes. Standing behind me, his lips gently caress the side of my neck as he unzips my dress and lets it slip from my shoulders. *Do you interview all your candidates like this?* I ask him. *GEMMA!* This time it wakes me up. "Gemma, you're late again!" Staggering to the window, I draw the curtains, look down to the street below and give Nat a wave. *The perfect neighbour. The perfect alarm clock!* She gives me a cheeky wave, walking off to the train station with a chuckle, shaking her head. I smile to myself and sigh. *One day it won't be a flippin' dream!*

Nat is a life saver. My interview is in an hour and it would be good to be on time to this one. I contemplate life while having my morning wee, still annoyed that my romantic encounter was just a dream (and over - I quite liked where it was going!). I jump into the shower to wake myself up. I must be especially tired this morning, because I still have my socks on. *Seriously, who does that?* I roll my eyes and sigh at my dizziness. Shower done, and still thinking of my dreamterview, I fling open my wardrobe doors. My eyes fall straight onto my silk red dress. Okay, so I had to search among my joggers and hoodies, but it still feels right. Rummaging around at the back of the wardrobe, I find my black heels. My previous job didn't have much of a dress code so I got away with wearing my Converse All Stars most days. As a result I've worn these heels only twice before; once for an auntie's wedding which they were bought for and once for the funeral of an uncle I never met. Dress and heels on the bed, I

2

head for my knicker drawer with a feeling of dread; Unless some higher power has fixed my washing machine overnight, there are going to be no clean pants in there.

Nope. No miracle.

I can't wear yesterday's knickers, I've been brought up properly, but I can't go commando either. *Sod it, I'll be GI Jane for today.* I slip on the dress - it feels good. A quick mirror check: I *look* good too. Hair above average. Make-up average. Mirror really dirty. *I'll sort it later.*

I have two minutes to catch my bus as I close the front door. I'm organised, ready to go and *very* confident about this interview. Life feels good. I even manage to avoid the present left by next door's cat in the middle of the garden path. I don't get cats; they serve no purpose. But if people must own one to satisfy their own insecurities of needing to be loved and wanted, why can't they train the flipping things to poo in their own gardens? *I'll sort it later.*

I close the gate at the end of the path and turn left down the street to the bus stop. I live on a quiet street and rarely pass anyone; today though, I have a rather dishy bloke walking towards me. I look down and, dragging a stray bit of hair back behind my ear, look coyly up at him as we pass. I get a cheeky wink. *An actual wink.* The day is already going well. As I approach the bus shelter, I look at the reflection in the advertising board to see Mr Cheeky looking over his shoulder at me. I conclude he is either checking me out or my dress is stuck in my knickers...oh.

It is option one then! *Note to self: wear red dress more.*

Unlike me, the bus is always on time. I board and take my usual space. Commuters and churchgoers have a lot in common when it comes to having their regular seats and woe betide anyone who messes with their system. The journey takes 15 minutes; Digging my iPhone 7 out of my handbag, it is just enough time to read the news headlines and see if there are any washing machines on Gumtree. It also means I can observe the rules for every commuter who has ever walked the face of the earth:

-Rule One: Make no eye contact with anyone.

-Rule Two: Expect death by a thousand cuts if you break Rule One.

When I'm not swiping my phone screen, I tend to look out of the window and 'people watch'. It's fascinating to see what people are up to and I enjoy the challenge of working out what they're discussing, buying, where they're headed or what they're arguing about. Today has less action, although I do pass a couple taking a selfie beside the road. I have never understood why people have to photograph themselves; when I was younger, a selfie only happened by accident when an elderly relative offered to take the photos at a family gathering. After photographing one's lunch and posting it on Facebook it has to be the most pointless and unnecessary exercise.

It's worth mentioning at this point that I am also strongly opposed to commercialisation. By that, I mean I can't stand major conglomerates who corner the market and push out the smaller boys. Tesco has helped to destroy the market trader and the humble tea shop has been conquered by larger brands. But with all that being said, Costa coffee is AMAZING. And the bus stops right outside, so I tend to shelve my views for this minor indulgence every morning. And when I do my weekly shop.

My usual cappuccino with two shots is in the making when I walk in - Sally the manager knows me, she knows what I like and cracks on as soon as she sees me.

"Looking good today, Gemma."

"I've got a job interview."

"Ooh, where at?"

"Marquis Cars."

"Very nice - good luck!"

4

As I walk out of Costa into the busyness of the town, I feel empowered. With a cappuccino in one hand, my handbag in the other and Gucci sunglasses resting on my head, I feel close to resembling Julia Roberts in Pretty Woman when she walks so elegantly up Rodeo Drive; Everyone looking, she is oozing confidence and walking with purpose. That is me. Right now.

Walking through the street, I review my life as it currently stands:

Looking and feeling sexy in my red dress and black heels. *Awesome.*

Making my way to a potentially life-changing interview. *Good.*

Thinking how dirty my bedroom mirror is and how I must sort my house out. *Average.*

Getting my heel caught in a pavement grate. *Bad.*

Having no spare hand to free said heel. *Worse.*

Having an underground train rush past at that exact moment, causing an updraft to lift my dress above my head. *Hell on Earth.*

Remembering that I have a broken washing machine. *Kill me. Kill me now!*

I still feel like Julia Roberts. Just from an earlier point in the film.

CHAPTER TWO

I approach the forecourt of Marquis Cars after eleven minutes' walk from Costa. I know the precise time because it's directly opposite the business who fired me last month. I never did see myself cutting my teeth in the laminate flooring industry but it still paid the bills so I was rather miffed to have been let go. Officially, I was made redundant. Unofficially, I don't think the boss liked the way I encouraged customers to try other places that had sales on.

Looking towards the building of Marquis Cars I have a good feeling; the place looks clean and fresh, appears to have been treated to a fresh lick of paint in recent weeks and has a number of small bay trees and hanging baskets around the perimeter. The owner clearly takes pride in his establishment, so with any luck he'll also look after his staff. I drain my cappuccino and put it in the bin outside the forecourt.

I walk between cars on the forecourt towards the entrance; all second hand, high-end motors. A salesman walks out to me, clearly thinking I'm a potential punter. I must look like I can afford one of these things, then - it's a start! "Lovely morning - is there anything I can help you with?" he asks, trying to look suave but coming across as rather desperate to hit his sales targets.

"Sorry to disappoint, I'm here for the job interview."

"Oh, you must be Gemma!" he exclaims brightly. "I'm Robbie, I'll take you in." He walks on ahead of me to grab the door. As he opens it for me he gestures with one hand for me to go in front of him. I can't work out whether he is a gentleman or if he's just wanting to check out my rear as I walk in. "Can I get you a coffee?" he asks, maintaining eye contact.

"That would be great, thanks. Milk no sugar." This is one of my weaknesses in life. I'm unable to ask "Is it instant coffee or nice coffee?" for fear of offending. So, I reply "Yes" in the hope that I will get the latter but risk subjecting myself to a teaspoon of granules in a mug of hot water.

I'm standing a little awkwardly inside the front door so I walk slowly to the Mercedes convertible just in front of me - I conclude it will do me no harm to look interested in the things I hope to sell. In the distance, Robbie has entered a side office where there is a chap working away on a computer. Robbie seems to be informing him that I've arrived and the chap looks up and over to me. He gives me a smile and a little jerk of his head which I take to mean he'll be right over. I smile back with a similar head jerk and get back to looking at the Mercedes. It's a 2016 C-Class, top of the range with a 3.0-litre diesel engine. That's what the sign on the windscreen says anyway. I hadn't suffered from interview butterflies until now but it has only just registered that I know sod all about cars and I'm trying to get a job in a car showroom. *I really should have done some homework.*

"She's a stunner, isn't she?" The chap who was in the office is now standing behind me. By the way he said it, I think he wanted to make me jump but I remain flinch-free.

"Yes, she is," I reply. *It's a girl? How do you tell?* "I noticed this is the 3.0-litre version. Have you had much interest?"

"She only came in last night, but I don't think we'll struggle to shift her - she's bulletproof with a full history and a year's ticket, a total steal." He laughs loudly. "Listen to me - I'm trying to sell to my interviewee now!" The chap looks around while finishing the sentence, as if to look for an amused reaction from other staff. No one reacts.

"I'm Mark, and you are Gemma, right?"

"Yes, that's right. I'm very pleased to meet you Mark."

"If you'd like to walk this way Gemma, we'll crack on with your

7

interview."

Mark is bubbly and chatty, a marked improvement on my previous boss who had less charisma than a corpse. Same as Robbie, Mark walks on ahead for me to follow. My heels make loud clacking noises as I make my way across the polished faux marble. The resonance is quite impressive as I pass a variety of convertibles and sports cars. Walking into the office, I sit down and place my handbag on the floor. As my head comes back up, I almost knock the coffee out of Robbie's hand as he sets it down on the desk in front of me. "Almost had you!" he jokes, with a little wink. Robbie leaves the office, closing the door behind him.

Mark then proceeds to chat about the business, how long they've been trading and what their aspirations are for the coming years. I give very interested nods with raised eyebrows at the right times while sipping my coffee. *Yep, granules and hot water.* He took the business on from his father so there was no pun in the company name to match his own, and his dad handed over sole ownership to Mark last year. Mark explains what my title would be if I were the successful candidate: Senior Relational Advisor. *So, a receptionist then.* It appears that, in addition to call handling, data management and sorting the post, there would actually be some car sales involved too. *Me. Selling cars!* Mark explains that he and the sales team would on occasion be on test drives with customers or at auction houses at the same time, so I might be called upon to step onto the sales floor.

"That shouldn't be a problem," I assure him. We do some more chatting, small talk mostly, and I happen to notice a picture of a man with a small boy on his shoulders in a chrome frame on his desk. "Oh, is that you with your dad when you were younger?" I ask.

"Oh, that. No, it's a new frame - that's just the photo it came with." Normally, such a question wouldn't have been that strange. Considering that the lad in the photo is black does make it rather stupid, though. Mark gives a smile when he clocks the boy in the photo but doesn't dwell on it. Instead, he comes round to the other side of the desk and perches on it so he is right in front of me. His knees are almost touching mine and his height difference makes him a little intimidating.

"Gemma, if you end up working with us, I guarantee you will enjoy your time here. We are fair with holidays, enjoy team times together and make sure everyone shares weekend shifts fairly. And, we make sure we have good coffee here - it sells the cars!" *Please tell me you're joking.*

"That's good to know. It certainly seems like a fun place to be."

"Oh it is, Gemma," he replies. "You'll be like...part of the family." Saying this while resting his hand on my knee is a little creepy, I have to say. I resist the urge to swipe his hand away - I could do with the job. His hand comes off my knee and extends it for me to take. He then pulls me to my feet in an impressively cool way and leads me out to the sales floor where we first met. It's nothing short of weird that we're both standing there, looking over the cars, holding hands. *The guy is officially a creep!* Mark then turns to me and takes my other hand too. It's like we're about to start a duet from a West End musical. "Gemma, it's been great meeting you. I'm seeing other girls this week but I'll make sure I let you know either way within the week."

I pull my hands away and reconnect by shaking Mark's right hand firmly. "Thank you Mark." *And I'll let you know if I want to be your dolly bird, you perv.*

Robbie is holding the same door open for me as he did when I arrived. "You survived it then?" Robbie asks. I can't tell whether it's a standard conversation-maker, or if he is acknowledging that his boss is a creep. "Just about," I reply. I pass the Mercedes as I get close to Robbie. He nods at it and says, "She's a stunner isn't she?"

"She sure is," I reply. "And she's a steal with full history and a year's ticket. Bulletproof." Robbie's jaw drops as I head back across the forecourt to begin my eleven-minute walk to the bus stop. As I get up to pace my stomach is a little knotted up. I can't tell whether it's a delayed reaction to the mild sexual harassment or that awful coffee.

Note to self: Avoid pavement grating on the way back.

CHAPTER THREE

Tuesday night is Mum Night where we both turn off our phones, keep the evening free and I allow her to cook me "A proper meal with proper vegetables" as she puts it. Her favourite dish is Toad In The Hole. In reality, every vegetable on the plate has been steamed to the point where it is virtually liquid and I end up farting for twelve hours straight. Mum doesn't like the word 'fart'. Or 'loo'. It is 'windy-pop' and 'toilet'. But I love her to pieces. She often sends me little parcels of things I don't need but which further cement how much she loves me. Like socks. And envelopes. And newspaper clippings of a cute animal doing something funny from the Daily Mail ("the only articles ever to be printed," Bill says, "which don't mention how much their houses cost or if they're an immigrant"). In short, she doesn't stop thinking of me and I'm truly indebted to her for what she does. Since losing my job last month, she has covered my rent as well - she's amazing. Dad took out insurance when they first married, meaning Mum would be financially healthy if he died before a certain age. That was Dad all over. Never fussed about money for himself but determined to make sure it wasn't an issue for Mum once he'd gone. When Dad died, Mum received the promised lump sum so paid off her mortgage and took early retirement. She also bought a property in Spain which returns a nice monthly profit as a holiday home. So, as Dad would have put it, "She's doing alright."

I did have a bottle of red wine to bring over on this particular evening, but after checking twice before leaving the bus, I establish that I must have left it at home. *I was certain I'd left the house with it.* From time to time I do get a little absent-minded. Or, as Mum would put it, I'm "a total airhead who'd lose her head if it wasn't screwed on."

I let myself in as usual, kick off my shoes and hang up my coat. Two steps into the hallway, my coat falls off the hook. That hook has rejected every coat I have ever worn. It loves everyone else's, it's just mine. I never attempt to rehook because it will mock me further with another coat-throwing gesture, so I always leave the coat where it falls. "Evening Love," Mum says as she makes her way from the kitchen at the end of the hall. Returning the salutation, Mum predictably walks straight past me with the quickest of air kisses to line up my shoes neatly against the skirting while asking me how my day has been. I could actually say what I like in reply because the question is always asked out of servitude as opposed to genuinely wanting to know - not that she's uninterested, it's just that scattered shoes and a coat on the floor will always dominate her thought process.

"Oh, you know," I reply as I watch in bewilderment how she hangs my coat on the demon hook every time with no issue.

Walking back past me to the kitchen, she follows up with "How did the interview go?" I follow her in slowly, looking back at my coat hanging perfectly in place. *How does she do that?*

I love Mum's kitchen: it's so light thanks to french doors and a massive skylight put in when it was extended. I always sit down at the small round table she has in the kitchen and pour us both a glass of whatever is sitting on the breakfast bar when I get there. It's usually the bottle I bring round from the previous week, and last week's offering was a bottle of Vina Maipo. I look distantly up to the ceiling wondering where on earth I left today's bottle of wine.

"I said how did the interview go?" Mum, with her back to me, is getting on with dishing up chicken and liquid veg.

"Fine, I think. He said he'll let me know."

He? Husband material?" Mum asks in a way that ends the sentence an octave higher than where it started.

"Stalker material."

"Did you make an effort with your outfit this time?"

"Well I didn't go naked."

"So you've fixed the washing machine, then?"

"Not yet."

"You'd better get onto that Love. You don't want to run out of fresh knickers."

Mums: Coat-hanging prophets.

She spends a few minutes discussing the interview and how, if I got the job, it could result in me running the company in just a few years. For the rest of the meal she tells me all about the cruise she will be going on during December. She tries to get away once a year on a massive boat. She loves the dressing up, the fine food, the total pampering and the fussing she receives for the duration of the cruise and how she can spend a significant time in the casino "because I'm on holiday." I'm not jealous, I'm really pleased for her. Dad's been dead for 15 years now and I'm delighted she hasn't become a multiple cat-owning mad recluse. I'm not saying all widows do that. Only most of them. Mum's week is spent largely catching up with girlfriends, having coffees in garden centres and visiting every clothes shop in a ten-mile radius at least twice. She's a sucker for bulk-bargains too, so Costco will feature most Saturdays. So with that and the cruises she is enjoying life.

While we are washing up, the usual conversation topics are ticked off: the weather, how there's nothing on the tv these days and how next door's cat keeps leaving presents in my garden. But, I also notice how Bill is being mentioned in greater measure. You remember how when you were younger and you saw a toy on the adverts that you *really* wanted for Christmas which you'd then keep mentioning around Mum & Dad

13

whenever possible until they got the hint? Mum seemed to have being doing this about Bill recently. I hoped she wasn't hinting she wanted *him* for Christmas (*thanks, Imagination, for putting that image in my head*), but he was certainly being mentioned quite a bit. Mum met Bill a few years back at a gathering for folk wanting to invest in timeshares abroad. As it happens, Mum followed Bill's lead and bought a property fairly close to his in Spain. They've remained close friends since and flew out together last year to check on both properties at the same time. I shared my concerns with her at the time but after meeting Bill a handful of times I've determined he's harmless. I've shown quite a bit of interest of late, because clearly Mum likes him and I have no issue with her falling in love again. *Clear off, Imagination!*

"I'd love for you to see him again soon. Why don't I invite him over for a meal? I can cook my Toad In The Hole."

"Or we could eat out." *Unless you don't like him, Mum.* "How about the new Indian in town at the weekend?" I'm quite protective about *Mum Tuesday* and would quite like it to stay sacred between the two of us.

"Ooh, good idea Love. I'll call him tomorrow."

We settle down for an evening of Bridget Jones' Diary - Mum's ultimate hint for me to sort my life out and find a bloke - then I make my excuses to leave. I can't work out whether she's dying to tell me more about Bill, but I conclude that there are plenty more Mum Tuesdays to come.

I force my shoes on without undoing the laces. "So I'll see if Bill can do Saturday, then?" Mum asks, through a look of bemusement that her daughter still puts her shoes on like a nine year old. "I'll see if he can bring Simon."

"Simon?" I ask non-inquisitively, while retrieving my coat from the demon hook.

"His son. He's about your age. Doing ever so well in his job, apparently."

And that's the penny dropping.

Rolling my eyes at another of Mum's match-making attempts, I return the air kiss from the beginning of the evening and follow up with a big embrace. "I love you, Mum. See you next week."

"Bye, Love."

I smile to myself as Mum closes and bolts the door and I walk down the path, taking care not to step on the cracks like I've always done. It's much harder these days with size fives, but just doable if I walk like an idiot. As I approach the path I glance over to my right to see the front lawn lit up with a yellow tinge from the street lamp. Whenever I look at the lawn I smile at a memory of Dad spinning me around in the garden to the point where I would almost throw up, then beg him to do it again. So many super memories of a super, super dad. Bill won't be a replacement, but he'll hopefully be someone to make Mum smile properly again. *Don't let me down, William!*

I make my way to the bus stop just a few yards from her door. It's only a short walk home but Mum's paranoid about every conceivable disaster occurring which her favourite tabloid suggests will happen as soon as I step outside. She's stressed enough as it is with me using public transport, regularly sending me new bottles of alcohol gel to use on my commutes.

Five minutes later and the bus turns into my street. It's getting worse, this street; almost every week some idiot has smashed a bottle of wine on the bend just before my house. *Ignorant.*

I text Mum before she sends for Search & Rescue:

I'm in. And I've just missed a pile of cat poo on the path x
I'll sort it later.

15

CHAPTER FOUR

Being unemployed has its perks. I can get up late, stay in my pyjamas, wait for the washing machine repair guy and watch junk on TV. Honestly though, I can't say I want to remain like this forever so I'm hoping the Marquis Cars job comes through. I've come to the conclusion that Mark isn't an intentional creep. I think he's probably more likely to be socially-awkward around women. I decide to give it a week to hear from him and then I'll sell my body - it should fund the odd cappuccino.

Making the most of this spare time, I've arranged to see Nat who has wangled a day off work. Aside from her occasional wake-up calls from the street below, we don't spend as much time together these days. We certainly don't cash in on her living two doors away. *Maybe I should establish Nat Thursday to complement Mum Tuesday.*

I spend the rest of the morning tidying up the house and making it look a little less like I've been burgled, and around lunchtime the doorbell rings. Mr Washing Machine Man has arrived to sort out my knicker problem. Fifteen minutes later, I'm £50 poorer but have an unblocked and functioning washing machine. To be precise, I'm actually £49.50 out of pocket considering he managed to retrieve the rogue 50p that had caused the blockage in the first place. Thanking him as he leaves *(For what exactly? For doing what he's paid to do at a rate of £200 per hour?)*, he gives me a leaflet to sign up to a maintenance contract.

'We'll fix all your household appliances for a low monthly fee'

I thank him again *(seriously?!)* as he walks down the path and I close the door. I put the leaflet to one side; *I'll sort it later*. The most important job right now is to retrieve every pair of knickers from the overflowing laundry basket and wash the life out of them!

I'm on my second load as Nat lets herself in. Mum gave her a key to the house a few months back because I was always locking myself out. I have no problem with Nat having a key, but I'm quite annoyed that she got it from my mother who considers me to be marginally incompetent. Nat knows this and enjoys winding me up, hence letting herself in just now. "Two shots" Nat says as she hands over a takeaway cappuccino. "I'll make lunch." She's amazing. It's her day off and she's the one doing all the work. I follow her to the kitchen, throwing the lid to my cappuccino in the bin as I go. I lift myself up to sit on the kitchen worktop to keep her company while she collects the necessary cutlery and crockery from various cupboards. *She knows my kitchen layout better than I do!*

"How's work going?" I ask her. Nat's an estate agent and by all accounts a good one.

"Really well." she replies. "They've just asked me to take on all commercial properties in our area. It's not many more hours and they're going to give me a car and..." Nat stops mid-flow and gets back to preparing the baguettes she's making for us.

"What's the matter?" I ask, scooping the frothy milk from my cup with a teaspoon.

"Here's me going on about how great my work is and you're here, jobless."

"I'm not destitute, Nat - well, not yet," I joke. "I'm delighted work's going well. Does the increase in hours mean you have to work weekends then?"

Nat proceeds to explain how the job will require a few night hours and the occasional weekend to show prospective clients around various properties. It seems that the company car and salary increase will soften the blow. I'm genuinely happy for her - she's a grafter so it's lovely that her company have recognised this and rewarded her commitment to the job.

"Anyway," I announce "I might have landed a new job myself."

"Of course! Marquis Cars. How did it go?"

I share how the combination of perv and naff coffee were diluted sufficiently by the warm atmosphere and decent wage. "If I get it I have to sell cars, Nat."

Nat puts down the knife and just looks at me. "Selling cars?"

I choke on my cappuccino and we both laugh at the prospect of me imitating Jeremy Clarkson. Nat hands me my plate and we head into the living room, still chuckling.

Nat knows how to make a decent baguette. She has bisected a tiger loaf and rammed it with cheese, ham slices, red onion and pickle. If I could live on one meal for the rest of my life, this would be it. No cutlery required, minimal hassle and not a single liquid vegetable in sight. We both fall back onto the same sofa and put our feet up on the coffee table in front of us. We chat about company cars, perverts and washing machines in between bites of baguette. "How shall we fill our afternoon, then? A long walk to get fit, followed by a healthy salad?" I ask, sarcastically. "Or...DVD and junk food?" *Tough call, as ever.*

I take the plates out and load the dishwasher while Nat heads back to hers for a DVD.

I walk back into the living room with a bottle of Vina Maipo and two glasses just as Nat walks back through the front door. "What's the movie of choice for today then, Nat?" I ask, as I sit back on the sofa.

"Fifty Shades of Grey," Nat replies as she bends down in front of the DVD player to load the disc.

"Okay, then." We're both rather out of touch with movies, so tend to watch blockbusters several years after they come out. It makes them cheaper to buy though - this one has a £4 sale sticker on the cover.

I've read the book already, so I suspect the film to be at a similar level of soft porn. I'm not disappointed, obviously, but ten minutes in and I think I could watch this with Mum in the room. I remember all the feminist posts on Facebook at the time about how FSoG degrades women and encourages them to be subservient in a violent relationship. I can't say I felt that myself when I read the book and as I watch the movie I can't take my eyes off Christian Grey. *I'd bite my lip too if it got me attention like that!* I try my best at reviewing the movie more as a critic rather than a relationship specialist and comment on how they have cleverly encouraged different emotions from the viewer by way of music, lighting and scene setup. Nat responds a little less creatively with "Christian Grey. I'd throw him on the table and give him one right there." *Nat is suited to the role of film critic almost as much as I am to selling cars!*

As E L James intensifies Mr Grey's relationship with Ana, a quizzical look appears on my face as I try to locate the source of the vile smell filling the room. Nat has obviously picked up the scent too, as she looks at me with a similar expression. Suddenly, Nat's jaw drops as she lunges forward to check her shoes. "Bloody cat! Sodding, bloody cat!" she exclaims. "I'm so sorry, Gem, it must have been on the path outside," she cries, taking off her shoes and throwing them outside. I assure her it's not a problem as we both rush to the kitchen for appropriate cleaning products, especially as the source is most likely what I've been meaning to clean up for ages. Technically then, I'm equally at fault. As we're both on our hands and knees scrubbing the carpet, we both share how little we regard the cat owners who have allowed their pet's business to enter my house. We continue to one-up each other's comments until we reach the point of discussing gun ownership and then discover the stains are virtually gone and the smell has dissipated.

"Seriously though, how do I stop cats doing this around my

property? Legally!" I add the extra bit to stop Nat suggesting anti-freeze or claymores.

"I think a hosepipe will work well." *Around its neck.* "Cats hate water, so next time you see it, get the hose and squirt the thing. It should get the idea after a while."

"Good thought. I'll do that next time."

"And if not, leave some bloody anti-freeze out!" Nat can't help herself, but it's largely because she's the careful one out of the two of us so is particularly annoyed that, not only had she stepped in the poo, but she'd forgotten to remove her shoes as well.

We get back into Fifty Shades just as Ana is having a tearful farewell with Christian. Nat and I look at each other with a similar expression to when we smelt the cat poo, wondering what we've missed. "Shall we start it again?" I ask, mainly because I'm wondering how much of Christian Grey's body I've missed.

"Can do, or we can get the next one and watch them back to back next time."

"There's another one?"

"There's another two."

I'm seriously out of touch. Ana clearly wants her backside smacked some more though, so the feminists had better watch Toy Story instead.

CHAPTER FIVE

The last couple of days have been largely uneventful, mostly filled with microwave meals and Jeremy Kyle, while exhausting every job searching site online and having various agencies remind me that it's a tough time to be looking for a job. *It wasn't a choice to be unemployed, people!*

I like to get up early on Saturdays to get the most out of my weekends. I appreciate that unemployment has temporarily taken me off the grid calendar-wise, but I don't want to break the habit. As I'm pulling on my joggers, I hear a noise in the back garden. Looking out of my window, I locate the source of the noise - next door's cat scratching at my bin bags. He's already torn one of them open and has clearly enjoyed the remainder of last night's microwave biryani. I think better of shouting at him from the window and waking up the whole street, choosing instead to head down to the back door where my hosepipe awaits. I slip on my flipflops and quietly unlock the back door. As I open it, it produces the loud creak it has given every day for the past six months, complaining how much it needs a squirt of WD-40. *I'll sort it later.*

I tiptoe, ninja-style, to the hosepipe just outside the door, turn the tap on and walk towards the cat, hose slowly unravelling. As I get close enough to the cat without disturbing it, I aim and fire. The cat has clearly known what I've been up to the entire time and simply sidesteps my shot. I continue squirting and the cat strolls just out of range. As he hops up and over my fence, he looks back at me. If cats were able to look smug, that's the look he would be giving. I let go of the trigger to the hose, but the thing won't stop squirting at full blast. It has been getting jammed for months, but a few smacks tend to fix it so I haven't got round to replacing it just yet. True enough, the trigger releases itself after half a dozen clouts

21

and I roll the hose back up and turn the tap off. *Next time, cat. Next time.*

As I'm closing the back door and removing my flipflops, the telephone rings.

"Hello? Oh, hi. Yes, I'm fine, thanks. How are you? Good...right...okay. Well, I don't know what to say! Thanks very much. Of course, yes. Next week, Monday, 9am. See you then. Thanks so much. You too. Bye."

And I have a job. Mark feels I would slot perfectly into the Marquis Cars family and would like me to start straight away. I knew I liked him. And his coffee.

I pull my phone from my joggers pocket and text Mum as I head upstairs to take a shower:

Got the job. Start Monday. See you tonight x

The rest of the day is spent buying new office clothes online. I head only for those on special offer and with free delivery; I'm not paying them to put it in their lorry as well. My iPhone vibrates at 6:15pm to remind me that I have an Indian to get ready for. I slip on some tight jeans and a white blouse. As I'm looking at myself in the mirror, through all the thumbprints and hairspray marks, I decide to change the blouse for a darker colour due to my track record with curries. And every other type of food. Top changed, I tie my hair back and allow a few strands to hang down the side of my face. I then chuck on a bit of makeup, add a light spray of Issey Miyake and slip on the same heels I wore for my interview. I can't help but notice how I've doubled the times I've worn them in a single week!

I make my way to the bus stop - no dishy bloke this time - and the bus arrives shortly afterwards, just as it starts to rain. As I board, I have a split-second panic attack due to an old chap sitting in my seat. *Of course! The Commuter Code doesn't apply on Saturday evenings.* I sit just behind him feeling it's close enough and crack on with the news app on my iPhone. Several notifications pop up to show me my various clothes orders have been dispatched. *Good to know.* A couple of stops later and the old boy gets off the bus. The rain is quite heavy now, so I feel for him as he pulls up the collar on his coat and walks slowly up the street. I'm faced with an even bigger quandary now - do I move seats? While I'm still considering feeding my OCD appetite, a young couple board the bus and take the seat instead. *Idiot.*

Twenty minutes later and I'm leaving the bus. The young couple also get off the bus and head in the other direction, sheltering under the same umbrella that the guy brought with him. It's only 100 yards to the restaurant from here, so I quicken the pace to avoid getting drenched.

As I get to the restaurant, I can see Mum standing inside with Bill. The windows are rather misted up due to the weather, but they notice me extending a brief wave to them both as I walk into the restaurant. Mum laughs at me "Didn't you bring an umbrella?" *Yes Mum, I did. But I can't bear to get it wet!*

I resist the urge to say it out loud and give Bill a peck on the cheek instead. "Hi Bill."

"Hi Gemma," he laughs, returning the kiss and looking me up and down to add to Mum's amusement at my dampness. I laugh too, out of politeness. A waiter comes over to take my coat from me and informs us that our table will be ready in around 15 minutes. Bill thanks him, then turns to us and says under his breath "Why book for 7pm then, if it won't be ready until 7:15pm?" I'm inclined to agree with him. "Shall we wet our whistles first, then?" Bill says, motioning to the bar. "Simon should be with us soon." Mum gives me a slow, single nod while widening her eyes and smiling the moment Simon's name is mentioned. *We're not at a school disco, Mum.*

As we approach the bar, Bill makes sure he's tended to by the barman - I like someone who is first to get the drinks in. "What's your poison, Gemma?" he asks.

"Red wine, please."

"A lager, gin & tonic and a large red wine please." I've decided I like Bill.

I thank him as he passes the glass to me, and his eyes catch someone walking up to the restaurant. "And another lager please, squire." I'm guessing the new arrival is Simon, so I turn to see him walk through the door. He's tall. I mean over 6 foot tall. And, in the words of Shakespeare, pretty fit. He stands still for a moment once inside the restaurant, scanning the room for familiar faces. As his gaze falls on us at the bar, he grins and heads towards us. *Lovely smile.* The waiter walks up and offers to take his coat, as he did with me, and Simon accepts. This guy knows how to dress. Smart jeans, a slim fit shirt and brown leather shoes. He reminds me a little of Christian Gray in Fifty Shades. *And now I can't stop wondering if Simon has a Red Room.*

"Evening everyone." Simon looks first at Bill, then gives Mum a nod and finally rests his gaze on me. "Nice to meet you Gemma," Simon says, with a little smirk as if to suggest Mum has already told him a lot about me.

"And you," I reply, blushing slightly. *I never blush.* I like men who are well groomed. Simon is well groomed. I like men who have an air of confidence about them. Simon has that air. And I like a man who has a nice bum. Without acting like a dog greeting another dog in the park though, I'm not able to confirm criterion three just yet.

"Pam, how has your day been?"

"Fine, thank you Simon. And yours?"

"Not too bad. A hectic day at work, but glad to be here now"

"What is it you do, Simon?" I ask.

"I'm a fireman." *Of course you are.*

The waiter motions to us that our table is ready, so we make our way over. Simon notices a guy at the entrance on crutches struggling to open the door, so he walks over quickly to help. *Criterion three is affirmative. And he helps cripples too, which is nice.*

I'm just sitting down as Simon returns to help push my chair in. "Thanks," I say.

"Actually, I was going to pull it away as you sat down, but you were too quick" he quips, sitting down and laying the napkin on his lap. *Okay, what's the catch with this guy?* We jump straight to ordering, and I'm all ready to order my usual Prawn Cocktail for starters and Chicken Tikka Jalfrezi for mains.

The waiter goes round the table, starting with Mum. "Oh, don't start with me, I want to see what everyone else is ordering." *Every time.* Bill orders Onion Bhajis and a Xacuti for Main. It sounds Japanese, but I'm sure it's very nice.

Next up is Simon. "Hi, I'll have the Prawn Cocktail and Chicken Tikkia Jalfrezi, please." *Shut up!*

"Same for me please," I reply, giving Simon a quizzical look. Mum takes forever to make her decision but finally rests on Vegetable Samosas and Lamb Biryani. As the waiter takes our menus back and walks off to notify the kitchen, Simon asks me what I do for a job.

"As of about six hours ago, I work for Marquis Cars."

"Oh, the used car dealership - I know it. In that case folks, may I raise a toast to Gemma's new job. Many congratulations, and I hope it's the start of something special."

"To something special" Mum says, her eyes switching between Simon & I. I roll my eyes before joining in with the glass clinking.

It's not long before our starters arrive. Before the plates come to rest

25

on the tables, Mum is already complaining how she wished she'd chosen the Bhajis. "Well, let's share" Bill suggests, as they trade Bhajis and Samosas.

Simon leans over to me and quietly says "Shall we swap too?" I giggle, probably too much. It was funny, but hardly a winner at the Edinburgh Fringe Festival.

"Hmm?" Mum says, wondering what we're laughing about. Bill engages Mum in another conversation, giving me a look that says "Leave her to me, Gemma, I'll get her off your case for a bit." I give him grateful eyes - I think he's sussed her out already.

As the evening draws on, we order more drinks and have a good time together. I mean, a *really* good time together. Conversation is flowing well and we all just *get on*. As the meal ends, Bill asks for the bill (*brilliant!*) and despite much protesting from all of us, settles up. We all thank him for his generosity and stand up to leave. The waiter comes over with our coats and we head outside. It's still raining, the raindrops lit up by the streetlamps, so we don't spend too much time talking outside.

Mum & Bill drove here together, but Simon had taken a taxi. "Where's your car, Gemma?" he asks.

"Oh, I took the bus. And here it is," as it's squeaky brakes bring it to a halt 100 yards away. I'm disappointed to have to end our evening so abruptly, but Simon says "I'll keep you company for the journey home, if that's okay?" I push my lips out and nod.

Bill comes towards me and gives me a warm hug and small peck on the cheek. "Gemma, it was a treat to see you again. Congratulations on your new job, and I hope to see you again soon."

"Likewise, Bill. See you soon." I give Mum a hug too.

"Be good" Mum says, as suggestively as all the other comments she has made this evening.

"You too," I counter sarcastically. Simon and I board the bus, and I sit in my seat. He sits next to me - it would have been weird if he hadn't I guess - and we chat about how well the evening went.

"Mum & Bill get on well don't they?"

"Yes, they do. Dad won't stop talking about your mum, dropping her into every possible conversation." I laugh and share how it's the same for Mum. "Your Dad died some years ago, is that right?"

I nod, looking down. I don't think I'll ever reach the point where I don't well up when Dad is mentioned. "And your Mum? Is she-"

"Humping some younger bloke in Sussex. Yes." Simon says it in a deadpan way, looking down. A mischievous grin spreads across his face as he turns his head back to me. We both erupt into laughter. The bus journey goes so quickly due to the conversations and jokes we're sharing that my stop comes up rather quickly. "I'll walk you to your door," offers Simon. I don't turn the offer down, and he waits for me to leave the bus first. *Assessing my credentials, perhaps? Do I care?*

It has stopped raining now, and Simon offers the crook of his elbow as we head up the street to my house. I put my arm through and hold on with the other. I'm beaming from how it's been such a perfect time together and how I've managed not to make a fool of myself all evening. "It's been great spending the evening with you Gemma," he says, warmly.

I look up at him with a serious expression. "Yeah, me too. I'm sorry about my Mum."

He laughs, "No, it was funny. Perhaps we should take a selfie of us both in your bath and send it to her."

"We can't do that" I reply, with a serious face.

"I'm sorry, it was just a joke," replies Simon, clearly devastated that he may have ruined any potential friendship.

"No," I reply. " I mean, I only have a shower." I keep looking at him, wondering who will laugh first. I win.

"Okay, you got me," he says. We chuckle the remainder of the walk.

"This is me," I declare, as we reach my gate. "Would you like to come in for a drink?"

"Next time, that would be lovely. I've got an early shift tomorrow, so I'll get on my way."

"Oh, I didn't realise. Sorry for dragging you across town."

"Don't be sorry, I offered...and I really enjoyed being with you."

"Me too."

Simon leans in, gives me a long kiss on the cheek and hugs me tightly. I return the hug. We both say "goodnight" at the same time, and as I turn to walk up the path my handbag gets caught in the gate which pulls me sharply back, and in an effort to maintain balance manage to kick off one of my shoes into the hedge. Simon is already walking away so I don't think he saw, fortunately.

I head over to the hedge to retrieve my shoe and head into the house, closing and bolting the door behind me. After removing the other shoe I hang up my coat and text mum:

I'm in. Got to go, I'm having rampant sex. x

I have a wee, brush my teeth, turn off the light, strip off and leave the clothes in a trail to the bed, collapsing under the duvet. My phone wolf whistles to tell me I've received a text. I rummage in my handbag to retrieve my phone and open up the message:

So am I. x

CHAPTER SIX

How can it be Monday already?

Sunday was a 'doing day' for me - I cleaned and tidied the entire house, did my weekly shop, removed the last bits of cat poo from the path and applied WD-40 to the back door for Operation Cat MkII. For the evening, I swotted up on various car makes and what the differences are between them. I still have absolutely no idea about cars, so my self-esteem had taken a bit of a dip by the time I went to bed. Still, someone has a new job starting today. *Self-esteem back in credit!*

I get up without the need for Nat this morning, keen to start as I mean to go on. It is a treat to step onto a clean carpet around my bed and not trip over socks, coat hangers and other things that typically occupy the bedroom floor. I shower, straighten my hair and head for the wardrobe to see what my first day's outfit should be. As I get into my room, the doorbell rings followed by a loud, abrupt knocking. I throw on my dressing gown and head for the door to discover a delivery driver with an armful of packages. *My outfits!* I thank him, sign the digital thing and close the door. Opening the first package, I'm presented with a grey trouser suit with a thin black pinstripe. I consider hanging out the creases but it doesn't look too bad so I decide to wear it today along with the white blouse I sidelined on Saturday night. A quick check in my HD mirror confirms the combo works, so I head downstairs to start the day. With muesli in my stomach and a freshly-charged iPhone in my handbag, I'm ready to face the world. *Marquis, here I come!* As I'm putting on my heels, there's another knock on the door. *Seriously? Now?* I fling open the door expecting there to be a sheepish delivery driver with an extra parcel, but I'm instead met by the largest bunch of flowers I've ever seen.

It's verging on obscene as I can't actually see the face of the florist delivering them. A hand appears between stalks with another device to sign and then we exchange goods. With a faceful of flowers I offer a muffled thanks and bring them into the kitchen. I find a small card amongst them, so put the flowers on the drainer while I see who it's from. My jaw drops a bit:

Best of luck for your first day. Thinking of you, Simon x
0077 15933408

He's thinking of me. Likewise, Mr. Fireman! I fill the sink with water and bung the flowers in. Lovely as they are, I can't be late for my first day arranging them. I pocket the card and leave the house with a spring in my step. No cat poo on the path this morning either *and* the sun is shining as I head to the bus stop. This is a good day! I hear the bus arriving as I get to the stop and the driver has the doors already open as I hop on. I give him a bright "Good morning" and I'm met with an oppositely-enthusiastic "Morning." I swipe my card on the payment reader and make my way to *my* seat. I catch the eye of someone in a seat opposite as I go to sit down and they look away awkwardly. I'm breaking The Code! But I got a massive bunch of flowers this morning - The Code can be broken!

I put my handbag on the empty seat next to me as usual and fish out my phone. Instead of checking the latest news headlines, I text Simon using the number he gave on the card:

Flowers are beautiful - thanks so much. Coffee soon? xxx

I press *send* and sit back in the seat with a wide grin. I feel everyone on the bus is looking at me and wishing they had my life. As I put my phone back in my bag I casually look around the bus to see how many people *are* looking. Not one. *They're in denial. I got a massive bunch of flowers!*

30

Two minutes into the journey and I realise that I haven't yet received an acknowledgement to my message. I get the phone out to check it's not on silent. *Strange.* I open up the message I've just sent to check I put the number in correctly. *Strange again.* I've got a strong signal as well. *Why hasn't he replied? Was the invitation to coffee too forward? Maybe I shouldn't have said 'soon' at the end. Oh, heck. It was the kisses. One is flirty, Two is commitment, Three is 'Stalker Level'. Three is 'Marry me and have my babies now or you'll find a bunny boiling in your saucepan.' I don't deserve a text...I deserve a restraining order!*

As I'm lamenting the one that got away, my phone gives a wolf whistle:

Or something stronger ;) Free tonight?

My jaw drops. *Is this actually happening?* I read it again, just to be sure. Yep, it definitely says that.

It takes me the rest of the bus journey to think of a reply because I want to get it just right, but I finally nail it:

Yep. x

I get off the bus and nip into Costa. No cappuccino in process today as there's a bit of a queue. While I'm in the queue, I get another wolf whistle:

Shall we make it dinner? Pick you up at 7?

If I had a weak bladder, I think I would actually wet myself. I complete the reply just as I get served:

Great. See you then. x

"Someone's looking happy, Gemma." I look up to find Sally preparing my cappuccino.

"You could say that."

"How did the Marquis interview go?"

"Really well. I start today!"

31

"Yay. Well done you!"

"Thanks," I reply, placing a fiver on the counter for the coffee. Sally slides it back to me.

"Keep that. It's on the house - a small congratulations."

I beam at her, retake the fiver and head for the door. I wave while walking away. "See you in the morning."

The eleven minutes to Marquis Cars goes rather quickly, probably because I'm floating most of the way. I don't have a ridiculous crush on Simon, yet. It's more that I've been bowled over by how - well - *perfect* he seems to be. Tonight will be a further test though. And I've no doubt he'll be testing me too. *Test away, Mr. Fireman.* In no time I find myself standing at the end of the forecourt, exactly where I was last week before the interview. I don't know why I'm making it so sentimental, but I close my eyes and take a deep breath. Exhaling loudly, I open my eyes and make my way towards my new job. *Please let this be a good thing.*

As I walk between two BMWs, my handbag falls off my shoulder. Attempting to catch it, it swings off my arm and knocks the wing mirror of the 3-Series on my right, setting off the alarm. Similar to the feeling you get when you set off the alarms in a shop doorway, I don't know whether to freeze or keep going. I look through the showroom to see if anyone has noticed. Everyone has. I decide to keep walking and I see Robbie opening the main door, just as he did last week. "Quite an entrance that, Gemma!" he says, chuckling. The warmth in his face assures me there is no harm done and I roll my eyes at my clumsiness as I walk past him.

Mark is already walking over to me as I get inside, extending his hand to welcome me. I reciprocate and he grabs it warmly with both hands. "Let me show you around," he says. "You've already met Robbie," he remarks, nodding towards him. I turn to see Robbie turning off the car alarm with the keyfob, giving me a cheeky grin in the process.

Git. "This is the lovely Tania." He gestures to a woman in her mid-20s chewing gum and tapping away on the computer. I can see the lime green skirt she's wearing through her glass desk, barely covering her modesty, complemented by a tight black v-neck top. As Dad would have said, *"her lungs are hanging out of that."* She looks up and gives me a warm smile.

"Hiya!" she says, in a pitch that would rival a dog whistle.

"Hiya," I reply. Her right wrist is a mass of bracelets and bangles. She doesn't strike me as a car burglar, but she will be heard a mile away if she ever considers a career change. Her left wrist is far more conservative with just a fitness tracker wrapped round it. I've never understood the things. For generations we have been able to work out for ourselves if we're unfit, fat or lazy. Now we need a watch to tell us that we need to get up and walk more. *It's not for me.*

Tania gets up, offers to take my coat and hangs it on a rack behind her desk. "You can leave that here for a bit if you want," she says, nodding at my handbag. I thank her and leave it on her desk. I'm not the best judge of character, but I don't think she'll nick it.

Mark places a hand gently in the small of my back and takes me round the showroom pointing at doors which are in the three available walls, explaining where they lead. I do my best to remember what each one is for but eventually confess to Mark that he may have to run them past me again at some point. "That's why we have it written on each door, Gemma," he says, with a slightly concerned face. *How thick am I?* I let him see me rolling my eyes again, to which he chuckles. "Don't worry - I know what first-day-nerves are like! And this...is you." There is a glass desk similar to Tania's resting in the corner of the showroom, the furthest point from the door and largely hidden from the entrance by a Silver BMW X5. I'm wondering if it is an intentional location until I can be trusted with new customers. "The computer has been set up already, but the rest is down to you." Mark points to a cupboard through the window in his office. "Stationery is in there. Knock yourself out, make yourself at home and I'll see how you're doing shortly."

I thank him and take a seat at my desk. I haven't seen the pervert side to Mark at all, so I put last week's performance down to nerves. I watch the life of Marquis Cars unfold around me; Robbie sliding back one of the large showroom windows, Mark sitting at his desk sifting through various documents, Tania filing down a rogue nail and a team of folk arriving to wash cars on the forecourt. They all greet Robbie who returns the salutation. He walks over to them, I guess to make small talk. He looks over to me and the team of washers give me a medley of smiles, nods and waves. I return all three.

Rogue nail sorted, Tania heads over to me with purpose. And my handbag. "Coffee?" she asks, resting my handbag on my desk. I hope to be in this job for a long time, so decide to be honest from the start. "I've just had one, but thanks anyway." *Half honest.* Tania shrugs her shoulders in an unbothered manner and heads through a door. I'm guessing that is the kitchen, but no doubt it says it on the door.

The rest of the morning is largely uneventful. Robbie talks me through various aspects of car sales and Tania shows me how various spreadsheets work to manage the inventory of cars. Figures aren't really my thing, so I'm relieved to discover I won't have to oversee invoicing or anything like that. It all seems pretty straightforward and largely relies on common sense. Robbie is in the process of talking me through how to arrange insurance for test drives when a well-dressed man walks in. Removing his sunglasses and putting them in the chest pocket of his suit jacket, he looks like a James Bond wannabe. *Simon looks way better.* Tania jumps out of her chair to greet the man, straightening out her skirt, and I establish that this is our first client of the day. She shares a few sentences with him and then begins to walk over to us. Robbie is leaning over me with one hand on the desk and the other on the back of my chair as his head turns to the client. "Ah, first job." He gives me a mischievous look "Watch and learn." I swallow hard. Tania joins me at my desk as Robbie walks purposefully over to the client who is looking through the open window of the Mercedes convertible I saw at my interview. *Full service history. Year's ticket.* Robbie greets the man with a handshake and engages him in conversation while opening various doors and lifting the bonnet.

"Robbie is a god at this," Tania gushes. She obviously likes him, although I'm guessing he has ten years on her. As Robbie makes gestures, cracks jokes and points at endearing features of the car, Tania explains how Robbie has a near-identical patter for every client. "He's perfected it over the years, and it works like a charm. When someone points out a scuff, he passes it off and changes subject. If it's a high miler he'll explain they're all motorway miles and the engine is barely run in." At this, the client spots something at the bottom of the passenger door. Robbie lifts his trouser legs slightly, crouches down, licks his finger and tries to rub out the scuff in vain. He then says something to the client which earns an understanding nod and Robbie heads over to a cabinet hanging on the wall beside the window to Mark's office. Opening it, there are dozens of keys hanging in neat rows. Robbie takes a while to find the one he wants, but eventually locates it and walks back to the client, giving it to him. He encourages the client to get in the driver's seat and walks over to me.

"Gemma, can you help me shift some cars so I can get the Merc out?"

I swallow hard. "Shift some cars?"

One side of his mouth lifts up, saying "You *can* drive, can't you?"

"Of course I can." *Well, I have a license. Driving is another thing entirely.* I haven't owned a car for years.

"Phew. That would have been a short career," he says with a wink. "Come on." I look at Tania, who is smiling at me as if to suggest this is a standard first day initiation. My heels resonate loudly as I make my way outside, passing the client in the Mercedes as I go. I offer him a warm smile but he's too busy trying to put a fancy cup holder back into place.

Robbie joins me with a handful of keys. "Bung that one over there for me," he says, throwing me a key and pointing at something over my shoulder. I turn to see a bright yellow Porsche convertible behind me.

I gasp. *Move that?* I turn back to Robbie but he has already got into another car. I face the Porsche again, take a deep breath and walk round the front of it. As I near the driver's door, I notice the price in the windscreen. £52,995. *Oh hell.* I try to open the door but it's locked. *Unlock it then, Gemma.* After pressing the first button on the keyfob, the boot pops open. After closing the boot, the next button I attempt does its job. I get into the car. *Man, this is low.* I establish quickly that there is a start button for the car and there is no keyhole. So, I put my foot on the brake and hope for the best. Pressing the start button the car roars into life, sounding like a jet fighter. As I prepare myself to drive, I realise that it's a real effort with heels on. I'm not desperate to launch the car into the rest of the stock, so I remove my heels and place them on the passenger seat. In barefoot, I engage first gear and crawl the car out of the way and into the space Robbie indicated earlier. *That wasn't too painful.*

Engine off, I open the door, grab my heels and slide my legs out to put my heels on. As I'm moving into position, I lean on the horn button in the centre of the steering wheel. I flinch so much that I throw my shoes under the car next to mine . I get out, lock the Porsche and proceed to go on hands and knees to retrieve my heels from under the adjacent sports car. *Ground, swallow me up.* Leaning against the Porsche to put on my shoes one at a time, I walk over to Robbie to see what car to move next only to discover that he has moved all the others himself.

He gives a chuckle at my car-moving performance and I reply with "I didn't want to knock a wing mirror *and* crash a Porsche on my first day!" He nods approvingly as he heads back to the client to commence the test drive.

The rest of the day is filled with more spreadsheets, eating my sandwiches in the kitchen with Tania, further offers of coffee and Robbie taking clients on test drives. At around 4pm, Mark knocks on his office window and motions for me to come in. I knock before entering and he encourages me to take a seat. "Sorry I haven't had a chance to see you yet. It's been a busy start to the week," Mark explains.

"Don't worry," I assure him.

"How has Day One been for you? Have Robbie & Tania looked after you?"

I share how friendly they've been to me and how the day has largely entailed being shown the ropes.

"So, what do you think of Marquis Cars? Will you come back tomorrow?"

"I will if you'll have me"

"I might have you," he says, with a suggestive look. *And there's the perv.*

I've established that they have a good sense of humour, so I decide to be a bit cheeky in return.

"Well, if there's nothing on telly in the morning, I'll come in for another day." Mark laughs loudly. "Love it. Love it!" *I think he loves it.* "You'll fit in really well here, Gemma" he says, still laughing. I laugh too. "Gemma, I don't think we're going to get any more customers through the door now, so let's call it a day." I give him a surprised look, but he assures me that things will balance out with longer shifts at other times. I nod, acknowledging this to be very fair. I get up, assure him I'll come back tomorrow while winking and head for the door.

"Just one thing, Gemma." With one hand on the door handle, I turn back to Mark. "Is there anything you would change here?" I pause, looking up to the corner of Mark's office where a spider has made an impressive home.

"Can I be honest?" I ask, looking back at him.

Mark leans forward onto his desk. "Please" he says, sincerely.

"Would you consider getting a coffee machine?" Mark relaxes his shoulders a little and his mouth opens slightly, suggesting I have really hurt his feelings. A smile then spreads across his face and he looks down to his desk, chuckling while shaking his head. I smile and turn back to leave.

As I'm halfway through the door, Mark calls out "Can I suggest something for you, then?"

"Please" I reply, in a similar way to his. Walking up to me slowly, Mark extends his hand and puts it round my shoulder. *This is weird.* He then pulls at the back of my collar until something snaps, which Mark then brings round to the front to show me.

"Would you remove the label from *tomorrow's* outfit before you leave the house?"

CHAPTER SEVEN

I get home around 5:30pm thanks to the early finish at Marquis Cars. I've really enjoyed the day and I'm looking forward to starting again tomorrow. It's already beating laminate flooring! I'm pretty hungry due to a poor lunchtime spread, but I want to stay hungry so I can have a good munch with Simon. *On Simon.*

It crosses my mind that Simon last time said he would take me up on a coffee next time I asked, so in case tonight's the night I decide to get my house in order. Thanks to yesterday's titivation, there isn't much to do. I arrange the flowers, separating them among three vases around the house and throw a duster around. I also fire up a playlist of acoustic songs in the living room, setting the mood for the evening. I head upstairs to get ready, carrying all the deliveries I received this morning. I rip open the remaining parcels and lay out all my purchases on the bed. I now have an impressive selection of work outfits, various tops, some new underwear sets and a Little Black Dress to replace the one I've had since the dawn of civilisation. *But what to wear tonight?* I established years ago that blokes have it far easier. They can chuck on jeans and a shirt and be ready for a range of formalities. Pick the wrong type of dress and a girl either says she couldn't care less or is charging by the hour.

I decide to chuck on my new LBD, with an old set of blue satin knickers and bra. I'm not wearing new pants until they've been washed, regardless of how well packaged they are! Considering I haven't worn this set for ever, they fit perfectly. *More self-esteem points, I haven't put on weight!* I don't tend to focus on underwear very much. They just serve a purpose to hold everything in and stop leaving embarrassing sweat marks on fake leather seats. But tonight though, I decide to make a bit of an effort. *They do it in the movies, so why shouldn't I?* I've never understood thongs or g-strings though. The idea of having something stuck up my bum crack all day long sounds like a form of ancient torture. I'd rather have bamboo shoots under my fingernails.

I look in Mirror HD and give a smile. *Mr. Fireman, you're gonna have to hose me down because I look HOT.* The smile falls from my face quickly when it dawns on me this may be too 'dressy'. What if he's just taking me to KFC and arrives in shorts and a t-shirt? I decide to keep things as they are but line up Saturday's tight jeans and a new top in reserve.

Time is already escaping me and I'm finishing off my make-up as I hear a car pull up outside. With my bedroom light off I peer through a gap in my curtains. Simon gets out of a white BMW *(I know my cars after all!)*, closes the door and walks down my garden path. As my security light comes on, I can see he is dressed in a smart grey suit with a blue shirt underneath. *An LBD complements that very nicely...and so does my underwear!*

I leg it downstairs like an eight year old hearing the ice cream van and then casually walk the last few feet to the door as Simon approaches. I open it to see him with one fist raised, ready to knock. We both laugh. "Wow" Simon says, stopping his laugh and looking me up and down. He exhales some air while looking me straight in the eyes. *He likes what he sees. Well, back at ya!* We're both standing there on the doorstep for almost an eternity when Simon snaps out of his trance and says, "Ready to go?"

"Pretty much," I reply. I sit on the stairs to put on my shoes. I'm aware I'm flashing my satin blues at him, but he is a gentleman and has looked away already. *I could have worn boring pants.* "Ready," I announce, grabbing my handbag from the table by the door. Mum says it's called a telephone table. My telephone is in the kitchen. I close the door behind me and we both walk to his BMW. He is already opening my door as I close the gate. I thank him and slide into the car as elegantly as I can. It's nowhere near as low as the Porsche but I still struggle to keep my legs together as I slide in. Once again, Mr Gentleman has looked away and closes my door which gives a solid thud to demonstrate how effective the car's sound proofing is.

Now, don't ask me why but I feel that simply *thinking* the following sentence isn't enough. I have to *say* it. Perhaps my subconscious thinks I will jinx the whole evening if I don't vocalise it. More likely it's my mild OCD telling me I have to do something once it's in my head. It's not like I want it to happen on a first date either - I'm not a slapper, I've been brought up properly. In fact, society would consider me old fashioned because I want to wait until I'm married before I jump into bed with my lifelong partner. Either way, as Simon makes his way round the front of the car to his door I say, in a strange South American accent, "I'm gonna get me some hot, crazy sex tonight!" Fine. I've said it, and he hasn't even reached his door yet. No harm done.

He gets in the other side and closes his door. "Are you ready to go?" he asks.

"Yep," comes the reply. But not from me. From Bill, who is sat in the back.

A quick glance round confirms I'm not imagining it - and I'm not imagining the huge grin that meets me either. "We're just dropping off Dad to his poker night and then the evening's ours," Simon explains.

"Super" I reply, sinking into the leather seat.

"Super" says Bill.

Simon asks me if I like Italian food, to which I nod keenly. *I LOVE Italian food.* "That's handy - the table's booked!" he jokes. I laugh, again

41

probably louder and more enthusiastically than it needs to be, but I'm still dying inside from my painful experience a few moments ago. I can feel Bill's eyes burning my back, no doubt assisted by the large grin he's wearing.

"How was your first day, Gemma?" Bill asks. He must have read my mind because he's asking it in a very normal way.

"Really well thanks, Bill. Everyone was really nice to me."

"That's because you're a nice girl, Gemma." Out of the corner of my eye I catch Simon peering at his Dad in the rear view mirror as if to ask him what his game is.

"Thanks" I reply.

A short while later we pull up to a small cottage in a quiet lane. "See you later, Dad - you're okay getting home?"

"Yep, all sorted," he replies. He shifts over seats to get out by the kerb, placing his hand on my shoulder. "Look after him, and be gentle," he says. Simon laughs. I laugh. Simon doesn't know what Bill really means. Bill laughs because he knows that Simon doesn't know what he really means. Bill closes the door and walks towards the cottage. Simon waits until someone opens the door to his dad, then drives off.

Simon sighs "Creature of habit, Dad. He's played poker with his old sparky mates once a week for nearly twenty years."

"Sparky mates?"

"They all used to work for a security firm installing alarm systems. Retired now, of course, but they stay in touch," I remark how nice it is that they still see each other, and Simon reels off a list of Bill's past colleagues who have already snuffed it. *Lively conversation, this.* Simon senses the mood has dipped a tad and turns on the stereo. I wonder what he's into. The first tune to play is Hedonism by Skunk Anansie. It reminds me of my college days, not a bad tune as I recall. Simon's fingers tap on his steering wheel in time with the beat. "So, tell me about you, Gemma. What has life delivered you up to now?" I inhale deeply and then share the most newsworthy parts of my childhood, explain how Dad lost his battle to cancer and how I do my best to "make every day count." Simon nods through it all (to prove he's listening, I think) and then I return the question. "My life has been utterly boring compared with yours, but I joined the Fire Service when I left school and have been doing it ever since." Simon explains that he is mostly office-based these days but will leap to action if there are any bigger 'shouts'. "I leave the physical stuff to the younger ones" he jokes. *I hope not all physical stuff.*

After exhausting all possible fireman questions, we pull up to a halt in a village side road. I look at Simon, confused. "It's round the corner, but we won't be able to park," he chuckles, probably thinking my expression was out of fear that he was going to dump my body somewhere.

As he gets out of his car, I roll my eyes at the expression I gave. I am out of the car before he gets round to me, but I can tell he was going to be the perfect gentleman and open the door for me. I've already established he's not into upskirt voyeurism. *I really could have worn boring pants.*

Simon offers me the crook of his elbow like he did on Saturday and we stroll to the restaurant. It's a warm and dry evening so no need for brollies or coats. As we approach the restaurant door, Simon skips ahead to pull the door open for me. I thank him by placing my hand on his arm as I walk past. It's my way of saying "Thank you for the evening so far, for my flowers and for being - well - *perfect.*" Simon responds by putting his arm in the small of my back as he joins me inside the restaurant.

A waiter comes over to us quickly. "Table for Simon?" he says. Simon nods and the waiter grabs two menus from the bookings table, beckoning us to follow him. I get annoyed how restaurants tend to cram diners together to save their staff running to all corners taking orders. For those wanting a quieter time, it's quite a mood spoiler to be sat amongst families with kids scraping their chairs and dropping cutlery all the time. We're led to the centre of the restaurant to where the cluster of diners are, but the waiter goes straight through and leads us to a small table in the furthest corner. *How refreshing!* "How is this for you?" he asks.

We both respond with "Perfect" at the same and then look at each other and giggle.

"This is on me, so spoil yourself rotten," Simon announces. I protest, reminding Simon that he has already spoiled me enough with the flowers. It's not really our first argument, but I lose.

Simon chooses a gorgeous bottle of red for us to share, although he only has one glass. *Of course, he's driving.* We then share a breadboard starter before digging into our mains. I offer Simon some of my dish, a pasta, chicken and walnut ensemble, but he refuses. I try to disguise that I'm a little taken aback but he then explains. "I have a nut allergy. It's not too desperate, but I come out in some impressive lumps and rashes if I come into contact with them." *My poor baby.* I have visions of me tending to an allergic reaction, mopping his fevered brow. In a nurse's uniform. *Ah, Imagination, my old friend. I haven't seen you for a while.*

Simon spends the next few minutes regaling stories of previous allergic reactions, all of them pretty humourous. I can see that it bothers him a little and that he's trying to show male bravado. I empathise with how restricting it must be from time to time, and he jokes how he's always wanted to know what Peanut Butter & Jam Sandwiches taste like. I fake a retch at the thought of such a vile combo and he laughs.

After more conversing, we both order desserts from the waiter as he comes over and I excuse myself to the ladies' to powder my nose. *I'm having a wee - no woman powders her nose in the loo!* I have *the* widest smile across my face as I make my way to the toilets. Walking in, I see there is a long line of cubicles with an equal number of basins which are flush mounted to a counter against a mirrored wall. A lady is there, powdering her nose. *Okay, some do.* She looks at me in the mirror and smiles. I smile back and head to the cubicle. As I hitch my dress up and sit down, I feel a rip. My jaw drops as wide as the Channel Tunnel. "Oh no."

"Was that what I thought it was?" asks the lady who is mid-powder.

"Yes. It was."

"I might have some pins," she offers.

I have the quickest wee in history and head out of the cubicle for more space to see what I've done. My toilet companion goes round the back of my dress to see the zip has ripped from its base which is at the middle of my backside. She explains the rip isn't massive but enough to enrage public decency. *Great. I'm flashing my satin blues after all.*

"Easy fix," she declares, as she digs through her Mary Poppins-esque bag to locate the necessary hardware. Five minutes later and I have a row of pins holding everything in place. "It will get you home, just don't put too much pressure on it," She sounds like she's just done a temporary fix on a car!

I hug her to say thanks and as she leaves I realise I haven't yet washed my hands. I look at myself in the mirror while washing, rolling my eyes. I can see this being mentioned at the wedding. *Slow down, Gem.*

I head back out of the toilets and walk over to Simon, just as the desserts are being laid on the table. Simon offers me some of his Knickerbocker Glory. Such a childhood pudding - he's obviously a kid at heart - and it tastes *amazing*. He then accepts an offer of a mouthful of my nut-free cheesecake, so I load up my fork. As I lean over the table, one of the pins in my LBD comes loose and jabs me in my backside, causing me to flinch and stab Simon in the face with my fork. I hold my position, fork where it was, not entirely sure that what just happened has actually happened, as Simon recoils from the pain. Sitting back in his chair, and his hand on his cheek, he looks at me much in the same way as a dog looks when you blow in its face. Or, the look someone gives you when you stab them in the face with a fork.

I'm still holding my fork where it was. "I am so sorry, Simon," I say, in utter disbelief at what has just happened. Simon picks up a napkin that has fallen on the floor and wipes away the cheesecake left on his cheek. He keeps looking at his napkin, expecting to see blood. There isn't too much, but enough that it's Actual Bodily Harm.

I roll my eyes and look down, shaking my head. It was nice while it lasted. And here begins the rest of my single life. I can't hear anything from Simon. No reaction at all. *He must be furious. Look at him, you idiot.* I pluck up the courage to lift my head and look at him. I'm met with the broadest grin from the most gorgeous man I've ever met. His shoulders are shaking from the silent laughter he is doing. "I'm so sorry," I say again, shaking my head while looking at him with pleading eyes to show my sincerity.

"You didn't strike me as the violent type, Gemma," he replies. "How much more of you is there to know?"

I look to the ceiling and then reply confidently, "I think that's about it." *Assuming your dad won't tell you what I said in the car.*

I confess to Simon why I stabbed him, which also explains why I took so long in the bathroom. By the end, Simon looks like he is close to having a heart attack from the amount of laughing he is doing. All the while, we're doing our best to be quiet so as not to disturb the other diners. "Coffee?" Simon asks, protecting his face in a pantomime fashion.

"I still owe you one at mine" I reply.

A warm smile spreads across Simon's face. "Deal." He motions to the waiter to bring the bill and in a few minutes we're getting up to leave. My chair legs give a high pitched squeal as I slide the chair back and, leaning on the table, manage to knock an unused knife onto the floor, making an enormous clatter as it settles. There's a momentary silence as all the other diners look at me. Simon stays quiet as we head for the door. I'm not drunk, but as we step outside and the cold air hits us I feel a little more wobbly than earlier. A suit jacket gets put on me and I hold it tightly around my front. "It's not just for the cold," he says, signalling with his head that it is also to preserve my modesty. I thank him, feeling my cheeks burning. Simon puts his arm around me as we walk down the unlit village road and I nuzzle into him as much as I can without falling over.

Simon's car appears to unlock automatically as you get close to it, so he just pulls my door handle to open the door. Keeping the jacket around me I slide into the seat and Simon closes the door, walking round to the driver's side. I look over my shoulder to check Bill isn't in the back but still choose to stay quiet this time. We spend most of the journey back laughing about the evening's events, cracking jokes and generally enjoying each other's company. No Doubt, Sash and The Corrs entertain us through the car's Bose system for the duration. *Tunes.*

When we get to mine, Simon parks up and turns off the engine. He looks at me, expectantly. "Coffee?" I smile.

"Coffee" he replies, exhaling and relaxing his shoulders like he needs one. "And a plaster" he jokes, giving me a wink. I roll my eyes again and head out of the car door, leaving Simon chuckling. I get round to the path as Simon is getting out of his side and as I head for my path he stops me from opening the gate. Facing me and moving in really close, I can smell his aftershave. *He smells good.* Grabbing both lapels of the jacket still around my shoulders, he pulls me in for the most passionate kiss I have ever experienced. It's simply divine, he holds me tight and I return the grip. *I think I have a boyfriend.* Frustratingly, the kiss comes to an end. I giggle while opening the gate and walk to the front door while holding Simon's hand.

Getting in the house, I hang his jacket over the newel post at the foot of the stairs, fill up the water container for my Gaggia and get the thing warmed up. Turning round, Simon is there to greet me with another kiss. It lasts as long as the water takes to heat. *I'm heating up a little myself!* We take our coffees into the living room and fall back into the sofa. I look over at the clock on the mantelpiece - it's 11pm, it's a weeknight and I'm still up. Putting the coffees down, we enjoy yet another snog and a really long, lovely cuddle. *I like this. A lot.*

I open my eyes and look over at the clock on the mantlepiece. It's 3am. I'm sure that can't be right, so I rub my eyes and allow them time to adjust before checking again. *It's 3am!* I sit up bolt upright, nearly knocking over our coffees that haven't been touched, waking Simon in the process. He has a wet shoulder from where I've been dribbling on his shirt. He looks at the clock, looks back at me and looks back at the clock again. He gets up in a bit of a daze, and staggers to the door. I follow him and make a rather out-of-character suggestion. "It's a good half an hour's drive home from here. Why don't you stay the night?"

Simon looks wide eyed at me, I think partly because he's still trying to wake himself up.

"I have a spare room," I add, confirming that I'm not that easy.

Simon sighs, looks at his watch, gives a weary chuckle and feebly replies, "That would be great."

I invite him to use the downstairs loo and fish out a new toothbrush from its packet in my stash under the kitchen sink. I run upstairs to check the spare room is decent. Apart from the odd box filled with things I still haven't found a home for since moving here three years ago, the room is good to go. A bit girlie for him, but good to go.

I complete my usual evening bathroom routine and come on to the landing to find Simon outside his room, shirt in hand. *He has THE hottest body.* I apologise and look away before remembering that it's my landing and he doesn't need to stand there with his shirt off.

"It's wet," he explains "so I'll leave it over here if that's okay?" placing it on the bannister. "Sorry, that's my dribble," I confess. *I think he knows that Gemma, well done.* I take the shirt from the bannister so that it can be hung up properly. I can't imagine Simon has a spare shirt in his car so it needs to be in good nick for work in the morning. *This morning.*

"So I'll see you in a few hours, then" Simon says with a smirk.

"Night" I giggle, my head reminiscing the evening's events up to now. He leans in and gives me a long goodnight kiss. I envisage him lifting me up into his arms and carrying me into my room for a night of passion, but my gentleman stays true to character and heads into his room, closing the door behind him. *I would have turned you down anyway. I'm a good girl!*

I close my door for the first time ever since moving in, still carrying Simon's shirt. Throwing it onto the bed, I remove my LBD, bra and tights. I collapse onto the bed and pull my duvet over me, my brain scrambled in a good way from all the amazing experiences the past few hours have thrown at me. I produce a massive grin. *I have a boyfriend - with an amazing body!* As I now have company, I feel it appropriate to put on some joggers and a t-shirt to sleep in. I'm so tired though, so I decide to stay where I am for a minute longer.

I'm dreaming about a variety of things, mostly involving Simon rescuing me from burning buildings, when I'm awoken by a familiar sound in the garden. My bedside clock confirms it's 6am and it's already quite light outside when I look to see the cat rooting through my bin bags again.

This time, Cat. Oh, it's on. As I open my bedroom door, I remember two things. Simon is in the room next door...and I'm standing on the landing in just my knickers! I don't want to miss the opportunity to get the cat, so I shoot back into my room to find something to throw on quickly. My eyes fall immediately on Simon's shirt, still lying on the bed. I put it on to check its level of decency and it just about covers my satin blues. My theory is that I'll be back up in my room in a matter of minutes. And besides, there are spare joggers and t-shirts in the utility room by the kitchen. *Job done.* Shirt buttoned up, I nip downstairs as fast and quietly as I can, making my way to the back door.

Door unlocked, I open it slowly. *No creaking.* A quick check and I can see the cat is still nose-deep in a bin bag. *Cat, this is your time.* I tiptoe over to the hose, turning on the tap, and quietly walk towards the cat with the hose unravelling as I go. I anticipate the cat's escape route this time, so I prepare myself for a moving target. I take aim and fire, full blast at the cat. It sidesteps my shot as before but I continue to deliver my attack and manage to hit my mark. This sends the cat into a panic and it darts in the other direction across the garden. I've prepared myself for him to go the other way so it leaves me a little off-balance but I maintain my onslaught. The cat has run almost an entire arc around the side of the garden with me responding accordingly. In the process of keeping up with the cat, my top half has reached a point of contortion where I can longer stay upright and have to put out a foot to steady myself. Due to the cat taking a different escape route though, my free foot has got entangled in the hose pipe. Ever tried walking with shoelaces tied together? Same thing here. As I fall over, I manage to twist my body so that I land on my back, hosepipe still running. I've somehow managed to tie myself up with the hose, unable to get up and unable to give my hose gun a good enough clout to turn it off. In short, I'm having an outside shower lying down in the garden at six in the morning. In Simon's shirt.

After what seems like hours - *it is certainly long enough* - I free myself from the hose and turn the spray away from me. I'm still lying down while clouting the gun and it eventually unjams itself. I'm panting like crazy, partly due to being saturated in cold water and also because it was a mini-workout. I look up to Simon's bedroom window and see that I've been spraying it while trying to turn off the gun, so retreat inside quickly before he wakes up. I get into the kitchen, close the door behind me and turn to face Simon standing by the coffee machine, glass of water in hand.

"Morning," he says, raising his glass slightly.

"Morning," I reply, a small puddle developing around my feet.

"Sleep well?" he asks, his head to one side with eyebrows raised.

"Yes thanks" I reply, doing my best to pretend everything is completely normal.

"Good, good. Shall I make you a coffee?"

"That would be nice."

Simon turns to prepare my caffeine fix, whistling a merry tune I can't quite place. *How is he keeping a straight face?*

I walk back upstairs to get ready for work, wondering why manufacturers make shirts that go transparent when wet.

At least I'm wearing nice pants.

CHAPTER EIGHT

Dressed and ready for work, I head back downstairs, holding Simon's shirt and a hoodie to substitute it. As I turn into the kitchen to put his shirt in the washing machine, Simon is standing over the hob topless, cooking. "I wasn't sure what you liked, so I guessed," he said. He is preparing beans in a saucepan with bread heating up in the toaster. The microwave pings and he removes scrambled eggs. He has already located a variety of herbs which get scattered on the eggs and he begins to dish up. "That looks amazing," I announce. He gives me a smile and gets back to serving.

I put the shirt in the washing machine and hand Simon my hoodie. He laughs and puts it on. As his head is still mid-hoodie I assure him it will fit because it's several sizes too big.

His eyes appear from the top of the hoodie. "Old boyfriend?"

"It was my Dad's." Simon makes a face as if to apologise while pulling the hoodie into place. I throw my arms around him, thanking him for breakfast. He pulls us apart slightly and kisses me passionately again.

"You're welcome," he whispers, once our lips separate. "Take a seat, madam."

The table has been laid with cutlery, pepper, ketchup and some other bits, and he has taken one of his flowers out of a vase and laid it at the space where I'm to sit. *He is perfect.*

As I sit down, a cappuccino is put in front of me. I gave him a surprised look, as few people ever know how to use a machine like mine. He then returns with our plates of breakfast and we sit down at the table together to eat. It's not the most amazing meal I've ever tasted, but the herbs in the egg is a lovely touch.

It's still quite early and I don't have to leave just yet, but I'm aware

Simon needs to. "I'm happy to drive you in this morning if you fancy a break from the bus," he offers. With a mouthful of egg and toast I nod approvingly. *I don't want a break from you, Mr. Fireman.*

Simon smiles and gets back to finishing his breakfast. We both finish around the same time, I thank him for the breakfast and he quips that he'll leave me to wash up. I giggle and nod to show how very fair this is.

"Your shirt won't be ready before we leave, but I can drop it to you in the week," I offer.

"It's yours now," says Simon. *A trophy?* "Besides," Simon says, looking at his plate as he collects his last bits of food onto his fork "it looked way better on you." He lifts his eyes up to me as he puts the fork to his mouth, winking. I roll my eyes and blush, smiling. He quietly chuckles.

I complete a few minor jobs and then announce I'm ready to go. Simon is putting on his suit jacket as I meet him at the door, and we kiss again. *I love this.*

We both head down the path and get into his car. No knicker flashing risk today as I'm wearing another trouser suit. Quite similar to yesterday's but different enough to prove to Mark that I do own other outfits.

As we head off down the road, I ask Simon how his work will take his hoodie.

"I have a spare uniform at the office, in case I have an accident with a hose," he says cheekily. *Git. Lovely, gorgeous git.* "I'm on flexi time anyway, so I can nip home to change and pretty much arrive when I like." *Cushy.* After hearing a little more about his job, it transpires Simon was being rather modest about his role. Essentially, all major responsibilities fall on this guy and he is often the chap to be seen on the TV when being questioned by reporters about a major job. That would explain the BMW then - he earns a mint, but works his backside off for it.

Simon drives us through a few side roads I didn't know existed, meaning the journey is much shorter than my usual commute. We end up driving past the bus stop where I normally alight, straight past Costa. I see Sally in there, preparing drinks for customers, but she doesn't look out. She'll be wondering where I am this morning - sorry *Sally, I've already had a cappuccino this morning!*

We pull up outside Marquis a few minutes later and I see Robbie sliding open the showroom doors. "Before you go, shall we swap a few more details?"

"Mmm," I reply, keen to get him on my grid. We swap Facebook profiles, alternative numbers and email addresses and then chuckle about how there's no escape from each other. *Not a chance, handsome. I'm all yours.*

"If it's okay with you," Simon asks "I'd like to change my status to 'in a relationship'." *I guess that's the new way of asking someone out.*

"I'd like that a lot," I reply, accompanied by a sincere look and slow nod.

"Have a great day," he whispers, as he leans in for a farewell kiss.

"Goodbye yourself," I whisper with a cheeky grin as I get out from the car. Simon drives off before I make my way across the road to commence day two with Marquis.

Robbie is getting up from his sliding position as I arrive and gives a double take when he realises it was me getting out of the car.

I walk in as coolly as possible.

"Personal chauffeur this morning?" says Robbie.

"Yep"

"Anyone interesting?"

"A Friend." I'm sure Robbie's not the village gossip but I've decided to keep my cards to my chest for a while at Marquis. *They don't have to know everything about me in the first week*

"He has good taste," Robbie says. I give him a quick inquisitive stare. "In cars," he clarifies.

I smile and walk onto the showroom floor. I receive a "Hiya" from Tania. I'm sure I can hear some dogs barking in the distance. "Hiya," I reply.

I place my coat on the same rack Tania did yesterday and head straight for the door marked "Kitchen" to unload my lunch into the company fridge. As I turn around to walk back out, I notice a large box. *No way.* It's a brand new Gaggia Classic. It's not the Rolls Royce of Gaggias, but it's just perfect for work-placed cappuccinos. I'm still drooling over it as Mark walks in.

"You like?" he asks.

Beaming at him, I reply "I like." *A lot.*

"Well, Robbie has his generous commission, Tania has an iPad. I thought you'd appreciate this."

"I do. Thanks so much." *I wouldn't have turned down the commission and bought one myself though.*

I offer to make everyone their favourite coffees and they all choose cappuccinos - *simple*. The car washers haven't arrived yet, so there are only three to make. The kitchen door has a wedge to keep it open so I use it in order to stay a part of the action. I decide to make the first cappuccino for Mark, it only seems fair. As the Gaggia is heating up I search for mugs in the cupboards and find one that says "Mark" on it in cartoon writing. My enviable ingenuity determines this must belong to Mark. I steam the milk to perfection, courtesy of the metal jug that has come with the machine. Creation complete, I walk it over to Mark while the next batch is staying warm on the heating plate. I knock and enter Mark's office. "Ah, a frothy coffee," he sighs, like it's the first luxury he has had in months. *Commoner*. "Thanks Gemma, have one yourself," he jokes. I laugh.

"I don't really like coffee," I joke. I can still hear Mark laughing as I walk away from the office. "I love it. I love it." *He still loves it.*

As I'm heading back to the kitchen, Mark calls me back. "Gemma, forgot to say before. We have a few perks here, one of them being you're welcome to borrow one of our cars if you ever need a flash motor. You know, for a wedding, or-"

"Or a job interview" I interrupt. More laughter, and more declarations of love. "Thanks, Mark." *I can't see me taking him up on the offer any time soon.*

Walking into the kitchen I hear an unmistakeable ping that tells me I have been tagged into a Facebook post. I pull my phone out of my handbag and scroll through the latest updates while trying to find mugs for Tania & Robbie. I've got hold of one for Tania when I see the the post:

Simon has asked to be your friend.

I smile and accept his request. Putting down Tania's mug I go on tiptoes to find Robbie's mug. Another ping sounds from the phone, just as I'm pulling a mug with my fingertips into a more manageable grip. Coming down from tiptoes with Robbie's mug in my hand, I see the post:

Simon is in a relationship with you.

I hold the phone and Robbie's mug close to my chest, closing my eyes and tilting my head upwards in a sentimental fashion. *I have a boyfriend. A super, gorgeous, gentleman of a boyfriend.* My little moment is interrupted by "Hiya!" and I drop both phone and mug. Fortunately, Robbie's mug strikes my foot giving it a soft landing. My phone has a protective rubber case around it due to previous butterfingered experiences so that also survives.

"Oh, sorry. Did I make you jump?"

Yes! " Don't worry, I was in a little world of my own," I share, with a wide grin.

Tania stops and narrows her eyes at me with a similar grin. "What happened to *you* last night?" The cards fall from my chest as I share almost everything with Tania. I didn't mention the surprise encounter with Bill on the back seat, but do share my involuntary wet shirt competition this morning.

"Oh, nightmare" she gasps, stifling a laugh. She seems unable to say 'Nightmare' properly. She pronounces it 'Nightmayer'. Still, considering her name is pronounced 'Tan-Eye-A', it probably seems perfectly normal to her.

She keeps me company while I finish making cappuccinos for her while telling me about her beau, John. They met at a club over the weekend and Tania seems ready to bear his children. I smile at how simply Tania appears to regard life. It's most refreshing, although not for me. Robbie soon arrives to take the coffees away with endless thanks. My official start time is almost upon me so I quickly update my status to match Simon's. He likes it almost instantly and so begins a barrage of pings from friends I forgot I had, showing how much they like my update. *This feels good. We must do a selfie next time we're together.*

I decide to turn my phone to silent until lunchtime so that I can be professional and avoid distractions. I've noticed Tania has adopted an opposite approach, spending more time on her phone than any work equipment, but I'll leave that with Mark to sort. This is a new me in a new job, *I'm going to make this work.*

The morning flies past and I'm largely left to deal with the spreadsheets I now oversee and maintain communication with previous clients. My main job for the day is to contact those who bought a car from us three years ago and enquire whether they're about to replace it with a newer model. I've got a pretty good phone voice and before long I've established a decent patter to get to the point quickly with those at the other end of the phone. I keep a log of all those who are interested and gauge how likely they are to visit. As well as having a few who agree to visit this week, one even says he would like to see our stock this afternoon. *My first potential sale!* I go and tell Mark, who is delighted (for me more than Marquis I think). "That's my girl - well done," he says. I can't fault his enthusiasm or support. He suggests that Robbie does the talking for this one while I stand with him and pick up the lingo. I share with Mark how relieved I am at this suggestion and he nods understandingly. "What's the time" asks Mark, quite randomly.

"It's almost 12pm," I reply.

"Lunchtime then," he says with raised eyebrows, indicating I've earned a break. I smile and go to the kitchen, grabbing my handbag on the way.

I've prepared a better lunch today after being so unsatisfied yesterday. Due to Mr. Fireman's breakfast though, I'm not famished by any stretch of the imagination. I get my lunch out of the fridge, sit down and see how many likes my status has received over the past few hours. *Quite a lot - I never knew I was this popular!* I notice that I have a couple of text messages, so I open the first one from my new man:

Missing you. Hope you're having a good day x

I miss you too, Mister. **It's going well - just booked my first enquiry this afternoon! X**

Well done you. Don't offer him any cheesecake, will you ;) x

Harsh x

I'll make it up to you x

Yes, you will ;) x

Tonight? x

It's Mum Tuesday. I can't give that a miss. I decide I'll phone Simon to explain. Before calling him I see who the other message is from and discover it's from Mum. *Maybe she's cancelling. She never cancels:*

Can I see you for lunch? Something terrible has happened.

My heart skips a beat. She never texts like this, so I'm wondering what the matter is. I decide to call her. She immediately answers the phone.

"Hi, Love," she says, sounding desperately upset.

"Hi, Mum. What's up?" *Has another uncle I've never met died?*

"I've lost everything."

"What do you mean, Mum?" I'm getting worried now.

Silence. I can hear Mum is struggling to catch her breath.

"Okay. Calm down, take some breaths and tell me what's going on." I can tell Mum is trying to compose herself. She eventually finds her voice.

"My property in Spain has gone tits up. I've lost all my money."

My jaw drops. I can't understand how a property she owns outright has gone under, but through her sobbing I pick up 'timeshare', 'fraud' and 'Bill'. *Bill! He's taken Mum's money somehow!* My heart skips a dozen more beats at the thought of my new boyfriend's dad shafting my mum out of her life savings.

I'm going to be sick.

CHAPTER NINE

My stomach regains control as I try to grasp the situation and be of use to Mum.

"Okay, where are you now," I ask her in an authoritative tone.

"On my way to the bank."

"Okay, I'll meet you there in half an hour."

I've been speaking quite loudly so that Mum will hear me through her state, so my colleagues have all realised something serious has happened. I turn to Mark and ask for an extended lunch, but he raises his hand to stop me speaking

"I got the gist. Go!" I shake my head at him with sincere eyes by way of an apology. *Who does this on their second day?* Tania offers to discard the remainder of my lunch and clear up, so I put my phone in my handbag and walk quickly to the door, leaving my coat. My pace turns into a jog as I near the end of the forecourt. Mum's bank isn't too far from my Costa bus stop, so I do my best to knock the eleven minutes down to as few as possible. All the way, I'm seething. I can't believe Bill would do this to Mum as he seemed so pleasant. *And what the hell am I going to do about Simon?* I can't go out with the son of a conman, especially a conman who ripped off my Mum. I keep thinking *Like father, like son* throughout the journey, wondering how on earth Simon could do the same thing. I then have a sudden panic, remembering that I left my purse at the restaurant last night while going to the loo. I turn on my phone to check my bank balance. *He hasn't taken anything yet.* I decide that I'll arrange to put a block on my account once I'm at the bank.

My panicking and fast walking mean I am in quite a state by the time I get to Mum who is standing outside the bank. When I get to her, we both embrace. Mum sobs her heart out, really loudly. Goodness knows what passersby are thinking. Eventually, Mum pulls away and says that she phoned ahead to the bank who have agreed to see her immediately. So, we both go in and are met at the door by the manager who introduces himself as Chris. He ushers us into an office, offering us both a coffee. I'm not in a place to care what type of coffee it is, so we both accept the offer. He leaves us alone to arrange our caffeine fix, handing mum a handful of tissues as he heads for the door.

"Okay, talk to me," I say, turning my chair to face Mum. She takes a deep breath and brings me up to speed.

"My property in Spain?" she begins. I nod. *Yes, I got that bit, get on with it!.*

"When I flew out with Bill to check on it last Summer, we looked into a timeshare investment. We went to a meeting where they laid on a spread of food and talked us through how it works."

"Who did?"

"Paraiso Estates."

"Okay..?" I shake my head slowly, indicating I have no idea who or what this is.

"They offered to trade my property for part ownership in a large timeshare of multiple properties on a new estate of villas nearby. I decided to go for it -"

"Without telling me!" I interrupt.

"Not now, Gem," she replies, with a pained expression to show she is suffering enough already without a hard time from her daughter.

"Sorry. Go on."

"It seemed an amazing investment, so I signed the apartment over to them and they drew up contracts for the timeshare. But there never was a timeshare. They've just taken my house and my money. I've lost

61

everything." She dissolves into another sobbing session to rival the last outside the bank. I sit on the very edge of my chair and hug her tightly. *That explains the BMW, Simon. I bet you're not even a fireman!*

"So, does Bill own Paraiso Estates outright?" I ask, although it hardly matters right now.

"What do you mean," Mum muffles, still firmly nuzzled into my shoulder.

"Is Bill solely to blame, or is there a large group of them?"

Mum pulls away from me, sorting out her nostrils and eyes with a tissue.

"What are you talking about? Bill invested in the same scheme. He's lost everything too."

I'm trying to focus entirely on Mum, but can't help breathe a sigh of relief that my man isn't crooked. *Oh great - now I feel guilt for judging him but elated that I'm so, so wrong.* I decide to put my own feelings to one side so I can be an effective support to Mum. As it happens, I'm thinking much more clearly now I know Mr Fireman isn't the son of Mr Fraudman.

Chris The Bank Manager comes back in with our coffees and I take a sip. *Not bad.*

"Mrs Sanders, I understand you may have been a victim of a timeshare scam, is that right?" *May have been! Look at her, you idiot.*

"Yes," mum sniffles.

"The police sent a bulletin to all banks in the country last night to say their Spanish counterparts were investigating a possible scam and to be prepared for a few phonecalls like yours this morning. I'm so sorry to hear your news, but it's looking like you have been added to the list of victims."

A list? "How many are there?" I ask. "Victims, I mean."

"We don't know for sure, but going by similar scams in the past it's likely to be dozens."

Mum and I both fall back into our chairs as the reality of the situation unfolds in front of us. Chris is very patient, allowing lots of silence for us to gather our thoughts. Either that, or he doesn't have a clue what to do. I decide to be proactive.

"Okay, so how do we get our money back?" Chris looks at me with a confused face.

I rephrase the question. "I mean, you're insured, right? If people clone a credit card you guys write it off, right?" Chris nods in agreement. "Yes, that's right, but -"

"So, you'll be able to get the money back for us. I appreciate it won't happen overnight, but you'll get it back," I nod keenly, to make sure I get an affirmative response. Chris leans forward from his leather seat, resting his forehands on the desk and linking his fingers.

"Miss Sanders - "

"Gemma." *We're way past formalities.*

"Gemma," he says, with a soft, compassionate tone. "I'll say it how it is." *About bloody time, Chris!*

"Your mum has been duped into part-owning properties that don't exist. The estate isn't on the map, it never will be. Paraios Estates is a phony company, set up by smooth-talking criminals who have spent the last twelve months convincing people to part with their hard earned cash, promising a lucrative return. As far as I understand, Spanish investigators have uncovered Paraios Estates and put a stop to its dodgy deals. Unfortunately for your Mum, she has already handed over her property so it's too late."

"But, the police have found them, so surely they can give it back." Chris shakes his head, looking so sorry for us.

"No. They have found the *company*. No doubt they will have

frozen the company assets but I'll bet it's worthless."

"So where are the gits who have Mum's money?" I demand.

"Soaking in a jacuzzi somewhere. Flying in their private jet to the Bahamas. Who knows, but I can promise you that the house has gone and you won't be getting it back. I'm sorry to be blunt."

We both continue to sit there, struggling to take everything in. As a million thoughts enter my head and I wonder how Mum is going to survive financially, I have a brainwave.

"Your house! The one here, our family home. There are all those adverts on the telly saying how you can unlock the equity and live off that."

"I can't do that Love," Mum sighs, looking down and shaking her head.

"You can! Sod the inheritance, it's your money. You can sell the house to the bank and live off the proceeds - you might do quite well out of it." I look eagerly towards Chris for him to back me up. He also nods to confirm the system. "Equity from homes has taken a hit in recent years, but we should be able to establish an attractive income for you." Chris' heightened enthusiasm is encouraging and we both look at Mum for her to see sense.

"Oh, Love," she says, exasperated. "I've already done that." My eyes widen to the size of saucers. "I sold it to the bank so that I could have a larger chunk of the timeshare." She breaks down again. "They said I'd be a millionaire in five years."

Oh, you silly woman. "Okay Mum, okay. Don't cry, we'll fix it." I look helplessly at Chris - he's busy tapping on his computer, and stops when he reaches the appropriate screen. He returns the same helpless look which confirms Mum has handed over ownership of the house to them. And then, awkwardly, he apologises that he has other customers waiting to meet him but tells me that he will notify the police and get them to make contact. I give an understanding nod and lead Mum out of the office with a tight grip around her shoulder. "Let's wait for the police and see what they have to say." Mum nods with a body language that suggests it will be a fruitless conversation.

I offer to keep Mum company on the way home, but she refuses. "You need to go back to work, Love. Don't worry about me, I'll be fine." I begin to insist, but she gives me the look Mums give when they don't want to be argued with. I smile, kiss her on the cheek and walk her to the bus stop.

The bus is already there when we arrive. Mum scoffs how her luck must be in.

"I'll be over later - it's Mum Tuesday." She turns and gives me a feeble smile and nod as she gets on the bus. I try to catch her eye as the bus departs, but she's looking down. The woman looks like she's aged 20 years in the last half an hour. I sob as I begin my walk back to Marquis Cars.

Passing my favourite coffee shop, Sally shouts from the doorway. "What's up, Lovely?"

I turn to her and assure her I'm fine and that I'll see her tomorrow.

She gives me a concerned face and mouths "Are you okay?"

I smile through the tears and give her a reassuring nod, then turn to continue my walk. I dig my phone out of my handbag to text Simon. As the screen comes to life, it reminds me that I've still to reply to Simon's text from earlier. I get busy tapping a reply:

Have you spoken to your Dad today? x

No. Why? x

I think you need to call him. x

CHAPTER TEN

As it happens, my time with Mum hasn't expanded much beyond my usual lunch hour which is a relief. Robbie is sat in the Porsche with a client as I cross the forecourt, opening and closing the roof. I can tell he is in mid-sale mode but still offers me a nod. I give a smile through pursed lips as I head into the showroom. Tania jumps out of her seat and walks quickly to me without adjusting her bright orange skirt. "Hiya" she says, in the lowest tone I've ever heard from her. "How's your Mum," she asks with a genuinely concerned face. *Tania's lovely.*

"Not good" I reply, shaking my head. I begin to explain the main details with her as Mark walks over and sits on the edge of Tania's desk, similarly concerned. They let me share as much as I know, interjecting with the occasional expletive or sharp intake of breath. Mark is the first to deliver a full sentence when I pause for breath.

"Look, let me know if you need anything - time off, use of the photocopier - whatever you need, it's yours." *They're both lovely.* I put my hand on his forearm to show my appreciation.

"This is not how I usually behave at work. And it's only my second day-"

Mark holds his hand up like he did earlier, showing me there is no need to apologise. *Really lovely.*

I take a huge breath and Tania jumps in with "If you need to cry, just cry." I explain that I think I did all the sobbing I needed to on the way over. "Well, if you decide you have more crying to do, just do it." It seems like Tania needs to see tears to add weight to the situation - I'm sure I'll deliver the goods at some point. In the meantime, I have a more pressing need.

"Coffee?" I say. They both look at each other and laugh, probably relieved that their new colleague is able to shelve personal dramas and get back to work.

"We both tried to get the machine working and failed," Mark confesses. "Seriously, I think you need a degree in operating the thing!" I chuckle through tears and get orders in for a round of cappuccinos.

The next couple of hours fly by and at around 4pm I get a text from my handsome man. My personal rule of turning off my phone at work has lasted all of 24 hours.

We're both coming over to your Mum's tonight to chat things through x

I'm delighted that I get to see him again so soon - I doubt it'll be a fun-packed time though.

Looking forward to seeing you x

Ditto x

As I'm sending the last message I notice a chap walking slowly around the cars. Tania is in the filing room sorting paperwork, Mark is busy in his office and Robbie is on a test drive. I swallow. Hard. I get up from my desk and walk over to the guy who by this point is almost at the showroom entrance. As he turns to face me, I give him a warm smile and continue with my purposeful walk. *Start confident, Gem.*

"Afternoon," I offer, and he responds with "Hi, I'm here to see Gemma." *Gemma? Why is he here to see me?* And then the penny drops. *He's the client I phoned earlier.*

"Of course, you must be Phil." He nods, appearing slightly annoyed that I may have forgotten he was coming. I continue unperturbed by talking about Phil's current car and if it fulfils his needs.

He explains that his current 3-series coupe has served him well but would like to consider an SUV as he now has two children. "Wow, you've

67

been busy," I exclaim. *Too forward, Gem.*

"Tell me about it - life is rather different to what it was last time I was here!"

We both laugh. *Not too forward, Gem - good girl.* I share that we have a number of SUVs around the lot and encourage him into the showroom first to see the X5 next to my desk. As we're walking through, I offer him a range of coffees.

"I'd love a cappuccino," he replies. *I am in my element.* I leave him to browse the car and encourage him to pop the bonnet - it has dawned on me that I haven't the foggiest idea how to open it, so it'll stop me looking like an idiot if I leave it to him. He thanks me and I nip off to get the coffee made. As I walk to the kitchen, Tania throws me a smile and looks excitedly at me. *I can do this.*

The Gaggia is a relatively simple system, although Mark and Tania would disagree, so I'm heading back to Phil with his cappuccino in just a few minutes. He is in the back seat checking out the anchor points for car seats and seeing how much room is available. "Big enough?" I ask.

"I think so," replies Phil "although I could do with having the car seats here to see what room we have."

"Well," I offer, "If you're up for a test drive we could swing by your home and put them in if they're there."

Phil steps out of the car and straightens up with a thoughtful look, as if accessing a diary in his memory. "The other half doesn't work on Tuesdays, so she should be at home. I'll give her a call." He walks out of the showroom to do the necessaries. I decide this is a perfect time to update Mark on things and see precisely what needs to be done to complete a test drive. Mark gives me a look to suggest he's impressed at my initiative and explains that I should ask Tania to make our insurance valid for the test drive. He then tells me to see which cars need to be moved from the forecourt to allow the X5 to get onto the road. I nod and head back out of the door, my heart beating a little faster than before, and see Phil coming back to the showroom.

"The wife is in, so we're good to go."

"Great." I reply. "I just need to do some juggling with cars and then we can get on our way" I explain.

Phil nods and I take him over to Tania to sort out the insurance details. Going out to the forecourt I notice there are only two cars that need moving; an Alfa Romeo Brera and an Audi S6. After retrieving the right keys from the cabinet, I decide to move the Brera first because it only needs to move a short distance and will help build my confidence. I am wearing flatter shoes today, so get straight into moving the car. As I'm completing my manoeuvre, I notice Robbie returning from his test drive. He appears to be encouraging the client into the showroom but he declines. I'm just getting out of the Brera as they shake hands and the client walks off to his car. Robbie is looking down until he is about 5 metres away and then looks up to see me throwing a key to him. "Here," I say, nodding to the S6. "Shift that for me."

He looks quite startled at what just happened, so he stops his walk and just looks at me with his jaw open slightly.

"You *can* drive, can't you?" I say, with a cheeky wink, and walk back to Phil who is still with Tania.

They have completed the paperwork as I get to them, so Phil follows me to the X5. Mark is putting trade plates on the vehicle as we get to it. *I've always wondered what those red number plates hanging off cars were for.* I gesture for Phil to get in the passenger seat and I walk round to the driver's side. I get the car off the forecourt without drama and we're soon at Phil's home. His wife is already standing outside the house with a car seat, so Phil introduces me and gets to work testing the space for the seats.

For anyone with baby twins, Phil can confirm the X5 has ample room to fit baby seats without parents contorting too much. Phil looks at his wife with keen eyes, as if to say, "Look, it's practical. Let's ignore the fact it's a gas-guzzling 4.0 litre petrol." His wife rolls her eyes in submission. I laugh at them both. Phil drives us back a longer way to Marquis so he can test the car on various roads. *He's not a bad driver.* He makes a variety of comments throughout the journey about how well the car copes in various situations. He especially seems to like how well it launches to a healthy speed from a standing start. I find myself holding onto my seat a few times as he performs this test a few more times, hoping he can't see. As we pull into Marquis' forecourt, Phil slows to a crawl to negotiate all the cars on our way back to the showroom.

As he brings the car back to its original space, Robbie walks towards my door looking concerned. Engine off, we both exit the vehicle and Phil hands me the keys. Robbie is about to say something to me, but Mark calls over to him.

"Robbie, can you help me with something for a sec?" Robbie's shoulders drop, he nods disappointedly and walks over to him.

"What do you think?" I ask Phil, as I return the keys to the cabinet. "Honestly? It's perfect," he replies. *Another bladder moment.*

"Great," I reply. "Grab a seat and I'll be right back." Phil nods and sits at my desk.

As I go to Mark's office I can see he and Robbie in deep discussion about something. I don't feel it's right to disturb them, but I'm keen not to leave Phil waiting. Mark fortunately sees me hovering through his window and beckons me in. "I need a little help. I think I've just sold my first car...and I don't know what to do!" I confess. Mark gives Robbie a look as if to say "See?" and Robbie looks down. He then chuckles to himself and looks back at me.

"Well done, Gemma," Robbie sighs, with a smile. "Really, well done. Come on, I'll give you a hand."

I look back at Mark, and he gives me a subtle thumbs up. I'm not sure whether it's to congratulate me on my first sale or to acknowledge that just a few hours ago I had a sobbing Mum in my arms at the bank. As we're heading over to Phil, Robbie explains that he lost out on the Porsche sale because the roof stopped working. "It was fine to open, but just wouldn't close. I'll get the garage onto it, it's probably a dodgy fuse."

Robbie is first to reach Phil as we get to my desk. He then pulls another chair around to my side of the desk and leads me through the process. Phil is very patient, and after half an hour we've established part exchange deals, deposits and finance arrangements. We agree to have the car ready next week, phoning Phil in a couple of days to confirm the exact date and time. Handshakes are exchanged and Phil makes his way back to his 3-series coupe for one of the last drives they will have together. *I've just sold a car.*

Tania walks hurriedly over to me from her desk without adjusting her bright orange skirt, and gives me a huge hug. "I don't believe it - well done you. When he turned up, and Robbie wasn't here, I thought 'Nightmayer'!" I laugh.

Robbie is next to congratulate me. "I have to say Gemma," he says "you owned it. Well done." I give him thankful eyes to assure him that we're not in competition.

I turn to Mark and I'm given a long, long hug. *Okay, you can let go now.* Releasing his hold, once Tania and Robbie are out of earshot Mark whispers, "Don't let a customer drive a car back onto the forecourt again, make them leave it on the road and we'll drive them in afterwards." I nod understandingly while looking down. He lifts my chin up with his finger. *Getting weird again.* "You did great," he assures, looking deep into my eyes. I give an appreciative smile.

The final hour is filled with Robbie talking me through the pile of paperwork that needs to be completed when a car is sold. Phil also has a personal number plate so I'm shown how to arrange the transfer to the X5. We then discuss booking in a valet and getting it taxed. I struggle to take it all in, but Robbie assures me that it'll sink in eventually. *He's lovely too. A full house.*

And that is the end of Day Two. Tania has already gone when I give my farewells and Mark wishes me all the best with tonight's discussions.

As I walk through the cars in the forecourt, I notice a familiar white BMW at the roadside. I beam as I open the door. "I was just passing…" Simon says, sarcastically. I chuckle quietly and get in the car. As I close the door, I see Mark giving me a double-take. He gives a comedy expression like I've broken his heart and follows it up with a broad smile.

Phew.

CHAPTER ELEVEN

"How are you?" Simon asks.

"I'm okay," I reply. *All things considered.* He nods. "How are you?"

"Well," he chuckles sarcastically, "I haven't done an awful lot of work today." I scoff too, knowing exactly what he means.

"I've found him Gem." *He called me Gem. He's using my nickname! It sounds lovely.*

"Found who?"

"The git who shafted them."

"Seriously?" *Let's go visit him and remove his testicles.* "Where is he?"

"Sorry, I mean I found him online."

"Oh." His Testicles are safe for now.

Simon doesn't give much more information because he wants Mum & Bill to hear it all as well, so I change the subject and tell him about how my first car sale went. I can tell Simon is happy for me and he squeezes my leg while saying "Well done, you." He then keeps his hand on my leg for the rest of the journey. *The perks of driving an automatic.*

It takes a while longer to get to Mum's through the rush hour traffic but The Charlatans, The Beautiful South and The Lightning Seeds keep us company. I also ask Simon to swing by an off license on the way so I can get a bottle of Vina Maipo. When we arrive, Bill's car is parked on the driveway so we have to park on the street. The house is on my side of the car when we pull up, so I wait for Simon to join me before walking up the path to Mum's. As he steps onto the pavement, he gives me a wide grin and pulls me in for a quick snog. His hands travel to my backside, giving both cheeks a little squeeze. *Two can play at that game, Mister.*

Snog complete, *(And very nice it was too),* I take Simon's hand and lead him to Mum's front door. I let us in using the key I've had since I was at school. Simon laughs at its Minnie Mouse rubber identifier. I give him a look like he's a naughty boy who will be punished. *Missing Fifty Shades, Gem?*

I can hear Mum & Bill talking in the kitchen so in we walk, holding hands. They both stop talking as we walk in. Bill gives us a smile. Simon has obviously told his dad we're an item already - Mum looks at me and her eyes dart between the two of us before a huge grin spreads across her face. I squeeze Simon's hand tightly. *She approves.*

"I'm so sorry to hear your news, Pam," Simon says. I look at Bill, nodding to echo the sentiment.

"Thanks Simon," Mum answers, dabbing at her nostrils with a tissue. *She's been crying all day.*

"Any luck, boy?" Bill asks Simon.

"Some," he replies, pushing out his bottom lip and producing some folded paper from his jacket's inside pocket.

We join them at the kitchen table once I get us all a glass of red wine to hear what Simon has to tell us.

"Okay," he says, unfolding the paper. "The man behind all of this is a Mr Steve Parsons. There are already a few websites accusing him of doing similar things in the past, and each time he has avoided the authorities."

"How?" enquires Bill.

"It's not entirely clear, but he seems to be using a mixture of aliases and fake companies to cover his tracks."

"So when his dodgy deals are uncovered, there's nothing on him," Bill confirms, beginning to understand how the cons work.

"In a word, yes. Some people tried to sue him a few years back and he was found to have no assets so it was fruitless suing him. And he stayed out of prison too."

"How?" I splutter, nearly choking on my red wine.

"Smart-talking lawyers and a few payments to the right people by the looks of things."

Mum swears loudly. I have never heard her use *that* word before!

"And do you remember that weekly documentary about dodgy traders last year?"

"That was *him?*" Mum says, burying her face in her hands. I know why it bothers her - we watched that episode together.

I try to bring us back to the present issue. "Okay, so where does that leave us?"

We all look to Simon for the solution. He sighs and looks down.

"Look-" Simon begins, before being interrupted by the doorbell.

As I was growing up, Mum would always ask Dad who was at the door if the bell sounded. He would often reply with a sarcastic remark to remind her that he isn't psychic. Mum looks like she wants to ask the same question now. I get up to answer the door. There is a well dressed gentleman on the step, smiling. "Mrs Sanders?" he asks, showing his police identification.

"No, I'm her daughter. Come in." He gives a nod of appreciation and enters the house, wiping his feet before walking through the hallway. The kitchen is rather crowded now and he refuses the offer of a seat, choosing to stay in the doorway.

He explains that details are still sketchy but confirms that everything the bank said is true: Mum has indeed been the victim of a scam and is to prepare herself for what they consider to be the inevitable. "I'm not cheapening what's happened to you, Love, it's awful. But, we've heard of

75

some people selling both their foreign properties AND cashing in on their own homes-"

He stops mid sentence, Mum's face telling him that she is one of them. He purses his lips and looks at all of us in turn sympathetically. *Silly, silly woman.* The policeman continues. "He has played the system so that he is untouchable. Spanish police are doing all they can, but their laws work differently to ours in various ways-"

Bill cuts in and explains that he too has been a victim. The policeman looks through some paper and confirms he is someone they are due to speak to in the coming days. He ticks his name off the list.

"So, what can be done to bring Mr Parsons to justice?" asks Simon, already knowing the answer.

"You've done some homework haven't you, buddy?" The policeman says. He takes a breath. "Short of the guy suddenly growing a conscience, there's nothing we can do. I'm truly sorry."

We've had it confirmed several times now so it's time to face reality.

The policeman hands mum a couple of leaflets about coping with the current situation and seeking debt advice, and I get up again to see the policeman out. Simon walks with us to thank him as he leaves. *I thank washing machine men for taking my hard earned cash, Simon thanks policemen for telling him our parents' money is all gone.*

"Don't do anything silly," the policeman warns Simon. Simon doesn't reply and closes the door.

"What did he mean?" I ask.

"He means don't fly to Spain and rip the guy's heart out." *He hasn't got one. Go for the testicles.*

The rest of the evening is a rather dull affair. Mum and Bill try to lighten the mood (stiff upper lip and all that, classic Brits!) and I'm in awe at their resilience.

Simon eventually says, "We need a change of scenery. Pub!"

"Sorry, Love. I don't really feel like it tonight. But don't let that stop you two heading out." Mum smiles at me. "Go on, have a breather - and thanks Simon for all you've done."

Bill chooses to keep Mum company, so Simon and I head for the local pub. For the first time since I can remember, Mum Tuesday hasn't happened.

On the way to the pub, my pocket wolf whistles. Simon gives me a strange look even though he knows what it's likely to be. *Cheeky boy.*

The text message is from Nat:

Saw a fancy car outside yours this morning. Hiding something from me? X

I apologise to Simon for replying, and he waves it off as completely acceptable. "Unless it's another bloke," he says. I return a slight grin and narrow my eyes at him.

My latest Facebook status will explain the car. But I've had a crazy day with Mum, she's been scammed out of loads of money by some git in Spain. Talk later. x

What??? That was on the news this evening! Awful! Let me know if I can do anything.

Fancy getting together Thursday night?

Done. I'll be over at 8. Unless you have other plans - I just saw your status ;) x

I smile, pocket the phone and resume holding Simon's hand. We don't talk much for the rest of the walk.

We're at the pub within a couple of minutes. Simon holds the door for me so I walk in first. As I enter the bar, I have a flashback. Mum & Dad used to come here all the time. Back then, the place was heaving with couples and friends socialising, lively music playing, the pool table crowded and karaoke nights often featuring too. As my eyes scan the room, I establish that we've just doubled the number in the room; and one of those is the barman, who is talking to the other patron. As I walk to the pumps, the barman pulls himself up from leaning over the bar to serve us. The other chap turns his head to watch a football match which is on mute. I've just realised I don't know what Simon's favourite drink is, although I remember Bill ordering him a lager at the Indian restaurant.. "What are you having?" I ask.

"A lemonade and lime, please." *I wasn't expecting that. Of course, he's driving again.* I order two of them, pay and carry them for us. I feel it's about time I bought Simon something. We find a quiet corner, although in reality all the corners are quiet, and talk some more about the day's events.

"How is your mum financially after all this, Gem?" Simon asks, sipping his drink.

"Well, she'll have her state pension but other than a small amount of savings, that's it." I get upset as I remind myself how Mum's life has suddenly changed. Simon hands me a napkin from an adjacent table.

"How about your Dad?" I ask, wiping my eyes.

"It's bad. He only rents because Mum took the house when she left him. The Spanish home was the only nest egg he has. He has some cash in the bank like Pam, but only enough to replace his car when it gets old in a few years." We establish that they will both survive but Mum will certainly have had her last cruise. Or new pair of shoes. Or takeaway. They will just exist, no luxuries. *What sort of life is that when someone has robbed you?*

"I'm tempted to go visit this Mr Parsons and have a little word with him," Simon says, with an air about him I've never witnessed before. I give him a concerned look.

"I've only just met you," I reply. "I'd quite like it if you didn't go to prison just yet." Simon chuckles.

"That won't happen," he assures me, picking up my hand to kiss it.

We spend around half an hour in the pub chatting about dishonesty and wondering how people can live with themselves before deciding it would be good to head back and check on Mum and Bill. Simon returns the glasses to the barman - *it's been a busy night for him, so it's good to save him the extra walk* - and we stroll back.

Once we get back to Mum's, we pop in on them to check they're alright. As I go into the living room, I notice they've both fallen asleep on the sofa in front of some junk on the TV. We both smile at each other and decide to leave them to it. Simon drives me home but explains that he needs to get home to be ready for a longer shift tomorrow. "I've got to catch up on all the work I didn't do today" he explains.

As he pulls to a stop outside my home, I lean over and give him a long kiss, squeezing his leg. "See you soon."

He waits until I'm in the house and closing the door before he drives off. *Such a gentleman.*

I kick off my shoes, tidy the house a little, turn off the lights and head upstairs for another evening bathroom routine. I'm collapsing into bed about half an hour later when I receive a wolf whistle from my new boyfriend.

Free this weekend? x

Yep. x

Good. We're going to Spain. x

Ok. x

I'm going to Spain. For the weekend.

CHAPTER TWELVE

After dreams of Spanish holidays and severed testicles, I wake up to my non-Nat alarm clock and jump straight out of bed. *Come on world, bring it on!*

I decide to repeat Simon's breakfast treat and get some more beans, eggs and toast on the go. While things are heating up and my cappuccino is being made, a wolf whistle fills the room.

Morning gorgeous! *Gorgeous. Me!* **Not sure I'll get to see you today. Drink tomorrow? x**

No! It's Nat Thursday!

I'm seeing Nat tomorrow evening :(But you can pop over before x

Sounds like a plan. Pick u up from work again? X

That would be lovely. Have a good day x

You too. See you tomorrow x

A day without my man. At least we have a healthy text life. I'm getting through my new purchases of outfits so decide to load the washing machine before leaving the house. I smile at my newly-discovered level of organisation.

The bus journey is uneventful and I manage to adhere to The Code throughout. Sally sees me get off the bus and gets my cappuccino in the making as I walk towards the door. *Second caffeine fix in an hour - I might need to cut down at work today.* She gives me a concerned look as I go in and I remember that she last saw me in quite a state following Mum's news. I explain all while I'm in the queue and she comments how, like Nat, she also had seen a news story about it.

"I'm so sorry, Gem. Let me know if there is anything I can do."

I thank her for her compassion, pay up and get on with my eleven minute walk. As I begin my familiar route, I wonder how many miles I'll clock up over the course of a week. *I should get a fitness tracker.*

The day starts with a mini-inquisition from Mark about my chauffeur last night. I confess that Simon is my boyfriend. "I thought you were saving yourself for me!" he jokes. "I tell you what," I reply, "if it doesn't work out between us, I'll give you a call."

Mark releases a loud chortle, going back to his office "I love it. I love it." *He still loves it.* As he closes his door and makes his way to his seat, he puts his hand to the side of his face to resemble a telephone. "Call me," he mouths, with a cheeky grin. I give him an overly-enthusiastic thumbs up which earns chuckles from Tania and Robbie who have been bystanders the whole time.

The end of the day arrives rather quickly, with Tania turning off her computer and going to the kitchen to collect her lunch things. Robbie and Mark both come onto the showroom at the same time so we start our farewells. There is a loud clatter as Tania drops a handful of cutlery walking back from the kitchen. "Nightmayer" she sighs, collecting them up. Her skirt length as it always is, she leaves little to the imagination as she bends over to pick up the utensils on the floor. Robbie buries his head in his hands out of disbelief that she has no inhibitions. I look over to Mark who also finds it amusing...and good viewing. *Perv.*

Once Tania has got herself together, I ask her what she's doing with all the cutlery. "I thought I'd take them home to give them a good clean." Robbie looks at her confusingly. "But, we have a sink and washing up liquid in there," pointing to the kitchen she has just walked out of. "Oh. Oh, yeah," she says with a giggle that resembles a chipmunk mating call. We all laugh as Tania puts the cutlery back in the kitchen and I head out to the forecourt to begin my walk to the bus stop.

"No Beemer today?" Mark calls out from behind.

"Not today," I reply. "I don't want to torture you any more than I already am," I tease. Mark laughs as he starts to slide shut the showroom doors. "I love it. I love it" can be heard as I cross the road.

I swing by Tesco on the way home to grab myself some dinner. I choose to go for a chicken salad tonight by way of a crash diet for my trip to Spain in a couple of days. *I can lose a stone in two days, no problem.*

Apart from the odd text to my man and phoning Mum to see how she is today - *she is doing well, all things considered* - the evening soon turns into bedtime. As I'm sliding between the sheets, my dressing table wolf whistles:

Night, gorgeous. X *I love this nickname!*

Ditto. Looking forward to seeing you tomorrow. x

Going to bed with a massive grin is a treat. It would be more of a treat going to bed with my man though. *Down, girl. You've got to marry him first, remember?*

No dreams of Spanish holidays and severed testicles this time. Weirdly, I can only recall dreaming of Tania's skirts getting shorter and shorter until they don't exist. Mark responds by giving her a payrise but it makes Robbie jealous. So, he starts wearing brightly coloured mini skirts to work too. *Dreams can get very odd, very quickly.*

Today becomes quite a blur, because I cannot get Simon out of my mind. *This is crazy, I've never felt like this about anyone before.* Fortunately, the day shoots past and I keenly look for my white chariot to collect me. *He's there. My man is already waiting.* We exchange a long, lingering kiss in the car. *Perhaps we should be apart more often!* The journey to my home is spent chatting mostly about Simon's plans for our trip to Spain.

"Gem, I've found out a bit more about Parsons."

"Go on," I respond, keen to know what Simon's thinking.

"He isn't in Spain anymore." My heart sinks.

"Where is he then?" Simon looks to me with a smile. "England."

My saucer eyes make an appearance at the revelation, although I'm not sure what difference it makes. "I guess we don't need to go to Spain at the weekend then," I say, in a matter-of-fact tone. I'm desperately disappointed, but don't want to show it. After all, it wasn't meant to be a holiday.

"Well, the tickets are booked and the villa is sorted." *Villa?* "There won't be much of a refund at this late notice, so I'm still up for going...if you are?" he ends, with a hopeful expression.

"I'm sure I can manage it," I joke. *We're still allowed to have a break together.* Simon's hand ends up on my knee again and I put my hand on top to make sure it stays there.

Simon explains that, although discovering Parsons is back in the UK, we can still find out as much as we can about him while in Spain. During his online research, he also found a support group for expats who have been stung by Parsons in the scam, so suggests it would be a good idea to attend a meeting they have planned over the weekend.

"Great idea," I announce, in awe at how clever my man is. *Compassionate, intelligent, a gentleman, nice bum...he has it all.*

We're soon at the house and I'm first onto the garden path. As I make my way to the front door, my feline nemesis bolts from a small hedge and up and over my fence. *Keep running, cat.* "You know, the best way to get rid of them is by spraying them with a hose," Simon says with feigned sincerity.

As I'm opening the door, I turn round to Simon with narrow eyes. "Really?" acting annoyed. "I must try that."

Simon chuckles quietly. "Let me know when you do and I'll have my camera ready!" Simon can't see me rolling my eyes as I open the door, but he can tell I'm still on the verge of mortification at the see-through wakeup call I gave him a few days ago. He taps my backside as I'm heading indoors and I make a mental note to wind him up when he cocks up in the future. *I can't see that happening though, my man is perfect.*

I make Simon dinner, opting to use the remainder of last night's chicken to make a Mexican stir fry with fajitas. Judging by his choices at the Indian restaurant, I decide to make it rather spicy. He goes through a pint of water in the process, so I tease him about being a lightweight. The reactions I get suggest he enjoys a girlfriend who will give as good as she gets in the Wind Up Department. *Good job, Mister!*

After dinner, I load the dishwasher while Simon makes us a drink and we head to the living room to enjoy the cappuccinos he has made. I remember how we didn't even touch the last ones that were made due to a snogging marathon; This time, we are far more sensible and enjoy the drinks with my playlist entertaining us in the background. It dawns on me that my song collection is not as plentiful as my man's and the days of mixtapes are gone. *Such is life.*

We discuss a little more about Spain while also discussing how our parents are holding up. One thing leads to another and I end up cracking a joke before I think it through. "What if they end up getting married?" Simon pauses, mid-sip. The corners of his mouth turn upwards and then he finishes his sip.

"That would be weird," he replies, with a thoughtful look. He then looks at me to clarify, "But I would have no objections."

I nod in agreement and take a large swig of coffee, Simon following up with, "That would make you my step-sister though." I spit my mouthful of cappuccino over the coffee table and myself. Simon roars with laughter and goes to the kitchen to get a cloth. He's still laughing while searching for cleaning products and I run upstairs to change my clothes for something drier. I throw on some joggers and a hoodie and head back downstairs with my blouse and skirt, putting them both in a washing-up bowl of detergent to soak.

I get back into the living room just as Simon is finishing clearing up. He looks at me, pauses and laughs some more. I roll my eyes. *When you eventually put a foot wrong, I'm going to revel in it, Chum!* He appears to read my thoughts, gets up and gives me a massive hug in the doorway. Ending up in a snog, I push him over the arm of the sofa so that we're both lying down on it. Giggling, we carry on our snog marathon until we're interrupted by the doorbell. *Nat!.* I roll off the sofa and pull Simon up to a sitting position. As I go to answer the door, he grabs his mug to finish off his cappuccino.

"All okay?" Nat asks, as I open the door.

"Fine, thanks," I reply, both exchanging mischievous smiles. I realise that Nat has noticed Simon's car outside, so walks past me to meet Mr Perfect.

"Hi. I'm Nat. You must be Simon."

Simon gives a confused look. "Who's Simon?"

Nat looks awkwardly at me and I play along with Simon's wind-up by looking awkwardly back.

"But-" Nat begins, looking back at Simon. She sees him smiling and laughs at being so gullible. Simon apologises for his sense of humour while giving Nat a friendly peck on the cheek.

"Coffee?" he offers, looking at us both. We both return keen nods and head for the sofa while Simon performs his barista skills for the second time this evening.

"Wow" Nat whispers. "This is *him!*" I nod in a way that says I need to pinch myself every half hour to check it's really happening. "Let's shelve this little convo for later," she whispers, with a wink. "Mum - what's the score?" I love Nat, she's so thoughtful and amazing at remembering everyone else's dilemmas. I bring her up to speed with the events and explain how nothing can be done. She shares her thoughts, adding a timely expletive every few sentences. Simon walks in during one of Nat's exclamations of illegitimacy, making him stop dead in the doorway. "Not you, Simon, this Spanish conman." Simon lifts his head to show the penny has dropped and continues walking into the living room to place our drinks on the table.

"He's not Spanish," I explain to Nat. Nat looks up to me while grabbing her mug with a look that suggests it makes it even worse that a Brit can rip off one of their own. *It makes no difference to me.*

Simon interrupts the moment by saying "I'm going to head off, Gem. Nat, lovely to meet you and I hope to see you again soon."

"Likewise, Simon," Nat says with a genuine smile. I walk him to the door and we have a quick kiss.

"I'll pick you up from work tomorrow. Remember your passport," he whispers with a wink. I watch him go up the path, close the gate and get to his door. He blows me a kiss as he gets in and I close the door as he drives off. Judging by the sound of the engine, I think it must be a straight-six. *Marquis has taught me a lot already!*

I walk back into the living room to be met with raised eyebrows and a cheeky grin from Nat. "Passport?" she asks with cheeky suspicion.

"Well, we have been seeing each other for *three days*. It's about time we had a mini-break in Spain!" I reply sarcastically. Nat laughs. "And why didn't you let yourself in like normal?" I question. She gives me a look with a raised eyebrow.

"I didn't want to *interrupt* anything. Are you packed yet?" I shake my head.

"It's not hard Nat - I have packed before." She shakes her head, looking down incredulously.

"Not for a holiday with a boyfriend, you haven't." *She's right.* I look at her and, without speaking, we both run upstairs to my bedroom like teenagers planning to go to a school disco. Nat flings open my wardrobe doors and starts rifling through my outfits. She selects my tight jeans, a variety of tops, a couple of short summer dresses and a pair of white three quarter-length trousers. I stand in awe at her ability to complete an assignment many women pain over for weeks. "Bikini?" she asks, looking around at various drawers it may be lurking in. *She'll struggle to find it.*

"I don't own one," I confess. Nat looks at me like I need a carer. I walk over to my knicker drawer and retrieve a rather sorry-looking swimsuit I haven't worn for some years. Nat takes one look, then at me, and we both laugh. *I can't take that.* "I'll have to head out tomorrow lunchtime and get something," I sigh, with a microscopic amount of enthusiasm. *This is the reason I do online shopping.*

"Hang on," Nat exclaims brightly, running downstairs. I hear a jangle of keys and a slam of my door, so I peer out of the window to see Nat running to hers. *She could have put her shoes on!*

I grab my small suitcase from the top of the wardrobe and manage to shower myself in months of dust and insects in the process. I decide to pack everything, minus swimsuit, in Nat's absence. I've just got to my knicker drawer when I hear Nat running back up the path so I decide to throw in all the new underwear I recently ordered. I add socks to the mix and I'm done, choosing to keep one of my summer dresses for the journey over. I turn round to see Nat standing in the doorway, twirling a yellow two-piece with black spots. Instantly, I get a song enter my head which Timmy Mallet covered in 1990:

"She wore an itsy bitsy teenie weenie

Yello polkadot bikini

That she wore for the first time today."

I give Nat an appreciative smile. *Maybe I will go shopping at lunchtime after all.*

I pack a few toiletries, making sure I stay under the liquid limit for airport security, and head back downstairs to join Nat who is busy loading the DVD player. *Of course - Fifty Shades!*

We chapter-hop the first movie so we can get the gist of the story (*lots of smacking, I remember now!*) and guess how we think the story will go into Part Two. The second is a very different affair, seeming more like a thriller than a soft porno for randy couples. EL James doesn't let us down though, and a few kinky toys make their appearance. Within a short time, we both conclude the movie isn't for us, citing a blend of mediocrity and repetition, and decide to turn some music on instead. *My playlist comes into its own yet again.* While demolishing a bottle of wine between us, we chat about what really makes us tick in the Romance Department. I establish that Simon is making things tick rather nicely so far, and Nat gushes how happy she is for me.

"Massage!" Nat exclaims, rather out of the blue. "Let him give you a back massage in Spain - see what his wooing skills are like." *Wooing skills? What are they?!*

"I can't just ask him for a back massage, Nat."

"Okay, then offer to give *him* one then." I raise an eyebrow at her. "A massage," she clarifies.

"Oh," I sigh, relieved. We both fall back into the sofa, laughing.

"Hang on!" Nat says, and rushes out of the door back to hers again. *I think she has worms.* She comes back in a flash with a bottle of liquid and throws it to me.

I read the bottle's label. "Massage oil?" I look at her with cheeky suspicion.

"I used it on a boyfriend last year for a Valentine's date night."

"Oh, yes - The Weirdo From Wapping," I recall, laughing. Nat groans and rolls her eyes painfully, also reminiscing. Nat hasn't had much success in the Romance Department. For an intelligent woman, she has managed to land herself mostly candidates for sectioning. I raise the bottle to her in appreciation.

"Do you know how to use that?" she asks. "It's not just a case of slathering it all over his chest, you know-" *Imagination - behave yourself.* "Although it's a start," she laughs, reading my thoughts. The rest of the evening contains mostly laughing, a chinese takeaway - *crash diet went well, then* - and demolishing another bottle of wine.

As Nat gets up to leave, she gives me a long hug. "Have a super time with your man." *My man!*

"I will. Thank you for the bikini." She laughs and waves it off.

As she's about to leave, she says, "Let me know if there's anything I can do to help your situation with Mum." I give her another hug to show my appreciation. After donning shoes and collecting her DVDs, she walks up the path and begins her short walk home, humming 'Itsy Bitsy Teenie Weenie Yellow Polka Dot Bikini'.

"Very funny" I call out. I load the dishwasher with the evening's things, noticing Simon's plate from earlier. I smile, get my phone out of my pocket and send him a text:

Nat thinks you're lovely. That makes two of us x

I chuckle quietly to myself as I press 'send' and rinse out my coffee-stained blouse and skirt to see what the damage is. I'm delighted to see the detergent has done its job and throw them both in the washing machine ready for my next load.

As I'm heading upstairs I get a wolf whistle. *This is becoming a routine!*

Pleased I passed the 'friend' test. See you after work tomorrow. Remember your sun cream.

Only if you rub it in. ;)x *Nat would be impressed at my ingenuity - a definite bridge to a back massage!*

As I turn on my bedroom light, I see all my holiday gear on the bed. I add Nat's massage oil to the suitcase, prepare my clothes for tomorrow and give the duvet a quick whip to remove the dust and insects from earlier.

To bed...

CHAPTER THIRTEEN

...and to work. Simon must have got up very early this morning as there is a single red rose waiting for me on my desk when I arrive. A small note accompanies it:

Can't wait to spend the weekend with you. Olé!

I look over to Mark who raises his eyebrows at me twice in quick succession. I roll my eyes in embarrassment, but secretly I'm loving the attention! I take a cappuccino over to Mark after a short while and he confesses that Simon had called him to arrange the early drop-off. "Hold onto him, Gemma. He seems lovely." He nods, with sincerity.

"He is," I confirm, blushing.

The day goes without drama and it is Tania who notices Simon pulling up outside. She trots over to me, adjusting her skirt as she goes. "He's here! He's here." She actually appears more excited than me.

"Well, it's not close of play yet, so he'll have to wait," I say dominantly. Tania is taken aback seeing this side of me, but I follow it up with a wink. She giggles and does a slow trot back to her desk. She's still giggling as she gathers her things. As I begin to shut down my computer, my office phone rings to indicate I have an internal call from Mark. *Strange.* "Hello?"

"Yeah, Gemma, sorry I forgot to mention it earlier. I need you to work this weekend because we have a few clients arriving." He says it with an authoritative voice.

"Okay..." I begin, wondering what on earth to do. I struggle to look at him, but eventually I cast my eyes over to him in his office. I'm met with the largest mischievous grin I've ever seen.

"You sod." More laughter.

"Have a lovely time - don't do anything I *would* do" he says, suggestively.

I give my boss, my wage-payer, a two-fingered gesture which he applauds, and make my way to the ladies to get changed. In a few minutes I'm in my summer dress with my office suit hanging in the bathroom for collection some time next week. *I didn't think that bit through.* And off I go to Simon, wheeling my case behind me. Simon gets out of the car as I walk across the road to him, takes my case from me and puts it in the boot next to his. I then receive a lovely, pre-holiday kiss. *I'm going to Spain with my man.* I giggle as I get into the passenger seat. As we drive off to the airport, I see Tania waving at me with both hands excitedly. *Nightmayer.*

The journey to the airport goes quickly as we talk about my first week at Marquis. I ask Simon how his day has been and he shares how he had to go on a shout today. He's selective in what he tells me, I guess because it hasn't been a pleasant experience. For him to have been called out, it must have been rather nasty. I put my hand on his leg and he glances me an appreciative smile. By the time we're parked and walking into the terminal, he's back to his usual self. We head to a small restaurant for dinner - I insist on paying, but Simon again refuses. "I can't take you away for the weekend and then expect you to pay for anything. So, no more protests!" he says with a half-serious look. I relent, and promise not to insist on paying any more. "Good," comes the reply.

After a quick meal together, we head for the departure lounge and the security search. I have already got hold of a plastic wallet for us both in which to put our liquids. I have brought a small stick of roll-on deodorant, shower gel and shampoo, so it takes little effort. Simon, on the other hand, has brought a small arsenal of toiletries with him including contact lens solution. *Who knew?!* He struggles to get all his items in his bag so I offer to take a few things from him. He jokes that I've taken a bottle of concealed drugs from him - I suggest it may be best not to make jokes like that in the security area of one of the busiest airports in the world.

After a small queue, we load our belongings onto the conveyor belts. Our suitcases are small enough to be hand luggage which is a huge timesaver. As I walk through the x-ray machine there is no bleep which is always a relief - *I remembered to leave my gun at home!*

As I walk to the end of the conveyor belt to collect my case, I'm told to collect it from another table. *Random search.* This hasn't happened to me before, but I've been with friends in the past who have had their entire contents removed as a course of practice. Highly embarrassing if you have lots of frilly knickers but I've packed mine in a logical fashion in anticipation. As a security guard opens my case, he asks me if there is anything I have in the case I haven't declared, such as excess liquids. I frown and confirm that I don't and that I have packed the case myself. As soon as the case is opened, my heart skips a beat. "Oh -" I begin. The security guard looks at me and then continues to root around my things. "There might be a bottle of oil in there." As I finish the sentence, he finds it and holds it out for me to see in a very accusatory manner. *Yes, I know it's there - I just told you.*

"Can you tell me what is in the content of this bottle, Madam," he asks in a very serious tone.

"It's massage oil." *It says it on the bottle.*

"Is it yours?"

"It's a friends, she lent it to me."

"For what purpose?" *Seriously?!*

I struggle to find an answer, and instead look incredibly guilty.

The guard opens the bottle, sniffs the contents, then offers it to another guard to sniff. They then walk away from me and show it to an official-looking chap who has been observing the entire affair from a distance. After a short discussion they walk over to me, binning the oil as they get close. After some advice on air travel, and reminding me how hard it is for the guards and how I should consider more carefully what I pack in future, they let me rejoin Simon in the departure lounge. He stands up from the seat he has been at and gives me a curious look. "Don't ask," I warn.

"Don't tell" he says, tapping my backside and putting his arm round me. *Blushing already. I feel like a terrorist!*

The flight itself is quick and simple and we are soon landing in Spain. As the plane doors open, a wall of heat hits us. We both close our eyes and put our heads back, enjoying the experience, before walking down the steps to the tarmac below. Getting through airport security is a hassle-free affair and we are soon in our hire car heading for the villa Simon has booked for us. I try to call Mum so she knows our plane wasn't hijacked, but there is no reply. *Strange.* Simon offers to call Bill to see if they're together, but there is no reply from him either. "They're probably making mad, passionate love to each other and can't hear the phone!" I shiver at the thought and then decide not to worry any more. *She's a grown woman - look after her, Bill.*

It's dark by the time we get to the villa, but it's lit up by a few security lights and looks stunning. *And it's all ours.*

Simon carries our cases to the door and calls out a 4-digit code for me to enter into a keysafe bolted to the wall. We let ourselves in, drop the cases and turn on the light in each room we inspect. The kitchen is one of the first rooms we come to and we find a large bowl of fruit and bottle of red wine as a welcome present from the villa owners. *Nice touch.* As we get to the living room area, one wall has french doors which open up to a patio. It strikes me how the large windows remind me of Marquis, only much, much posher. As I cup my hands to the glass to peer out, Simon locates the switch to turn on the exterior light. My jaw drops as the patio is bathed in tungsten, leading to a gorgeous blue swimming pool with a jacuzzi at one end. The underwater lights shine through the steam rising from the water. We both look at each other and produce wide grins while sliding open the french doors. I can't help thinking that we're Brits, in Spain, opening French doors. I'm the first to the pool and I kneel down and put my arm in to see how warm the water is. *Perfect.* Simon is looking at other parts of the patio area, so I call him over.

"Thank you," I whisper, hugging him tightly. *For the treat, and for being you.* My hands wander around his waist, which he seems to like. As it happens, I'm searching for phones, keys and anything else that may not be waterproof before exacting revenge on his smugness at my impromptu shower a few days earlier. As I pull out of the hug, I do a double-take to a spot at the bottom of the pool, adopting my best drama skills from high school. "What's that down there" I ask, pointing at the spot. As Simon turns to see it, I seize my moment and push him in. I've underestimated his athleticism though, because he manages to spin round while falling and pull me in with him. *Not what I had planned.* As we both surface, Simon gives me quite a surprised look and then starts laughing.

"I'm learning quite a bit about you, Gemma." "Good or bad," I ask him, treading water.

"All good," he says, as he moves in and kisses me passionately. *Okay, this isn't how it was supposed to end up, but I'm not disappointed at the outcome!.* After some more lengthy snogs in the pool, we both get out and dry ourselves using towels from an undercover store on the patio. It's a warm evening so neither of us feel especially cold, but Simon removes his jeans and shirt and puts on a robe from the same store. I don't overt my eyes during his stripping routine and am pleased to see everything in the right place, in healthy measure. I decide against stripping in front of Simon, in part due to me being more of a prude, but I'm also suspecting my white underwear will be more revealing than his black boxers.

Simon heads indoors to retrieve the red wine so I grab the opportunity to quickly strip and jump into a robe. I'm just resting back onto a sun lounger as Simon returns. He sees my discarded dress and smiles. "To a super break - and finding out more about Parsons," he says, clinking our glasses of wine together.

"To us," I add. He smiles warmly.

A patio heater keeps us warm as we finish the bottle by the pool, then we head into the living room to see what Spanish TV has to offer. *Not much.* We both look at each other after a few minutes of channel-hopping and chuckle. "Shall we just go to bed," suggests Simon. "We have a long day tomorrow." *Bed!* It dawns on me that we haven't discussed our expectations of each other this weekend. Simon, as ever the mind-reader, chuckles and reveals that there are two separate rooms, "before you have a cardiac arrest!" I feign insult, making out that I wasn't worried. He chuckles again, seeing right through me. *Am I that predictable?*

He walks over to both our cases and picks them up from where we left them by the door. "Come on you," he says, and I follow him down the short hallway. "Take your pick," he says, putting down my case and standing with a bedroom door either side of him. Blushing, I pick up my case and take the room on the right. As I hoped, it has a window overlooking the pool which means I should have the sun waking me up in the morning. It transpires that it's the bigger of the two rooms with an ensuite and sunken bath. *This is very cool.*

"I'll have this one then," Simon teases, walking to the other room. I grab the belt at the back of his robe, pulling him back to my doorway. He turns round and, smiling, puts down his case to embrace me.

"Good night. And thank you again," I say. *For being a gentleman in every way.* It may not be the world's best kisses of appreciation, but it has an effect on me so I decide to call time before we end up sharing a room.

"Goodnight," he whispers, giving me a wink. I close my door and begin to unpack my case. *Oh no, please no.* In my haste to pack yesterday, I discover that I haven't packed any loungewear or pyjamas. I can't wear my only dry dress to bed, my three quarter lengths will get irreparably creased and my jeans will deliver the most uncomfortable night's sleep in history. Through my anguishing I hear Simon lock up and turn off lights, eventually making his way to his room. I conclude that it's acceptable to sleep in my undies, and with no aircon in my room the sheets don't stay on me for too long either.

I'm in mild slumber when I hear my bedroom door open. I sit up to see Simon walking towards me in his boxers, still wet from the pool. His hair is slicked back and beads of pool water make their way down his ripped chest to join the rest of those making his boxers glisten.. He lifts one knee up onto my bed and puts an arm around my waist. Pulling me towards him, I melt into another knee-buckling kiss. After running my hands up and down his back a few times, I deliver enough force to drag him down on top of me. His knees eventually relent and I enjoy a damp embrace, quite refreshing considering the temperature.

"Gemma," he whispers into my ear as he brings his face close to my cheek.

"Simon," I sigh, my temperature rising much quicker than a damp boyfriend can counter.

"Gemma," he repeats, a little louder and more authoritative than before. *Alright, chum, don't spoil the moment.* "Gemma!" I sit bolt upright. "I've made you breakfast, it's ready when you are." I control my panting before mustering a reply.

"Okay….thanks," I say to the voice outside my door. *Imagination - you took the flight over too, I see.* Sitting up in my bed, I lay my hand on my chest to help calm my hyperventilating. "Do you want a coffee, Gem?"

"Yes please."

And a cold shower.

CHAPTER FOURTEEN

I decide to have a quick freshen-up in order to get to breakfast. I'm met with a medley of aromas as I make my way down the hallway. As I reach the end of the hallway, I turn into the kitchen to see Simon cooking. *Flashback to the other night - breakfast chef!*

"She's awake," he exclaims, giving me a beaming smile. He doesn't stop frying, but offers my cheek for him to kiss as I walk over to him. As my lips are about to make contact, he turns his head quickly so that I get his lips after all. I smack his backside at his cheekiness.

Simon invites me to sit at the table he has laid. There are croissants, orange juice, my cappuccino and a range of things to spread into the pastry. "Someone has been shopping," I say.

"Someone emailed a local company to deliver it before he left England," he corrects. *Does this guy ever run out of surprises?* Simon reduces the heat on the hob and walks over to join me. As he walks past to sit down, he puts his hands on my shoulders and gives me a kiss on the cheek. I put one of my hands on one of his and push my cheek into his lips. "Morning," he whispers.

"Mm-mm" I reply, with a mouthful of croissant.

As he sits down, he begins to add various spreads to his croissant. "Did you get off alright last night?"

I choke on my croissant.

"So, what's the plan of action for *Operation Gitface* today?" I ask. Simon chuckles at the title, sipping his orange juice.

"Well," he replies, draining his glass. "We should go to this expat meeting which is at 2pm. It's around an hour's drive away, so we can veg out here for the morning...if that's okay with you?" I nod in agreement.

Sun. My man. The pool. The perfect weekend!

The croissants tag-team with a Full English Breakfast which is absolutely delicious. *I guess it's too early for Paella.* I get up to clear the plates, but Simon insists it's "a full-service breakfast which includes washing up," so I head back to my room. We're all different, but I find a bath makes me feel sleepy so I only take showers in the morning. It's a shame because my sunken bath looks very inviting. I don't spend long in the shower, just enough to ensure I have done enough shaving so the Spanish Forestry Commission don't put me on the map. I also can't wait to get the most out of the patio. And Simon. As I walk from the ensuite with a towel wrapped round me, I have another panic moment. *I never bought a new bikini!* I can feel my heart beating louder as I walk, in slow motion, to the bikini in my Spanish chest of drawers. Laying the two-piece on my bed, the IBTWYPDB looks small enough to be tight on a barbie doll. I shake my head in disbelief at forgetting to buy a new bikini and make a mental note to use the reminder function on my phone regularly from this point forward. Still in my towel, I have one hand on my hip and the other across my mouth. *I can't go in the pool in clothes. I mean, not again.*

I pull myself together, convincing myself that I don't have bigger muffin tops than a bakery, drop my towel and get on with making Nat proud. I choose not to look in the mirror until the last moment, turning around to see how ghastly I look. My jaw drops at the revelation. *I look freakin' hot!* The bottoms are just right and the top allows the right bits to overflow a little. I still put on the robe I wore last night though, deciding I can't stroll through the house in a bikini with a boyfriend of four days. *Four days - longest relationship ever!*

Donning some flipflops that are in the room, I head out to meet Simon on the patio. He has already got changed and is relaxing on the sun lounger, wearing bright red shorts and dark sunglasses. *Looking good, Mister.* I lie down on the lounger next to him, a small table separating us, choosing to keep my robe on. Simon lowers his glasses and gives me a wink, pretending he is some Hollywood movie star. I place my hand on my heart, pantomime-style. "Be still, my beating heart!" He chuckles, returns his sunglasses to position and continues with his Vitamin D overdose. I notice that he has poured a couple of glasses of something fruity. I take a sip. Non-alcoholic, but it is only 10am.

The sun has been warming up the area for a couple of hours already, so it's heating up well. Too well, because I'm beginning to melt in my robe. So, I have a choice: pass out, or get them out. I choose the latter. I decide to undo my robe and allow it to fall open quietly without disturbing Simon. As I continue my ninja tactics, I pull my arms out of my robe. I find myself contorting to a bizarre shape in order to be as quiet as possible but in the process I lean on a metal part of the lounger that is hotter than the surface of the Sun. We all flinch if we touch something hot without meaning to. I react with my foot, causing the table between us to perform a vertical take-off. Table, drinks and glass create the biggest noise the world has ever heard, causing Simon to jump bolt upright out of his lounger. This in turn makes his sunglasses fly off his head and join the new mess on the patio. Mouth agape and panting, he looks at me, then at the mess, then at me again. I slowly put my robe back on, do it up and head to the kitchen to find a dustpan, brush and the villa's accidental damage policy. Ten minutes later, I resume my sunbathing with new glasses charged with the same fruity concoction and decide to remove my robe entirely, throwing it on a spare lounger. I lie on my front to keep Simon's temperature down for as long as possible. And then I remember my sneaky plan...*this is my moment!*

"Simon?" I ask innocently. "Mmm?" he says, mid-sunbathe.

"Would you do my back, please?" I've never seen the guy move so quickly, and he is soon sitting at the side of my lounger squirting his palms with the white stuff. I adjust the lounger so that it's horizontal and keep my arms down by my side. *Do your worst. But make it your best.* I give a slight flinch when the cold suncream makes contact for the first time, but mildly enough that the patio table is safe. Simon starts at the small of my back and makes long, firm strokes with the palms of his hands either side of my spine, working up to my neck. His fingers catch the straps of my bikini top each time he passes, so I undo the clasp and allow the straps to fall to each side. The massage is heavenly as he goes from the top of my backside up to my shoulders and down again, so I can't help but to close my eyes. After a short while he shuffles closer to my head and, recharging the cream, gives my shoulders a lot of attention. I don't have a lot of stresses in life, but any that exist get massaged away. He expands on the shoulder focus by running his hands down my arms and to my fingertips. *They must have had GCSEs in massage when my man was at school. This is amazing.*

After a few minutes I suddenly lose Simon's touch and wonder where he has disappeared to. I'm just about to roll over when the super-gifted hands return to my feet. Considering my ability to level a patio table, he would have been well advised to check I wasn't ticklish before massaging my plates. Fortunately, my feet are immune to tickling and I revel in the moment. As before, his hands eventually move up from my feet to my calves and up my thighs. I raise an eyebrow as his fingers get rather close to unchartered territory. *How high are we going, Mister?* Simon clearly spots the No Entry sign on his route and performs a U-turn. He repeats the drive-by many more times and I relish the experience, knowing he is still the perfect gentleman. As I'm melting in the moment, and the Spanish heat, I receive a sudden smack on the backside which makes me jolt my head up. "Done!" he says, and lies down on his sun lounger. I'm not sure about the abrupt ending, but I mumble a "thank you" before closing my eyes and focussing on the mass of post-massage tingles coursing around my body. *Mmm, that was lovely.*

The rest of the morning is spent doing more sunbathing (I massaged my front myself!) and having the odd dip in the pool. We both agree that the jacuzzi adjacent to the pool is too hot for the daytime sun, but agree to test it out tonight. Before we know it, it's midday and time to get ready for the trip. I don my summer dress, apply more suncream in my room and meet Simon in the hallway. He has already started our hire car to get the aircon working, so we jump in and allow the satnav to guide us to our destination. We both decide that we are still full up from breakfast so skip lunch. After about an hour's driving, we find ourselves in a quaint town with a cobbled market square. We park up and walk to our meeting place, a small bar on the edge of the square. As soon as we walk in we are greeted by a couple of Brits and within a few minutes have exchanged pleasantries with a couple of dozen people. The spokesperson for the group is a woman called Beryl who has organised for us to gather in a function room at the rear of the premises. She strikes me as an assertive woman who gets down to business. The meeting isn't too intense, but more of a support group for those who have been stung by Parsons' dodgy dealings. After a few minutes, Beryl shares how every victim has now been located and she is in the process of making contact with those who are unable to join us today. Through the range of comments filling the room, no one needs to be educated on the likelihood of getting their money back; instead, the group decides to focus on preventing Parsons from committing further crimes. "We've already managed to shut down one of his companies in Portugal," explains Beryl, "due to the local press running a front page spread on his activities and us contacting expat forums for those living in the area."

"He can't carry on, surely," I announce. This is met with a couple of scoffs and I look to Simon helplessly. *He can't, surely.* Beryl gives me sympathetic eyes, as if I'm an innocent child being introduced to the 'real world' for the first time.

"He's been doing it for years...and he's already got another business on the go!" My jaw drops.

"What, in Spain?"

"Not just in Spain," calls out another chap who has been sat with his arms folded the entire time. "About ten minutes' drive from where he was before." *How can someone do this?!*

"But surely no one will go to him for their investment?"

More sympathetic eyes - *poor, sheltered child.*

"There are loads of timeshare businesses on the continent. All it takes is a fancy website implying you've been trading thirty years and some glossy leaflets sent to expat communities and you're ready to fleece some more."

"They don't go to Parsons," Beryl explains, "They go to the *company*. Parsons' name is never mentioned."

I nod my head slowly as I understand, then shake it slowly out of disbelief that someone could be so calculatingly callous.

I decide to stay quiet for the rest of the meeting and listen to other people's outbursts instead. Mum and Bill have got it bad, especially Mum, but it transpires that some people have lost their properties altogether and have had to move back in with family. Another group share how they have heard of others committing suicide over similar scams in recent months. In total, Beryl has worked out that Parsons has got away with around five million euros from the people in the room, including Mum and Bill. *Five million.* The enormity of what Parsons has done is heartbreaking. I can feel anger building inside me and start to tense up in my seat. Simon, who has been quiet as a mouse the entire time, puts his hand on my leg to calm me down. The meeting lasts just under an hour and we spend time afterwards exchanging stories over coffee and tea which the bar have provided free of charge. *Proper coffee too. Nice touch.* Beryl offers to send us each other's contact details so we can stay in touch in case we have updates on news. We all agree to share the information, keen to see Parsons cease trading for good.

As a contact form is being circulated, the chap who had his arms folded comes over and introduces himself. Gary, a police officer from England, invested a similar amount to Mum so we chat at length explaining what happened to Mum and Bill. It transpires that Gary knows Mum and Bill well as they bought their properties at the same time. *If a policeman can be shafted, Joe Public has no hope.*

"How did you discover Parsons is still trading nearby?" I ask him.

"The internet is a clever thing - add a few phonecalls to the mix pretending to be potential investors and you get the info you need. Plus, I have a few police contacts over here." *Of course - he's a copper. He must be quite high up in the force.* I smile at his ingenuity.

"Conning the con artist, then?" I say with a wink.

"For the greater good" he assures, to which we both agree.

Simon speaks for the first time. "So, where is this new place Parsons has set up." Gary gives a suspicious look to Simon then chooses to divulge the necessary information.

"Be careful, mate. He hasn't been caught for a reason, and I'm sure your Dad doesn't want to visit you in the nick." Simon nods with the same assurance he did to me when the policeman warned him a few days earlier.

"I just want to find out a little more about the company." Gary pushes out his lips and muses there would be no harm in doing that, "especially as he's back in the UK," and shares some details with Simon. I look up at Simon, smiling at his determination.

After a short while the group begins to disperse so we also make our leave, promising to keep Beryl updated if we uncover any new information. Gary also leaves and asks us to send his regards to Mum and Bill.

We sit in the car with the doors open for a while to allow the car's ambient temperature to drop, then turn on the aircon and make the short trip to Parsons' new company, Villa Lujo. As we arrive, we are slightly disappointed that it looks so shabby. It is essentially a portacabin in the middle of a small building site, although some bay trees in pots either side of the entrance and a carpet running over the mud to the gravel car park improve its appeal a little. We hold hands and walk straight in, both taking deep breaths as we step foot on the carpet. We walk into a single room with dozens of large framed pictures of sun-drenched properties hanging on the walls. Behind a single desk is Tania's Spanish cousin; short bright blue skirt, heels and a top that exposes a cleavage ample enough to create an echo. The "Hola!" we receive is not quite at dog whistle level, but not far off. We both return the salutation in English and say how we are looking to invest in a property in Spain, wondering if she would be able to provide information on how to make this possible.

"We can do better than that," comes a voice from a door in the opposite corner. Out walks a gentleman in smart knee length chino shorts and tight shirt. Very handsome and with a perfect hairstyle, he reminds me of a stereotypical premiership footballer. *He could do shampoo commercials too with that barnet.* As he walks over, Simon steps forward a little, slightly putting himself between us. *This is Steve Parsons!*

"Steve Andrews," he announces, holding his hand out to Simon. Simon musters an impressive poker face and returns the shake. Parsons nods keenly and extends the handshake to me. I never realised how hard it is not to give your name when someone tells you theirs, but following Simon's lead has made things easier.

"Why don't you come through and we can talk business," he says, gesturing to the door. We both walk through, holding hands, into another office which is much cosier. Leather chairs, plants and a posh desk adorn the room, along with a Gaggia in the corner. No one can deny his gifting in interior design. In addition to the office attire, there are four large silver cases in a neat row against the far wall. Parsons catches me looking at them and smiles. "Coffee?" he offers. We both refuse, sitting on the chairs we've been directed to. It would be like accepting a lift from someone who has nicked a car. Parsons - *Andrews* - sits behind his desk and explains how he only flew over this morning to secure a deal on a new plot of land, heading back to the UK tomorrow. Moving on, he asks us exactly what we're looking to invest. Simon spins a yarn which makes Parsons reveal how the process works. I'm wondering how long Simon can keep up the facade when he suddenly drops the act.

"We're not here to invest, Parsons." The shampoo model leans back into his chair, and a smug grin appears on his face.

"Oh, it all makes sense now. You're here with chips on your shoulders! Come on then, what am I supposed to have done?"

Simon reveals Mum and Bill's names and is met with an expressionless headshake. "Can't say I remember them, but I have - *exchanged contracts* - with a lot of clients over the years." Simon looks about ready to reach across the desk to rip the smug look from his face, so I place my hand on his forearm to hold him. Sensing the potential bust-up, Parsons continues his performance.

"I wouldn't let your emotions get the better of you, my friend." He leans forward on the desk, almost goading Simon. "You see, the authorities have nothing on me, both here and in the UK, but if you lay a finger on me you'll land yourself in a Spanish jail in no time." He points to a security camera aimed at us from the corner of the room which, until now, we hadn't noticed. He sits back again into his chair and puts his hands behind his head. "As you can see," he concludes, "I'm quite literally untouchable."

Simon inhales deeply with pursed lips and stands up quickly, making Parsons flinch. My man then holds his hand out to help me out of my seat. As we leave, Simon turns back to Parsons as if to give him one last chance to redeem himself. "A lot of people have given you millions of pounds and received nothing in return. Does that not create an ounce of guilt in you?" Parsons looks thoughtful for a second, begins to nod and then shakes head with a wide, smug grin again.

"You are going to give all that money back, Parsons." Simon promises. We both walk out to a send-off of raucous laughter.

"I'd find a new boss," I say to Tania's cousin as we walk out of the portacabin, almost knocking into two official-looking folk making their way in, complete with sunglasses, briefcases and serious clothing. *Spanish police?*

"And here are my two favourite people!" Parsons exclaims. We turn round to see him ushering the man and women in, then turns to us one last time, announcing "These guys are about to sell me a lovely plot of land. They don't believe in banks, like me. They believe in Euros. Five million of them, sat in those cases as it happens." *The money. We were sat right next to it!* "Nice round number, don't you think?" he quips, giving us a cheery wave as he closes the door behind him. Simon starts to walk back into the cabin, but I stop him.

"That's what he wants. He's had enough out of us already." Simon nods and sighs through gritted teeth as we head back to the car.

We don't talk to each other for the majority of the journey back, but I eventually break silence by asking "What are we going to do?"

"We're going to go to a tapas bar. Then, we are going to drive back to the patio and get back in that pool. With an unhealthy amount of alcohol!"

I chuckle and place my hand on his leg. It's not what I meant and he knows that. Tapas sounds good.

Our experience of Spanish cuisine is amazing. Washed down with a gorgeous rioja, we carry our glasses to drain them outside. The tapas bar extends to the beach, so we remove our shoes and walk hand in hand to the sea a few hundred feet in the distance. The sun has made the sand almost unbearable to walk on, so I try and dig in with every step to find cooler bits. Simon seems to cope ably. *Of course he does, he's a fireman!* Paddling in the sea, we playfully kick some water at each other and my difficulty in staying upright on one leg shows the rioja has gone to my head rather quickly. Draining the glasses, we stroll along the beach a little longer and then Simon turns to me.

"I have never met anyone like you before, Gem. You are caring, thoughtful, intelligent, funny and so, so beautiful." *Where did that come from?* "I know it's crazy to say it when we haven't even known each other for a week yet." *Oh no. He's going to propose, isn't he?* "Gemma…"

Yes? Yes???

"Would you like some dessert?" he says with a wink.

I hit him. Twice. Very hard. He laughs and wraps me up in his arms. "Sorry, couldn't resist!"

"Try harder," I retort, in a way to show I'm a little miffed.

He reduces his chuckles until they subside and faces me again. "But seriously, I think you're amazing and I'm so pleased to be your boyfriend. Honestly, this has been the best week of my life and I really hope you'll have me for another one." *You're forgiven.*

"I think I'll be able to stretch to that," I whisper. I go on tiptoes to wrap my arms around Simon's neck and he gently places his hands on my waist. I then try to suffocate him with the longest snog yet. This region of Spain must have issues with gravity because Simon's hands get pulled down to my bum cheeks. *I love this gravity!*

We drive back to the villa, both with massive grins. I'm not sure about his, but mine is out of pure excitement that there's another week of relationship to come. And another. And another. *Please!*

"So what are going to do about him?" I ask Simon. "I know the money's gone, we've been reminded that enough times now. But how can we let him get away scot-free?" Simon replies with the obvious.

"You heard him, Gem. He's untouchable. He knows the system and he knows how to stay one step ahead." As he pulls up outside the house, he concludes, "I think we just need to put it down to experience. A horrid, horrid experience." *As usual, my wonderful man is right.*

Simon opens the door, and I walk to the kitchen. "Copious amounts of alcohol in the pool, then?" I announce, reminding Simon of our deal early. He nods with a grin and walks to his bedroom to get changed. I dash to my room as well to put on my IBTWYPDB which I left soaking in my bathroom. *I can't stand the smell of chlorine on my clothes, in my hair, anywhere in fact.* Putting on a wet bikini is not the most pleasant experience, but I'm conscious that the sun will dry it out in no time. As I head down the hallway, I collect the wine bottles and glasses on a tray and go to the patio. Simon is already on the lounger like before so I pour him a large rioja, giving him a kiss with the glass. He returns the kiss without getting up. I move my lounger round beside his and lie down next to him, enjoying the last of the day's sun whilst holding his spare hand. *I love this.*

Around an hour later I ask Simon how he is. "I'm okay, just rather tense." *Tense? I might be able to fix that.*

"Would you like a back massage?" I offer. He lowers his glasses to look me straight in the eyes.

"You give back massages?" I shrug my shoulders and give a nod. "Are you any good?" he asks, teasing me.

"Well, roll over and you'll find out," I tease back. There isn't too much suncream left in the bottle so decide to save this for potential sunbathing tomorrow. I'm keen to use some kind of lubricant to avoid friction burns, so I explain to Simon that I'm on the hunt for something appropriate.

"Proper job, then?" he adds. "I'm impressed." As I root around bathroom cupboards, dressing tables and other places where there may be leftovers from previous tenants, I discover a large bowl on top of a cabinet. Using a chair to reach, I bring the bowl down to find a mini treasure trove of small bottles. Shampoos, shower gels, conditioners and many other products fill up the bowl, and amongst the collection I find what I'm looking for. *Massage Oil. Perfect.* I kiss the bottle, not sure why, then wonder how many other mouths have been on it. As I'm walking into the living room on my way to the patio, I jump at the sight of Simon on the rug in the middle of the floor.

"There were loads of midges appearing, so thought the massage could happen in here," he explains. I look outside to see a few small clouds of insects hogging our suntrap.

"Good move," I admit. Simon takes a large swig of his wine, so I copy him. He then lies on his front in the same way I did this morning, ready for me to resume. I swallow, exhale some air and get down to business. I begin by kneeling by his side and apply some oil to my hands to work up and down his back.

"Mmm, that's really nice," he mumbles into the rug. *I'm a pro and didn't even realise!* After a few more minutes of oiling him up, my back begins to ache from the awkward position. I decide to straddle my man so that I can be more square on. He doesn't seem to mind. I crack on with the massaging, working on his shoulders and down his arms as well. After massaging his legs, I eventually am all massaged out so decide to hug him from behind and nibble his ear. He wakes up and gives a mumble of appreciation. He comments on how lovely it was, and how hot he has started to feel. I offer to put the aircon on a little and as I head to the remote control he complains that he's getting even hotter. "Gem, I'm burning up," he announces with a worried tone. I look at him nonplussed, and then his jaw drops.

"What was in that massage oil?" he asks.

"Nothing," I reply, "it just says 'pure Almond Oil'. ALMONDS!" *Oh no. Oh no, oh no.*

Spanish paramedics are so professional. I mean *really* professional. You'd think they would at least raise an eyebrow or have something to say about various predicaments. Nothing. Just a few questions about Simon's level of allergy, assessing the affected areas and injecting some antihistamine. Done. I share this observation with Simon while I help him walk to his bed and he gives a kind of grunt in response.

I think I had better make breakfast in the morning.

CHAPTER FIFTEEN

I wake up to a knock on my bedroom door. Still half asleep, I call out "Who is it?" I roll my eyes at the question. *You know who it is you pillock!* "Er..it's Simon," comes the reply. "Sorry, I meant, 'Come in'." The door opens slowly and in walks Simon. He is wearing joggers and a t-shirt. *Still looks good.* He clears his throat and looks down, smiling. I eventually pick up the hint and remember I'm lying here in my underwear. *Crap.* I reach forward to pull my duvet up to my neck, only to discover it is on the floor. *Double crap.* Simon is still looking down and laughing, seeming to enjoy my predicament. I try and pull the duvet towards me but it appears to be caught under the bed. I'm still in my smalls and Simon is laughing more by the second. He eventually puts me out of my misery by leaving the room and closing the door. From behind the door he calls, "I came to see if you wanted breakfast yet?"

"I should be making *you* breakfast after last night," I reply, trying to sound like I'm unfazed by what just happened.

"I'll do you a deal. You make the coffee, I'll make the breakfast."

"Okay, I'll be out in a minute."

"Take your time," he says in a cheeky tone, laughing as he walks down the hallway. I roll my eyes.

I have a shower to freshen up and get changed into my IBTWYPDB. It's only as I'm walking back out of the bathroom that I realise I haven't once taken advantage of the sunken bath while we've stayed here. *Next time, bath.* Washed and clean, I put the robe back around me and search for Simon. Predictably he is in his usual spot, soaking up the sun on the lounger. My man has already got a red wine out for us to enjoy, so as I remove my robe I take care not to dropkick the table's contents across the

113

patio. I stay on my back and work my suncream into my front. *You use a lot more cream when you wear less clothes.* I look over to Simon who hasn't said a word to me so far and discover that he is dozing.

"Simon?" I whisper. The lack of reaction tells me this boy is fast asleep. A mischievous smile spreads across my face as I grab the sun cream again. Tiptoeing around the back of his lounger, I flip the lid to the cream and get to work creating my masterpiece - a heart shape just above his left pectoral. I giggle silently to myself while doing it, so I struggle to stop the bottle from shaking. As I'm tiptoeing back to my lounger, I catch my foot on one of its legs causing Simon to stir.

"What are you doing?" he mumbles.

"I'm just...going for a dip," I reply. Simon nods and resumes his dozing. I stay on the lounger in the hope he won't notice and have a doze myself.

I wake around an hour later and roll over to see how Simon's tan is taking shape. *Oh wow!* The suncream prank has worked better than imagined and Simon, now awake, is sporting a stunningly white heart on an impressively tanned body. I bite my lip to stop laughing. Simon gives me a suspicious stare so I perform some distraction therapy. "Jacuzzi?" I nod with an unbothered expression, but as soon as he passes me I silently giggle some more. *This is brilliant!* We both sink into the jacuzzi and I enjoy the countless jets massaging my body. Simon looks similarly relaxed, his white heart just above the water line. *I'm going to wet myself.*

"What?!" Simon demands, seeing my doing my best to stop laughing.

"The bubbles are tickling me, that's all," I fib. He nods in acceptance of my excuse, but still gives me a suspicious look for a while longer. I decide the best way to hide my face is to reverse into Simon and sit on his lap. He seems to enjoy it a lot, and we sit for ages with his arms and legs wrapped around my body talking about almost every topic that exists in the world. I am excited how we have such similar views and we reach a point where we are almost ending each other's sentences. I'm relishing the jacuzzi moment and that we seem so suited. *I think I'm falling in love with this man.* Throughout our conversations, I can't stop thinking about Parsons and the fact we were inches away from all the money he stole. It was now gone, invested in his new plot of land ready for more victims. "How can we get the money back from Parsons?" I ask Simon.

"Legally?" he checks.

"Not necessarily," I reply, waiting for the reaction. He turns me round to face him.

"Are you serious?"

"I'm just thinking about all the people who have been affected because of Parsons, while he can laze in *his* jacuzzi living off the proceeds."

"I'm not disagreeing with you. I just don't want to end up in prison." He says it firmly, taking me back a little. I look down nodding, and can't help stop a few tears forming. Tutting and rolling his eyes, he kisses me on the forehead and gives me a comforting hug. I blame tiredness, and perhaps a little too much wine. Either way, I find myself bawling on his shoulder. I mean, serious wailing like there's something wrong with me. Simon just keeps his tight grip on me until I run out of sobs.

After several minutes, Simon says "Come on, we need to get back to Blighty."

"Thank you for an amazing, amazing time," I sniffle.

"Thank you for making it amazing. I wouldn't change a thing about it - I wouldn't change a thing about you."

"Well, maybe my plans to be a master thief."

"Not even that - it's not even your money, you're just wanting to make things right for others. It shows how lovely you are."

He then lands an almighty smacker on my lips and walks us back into the house to start our packing. Walking into my room, I walk straight to the sunken bath. *You & me, it's happening now.* I fill the bath as quickly as I can, using almost half a bottle of bubble bath. I strip off my bikini and get into my indoor jacuzzi. With the bubble jets on full blast it is a wonderful sensation! I treat myself to a couple more minutes to make sure all the chlorine is off and then get out to dry myself. There is more space in the bedroom so I choose to dry myself there instead. As I'm getting dressed, I glance at myself in the free-standing mirror in the corner of the room and my heart skips a beat. *What is THAT?!* Walking closer to the mirror in my jeans and bra, I can see more clearly that I have a heart shape just about my left breast. It's as if the sun hasn't tanned there as much as the rest of me. Then the penny drops.

"Simon!" I walk through my door straight into his bedroom. Simon, with a towel round him, is busy loading his suitcase with clothes.

"Did you call, Darling?" he says, in an unassuming fashion.

"What do you have to say about *this*!" I declare, pointing at my chest.

"They're very lovely, Gem. Really, they're perfect," he replies with the straightest face he can achieve. Trying not to laugh, I give him a formal Sanders warning.

"This is war, Mister" I announce, and storm back into my room. Door closed, I look at my heart. I establish that he must have been aware I was drawing the heart on *his* chest the whole time, pretending to be asleep. Then when I dozed off, he got his own back. *Sod.* I giggle a little to myself. *For sure, this man is a keeper - he certainly isn't boring.*

I finish dressing and get packed quickly, deciding to leave most of my toiletries in the bowl above the cabinet as it seems to be *the done thing*. Besides, the less things in my suitcase that can leak or cause me to be stopped at the airport, the better. After some dishwashing and bin emptying, the house is ready for the next weekenders. Jumping into the car, I look up to the villa one last time before leaving the driveway. *Thanks for the memories.*

The trip back to the airport is as simple as the journey here, and within a short time we've handed the hire car's keys back and are entering the departure lounge. With no security scares, and flights on time, we get back to England as it's beginning to look dusky. Simon and I have spent the majority of the trip talking non-stop, just as we did in the jacuzzi earlier. As we get through customs and start walking through the car park, I text Mum:

> **The plane didn't crash and we're back in the UK x**
> **Good to know x**
> **And, where were you yesterday? Tried to call you and Bill x**
> **We had a little break ourselves. Catch up soon x**

The sly old couple! I show the texts to Simon. "Good on them," he laughs. I join in with the giggles in agreement, although I'm not desperate to know what they got up to. *Hola, Imagination!* Simon's BMW gives a brief flash of its indicators as we get close. Simon stops and turns to me. "Gem, I really have had an amazing experience with you."

"Me too," I reply. I never thought snogging in an airport car park could be that romantic. I was wrong. It doesn't last too long, but enough for anyone watching the car park's security cameras to wish they had popcorn. I smile as I get into Simon's car to begin the journey home.

Before long, we're turning into my street and pulling up outside my house. *Back to reality.* Simon gets out to retrieve my case from the boot and carries it to my front door. One more cuddle and the weekend trip is over. We agree to catch up with Mum and Bill tomorrow and update them on our discoveries, not that it will make any difference to the outcome. "Have a good day tomorrow," I say.

"You too," my man replies. "And no bank robberies in your lunchbreak." I return a comedy scowl which earns a wink. *Git.*

Simon waits until I get inside the house and then drives off. *The gentleman has left.* I shut the door, leave my case in the porch and head to the kitchen to make a cappuccino. As I'm preparing the first caffeine fix I've had since this morning, I reflect on how organised Simon is. It's about the only thing we don't appear to have in common. It's amazing how much one contemplates life while making a coffee, but at that moment I make a pact with myself: To get up earlier, never go to bed with a messy kitchen and to always put clothes away. I'm still heating the water when my pocket wolf whistles:

You're back then. Good time? *Nat, you curtain-twitcher!*

Amazing! Come over if you like. X

I don't get a reply from Nat, I just hear her key turning in the lock around 30 seconds later. I smile to myself and carry on making the coffee.

"So, good time then?" she says, in a suggestive manner. I turn to nod and her jaw drops. "Serious tan, lady. Looking *good!*" I look down, grateful that my white heart is undercover, then turn to get back to making our cappuccinos. So far, I haven't uttered a word but the grin says it all.

"Come on then, what happened?" Nat asks. I decide to torture her with suspense for a little while longer, until the drinks are ready. Eventually, I turn to her and assume a poker face.

"Shall we drink these in the living room?"

"We're not going anywhere until you give me some news, lady!" she says, laughing. I can't get past her as she has blocked my route to the living room, so I decide to disclose a bit of information.

"The massage happened," I reveal, which allows me a pass to the living room with the drinks.

"And?" Nat pushes, following me. "And, I got one back," I reply, still maintaining my straight face.

As we both fall back into the sofa with our drinks, I realise I can't keep up the facade any longer. "Nat, it was *awesome*. He is romantic, a gentleman, an amazing kisser, a comedian...I think I love him."

It's Nat's turn to be silent.

"Well, say something," I demand, nudging her. Nat turns to me and, with the most sincerity I have ever witnessed from her, replies "Girl, you deserve it. I am SO happy for you......can I be your chief bridesmaid?" I pretend to choke on my cappuccino and we both erupt into laughter.

I share more stories with Nat to give her an idea of how well it went. I decide to keep a few things to myself, like the visit from Spanish paramedics and my white heart; it's not that I don't trust Nat to keep secrets, she's amazing. But some moments are just for me and Simon to know about...and I'm sure he would agree.

After a while the conversation turns to Parsons and Nat asks if I managed to find anything out. I share what we discovered about Parsons and paint him in an appropriate light. Nat provides a few more declarations of illegitimacy at the right moments. "But, that's the end of it," I declare. "We gave him a chance to make good, it hasn't happened, and we're certainly not prepared to rob him at gunpoint. It's just so annoying that he's got away with i,t" I finish. Nat nods in agreement, sipping her coffee. Her eyes then widen with an idea.

"Why don't I see what properties he owns. It might be he has some that the authorities don't know about, and there could be a chance of freezing assets or reclaiming some of it as proceeds of crime." I give Nat an impressed look. *She knows her stuff.*

"It won't hurt," I muse. "Do your worst." Nat smiles, drains her coffee and stands up.

"Right, leave it with me!" she announces.

"What, now?" I blurt out.

"Not now" she laughs, "I'm going to bed. You look knackered too. And you have work tomorrow." *I forgot.* "So, it's time for you to hit the hay as well." At this, I yawn. Nat is very observant.

We hug and I see her out, promising to catch up again soon.

I lock up, put my coffee cup on the kitchen counter, turn off the lights and head upstairs to bed. *It's weird being on my own again.* As I turn at the top of the stairs I see my suitcase still lying in the porchway.

I'll sort it later.

CHAPTER SIXTEEN

Monday mornings come round quick.

My alarm's snooze function is a welcome invention, but it means I get up half an hour later than I want to. *Not good.* To catch up on time I skip having a shower and decide to buy lunch on the way to work. *Back on schedule!*

The bus journey consists of the same Code adherence and I'm soon getting a cappuccino courtesy of the lovely Sally. "Good weekend?" she asks. I share a few Spanish tales, although not as many as I did with Nat. Sally's eyes light up during the conversation and she endorses Nat's comments from last night by saying how happy she is for me. It's starting to sound like even my friends didn't think I could land a bloke! I buy a baguette, some crisps and a cake from Sally too, explaining that I got up too late to make lunch. She laughs, "Most of our lunches get sold for the same reasons! You should make a pact with yourself to get up earlier." *Thanks Sally.*

As I get to the forecourt eleven minutes later, I notice the cars have been juggled around a little to make room for some new additions. There are another couple of Mercedes and a Tesla people carrier. This thing looks like a spaceship, so I go up and peer in through the window. *It doesn't even have a gearstick. What?!*

"Welcome to the new members of the family," Mark announces next to me, making me jump; He clearly enjoys creeping up on people. Or just girls.

"It's something else, isn't it?" I reply, looking back through the window. "It's electric," he explains, opening the rear doors to show me how they fold upwards like a supercar. *This thing looks amazing.* Mark smiles at the look I give.

"She's becoming a petrol head," he sings. "I'll take you out in it later." I nod keenly.

As we walk into the showroom, I'm met by an excited-looking Tania who trots up to me, straightening her skirt as she comes. "Hiya! How was Spain?" she asks. "It was lovely, thanks. Great weather, great company - a lovely time." Tania puts her hand on her heart. "When I saw that rose he brought you on Friday, I knew he was a real gentleman" she gushes. "I had a boyfriend who brought me a present to work once."

"Really?" I ask, still standing in the doorway with my coat and holding my handbag and lunch.

"Yeah, he did. He said I was to bring them on our first date. But when I unwrapped it, it was a load of condoms. One of them was mango flavoured!"

"Nightmayer" I reply. Mark disguises a laugh well when he needs to.

"I know, that's what I thought. I don't even *like* mangos."

I hang up my coat and excuse myself to the kitchen. *Imagination, please don't add to what is already in my head, thank you.*

Cappuccinos created for Tania and Mark, I notice Robbie isn't around. Mark explains that he has gone to an auction house to collect a car. "He's been busy all week," he continues, "that's why we have all this stock." I nod, hoping he doesn't continue the sentence. "I'll get you to an auction house one weekend, Gemma. See what your bidding is like." *He did. Oh good.*

The rest of the morning consists largely of tyre-kickers browsing the stock, although I take a couple of people on test drives with no dramas. Mark appears impressed throughout, so I'm pleased I've been able to show him what I'm capable of. And myself, for that matter. During lunch, my handbag wolf whistles. *Nat must be bored.*

I've found out a little about your friend Parsons

?

He has a large town house on Park View. *Of course he does. One of the wealthiest streets in the area.* There's a posh restaurant at the end of Park View called The Sunset which an old boyfriend once took me to. He thought that I would put out because the meal was so expensive. He was wrong.

My heart bleeds for him x

He also had planning permission for a large vault to be installed eighteen months ago. He must be minted! x

You can stop texting now, Nat. **Thanks, hun x**

With my office jobs complete, I find myself browsing the internet a little. After looking at a variety of videos on YouTube, mostly involving cats with cucumbers, I decide to search for Spanish law on fraud. After a short while I am fairly swotted up on timeshare swindlers and within the hour have a good grasp of how the authorities can freeze assets. I didn't doubt my super man for a second, but he's right. Parsons, it seems, is untouchable. When it comes to fake names, dealing mostly in cash and owning bank accounts in other countries, the authorities are powerless. *He mustn't get away with this.*

Mark must notice that I'm down in the dumps because, with about half an hour of the day left, he walks over to me. "Come on, I promised you a test drive. Tania, hold the fort," he says to her, with a wink. Tania nods keenly, I think enjoying her half-hour of management.

As we're walking out to the forecourt, my phone wolf whistles again. I look apologetically at Mark. "Read it, this isn't a prison," he says. *He's a good boss.* It's from Simon.

Free tonight? X *Typical.*

Sort of. Nat's coming over but it would be nice for you to see her properly.

Sounds good. I'm leaving work now if u want me to pick u up x

I love this man. **Yes please x**

I text Nat quickly to tell her we have company. The reply is almost instant:

Looking forward to having a proper chat with Mr Right ;)

We jump into the Tesla, a Model X. The doors pop open for us and, as we close them, they have a function where they complete the close by themselves. *This is very cool.* Mark then shows me the dashboard which resembles a large iPad. He dials in a series of commands including temperature settings, and he sits back to get driving. We cruise silently around the town and I notice how a few people flinch slightly as we suddenly appear in their peripheral. "That's one of the drawbacks of an electric car," Mark explains. "They're virtually silent, so people are more likely just to step out in front of you." After a while, we reach a roundabout with a dual carriageway on the other side. Mark crawls around the roundabout and, checking his rearview mirror, pulls to a complete halt. "Watch this," he says, with a grin. Putting the right pedal to the floor, the car accelerates faster than anything I have ever experienced before. You know the pain you get when you've suddenly been shocked by a thought or a loud noise? Same pain. I don't get to see the speedometer but I suspect we are travelling fast enough to lose Mark's license. We get to another roundabout rather quickly and Mark returns to a sedate form of driving. "Impressive, isn't it. 0-60 in just over 3 seconds. That's supercar speed. And it's a people carrier!" he laughs. I laugh along. The experience is exhilarating, but I can't imagine any responsible parent would do the school run like that.

The journey back is similarly sensible, but I can't help but think

Mark is trying to make people jump as we drive past. He manages it a couple of times. Parking up, he walks back to the showroom spinning the keys around his finger, whistling. I think he enjoyed his little moment with me. "Any action, Tan?" he says. Tania gives a disappointed shake of her head, sighs and packs up to leave. I think she was hoping to double Marquis' annual turnover while we were gone.

As Tania leaves, Mark comes over to see how my day has been. "So-so. I didn't have a lot of work to do this afternoon, but it's been quiet, hasn't it?" Mark agrees, saying Robbie has chosen the perfect day to be at the auction house. Mark then walks over to the showroom windows to close them.

"Your taxi is here Madam," he says, noticing Simon's parked across the road. I blush.

As I get into the BMW, I look over to Mark who is air driving on the forecourt. My scowl is met with laughs.

"Good day?" I ask Simon. "Not too bad, thanks. You?"

It's been fine, I've been Googling ways to kill Parsons. "Not bad."

CHAPTER SEVENTEEN

We're soon back at mine and Simon rustles up some food for us while I make a cappuccino. After dinner we enjoy a bit of chill time before Nat arrives.

As before, she rings the doorbell rather than letting herself in. I can't fault her tact.

She joins us in the living room and after a bit of small talk gets straight into sharing what she has found out about Parsons. She confirms that he owns this property in Park View which had the planning permission for a vault room. I comment on how much money could be in there, which earns a cautionary look from Simon.

"And that's not all," adds Nat. We both brace ourselves for what is to come.

"He appears to be forming another timeshare business, this time in Portugal." Simon groans.

"He's doing it again," he mutters, remembering the expat meeting where they shared how a recent Portuguese scam had been shut down.

I've had enough by this point. I slam my coffee mug rather hard which makes Simon and Nat both jump. "Enough's enough. I'm sorry Simon, but I have to do something."

"What. What are you going to do?" he asks, his voice raised.

"I'm going to get into that vault and get the money!"

"How?" he asks, in a way that suggests a woman can't achieve such a challenge.

The truth is, I haven't a clue how to get the money, so I slump back into the chair. "I don't know, but I'm going to get it!"

"You're not, Gem. I won't allow it." Nat is watching our spat like a wimbledon spectator.

"But I HAVE to!"

I can't help but notice how, a few days ago, it was me restraining *him*. I burst into tears, helpless.

Simon tuts and grabs me, hugging me tightly. Another sobbing session on his shoulder.

Silence. Apart from lots of sniffing.

Simon eventually lets go of me and looks me square in the eyes. "Okay. You have 24 hours to work out how you would do it." *What?* "Let's get together at your mum's tomorrow and you can share what you're thinking. If it sounds dangerous, or risky, you have to promise to drop it." I give Simon a surprised look, not quite believing what I'm hearing. "Look, I'm a bloke," he continues. "I hate losing! And it breaks my heart to know that this has happened to my Dad." He fills up. "But, I'm not going to sit back and let you get into serious trouble."

I put my hand on his leg. I like how he feels able to share his emotions, although the 24 hour deadline is a little Christian Greyish. I'm sure Nat is wondering if we've forgotten she's in the room.

"Thank you," I whisper. Simon scoffs, "Like I have a choice," and hugs me. I text Mum once the hug is over:

Simon & Nat are joining us tomorrow. I've got something to talk to you about. x

I'm intrigued! I'll invite Bill over too x

Nat shares how she is keen to help as much as possible "without actually robbing the guy." I give her a warm smile of appreciation.

"What can I do?" asks Simon with a teary smile. "Just keep being you," I reply. Sitting back in our respective seats, we take on board what we're about to do.

Nat decides to break the mood. "Film?"

127

We both nod and head out to prepare snacks and drinks. As I'm retrieving a bottle of wine from an overhead cupboard, Simon comes out with "Gemma. I love you." I'm wondering what else he thought would happen as I drop the bottle of wine onto the kitchen worktop causing it to smash and spill its contents everywhere. "Sorry," he says.

"No, it's fine. Say it again." He chuckles to himself and paddles through the wine to put his arms around me. "It's crazy after only a short time together, but I've never felt like this about anyone before." *Did he just say that? My turn, then.*

"I love you too." We both agree that, due to our newly-declared love for each other, it would be really handy if we didn't go to prison. We both chuckle and kiss some more as Nat walks in. She's standing in the doorway, looking at Simon and I cuddling in the middle of our indoor alcoholics pool and does a comedy turn to walk out again. We both laugh as Simon removes his socks and takes things through to the living room while I clean up.

We sit down to see that Nat has put on the 2003 remake of The Italian Job. Noticing my unimpressed face, she responds innocently with "What? It's research!"

Even Simon laughs.

As it happens, the film does provide some amazing tips so I make a mental note of ideas. The film is slightly tainted by the fact that the money wasn't theirs to begin with, but as the crew are stealing it back from a character like Parsons, it makes it almost defensible. *They got away with it, and it wasn't even theirs in the first place. I can't fail!*

After the movie, Nat gets up to leave. We invite her to join us tomorrow night at Mum's, considering she is now part of *our* crew. She chuckles and assures us she will be there. *Nat's amazing. Alarm clock, friend, accessory to grand theft.*

Once we're on our own, Simon can tell I'm distant in thought. He chuckles and gets up to leave as well. "I'll leave you to your plotting. Try and get some sleep and I'll see you tomorrow night." He gives me a kiss and I walk him to the door.

"I love you," I call out as he reaches his car, desperately hoping he replies in kind. He smiles and blows me a kiss. *Why didn't he say it? Has he gone off the idea? Maybe he can't love a thief.*

As I walk around the house in a daze, my pocket wolf whistles.

I love you too. x

Didn't doubt him for a second.

I make myself another coffee and head back into the living room to make a few Parson plans.

First challenge - how do I get inside his flipping house?

CHAPTER EIGHTEEN

Going to bed when the sun is already rising is not conducive to a good night's sleep. Fortunately my alarm clock has done its thing and, surprisingly, I haven't taken advantage of the snooze function. Looking like I'm auditioning for a remake of Dawn Of The Dead, I get to the kitchen to wake myself with coffee. I get the Gaggia's water heating before heading back upstairs to shower and get dressed. As I'm soaping up, I reflect on the plans I made last night. I have already got most of the plan worked out but I'm hoping I have a quiet day at work to help fill some holes.

Coffee and toast inside me, I leave the house with a decent packed lunch. It appears my master thief aspirations have made me a little better organised. *Go figure.*

I decide I need another caffeine fix to counterbalance minimal sleep and Sally, as ever, is preparing the goods as I enter Costa. "No lunch today, Lovely?" she asks. She's either got an amazing memory, or very few customers.

"Not today," I reply, holding up my carrier bag of packed lunch. She chuckles.

I take my Cappuccino and begin another eleven minutes of masterplanning. I've sussed out an elaborate way to get into his property, but I will need some help from my crew. *Listen to me.* From there, it should be plain sailing. As I complete my walk to Marquis, I begin to doubt the success of the exercise and recall Simon's words from last night:

"If it sounds dangerous, or risky, you have to promise to drop it." *It's all of the above!*

As I get to the forecourt I have to walk sideways between some cars due to an increase in stock taking up more space. Robbie is sliding the showroom doors open as I get closer, so I comment on his obvious successes at finding good deals at the auction house. With all the new stock attracting more clients, the chance of it being a quiet day is rather unlikely. I resign myself to plotting in my lunch break.

Tania welcomes me with her usual 'Hiya' which I reciprocate, albeit a couple of octaves lower. As I get to my desk I can see Mark is on the phone, but I motion to him the offer of a coffee which earns me a thumbs up. Robbie and Tania also accept the offer, so I get into the kitchen to perform my barista skills. Coffees made, I return to the kitchen to unpack my lunch and get my own cappuccino. As I step out to the showroom, there is already a couple peering into a BMW not far from my desk. I look around for Robbie but notice he is working with a client on the forecourt. Mark, still on his phone, gives me an encouraging nod to get selling. I swallow and approach the couple. They are incredibly friendly and keen to know everything about the 1-series they are looking at. I surprise myself at how much I already know about the car, but I do have to refer to the manual in the glovebox to find out where the battery is. I mean, seriously. There is a massive bonnet at the front of the car in which to put a chunk of acid. *Why do the Germans feel the need to put it in the boot then?* The couple are very kind though, and don't make comments about how I should know these things. I think they were just as surprised. I pretend to search for the service history while discovering where the spare wheel goes, considering the battery has hogged all the room. It transpires that this car has 'run-flats' - I haven't a clue what that means, but it's clearly a form of witchcraft that negates the need for a spare tyre. I decide to keep this observation to myself. The couple turn down the offer of a test drive, citing a lack of time, but promise to return later in the week.

The rest of the morning runs in a similar fashion: lots of interest from various folk but no commitment. Mark looks rather deflated by lunchtime - in need of run-flats himself - because he has invested several thousand pounds in the past few days and there appears to be no real interest. I offer to make him another cappuccino which he accepts.

I decide to eat my lunch in the kitchen to have a bit of privacy in order to keep working through Operation Parsons. I realise that I'm struggling for inspiration in getting Parsons' house keys, the first hurdle, so begin to feel despondent. At that, Mark joins me in the kitchen to return the mug. "What's up, Gem," he asks, noticing my frustration. *I'm struggling to work out how to rob a git and return millions of euros to the people they belong to.*

"Oh, nothing," I reply, deciding it's a better answer. Mark smiles and heads back out the kitchen. As he is halfway through the doorway though, I have a brainwave.

"Mark?" I ask, in a brighter voice. "Can I ask a favour?" He reverses back into the kitchen in a comedy fashion. I giggle. *It's not that funny, but it deserves acknowledgment.*

"Anything" he replies.

"Last week you said I could borrow a car if I ever wanted to. I would like to give Simon a treat to say thanks for the trip to Spain. Could I borrow one of our cars tonight?"

The question is met with a big smile. "I know just the car," he says with a mischievous grin. "Not the Tesla," I say, with a horrified tone. He pretends that his feelings are hurt by placing his hand over his heart and looking devastated. His smile returns quickly, and he assures me he will provide an appropriate vehicle.

"Thank you, Mark," I say, with sincerity.

"Not at all," he replies. I'll have the boys valet it so it's gleaming tonight."

As Mark begins to leave, he stops again. "How are things going with your Mum and the money situation?"

"Oh, we're doing all we can to get the money back for her." *It's the truth.*

"Well, best of luck with that," he says with a sympathetic smile, and walks towards the doorway for the third time in 60 seconds.

I text Simon to see if he would like a taxi driver:

I'm picking you up tonight. X

I'm intrigued. Would you like to know where I live? ;)

Gemma. You are officially an idiot.

Yes please x

When I return from lunch, I see Robbie shaking hands with an older gentleman who then leaves. Robbie punches the air once the chap has gone. *Good boy - he's sold a car.* "The old boy wants a toy for the weekends so has bought the MX-5 I got in yesterday."

"Wow, well done you!" I gush. Robbie is very pleased with himself and walks to Mark's office to share the good news. With all the hard work Robbie has gone to in getting the cars in, it's great to see that the gamble is starting to pay off.

The rest of the afternoon follows a similar pattern with Mark, Robbie and myself all caught up with sales and test drives. As we approach the end of the day, the couple I chatted to earlier return to ask to test drive the 1-Series. It all goes smoothly and, after a degree of haggling and several trips to Mark's office to agree warranty deals and deposits, I make a sale. Once they have left, Mark comes over to congratulate me. Robbie is equally pleased and I'm sure relieved that he's shifted another of his stock. "I think I'm getting the hang of this!" I announce. Mark laughs.

The mood at Marquis is much better as we near the end of the day, which is a relief. Mark has his smile back, and still resisting the urge to make sexual comments at every opportunity. Robbie, certainly, is happier and sliding the showroom doors while whistling. And Tania is, well, herself.

Tania!

My eyes widen at the flash of inspiration coursing through my brain cells. "Tania?" I call as she's walking out of the showroom to go home. She walks over to me.

"Yeah?" she asks.

"I've been meaning to ask for ages. Where do you get your skirts from?"

Tania produces the widest grin I've seen on her and her chest swells with pride that I'm wanting to replicate her fashion sense. *I didn't think her chest could swell any more.*

"Well, I go to Rizzlerz on Hay Street. Just past the bakery up the alley." *I know it.* "Make sure you text me what colour you're going to wear tomorrow though, because we can't have the same ones on. Nightmayer!" she laughs.

"I might not be wearing it for work," I scoff. Tania's grin disappears, so I try to dig myself out of the hole I have just created. "What I mean is, I would hate to get oil on them or make them dirty. I think I'll save them for special occasions." The smile comes back. *Good save, Gem.*

I'm just collecting my lunch things from the kitchen when Mark walks in with a cheeky grin. "Enjoy," he says, and throws a single car key to me which is attached to a leather fob. I turn the fob round to see the Porsche logo. I look up at him. "You deserve it for your sale today. Don't crash it!" he warns, with a level of comedy that shows he is deadly serious. *I won't take it out of first gear.*

As I get outside I realise Mark hasn't told me which of the Porsches the key belongs to, so I press the unlock button in the hope it will flash its headlights to reveal itself. A split second later, I hear an alarm chirp to my right and as I turn to see the source I notice the boot of the yellow Porsche finishing its opening. I roll my eyes, in part due to me pressing the wrong button, but mostly at the thought of driving such a conspicuous vehicle. As I start the car, with my heels off, the roar is rather addictive. I blip the throttle a little more and the roar tells me the Porsche is ready to impress Simon. Fortunately it isn't blocked in so I crawl the car off the forecourt, the freshly-valeted tyres giving slight squeaks on the tarmac. I can see Mark in my rearview mirror doing some more air driving as I turn right and roar up the main road to Rizzlerz.

CHAPTER NINETEEN

The car is either very loud or Simon has already been waiting for me, because he is standing on his front step when I reach his house. He is chuckling to himself while shaking his head as I get out of the car. *Another great day to wear a skirt, Gemma.* As I walk up the path to his house, I take in how stunning it is. It's a new-build with a double garage at the end of a quiet cul de sac of large houses. It's clearly a very lovely area filled with people mostly working in the City. Simon greets me with a kiss and cuddle, saying, "Nice car," as his chin rests on my shoulder. "Well, I wanted to get something subtle..." I joke. Chuckling some more, Simon offers me a tour of his bachelor pad which I keenly accept. This guy has no junk, anywhere. Not an ornament out of place, no unwashed crockery, no scuffs on the walls from overuse. The living room is a very large space with a lovely corner sofa and widescreen TV on the wall. *He is very smooth, this guy.* As Simon takes me upstairs for a guided tour, I can see his bedroom through the gap in the bannisters. It is equally minimalistic, the bed is massive and everything is perfectly neat. The bathroom is a similar affair, along with every other room in the house. Even the double garage is pristine, walking to it from the kitchen which has a stunning island bar and recessed lighting around the floor plinths. I reflect on how much I considered us to have in common while we were in Spain. *Everything, it seems, but domestic cleanliness!* Simon senses what I'm thinking and jokes, "This house was a right state five minutes ago, but I've bunged everything in the loft."

"I bet that's just as perfectly laid out as every other room," I retort. His face tells me that it is.

"Ready to go?" I say, needing to change the subject before I feel utterly disorganised.

"Ready when you are, Ronnie."

"Ronnie?" I query.

"Ronnie Biggs. The Great Train Robbery?"

I show Simon how utterly hilarious he is by pushing him into his perfectly organised shoe rack. As we get into the Porsche I can tell Simon is impressed, although handing him my shoes spoils the mood a little. I start the engine and press the button to open the roof. Simon's wide grin widens.

Doing a three-point-turn turns out to be rather tricky in the car due to its blind spots, so I no doubt have the entire street's attention by the time I'm facing the right way and roaring towards Mum's house. "So, why have you got this car, then?" Simon asks suspiciously.

I tease him by saying, "It's Mark's reward to me for doing so well today." I get a mumble rather than a reply. *I think my man is a little jealous.* I chuckle and put him out of his misery. "I asked if I could borrow it overnight." Simon relaxes a little despite looking confused that I would borrow a fancy car in the middle of the week. I smile to myself as we pull up outside Mum's house. Bill's car is again on the driveway, so I park up outside. *I hope no one bumps into the Porsche.* Before switching off the engine, I press the button to close the roof. There is a series of whirring, and then nothing. *Oh, great.* I explain to Simon this happened to Robbie earlier in the week and he mumbles something sarcastic about cheap German cars. After a few more attempts, the roof eventually completes it close. I roll my eyes, mostly out of relief.

As we're getting to the front door, I turn around to see Nat arriving on foot, panting. "You didn't have to run the whole way," I tease. She laughs and explains she didn't want to miss any of the action. Simon glances her a serious stare, as if she is giving away our illegal intentions to the entire street. Simon takes my coat as we enter the house and hangs it, first time, on the hook. *Great. He can do it too.*

"We're in here," Mum calls, showing that our usual Mum Tuesday kitchen table has been replaced with Everybody Tuesday living room sofas.

Mum and Bill are looking very chilled on the two-seater sofa. I choose to sit on the single seat while Simon and Nat head for the larger sofa. Mum is looking at me like she wants me to explain why we're all here before the evening continues. Glancing at Simon and Nat together on the sofa, I get the impression that she thinks we're going to announce some open relationship agreement between the three of us. I decide to get on with it before Imagination makes an appearance.

"Mum, I'm going to get your money back for you." I'm met with a surprised look from Mum, who looks at Bill before replying.

"And how are you going to do that, Love?" *She is so patronising at times.*

"I'm going to steal it back from Parsons!" I announce, waiting for the inevitable. But it doesn't come.

"Okay," she says, calmly. *What?!* "How are you going to do it." I'm a little taken aback by her response, so I stutter my way through my introduction. "Right, well this is what I have so far," I announce, while opening my masterplan notebook:

"Nat has found out that Parsons has a house on Park View, and it has a vault." Mum's eyebrows raise, as if surprised that my plan has even got this far. I carry on, unperturbed.

"It's got to be full of cash, so I'm going to take back what's yours." I look to Simon for encouragement. There isn't any as he appears too busy counting the weaves in Mum's carpet.

Bill decides to take the lead in critiquing my plan.

138

"How will you get into his property?" he asks.

"I will get his keys off him."

"How?" I clear my throat. *Here goes.*

"I'm going to go on a date with him, and at some point in the evening I'll get the keys off him."

"Okay. Well, you'll need to get them cut while on the date because he'll notice they're missing as soon as he heads home."

I love Bill. He isn't judging me, he isn't making any faces. He's taking me so seriously. Which is more to be said than the duo who have joined Simon in a weave-counting contest.

"Well, I need to hand the keys to someone who can get them cut while I'm with Parsons and get them back to me before we leave." *It worked for Rene Russo's character in The Thomas Crown Affair.*

"So, it needs to be someone in this room, really Is there an all-night key cutter close to a bar?"

He's really taking me seriously.

Nat almost makes us jump by breaking her weave-counting with a suggestion. "I might be able to help you there."

My eyes widen. "How?" I ask.

"We have key cutting gear at work. We're always making duplicate copies for new owners. Find a bar near my work and I'll get them cut and returned in minutes."

"Really?" I ask, doing my best to show Nat this gets her a little more involved than we originally agreed.

"It's you nicking the keys, not me," she says, with a wink. I give her an impressed look, showing that I haven't seen this side to her before.

"What about The Highwayman," I suggest, which earns a positive response from Nat. It's a five minute walk from Nat's work so would be perfect.

"Okay, so you have the keys. Now what?" Simon asks sharply. I take a breath before continuing, desperate for Simon to take the plan seriously.

"I'll ask him on another date so that he'll be miles away at another bar. By the time he realises he's been stood up, I will already have the money. But, I need all of you to be my alibis." This earns me a roomful of inquisitive faces, so I explain.

"There is a posh restaurant a few hundred yards from Parsons' house. The Sunset? We are all going to have a meal there and, during the meal I'm going to sneak out and do the deed." Everyone looks at each other, waiting for someone to spot a hole in the plan's simplistic genius. Bill is first to suggest a flaw.

"What if the vault has a code rather than a key? It might even be an eyeball scanner!"

"Cut his eye out!" shouts Mum.

"Too messy," says Bill with a deadpan face. It's probably mostly nerves but we all break into laughter, even Simon. Once again, I marvel at Bill's ability to control the mood of a room. As the laughter subsides, I get back to my plan.

"I'll be able to tell if any of the keys I cut is a security key," offers Nat. Bill nods. *The plan is still working.*

"What about an alarm?" asks Mum, her first rational comment of the evening so far. "He's bound to have an alarm if he has a vault with millions of pounds inside." *Good point.*

I spot Simon looking over at Bill, who returns with a mischievous grin. *Of course!*

"Bill, you did this for a job before you retired, didn't you?"

"Yes I did, Gemma," he replies, looking over at Simon wondering what else he has shared about his father.

"So, can you disable any alarm system that Parsons has?"

Bill leans forward to the coffee table and picks up a mini battenberg from the selection Mum has laid on plates, which up until now I hadn't noticed. Bill savours the battenberg, sitting back into the sofa and inhaling deeply through his nose. I can't help but notice how much he is enjoying building the suspense. Eventually, I can't take any more.

"Well?" I push.

Bill smiles and, nodding at the half-eaten battenberg in his hand, whispers, "Piece of cake," with a wink at me. More laughter. Bill then offers to do a reccy of The Sunset to find a suitable place to hide his tools for easy retrieval. Simon starts to nod, as if to show that the plan is looking more feasible by the minute. He is next to ask a question.

"So, what will you do with all the money? You can't walk back into the restaurant with it all." I smile at him for starting to believe in me.

"There is a private road behind his property, lined with bushes. I will drop the money out of the window into the bushes for us to collect a few hours later. We just need to hope he doesn't check his money every time he comes home."

I lift up my hands to indicate I've finished, and interlock my fingers waiting for final hole-picking.

"I like it," declares Nat. I give her a thankful look.

Mum nods in agreement. "Just be careful, Love." Bill echoes her comments. I look to Simon with puppy dog eyes for several seconds until I get a response.

"Okay, I admit. It looks like it could work, assuming everything works the way you hope," he adds with a serious look. I nod to show I'm listening. "You just need to promise that you won't venture from the plan. If it doesn't work first time, we walk away. We forget about it and we move on. Agreed?"

I run over to Simon and throw my arms around him. I thank him through sniffles. Bill breaks the mood with one more comment.

"Just one slight problem in all of this though, Gemma." *Just one?* "How are you going to get a date from him?"

I smile.

CHAPTER TWENTY

A week ago, if anyone had asked me what I would be doing today, I can't say I would have expected to be bending over a yellow Porsche's engine bay in a mini skirt at seven in the morning. And certainly not outside Steve Parsons' Park View house. I have no idea if he's in, if he sleeps in until Noon or if he's even in the country, but I've decided to play the odds and see if I can get some attention. For the past hour, I have given the yellow beast a few croaky revs every five minutes, before returning to my engine bay position. So far, I have received a couple of curtain twitches from neighbours and the odd taxi driver has slowed down to get a good look down my blouse. *Things haven't gone as planned.* After promising to allow myself ten more minutes of revving however, I am startled by a voice behind me.

"You look like you need some help." I spin round to see Parsons checking out my legs. His eyes slowly make their way up my body until they get to my chest, staying there for a moment before finally meeting my own. "What seems to be the problem?" he asks, with a smarmy grin. Mark is like a vicar in comparison to this creature.

"I'm not sure," I reply, turning back to the engine bay. *He hasn't recognised me!* "It just isn't running properly." And it won't, seeing as I've removed the plug to the Mass Air Flow Meter. Google doesn't just show you how to *fix* cars.

"Allow me" Parsons offers, leaning in to have a look. Despite a large engine bay, and the fact he could have looked from the other side, he brushes right up to me in order to take a look. He finds the fault within a few seconds, pushes the sensor's plug into position and encourages me to start the car, following me to the driver's door. With the roof off it's very easy to see into the cockpit and rather obvious that Parsons is wanting a cheap upskirt thrill as I get in. I feign surprise and elation when the Porsche delivers its well-tuned voice and get back out of the car to show my appreciation.

"I don't know how to thank you," I gush, fluttering my heavily made up eyelashes.

"Well..." Parsons begins, as I had hoped, "why don't you let me take you out for a drink?"

"Let you take *me* out for a drink, when it's you that has helped *me*?" I query, doing my best to flirt with a guy I'm keen to turn into a eunuch. He chuckles, leaning against the car.

"How about tomorrow at 8pm?" he suggests.

I look upwards as if to consult a diary and then say, "That's fine. What about The Highwayman?" I'm hoping he doesn't raise suspicion that I already have a venue in mind but it seems to go over his head.

"Done! I'll pick you up at 7:30pm if you tell me where you live." *I wasn't expecting that. Think fast, Gem.*

"No offense, but I don't know you. I'll meet you there, 8pm." Parsons appears a little taken aback by this, but eventually relents with a smirk. I think he regards my reservation as a little challenge, so he nods to accompany the smirk.

"See you tomorrow, then." I nod and begin to close the boot.

"Wait!" he says. *Oh no, he's made me.* "I don't even know your name. I'm Steve," he says, offering his hand.

"I'm Tania," I reply. I feel the name complements the look.

"Tania," Parsons echoes, as if to check it suits me. We shake hands. "So, what are you doing now, Tania?" I explain that I'm heading out for the day to see friends.

"And you?" I counter. *It's worth finding out a bit more about this git.*

"Nothing much." he replies. "I'm going to walk the dog and then do some business in town."

"What is it you do?" I ask.

"A bit of this, a bit of that," he says, with a similar smirk to earlier. "Right, well I'll see you later, Tania." I sign off and get in the car, roaring off to Marquis. He's bitten the bait!

Two things cross my mind. The first is that I hadn't considered Parsons might have a dog. The second is that I really should have brought a change of clothes with me for working at Marquis today.

As I drive away from Parsons, I press the button to close the Porsche's roof but nothing happens. Nothing. Not even a whir. I repeat the procedure a couple of times to discover the roof is not going to perform its duty. I decide to leave it and inform Robbie when I get to Marquis.

You know that feeling you get when a police car appears in your rear-view mirror and you instantly feel guilty? I can confirm that the feeling of guilt is far worse when you have just begun the first stage of robbing someone. After a short while I approach a pelican crossing but stop at the green light purely out of nerves at being followed by Plod. After realising my error, I start to drive off but stall the car and look down at the gearstick to rectify the issue. Granted, I don't drive every day but I know the order in which gears go in a car. Right now it's different though because I still have a police car in my rear view mirror. Right now, brain surgery would be an easier task than selecting the right gear. I'm not sure how long I've been here, but it must have been at least a month. I hope that maybe the policemen have moved on. Or retired. *A quick check - nope, still there.* I take a deep breath, compose myself, find gear one and, after a fair bit of crunching, pull away. Through what is now a red light.

If you ask me, I don't think mobility scooters should be on the roads anyway. It's not the vehicles per se, but rather the aged has-beens who are driving them. Mum or Dad gets too naff at driving in their old age, so what do the kids do? Put them in a plastic-covered gokart which can trundle round Tesco's vegetable aisle or the North Circular so that they can still 'live an independent life'. All that being said though, the chap driving this scooter does a great job of avoiding me. He continues his original route past the front of my car, giving me one of those disapproving looks only old people can give.

The "Are you okay, Miss?" that comes out of nowhere makes me jump clean out of my seat. But when I turn to see a policeman standing next to my car, I nearly wet myself. "I said, are you okay, Miss?" he asks again. I swallow and stutter my way through explaining how it's not my car, quick to add that it's not stolen. After sharing a lot of personal information and receiving a bucketload of advice similar in tone to that which I received in the airport, the policeman appears content that I'm not a major threat to pensioners in the area. He does however recommend that "perhaps a lady like you who is not used to high performance vehicles" should stick to plain old hatchbacks. It pains me to nod in agreement but feel it's the best way to end the torture. Satisfied that he has belittled me enough, the policeman heads back to his car and they drive off to save the day elsewhere.

I puff air through my lips at how much action my morning has already had. I conclude that nothing else can happen to me today.

Oh good. It's raining.

CHAPTER TWENTY ONE

I was initially relieved to be driving into work this morning. I knew the Porsche would receive a lot of attention but I suspected far less than my skirt would have had on public transport. Things are a little different though when you're driving a bright yellow convertible with its roof down in the pouring rain. Robbie is already looking out across the forecourt as I arrive, I suspect because he can hear the engine from some distance. His jaw drops as I pull up and I can see him motioning for Mark and Tania. *Oh, please no.* Mark walks over slowly to join Robbie, as does Tania, and they all stare at me through the showroom windows. I press the roof button one last time in a feeble attempt to fix it - the flipping thing closes first time. I roll my eyes, take a deep sigh and pick up my handbag ready to get out of the car. I conclude there isn't much point running for cover and risk falling in my heels due to my already damp state, so I open the door slowly and get out. As I close the door and head for the showroom, Robbie's jaw is even wider as he sees the skirt I am almost not wearing. Tania gives an impressed look and Mark...multiple Christmases arriving at once.

By the time I reach the showroom, Mark has managed to compose himself and innocently says, "Good Morning, Gemma."

"Don't ask," I reply, handing Robbie the keys to the Porsche and walking to the toilets to dry myself as best I can. As I close the toilet door, wishing the ground could swallow me up, I hear Tania's heels clacking their way towards the toilet door.

"Hiya!" she exclaims. I don't answer, but continue to remove my makeup. "Is there anything I can do, Gemma?" I'm about to ask for a large brandy when my eyes suddenly widen. *Of course!* I spin round and head to the cupboard in the corner and there, hanging majestically, is my trouser suit which I left here before I went to Spain. For the first time ever, I'm delighted at my absent-mindedness - if I was organised, it wouldn't be here. I quickly change and Tania offers to hang up my skirt. "It's a shame you couldn't wear it today. We could have been skirt buddies!" *Shame.*

Mark & Robbie are both watching from the other side of the showroom as I emerge from the toilets. Looks of disappointment appear, I guess because the day's worth of wind-up material they have been creating is now superfluous.

"I'm sorry about the car, Mark." He walks over while looking at my new outfit and smiling.

"No problem, Gemma. It'll dry. Besides, I'm glad it happened to you rather than a customer." *I bet you are.* "How did Simon like it?" I shake my head apologetically for not mentioning it first.

"He loved it. Thanks so much."

"Any time," he says warmly. *Mark's great.* I've just given one of his most expensive cars an internal wash and he seems unfazed.

I offer to make coffees by way of a conversation changer and soon return with Mark's cappuccino. "So, hopefully we'll have more of the same today," I say, referring to the amount of customers we saw yesterday.

"Here's hoping," Mark replies, sipping his coffee.

Conscious that I need to speak in code in case the police ever get involved, I send Simon a text:

All went well this morning. Meeting sorted for 8pm x

I then ponder the latest addition to Operation Parsons: The dog. A guy like him must own quite a beast, but it could mean that there is no alarm system activated if his canine chum is free to patrol the house. I conclude that I'll either have an alarm to contend with or something that can tear me to pieces. *Oh good!*

"You okay, Gem?" asks Robbie, noticing that I'm looking distant.

"Fine, thanks," I reply. *I'm just plotting how to rob someone.*

"Could you move the Porsche for me, so I can get it off the front of the forecourt?"

I get up to move it, but notice a woman checking out a Mercedes SLK so decide to deal with that first. As it happens, the woman owns an older version of the same car so would like to do a part exchange. This is good news because it makes the process much simpler, as opposed to indecisive folk who test drive a dozen different cars. We go through the car's range of switchgear and make sure everything works - especially the roof - and the woman takes it for a test drive. It's comical because she has decided to buy it before the rear wheels have left the forecourt. In fairness, it's exactly the same as the car she's trading in except this one is cherry red so she's satisfied as soon as she knows there are no suspicious clunks or groans. Within half an hour of us returning to the forecourt, she has signed the appropriate paperwork and agreed to collect the car early next week. I wave her off before returning to tell Mark the good news.

As I'm making my way back into the showroom, Robbie is giving me the same kind of look a disappointed parent gives. "What?" I say, rather abruptly.

"The Porsche?" he replies with raised eyebrows. *Oh, yes. I forgot.* I turn to move the car as Mark appears from his office.

"How did it go, Gemma?" I turn back to share the good news with Mark, deciding it's more important to deal with the boss first. I can't see Robbie's reaction, but I guess his 'disappointed parent' look will be even more exaggerated in a while.

"So, how did it go?" Mark asks again, sitting at his desk. I tell him the good news, and he is overjoyed. I honestly think he is more happy for me than the fact his company has made a few more grand this week.

Despite the occasional perv moments, I can't fault his support. "Well, I won't keep you then, sales guru!" I blush. "Best you get out there and sell some more motors - but I'll have a coffee first," he adds, with a wink. I smile appreciatively and nod. Heading to the kitchen there is no sign of Robbie, so I'm off the hook Porsche-wise for a little while longer. As I emerge a few minutes later with Mark's caffeine fix, I discover Robbie's taken a client on a test drive. *This week could be a good earner for Mark after all.*

Sitting back at my desk, I organise paperwork and then get back into a minor daze considering how best to deal with Parsons' dog. I smile to myself thinking the canine is most likely his only friend - and even then, it has no choice. I get so caught up with my head-plotting that only a text from my man tells me it's the end of the day:

I'm outside x

I decide not to tell Simon I forgot he is picking me up today, so I gather my things, along with my less-damp skirt in the toilets, and head out to see Mr. Fireman. As I'm crossing the forecourt, I hear an exaggerated cough from behind me. Turning round, I see Mr Disappointed Parent giving me his now well-practised look. I roll my eyes and look apologetically at him. I put down my things, hop into the Porsche and discover that car seats need a lot longer to dry. I've never sat on a sponge but I suspect it's a similar experience. I look over to Robbie who gives a satisfied smile before closing the showroom windows. *He knew the seats were wet all along. Revenge is sweet, my friend.* I move the car, collect my things and head to Simon. I lay my coat down on his passenger seat to save his leather getting similarly damp. I'm greeted with a lovely kiss.

"Good day?" he asks. *Where do I start...?*

As we make the journey to mine, it occurs to me how many times I've got involuntarily soaked in the past week alone. Any more exposure and I think I'll turn into a fish.

Once at mine, I nip upstairs to change while Simon makes himself a cold drink. I'm down within a couple of minutes and I walk to collect Nat from her house. I'm glad Simon suggested we do a reccy of the pub where I'm taking Parsons tomorrow as it will help establish the best place for me to nick his keys without being seen by others.

"Nice car," Nat says as she slides into the back. I say 'back', but Nat has to pull her legs almost up to her chest in order to fit in. Simon gives a little grin. It takes us quite a while to get to The Highwayman due to it still being rush hour for many, but it means we're able to chat as a threesome. To begin with, it proves difficult to talk about anything but Operation Parsons but before long we're chatting about normal life. *How refreshing.* I strikes me how well Nat and Simon get on which is lovely to see. At one point they're busy chuckling over something they both saw on TV which makes me feel a little out of the loop, but I decide to let them have their moment without interrupting. *This can't be what jealousy feels like. I don't get jealous.*

They're still busy talking about some reality TV show that has recently come on air as we approach The Highwayman. I have never understood why millions of people tune in to see how other people live, but as life draws on I realise how often I find myself in the minority. *It's even happening in this flipping car!*

The Highwayman has a massive gravel car park and the pub itself is glowing with an array of accent lighting shining up its exterior walls. At the rear of the pub I can just make out the river glistening slightly in the moonlight. It's the perfect Sunday afternoon venue for families to have some time together. Or, just right to rob a conman on a Thursday night.

I think for the first time since we've been an item when walking together, Simon doesn't take my hand. I pass it off as him not wanting Nat to feel like a spare part, forever the thoughtful gentleman. *I'd still rather he held my hand though.*

The Highwayman is nicely laid out as a country pub with a large wood burner at one end flanked by a couple of mock Chesterfield sofas. To our left is the dining area, but the area of focus for us is the bar area to the right. I open my mouth to see what everyone wants to drink but Simon, yet again, beats me to it. I smile. Nat and I both choose a red wine while Simon heads for a Hoegaarden, a cloudy belgian beer which looks like a diabetic's sample for their doctor. He takes a sip and seems to enjoy it. *To each their own.*

The three of us turn our backs to the bar to assess potential robbing areas. I am racked with nerves feeling everyone knows what we're up to. After a quick scan of the area I realise we're mostly alone except for a few diners and the barman who has gone to collect empty glasses. Simon kicks things off by suggesting one of the Chesterfields as a good spot. It's a good idea, but I comment how if anyone else sits on the other sofa I will be quite overlooked. Simon nods in agreement. Nat is the next to offer the suggestion of a quieter area in the corner, so Simon and I crane our necks to see where she is referring to. *Perfect.* It's not overlooked and seems just right. Simon also is pleased with the suggestion because he and Nat can sit on one of the Chesterfields and keep a protective watch over me without Parsons realising.

"Well that didn't take long, then," I joke. Simon and Nat both laugh but it appears to be an effort for them. "Guys, I'll be fine," I assure them, understanding their reservations. "You're a stone's throw from me. If things get silly, we can get out easy." Simon nods with an expression to suggest he is acting under duress. I put my hand on the forearm he is using to lean against the bar and give him a look of assurance. "I'll be fine," I confirm. He nods and smiles.

"Okay," says Nat, realising we need a change of subject. "Let's get our money's worth out of this fireplace."

Winter is still a way off, but the Autumn evenings of late have got decidedly cooler. The fire isn't roaring, so it's just right at taking the chill off an otherwise cooler temperature. The three of us do the classic British thing of finding lots to laugh about without once mentioning the elephant in the room. I'm relieved not to hear any more discussion of reality TV or other 'in jokes' that only 66% of the party can relate to.

As I go to get a second round of drinks in, Nat suggests we have a meal which earns her a look from both of us, suggesting it is verging on inappropriate. "Hey, we're here aren't we? And I haven't eaten yet."

I'm about to find us a table when Simon stops me. "Better not, Gem. You're back here tomorrow chatting up another bloke. What if someone recognises you?" I take a breath, considering the question. I then feel a grin spread across my face before replying to my special man.

"I'll be looking rather different tomorrow, won't I"? Simon looks down and laughs. He forgot that it's Tania seeing Parsons tomorrow.

We head to the dining area and enjoy a lovely meal together before heading back home. The roads are virtually empty due to the time of evening so we're back in good time. Nat and Simon both decide to turn in early, with Simon suggesting I also get an early night's sleep. "Big day tomorrow, Gem," he says. *Thanks for the reminder*. Nat has already said her goodbyes and gone to her home as I'm kissing Simon goodbye. As usual, he waits for me to get in the house before driving off.

As I'm locking up, my handbag wolf whistles.

Sleep well. I love you x

I love you too, Mister.

I collapse into bed.

CHAPTER TWENTY TWO

It appears Insomnia is the solution to sleeping through your alarm. I've been awake since the small hours, my brain buzzing with dreams about robbing Parsons. Robbie didn't feature in a skirt but he was replaced many times over by Parsons' dog cornering me in an alley. I switch the alarm off immediately and stagger to the curtains to let some light in. I notice my intact bin bags at the end of the garden and it dawns on me that I haven't had any feline presents since last week's soaking. *Nat was right - it works!* I chuckle to myself while shaking my head as I relive 'Hosegate'. *How embarrassing.*

I get dressed for work and prepare tonight's outfit for my alter ego. I lay out the second of the two skirts I bought from Rizzlerz. Its vivid colour makes it look almost radioactive so I decide not to add more colour, opting instead for heels and a tight black v-neck. In all the years I have bought and worn clothes, this is the first time I've prepared an outfit hours before needing it...and it's not even for me. It's for Tania, the yellow Porsche-driving seductress.

Showered, lunch made and breakfast eaten, I find I have spare time to sit with a coffee before heading off to work. A wolf whistle breaks the morning silence. *My man is awake!*

Be careful today x

Correction. My mum is awake.

Since I've been able to understand the English language, Mum has told me to be careful in everything I do. As I'm considering a suitable reply, I get another wolf whistle. *My man's awake now!*

Morning beautiful. Pick you up from work again? X

Yes please, handsome. x

And it's time to leave. I give up on the sarcastic reply to Mum and choose to send a simpler message.

x

I adhere to The Code all the way to my next caffeine fix and I'm greeted with a broad smile from Sally. "Got much on today, Gemma?" *You wouldn't believe me if I told you.*

"So-So," I reply. She smiles and narrows her eyes at me suspiciously. Starting my eleven minutes, I reflect on how I'm beginning to enjoy being a woman of mystery and how I should keep it up in future. However it does strike me that in doing so I'll be a step closer to people I can't stand on social media; the ones who hint at a personal dilemma, but when others post concerning questions like, "what's up hun?" the original poster says, "I can't tell you." *Then don't start!*

My opinionated musings occupy the majority of my walk, so I soon find myself greeting Robbie sliding open the showroom windows. Tania is already settled and sitting at her desk, suggesting she also got up early. "Morning Tania," I offer.

Tania gives little more than a grunt. *The dog whistle is broken.*

"What's wrong?" I ask, with genuine concern.

"Phil dumped me last night."

"Phil? I thought it was John."

Tania rolls her eyes at me. "That was *last* week."

Of course. I conclude Tania's life isn't as simple as I once thought.

"I'm sorry to hear your news, Tania. I make a good Cheering-Up Coffee," I say, catching her eye.

Tania smiles back through a few sniffles. "That would be lovely, thanks."

She then dabs her eyes with a tissue and tuts when she realises her mascara is running. "Nightmayer!" she declares, and heads for the toilets.

And that is the highlight of the entire day other than trying - and failing - to create impressive latte art on everyone's coffees.

Mark walks out from his office to the showroom around an hour before close and declares that we can go home. "There's no point sitting around waiting for nobody to turn up," he explains. *Good logic.* I grab my things and head for home, texting Simon that he no longer needs to collect me. Between our text exchanges, I determine he hasn't had much of a lunch so buy some ingredients on the way home to create a lasagne.

With my journey added to the mix, Simon arrives at mine around 15 minutes after me. I'm still in my work clothes when I answer the door. I give my man a cheery "Hello, you!" He doesn't reply. Instead, he walks straight up to me, grabs me around the waist and pulls me in tightly for a passionate kiss. *This is nice.*

"Hello yourself," he replies, once his tongue is back in his own mouth. Simon lays the table while things are cooking in the oven and then we both sit to chat through final details for tonight.

We establish that Nat is coming over at 7pm, giving us ample time to get to The Highwayman and settled before Parsons arrives. The last thing we want is him seeing us arriving together, as that would ruin the whole thing. My man then goes quiet and looks down thoughtfully to the table, lining up the cutlery in front of him perfectly beside the placemat. "Gem..." Simon begins. *I know what's coming.*

"Yep?"

"You really don't have to do this."

"I know I don't. But I want to."

He smiles and nods. I can tell this is the last time he will give me a get-out.

We discuss final plans once more which ends just as the oven beeps to tell me the lasagne is ready. I'm far from a culinary expert but Simon appears to enjoy the result served with salad and garlic bread. With my playlist accompanying our chats about Life, The Universe and Robbery, 6pm comes round rather quickly. *Time to get ready.* Simon makes himself comfy watching the tv while I go upstairs to change. It takes me quite a while to perfect my creation due to having to curl my hair as well as apply shedloads of makeup. I eventually emerge from the bedroom and head downstairs, walking into the living room.

"What do you think?" I ask, putting one hand on my hip and another behind my head in a comic attempt to pose like a model.

"Who are you, and what have you done with my girlfriend?" Simon demands in jest. We both laugh, probably out of nerves more than anything else.

I step back into the hallway to collect my heels and choose to sit down on the stairs to put them on. As I'm partway through Shoe #1, I hear Nat turning her key in my lock to let herself in. *The first time she hasn't knocked when Simon has been here.*

"Blimey!" she announces, seeing me in my revealing garb. I stick my tongue out at her and finish buckling Shoe #2. I stand up, straighten my skirt and declare that I'm ready. Nat walks back out through the front door she hasn't yet closed, followed by Simon. I lock up, grab my handbag and bring up the rear.

Once we're in the car, Simon turns round to Nat to check that everything is in place with the key cutting part of the evening. She gives him a reassuring smile. "It's all ready and waiting. I can have them cut and be back within fifteen minutes."

Simon pauses for a while and then turns back to her. "Take my car, it'll halve the time." I look at Nat to show this is a good idea, and she agrees.

"It's all sorted then," I announce, earning a mean look from Simon.

"Apart from stealing his keys and returning them without him knowing, I mean." Cue more nervous laughter from the three of us.

As we're approaching The Highwayman, my phone vibrates. I decided earlier that it may be best to avoid wolf whistles during the evening. I smile at the predictable text from my mother:

Be careful x

I'm glad she reminded me.

Simon and Nat walk into the pub first, as agreed, with me following a minute later. By the time I walk in, Nat is already sat at the Chesterfield sofa and Simon is at the bar. He is busy putting an order in with a barman, different to who was serving last night. I'm standing around a metre away from Simon when another member of staff walks behind the bar and looks at us both .

"Are you together?" he asks. We both reply "No" quickly and abruptly which takes him back a little. He then asks me what I would like to drink, so I order an orange juice. *It would be handy staying sober tonight.* Orange juice served and paid for, I head over to the table we agreed upon last night while Simon is still having his order completed. Once at my table I decide to get my phone out to look more relaxed and look at my news app, although I'm unable to concentrate on any of the articles. Out of the corner of my eye, I look over to see Nat and Simon sitting on a sofa each. This is a good move because it has given them an opportunity to talk together without anyone else listening nearby. Simon has sat so that he can look at me and Nat is facing the door. I've noticed that her legs are crossed in such a way that her foot is almost touching my man's leg. *Not now, Imagination.* I try to concentrate on my news app but keep being drawn to Nat's foot. After a few more seconds, I notice that she gives Simon a small kick. *Did she just boot my man?* She then does it again, only harder. *What is she doing?* As I'm wondering how much longer Simon is going to stand for it, a familiar figure walks into the bar area. I roll my eyes when I realise Nat is signalling to Simon that Mr Gitface has arrived. *Parsons is here.*

He stands in the doorway and scans the bar area until his eyes fall on me. I give a small wave and his smarmy grin spreads across his face. He walks over to me, so I stand up to greet him. He is already looking me up and down as he gets closer, eventually opening his mouth to produce words. "Tania, I thought you'd stood me up when I couldn't see the Porsche."

"I took a taxi," I lie. He gives me a small peck on the cheek. *Sorry, Simon.*

"Of course, you can have a few drinks then, can't you," he says, increasing the suggestiveness in his tone. I smile, feeling it's better than giving an answer. "What are you drinking?" he asks.

"No, it's me buying *you* the drink," I interject. "You helped me, remember?" Parsons pauses, taking stock of the deal.

"Okay...you can get the next round in. So, what are you having?"

"I'll have a small red wine please." *I'd better keep it small if there's another round coming.*

"Large red wine it is then," he says with a wink. The guy talks like he has had it confirmed he is God's gift to women. He has been misinformed.

As Parsons walks to the bar, I give a quick glance to Simon who responds with a subtle wink. *I'm so pleased you're here.* Despite the company, I feel very safe with my man just a few yards away. A couple of minutes later and Parsons walks back, sits down opposite me with his back to Nat and Simon and places his keys on the table. *The keys!* I imagined a few scenarios of where the keys may have ended up. Obviously, staying in his trouser pockets would have ended the deal there and then; there was no way I was going near them! Considering he is not wearing a coat, the table was the only other alternative. Relief that the keys have ended up where I hoped is soon replaced by trepidation at the plan still going ahead. I place my handbag on the table in which to put my phone and, as rehearsed so many times over the past few days, place it beside his keys in order to block them from view. I then slide the handbag (and keys) further down the table to imply it gives me more elbow room to lean on the table. Any suspicion that may have been aroused is replaced by another sort of arousal as my leaning forward gives Parsons an eyeful of my 34D assets. Despite the discomfort, squeezing them into a 34C plunge bra has proved to be a good move.

One of the first conversation topics instigated by Parsons is to enquire what I do for a living. I can't work out whether he's genuinely interested or wants to know how I can afford a Porsche.

"I am an accountant," I reply, exactly as I had rehearsed.

"Oh, where abouts?" *I wasn't expecting that.*

"In the City." *Please don't ask me what the company is called?*

"Cool. What company is that, then?"

Oh good! "I'm, er, freelance. I work for a variety of companies." I'm not sure how accountancy works, but it sounds believable to me. Either way, Parsons appears to buy it. I then return the question, wondering if he will elaborate on his "This and that" answer a couple of days ago. He doesn't. He's very vague and clearly wants to be cagey about what he does. I give a look that shows disappointment at his secrecy - we are supposed to be on a sort of date, after all, but he attempts a reassuring smile.

"It's all legal."

You haven't been put in prison, Parsons - that doesn't make it legal.

Giving him credit, conversation never dries up and he appears to have an endless supply of questions to ask in order to keep us chatting. Eventually our drinks run dry, so I offer to buy him another lager. "Go on then. While you do that, I'll go and have a slash." *God's gift.*

Parsons gets up with me and we walk together towards the bar with his hand in the small of my back. I half expect Simon to throttle him, but my man appears to be composing himself. Either that, or Nat has wrestled him to the ground. *Not now, Imagination. Please!* As I stop at the bar he continues his walk to the toilets. After seeing him turn a corner, I pray like mad that Nat has taken the opportunity to do her thing. It takes everything within me not to turn around to check. Drinks poured and money exchanged, I turn to walk back to my table. As I get closer to it, my handbag comes into view but I'm unable to see beyond it. Once I've sat down, I return my purse to my handbag and see that the keys have indeed gone. I glance over to Simon who is now sitting alone. My stomach turns with a surge of adrenalin. *Nat's doing it!* I find myself breathing faster so take a quick sip of my wine to calm me down. I do remarkably well to stop my shaky hand from spilling my wine everywhere and replace my glass to the table to take a deep breath of composure.

My breathing is largely back to normal by the time Parsons rejoins me at the table. I immediately slide his lager over to him by way of eliminating his gaze from going anywhere else. Giving an appreciative smile he takes a long sip. He gives a loud exhalation of satisfaction and returns the glass to the table. "Drinks are always nice...when someone else has paid for them," he jokes.

I laugh. It stops me from punching him.

It's my turn to keep him talking now so that he doesn't have any reason to look for his keys. Favourite football teams, childhood memories, best holiday destination, previous relationships - I get a conversation going from every topic that enters my head, to the point where Parsons appears to be enjoying my company less. After around ten minutes of waffling, he dives in to change the subject and asks me if I'm seeing anyone at the moment.

"Nothing serious," I reply.

He delivers his signature smile again, sighing "That's good. I'd love to see you again, Tania." I determine that he must be desperate, considering my painful topics of discussion over the past fifteen minutes. *Fifteen minutes! Where has she got to!* "Do you want another drink?" offers Parsons. I know that if I decline we will be heading off and Parsons will know his keys are missing straight away. So, I accept the offer with the added thought he will no doubt need to visit the facilities again. The trouble is, I'm rather keen for the loo as well. Parsons gets up and says, "Red wine again?" to which I nod, emphasising that I want a small one. "Large red wine coming up," he replies with a smirk. *He's trying to get me hammered. And he's succeeding.* As he heads to the bar for our third round of drinks, I glance to Simon who gives me a similarly clueless expression to show he has no idea where Nat has got to. *Has she been rumbled? Has she crashed Simon's car?* As a ton of thoughts course through my head about what could have happened to her, the bar door opens with a rather out of breath Nat appearing. She composes herself quickly and walks over to resume her seat with Simon. The looks of relief on mine and Simon's faces would be noticeable to anyone who has been looking, but the bar fortunately is still empty of other patrons. Simon gives me a subtle nod to indicate that the deed has been done and I return to character just as Parsons is walking back to the table.

Laying down my drink and his own, he announces, "Back in a mo. I need another slash." I nod, rolling my eyes once his back is turned. He seems to take a lifetime to make his way to the toilet corridor but as soon as he turns the corner Nat leaps from her chair and makes her way over to me. While playing the scenario over in my head this week I had visions of the handover requiring far more stealth and finesse. As it happens, Nat is able to walk straight over and hand me the keys without anyone noticing. She gives me a wink and says, "All done. And there is a security key!"

This means that the vault almost certainly has a regular keyhole as opposed to any other form of gadgetry. *Result.* I put the keys back where they were behind my handbag as Nat returns to her seat. Parsons returns around a minute later and joins us. He leads most of the conversations this time - *I can't imagine why* - and drinks his pint rather quickly. Despite being rather squiffy by this point, I still down the third drink in good time due to not wanting to spend any more time than necessary with Mr Gitface. Drinks done, Parsons takes a breath.

"So, I've had a good time tonight, Gemma. Thank you for your company."

"Me too," I reply. *That was easy.* "We must do it again" I add. His eyes light up.

"Great. How about now, back at mine." *No chance, Mister.* I use the excuse of having to be up early in the morning but ask him if he's free Saturday night, as agreed between us at Mum's a few days ago. Parsons pauses, then shakes his head.

"I'll be out of the country on business." My heart sinks at how the date can't go ahead, and then it jumps for joy. *He's out of the country altogether. Much better!* I pretend to be disappointed and offer to catch up with him when he's back. "Yeah, sounds great. Give me your mobile number," he says, getting his phone out of his pocket to tap in the numbers. *Think fast, Gem.*

"Why don't you give me *your* number and I'll call *you*?"

Parsons smiles. "Still don't trust me, then?" he teases.

"It's not that. I just don't give my phone out to people until I've known them for a while. It's a rule I have." Parsons makes some sideways comment about rules being broken, but agrees to give me his mobile number.

He then offers to drive me home but I decline, saying I have ordered a taxi for 11pm. It's only 10:30am, so I consider it a suitable answer. "Well, I'll stay with you until it arrives," he offers. *Great.* Despite all the planning, all the Plan Bs I have had in place, I'm completely unprepared for this outcome. I pretend to be positive about Parsons' suggestion and then excuse myself to the toilets, taking my handbag with me. Once safely in the powder room, I text Simon:

Help! He's going to stay until my 'taxi' arrives.

Silence, for what seems like an eternity.

Sorted. Come back and play along. X

I'm seriously trusting you now, Simon. I consider the next few minutes to be the deciding factor for whether Simon is a keeper or not. I'm busting for the loo anyway, and once I'm finished I head back to the table. "I thought you'd fallen in!" jokes Parsons.

"There was a queue," I fib. Parsons laughs.

"There are never queues in the gents. We just whip it out and get on with it." *Thanks for that.*

As Parsons begins to reel off other differences between men and women, I'm beginning to wonder what on earth Simon has planned. Then, with the bar's clock nearing 11pm, Nat and Simon both get up and walk out of the pub. Both of them. Straight out of the pub. *Great plan, guys. I'm alone.* I'm wondering what on earth to do as Nat walks back into the bar and loudly says "Taxi for Tania!." *Utter genius.*

I sigh, "That's me then," and collect my things to leave.

"I'll walk you out," offers Parsons. He puts his hand in the small of my back and leads me out of the pub. There, parked perpendicular to the entrance, is Simon's BMW.

"Blimey, that's a taxi and a half," announces Parsons.

"Yeah, it's the boss's," explains Nat. "All our other cars are on jobs, so I used his for this last pickup." No suspicion from Parsons, huge elation from me.

"Well thank you for a lovely evening Steve," I say, offering him my cheek. He kisses it and attempts to turn into something more passionate but I pull away. He smiles again at my implied frigidity with a look that says, "I'll break you eventually." *I forgot. He's God's gift..*

Parsons opens the rear door for me to step into, and Nat drives us away.

"Thank you, thank you, thank you," I exclaim.

"No worries," Nat chuckles. "Me and Simon were talking about this maybe happening with about half an hour to go. I can't believe we didn't think of it sooner. Still, no harm done. You're out now."

"And you've got the keys!" I announce.

Nat reaches down to her side and jangles a bunch of freshly-cut keys in front of me. We both laugh. Nat drives a few hundred metres to a bus stop where Simon is waiting for us. He and Nat swap seats and I remain in the back.

"Hello," Simon says to me, like we're old friends on a regular night out. I reply in kind and we all laugh again. Simon quickly spins the car round and drives quickly to the bypass. "I thought it would be a good idea to be waiting for Parsons when he gets home. We might see if he has an alarm system or not." I nod at my man's brilliance, yet again. "Did you get another date out of him," he adds.

"Better than that," I grin. "He's out of the country."

"Of course" exclaims Simon. "He's going to want to check out this new plot of land he's just bought." I shake my head again at how he has been able to get away with robbing so many people.

We pull up across the road from Parsons' home around twenty minutes later, turning off the engine and lights. "Of course, he may not be coming straight home," Nat suggests. At that, the street gets lit up by a pair of xenon headlights approaching us from behind. It slows as a black Lexus gets closer, parking up across the road from us. *It's him!* We all crane our necks to see Parsons hop up the steps to his house. He pauses for a moment looking down to his keys, I suspect to find the right one, and then opens his door. We try our best to see if there is a form of alarm system, but Parsons simply closes the door behind him.

"Looks like we need your Dad then," I say to Simon. He sighs, nods and drives off back to mine. I then turn my attention to Nat. "You, girl, are a superstar. On two counts! Amazing effort with the key cutting, and again for saving me with your taxi plan.. Just brilliant." Nat turns round to me.

"That was Simon's idea. I was wetting myself because I didn't know what to do." Simon winks at me in his rear view mirror. I respond by blowing him a kiss. *You'll be getting a proper one in a minute!*

As we pull up to mine, Nat begins to give her farewells but I insist she join us for a drink, which she accepts. Kicking off our shoes, we all fall into the sofa and demolish a bottle of wine. I have consumed several glasses of wine now, so speech isn't as coherent as it normally is. Around half an hour later Nat takes her leave so I see her out, giving her a massive hug before closing the door. *What a superstar.* Simon is already standing up and about to leave when I turn round.

"Gem, you were amazing tonight. You handled everything brilliantly. I'm so proud of you, you little thief!"

I chuckle. "You weren't so bad yourself, you accessory!" We share another super smooch in the hallway followed by a long cuddle. As I open the door, I think Simon can sense my reluctance at being alone.

"I have kept a change of clothes in my car following last week's impromptu sleepover..." he begins, not needing to finish the sentence.

I smile and close my eyes. "That would be lovely," I confess.

"I'm going to bed now, but I'll text my dad first and tell him we need his alarm deactivating prowess." I nod nervously. *It's really happening.*

Within ten minutes, Simon is in the spare room and I am in mine, rather sozzled. Just before turning off my light, I decide to text Mum that all went well:

Ive got kyes. All srtoed. Spaek sono z

Texting while drunk is always a challenge.

CHAPTER TWENTY THREE

"Gemma!"

I wake up with a start - and a bit of a headache - taking a few seconds to establish my whereabouts. I'm used to being alone in this house so the extra voice has thrown me. I close my eyes when I remember I have an overnight guest. "Come in," I call with a smile. The door opens slightly and Simon peers through the gap.

"I just wanted to make sure you're decent this time," he jokes. *Git.* I'm suitably dressed in nightshorts and t-shirt.

"Yes I am, thank you," I reply, feigning annoyance.

He chuckles quietly to himself and walks in, holding a cappuccino. "I thought you'd like this," he says.

I give him an appreciative look. *I've never been given a coffee in bed before. I like.*

Simon gives me a super morning kiss and walks back out of my room while telling me breakfast will be ready in ten minutes. *I really like.* I relish my caffeine experience before throwing a hoodie over my t-shirt and heading downstairs.

By the time I walk into the kitchen, Simon is dishing up. I'm impressed how this man can create a super meal from what I consider to be poorly stocked cupboards. *I must go shopping today.* As I'm putting the last piece of fried bread in my mouth, I give Simon a deserving look of appreciation. *Seriously tasty, Mister. And the breakfast isn't too bad either.*

We're both showered - *separately!* - and dressed, ready for work in ample time so it gives us a chance to sit in the living room and chat some more. I love being with this man; whether we're walking, snacking or robbing people, he is such wonderful company. *Lucky girl.*

I'm soon at work thanks to Simon's knowledge of backroads, and ready to face the day. I'm surprised to see Mark opening the showroom doors this morning and he seems similarly surprised that I have a morning chauffeur. I give Simon a kiss goodbye and wish him a good day. "You too, gorgeous," he replies.

As I lift myself out of his car and smile at Mark, Simon leans over and pinches my backside, making me jump. I close the door, narrowly missing his hand. *Shame.* I glance him a comedy glare as he drives off.

As I get to the forecourt, I call over to Mark, "No Robbie today then?"

Mark returns an annoyed shake of his head. "He has just phoned in sick. Dodgy kebab, by the sounds of it." *Nice.*

Tania greets me with a bright "Hiya!" as I get in. It's great to see that she's back on form and she explains how she and Phil have patched things up.

"Oh, that's great news," I reply. "It's lovely to see you smiling again."

Tania giggles some more and nods keenly when I offer to make her a coffee. As I head to the kitchen, I can sense Mark walking behind me. I hold the kitchen door open for him and ask how he is. "Not bad, thanks," he replies, "but I'm going to need you to work tomorrow."

Not good. "Is Robbie too sick?" I ask.

"It's likely he won't be better, and I'm out all day at a car show. I hope you didn't have anything important planned."

"No, it's fine." I reply. *I was just going to make final preparations for breaking into a house tomorrow evening, that's all.* "Will I be on my own?"

Mark gives an apologetic nod but confirms that, with locking up, I

169

should still be away by 6pm. Our table at The Sunset is booked for 8pm so that will still give me ample time to get ready. I would have rather had the day spare though. I tell Mark it's not a problem, although it doesn't look like I have much of a choice. Mark senses my frustration.

"Look, I'll try and get away from this show in the early afternoon and get over to you. And I won't expect you to do any test drives tomorrow; just book clients in for one later in the week." I nod in understanding, to which he chuckles and lifts my chin up with his hand. *Weird.* "You'll be fine, Gemma. Don't worry! Oh, and I noticed that you had Simon bring you in this morning."

"Yes that's right. Beats taking the bus," I kid, moving away from him a little.

"Yes, of course," he says, gearing up for another leading question. "He, er, stayed over last night then?" he asks, in a suggestive manner.

"Yes, he'd had a drink so he stayed over," I reply in a harsh tone to remind Mark that it is none of his business.

"All going well between you, then?" he continues.

"It looks that way, doesn't it?" I respond, giving him another opportunity to read the signal to shut up.

I think Mark gets the hint, because he innocently replies, "Good for you" and heads back into the showroom. *I'll work this guy out one day.*

While the water is heating up I grab my phone from my pocket to update Simon on this latest development, only to discover that I already have a text waiting for me. *Idiot, I've left my phone on Silent since being at the pub last night.*

Dad is all good for his little job tomorrow x

I smile while replying:

Good news. Glad I'm leading him astray too ;) Got to work tomorrow, should be done by 6 x

Will you be on your own?

Looks like it.

I'll bring you lunch tomorrow then x

You read my mind! Have a good day x

I finish making the coffees and deliver them. As I hand Tania's over, she is next to engage in a grand inquisition of my activities last night. "So, Simon stayed over last night, then?" she says.

"That's right," I reply, growing a little tired of the limited range of topics this morning. I walk back to my desk, hoping the conversation will die an appropriate death.

"Things are going well between the two of you then?"

I decide not to answer, pretending that I haven't heard, and finish my cappuccino.

As Tania is gearing up for another round of questions, I happen to notice a couple walking onto the forecourt. *Perfect getout!*

I walk over quickly before Tania presses me for more details about my love life, greeting the browsers with a smile. The man and woman appear very keen to purchase a Mondeo ST220 nestling in a corner of the forecourt. The model itself is one of the older vehicles we own, but Mark explained recently how they are starting to grow in popularity as a future classic; as such, he expects it to sell soon. It turns out they have cash to purchase the car outright which I've established is a far less stressful experience for both parties. The man jumps at the offer of a test drive and within a couple of hours has committed to buying it. On completion of contract signing and the handing over of a sizeable deposit, we agree to a collection date and I book it in for a full valet. Tania gives me an excited look to congratulate me as I see the couple off the forecourt.

The process has taken me beyond my lunch break, so I head out to the kitchen to enjoy my sandwiches.

Stomach filled, I step back into the showroom to deliver freshly-made cappuccinos to my colleagues; Mark calls me into his office when I deliver his and explains how he needs to run a few procedures past me for tomorrow, seeing as I will be working solo. Within half an hour, I've been shown how to open and close the showroom, secure cash and keys and sign off various documents. I make a few written notes to remind me in the morning and as I turn to leave I fire a question back at him.

"I'm obviously very happy to do this tomorrow Mark." He looks up, waiting for the 'but'. "But," I continue, "is Tania not available to help as well?" Mark looks over at Tania through his office window, I guess to check she can't hear, and leans over his desk to speak quietly to me.

"I asked her once to hold the fort, and she sold a twenty grand car for two grand."

"How did she do that?"

"She left off a zero on the contract and then didn't query it when the guy transferred the money over."

I put my hand over my mouth, partly out of shock and also to stifle a laugh brewing inside me.

"Needless to say, I keep her well within her comfort zones from now on," he whispers. "And you're allowed to laugh just this once," he adds, seeing me fit to burst.

I apologise and then giggle nervously. "What did you do?"

"Fortunately, the chap was honest so I was able to sort it when I got back, but I decided to keep Tania away from contracts after that."

I can't imagine why!

"Anyway, seeing as I've sprung tomorrow's shift on you, why don't you call it a day? Especially as you've made us a few quid with that Mondeo!" he adds.

I smile appreciatively, wish him a good evening and within a short while am beginning my eleven minute journey to the bus stop. The streets are much emptier than usual, I suspect due to most people being still at work, so I enjoy the quieter stroll and collect my thoughts for the next 24 hours. It strikes me that I should probably be a lot more nervous than I'm feeling, but it hasn't really registered that I will be robbing Parsons tomorrow. I'm reluctant to perform a dry-run in my head for fear of the reality suddenly hitting home - I suspect my bladder may not be able to cope - but I have a flash of inspiration as I'm heading through the high street. *My secret weapon.*

Once home, I text my man to tell him I'm available for company and go upstairs to change into more comfortable clothes. With Simon here, we can talk things through once more and iron out any creases in tomorrow's plan to make up for being at Marquis tomorrow.

As I'm hanging up my trouser suit my phone wolf whistles to me from the kitchen, making me smile. I head downstairs to see what my man has to say:

On a big shout. Not pretty. Doubt I'll get to see you tonight. X

I push out my bottom lip like a spoiled child. I manage a reluctant response:

Stay safe. See you tomorrow x

Sure thing. Pick u up for work in the morning and we can talk x

The lip goes back in. *I love this man!*

After stashing the secret weapon I look in my cupboards to see what I can rustle up for dinner; there is only enough to satisfy me if I'm anorexic. Despondent, I reflect on the irony of how, for the first time in years, I have a boyfriend...and I'm lonely on a Friday night. I text Nat:

Film fest and takeaway?

A wolf whistle sounds almost immediately:

Coming now x

CHAPTER TWENTY FOUR

It feels like I have hardly slept when another wolf whistle wakes me up. *I don't half get a lot of texts!*

I'm bringing you breakfast x

Bringing? My cupboards' resources are too depleted even for my man.

I decide to get showered and dressed in time for breakfast, laying the table and making fresh coffee in the process. I'm still tired from my session with Nat just a few hours ago; it wasn't a late one but it was full-on as we discussed every detail of Operation Gitface. *It's happening - tonight!* My brain had a full assortment of dreams overnight, accompanied by seriously heavy rainfall. It was relentless, along with most other nights this past week; no doubt the government will still impose a hosepipe ban next summer.

I dig out the notepad on which I have written down the running order of tonight's performance. I'm relieved how simple the plan is - the complexity is in the balls required to pull it off. I concluded some time ago that, figuratively speaking, I do have the balls. That's not to say my stomach doesn't knot up every time I think about what I'm going to do.

With the coffee sitting on the heating plate, I decide to nip back upstairs and prepare my outfit for tonight as well. With time being far more limited due to my surprise shift, it makes sense to be as ready as possible. I've just selected an appropriately inappropriate top when I hear Simon knocking at the front door. I smile to myself. *Will I ever get tired of wanting to see him?*

I jog down the stairs to open the door and by the time my man is in the hallway he looks like a drowned rat. It's rather amusing to see him so wet just walking from the car, but his look of annoyance suggests I should refrain from making a smart comment. "Coffee?" I ask, receiving a damp nod of approval. We both walk into the kitchen and I place our coffees on the kitchen table while Simon prepares our takeaway breakfast. He has bought croissants, jam, strawberries and fresh orange juice. Just looking at the food in their respective cellophane wrapping makes me salivate.

As we're tucking into the food - which tastes amazing - I ask Simon how his shout went last night.

"I haven't gone home yet," he replies without looking up.

I almost choke on a strawberry. "What?! Oh, darling. It must have been a bad one then," I comment in a leading way, expecting him to tell all. I'm not hungry for gory details, it's more that I want to be a loving counsellor.

"It was a big one. Not very nice." And that is the end of him opening up his heart to me.

The silence is a little awkward so I feel the need to fill it with my voice. "I'm here if you ever need to talk."

He stops eating and looks straight up to me with a warm smile. "You're a super, bright, beautiful, amazing woman." *Oh stop. Okay, carry on!* "I will always share when I need to, I just don't see the point in bringing you down with me." He nods at the end to show this is the way he deals with this kind of thing. *If it works for him...*

Simon then asks me how my day was, making me feel rather inadequate; the selling of a Mondeo is definitely not worthy of a counselling session, but Simon gushes with praise and delight at how well I'm doing at Marquis.

I finish my breakfast with a huge grin, such is the mark his praise has left, and enjoy copious dollops of strawberry jam. I'm just entering a daydream about Simon and strawberries when he snaps me out of it to remind me what the time is. "We've got to go, gorgeous." I nod while blushing. *I'll be back later, Daydream.*

The journey to Marquis is very quick due to the lack of rush hour traffic so we're pulling up outside the forecourt in no time. I'm a little disappointed that my time with Simon has ended, but pleased he is able to go and get some sleep for a few hours. Suddenly I have a mini-brainwave.

"You're welcome to sleep at mine if you like," I offer. "It's closer, so you can get more sleep in." His grin tells me that it is a good suggestion, so I pass him my house keys. Leaning over, I give him a kiss, which he returns. "Pleasant dreams," I whisper. It really wasn't meant to sound suggestive, but on reflection it could have been Mark speaking. The look Simon gives me also suggests that it was most unexpected, although it's probably tinged with fear that I'm about to rub almond oil onto his essentials. *Your essentials are safe with me.* It continues to be a good job Simon can't read my thoughts. *Imagination, please have a day off!*

It is still throwing it down with rain, so Simon has parked as close as possible to reduce the dampness. He then leans over to the back seat to grab his jacket which he gives me. *This is a proper relationship now!*

"I won't expect to see you at lunchtime," I announce, deciding it's more important he is fully awake later. He smiles and nods.

I decide to hold Simon's jacket above my head, open the door and make a dash for it. Jogging in heels is always a challenge but dodging puddles certainly makes it a little harder. I manage to hop my way to the showroom doors, coat still suspended over my head like a tarpaulin with pockets. I fish out Mark's keys from my handbag and let myself in the small access door around the side of the property which fortunately is undercover. Once in, I get to work completing the entire setting-up procedure Mark gave me yesterday. Sliding open the large showroom doors is the last job, so I calm my breathing and head to the kitchen for a well-earned cappuccino. As the noise of the rain resonates loudly around the showroom, I can't help but think it's going to be a quiet shift - *other than that racket*. A wolf whistle accompanies me to the kitchen.

I may not wake up for lunch. x

I sigh at the prospect of being alone all day, although I'm pleased he feels able to be honest.

As I begin to froth up the milk for my cappuccino, my eyes light up at the opportunity to pay extra attention to my latte art. I tend not to go to town with the fancy extras on a normal day because it means I will have to do it to everyone else's, and my creations would be wasted on these coffee commoners. Once the milk is steamed to the right consistency, I start to pour it into my mug just like the YouTube tutorials I have watched over the years. My favourite is a leaf design which is made to look so easy by these online baristas, so I get to work. Mid-creation, I consider it typical that there will be no one to witness my masterpiece so I prepare my phone ready to photograph it for Facebook. By the time I've finished, the milk artwork resting on top of my coffee looks exactly like a maple leaf. After a forest fire. I put my phone back in my pocket. *At least I have a hot boyfriend.*

Over the noise of the rain I can just make out a loud diesel engine making its way round the side of the property. I peer out to see the car washers have arrived and, taking advantage of Simon's coat as before, go out to greet them. We exchange small talk, mostly joking about how their services are largely superfluous today, and it concludes with them asking for a round of coffees. They don't strike me as coffee connoisseurs so I opt to head down the 'hot water and granules' route. As I'm heading back to the kitchen, one of them hops out to raise a massive garage door. It looks like a large version of what you get at a regular house, but it requires a huge chain pulley system to open it. I then roll my eyes, remembering this was on the list Mark gave me as part of the setting up procedure. *Oh well, no harm done.* As I deliver the freshly-made coffees a few minutes later, I notice they have already driven the Mondeo I sold yesterday into the garage to begin its full valet. *I love hard workers.*

I return to my cappuccino at my desk and as I take the weight off my feet I suddenly find myself in silence. *The rain has stopped.* With the deluge ended, I realise how loud the rainfall was. I lean back into my office chair and drink my cappuccino, holding the mug with both hands and sighing loudly after each sip. Before long, my first post-rain customer arrives, browsing a TVR on the forecourt. It only arrived a few days ago so I leap into action, seizing the opportunity to do Mark proud (and perhaps get a little payrise).

"Morning. Can I help at all?" I ask in a cheerful manner.

The chap looks me up and and down then scoffs, "No, you're alright, Love," in a tone that suggests he doesn't feel women should be selling cars. I'm a little surprised I haven't received a similar reaction already in this role, such is the ignorance of many blokes in the country, so I'm ill-prepared with a response. "Well, let me know if you need any help Sir," I reply, turning to walk back to the showroom.

I hear another scoff from the chap as he says something under his breath; I can't hear the entire sentence but I determine that he is - in technical terms - a sexist git. Incensed, I spin round and walk straight up to him, wondering if I should deliver an appropriate verbal response or just reverse over him. I notice he is trying to find the door handle to get into the TVR. I smile broadly. *Justice is about to be served without leaving tire marks on his face.*

I lean between him and the car to activate the door popper hiding underneath the wing mirror, making as big a meal of it as I can. Pulling the door open for him, I cheerfully announce, "There you are, Sir."

I receive a grunt as he gets in and closes the door behind him.

"Let me know If you need anything else," I call smugly through the glass. I walk off with an even broader smile; he isn't to know I only discovered the popper myself yesterday.

I decide to locate paperwork for the TVR in case Mr Sexist wants to view its history. Going to the filing cabinet where all vehicle documents are stored, my jaw drops at the state of its disorganisation. Fortunately, the TVR's paperwork is near the top of the mess so I'm able to retrieve it quite easily.

I drop the paperwork at my desk and as I'm walking back to Mr Sexist, it takes everything within me not to roar with laughter; he is still in the driver's seat struggling to exit the car. Composing myself, I walk over to him and tap on the window, making him jump.

"Is everything alright, Sir?" I ask, wondering how he will respond. He motions that he is trying to get out of the car, so I pretend not to understand at first. "I'm sorry sir, are you saying you can't get out of the vehicle?" I shout, so that passersby turn round to watch. "You need to twist the knob, Sir...No, the other way...I tell you what, why don't I let you out from the outside...Hang on." Confident that I have shown him up enough, I pop the doors in the same way I did earlier and let the man out. He gets out, looking a little irate but decidedly smaller than before. He makes a comment about how the door poppers are a stupid design and I agree, saying how I'm amazed I managed to work it out for myself, "being a woman."

I am busy urging him to let me know if there is *anything* else I can do for him, but he appears keen to leave. I've already enjoyed the moment enough, but the fact he also steps in a large puddle on the way back to his car seals it. I get the impression he may not be returning. *It was worth it though - very satisfying.*

It starts to rain heavily again as I chuckle my way back to the showroom. With the weather as it is, I guess that I'm unlikely to get any customers for the time being. So, I grab the TVR documents from my desk and head to the filing cabinet. *Sorting time!* I get to work emptying the cabinet of all paperwork and adopt a logical system to locate files more efficiently. The entire job takes me several hours to complete but by the end it looks amazing. I have a couple of mock run-throughs to see it in practice and giggle to myself when I see how slick it is in action. I decide that I need to be more organised at home from now on, so make a mental note of which cupboards to organise first when I return. *Once I've robbed Parsons, of course.*

Due to being so engrossed with my new system and organising my entire house in my head, I don't realise how much time has passed. A quick glance at my phone tells me that the day is almost over - one customer for the entire day - so I begin running through the closing down procedure Mark left me. Within 15 minutes everything is done except for the large garage doors which the car washers opened. They never said goodbye, but I suspect they have done all they needed to do for the day. It's also pleasant to see that it has stopped raining again, so I nip out quickly to shut the garage doors before Mother Nature changes her mind.

I remember Mark telling me I must have a good grip on the chain while pulling the doors shut, otherwise the entire system will crash down and damage its runners. The chain is positioned at the very centre of the doors, which I suspect helps users to know how quickly the doors are falling. As the weight of the garage starts to take hold, I really hold on tight to the chain so that it doesn't fall quickly. Now, I'm aware it has been raining all day; I realise this because I'm the one who has been accompanied by the cacophony of rainwater for hours on end. So, you would have thought that I would have had the presence of mind to know that the garage doors would be supporting a vast quantity of rainwater. Having said that, my brain is rather elsewhere at the moment because it is focused on this evening's events. As I'm lowering the door it begins to gather momentum and, once it is at the point where I cannot let go of the chain, I feel an increasing amount of drips falling on my head. I already know what's coming, so I have a choice to either let go of the chain and risk breaking the doors or receive a most unwelcome shower. Rather reluctantly, I choose the second option, closing my eyes for the inevitable. But it doesn't come. I open my eyes to see Simon standing next to me, supporting the weight of the doors with the chain. *My hero.* This gives me a chance to step aside while Simon's additional strength is able to let the doors down slowly, enabling the collected water to drain away without soaking either of us. "You came just at the right time," I gush, which is met with a smile from my man.

As I complete the lockup and walk to Simon's car, I can't help but think I missed a huge opportunity to get Simon soaked. *Your day will come, Mister.*

"Good day?" he asks as we head to his car holding hands.

"It was okay," I reply. "Quiet though. How was your sleep?"

"Just what I needed," he sighs. "Thank you for saving me a journey home."

I smile and squeeze his hand tighter before we separate to get in the car.

Neither of us wants to mention that elephant in the room, but Simon eventually breaks the silence. "Are you ready for the next few hours?" he asks, in a surprisingly upbeat tone.

"Not really," I admit, "but it's the right thing to do." I see him nodding sincerely, showing that he understands why I'm doing it. This is accompanied by a squeeze of my thigh to show that I also have his full support. I put both my hands on his for the rest of the journey.

As we pull up to my house, I glance at the BMW's clock: 6:30pm. In an hour we'll be leaving.

In two hours I'll be robbing Parsons!

CHAPTER TWENTY FIVE

Simon and I don't talk much during the hour. It's probably mostly down to nerves, but also because we don't have much time to get ready. Simon took the initiative to collect his clothes earlier, so he is ready fairly quickly. Me on the other hand, I have a taller order because I'm busy dressing as Tania again. My theory is that Parsons may well have security cameras in his home, so it will pay to look as little like me as possible. Once dressed, I meet Simon in the living room who is relaxing with a coffee. He stands up and smiles at me when he sees me in my getup. I roll my eyes. He is dressed in beige chinos and a pastel green slim fitted shirt which shows off his bulk nicely. I can't help but think people at The Sunset will think he has paid for my company for the evening, but I remind myself this is for the greater good - and no one will recognise me anyway!

As we head out of the door, I gasp and run back into the kitchen to get my secret weapon. *I can't believe I nearly forgot it.* Rejoining Simon on the doorstep, I hold open the bag to show what's inside. He looks at me with a big grin. "Oh, very good," he whispers. *Why thank you, chino man!* Simon opens the car door for me, looking away so I don't give him an eyeful as I get in. I smile to myself as the perfect gentleman makes his way round to his own door and gets in. The Sunset is a fair trip in the car so my man fires up the MP3 player. Kula Shaker, Fatboy Slim and Sash keep Celine Dion company for the journey; I can't help but think that would make for an interesting concert.

My Heart Will Go On is coming to a depressing end just as Simon is driving past Parsons' house. Neither of us says the obvious as Simon continues past, and after another minute he turns into the car park for The Sunset. Dozens of posh cars are bathed in white tungsten, making it look like an organised version of Marquis' forecourt. *Perhaps that's the next thing I can sort out at work!* Simon parks towards the rear of the property where there are less cars and I retrieve my secret weapon from the back seat. Bill's reccy earlier in the week has determined there is an unlit patch under the toilet windows where he is going to stash his tools, so I decide to leave my secret weapon and the cut keys there after checking no one is watching. I notice a small bag of tools as I'm mid-stash, telling me that Mum and Bill must already be in the restaurant. The butterflies begin to flap in my belly.

As we walk hand in hand towards the restaurant's entrance, I can't help but notice how stunning this place is. The cars alone are an indicator as to how expensive it is, but its appearance and postcode confirm the fact. The main door is opened for us as we enter and we are greeted by a waiter. As he is about to ask us if we have a reservation, Mum and Bill wave to us from a table in a far corner so we are escorted over. They both look decidedly nervous, which I'm guessing is down to our imminent lawbreaking rather than the price of the meals. Glancing at the menu as I sit down though, it looks like grand theft is being committed already in the shape of steak and chips. *This place is extortionate.*

Bill is first to behave normally out of the four us, getting up to greet me with a kiss. "Great to see you both. Good day?" he asks, looking as normal as possible.

"Yes, thank you. It's good to see you too," I reply, returning the kiss. I then lean over to Mum and kiss her too, whispering "Relax, we're having a meal!" She nods nervously, then looks up to see Nat walking over to us. *We're all here!*

"Good spot Dad," Simon says, referring to the table he chose.

Bill gives an appreciative look. "I thought it would be good not to be overlooked and be as close to the toilets as possible." he explains. *Good lad.* "Especially as some can't help but look guilty," he teases, nudging Mum. Three of us laugh. Mum doesn't.

I'm impressed at how calm Bill is, and he's certainly helping my nerves. Before long, we have ordered our starters and main meals, along with a couple of bottles of red wine. While the three of us are getting into the swing of feigning normality, Mum still looks like she is hiding a headless torso under the table, so I motion to her to drink her wine. *She's not even the one breaking and entering!*

We've already agreed that myself and Bill will do the deed immediately after the main meal, due to the fact waiters usually allow a long gap before desserts to allow room for overindulgence. As a result, the meal itself is little more than a vague memory. When the waiter lays out starters in front of us, I cannot even remember what I ordered. It matters little though because I push the majority of the food around the plate due to a lack of appetite. When my main meal arrives, a steak which I also don't remember ordering, I manage only a few chips and the smallest bit of meat. Nat looks over to me, mouthing, "Are you okay?" I give her a reassuring smile to show that I'm not going to back out of my upcoming challenge. Bill sees my lack of desire to eat and makes a quip about whether the restaurant provides doggy bags. *I think not, William.*

"Right then," Bill announces once he has finished his meal. "I'm off to the toilet." My stomach knots up tighter than I have ever known. Until now, *Operation Gitface* has been just a suggestion; it has been largely words, grand speeches about Right vs Wrong. But right now, at this very moment, it's three-dimensional. It is happening; I am about to break the law with my boyfriend's dad!

I have a sudden rush of guilt at how I'm going to be stealing from another human being, but Simon leans over, squeezes my thigh and whispers, "Go get him!" So, I take a deep breath and excuse myself to the toilets as well. I don't look at Mum for fear of her suddenly screaming or having a cardiac arrest.

I am the only one in the toilets as I head for the end cubicle which has my escape route in it. I fold down the toilet seat, remove my heels and stand on the toilet to get access to the window latches. Once open, I throw my heels through the window and then lift myself up. I have to go headfirst due to a lack of opportunities to turn round, so I jump when I see Bill looking up at me from outside. He gives me a cheeky grin, suggesting he is enjoying this post-retirement adrenaline fix.

The window is very wide albeit lacking height, so once my 34Ds have made it through the gap I begin to turn myself around so that I can exit feet-first. It occurs to me that, should someone walk into the toilets at this very moment, I will have to deliver an impressive excuse. I eventually reach the point where my head and chest are back inside the toilet area with my bottom half hanging down the outside of the building. Bill whispers to me to let myself down and he will catch me. As I'm building up the confidence to let go, I'm hoping that Simon has inherited his gentlemanly manners from his father and that Bill isn't enjoying the view. "Let go!" whispers Bill, more authoritative than before. I take a deep breath and allow myself to fall, straight into Bill's arms. *For an old boy, this guy is strong.* I straighten my skirt that has worked its way up to my backside, put on my heels and bend down to retrieve Bill's tools, the keys and my secret weapon. Bill peers into the bag and then gives me a nod to confirm that I am a genius. I smile back, handing him his tools.

"Right, let's do this," says Bill. I swallow, which is hard to do when sheer terror deprives you of spit. We walk out from behind the building to the car park and out onto the street. I put my arm through Bill's and he sets a brisk walking pace. We don't talk for the duration as we play through our minds what jobs we need to complete:

Open door

Disable alarm/Beware of dog

Open vault door

Grab money

Throw money out of window

Leave

We're soon at Parsons' house and I'm first to walk up the steps to his front door. As yet, we haven't seen anybody in the street which has been a relief but I decide that if someone walks within earshot, I'll moan to Bill about a rubbish movie we have just seen in order to look less suspicious. It's the best I can think of, considering all the other thoughts currently racing around my head.

I scan the bunch of keys and select the one most likely to open the front door. As I'm about to insert the key, Bill stops me. "Put these on," he says, passing me a pair of latex gloves. *Of course - fingerprints.* Exchanging smiles, I turn back to the door. Putting the key in, I turn it and hear the door unlocking. *It's the right key!*

I turn to Bill and whisper, "Get ready." He smiles.

I open the door quickly in order to get out of Bill's way and we both wait a few seconds for any telltale noises. In the silence, we both spot an alarm keypad on the wall so Bill goes to look at its display and confirms that it's deactivated. I breathe a sigh of relief but it's soon replaced by the realisation that there is likely to be a rabid beast prowling the property instead. I look to Bill. "You should go," I whisper.

"Good luck," he whispers. "I'll see you soon." I close the door behind him and, as I'm about to turn round to look for the vault, I hear a soft padding of paws coming up behind me. I freeze for a moment waiting for teeth to sink into my bum cheeks. The suspense builds to the point where I force myself to turn round slowly. And there it is, looking up at me. A jet-black, fully-grown, gorgeous cocker spaniel. My shoulders seem to drop six inches out of relief and I bend down to stroke the dog. It is the soppiest thing I've ever met and it rolls onto its back to allow its belly to be rubbed. The dog's nose then twitches as it picks up a scent from behind me, so I bring my secret weapon from behind my back to reveal the source of the aroma in a carrier bag. The bone I have brought with me is almost as big as the dog itself so it's amusing to watch it grab the bone from the bag and drag it a few feet away from me, giving it a thorough licking. I chuckle to myself as I remember how much I stressed about this moment. *I've met far scarier people.*

I stand back up and look around the open plan room to see if I can spot an obvious route to the vault. Spotting a small door in the corner of the room, I walk over to it and notice it has a unique keyhole. My eyes widen as I realise what it is. *Parsons doesn't have a vault full of cash...he has an entire room!* Next to the door is a window which leads out to the private road I discussed with the team; it has no lock, so this will be where I can throw the money for collecting later. I sort through the bunch and locate the security key which Nat identified earlier in the week. Bringing a shaky hand up to the lock, I put the key in its hole and turn while closing my eyes, pleading for it to work. The key turns without resistance and is accompanied by a series of clicks as I hear a number of small bolts being released from around the doorframe. I turn the handle and pull the door outwards towards me. *This is it.*

The door-opening moment seems to happen in slow motion as my brain processes the poetry of this defining moment. I step back a little to allow room for the door to open fully and then I step into the room to observe its contents. Still in slow motion, my eyes scan from one side of the room round to the other. My gaze takes a second flyby so I can be sure that there is indeed nothing in the room. Nothing. Not a coin. My heart sinks as it dawns on me what has happened. *Nat confirmed there was planning permission granted, not that it was actually built.* It seems Parsons has been so busy shafting people that he hasn't got round to building it.

All our work - not to mention the risk - has been for nothing. I feel a lump in my throat as I establish why this has all been surprisingly simple: it was never meant to be. As tears start to form, I turn round to stroke the dog that appears to be walking up to me and there, instead, is Steve Parsons. I would scream, but I am too shocked to make a noise. He just stands there smiling.

"I knew I'd seen you before," he explains, "but when I went to open my door after our date I noticed that my keys were in a different order. I remembered you wanted to go out with me tonight, so thought I would postpone my trip until tomorrow. It seems my hunch was spot on."

I am at a loss for words.

"Very clever," he adds. "Just not clever enough." Parsons then pushes past me to walk into the room. "Did you really think that I would leave my money behind a simple door?" he asks. It's a valid question, all things considered. My face is still one of shock as he continues to gloat. "And you know the *really* funny thing?" Parsons whispers sinisterly as he walks up to me. "You're going to get banged up...for stealing nothing," he laughs.

As he goes to restrain me, I instinctively push him back into the room. He pauses for a second and then an evil glare appears on his face as he storms towards me. Without thinking, I slam the door and quickly lock it. As I hear him retrieving his own keys from his pocket, I make a dash for the front door and close it behind me and head out onto the street. I can't see anyone in the vicinity, so I remove my heels and run for all I'm worth. My heart is beating so hard I feel it is about to break through my skin, but I continue to run. After around 100 yards, I look behind me to see how close Parsons is. *He isn't there.* I suspect he has thought twice about chasing a girl up the street and instead is on the phone to the police, so I throw the copied keys down a drain. I pause for a moment to put my heels back on and then walk briskly for the last few yards to the relative safety of The Sunset's car park. Making my way round to the toilet window area, I notice there is now a wheelie bin under the window to allow me to climb back in. *Bill, you superstar!*

I remove my heels, climb up onto the bin and stand on tiptoes to peer over the window ledge. After establishing the toilets are empty again, I throw my heels through the window and lift myself up, turning round as I did before so my feet go in first. In my haste to get back inside, my blouse catches on a loose screw on the ledge causing it to ride upwards. Deciding to sort it once I'm fully in the toilet, the thing comes off over my head entirely as I lower myself down onto the toilet seat. I catch my breath and try to calm my heartbeat a little before retrieving the blouse. In doing so, I take stock of the situation:

Parsons has no idea who I am or where I am. If he does indeed have cameras in his house I don't really look like me, so provided I don't get arrested before I get home I'm in the clear. We'll still have no money, but I won't be in prison either.

Composure complete, I reach up to grab my blouse, only to find it's snagged quite a lot. I stand back up on the toilet seat and push the blouse further away from me to release it from the screw. Now, if I was watching this unfold in a movie or reading it in a book, I would know what's coming next. When you're in the situation yourself though, you can't imagine it will happen to you. So, it does come as a huge shock when I accidentally release the window from its latch, pull my hands in quickly to save them being crushed...and let go of my blouse in the process, allowing it fall back onto the wheelie bin. *Oh no. Oh, NO!*

I look around the toilet cubicle in a vain attempt to find something to help me. I have no phone. I have no blouse. I decide my only option is to climb back out and start again, but as I'm returning to the toilet seat to begin my descent, I hear someone coming into the ladies. I quickly drop down and sit on the seat. Whoever it is is just standing near the door and hasn't chosen a cubicle. I sit in silence, hearing my own heartbeat fill the room. *Who is it out there? Is it Parsons? Is it the police?* I jump clean off the seat when the person breaks the silence. "Gemma?"

"Mum!" I gasp, out of relief. "I'm in here," I continue, opening the cubicle door. As she comes into view, her smile is replaced by a look of confusion. I decide to answer her question before she asks it. "My blouse came off as I climbed back in."

Mum stands still for a moment and then retrieves her mobile from her handbag as she gets a flash of inspiration. After a flurry of taps on her screen, she assures me that Bill will save the day. I nod with full confidence in the wonderful man; *after tonight, I'll trust him with anything.*

She then looks to me with expectant eyes, so I decide to answer another question before she asks it. "There was no money there, Mum," I tell her. Her jaw drops as she processes the information in much the same way I did, then nods.

"I'm so proud of you, Love" she whispers. "I'd better get back. See you in a mo."

As I hear the door close, I can't help but feel I've let her down. I'm doing my best to be reflective and contemplative, but it's always hard to do when a blouse flies through a window and lands on your head. *Thanks, Bill.* I quickly get dressed, take a deep breath and head outside to rejoin the folk. *This restaurant had better do good desserts, and I'm definitely*

191

having another wine.

As I head back to the table I notice two men standing over our group. I assume they're restaurant staff, but as I sit down they both turn to me.

"Miss Sanders?" one of them asks.

"Yes..?" I reply, trying to look innocent.

"Police," the other one says, producing identification. "Would you accompany us to the station?" He continues. "We'd like to talk to you about an attempted robbery."

CHAPTER TWENTY SIX

"I asked you a question, Miss Sanders," Sergeant Cocky repeats, with more aggression this time. "Would you mind explaining this?"

I look at the bone through the evidence bag, wondering if all my DNA has been licked off by the cocker spaniel, and decide that silence is a good option just now.

"Okay, I'll do you a deal." he says, clearly frustrated at my refusal to cooperate. "If you own up now, I'll make sure your other friends don't go down for it too." My heart skips a beat. *Oh no, not them.* "I'll leave you to think about it for a few minutes," he concludes, walking out of the room and closing the door behind him.

My mind is now spinning at a rate of knots. I'm wondering if he is able to prosecute anyone else without evidence, or if he does indeed have evidence that incriminates the others. *Maybe they have found the keys and Nat's DNA is on them. They might have Bill on camera entering the property with me.* My jaw drops. *Maybe those policemen who visited Mum's house planted bugging equipment!* By the time my imagination has incarcerated all of us, my mind is made up: I need to confess, for everyone's sake. I take a deep breath and wait for Sergeant Cocky's return.

I don't have to wait very long as he bursts into the room moments later. I inhale deeply to deliver my confession, but Sergeant Cocky is first to speak. "You're free to go," he says, clearly annoyed that he is having to make the announcement. "Go on," he shouts, "sod off!" I decide to sod off quickly.

I walk, confused, down the police station corridor towards the main reception area. As I see the main exit in the distance, I fully expect to be grabbed as they realise they've made a mistake. With just yards to go, I brace myself for the inevitable. When a hand eventually falls on my shoulder, it doesn't make me jump due to it being expected. I turn around to see a chap in plain clothes giving me a cheeky grin. I don't return the smile, but I narrow my eyes at him as I try to remember how I know him. He waits patiently as I scroll through my cerebral address book. Eventually my eyes widen when I remember his name. *Gary!*

"You were in Spain last week at the meeting for expats," I tell him, although I suspect he knows that. He chuckles, puts his arm around my waist and leads me out of the police station. I am utterly bemused so allow him to take the lead. Once we're outside, I turn to him. "Okay," I snap, "what's going on."

He chuckles some more. "Your Mum called me a couple of hours ago. Said you might be in a bit of bother. It sounds like you've been busy!" he jokes. This revelation feeds my bemusement further.

"But, how did you get me out?" I blurt.

"You don't spend your entire career in the force without having a few people who owe you a favour," he explains.

"But, I was in his house - he caught me red handed," I confess, knowing favours don't stretch to blatant corruption.

"Mr Parsons has been advised that we have just been made aware of a variety of properties he appears to own that we may be seizing."

I smile broadly. *Good old Nat!*

"So," Gary continues, "I suspect Mr Parsons will be too busy trying to hide his assets to worry about pursuing someone in his house." My broad smile broadens as Gary continues. "Besides, you were only in there because you're madly in love with him, aren't you?"

My smile drops. *Is he serious?*

"So intense is your love for him, you even brought a bone for his dog." *Okay, I get what you're doing now.*

"Luckily for you, a stalker usually just gets a warning for their first offense!" he concludes, with a wink. We both grin. Somehow, I've managed to break into someone's house and get away with it.

I accept Gary's offer of a lift when he tells me everyone is at Mum's house. During the journey, we chat more about Parsons and the money which has been taken. "It still means he's got away with it though," I say despondently.

Gary turns to me and reassures me with "It'll sort itself out. Things like this always do." I admire his confidence. I'm more realistic, but right now am utterly relieved I'm not going to prison. *Thank you Mum!*

Gary declines when I invite him in, but he promises to update me on the stalker situation in due course. "Honestly, I think it's the last you'll hear from the police," he asserts. *I'm indebted to this man!* I lean over to give him a well-deserved peck on the cheek before I get out of the car.

"Thank you," I whisper sincerely as I walk to the front door.

"Be good!" Gary shouts. I roll my eyes as he drives off, chuckling.

Simon opens the door before I reach the doorbell and we stand there for a few seconds without speaking. He is first to break the silence, laughing and enveloping me in a tight embrace. I sob my heart out on his shoulder, a serious snotfest. When I've gathered a degree of composure, we pull apart and kiss. *I am so relieved this isn't a goodbye kiss before I start 20 years' hard labour.* Once our tongues are back in our own mouths, Simon takes my hand and leads me through to the living room where the other three are. They all stand to attention as I step into the room and pile countless hugs on me. They are acting like I have just returned from a tour of Afghanistan and I'm quite enjoying the attention. Hugs compete, I turn to Mum to thank her for calling Gary.

"We didn't know what to do," she explains. But Gary told us he would sort it and to wait here. *Mum did as she was told - wonders will never cease!*

"Well, the plan is over," I sigh. I feel it's worth mentioning the obvious before anyone else does. "There was no vault after all, so goodness knows where the money is."

Silence.

"And thank you for the wheelie bin Bill," I add, winking at my man's dad. He winks back.

"I've certainly got a lot of stories to tell the grandchildren," he teases. Simon laughs and squeezes my thigh. *Slow down, William!*

The next half an hour is filled mostly with nervous laughter, relief and a few tears, the latter being mostly from me.

Simon offers to drive me and Nat home, so we get on our way.

"I'm going to burn this skirt when I get in," I comment as I try to pull the material to my knees once sat in the car.

"I was beginning to get used to it," he teases, giving me a mini-Mark look. *Perhaps I'll hold onto it a little while longer.*

Once home, Nat hugs us both and heads for the door. "I love you guys," she says. "Catch up with you soon."

"Stay over?" I suggest to Simon.

He pulls me in for another smacker. "I thought you'd never ask," he replies. I then have a mild panic that he thinks his luck's in, but my wonderful man reads my mind chuckling, "The spare room awaits." *I love you, Mr Fireman.*

Realising that dawn isn't too far away, we head straight to our rooms for a sleep-filled, non-intercourse slumber.

I take a deep breath, reflecting on the day's content before settling down.

Definitely something to tell Bill's grandchildren!

CHAPTER TWENTY SEVEN

I have struggled all night to get to sleep, waking up every half an hour or so. I guess it's down to my brain processing everything that has happened over the past 24 hours. In part, I'm relieved things are over, but bitterly disappointed that it was all in vain. I sigh and roll over to check the time displayed on my alarm clock. 6am. *I give up - you win, brain.* I drag myself out of bed and tiptoe downstairs to make myself a coffee. I decide it will be a good idea to wake Simon with a coffee, but not for another couple of hours. He deserves a bit of a lie-in.

"Morning!" he says, making me jump. Simon is already awake and making coffees for the pair of us. *Will I ever wake up before him?!*

He stops what he is doing, walks over and embraces me. We both hold onto each other for ages. When we eventually pull apart, Simon gives me the warmest smile I have ever seen; a look of reassurance, of respect and of deep affection for me. Not bad for six in the morning - I look like a sloth that has demolished a bottle of prosecco.

"Breakfast?" my amazing man asks. I nod my head.

"Yes, but I'm making it," I reply. "You go and chill."

He nods and heads into the living room. *You could have chilled with me in the kitchen though!*

As I'm getting hobs turned on and oil warmed up in their pans, Simon calls out to me. "Gemma, you need to see this."

"Hang on," I reply. Unless he has his clothes off, I suspect he wants me to see the latest characters on Jeremy Kyle. *I can can cope without seeing them Simon, really.*

Simon walks back into the kitchen with purpose. *Nope. His clothes are on.* He grabs my hand and pulls me into the living room. "You need to see this," he says again, authoritatively.

We come to a stop in front of the TV which is showing a news report. It takes a while for my eyes to focus on the screen, but I begin to read the scrolling tickertape headline at the bottom:

BREAKING NEWS: Victims of recent timeshare scam reunited with money.

I blink. A lot. After rereading the headline several times, I eventually turn to Simon with mouth agape. Simon returns the look, similarly at a loss for words. The studio presenters then hand over to a reporter who is standing at the end of someone's property. The words 'LIVE FROM SPAIN' slowly pulses at the top-right of my screen as the reporter begins to speak.

"Yes, good morning. We were the first to report on a timeshare scam last week, where dozens of expats in Spain fell victim to an elaborate con. Many people lost thousands of euros in the scam…some lost everything. But, one victim of the scam received an extraordinary surprise early this morning."

The reporter walks up the path to greet someone standing in the doorway.

"Beryl, you have been offering support to a number of people who were caught up in the scam, haven't you?"

"Yes that's right," the other woman replies. We instantly recognise her as the spokesperson for the expat group we met last weekend. Beryl continues, "We have been staying in touch via email but also managed to get most of us together only last week to talk things through. But yesterday I received an anonymous letter with instructions to access a bank account. The account had five million euros in it."

Cue serious open mouth action from me and Simon as we turn to each other, then back to the screen again.

"And did the letter ask you to do anything specifically with it?" the reporter asks, trying to move things on.

"Well, yes. It told me to repay everyone who had been conned, with any left over to be given to charity."

The reporter glances a look at the camera, as if to authenticate the story, and no doubt to remind her boss she's overdue a payrise.

"And Beryl, you have no idea who this was from?" the reporter clarifies.

"I haven't a clue."

"So, you are now in the process of repaying the money to everyone?" Beryl nods.

"I have contact details for everyone in the group, so I'm busy getting in touch to pay the money into their accounts, as per the letter's instructions. I've already transferred around two million euros so far, so I'm sure it won't take long before everyone gets paid." The reporter thanks Beryl and turns back to the camera.

"Police are still to issue an official statement, but currently there have been no reports of a theft or any illegal activity which could point to the source of this money. Right now, it looks like either someone wanted to share their wealth with this unfortunate group or, perhaps, someone has grown a conscience and paid it all back. Back to you in the studio."

We both keep standing there looking at the screen, which is now reporting on something to do with a rat infestation at a fast food restaurant in Scotland. I'm not sure I want to move in case I undo what has happened. Simon is the first to move and grabs my shoulders to turn me towards him.

"Parsons has paid all the money back," he declares.

I shake my head in disbelief, but can't think of an alternative explanation.

"You need to phone your mum," he says. I nod slowly, still with a mouth resembling the Channel Tunnel.

I go to get my phone from the kitchen, turning off all the hobs at the same time. *I think breakfast can wait a while.*

As I get my phone in my hand to call Mum, it lights up to say she is calling me. Clearly she has just been watching the same report.

"Mum!" I finally find my voice. "I've just seen the report on the telly."

"We're getting all our money back!" she shouts. "Beryl woke me up a couple of hours ago and told me she's transferring the money." I look up to the ceiling and mouth 'thank you'. I'm just about to ask a series of questions, but Mum speaks again. "Come over!"

"We'll be there soon," I reply, which is met by a vigorous nod from Simon. I hang up the phone and have another Channel Tunnel moment in the kitchen.

"Well?" Simon asks, already knowing the answer.

"Mum has got all her money back."

"And Dad?" *I forgot to ask. Shameful.*

"I suspect so."

"Right. Get dressed!" he orders. I nod as a massive smile spreads across his face. As I go to rush past him on my way up the stairs, he blocks my exit with his arm and lands another massive hug on me. We then break apart and crack on with throwing some clothes on us. I don't pay much attention to what I put on, although I have enough presence of mind not to dress like Tania.

As we head out of the front door to Simon's car, I take a quick detour to Nat's house. I knock multiple times on Nat's door in quick succession, but there is no answer. As I step back from the door, I hear her bedroom window opening from above - I've obviously woken her up.

"I'm off to Mum's," I shout. "She's got all her money back!"

"How?" Nat shrieks, with wide eyes.

"I don't really know. Turn on the news." I motion to her with my fingers that I'll call her when I know more.

On the journey over to Mum's, Simon finds an off-license to get some champagne. I giggle. It's definitely worth a celebration, despite the fact it's only breakfast time.

I begin to mull over what Simon said and wonder whether Parsons has indeed grown a conscience. *Did our attempt to steal back the money make him realise how awful he has been? Or, has some millionaire decided to make things right instead?* I look over to Simon. He is grinning like a boy who has been told he's going to Disneyland.

When we get to Mum's, Bill is already there. Perhaps he stayed over. *Okay, Imagination, you can stay - just this once.*

Mum has opened the door before we get there, running out to give me a hug. We both exchange snot on each other's shoulders for a while, then unlock for Mum to give Simon a kiss. He responds while I go indoors to hug Bill.

"I can't believe it," I gush to Bill. He just smiles, while Mum and Simon walk back into the house to join us. The three of us head into the living room while Simon finds some glasses for the champagne.

"So, tell me what you know," I demand from Mum as we sit down.

Mum sits upright, puts her hands on her knees and begins to relay the story to us as Simon arrives with our drinks.

"Beryl called a couple of hours ago to tell us the news. The money should be in our accounts later this morning!"

"Just like that?" I clarify.

"Just like that," Mum echoes. "Lovely, isn't it?"

Mum ends the sentence in a way that makes me go from joy to

suspicion. I narrow my eyes at her, trying to read her thoughts. "You're not telling me something," I announce slowly.

"I don't know what you mean, Love," she replies, much in the same way a parent winds up their child at Christmas when they're challenged about the authenticity of Santa. *You're definitely hiding something from me!*

"Mum!" I say, demanding she spill the beans.

Mum and Bill look at each other, obviously enjoying the suspense they are building. Bill nods to give Mum permission to continue so she takes a deep breath and turns to me and Simon.

"You know when you were in Spain with Simon and you couldn't get hold of me?"

"Yes, you said you had a little break," I reply. *Get on with it.*

"We did. In Spain." My eyes widen.

"You were in Spain at the same time as us? Why?"

"We went to visit Parsons."

"Go on..." I reply slowly, wondering where on earth this may be headed.

Mum stifles a chuckle, clearly enjoying the moment. "Well, we thought we would find an empty plot of land and sell it to Parsons for the amount he stole from everyone."

"Although it wasn't ours to sell," Bill interjects.

"Although it wasn't ours to sell," Mum echoes.

Simon and I exchange looks of utter perplexity as we wait for them to continue.

Mum decides to move to the finale. "With a bit of surfing online, we discovered that the landowner was out of the country on business."

"The Internet is an amazing thing," Bill jokes.

Mum continues, "So after discovering the plot would be deserted for a few days, we obtained contact details for Parsons, juggled a couple of phone numbers and got him in touch with us instead. Then it was a case of printing off a fake contract and letting him talk us into doing a cheaper deal in cash to avoid the taxman."

"Which we knew he would do because he's a greedy sod," adds Bill.

Mum makes it sound like she does this every week. Suddenly, my jaw drops as I realise something.

"That was you! We passed you outside Parsons' office."

"We know! We thought you'd recognised us," admits Bill. "We didn't realise our getup was *that* good!"

Simon and I look at each other, dumbstruck that our parents are masters of disguise.

"So, let me get this right," Simon says, finding his voice again. "You convinced Parsons that you represented the landowner and then he convinced you to do a dodgy deal in money, but all the while you knew he was going to do that anyway?"

Mum and Bill look each other, then turn back to us and nod. "Pretty much," confirms Bill.

"So he parted with all the cash in the silver briefcases we saw?" I confirm.

More nodding.

"But what did you do with the money?" asks Simon.

Mum takes the lead again. "We found out how to open a spanish bank account without identification and deposited the cash later that day, contacting Beryl anonymously with appropriate instructions."

We knew she could be trusted," Bill adds, "and sure enough she hasn't let us down."

It is actually worrying how simple Mum and Bill have made this all sound. And, by the fact that it worked, it clearly *was* that simple.

Bonnie and Clyde continue to enjoy the moment, and the looks on our faces, as Simon and I sit in stunned awe of our parents' brilliance. But then my eyes widen as I have a realisation.

"Hang on! Bill, you helped me break into Parsons' house. You were *both* part of my plan, even though you had already taken the money. Why would you do that?"

"Plausible deniability," explains Bill. "If things went sour while we conned Parsons in Spain, you wouldn't have had to pretend you knew nothing about it." *That makes sense. I think.* "We just weren't expecting you to come back from Spain and announce you were going to rob Parsons as well. It was clear that you couldn't be talked out of doing it, and by that time we already had the money, so we decided to play along with your scheme."

"So to protect me, you helped me break into a house," I clarify.

"Exactly."

I can't help but think I would have rather known about their con. It would have kept my grey hairs at bay for a little while longer, and eliminated the risk of me going to prison. *And this was masterminded by a woman who has the cheek to tell me to be careful every five minutes.*

Simon is clearly thinking the same as me, judging by his face. Between us, we almost robbed Parsons twice!

Once realisation sets in that this has actually been a success, but not in the way I was expecting, I begin to chuckle. I'm joined by Simon, and finally by Bonnie and Clyde, until the chuckling becomes full-on belly laughs. Loudly. For ages.

After more champagne pouring, and ample teasing from Bill, I have another serious moment.

"There is just one thing," I share.

Mum's face turns to one of concern. "What's that, Love?" she asks.

A wide grin spreads between my ears. "I would *love* to have seen Parsons' face when he discovers the land isn't his..!"

- THE END -

EPILOGUE

Steve Parsons gets out from his hired Mondeo and looks over at the large plot of land. He hasn't visited it for some time so is keen to remind himself of what the view is like in each direction to determine how he will site his new properties. *It was worth the five million*, he muses. *I'm going to make a fortune*. The car is just outside the perimeter of the property on firm gravel, so he takes care to walk around the wet mud patches of the building site. As soon as he gets inside, a confused look appears on his face at the sight of several workmen and an array of machinery dotted around the site. Parsons knows he hasn't hired these men, so suspects that they are trying their luck to convince him they are hireable.

Parsons will not be told what to do, so makes his presence known immediately. "Oi!" he shouts to the workman nearest him. "What are you doing on my land? Clear off!"

There is an obvious language barrier as the man shrugs his shoulders at him. This infuriates Parsons even more as he walks closer to him. Parsons over-enunciates and shouts "OWNER" to try and get him to understand, at which point the workman says "Ah! Owner," and lifts up a hand to indicate that he will return promptly. Within a short while, the workman trots back from a small demountable with a well-dressed Spanish gentleman. "Can I help you?" The Spaniard asks, in good English.

Parsons is incensed. "Who are you, and what are you doing on my property?"

Confused, the man replies, "Señor, I can assure you it is not your property."

Quietly and sinisterly, Parsons replies. "What…?"

"Señor, I have owned this property for the last two years. I'm busy preparing the land for a new holiday complex," the man explains, somewhat confused, pointing to a new sign in the distance advertising its expected opening date in 3 years' time.

"But, I bought it from you," stutters Parsons, his voice raising slightly.

"I've never seen you before," explains the Spaniard, beginning to find the situation amusing.

"Okay, not from you," Parsons responds, getting more flustered, "but from your associates."

"I don't have associates."

Parsons leans back against a digger, bewildered. Then his eyes light up.

"I have a contract!" he says, pointing back to the Mondeo.

"Well unless it has my signature at the bottom, which it won't, it's just a piece of paper."

Parsons does his best impression of a fish gasping for air. "I'm calling the police," he blurts.

The Spaniard takes a step closer and, speaking calmly and quietly, responds to Parsons' threat. "You do that. But right now, it's time you got off *my* property." He signals to two larger workmen who walk up to him.

As Parsons begins to protest, the workmen each grab one of Parsons arms and march him to his hire car. Parsons shrugs them off as his feet return to the ground.

"You haven't heard the last from me," Parsons shouts. The Spaniard has already walked back to the demountable, suggesting he probably has.

Parsons gets back in the car, rifles madly through a briefcase and uncovers the contract he signed last week. Scanning it quickly, his jaw drops as his gaze fixes on the signature at the end.

Mickey Mouse was never known for his property investments.

Hello reader!

Thank you for reading my novel – I hope you enjoyed it
as much as I did writing it.

Publishing *Coffee, Cats & Conmen* is the realisation of a lifelong
dream, another item ticked off my bucket list. I would be so grateful
if you could find the time to write a review of this book and share it
on social media **@mbagerauthor** if you feel it would raise a few
chuckles in other readers.

Assuming the reviews go well, this will be the beginning of many
more novels. So, please join my online community and be a part of
what I hope will be an exciting new journey.

With love and thanks,

M x

www.mbager.com

23882216R00125

Printed in Great Britain
by Amazon

The Galloway Highlands

The Galloway Highlands

Dane Love

CARN PUBLISHING

© Dane Love, 2014.
First Published in Great Britain, 2014.

ISBN - 978 0 9567550 7 0

Published by Carn Publishing,
Lochnoran House,
Auchinleck, Ayrshire, KA18 3JW.

www.carnpublishing.com

Printed by Bell & Bain Ltd,
Glasgow, G46 7UQ.

Contents

List of Illustrations

Introduction

The Galloway Highlands are beloved by many. The folksong, 'Bonnie Gallowa', makes reference to the 'fell and forest free' and the 'bonnie hills'. Another song named 'Gallowa' Hills' has the singer wishing to head to them in order to experience the 'heather bell in bonnie bloom'. Since man began to appreciate the rugged landscapes of the hills, the sparkling burns flowing in the glens, and the numerous lochs amongst the heather, the hills on the border between the Stewartry of Kirkcudbright and Ayrshire have lured him in.

My first real recollection of being introduced to the Galloway hills occurred at a young age, being taken on family days out to Loch Doon, or else to Loch Bradan, where the construction of the present dam is one of my early recollections. My grandparents lived in Newton Stewart for a time, and as a youth I often accompanied them on runs in the car from Ayrshire over the 'Hill Road' to Newton Stewart from Straiton, or via Carsphairn and New Galloway.

My grandfather was always one to try to find out more about places he read about or else discovered for himself, and on many an occasion he would say, 'We'll just knock this door and speir the man or woman who answers.' He often told me, 'You've a guid Scotch tongue in your heid, so don't be feart to ask.' Many a time I recall waiting on someone answering their door, and I was glad and pleasantly surprised to find that their love of the area was such that they were more than willing to tell of what they knew.

Over the years since then, my discovery of the Galloway hills has continued, from days driving around the hills, stopping to look for places of interest, to times when I and various friends have walked the mountain tops, crossed the valleys and explored on foot. On many other occasions I have cycled the byways and forest roads, either camping or staying in the bothies that were more common at that time. I have even canoed to the Castle Island on Loch Doon in order to experience it at close hand.

This book is the result of many years of exploring – looking for monuments and graves to lost shepherds or Covenanters, searching for the Deil's Dike, locating stones in the forests or hillsides and finding former cottages where once the shepherd and his family made their home.

The title, Galloway Highlands, comes from the fact that the area covered by the book is only that part of the central Galloway hills, where the highest summits are found. In the past they were often described as the Galloway Highlands, whereas today 'highland' is usually only used when referring to the mountains north of the central belt. To me, however, these mountains and glens are truly highland.

I trust that other lovers of this area will find much of interest in this volume.

Acknowledgments

The author would like to thank the numerous people who have assisted him in hundreds of different ways over countless years in the compilation of this book. Many of the pieces of information have been garnered decades ago, not necessarily for this volume, but for the author's own collection of notes and scraps of information that he has hoarded until this time! To name them all would be both impossible and unfair – impossible in that I cannot remember everyone who helped in many ways to extend my knowledge of the hills, and unfair in that someone who perhaps answered a query for something relevant in the writing of this book is still remembered, and yet many others who supplied more information in the past have been forgotten. In any case, thanks to all who have helped me over the years.

Nevertheless, there are a few acknowledgements that need to be noted. For *The Modern Raiders*, taken from *Winter and Rough Weather*, by W. G. M. Dobie, published by William Heinemann, my thanks are due to The Random House Group Limited. I must also thank Angela Lawrence for the use of her paintings for the cover. Her studio in Castle Douglas has many evocative images of the Galloway Hills and readers can find out more by visiting her website, www.cliencestudio.co.uk

Dane Love
Auchinleck, July 2014

1 Discovery and Pleasure

Writing in *The Martyr Graves of Scotland*, Rev John Henderson Thomson (1824-1901) describes his first journey to Loch Trool, which he was visiting in order to see the martyrs' tomb at Caldons. He was taken by horse and cart from Newton Stewart by way of the road alongside the east of the River Cree, before turning up into Minnoch dale. After noting the inscription from the stone, he appears to have spent the night in a lodge, perhaps Glen Trool or Buchan Lodge, by the side of the loch, for he refers to having rested there. In a later edition of the book, visiting the wild rugged glen had grown in popularity, and he writes that 'since we visited Loch Trool it can now be pleasantly reached from Dumfries in the summer months on Mondays by the early train to Newton-Stewart, where a conveyance waits for passengers, and returns from the loch in the afternoon.'

The introduction of tourism to the hills had begun. Apart from a few early guides such as *Scotland Delineated* (1791) or Pennant's *Tour in Scotland* (1769), the first guidebooks appeared in the early nineteenth century, when travel became more possible, and folk were interested to find out about places mentioned in the popular works of Sir Walter Scott.

One of the more common guidebooks used was Robert Chambers' *Picture of Scotland*, published in 1827 by William Tate of Edinburgh. He described some of the periphery of the Galloway Highlands, such as Loch Dungeon:

> A few miles to the west of the road from New Galloway to Dalry is situated
> Loch Dungeon, a little mountain *tarn* of singular sublimity. It is encompassed
> by high and precipitous rocks, which have been for ages the dwelling-place
> of the eagle, whose eyry has seldom been disturbed by the approach of man.
> In the immediate neighbourhood of the loch there is a *rocking-stone* of vast
> size, which may be moved by the slightest impulse.

His description of Carsphairn wouldn't attract many folk to the delightful little village:

> The Ken takes its rise amidst the wilds of Carsphairn, which is the most
> northerly and mountainous of all the parishes of the Stewartry. The aspect of
> the country is here as desolate as the wildest Highland tract; and indeed it is
> scarcely possible to conceive a scene more hopelessly, miserably bleak, than
> what is presented around the little clachan of Carsphairn. The clachan itself

consists of a few scattered houses, with its kirk and modest white manse; and, on casting the eye around, though a circuit of about eight or ten miles can be seen in almost every direction, not a single house or shealing is to be discerned. The country stretches away in extensive flats on various inclinations, towards the hills, which rise in vast round protuberances. The hue of the whole region is a mixture of green and yellow - the colour of melancholy, according to Shakspeare - with no interruption or variation except the black seams formed by the torrents in the hills, and which descend their great round sides somewhat after the fashion of the longitudinal lines of an armillary sphere.

One of the early influential guidebooks that attracted Ayrshire folk south to the hills around Loch Doon was *Ayrshire Streams*. Published in 1851, this book had two chapters about the River Doon and Dalmellington area, and it extolled the beautiful scenery that existed thereabouts. The book had as its genesis a series of articles in the *Ayr Advertiser*, published over a number of weeks in 1849-50 by William Howie Wylie. Wylie extended the articles for the book, published in London, and the tourist rate began to increase.

Wylie was originally the Kilmarnock correspondent for the *Advertiser*, but in 1850, at the age of eighteen, became the sub-editor. He was born around 1832, and from his work in news editing in Ayr, moved on to take up other journalistic positions in Nottingham and Glasgow. He found himself called to be a man of the cloth, training to become a Baptist minister. His journalistic and editing skills did not disappear, for he was sub-editor of the *Christian World* before he founded and edited *The Christian Leader*. In 1854 he published *Old and New Nottingham* and later came *Thomas Carlyle, the Man and his Books* in 1881. He was never a very fit man, and he resigned his pastorate. He continued writing however, before dying on 5 August 1891.

Wylie tells of a trip that he undertook to Loch Doon. He boarded 'The Crown', a horse-drawn coach, in the High Street of Ayr and set off. On board were other passengers bound for the hills and lochs – 'the appearance of not a few of the passengers plainly proclaims that they are bound on excursions of pleasure.' Many of them were fishermen, heading for Loch Doon, and it was noted that the loch and surrounding hills were already attracting visitors from Manchester, Liverpool and even London. He wrote that Dalmellington 'possesses a bustling air: the two leading inns seem well-filled – principally, too, by professors of the 'gentle art', who enjoy their favourite recreation on Loch Doon. The number of visitors to the loch is very numerous, and appears to be on the increase.'

Many folk came to the periphery of the Galloway hills and stayed in a variety of inns, which catered for them. In the villages around the hills inns and hotels were established, or extended, to cope with the influx of visitors, here to enjoy the scenery, or take part in country sports.

In Dalmellington the Eglinton Hotel, handily located near to the railway station, was enlarged sometime before 1889. The proprietor at that time was James MacDonald, who advertised the fact that he kept eight boats on Loch Doon for the use of tourists and anglers. Similarly, the Black Bull Hotel in the village – Mrs Wallace, proprietrix – had recently been rebuilt and extended to provide ten bedrooms.

In Carsphairn, the Salutation Hotel was a three-storey building which appeared to be rather large for the tiny village, but it needed the number of bedrooms to cope with the influx of visitors. The hotel had been enlarged in 1900 and was 'replete with every modern convenience'.

In St John's Town of Dalry the Lochinvar Hotel was erected in the late Victorian period to cater for visitors. A typical old coaching inn, the hotel was extended considerably in 1900 to provide accommodation for the increasing numbers of visitors, a 'handsome new dining room with separate tables' being added. By 1915 it had thirty rooms. The proprietors arranged coaches and horses, driven by liveried footmen, to pick up tourists at the nearest railway station, which was nine miles to the south at either Parton or Mossdale.

The House o' Hill is another roadside inn located between Bargrennan and Glentrool villages. In 1841 the innkeeper was John McNeiron. At one time an older 'House o' Hill' was located east of the current inn, half a mile into the present forest. This was in ruins by the time of the first Ordnance Survey of the area, carried out in 1849.

In addition to these larger inns and hotels that survive today, there were a fair number of smaller inns or hostelries that existed in the glens around the highlands over the years. At Suie Toll, which was located five miles north of Glentrool village, just south of the county boundary near to Kirriereoch, on the Straiton hill road, the toll-keeper also offered sustenance to the few passers-by that came that way. In 1841 the occupant of the toll-house was William Gracie, listed in the Census as an innkeeper, rather than a toll-keeper. In 1878 the turnpikes were abolished and maintenance of roads was passed to the county road trustees, followed by county councils in 1889. Toll cottages were no longer required along the roads, and many of them became occupied by roadmen, employed for highway maintenance.

In the Palnure Glen a small public house existed at Craigdews, near to Murray's Monument. This remote place was actually busier than one would imagine today, for in the nineteenth century quarrying was still undertaken at Craigdews, and thirsty quarrymen would have used the inn. In 1841 the publican was Barbara Heron, at that time 58 years old.

Coach trips were offered from Newton Stewart and other places into the hills, allowing visitors to see some of the sights. In the early twentieth century coach trips went up the Palnure Glen as far as Murray's Monument, where they turned about and returned to Newton Stewart. Visitors could wonder at the rocky grandeur of the glen, as well as climb the Big Doon to the tall obelisk, from where the view was particularly highland in effect.

The invention of the motor car, and its increasing popularity, resulted in rising numbers of visitors to the hills and glens. Consequently, popular tourist haunts have required the creation of parking spaces, and a number of minor roads in the glens have been surfaced with tarmacadam.

Artists have also enjoyed the views in the Galloway Hills, and among those who have painted scenes of the mountains and lochs is James Faed Junior (1821-1911). He visited the hills over a period at the turn of the twentieth century, and in 1919 a collection of his water-colours was published as a book. The scenes from the highland hinterland include The Cooran Lane, On a Galloway Moor, Minnoch Roman Bridge, Loch Dee, Loch Trool, Loch Neldricken, Loch Enoch, Source of Dee and Round Loch Dungeon. James' brother, John Faed RSA (1819-1902), used to say that, 'No hills are as paintable as the Galloway Hills.'

To the early Victorians, the Galloway Highlands, as was the case with the rest of the Scottish highlands, were thought to be rugged and frightening, a place that instilled horror and terror in the minds of those who saw them. At first it was this rugged grandeur that attracted some of the early tourists, there to be affected by what they saw.

1.1 Lochinvar Hotel, St John's Town of Dalry

One of the main attractions for tourists in the mid Victorian period were waterfalls, and though Galloway has few major cataracts, even on a Scottish scale, there were sufficient of reasonable height and appearance to be mentioned in guidebooks. In fact, almost every guide book to the Galloway uplands from the period refers to the waterfalls that exist, and visitors were wont to make an effort to visit them.

The largest, and thus most popular, falls in Galloway's highlands are the Grey Mare's Tails (of which there are two) and the Buchan Falls. Other major cataracts, which sometimes required heavy rain to make them more appealing, were the Black Linn, on the Water of Minnoch, and Tairlaw Linn, on the Water of Girvan. More about the waterfalls will be found in the chapter on Lanes and Linns.

1.2 House o' Hill Hotel, Glentrool

A lover of the Galloway Highlands was James MacBain, whose book, *The Merrick and the Neighbouring Hills*, became a standard work on the uplands. MacBain was an Ayrshireman who spent over fifty years exploring the hills of Galloway, walking amid the wild uplands, observing and recording the flora, fauna, geology and natural phenomena of the area. His accounts of the various hills and lochs are comprehensive, and he often became involved in wonderful exploits, such as the time when he measured the depth of Loch Enoch, discovering for the first time that it was the deepest loch in the Galloway uplands. The account was published in the *Ayrshire Post* of 27 June 1919. MacBain's book was published in 1929 by Stephen and Pollock of Ayr and was quickly snapped up by lovers of the hills. As more modern hill-walking and exploring became popular, copies of MacBain's book became scarce and much sought-after in the antiquarian market. To satisfy demand, a reprint of the book was issued by Jackson and Sproat of Ayr in 1980.

James MacBain's love of the hills shines through in every page. There doesn't seem to be a stone or mossy hollow that he has not visited and reported on in his book, subtitled 'Tramps by Hill, Stream, and Loch.' He wrote on other subjects, such as his account of 'Burns's Cottage', and he was elected as a Fellow of the Society of Antiquaries of Scotland. He contributed to a number of local newspapers, such as *The Ayrshire Post*, *The Kirkcudbrightshire Advertiser* and *The Gallovidian*. *The Merrick and the Neighbouring Hills* was mainly written in his 81st year.

MacBain's interests were wide and varied. He was a lover of literature, geology, music, astronomy, botany and history. Brought up in Aberdeen, he had left school at the age of thirteen and found work in a woollen mill. Yet he was a keen learner, and commenced self-education by reading books in the city's Mechanics' Institute. MacBain read omnivorously, and taught himself to speak in an educated English. He learned shorthand and trained to be a journalist. His first job was with the *Kelso Chronicle*, after which he worked with the *Edinburgh Courant*. He moved to work with an Irvine paper for a short time before moving to Ayr, settling in the town in 1878. There he was the representative of the *North British Daily Mail*. He was later to be a proprietor of the *Ayrshire Post* in its early days.

MacBain became the official shorthand writer for the Ayr Sheriff Court, a position he held for about five years. He was also the first person in Ayr to introduce the typewriter into business. He continued to be the local correspondent to a number of newspapers, such as *The Scotsman*. He often reported on golf competitions, a sport that he had a keen interest in.

A strange connection links James MacBain with the formation of the golf course at Turnberry in Ayrshire. At one time he wrote to the *Glasgow Herald* about the suitability of the dunes and links there for a championship course. Whether or not this was noted by the landowner, within a short period of time the Marquis of Ailsa had decided to invest in the formation of a course there, which was to become one of the finest in the whole of the world.

MacBain was noted as being a man of strong opinions, and one that had a mind desperate to find out things that he reckoned would be of interest to his fellow man. According to his obituary in the *Ayr Advertiser*, 'He did not suffer from shyness; rather the reverse. He was ever disposed to probe into matters, and to probe with a thoroughness that left, at least in his own mind, no doubt as to the attitude he was to take with regard to men and affairs. But he probed only into matters that were worth obtaining information about. He was no quidnunc, but he was ever on the alert for news that would be of benefit to him intellectually and of benefit to his fellow-men. He was a man of strong opinions – pronouncedly strong – and for these opinions he would fight to the utmost of his powers. To these opinions he was never frightened to give expression, and it was perhaps as a result of his fearlessness of expression that he, on some occasions, drove from him men of the 'yes' type. But to those most intimately associated with him Mr MacBain was at heart a really kindly-natured man, although some will declare to-day that he was almost perverse. His outspoken nature may have resulted in his not being *persona grata* with quite a number of people, and his kindness of heart may have been known to only a few.'

Always small in stature, MacBain was a hardy man, with courage to tackle various climbing exploits. Even between the ages of seventy and eighty he was still scaling rocks that many younger men could not attempt. It was noted that he could make his way up precipices with ease, often clinging precariously to a tuft of heather that any heavier man would probably drag out by its roots.

MacBain was so keen on climbing the Galloway hills that he made his final ascent of the Merrick at the age of 83 years. It is noted that he climbed the steep slopes to the summit with relative ease, gazing at the view fondly. It was during the descent that his body began to weaken, and his legs began to give way under the strain. It took great courage and stamina to make his way down to Culsharg, the highest cottage in Galloway, where he could rest awhile, before making the last drop to Glen Trool. It was to be his last major ascent.

Culsharg is today a roofed ruin, used as a shelter by walkers, but in MacBain's day it was still tenanted and he wrote of staying there with the shepherd for up to ten days at a time.

MacBain's mind remained clear until he died, though his body had started to give up. His limbs lost much of their strength, and he was almost totally blind. Yet his mind remained so sharp that he could argue points as though he had the mind of a forty-year old. It was said that he had a photographic memory, and his brain could recall many places he had been and things he had read, resulting in him taking comfort from his memories when his body was old and infirm. He was also able to quote great lengths of *Tam o' Shanter* and other works right until the end. Although he enjoyed Burns, MacBain reckoned that his favourite poets were Byron and Shelley.

His last few months were spent in failing health. A few weeks before he died MacBain realised that his time was coming to an end, even although his mind was still active. It was as though when his mind began to accept that his life was finishing, his death arrived quicker. James MacBain died at his home, Waterloo, in Ayr, on Tuesday 14 January 1941, at the age of 91 years. His funeral took place at Masonhill Crematorium, near Ayr. His last request was that his ashes be scattered across the hills.

The Merrick and the Neighbouring Hills reflects MacBain's inquisitive mind. There are those who reckoned that the book was rather too staid, and lacked some imagination, but he was a recorder of what he saw, and he was rather keen on facts and details of nature to be bothered with the traditions of the uplands. His obituary noted that 'He might have made *The Merrick and the Neighbouring Hills* more attractive to those who are not particular about facts, as long as the story is presented to them in pleasing fashion, but he had no use for embroidery and adornment; that he left to other individuals who appeal to popularity through these channels. Hard fact appealed to him all the time, and it is hard fact and truth that he presents to the reader of his book which is, in our opinion, an out-standing contribution of its kind to Scottish literature.'

MacBain was influential in persuading another classic book on the Galloway Hills to be published. Andrew McCormick had been exploring the area for many years, usually from the south, where he lived in Newton Stewart, whereas MacBain was exploring from the north. McCormick wrote in his preface, 'Some time ago Mr MacBain published an excellent book, *The Merrick and Neighbouring Hills*, which deals largely with the same countryside [as his book]. The author takes this opportunity of thanking Mr MacBain for urging him to put his gleanings in the same field into book form.'

McCormick had written some of the chapters as standalone articles for various magazines and newspapers, such as *The Glasgow Herald, The Galloway Gazette,* and *The Gallovidian Annual.* He pulled them together, and wrote a number of additional chapters to form the book, which was published in October 1932. The book sold out within weeks, and it was to be reprinted in December the same year. Five years later a second edition was issued, followed by another in 1947. Like MacBain, this book was to persuade many folk to explore the Galloway uplands, and it became a popular guide to the area.

Andrew McCormick was born in 1867. In the 1890s he started to practise as a solicitor in Newton Stewart, setting up his office within the British Linen Bank building at 66 Victoria Street. He was to be joined in partnership at a later date by David William Nicholson, and the firm of McCormick and Nicholson continues to practise from the same office to this day. McCormick was the town clerk of Newton Stewart and for a time he served as provost.

The first edition of *Galloway* was dedicated to his son, Donald, 'who aspires to climb', but unfortunately Donald was to take ill suddenly, and died at the age of fifteen years. Within the park in the town two trees were planted in his memory, and as 'Donald's Trees' they were known for many years.

Captain Andrew McCormick loved Galloway, and he was instrumental in persuading the authorities to erect the huge boulder in Glen Trool that commemorates the Bruce's victory over the English. This was right in what McCormick called, 'the cradle of Scottish independence.'

McCormick's other claim to fame was his knowledge and research into the gypsy population of Europe. As a teenager he travelled with the tinklers around Galloway, taking amazing pictures of their lifestyle. He learned the Romany language, and he spent many summer months in Europe prior to the Second World War, especially in the Balkans, where he mixed with gypsies. Gypsies came to respect him, and on many occasions they would pay him a visit at Newton Stewart. After Hitler tried to wipe out the gypsies in Europe, McCormick became the world's leading expert on the Romany language. Indeed, it is reported that many gypsies from all over Europe travelled to Newton Stewart to ask him to translate old family documents for them. Before he died, an American university recorded many hours of conversation with him, he being concerned that the knowledge he had gathered would die with him. McCormick's work in gypsy research resulted in a popular book, *The Tinkler-Gypsies of Galloway,* published in 1907. Many years after McCormick's death, and after the fall of President Nicolae Ceausescu of Romania in 1989, a group of elderly gypsies travelled to Newton Stewart to pay their respects, such was their love for him.

Andrew McCormick also wrote other books, including *Words from the Wild-Wood – sixteen Galloway Tales and Sketches,* published in 1912 and *The Gold Torque – a story of Galloway in early Christian Times,* published in 1951. He died in 1956.

From 1932 until 1965 a regular series of articles appeared in the *Ayrshire Post,* written by one who styled himself 'The Highway Man'. These stories told of adventures on bicycle across much of south west Scotland, and in particular through and across the Galloway hills. The articles were eagerly awaited by the readers of the newspaper, and the author contributed them regularly for 33 years.

A rather shy writer, in time it became known that the author was one Davie Bell. He was a member of various cycle clubs in Ayrshire, and lived at different places. Born at Brydekirk, a small village in Annandale, Dumfriesshire, in 1907, David Ernest Thomlinson Bell was educated at Noblehill, in Dumfries, where he was to win the dux medal. On leaving school Bell worked as a gardener then nurseryman in Dumfries. He moved to Ayrshire with his family in 1924, settling in Prestwick. Three years later his love of the bicycle commenced, his mother having saved hard to buy him one for £6. On one of his first excursions he cycled as far as Stirling, a distance of over 100 miles.

Davie Bell was a founder member with Tom MacKean of the Ayr Roads Cycling Club in 1933, a club that still survives. He was to remain a member for just one year, for he was married and moved to the mining village of Drumsmudden, in the parish of Ochiltree. The local Arran View Cycling Club was based in Drongan, and Bell became one of its most active members until it was disbanded in 1936. At that time he joined the Ayrshire Clarion Club, also based in Drongan, but he was also to re-join the Ayr Roads C. C., remaining a member until he died.

Bell loved to cycle, and spent many days touring across the routes of south west Scotland. He was an early lover of off-road cycling, and often he could be found pushing his bike along some mountain pass, or even up to the summit of a hill or peak.

Bell's first contribution to the *Ayrshire Post* was in 1932. Soon after he contributed a regular series of cycling notes which he wrote under the pen-name of 'The Nomad'. In 1934 his articles became much longer, and he changed his nom-de-plume to 'Highway Man'. The stories told of his cycling exploits, often traversing the wilds of south-west Scotland, staying in youth hostels or bothies. At other times his journeys took him further afield, to the highlands of Scotland or south into England's Lake District. In the period 1927-34 he climbed ten of the Galloway mountains, accompanied with his bicycle.

A great lover of literature, Davie Bell read extensively. He was an avid reader of the Galloway novels of S. R. Crockett, and he enjoyed anything that gave him more information on his beloved south-west, especially Rev C. H. Dick's *Highways and Byways in Galloway and Carrick*. Other authors and poets he loved included Robert Burns, Thomas Carlyle, Zane Grey, Lord Byron, Robert Service, Percy Bysshe Shelley and John Keats.

Davie Bell had a love of nature, and from 1938-39 he contributed some 'Nature Notes' to the *Ayrshire Post*. He returned to nursery work once more, getting a job at Prestwick.

A story is told of the time that David Bell arrived at a farm steading in the valley of the Minnoch Water. As he made his way into the steading on his bicycle, he was greeted by the shepherd. A regular reader of his articles in the *Post*, he said, 'It's been grand to see you, but you've been a queer while in getting here; I've been expecting you for the last five years!'

Bell loved to seek out the historical places he read about on his cycles. He spent many years tracking down various stretches of the De'il's Dyke, and to other obscure places, such as the Wells of the Rees, or The Nappers standing stones.

Davie Bell died in April 1965, at the early age of 58. His readers spontaneously raised funds to erect a memorial to him, and the appeal was closed in November 1965 when over £180 had been donated. The memorial was placed at Rowantree Toll, on the hill road between Straiton and Newton Stewart, one of his favourite cycle runs. It stands above the Rowantree Burn, between the two bridges across the stream made by the minor roads which meet just south of the monument. The base is built with stone, but on the top is a bronze relief map of the Galloway Highlands, depicting the main ridges and the numerous lochs, sculpted by Bert Cooper. The inscription is simple:

In Remembrance of David Bell, 'The Highwayman', who knew these hills so well. 1907-1965.

The memorial was unveiled by his widow, Georgina Bell, on Sunday 3 April 1966.

In 1970 the *Ayrshire Post* published a collection of Bell's articles, entitled *The Highway Man*. Three of Bell's companions selected the stories for inclusion. This was so popular that a second edition had to be printed the following year. In the book there was a comment made that it was hoped to publish a second volume of cycling memories in the future, and this came to fruition in 1990 when Peter Blane collected and edited *The Highwayman Again*. The profits from the book, which was again a best seller locally, were given to cancer research. In the second volume reference was made to my grandfather, who was a keen cyclist in his youth. Bell writes, 'In the course of tea a scooter drove up. The driver was an old acquaintance of thirty years ago. Finally I placed him as Tom Love of the old New Cumnock C.C.'

Some of Davie Bell's cycling exploits became quite legendary in the area. One of his more notable was the time that he took his bicycle to the summit of the Merrick, climbing from Kirriereoch farm over Kirriemore Hill and the western flank to the summit. This was in pre-mountain bike days, when frames were made from solid steel and not lightweight duralumin. The climb took three hours to complete. After studying the view, Bell and his fellow cyclists descended over the Broads of the Merrick to the Neive of the Spit and thence up Benyellary. From there a sudden descent, with broken milometers and mudguards, led to Culsharg and down to Loch Trool, six hours from Kirriereoch.

In my youth, the story of The Highway Man on the Merrick was something of an inspiration, and one day, whilst leading younger boys on an ascent of the Merrick, my friends and I decided to make it a bit more exciting for ourselves. 'Why not copy Davie Bell?' was the suggestion, and thus we set off from Buchan Lodge up the Merrick, complete with bicycles. We quickly realised that the bicycle was not for cycling on this occasion, and soon they were being strapped to the back of our rucksacks. The added weight and projecting handlebars and pedals were troublesome, but we soldiered on, through the woods to Culsharg and then up the steep face of Benyellary. There was a stretch from Benyellary towards the Merrick, across the Neive of the Spit, where we could actually cycle on our bikes, and the speed at which we crossed the ground made up for the added weight.

The summit of the Merrick was duly reached, and photographs of the cycles perched by the trig point were taken as evidence. Other walkers were amazed at our daft notion, but we were pleased with ourselves. Instead of returning by the same route, we dropped to the east down to the shores of Loch Enoch, then across the shoulder of Craig Neldricken to the Murder Hole at Loch Neldricken. A short descent by the Mid Burn brought us to Loch Valley, from where the path down the Gairland Burn valley brought us back to Buchan Lodge. The total route must be around eight and a half miles, of which we cycled half a mile at most!

Another lover of the Galloway Highlands had three different volumes of his collected writings published. Dan Kennedy enjoyed traipsing round the hills, passing through the glens, and searching out the odd places and those with tales to tell. Like Davie Bell, Kennedy had many of his articles published in the *Ayrshire Post*, starting in 1939. Other articles and poems were published in the *Galloway News*. In 1967 a selection of these articles were issued under the name *Galloway Memories: Hill-*

1.3 David Bell's Monument

climbing adventures in the Southern Uplands including a selection of various other articles, poems and sketches. In 1970 the book was revised and extended, being reissued under the name *Tales of the Galloway Hills.* Again sales were good, and the Ayrshire Post decided to extend the book further, reissuing it as *Climbing the Galloway Uplands,* in 1972.

In his books, Kennedy tells of his meetings with the shepherds at various lonely cottages, many of which are now unoccupied and ruinous, or else converted into bothies for the use of hill walkers.

Daniel Kennedy was a wine and spirit merchant who ran a licensed grocery at 110 Main Street in Newton-upon-Ayr from the 1950s until 1969. His father had previously been a grocer at Ayr's Malt Cross. Dan Kennedy used to travel around the southern part of the county on his bicycle, collecting orders for alcohol, which was later delivered. He lived for a time at Monument Road in the town, followed by Springvale Park for many years. Dan was described as being 'small of stature but strong – in fact, Ayr's Strong Man – complete with leopard-skin, Tarzan style!' He compiled a small book on how to become Mr Universe. He was married to Kate Margaret MacIlwraith. Their only son, Captain Graham Kennedy, served with the Royal Electrical and Mechanical Engineers during the Second World War. He died in action on 19 July 1945, during the closing weeks of the war, and was buried in Becklingen War cemetery, Niedersachsen, Germany. Dan Kennedy himself died on 25 May 1977 and was buried in Fisherton Cemetery, Dunure, overlooking the Ayrshire coast.

In 1947 much of the Forestry Commission land across the Galloway Highlands was designated a national forest park. At the time there was only one other of these parks in Scotland – Argyll - but there are now six, Galloway being the largest in Britain. To begin with it was named Glentrool Forest Park, a name that was something of a misnomer, especially to locals who appreciated that Glen Trool formed only a minor part of the extensive park, and so in 1973 the park was renamed Galloway Forest Park. Some current maps and guides still refer to it as Glentrool Forest Park, however, names taking some time to get out of the system.

The Forestry Commission established visitor centres to enhance the public's appreciation of the natural beauty and wildlife of the park, these being located at Glentrool, Clatteringshaws, and Kirroughtree. The latter is beyond the area covered by this volume, but the centres at Glentrool and Clatteringshaws are, and are open to the public from Easter to October. Visitor numbers have grown over the years, and though it is difficult to put exact numbers on the number of tourists enjoying the park, it is reckoned that there are over 800,000 visitors each year.

In 1954 land at Caldons, at the foot of Loch Trool, was designated a campsite, and this quickly grew in popularity, resulting in it being extended, and caravans being welcomed also. Operated by the Forestry Commission, Caldons campsite was leased out in 2002 but this only lasted a short while and the site was permanently closed in 2006, the facilities being demolished. The name Caldons is thought to derive from the Gaelic *caltuinn,* meaning hazel, there being numerous hazel trees in the vicinity.

A second campsite was established at Talnotry, at the head of the Palnure glen, in

May 1971. This was to cope with an increasing number of tourists who wished to park their caravans within the upland area. This too has now closed.

With a tradition of hospitality, the wilder cottages in the Galloway Highlands have always welcomed the walker, offering a bed for the night or a meal round the fire. As these cottages became abandoned, the walker adopted them, and soon they were being used for overnight stays on expeditions to the high tops. The notion of preserving the cottages was discussed round the fire one night at Backhill of Bush, which was in 1964 repaired and made available for walkers. Alan Murdoch of Ayr had written in the bothy log book that some sort of organisation might be of benefit in preserving the shelters. The discussion was productive, and it was decided that a voluntary organisation should be established to look after the remote bothies, making their shelter available and open to all.

The meeting was to be the birth of the Mountain Bothies Association, which was founded in 1965, 'to maintain simple unlocked shelters in remote country for the use of walkers, climbers and other outdoor enthusiasts who love the wild and lonely places.' Negotiations with the Forestry Commission commenced, and the first major project was the restoration of Tunskeen, another lonely cottage at the north-west end of the Galloway hills. This old shepherd's cottage had been abandoned for some time, and much of the building was demolished. However, there were still sufficient walls to allow a new roof to be constructed over the remains, creating a small, but readily usable bothy.

The work was carried out in the summer of 1965 by two of the MBA stalwarts of the time, Bernard and Betty Heath, with a group of friends. The Heaths were to be active in promoting the association for many years thereafter, and Bernard was to write in 1972, the 'members' only reward will be the knowledge that their efforts have helped save a bothy from ruin.' Always keen to support the work of the association, the Heaths would often arrive at work parties from their home in Huddersfield, in the Midlands of England, and latterly Thurso and Dunnet in Caithness. Their work within the association, which became registered as a charity in 1975, was finally recognised on 5 October 1991 when they were both presented with British Empire Medals for service to outdoor education.

Tunskeen was used by many climbers and walkers thereafter, its remoteness an attraction, allowing hikers to spend the night on the edge of the hills, allowing early rises and a quick ascent Shalloch on Minnoch, which climbs immediately to the west. On a couple of occasions, however, its remoteness has meant it has suffered in the wild winds that blow in these parts, and its roof has been blown off more than once.

In 1986 a 'work-party', as the MBA styled them, was arranged to construct a new roof over the walls of Tunskeen, the old one being damaged. Timber joists and corrugated aluminium sheets were dropped off at the end of the forestry road, near to Slaethornrig, and these were carried in by association members. Over a weekend the new roof was constructed, and the author took part in this, staying overnight and assisting in the erection. The roof proved to be serviceable for many years, until again it was blown off in the storms.

A public meeting was held in December 1965 in the village hall in Dalmellington, at which 32 interested people turned up and founded the group. Local Scoutmaster, Tom Riggans, took the chair and the Mountain Bothies Association was officially formed.

The success of Backhill (which was adopted by the MBA and was the subject of a renovation in 1966) and Tunskeen resulted in other bothies being created at other former steadings or cottages. In 1973 White Laggan was rebuilt, the walls having a slate roof over them with a sleeping area within the roof-space, an open balcony looking down to the living room and fireplace below, later changed to house a wood-burning stove. Adjoining was a store room, and White Laggan was different in that it had a small kitchen with a large window gazing across the glen and down to Loch Dee along one side. Whether or not the stories that the work party that was originally going to rebuild Black Laggan until they were frightened off by the ghost were true or apocryphal is not known!

1.4 Tunskeen Bothy

Shiel of Castlemaddy, located in the Polharrow Glen, east of Corserine, was converted into a bothy in 1974. A larger cottage, similar in size to Backhill, it had two main rooms on the ground floor and two sleeping rooms in the roof-space.

Although the MBA had other bothies in south-west Scotland, this was all that they had within the area covered by this book. Another bothy existed, however, that was erected by the Forestry Commission. A competition was held to design a new mountain refuge, and the winning design became known as the 'Wigwam'. The refuge got its name from its shape, for it was a polygonal pyramid made from timber and plywood, a cross between a lunar landing module and an Indian tepee. The door was angled, the windows were like those used in caravans, and in the middle of it was a wood-burning stove.

It was said that the site chosen was to remain a secret, its erection to have no publicity, and the bothy would be discovered by walkers. The site picked was on the western side of the Merrick range, at the foot of Kirriereoch's long finger. The refuge was officially named Crossburn Bothy, from the adjoining watercourse.

The Wigwam proved to be popular with climbers on the Merrick and Tarfessock range, but the wooden structure with a fire within proved to be its undoing. The shelter went on fire and was burned to the ground, whether deliberately or by accident is not known. It was decided by the Forestry Commission that it should not be replaced.

The other bothies also suffered from misuse over the years. The larger and more accessible bothies became the haunt of motorcyclists who would get their bikes over the locked forestry gates and drive to the bothies, loaded with alcohol. Other groups were too lazy to gather firewood from the forest, or else cut up sticks that the Forestry Commission kindly left nearby to try to prevent them from ripping up floors and other

1.5 Crossburn Bothy

25

parts of the building to burn on the fire. Vandalism became so bad that the volunteers of the Mountain Bothies Association couldn't keep up with the maintenance, and with regret had to give up Backhill of Bush and Shiel of Castlemaddy. The Forestry Commission then decided that it would be best to remove the latter, and thus, in March 2011, Shiel of Castlemaddy was flattened. Only the footings of the walls were left, marking where once families lived and worked on the land.

The other bothies remain, but Backhill is under threat, no organisation maintaining it any more. Tunskeen and White Laggan are still MBA bothies, but both have been susceptible to unsavoury residents and damage to them. The real outdoor enthusiast has lost out to the vandal who cares little for his fellow hills-man.

The rise in the number of walkers on the hills has resulted in an increase in injuries and accidents taking place. The Galloway Mountain Rescue Team was established in 1975 to assist in rescuing those who were unfortunate enough to have an accident. At that time it was known as the Galloway Hill Search and Rescue Group, but they changed their name in June 1983 and became affiliated to the Mountain Rescue Committee of Scotland. The group cover an area extending to over 3,000 square miles and their work includes assisting hill-walkers who have had injuries, become lost, or travelled beyond their abilities. They also help the police in searching for missing persons all over the area, or searching for bodies washed up on the shores of the Solway. The team has also responded to six aircraft accidents. The group comprises of volunteers, and they remain on call all day, every day. There are forty members of the team, and they have two trained search dogs. The principal base is at Newton Stewart and a secondary outpost is located at Castle Douglas. The costs of running the group have to be met by donations, and the team have arranged charity ascents of the Merrick, the first one being in 2012, when over £5,000 was raised by 141 walkers.

The use of public art has increased in recent years across the Galloway Highlands. In a number of remote locations there can be found sculptures and carvings, often appearing to be quite historical, now that time has rubbed its hoary hand over them. Many of these were commissioned by the Forestry Commission, to add interest to some of their walks, whereas others were the work of local artists, keen to have a public location in superb scenery in which to display their work.

One of the more intriguing examples is the Giant's Axehead, which is located by the side of the forest track between lochs Trool and Dee. This massive boulder is one of the 'Seven Stanes', a series of large blocks of stone that have been positioned in seven different forests, specifically on mountain bike trails. As well as at the Dargall Lane above Loch Dee, the other stones are located at Kirroughtree, Mabie and Dalbeattie forests in Galloway, Ae in Dumfriesshire, in addition to ones at Newcastleton and Glentress in the Borders. Each of these stones has a mysterious carving on it, and the cyclist, or anyone else visiting for that matter, is encouraged to study the stones and try to work out the mystery. When the visitor has gathered together all the letters required, they can arrange them into a significant phrase which, when sent to the Forestry Commission, will result in a tree being planted in the name of the person in one of southern Scotland's forests.

The Giant's Axehead stone is shaped like a massive Stone Age axe. It lies to the north of the track that makes its way along the southern side of Loch Dee before climbing over the pass into Glen Trool, south of the Dargall Lane. Lying prostrate on the moor, the stone measures around six feet six inches in length, by four feet wide and around one foot in thickness. The stone has been calculated to weigh around two tons. It is inscribed with a runic text, based on what is thought to be the oldest poem in Ireland – 'Amergin'. It translates as:

> I am the wind which breathes upon the sea,
> I am the wave of the ocean,
> I am the murmur of the billows,
> I am the ox of the seven combats,
> I am the vulture upon the rocks,
> I am a beam of the sun,
> I am the fairest of plants,
> I am a wild boar in valour,
> I am a salmon in the water,
> I am a loch in the plain,
> I am a word of science,
> I am the point of the lance in battle,
> I am the God who created in the head the fire.
> Who is it who throws light into the meeting on the mountain?
> Who announces the ages of the moon?
> Who teaches the place where couches the sun?

The Seven Stanes mountain bike trails were developed to encourage mountain bikers to cycle in their own designated areas, for often mountain cyclists are blamed for churning up open tracks on the hillsides or else disturbing walkers on narrow footpaths. The routes are some of the finest in Scotland, and that at Glen Trool takes riders through some of the most spectacular countryside. The International Mountain Biking Association, which presents awards to the tracks, has designated them as being of Global Superstar status. Starting at the Glen Trool visitor centre, the longest route here totals 36 miles in length. Known as the Big Country route, it takes in some magnificent scenery on its way through forest roads, minor public roads, and tracks. Riders may not appreciate the scenery at all times, for there are some difficult ascents which require the full effort of the cyclist, and some rough stretches where concentration is the order of the day.

Another significant sculpture is 'The Eye', a tall red cone constructed by the side of the Black Loch. This was commissioned in 1997 when a three-year-long art project was established to mark the fiftieth anniversary of Galloway Forest Park. This loch is easily accessed from the Queen's Way, a few miles west of Clatteringshaws Loch. A forest road leaves the public road just to the east of Craigdews Bridge and ascends the valley of the Tonderghie Burn, crossing the stream as it climbs to the loch. Near to the eastern end of the little loch is a parking area. 'The Eye' is a very pronounced cone, almost like the steeple of a church, and comparable to 'eye-catchers' or follies that seem to be dotted around England on landed estates, where the landowner constructed them to pretend that they were the parish church.

1.6 Giant's Axehead, Loch Dee

Designed by Colin Rose, 'The Eye' (of the needle) was built on a circular plan using red quarry tiles. It was completed in 1999. The needle stands around thirty feet in height and it gets its name of 'The Eye' from a hole at eye-level through the base of the structure. Looking through this small aperture hones in on a lonely part of the countryside, rather than a specific item or location. Colin Rose has worked extensively in the Newcastle and Sunderland area, lecturing on sculpture at various universities and colleges. He now lives and works in Northumberland.

To the west of the Black Loch, at an old set of sheep buchts by the side of the Grey Mare's Tail Burn, are a series of six carved heads, built into the remains of the stone dikes that formed the enclosures. These heads collectively form a sculpture called 'Quorum', the work of Matt Baker and Doug Cocker.

Slightly further is the 'Prolonged Exposure' artwork, also the work of Matt Baker, dating from 1997. It comprises of a series of 'cameras' made from salvaged forestry machinery The group are tall and elongated, rust-red in colour, with etched copper plates. According to the artist, the sculpture 'explores a sense of time, focusing the viewer on the shifting nature of landscape in both material and political terms.

The Forestry Commission were quick to establish forest trails when the trees grew to a reasonable height, encouraging visitors into what is publicly-owned land. The first forest trail to be created in the Galloway area was the Loch Trool trail, which opened in 1966. The second trail was located a couple of miles further down the valley, known as Stroan Bridge Forest Trail.

Other paths and trails have been developed across the uplands, from simple walks of a few hundred yards to places of interest or notable viewpoints, to longer through routes. In recent years the Ness Glen pathway has been rebuilt and opened to the public, with further routes heading north down by the side of the River Doon towards Dalmellington.

Way-marked walks established in Forestry Commission land can be followed in the vicinity of Glen Trool, where four walks varying in length from 1½ miles to six miles have been made. At Clatteringshaws a walk of two miles makes its way to the summit of 1,270 feet high Benniguinea, from where a view of the loch can be made. At the northern end of the park is a walk from Stinchar Bridge to the Cornish Loch and back, a distance of three miles. The walk makes its way alongside the Water of Girvan and over Cornish Hill.

The long distance path, the Southern Upland Way, passes through part of the Galloway Highlands on its way from Portpatrick in the west to Cockburnspath in the east. It was established in 1984 by the Countryside Commission for Scotland. Popular with long-distance walkers, the 212-mile route takes one through some of the remotest stretches of countryside in southern Scotland.

The Way enters the Galloway Highlands on crossing the River Cree at Bargrennan, from where it meanders alongside the Water of Minnoch and Water of Trool, passing through old birch and oak woods, before arriving at Caldons. From there it makes its way along the southern side of Loch Trool, passing the Steps of Trool and affording fine views north across the loch towards the Bruce's Stone and the Fell of Eschoncan. From the head of Loch Trool the Way makes its route eastwards, through the Glenhead glen and over the pass towards the upper reaches around Loch Dee. Following a forest road, the walk circles around the glen south of Loch Dee and arrives at the bridge over the Black Water of Dee. On the north side of the Dee, the Way follows the forest road eastwards to near Mid Garrary, before heading over the low hill of Shield Rig before dropping to Clenrie in the Garroch Glen. Picking up the minor road up through the glen, the Way makes its way into St John's Town of Dalry.

A couple of forest roads have also been opened to vehicular traffic, on the payment of a toll. The first of these routes to be opened was the Raider's Road, which makes its way alongside the Black Water of Dee from Bennan to Clatteringshaws. Opened in 1976, this ten mile routes is outside the area of this book, but it attracts visitors to the remote forests. The route was named after *The Raiders*, the novel by S. R. Crocket, written in 1894, in which the Faas and Marshalls stole cattle from the Maxwell estates and drove them into the fastness of the highlands around Loch Dee.

A second forest drive, and one within the area covered by this volume, is that from Loch Doon to the Straiton hill road. This road had existed for a number of years as a forest road, only used by forestry workers, walkers or cyclists. When it was opened to the public motorist, a parking area at an elevated viewpoint overlooking Loch Riecawr was created. The route covers five miles from the public road-ends near Craigmalloch on Loch Doon and Ballochbeatties near Loch Bradan.

Cycling has become a major sport once more, with off-road routes becoming extremely popular. Cross-country long-distance routes have been developed, The National Cycle Route number 7 being way-marked through Galloway, following tracks

1.7 'The Eye', Black Loch

in the Clatteringshaws and Glentrool forests. The route enters the area covered by this book at Clatteringshaws dam, follows the minor road alongside the west side of Clatteringshaws Loch, then by forest roads past Loch Dee and Loch Trool, before dropping down to the Water of Minnoch. The route then follows the hill road to Straiton as far as Rowantree Toll, leaving the area in this book at David Bell's Monument, taking the Nick of the Balloch route via the De'il's Elbow and Maybole to Ayr.

There are a few visitor centres and museums that have been established within the Galloway Highlands area. One of the better known is located on the shores of Clatteringshaws Loch. This was originally the Deer Museum, but it was re-developed as the Clatteringshaws Visitor Centre, with displays relevant to the deer, as well as other natural animals and birds, geology and archaeology. It was extended in 1976 to house a stained glass window by the painter and designer, Brian Thomas. Entitled 'The Hills of Home', it shows Galloway's lochs, hills, wildlife, as well as Murray's Monument. In

2012-13 the visitor centre was expanded, adding a new glazed front which looks over the extensive loch.

Another visitor centre was established at Stroan Bridge, known as Glentrool Visitor Centre. This replaced two smaller centres, one nearer Bruce's Stone, which was limited and cramped, and the older Stroan Bridge centre. The Glentrool Visitor Centre is popular with mountain bikers, the Glentrool part of the Seven Stanes mountain bike trails being based here.

1.8 'The Hills of Home' window, Clatteringshaws

A small heritage centre was erected at Carsphairn and opened in 1992 by the Carsphairn Heritage Group. The group was formed in 1987, but the seeds for it were sown when a local heritage exhibition had been put on in the village hall in 1982. This centre also contains a small selection of local books, articles and family history material that is invaluable for descendants of people who lived in the parish. The exhibition area is used for different exhibitions each year, most of the artefacts being sourced from local residents, who often have items that have been handed down through the generations. Examples of recent exhibitions include 'Legacies from the Loft', 'The Sporting Life' and 'Coming Home'. The exhibition centre is open at weekends from Easter to the end of May, then daily to the beginning of October.

Numerous other arts projects have been carried out in the uplands area. In 2008 the poet Mary Smith and the artist Silvana McLean were commissioned to produce a book celebrating the stories and memories of the hills. Entitled *Voices from Glentrool and Merrick*, the original book has etchings of upland scenes, with poetry printed on clear sheets, allowing the reader to see the etchings beneath them. The original book is held by the National Library of Scotland in Edinburgh, but some other copies were made and distributed.

2 Geology

The geology of the Galloway Highlands is a fairly complex matter, but one which can be simplified slightly to explain the formation of the mountains, lochs, glens and associated landscape.

The oldest rocks in the region covered by this volume date from the Lower Palaeozoic era. These rocks can be subdivided into some that were formed in the Ordovician period (about 500-435 million years ago) and others created in the Lower Silurian period (about 435-405 million years ago). These rocks form much of the Southern Uplands in general, extending from the north-east and following the Southern Uplands Boundary Fault to the south west, ending around Stranraer in Wigtownshire. The Southern Uplands rocks are extremely thick and have been deposited in geosynclines, which could be described as deep elongated basins. The rocks were formed by the compression of extremely deep silts laid down at the bottom of oceans. The Galloway Highlands covered by this volume are in the main comprised of rocks of this type, apart from the central range, created when a granite intrusion forced its way into these base rocks.

The Lower Palaeozoic rocks were folded over and fractured during the turbulent times of the Silurian and Lower Old Red Sandstone periods. The result is that the rocks at the north-west end of the Galloway Highlands are, in fact, older than those to the south-east.

During the Ordovician period, the land forming the Galloway Highlands was actually located near to the equator, and was gradually moving northwards as the plates on the Earth's crust moved. The Ordovician rocks are in the main made up of greywackes and associated siltstones and shales. The beds of strata are noted as being very steep, the rocks having undergone major disturbances, such as folding. The compression of the rocks occurred mainly in a north-west to south-east direction. In some cases the folds have resulted in beds of rock that are almost vertical, or at least, in many cases, extremely steep.

The bulk of the Galloway hills were thus composed of Ordovician siltstones and shales. However, there are some small areas of older rocks, dating from the Arenig to Llandello period. There are a few small outcrops of rock of this type appearing on Curleywee, Lamachan and Larg hills. Again more outcrops of Arenig chert are found in a band spreading across Corserine, from Meikle Craigtarson to the south-west of the mountain, to near Garryhorn farm to the north-east. A third outcrop is found on the slopes of Buchan Hill, above Loch Trool. The prevailing dip of the strata of these rocks is generally to the south-east, suggesting to geologists that the strata were subject to isoclinal folds.

Around the Arenig rock are larger areas of rock from the Caradoc period, comprising of what are termed Glenkiln Shales, that is, black shales with Glenkiln-type fauna identifiable within them. In each of the areas mentioned above, this rock is more widespread, although it also occurs in other areas, such as near Forrest Lodge and on the Redstone Rig of Merrick.

Geologists who wish to collect Graptolite fossils will find them in the Garryhorn Burn, south-east of the farmhouse, in places near to Forrest Lodge, on the cliffs above Loch Dungeon, or else on the gairies at the head of the Polmaddy Burn. In Glen Trool, graptolites are more readily discovered in the glen formed by the Pulnabrick Burn, in the Torr Lane, or else by the Minnoch Water, above Stroan Bridge. Another spot where the fossils can be found in the shales is in the old quarry located near to the site of the old Craiglure Lodge, north of Ballochbeatties, on the southern shores of Loch Bradan.

Younger than the Ordovician bedrock, of which much of the Galloway hills are composed, is the Silurian greywackes of the Llandovery period. These rocks exist in a stretch of hill across the southern edge of the Highland area covered by this volume. From the south-west at the River Cree they extend in a band almost two miles wide to the south of Garlick Hill, Black Benwee, Munwhul and Bennan of Craigenbay. The heights of Talnotry, Darnaw, Craignell, Bennan and Dunreoch Hill are composed of this stone. Lesser areas of the Silurian rock occur in lengths, trending north-east to south-west, forming the hills of Cairnbaber and Cairngarroch.

It was into these older sedimentary rocks that a series of igneous or molten rocks were pushed, forming granite and granitic rocks, formed when lava bubbled up into the softer rocks of the Earth's crust. The granitic rocks cover an area of 47 square miles. The proper granite rocks don't cover so large an area, being located in the centre of the region, forming the range of mountains from Hoodens Hill south towards Craiglee of Dee, measuring around six miles long (north-south) by one mile wide. In many circles this rock is referred to as Loch Dee Granite. This igneous intrusion is usually ascribed to the Old Red Sandstone Period, which occurred around 400 million years ago. It is thought that the intrusion occurred in three phases, with each phase producing rocks increasingly acidic in composition.

The molten rock was pushed into the parent rock, without breaking the surface, where it eventually cooled down. Over millennia, the softer rocks above the granite mass were worn away, revealing the harder rocks below. Some people have speculated that the molten granite reservoir formed the base of volcanoes that have long-since been eroded away, and of which there is no trace.

The first intrusion produced a rock known as norite, though evidence of this rock only appears at the surface in the north-western, eastern and southern extremities of the intrusion. The norite comprises plagioclase, rhombic pyroxene and augite. It can be found on the ground to the south of Loch Dee, where a band around half a mile wide and two and a half miles from east to west breaks the surface. The north-eastern slopes of White Hill and the Black Laggan Ward are formed of this rock. The second place in the highlands where it can be found is to the west of Loch Riecawr, where the eminences of Craigmasheenie, Shiel Hill and Waterhead are formed of norite. The third, smaller, outlier of norite is responsible for the southern slopes of Bennan Hill, east of Loch Minnoch, at Forrest Lodge.

The second phase, which was the largest, comprises of an igneous rock known as tonalite, which extends from the ridge forming Craiglee of Loch Doon south to Craiglee of Dee, as though the two hills were named to mark the extremities! In width this tonalite, or quartz mica diorite, boss extends to around four or five miles - from east to west the rock is buttressed between the slopes of the Merrick range to the west and the Rhinns of Kells to the east. Excluded from this area is the central range of hills, where granite proper is found. The rock is a darker grey colour than the granite it surrounds, described more precisely as comprising oligoclase, biotite and quartz.

The final phase of granite intrusion produced the biotite-granite, a white-coloured rock with speckles of black within it. It consists of quartz, biotite, orthoclase and has oligoclase and microcline within it. This forms the centre of the highlands, extending from Snibe Hill to the south, through Craignaw, Dungeon Hill and Mullwharchar, in a narrow ridge to just beyond Hoodens Hill to the north.

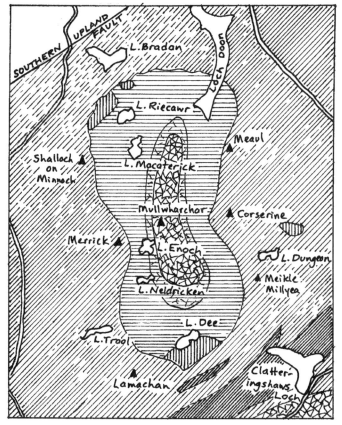

2.1 Sketch Map showing Geology of Galloway Highlands

35

Around the granite centre is a ring of rocks that are transitional between granite and tonalite, approximately half a mile in width. The intense heat of the molten lava bubble altered the surrounding bedrock, melting and re-crystalizing it. Some of the granite was changed into mica-schists, containing various minerals such as sillimanite.

When the main granite bubble was pushed into the parent rock it would have contorted it so much that cracks and fissures would have appeared. These were subsequently filled with molten lava which gradually cooled, creating a number of veins and dykes. As the mass of lava in the dykes was much less than the main blob of lava, the dyke lava cooled much quicker, creating rocks of a different form. It is thought that the dykes were created at a later period than the granite.

Over many millennia the covering rocks have been worn away by glaciers to reveal the dykes. In the Ordovician bedrock, one can find numerous dykes of intrusive rocks, in particular Porphyrite (a light buff coloured rock), but in some rarer instances, dykes of Felsite and Lamprophyre can be discovered. Within the metamorphosed rocks can be found garnet, biotite and cordierite

The granite intrusion also caused there to be veins of haematite, lead and nickel-bearing mispickel. These veins have in some cases been wrought.

These igneous intrusions right in the centre of the uplands were responsible for heating the surrounding parent rock, the greywackes. The immense heat changed these Ordovician rocks somewhat and altered their properties. This formed the aureole of metamorphism, where the rocks were baked. As a result, the Kells and Awful Hand range are harder rocks than the granite core, and this explains why these two ranges are in general higher than the Mullwharchar or Dungeon range. Within this aureole it is possible to find rarer minerals created by the intense heat. These include chiastolite, cordierite, sillimanite, tourmaline and garnet. The chert along the hill tops has a sheen indicative of heating, and are lighter in colour than the unheated rocks. Right at the junction of the two rocks, brown quartz crystals have been created, often gathered by hill-walkers and formed into small cairns.

There are a few other granite intrusions across Galloway. The Cairnsmore of Fleet intrusion is similar in size to the Loch Dee granite, and another large intrusion has resulted in the hill of Criffel, south-west of Dumfries, and the granite around

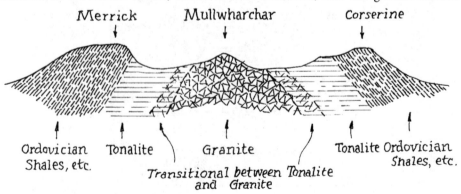

2.2 Sketch Section through hills from Merrick to Corserine

Dalbeattie, at one time famous for building stone. Lesser intrusions in south west Scotland exist at Cairnsmore of Carsphairn, Glen Afton and the Knipe, south of New Cumnock.

The granite has not been quarried to any extent within the central upland area, access being the main obstacle. More readily available sources of granite, such as above Creetown, have been quarried in preference to the more remote Galloway Highlands. However, the stone has been used over the centuries for various building purposes.

At Craigdews, or Craigdhews as older accounts spell it, the granite rocks of the Cairnsmore of Fleet mass appear at the surface. Numerous large boulders lie across the countryside, and at one time these were often taken or cut up for use in building, being of a high quality. The front pillars of the portico at Cally House, or Palace as it has become known in recent years, were quarried at Craigdews. The architect John Buonarotti Papworth (1775-1847) designed a massive *porte-cochere* for the house, added between 1833-8, when large extensions were made. The blocks of stone used for the pillars are upwards of twenty feet in height, the single stones shaped by masons into the finely polished Doric columns that make such a distinctive feature of the mansion. The quarries at Craigdews only operated for a few years. In 1841 William Campbell (b. 1806) lived there and according to the Census he was a 'stone-cutter'.

A number of geologists have investigated the rocks of the Galloway Highlands over the years, gradually improving the knowledge of how the hills could have been formed. Professor Charles Lapworth drew up the first detailed account of the rocks of the Southern Uplands in the Victorian era, his work discovering many features that became recognised as fairly obvious in later decades. In the 1920s, two geologists, Charles Irving Gardiner and Professor Sidney Hugh Reynolds, were responsible for identifying that the central granite intrusion was actually made up of three injections, resulting in different types of rock.

In addition to studying the parent rock, many geologists have looked at the landforms to try to work out how they were formed into the landscapes we know today. Much of this is due to the influence of ice, the hills being covered with deep coverings of frozen water at one time. As the years passed, the thickness was greatly reduced, and it wasn't until the last ice left Scotland that the shapes of the hills and glens were formed and subsequently revealed.

That the whole of Scotland was at one time covered by thick ice-caps is not in doubt, and as time passed the ice began to recede. At various times the earth cooled and small ice-caps returned, with associated glaciers. The principal Southern Uplands ice sheet melted around 12,000 years ago, having lasted for 70,000 years beforehand. The last 'ice-age' to affect Galloway probably ended around 10,000 years ago, in what is termed the Wurm-Weischel glacial period. At that time the highest of the Galloway Highlands were covered with ice, and small glaciers spread from this hinterland out onto the surrounding plains, where they gradually melted. These last glaciers created the valleys and corries of Galloway which we see today, previous ice coverings being on too large a scale to be responsible for any recognisable features. The melting ice also caused a run-off of sand and gravel, in some cases blocking the valleys and forming temporary lochs.

As well as scouring out valleys from the rock, the glaciers have been responsible for the creation of some of Galloway's lochs. Lochs Doon and Trool are two classic examples of this, the ice flow being held between the mountains and as a result the ice has deepened the valley further. When the ice melted, these deeper sections filled with water, leaving us with the lochs we know today.

The variable cutting strengths of the glaciers resulted in valleys of different depths being formed. Often these glens appear to be too large for the small streams that flow in them to have been responsible for their creation. Once the ice melted, and the valleys were drained by burns, a number of 'hanging valleys' were formed. These are glens located at a higher level than the parent valley. In the hanging valley the bottom of the glen suddenly comes to an end, the watercourse flowing within it tumbling in a series of falls to the bottom of the valley below. One of the better examples of these can be found off Glen Trool, where the glen of the Buchan Burn is relatively flat to below Culsharg, before the stream tumbles over the Buchan Falls down to the level of Loch Trool.

Although the corries of the Galloway Highlands are not so great as those to be found in the Highlands, or of Wales, there are a number of fair-sized examples of scoops of hillside that have probably been removed by the force of the ice. Some of the more significant ones include that to the north-west of Curleywee, the Caldron of the Merrick, Kirshinnoch (which probably means corrie of the fox in Gaelic – *coire shionnach*) or the Polmaddy Gairy on Corserine. The corrie to the north-west of Curleywee is regarded as being the finest example of such in Galloway. It measures around one mile across, from Bennanbrack to White Hill. Its semi-circular scoop has the vestiges of a corrie lochan on the floor, itself high above the Glenhead Burn.

Corrie lochans are rare in Galloway, the ice not being strong enough to scoop out a depression which later filled with water, but Kirshinnoch almost has one – the Bog of the Gairy – and perhaps Balminnoch Loch, north of Kirriereoch Hill is another.

Evidence of ice flows from the Galloway Highlands is seen in the striae, or scored grooves in the rocks. These lines were usually caused by rocks and stones being carried slowly by the ice cutting grooves into the parent rock below, the repeated flow of ice in a similar direction resulting in rock surfaces that have lines indicating the direction of glacial flow. If one goes to some of the old quarries by the side of the Loch Doon road, the flat beds of rock show these striations. A. S. Alexander wrote in *Across Watersheds*, 'In the floor of a roadside quarry of glacial drift used for road-metal, I observed a fine illustration of glaciation, or "ice-scratchings", the parallel scratches or striae running north and south in the direction of the trend of the glen, and indicating the direction of the ice-flow which was here northerly.' Similarly, an early student of Galloway glaciation, William Jolly, writing in the 1860s, identified excellent examples of striae at Craigencallie, Polharrow Burn, but noted that those in Glen Trool were poorly preserved.

Similarly, the glacial flow of ice carried with it large boulders which were dumped where the glacier either melted or could not carry the weight. This explains why there are a number of granite boulders across the Ayrshire plain and south into Wigtownshire and Galloway's lower farmland, where the parent rock is of a different type. The boulders were carried there by the ice flows and dropped when they could carry them no more. Of well-known erratic boulders left by Galloway ice is the Baron's Stone of Killochan, located in the midst of a green field to the north-east of Girvan. Standing alone, this massive boulder is thirteen yards in circumference and is reckoned to weigh 37 tons. The nearest granite to the stone's present location is thirteen miles away. It has been calculated that boulders of Loch Dee granite can be identified across

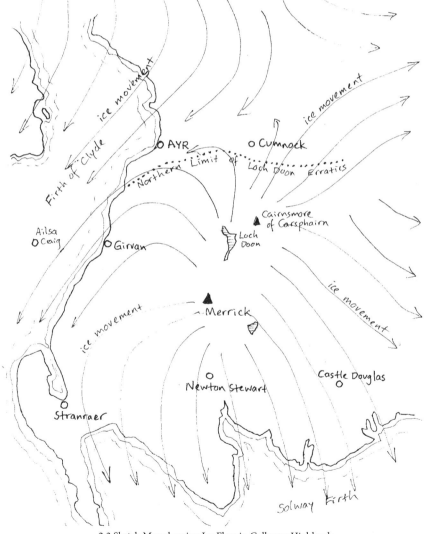

2.3 Sketch Map showing Ice Flow in Galloway Highlands

an area of around 1,300 square miles, indicating the extent of the ice flows. Even more spectacular are the blocks of granite that are known to have come from the Criffel mass which have been identified as far south as Birmingham and Pembrokeshire in South Wales.

The glaciers were also responsible for dumping stones and clays, in some cases in moraines, which could be formed at the sides, middle or termini of glaciers. In a few cases these moraines form what are known as drumlins, and various parts of the lower Galloway uplands are covered with these. On the periphery, located on the moors, these drumlins were often composed of a better soil than the surrounding peat bogs, and being higher allowed some drainage. This meant they could be cultivated more readily, and often farmsteads were erected on them. Today, examples of farms perched on low drumlins can be seen in the valley of the Cree or in the valley of the Carsphairn Lane, where many of the drumlins were at one time assumed to be motte hills and were marked as antiquities on older Ordnance Survey maps. Among these were 'motes' at Lamford, Brockloch and Holm of Daltallochan. On the Machars of Wigtownshire are numerous examples of drumlins, their elongated shaped being an indicator of former ice flow direction. In the wilder valleys, drumlins are uncultivated, and the small rounded form that the hillocks take is often described as 'basket of eggs topography'.

2.4 The De'il's Bowling Green, Little Craignaw, with Dungeon Hill behind

A rather impressive example of the work of the ice can be seen just to the north of the summit of Craignaw, right in the centre of the highlands. A flattish granite slabbed extent of the hill, known as Little Craignaw, is covered with hundreds of large granite boulders. These boulders were plucked by the ice from the parent rock and rolled or pushed across the flat slabs. When the ice eventually melted, the boulders were dumped as far as the ice had taken them. The random sprinkling of the stones has given rise to the term of the De'il's Bowling Green, as though the devil had been playing a game of bowls with the large stones when he was disturbed and had to abandon the game in mid-play.

Similarly, within the same vicinity, is a larger block of granite that has been given the name the De'il's Loaf. This stone has fairly straight sides, one of them straighter than the rest, so that it looks as though it has had a slice taken from the loaf. To make the appearance of a loaf of bread more apparent, the top of the rock is domed, like the crust rising whilst it has been baked.

One who investigated the geology of the Galloway Highlands was A. S. Alexander, already mentioned, who lived in Ayrshire, but whose book, *Across Watersheds*, was a popular publication in the 1930s. Born on 22 August 1860 at Balhearty farm, near Tillicoultry, he was educated at Dollar Academy and St Andrews University. He became a teacher, firstly at Newton Stewart Academy, followed by schools at Canonbie, Alva, Harris, Dunfermline, and Grangemouth. He lived in Canada for a time before returning to Scotland and recommenced teaching at Annan, Girvan and Ayr. Over the years he made a personal collection of natural history items, which was placed on display at Belleisle House in Ayr for five years, from 1927 until 1932. They were thereafter relocated to the town's Carnegie Library. *Tramps Across Watersheds'* first edition (published in 1934) sold 2,000 copies, and a second printing, retitled *Across Watersheds*, was issued in April 1939.

Like many of the early visitors to the hills, Alexander put up with shepherds and country folk. On a visit to the Merrick, he wrote:

... I swung down Minnoch vale for two or three miles to the ruins of Rowantree Toll, where a road branches north to Straiton, twelve miles distant; and soon thereafter I reached Rowantree School and Schoolhouse on the roadside, and in the shadow of Polmadie at sunset. The teacher invited me to accompany him across Minnoch water to his lodging with a shepherd's family. The shepherd pointed out the way to the top of Merrick, now aglow in the setting sun. After tea, talk, sleep, and breakfast, I marched at 3 a.m. over the dim, over-shadowed, dreary, moss-hag moor, stretching to the base of Merrick. I kept the round-headed, mound-like Kirriereoch, silhouetted on the brightening eastern sky, on my left, and the five-mile-long ridge of Merrick on my right. I had my eyes directed towards the stone dyke in the gap between these two hills, as advised by the shepherd. For two hours I struggled, steeplechased, and dodged around the white, spongy sphagnum 'hags', and felt quite in sympathy with the hardships of the 'Men o' the Moss Hags' of Covenanting times. I reached the burn flowing down between Kirriereoch and Merrick; and crossed the boulder dyke at the point directed. The dyke is on the march between Carrick and Kirkcudbright.

At 5 a.m. I sat on a big granite boulder on the ridge of Merrick to replace my wet socks with dry ones, and to watch the sun lighting and creeping down into Minnoch vale. The dazzling white disc at last appeared on a white cap of mist crowning Kirriereoch. This white cap or band of mist was the breadth of the disc. The sun shone brightly on the precipitous northern face of Merrick. The rounded, smooth, green Kirriereoch and the green sedgy slope of Merrick seemed covered with a shiny green velvet carpet spreading down into the grey marshes of Minnoch Glen, away over Wigtownshire, and up over Barr and Polmadie Hills to the 'Nick'. The sun gleamed on Trool lake in the south-west, and on whitewashed homesteads and shepherd sheilings scattered over the landscape. A cool breeze was blowing and I made steady progress upward, pausing every little while to look down on the vale, examine plants, lap with 'Adam's cup' a little water or rest a brief space on a grey granite boulder. The granite boulders bestrew the hill slope and point usually towards the south-west in the direction of Loch Trool, where probably the pressure of the ice that scooped out the lake was greatest.

Alexander studied the rocks of the district. He wrote of the dark grey schist of which the Merrick is composed – 'not quite so schistose as that of the Highlands of Scotland generally, nor so silvery or micaceous as that near Pitlochry or Pass of Killiecrankie in Perthshire.' Near the Merrick's summit he found a huge boulder, fourteen paces round and six feet tall. This had been worn smooth by the ice, abraded after being dumped by the stronger flows, only to be rubbed smooth by lesser ice during the Pleistocene period.

3 The Mountains

How one determines what constitutes a 'mountain', as opposed to a 'hill' is quite difficult. Some claim that only those summits in excess of 3,000 feet count, this height being chosen by Sir Hugh T. Munro, and which subsequently became known as 'Munros' amongst the hill-walking fraternity. My own dictionary simply describes a mountain as 'a high hill', without adding any figures. Certainly, in the Galloway Highlands the high hills of the central area should be classed as mountains, being rugged summits, in many places covered with rocks and boulders left by a receding glacier, and high cliffs, often known as 'gairies' in Galloway.

The highest mountain in Galloway, indeed in the whole of the south of Scotland, excluding the island of Arran, is the Merrick. Most maps simple name it 'Merrick', but to almost everyone who knows the area it is usually referred to as 'The Merrick'. Where the name came from is no longer known, but most agree that it derives from some form of Gaelic words, as do almost every other hill and loch in the area. Rev James B. Johnston, in *Place Names of Scotland*, published in 1934, reckons that the name derives from *meur* or *meurach*, meaning branched or fingered. Another derivation takes the name from the Gaelic, *Tiu Meurig*, which also means 'the (little) finger'. This is descriptive of the shape of the mountain, for there are various rigs, or ridges, striking off from the summit. Pont's map of 1654 names it as 'Maerack hill' on one sheet, 'Bin Maerack' on another, perhaps indicating that at one time it was Ben Merrick. John Ainslie's map of southern Scotland, dated 1821, names the mountain as 'Morrick'. John Thomson's *Atlas of Scotland*, published in 1832, names the summit as 'Mirrick' on one page, as 'Merrick mountain' on another. On the latter it claims the summit to be 2,751 feet in height, just short of its actual height. The *New Statistical Account* of the parish of Minnigaff, written in 1842, names the hill as 'the Meyrick', a spelling used by Maxwell in his *Guide to the Stewartry of Kirkcudbright*, published in 1884. Armstrong's map of Ayrshire, dated 1775, notes the hill as 'Merick'.

In recent years the name 'Awful Hand' has been derived for the range of mountains that includes the Merrick, stretching from Benyellary north to Shalloch on Minnoch. This name was perhaps first given by John MacTaggart in his *Scottish Gallovidian Encyclopaedia*, written in 1824. There, under the entry for 'Merrick', he writes:

> Five large hills or mountains [even he is not sure what they should be called!] in Galloway; they lay beside one another, and gradually rise, the one a little higher above the other; in the morning and evening the shadows of these

hills on the level moors below seem like the fingers of an awful hand; hence the name *Merrick*, which, in the Gaelic, signifies *fingers*. How expressive that language must be. O! that I were the master of it.

Perhaps an older name for the range was 'Kraigenny Hill', as Thomas Kitchin's map of the south part of Ayrshire names the hill range extending north from Loch Trool. This map, which is not a particularly detailed one, was published in 1749 and this is the only hill named thereon. This may be the modern Craigenrae, though it is probably a reduction of Craigenreoch, as some older maps name it.

The Merrick is 2,764 feet (843m) in height, the summit cairn having an Ordnance Survey triangulation station alongside. The summit, when approached from the south and west, which is the most common direction of ascent, is a fairly steady climb over flattish ground, becoming stonier the closer one gets to the top. However, a few yards in any other direction from the summit cairn leads one to steep gairies, or rough cliffs. The northern side of the Merrick has the Black Gairy extending westward for over one mile, in some places 600 feet in height. Snow remains in the gullies of this gairy long after it has melted elsewhere. One gully has been named the Black Gutter.

To the north-east is a small corrie, known as the Howe of the Caldron, again surrounded by a ring of rocky slopes. The south-eastern slopes are less steep, but there are still some stretches of rocky surfaces. Here is the Redstone Rig, which drops down to Loch Enoch.

The view from the Merrick is one of the finest in Scotland, assuming that one arrives at the summit on a clear day. When the atmosphere is clear, and the clouds and mist are absent, one can gaze out in various directions at distant peaks. Almost due north from the summit is Ben Lomond, 74 miles distant. By its side one can make out Ben Ledi and Ben Venue, summits in the Trossachs. Goat Fell on Arran is seen 43 miles to the north-west. The Mountains of Mourne can be seen to the south west, 100 miles away across the North Channel in County Down, Ireland. The peaks of the Lake District, or Cumbrian Mountains, can be seen sixty miles or so to the south-east.

It is claimed that the summit of the Merrick has the longest-possible view in the whole of the British Isles. Jonathan de Ferranti, from Newburgh in Fife, has used a computer programme to generate panoramas as seen from various locations around Britain, as well as across the world. These panoramas have been published on his website, viewfinderpanoramas.org, each summit, coastal headland, town or feature that is theoretical to see being indicated on the views. Theoretical is the word, however, for in many cases it requires binoculars and the clearest of skies to observe the farthest distances.

According to de Ferranti, his panoramas were designed to be printed off and carried up to the summits so that the climber could identify what he sees. His panorama as seen from the summit of Merrick indicate distant summits that it is possible to see include the Mountains of Mourne – Slieve Bearnagh at ninety miles. Beyond Kintyre are the Paps of Jura – Dubh Bheinn, Beinn a' Chaolais and Beinn an

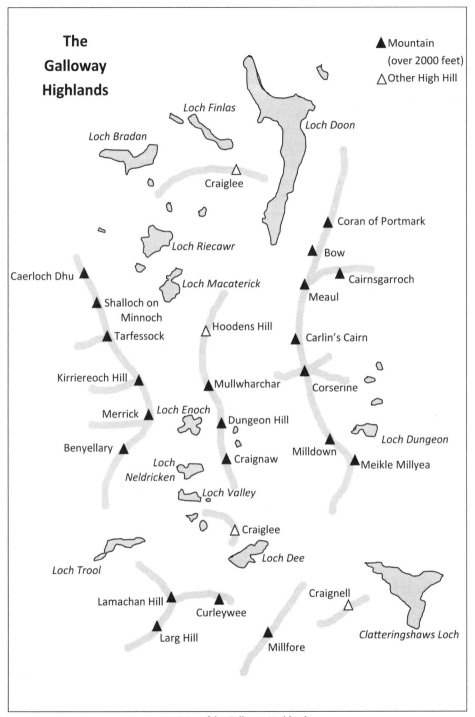

3.1 Map of the Galloway Highlands

Oir, which are up to eighty miles to the west. Further away, it should be possible to spot Ben More on Mull, 108 miles to the North West, though this is unlikely.

Ben Lomond can sometimes be seen to the north, 73 miles away. Just to the left of it, on a clear day, it would be possible to spot Beinn Dorain, 95 miles off. Above Kilmarnock is Stob Binnein, 85 miles to the north, with Meall Ghaordie a bit to the right, 96 miles away. In the same general direction Ben Lawers should be possible to make out, 98 miles to the north.

To the north-east, above Cumnock, Ben Cleuch, the highest summit in the Ochil Hills should be possible to spot, 77 miles to the north-east. To the north-east, Cairn Table, on the border of Ayrshire and Lanarkshire, stands up 30 miles distant. Blackcraig Hill in the Afton Hills is 19 miles away, and to the immediate right of it is Tinto, 45 miles off. Hills to the east, over Carlin's Cairn and Corserine, are in general 30-40 miles off, such as Queensberry (36 miles). Behind Meikle Millyea can be spotted the northern Pennine hills - Cross Fell, just to the left of Criffel, being 85 miles away.

In the Lake District, Skiddaw is 63 miles off, and Helvellyn is 72 miles away. Scafell Pike, the highest mountain in England, should be visible, but it is difficult to distinguish it in a myriad of peaks that include Great Gable.

If the Isle of Man is clear, have a close look at the eastern end of the island, on the horizon, for there the longest possible view in Britain may be seen. Due to the curvature of the Earth, and the relevant heights of the two mountains, a small peak appearing just off the Isle of Man and to the west of the summit of Lamachan Hill, would be Snowdon, 144 miles to the south.

Whether Snowdon has ever been seen from the summit of the Merrick is unlikely. Jonathan de Ferranti writes that this is the longest theoretical line of sight that is possible in the British Isles. He has tried to find longer ones, using different peaks, but was unable to get one. He also writes that Chris Jesty, a topographic researcher, also tried to find a longer sightline n the 1980s, but was unable to do so. Accordingly, this sightline was listed as a Guinness World Record.

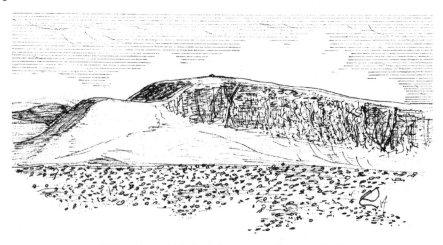

3.2 Merrick and Little Spear from slopes of Kirriereoch Hill

The view from Merrick to Snowdon is regarded as being more possible than the other way round, for de Ferranti writes that 'Merrick would be practically impossible to observe from Snowdon, because of the very thin aperture it shows behind nearby Lamachan Hill.' He continues, giving an analogy to explain his thinking: 'If a colleague and I were in neighbouring rooms, and I were at a desk but the colleague were looking through an empty keyhole, he would probably see me clearly, but I would not see him. The "keyhole" is Lamachan Hill, which is much closer to Merrick, so an observer on Merrick would see Snowdon much more easily than vice versa. In fact Merrick would be impossible to see from Snowdon other than with a telescope, and then only if there were a suitable contrast with Lamachan Hill (e.g. snow or sun on one, but not the other).'

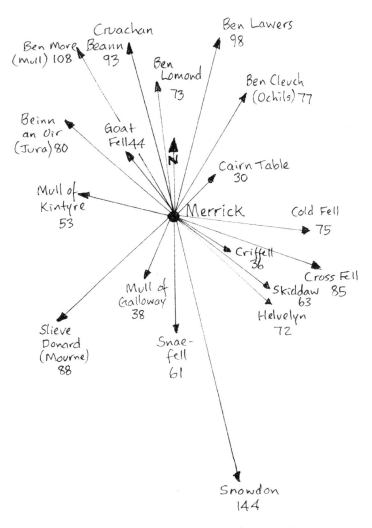

3.3 Sketch Diagram showing Panorama from Merrick

On the south side of the Merrick is Benyellary, or Ben Yellary as it is also written. This summit is usually crossed on ascents of the Merrick from Glen Trool, its summit cairn 2,360 feet (719m) above sea level. Over the top of the hill a stone dike makes its way, continuing over the Neive of the Spit, or ridge that links Benyellary with the Merrick. The south-eastern slopes of the Neive are rocky – the Scars of Benyellary. Most of the remainder of the hill is fairly rounded and grassy, though there are some outcrops of rock to the north, in the little corrie of the Kirkennan Burn, and lower down the slopes to the south-east – the Scab Craigs.

The name is reckoned to mean 'mountain of the eagles', Benyellary being a simple rendering of the Gaelic *Beinn na h-Iolaire*. On Thomson's *Atlas* the name is rendered Ben Yetter and on Pont's map of 1654 it is shown as Bennellury Hill.

To the north of the Merrick is Kirriereoch Hill, which has the distinction of being the highest summit in Ayrshire. The hill is located on the boundary with Kirkcudbrightshire, however, so Ayrshire has the problem of deciding whether or not to adopt this as its highest mountain. This is even more muddied when one studies more detailed maps and finds that the highest point on the mountain is actually 2,578 feet above sea level (786m), and is located 400 yards south of the boundary dike. The highest point on the boundary is in fact 2,565 feet.

The name Kirriereoch is descriptive of the great corrie that lies to the south of the hill, as opposed to the hill itself. Thomson's *Atlas* and Ainslie's map names it as 'Carroch Hill', and often locals say the name as 'kirrie-och', missing the extra syllable. *Coire Riabhach* is Gaelic for 'grey corrie', a very apt descriptive name for the huge corrie between Kirriereoch Hill and the Merrick. The Kirriereoch side of the corrie comprises a long slope covered in scree and rock outcrops, the Cantin Heads and Torrs of Kirriereoch. At the foot of the corrie is a flat glacial valley, drained by the Kirshinnoch

3.4 Benyellary from Merrick

Burn, and the Bog of the Gairy, probably at one time a corrie lochan. On the north-east side of Kirrireoch Hill is a high corrie, known as the Green Holes.

On the north side of Kirrireoch Hill is another lengthy scree slope, known as Balminnoch Brae, overlooking the corrie of Balminnoch. At the foot of the Brae is the Balminnoch Loch, a corrie lochan that survives, measuring 800 yards by 400 yards. This drains into the Cross Burn, which joins the Kirshinnoch Burn to form the Kirriemore Burn. The name Balminnoch is perhaps a derivation of Ben Minnoch, the mountain above the Water of Minnoch, and this is probably Kirriereoch Hill's original name, one that appears on Pont's map of 1654 as Bin Meanach Hill.

The next mountain heading north of Kirriereoch Hill in the Merrick range is Tarfessock. The name is thought to derive from the Gaelic *Torr Fasach*, which means the 'grassy or bushy hill'. The summit is far from bushy, being a prominent summit with numerous rock outcrops and scree slopes on it. Another possible derivation is *Torr Fasaich*, Gaelic for the 'desolate mountain', or even *Torr Faisgeachd*, the 'mountain of the narrow neck'. The main ridge of the 'Awful Hand' joins the hill on a north-south axis, but the western ridge of Tarfessock is much longer, forming the second finger. The summit cairn is located 2,282 feet (697m) above sea level.

On the southern side of Tarfessock is a long ridge known as Carmaddie Brae, linking it with Kirriereoch Hill. This ridge is in excess of one mile in length, an elevated stretch of hillside which averages 1,900-2,000 feet in height. To the south of Tarfessock itself is a smaller eminence on the ridge, perhaps a 'south top' to Tarfessock, or else the 'summit' of Carmaddie Brae, which rises above 2,000 feet and tops out at 2,034 feet (620m). Along this ridge are a number of lochans of various sizes. One of them is simply named on the Ordnance Survey map as 'Lochan' – most have no name although one has earned the name Loch Brough.

From the summit of Tarfessock the northern flank drops 226 feet to the pass between it and Shalloch and Minnoch, known as the Nick of Carclach. 'Nick' is a fairly common term in Galloway for the pass between two mountains or hills, and numerous others exist, such as the Nick of the Balloch, through which a road passes, or the Nick of the Loup.

The furthest north of the Merrick, or Awful Hand, range of mountains is Shalloch on Minnoch. This is one of the larger of the Galloway Highlands, and in fact is one of the largest hills in Ayrshire. It forms the third finger and pinkie of the Awful Hand range. It forms two digits as there are in fact two summits to the hill, Shalloch on Minnoch itself as well as a lower top to the north, sometimes referred to as Caerloch Dhu.

Shalloch on Minnoch's main summit rises to 2,543 feet (775m), a great whaleback, the eastern face of which has a steep but shallow corrie on it, dropping considerably in a short distance (around 1,000 feet in half a mile) to the level moors around Tunskeen and Loch Macaterick. This eastern cliff has on it a rock known as the Maiden's Bed, a considerable slab of stone. The summit of the hill has two eminences, one marked by an Ordnance Survey triangulation station and a fair-sized cairn, the other, higher top, by a small cairn.

The north summit of Shalloch on Minnoch, or Caerloch Dhu, is 2,162 feet (659m) above the level of the sea. A fairly bland hill, the summit is rather flat and seems to be little more than an eminence on the moors hereabouts, despite its considerable height. A small cairn about one foot in diameter by one foot tall marks the summit.

The eastern side of Shalloch on Minnoch is rocky in many places, and in addition to the corrie already mentioned, there are considerable outcrops at The Cargaie, to the north of the summit, as well as at Carglas Craig and lower down the eastern slopes. Above the forests to the east are various outcrops known as the Big Meowl and the Wee Meowl, obviously both derivations of the Gaelic *meall*, meaning lump. Here can also be found the Corbie Craig (rock of the crow), Rowantree Craig, and the Tailor's Stone.

The Tailor's Stone is a massive boulder located on the moor to the south of the ruin of Slaethornrig. Who the tailor was that it was named for is not known, nor why a tailor should be associated with so remote a spot.

The west side of Shalloch on Minnoch is more rounded and hill-like than the eastern flanks. It drops steadily down towards the Minnoch valley, the lower slopes clothed in forestry plantations. Among the lower summits thereabouts, and lower shoulders of Shalloch on Minnoch itself, are Shalloch, Rig of the Shalloch and Mount Shellie, all probably deriving their name from the great summit. In fact, Thomson's *Atlas* of 1832 indicates 'Shalloch Hills' rather than any particular name for the summit, though Pont in 1654 names it as 'Schelach of Minnock'. On Armstrong's 1775 *Map of Ayrshire* the hill is shown as 'Shalloch Cairn'. Ainslie's map of 1821 calls it 'Cairn Shalloch'.

The central range in the Galloway Highlands is known as the Dungeon range. The highest summit here is Mullwharchar, probably the most remote mountain in Galloway, being a rough four and a half miles from the nearest public road, which is located at Bruce's Stone in Glen Trool. The mountain is conical in shape, rising steadily to its summit cairn, which measures around six feet in diameter by five feet in height, perched 2,270 feet (692m) above sea level. A granite mountain, the soil is thin over it, and in many places the natural rock breaks through to form slabs and boulders. On its north eastern slope the hillside becomes ever rockier as one descends, until eventually it breaks out in a series of cliffs, known as The Tauchers. These are some of the steepest cliffs in Galloway, plunging headlong down to the level moss around the head of the Gala Lane.

The name derives from the Gaelic *Meall Adhairce*, which means 'hill of the huntsman's horn.' Thomson's *Atlas* spells it 'Millwharcher'. Pont's map has a rather strange version of the spelling – 'Mayblhorkun hill'. On Armstrong's *Map of Ayrshire*, dating from 1775, the mountain is spelled 'Milquarhar', and on Ainslie's map of 1821 it is spelled 'Mill Wharker'. Located in Ayrshire, the county boundary makes a detour south along the Pulskaig Burn and the Eglin Lane to claim the mountain as its own. Historically, the boundary between the Stewartry of Kirkcudbright and the county of Ayr was very much disputed hereabouts, and it was only in later years fixed across the Galloway Highlands.

To the south of Mullwharchar is Dungeon Hill. It is by no means the highest, but certainly one of the most attractive. The view of the cliffs on the east, rising from the moss of the Silver Flow, to its diminutive flat summit is one that is very distinctive. A granite mountain, like Craignaw to the south and Mullwharchar to the north, the Dungeon Hill rises to 2,031 feet (619m).

As mentioned, the eastern slopes of Dungeon Hill are occupied by cliffs – a series of upended slabs rising above the Round Loch of the Dungeon.

South of the Dungeon Hill is the wide corrie known as the Nick of the Dungeon. This name is shown on more detailed Ordnance Survey maps, but James MacBain, writing in *The Merrick and the Neighbouring Hills* in 1929, notes 'but that name is not to be found on the maps, and I never heard the pass so designated by the shepherds or given any other name by them. So far as I am concerned I invented the name.' That may be so, and MacBain certainly earned the right to give names to features in the highlands that bore no name, yet merited one. However, he must have heard the name somewhere, for the Six Inch Ordnance Survey map of 1853 clearly names the pass as such.

Lying on the moor at the north-east of Dungeon Hill is a huge granite boulder that has become known as the Dungeon Stone, named as such on larger-scaled Ordnance Survey maps. James MacBain reckons that he gave the rock its name. The boulder rises around eight feet in height, and it is difficult to climb onto. The top of the boulder is fairly flat, and on it is an area of heather and blaeberry. The stone is 78 feet around the waist and it is reckoned that it weighs around 300 tons.

3.5 Tarfessock and Shalloch on Minnoch from Kirriereoch Hill

Across the Nick of the Dungeon rises the granite mountain known as Craignaw. The name is one that has been difficult to explain satisfactorily. Even that doyen of Galloway place names, Sir Herbert Maxwell, couldn't make up his mind and decided that it could quite easily be explained as one or two things. One of these was from the Gaelic *Creag an Atha*, 'craig of the ford', the other from *Creag na Atha*, which means 'craig of the kiln'. Neither is particularly descriptive of what is seen today. Pont, on his map of 1654, shows the hill as 'Kraigna hill'.

The mountain is one of Galloway's pure granite eminences, the rocks bursting through the heather and heath to form considerable cliffs and slabs around its sides. The eastern flank is the steepest, for here the long wall of rock extends from the Nick of the Dungeon corrie southwards for a mile and a half to the Point of the Snibe at the southern end of the Snibe Hill, itself just a lower shoulder of Craignaw. The top is 2,115 feet (645m) above sea level. The summit of Craignaw has extensive stretches of granite slabs across many acres of the hilltop. The striae and grooves in these run on a roughly north-south direction, indicating the direction of ice flow when the Galloway Highlands was still covered by glaciers and ice-caps. The western side of the hill is also rocky, but not just so steep, the Black Gairy overhanging Loch Neldricken.

Many of Craignaw's rock faces have been ascended by rock-climbers, the smooth granite slabs proving to be extremely difficult to climb. The Memorial Craig rises above the monument to the F111 air crash, overlooking Loch Neldricken. The large granite cliff has numerous difficult routes up the many cracks and arêtes on it. On the east side of the hill are a number of slabs – steep flat rocks which allow some simpler climbing.

Some of the best climbs are located on the Point of the Snibe, at the southern end of Snibe Hill, where climbs such as 'Beltie' have been made, graded E3 in the climber's scale. This route ascends a sheer granite slab, with only a couple of cracks to allow the climber to gain a hand and foot hold.

Ice-climbers too also enjoy the ascent of the east face of Craignaw, where the Dow Spout, Shot Cleugh and other gullies provide good ice in cold winters.

The Dow Spout is a considerable waterfall after heavy rain, tumbling over rough cliffs down to the Silver Flow bog below. In summer, if the rainfall has been lower, it provides a steep scramble to the top of Craignaw, the route often requiring the climber to get wet in the spray from the falls. The Dow Spout, or *Dubh Sput* in Gaelic, rises from the Dhu Loch, itself a derivation of the Gaelic *Dubh Loch*, meaning 'black loch'.

The eastern range of mountains is known variously as the Kells range, Rhinns of Kells, or Rhinns of Carsphairn. Only the southern half is properly described as the Rhinns of Kells, for the summits from Carlin's Cairn northward are not within Kells parish, being instead in the parish of Carsphairn. On driving or cycling up the minor road from Glen Muck towards Loch Doon, one turns the corner and there in front of you is a grand vista across Loch Doon and the northern end of this range. The view from the foot of Loch Doon looks up the length of the loch towards two prominent summits, the Paps of Loch Doon, to some extent. These summits are Black Craig, which is 1,730 feet (533m) high, and Coran of Portmark, which is 2,042 feet (623m) tall. Coran has a cairn nine feet in diameter by three feet in height marking the summit.

The name is something of a mystery, and both parts of its name have been varied over the years. On some maps it is shown as Coran of Polmark, and on others, Corran of Portmark. This is the case on two-and-a-half inch Ordnance Survey maps, as well as Thomson's *Atlas* of 1832. Polmark or Portmark is the name of the former farm that lies at the foot of the hill on the eastern shores of Loch Doon, and which now lies in ruins, its land afforested. Coran may derive from the Gaelic *Coran*, which derives from *cor*, a round hill. On Kitchin's 1749 map, Portmark is shown as 'Partmarl'.

Coran of Portmark is the most northerly of the Galloway Highlands, and walkers tend to climb it from the east, there being more open access to it from the old lead mines above Garryhorn farm, near Carsphairn. Its summit is fairly rocky, the thin soil having been blown away. On the uppermost point is a smallish cairn, but on clear days the view is extensive. Access to the mountain from the west is more difficult, the east side of Loch Doon being quite inaccessible, and much of the slopes are clothed in blanket forest, making the walk to the summit more dreary.

The next summit to the south that gains the 2,000 feet contour is known as Bow, or the Bow. This long summit actually has three tops on it, difficult to discern in mist, so that many climbers will have arrived at what they assumed was the summit, but which was in fact one of the other tops. More detailed maps indicate that the northernmost of the three summits is the highest, but only just. This is 2,011 feet (613m) in height and is topped with a stone cairn, measuring around six feet in diameter by three feet in height. The middle lump is the lowest, and cairnless, and the southern lump is 2,008 feet (612m) high, with a small cairn. A boundary fence passes over the three lumps, dividing the forestry land to the west with the sheep hill ground of Garryhorn farm to the east.

The name Bow is thought to derive from the Gaelic *Bo*, which means cow. This is probably quite a descriptive name, the long ridgeback of the summit being not unlike the back of a cow when viewed from the side. A fairly rounded hill, only on the north-east slopes does there appear anything of interest, for there a small corrie with rocks and boulders has been carved by ancient ice-flows. On a boulder in this corrie one can find a small plaque commemorating an aeroplane crash that took place in 1975, the details of which will be related in a later chapter.

South of Bow the mountain of Meaul rises to a greater height than its northern neighbours. Meaul is a tall rounded summit, the shape of which is typical of the summits described in Gaelic as *Meall*, which signifies a rounded hill, mass, or lump. The Gaelic, as well as the local pronunciation, is 'miawl', and some call it Miall. Maxwell also claims that it derives from *maol*, meaning bald. In most cases this name is joined with other words to describe the rounded hill, such as Mullwharchar and numerous other examples across Galloway and in the Highlands, but Meaul seems to be a rounded hill *par excellence*, and simply bears the single description. Quite a high summit, the Ordnance Survey triangulation station is 2,280 feet above sea level, or 695m.

On the north-eastern slopes of Meaul, just to the north of the old dike and fence that makes its way to Cairnsgarroch, can be found the King's Stone and King's Well.

These have traditions associating them with Robert the Bruce.

A stone on the northern slopes of the hill, not far from the fence that links the summit with Bow, marks the spot where John Dempster, the Covenanter, was shot and killed by Grierson of Lag's dragoons. More about these antiquities can be read in subsequent chapters.

3.6 Dungeon Stone

The western slopes of Meaul are in general grassy but here and there, especially lower down, break out into rocks and scree slopes. In the col between Meaul and Carlin's Cairn are a couple of small lochans. These are only a few feet deep, and have neither an inlet nor outlet. On occasion, the walker will find the lochans completely dry, their bed empty of water. Apart from drier weather, the lochans can also be emptied by strong winds, which blow the water from the pools across the hillside.

Cairnsgarroch stands apart from the main Rhinns range of mountains. It is joined to the eastern side of Meaul. The name probably derives from the Gaelic *Carn Sceirach*, which means rocky cairn. Thomson's *Atlas* names it as Cairns Corroch. The summit, which is quite prominent in the district, is 2,155 feet (659m) above the level of the sea, topped by a cairn around three feet in diameter by two feet tall. The summit has a few rocky outcrops around it, and the northern slopes have a number of cliffs and scree runs, known as Roys. On the southern slopes is a lower shoulder known as Craigchessie, where again the rocks break through the grassy slopes. All of the southern slopes are afforested.

The Carlin's Cairn is one of the finest mountains in Galloway, located south of Meaul. It is one of the high summits on the northern continuation of the Rhinns of Kells, although it is the first of the tops to be in Carsphairn parish. A long and narrow hill, the highest point is crowned with a massive prehistoric cairn, one that has a traditional tale associating it with the time of Robert the Bruce, when he was still fighting for the country's freedom. More of this tale will be related in the chapter on the Wars of Independence.

The cairn itself is massive, and measures around fifty feet in diameter by ten feet in height. Whether or not it had its origins as a prehistoric burial cairn is not known, but recent maps no longer indicate it with Gothic writing, indicative that modern thought is that the cairn is not prehistoric. MacBain reckoned that the cairn contained over one hundred tons of stone within it.

The summit of Carlin's Cairn is 2,647 feet (807m) above sea level, the col to the south dropping to 2,323 feet before rising again to the higher summit of Corserine to the south. To the north the hill drops to 2,037 feet, near to the Goat Craigs, before rising again to Meaul.

Although the summit ridge of Carlin's Cairn is fairly flat and rounded, the sides of the hill have extensive areas of rock and stones along them. To the west are the scree slopes of Lochhead Gairy, dropping quickly to the forests beyond the head of Loch Doon. To the east are the rockier slopes of Castlemaddy Gairy, as well as the small corrie known as Dirclauch Howe.

Pont's map of the mid seventeenth century indicates the hill as 'Karling Kairn'.

Corserine is the second highest mountain in the Galloway Highlands, rising south of Carlin's Cairn. The three tallest mountains in the three Galloway ranges – Merrick, Mullwharchar and Corserine – are almost in a straight line with each other, as though the highest points should be arranged thus. Corserine rises to 2,668 feet (814m), the highest summit in the ridge of mountains known as the Rhinns of Kells. From the south the hill is a massive grassy lump, but to the north and east it is more mountainous in appearance. To the north the hill adjoins Carlin's Cairn, to the east of this ridge being a large corrie surrounded by the rocky slopes of the Polmaddy Gairy. To the west is a lesser corrie with scree slopes known as Fallincherrie Scar.

Corserine extends three fingers east and west of the summit. To the west is the ridge known as Meikle Craigtarson, the name meaning the 'large oblique rock', from the Gaelic *Creag Tharsuinn Mor*. Meikle Craigtarson itself is just over 2,000 feet in height, though it doesn't have a large enough re-ascent from Corserine in order for it to be listed as a separate summit.

To the east a high ridge extends to the head of a corrie, the sides of which have rocky screes, known as the Scar of the Folk. To either side of this corrie are high ridges, Craigrine and Craignelder to the north – Craignelder Gairy being a considerable rocky termination to this ridge. To the south of the Scar of the Folk is the ridge known as North Gairy Top, dropping steeply to the forests around Loch Harrow and Loch Minnoch.

The name Corserine is thought to mean the 'crossing of the range or ridge'. On Pont's map of 1654 it is shown as 'Krosraing hil'. The highest point has an Ordnance Survey triangulation station and a smallish cairn adjoining it.

To the south of Corserine is Millfire, a hill that rises to 2,350 feet (716m) in height. Although this is a considerable height in itself, the hill only has a re-ascent of 75 feet from the taller Milldown to the south. Millfire is said to come from the Gaelic *Meall Fuar*, which means cold hill. The eastern slopes of the hill have a number of rocky outcrops on the steep descent to the Hawse Burn, which runs along its foot into Loch Dungeon. To the west the more gentle slopes of the hills are afforested almost to the summit. The top is marked by a cairn five feet in diameter by three feet tall.

The name, Milldown, is a derivation of the Gaelic *Meall Donn*, which means brown hill. Thomson's *Atlas* shows it as Mill Doon on the map. The summit rises to 2,421 feet (738m). The eastern side of the hill is very steep and rocky, plunging headlong for 1,400 feet or so into the deep western pool of Loch Dungeon. Whereas many of the rock outcrops on other Galloway hills have names, these cliffs and slabs don't seem to have merited one. The western side of the hill is in complete contrast to the east, for here there is hardly a boulder or outcrop to be found, and the grassy slopes have been planted with conifer trees, which reach to within a hundred feet or so of the summit, although many of the trees are stunted due to the thin soil and altitude.

3.7 Carlin's Cairn from Corserine

The mountain of Meikle Millyea rises to a height of 2,454 feet (748m), although the Ordnance Survey triangulation station erected on it was not positioned on the highest spot, being located slightly to the north east, in order to gain the extensive views over the Glenkens and beyond. The highest point is 1,600 yards to the south west of the trig point, though the summit of the hill is fairly flat.

The name derives from the Gaelic *Meall Liath*, which means grey hill, meikle being the Scots word for big. To the south west of Meikle Millyea is Little Millyea, a lesser hill that rises to 1,898 feet.

Between Meikle Millyea and Milldown the ridge drops to around 2,129 feet, where the Lochans of Auchniebut can be found. These are eight small pools of water located in the saddle, only one of which is really large enough to be considered a lochan.

A ridge drops from the summit of Meikle Millyea to the north-east, known as Meikle Lump, before turning to the south east and dropping further where it is known as the Rig of Clenrie. On the Meikle Lump is a Rocking Stone, though old maps indicate that it has been 'displaced' for decades. Much of the northern and south-eastern slopes of Meikle Millyea are rocky, only the western slopes, known as Straverron Hill, being free from rocks near to the summit.

The mountain of Millfore is a fairly solitary summit in Galloway, standing quite unconnected to other hills in the district. The summit is 2,152 feet (656m) above sea level, marked by an Ordnance Survey triangulation station. As with Millfire in the Rhinns of Kells, Millfore is reckoned to mean the 'cold hill', from the Gaelic *Meall Fuar*.

There are a number of lesser shoulders and adjoining hills to Millfore. To the north-east the summit drops to the Nick of Rushes, before the land climbs once more to Cairngarroch, which is 1,829 feet (557m) tall. On the ridge heading towards Cairngarroch, on the south-eastern side, is a very steep slope and almost vertical cliff, known as the Buckdas of Cairnbaber, Cairnbaber being the name of the ridge. These cliffs are particularly high for Galloway, plummeting hundreds of feet in sheer slopes. The rocks forming the cliff are mildly calcareous and due to their inaccessibility provide a safe haven to numerous upland plants. As a result the cliff was designated a Site of Special Scientific Interest in 1987 for its upland habitat. Extending to 89 acres, the cliff's thin ledges and crevices are home to wood bitter-vetch, maidenhair spleenwort, and a variety of upland ferns, including oak fern and brittle bladder-fern. In some of the damp gullies common butterwort is joined by the rare alpine cinquefoil, *Potentilla crantzii*.

To the south-west of the summit of Millfore is the lower shoulder of Drigmorn Hill, which doesn't really have a separate summit of its own. A small lochan, known as Fuffock, can be found there.

The shoulder to the west of Millfore's summit is known as Meldens, the gap between it and Millfore itself, where the Black Laggan Burn flows, is known as Habbie's Howe.

On the shoulder of Meldens can be found a number of lochans, two of which merit being named on the Ordnance Survey map – Black Loch and White Lochan of Drigmorn. Although the latter is named as 'lochan', implying that it is a small loch, it is actually the largest of the lochans hereabouts. The lochan is quite well known for having been a place where curling was played regularly during the winter months, its elevation (around 1,834 feet above sea level) meaning that the water was often frozen. By the side of the lochan can be seen the remains of a foursquare building, the stone walls long-since crumbling back into the ground. It was built with rough-dressed stones, gathered from the hillside, and roofed with slate. This was the hut used by the curlers to store their stones and brooms when not being used and it is said that it was originally built by military officers stationed in Newton Stewart at the time of the Crimean War. The building was also used for shelter after the games, and a wee dram was passed around the curlers in order to heat up what must have been cold bodies. Curling stones weighed on average forty pounds, so carrying them up and down the hillside was rather troublesome and the players of the 'roaring game' preferred to leave them here.

Curleywee is often regarded by hill walkers as the finest peak in Galloway, for its steep conical shape makes it stand out from the rest, and the rugged and rocky slopes adds to the feeling of it being a true mountain. Indeed, MacBain says that it 'must be regarded as the Matterhorn of the uplands'. Curleywee is by no means the highest of the Galloway hills, for its summit is just 2,212 feet (674m) above sea level, but this is still a respectable height, and the mountain's remoteness and ruggedness means that it needs to be treated with respect.

The name is thought to derive from *Cor na Ghaoith*, Gaelic for 'windy peak', though this is by no means certain.

A couple of lower shoulders to Curleywee are found to the north and south of the main summit. To the north is the White Hill, there being little re-ascent from the main peak, though the height of the hill from the lower slopes of Loch Dee make it a considerable eminence. To the south is Bennan Hill, this ridge continuing to drop over White Benwee Hill and Stronbae Hill. The east side of Curleywee drops to a high shoulder known as Gaharn, the south-eastern slopes of which are rugged and scree-strewn, known as the Scars of Gaharn.

The west side of Curleywee drops steeply to the Nick of Curleywee, a high pass at over 1,800 feet, before ascending over the little peak of Milldown and up to Bennanbrack (2,247 feet), a shoulder of the main summit of Lamachan Hill. Between Curleywee and Bennanbrack is a high corrie, almost a hanging valley, the base of which looks as though there may have been a corrie lochan in it at one time, for there is a stretch of marshy ground, and a tiny lochan still existing. The head of the corrie has some rock outcrops and scree slopes known as the Scars of Bennanbrack.

Lamachan Hill is the highest summit in what is known as the Minnigaff Hills, four mountains of over 2,000 feet in that parish. The summit, which is actually quite a flat plateau, is 2,352 feet (717m) in height. To the south side of the summit the hill tumbles away quickly, into a wide corrie known as Nick of the Brush. The Scars of Lamachan are the steep rocky outcrops that mark its head.

To the north west of Lamachan the whaleback of the hill drops to Cambrick Hill, and then drops further to the Nick of the Lochans, where two fair-sized pools of water can be found. The land rises once more to the summit of Mulldonoch, the hill to the south of Loch Trool, which is 1,827 feet in height.

The name Lamachan is something of a mystery, no real explanation of its meaning having been made. Some maps name it as Lammachan Hill, with a double 'm', and Lamachan farm, sometimes named 'Lamachan House' is located in the valley of the Penkiln Burn to the south. Another version of the name, used in *Maxwell's Guide to the Stewartry of Kirkcudbright* is 'Lommachan'.

The summit of Lamachan was sometimes referred to as Cooper's Cairn, or Cupar Cairn, in older accounts, but today this name has almost been forgotten, However, more detailed maps indicate that some of the rock faces above the Nick of the Brush are known as Cooper's Scar. The Cooper after whom the summit was named was said to be one Couper, Bishop of Galloway, who, along with Archbishop Maxwell, was one of the main compilers of the new prayer book that was submitted to King James in 1619. This prayer book was never brought into use.

It is claimed that Ben Lomond can be seen from the top of Lamachan Hill. The mountain comprises of shales, but here and there along the summit plateau can be found granite blocks, some split in two, no doubt pushed here by the ice from Mullwharchar and the central granite boss.

3.8 Curleywee from Bennanbrack

To the south west of Lamachan Hill rises Larg Hill, which attains a height of 2,216 feet (676m). It is separated from Lamachan by a high pass known as the Nick of the Brushy. The name Larg is reckoned to be a derivation of the Gaelic *Learg*, which is a descriptive term used to describe a hillside. Older maps, such as Ainslie's map of 1821 and that in the *New Statistical Account* (1845), depict the hill as Larg Fell. Larg comprises of a ridge running in a north-east to south-westerly direction, each side having steep rock scars and screes dropping into high corries. That on the west is known as the Larg Scar, at the foot of it the Strife Land. To the east side is the Lamachan Scar and Cordorcan Craigs.

In addition to the 22 mountains over two thousand feet in the central Galloway Highlands, there are many other hills of lesser heights, some of which, such as Craiglee of Doon and Craiglee of Dee, Darnaw and Hoodens Hill being significant eminences in their own right, worth ascending for their character and views.

4 Lochs

There are dozens of lochs in the Galloway Highlands, each of a different form and appearance. The largest of these lochs is Loch Doon, located at the northern end of the mountainous country, and forming part of the boundary between Ayrshire and the Stewartry of Kirkcudbright. The loch today is dammed in two places – at the northern, natural outlet, from where the River Doon emanates, and to the east, at the Muck Burn Dam, preventing the waters from spilling over the low pass into the Glenkens. Although the latter dam prevents the waters from passing that way, the controlled waters in fact are tunnelled beneath Cullendoch Hill to the Drumjohn Power Station.

Loch Doon is currently 5½ miles in length, and in width varies from ½ to 1 mile. The deepest section of the loch is that part that lies between Black Craig and the Wee Hill of Craigmulloch, calculated to be 96 feet in depth. The measurement was made some time ago by Sir John Murray, a notable geographer, who plumbed the depths of many lochs across Scotland for the first time. He appears to have been financially backed by a gentleman who had an interest in the depths of Scottish lochs. This measurement varies somewhat, for the level of the loch can rise and fall, depending on how much water is released in order to supply the Galloway Hydro Power stations, and how dry or wet the summer can be. When full, Loch Doon covers 2,250 acres.

The name, Loch Doon, is thought to derive from the Gaelic, *Loch Duin*, which some say comes from the word *dun*, which can either mean fort or hill-fort. The name, however, may refer to the castle in the loch, but the loch was probably named Doon long before the castle was erected. Other derivations included 'loch of the mountain ridges,' or 'loch of the nation'. The latter two were suggested by John Kevan MacDowall, a keen Scottish place-name etymologist.

In the late 1780s some tunnels were formed at the foot of the loch, allowing water to be drained from Loch Doon into the River Doon. The purpose of these tunnels was to try to control the water level in the loch, and to ensure that the River Doon was less likely to flood, destroying the meadow lands north of Dalmellington. The creation of the tunnels was also expected to lower the level of the loch, and thus reveal some good quality farmland around the shores, but this proved not to be the case. Indeed, all that was revealed was 'barren sand, gravel, and stone.' A short account of the construction of the tunnels is given in the *Statistical Account* of the parish of Straiton, written in 1791. There, William Crawford writes:

The rains used formerly to raise the loch in such a manner, that the river, receiving an accumulated water from this reservoir, frequently overflows its banks, and destroyed the meadows. The rock, over which the loch discharged itself, has lately been cut in two places at considerable expence, by the Earl of Cassillis, and Mr MacAdam of Craigengillan, the proprietors on each side; so that, by means of sluices, not only the damage is prevented, but some land is gained, by a diminution of the extent of the loch.

Prior to the cut being made, there was a 'beautiful natural cascade' of water over the rock ledge and down into the Ness Glen, which may have gained its name from the falls, *Gleann an Eas* being Gaelic for 'glen of the waterfall'. On Ainslie's map of 1821, the mouth of Loch Doon has the term 'New Cut' written there, indicating the drainage channel.

Some of the shores of the loch are comprised of clay, or, as the same writer of the *Account* noted:

On the margin of Loch Doon, there are beds of a very singular soft bluish clay substance, which, when taken up, and exposed to the sun and atmosphere, becomes as white as any fuller's earth, and acquires the consistency of chalk. It has been examined chemically by the celebrated Dr Hutton, who can give the fullest and best account of it.

In other words, William Crawford could not tell what the clayish substance could be of any use for!

In 1885-6 a new sluice was constructed across the mouth of the loch which raised the water by eighteen or twenty feet – at flood-times the loch level flowed over the top of the dam, whereas at drought times, the loch level lowered, and any outflow was by means of the tunnel through the rock, regulated by sluices.

Loch Doon had its very own Eilean Donan at one time, though the defensive building on it was far less impressive than the castle of the same name in Lochalsh. Loch Doon's Eilean Donan was a smallish island half way along the west side of the loch, just south of Lambdoughty farm, on which were buildings of considerable antiquity. In recent years the island has been called Donald's Isle, but on Timothy Pont's map of 1654 it is shown as 'Ylen Donen', a literal pronunciation of the original Gaelic.

Who Donald or Donan was is no longer known, and there is no real traditional tale to give us a reason for either name. The Ordnance Survey Name Book of 1858 relates a claim that Donald was an ascetic local who died here – a drunkard, he may have lived on the island. It continues – 'Tradition has it that Donald's bones lie bleaching in the water that encircled him in life. Donald's notorious weakness for a less gentle liquid is still deplored in the neighbourhood.'

Older accounts, such as John Smith's *Prehistoric Man in Ayrshire*, state that the remains on the island were known as monks' graves. Smith, however, stated that 'although called graves they may have been Monks' cells; some of the Monks having probably been buried in or near them. When they were opened, several relics of antiquity were obtained, including a bit of red and yellow bead, a polished stone, fragments of pottery, bits of iron, etc.' The connection with monks may give the island a link with St Donan, an ancient saint, a name that was gradually changed to Donald. There are a few places associated with St Donan in Ayrshire, such as Chapel Donan, which lies to the north of Girvan. Perhaps this island was his secret cell, a place of solitude where he or his followers could study the scriptures in peace.

The island, which today is only visible when the level of the loch is low, comprises of a boulder strewn moraine. Prior to the level of the loch being raised, it was 190 yards from north to south and 95 east to west. Almost immediately west of the main structure's entrance the foundations of an old jetty were discovered, a line of boulders stretching into what was the loch, prior to the water level being lowered in 1823.

In 1933-6 the remains on the island were excavated once more by Archibald Fairbairn and a small group of archaeologists. The main building, which measured 52 feet by 20 feet, was excavated firstly. It seemed to have an entrance on the west wall, and within inches of the surface mediaeval pottery sherds were found. Lower down pieces of flint were discovered and ash found on the floor. To the south of the main building a secondary structure was excavated, and within the soil a silver penny of Edward I, minted in London in 1260, was found. It was reckoned that this building had been in ruins for many years before the coin was lost. It was surmised that this building was a prehistoric hut. On the flat clay floor a fireplace was discovered. The walls around this hut were from eight to twelve feet thick, and when excavated were found to still be around four feet in height. Internally, the hut had a floor-space of around eight feet by fifteen feet.

Further excavations took place to the north of the main building, where low circular walls in keeping with a hut were found – indeed the central socket for the upright pole was discovered. On the floor the archaeologists discovered various flat-headed iron nails, as well as some other iron objects, including a blade, arrow-head, piece of iron pot and other relics. A fragment of a glass armlet was discovered on the island, and this was subsequently dated to the 1st-2nd century AD.

Between the years 1916 and 1918 one of the British government's biggest waste of money occurred at Loch Doon. So much so that it became known as the Loch Doon Scandal. The gist of the story was that some mandarins in Whitehall thought that Loch Doon would make an ideal location for a school of aerial gunnery. However, the locals advised them otherwise, but it took the authorities two years and over £3 million to accept that they were wrong, and the project was abandoned. Fragmentary remains of the major scheme can still be found today, a memorial to what a government committee later reported as 'one of the most striking instance of wasted expenditure.'

Colonel W. Sefton Brancker was the man credited with the idea of establishing the school of aerial gunnery, having studied an example at Cazaux in France. Following surveys throughout Britain, Loch Doon was selected in early 1916. Over 16,500 acres of land was requisitioned for War Office use, 8,320 owned by the Marquis of Ailsa, 4,483 acres owned by Mrs Charlotte MacAdam (88 of which were at Bogton), 2,784 acres of which were owned by Major F. A. Cathcart and 1,000 acres owned by W. C. MacMillan. By August that year the War Department authorised the spending of £150,000 on the scheme. By September the Department of Fortifications and Works visited the loch, along with representatives from R. MacAlpine & Sons, who were to carry out the work. Reservations were soon being made regarding the proposals to drain the moss near to the foot of the Garpel Burn, as well as the conditions for flying in the vicinity. Brancker, however, dismissed these, and MacAlpine's commenced work before the end of September. To house their workers, camps were created on the northern side of the Garpel Burn, capable of accommodating the 1,500 contractors on site.

Camlarg House, to the east of Dalmellington, was requisitioned to be the headquarters for the school.

4.1 The road to Loch Doon from Glen Muck

The first aeroplane was sent to the loch on 19 January 1917. The plane, a Short 827 8560, was brought to Dalmellington by rail and transferred onto a lorry for the final stretch to the loch. Many more train loads of equipment arrived at Dalmellington and were sent up to the loch, up to 150 tons of equipment per day. Work had commenced on draining the moss, where an airfield was proposed. By February 1917 over fifty miles of drainage pipe had been laid, the peat was covered with many tons of soil, and the whole area seeded. However by March it was decided that the moss could never be drained and the airfield here was abandoned. Instead, new plans were drawn up to have the airfield located at Bogton, west of Dalmellington, the nearest suitable location to the loch. On 4 March a branch railway was commenced to the site, the first aeroplane travelling across it on 16 March. A light railway was also built from Dalmellington through Craigengillan policies to Dalfarson, saving the need to transfer the cargo to lorries. It was opened on 20 April 1917.

At Loch Doon work went on at great speed. A double hangar was constructed near the foot of the Garpel Burn, and barrack-houses were constructed at Macnabstone for eighty flying officers. Here also were stables. Across the foot of the loch a new dam was constructed, raising the water level by six feet, which allowed a hydro-electric station to be formed, supplying power both to work the bogies on which the targets were mounted and light for the camps. A second camp was established near to Lambdoughty to which German prisoners of war were brought on 17 March 1917.

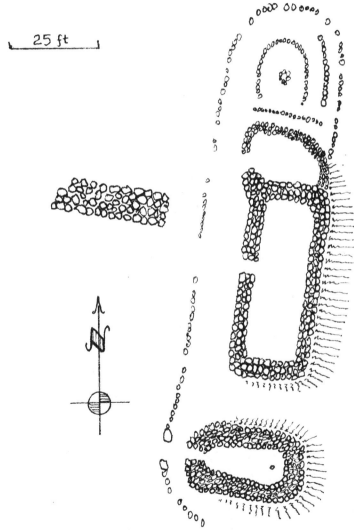

25 ft

4.2 Donald's Isle, Loch Doon – plan after that in the
Proceedings of the Society of Antiquaries of Scotland, vol. 71, (1936-37)

They were used in the construction of access roads and other civil engineering works. At one time there were over 1,200 here. Also in 1917 Craigengillan House was requisitioned as an officers' residence, Mrs Charlotte MacAdam being unsuccessful in her objection. Her niece, Lavinette MacAdam who lived at Craigengillan, as her companion, was so upset by the quartering of troops in the house that she committed suicide. Other accounts, however, claim that she became pregnant by an officer from the sea-plane base and she killed herself at Craigengillan's gasworks. At Bogton two hangars were erected, these being steel-frame structures with canvas roofs. There were also stores, workshops, and eighteen barrack blocks which were home to 500 men.

At the foot of Loch Doon, near to the new dam, a wharf was constructed, to allow boats to be tied up. A further motorboat dock was created to the south of Beoch farm.

The school and aerodrome had been under the command of Lt.-Col. Louis Arbon Strange (1891-1966), but he moved on to the Central Flying School at Uphaven. He was replaced by Lt.-Col. Evelyn Boscawen Gordon DSO (1877-1963). Work continued, the monorail constructed along the shore of the loch and alongside Muckle Eriff Hill was completed. On Cullendoch and Craigencolon hills the mobile targets were erected. The idea was that targets representing German aeroplanes would be released on bogeys that ran down a zigzag railway from the top of the hill. Approaching aeroplanes could fly up the loch and the impression given to the gunners on board was that a German aeroplane was approaching, allowing them the chance to fire at moving targets. On the opposite side of the loch, at Beoch, a cinema capable of seating 400 and a sewage treatment works were finished. By the end of May 1917 over £350,000 had been spent on the works.

A request for additional funding to allow an extension of the railway from Dalfarson to the northern end of the loch, passing through a proposed 1,150 feet long tunnel, brought about a change in direction. The Director of Fortifications and Works noticed the request, and the Duke of Connaught visited the scheme on 1 October 1917. A survey was ordered, to be carried out by the Institute of Civil Engineers, and their report was not favourable. It was presented to the Air Ministry in January 1918. Almost immediately the Under Secretary of State, Major J. L. Baird, and the Administrator of Works and Buildings, Sir John Hunter, were sent to the loch to look at the whole scheme. When they returned with their report the government ordered an immediate stop to the project. A Select Committee was formed to investigate, and stated that the project should have been abandoned earlier when it was realised that the targets could only move at around 25-60 mph down the hillside - too slow to represent enemy aircraft. The report stated that had the scheme been abandoned then, 'a great part of the waste of money which has occurred would have been obviated. We consider that the failure to do this was even less excusable than the original error in the selection of the site.' In conclusion the report stated that:

> Loch Doon and the country around it will soon return to the solitude and silence from which it was aroused by the introduction of thousands of men over a period of 15 months, at a cost of thousands of pounds of public money

on an enterprise which was misconceived from the beginning, and which, even if once begun ought never to have been continued. Its name will be remembered as the scene of one of the most striking instances of wasted expenditure our records can show.

How much the whole scheme had cost was never fully revealed. When Lord Curzon, Chairman of the Air Board, raised the question in the House of Lords he was told £600,000. Not fully believing it, he made local inquiries which revealed that during the time the work was underway over three million pounds had been paid through the Dalmellington bank. As laid down in the original agreement, after the war all the main structures were demolished, leaving only concrete foundations here and there.

Along the west side of the loch runs a public road, as far as Craigmalloch. At Craigmalloch was a public school where local children were educated. In January 1912 a great storm in the district caused considerable damage, and at the time the wall round the school and schoolmaster's house was washed away. The school was closed in February 1931, by which time the roll had fallen to one pupil. The building was later used as an outdoor centre but it is now closed and the building converted into a house.

When the level of the loch was raised in the 1930s, the Pickmaw Island was submerged, destroying what had been a breeding colony of seagulls for many years. The island was located at the southern end of the loch, near to Starr, and its name comes from 'Pickmaw' or 'Pickmire', the local name for the nesting black-headed seagulls. These often resorted away from the coast to upland lochs for breeding. Pickmaw Island was one of the larger in the district, and MacBain wrote that he landed on the island during the breeding season, only to discover that it was difficult to walk about as the nests were so close together. When the loch level was raised the birds had to find a new place for nesting. The island still appears when the level of the water in the reservoir is at its lowest, revealing a rocky granite islet, surrounded by granite sands and clays.

In addition to the Pickmaw Isle, as it was named on the Ordnance Survey 1858 Six Inch map, there was a Wee Pickmaw Isle immediately to the north of it, and slightly further to the north again was the Ducker's Stone, a large granite rock that broke the surface of the water.

Fishing on Loch Doon is free, the proprietors of the loch long ago having gifted it to the public. The loch has brown trout in it, as well as Arctic char, perch and pike. The char is a fish that can be traced back to prehistoric times, and though it is rare to catch one in Loch Doon, some do live in the waters. The dam allows salmon to reach the loch, but these fish are rare to catch in the deep and murky waters. The average size of trout caught is eight ounces, although some fish up to fifteen pounds in weight have been landed. Although the fishing is free, boats can be hired locally.

A few pleasure boats can be seen on the loch, but these are not particularly common. Canoeing is sometimes enjoyed, often by youth groups. The waters can become choppy at times due to the wind, resulting in some accidents. On 16 August 2001 William Nugent, aged 20, capsized his canoe in the loch and was unable to be rescued by his companions. He slipped under the surface of the water, around 250 yards from the shore. Next day a group of police divers searched the area and recovered his body.

The lochs of the Doon basin are varied in character and size, and number thirteen in total. If we start at the southernmost point, the first lake is Loch Enoch, one of the Galloway Highlands' most enigmatic lochs. This is the highest of the large Galloway lochs, located immediately east of the Merrick. The derivation of the name is unknown, though some think that it came from the Gaelic *Loch Eidheannach*, meaning 'icy loch', or perhaps from *Loch Eunach*, 'loch of the birds', or *Loch Aonach*, loch of the moor. In any case, the proper pronunciation of the name is 'loch ennoch', though in recent years 'loch eenach' has become more popular. Some say that the name is a variation of 'Loch in Loch', for there is an island in the middle of Loch Enoch on which a smaller loch can be found. Why the greater loch should be named after the little loch is unclear.

On some older maps it is spelled as Loch Ennock, or Loch Ennoch (Armstrong – 1775). When Timothy Pont produced his map in 1590, the name was spelled 'Loch Aingoch'. The surface of the water is reckoned to be 1,617 feet above sea level – when the Ordnance Surveyors were making the first detailed maps of the area they visited the loch on 2 August 1894 and on that day the surface of the water was 1,616.9 feet above datum.

The loch is fed by few streams – only minor burns running off the granite hills into one of the many pools. Not one of these appears to have a name, at least according to the Ordnance Survey. The loch empties into the infant Eglin Lane, a watercourse that grows in size until it reaches Loch Doon. The northern shore of Loch Enoch is in Ayrshire, though the bulk of the shore, and the entire water surface, is in the Stewartry of Kirkcudbright, even although the loch drains into Ayrshire.

The periphery of Loch Enoch is jagged, the water surface broken into a variety of basins. That to the south-east is almost totally shut off by a promontory projecting from the southern shore. It has been claimed that even although the circumference of the loch is around three miles, no part of the water surface is more than 150 yards from the shore.

That the loch is the highest in the Galloway Highlands is clear, but there have been claims that it is the highest in Scotland – indeed, a recent book about the Glenkens goes as far as to state that it 'is the highest body of water in Britain'. MacBain states that the next highest is Loch Muick in Aberdeenshire, which is 1,310 feet above sea level. This is, of course, nonsense, for there are dozens of lochs in the highlands that have surface levels that are considerably higher. If we look at the Cairngorm mountains we find the similarly-named Loch Einich, which has a surface level almost the same as Loch Enoch. Further east there is Loch Avon, the surface of which is around 2,340 feet above sea level. Higher up is Loch Etchachan, which is around 3,000 feet above sea level. These lochs are getting smaller, and below Braeriach is Loch Coire an Lochain, which is 3,230 feet above sea level, and between Ben Macdhui and Carn an Lochain is Lochan a' Buidhe, over 3,600 feet above sea level. The latter, however, is a tiny lochan, comparable to Galloway's Loch Twachtan. Indeed, if we count small lochs, in the

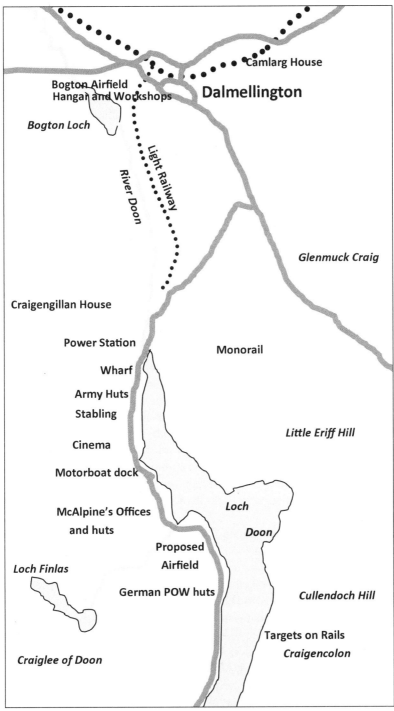

4.3 Sketch Map of Loch Doon showing Aerial Gunnery scheme

Galloway Highlands the Balminnoch Loch below Kirriereoch Hill itself is higher than Loch Enoch.

If Loch Enoch is not the highest in Galloway, it is certainly the deepest. The south-western basin is around 120 feet deep. The first person to measure the depth was James MacBain, and he tells the story in a chapter of his *Merrick and Neighbouring Hills*. MacBain had planned to measure the depth for some time, and awaited a day when the surface of the loch was thick with ice, thick enough to allow him to walk across it. When the temperature was suitably low he tramped seven miles in thick mist from Loch Doon to the shores of the loch, only to find that parts of the surface still had open water on it.

It was on MacBain's third attempt that he was finally successful in his task. In a period of prolonged cold, in March 1918, he made his way from Loch Doon back to the loch. He followed the Eglin Lane, many of the pools thick with ice, a hint at what was to come. At the loch he found much of the surface was frozen over, though there were still some open pools to be seen. The south-west basin was mostly frozen, however, allowing the expedition to proceed.

Checking the thickness of the ice, MacBain chiselled a hole through it to the water, and discovered that it was four inches thick – safe enough to walk on. As he made his way across the ice, which had strands of wisping snow blowing across it, MacBain thought with exhilaration of the 'abysmal deeps' below him, and of his safety in such a place by himself.

At the spot where he proposed plumbing the loch, he began chiselling a hole through the ice. As he did, a loud snap resounded, but this was a deep sound, indicating that the ice was thick, even although a crack appeared in it. MacBain repeated the cutting of the ice and dropping a weight to the bottom of the loch six times, across the basin. He obtained readings of 63 feet, 85 feet, 96 feet, 127 feet, 105 feet and 57 feet.

In the south-eastern basin, MacBain was able to plumb the loch again, finding depths of 50 feet, 56 feet, and 64 feet, the last-depth recorded at the centre of the lagoon. The freezing wind and cold night drawing closer, MacBain then made his way east through the Nick of the Dungeon to Backhill of Bush, where he was able to get lodgings with the shepherd.

An early account of Loch Enoch is given by Rev Thomas Grierson, writing in *Autumnal Rambles*, published in 1850. He visited in the autumn of 1846. He writes:

> Loch Enoch is in some respects one of the most remarkable anywhere to be seen. It contains several islands, in one of which is a small lake, said to be well stocked with trout; and it is so indented by headlands, that keeping close to its margin would perhaps double its circumference, which may be estimated at about three miles. A more desolate, dreary, unapproachable scene, can hardly be imagined. All its shores are of granite, bleached by the storms of ages, which, in such a region, probably 1,200 feet at least above the sea, must rage with tremendous fury. It is intersected by dykes of granite, resembling artificial piers; and, as there are no weeds, and deep water from

the very edge, it is particularly favourable to the angler, who may in the course of a few hours fill his basket with trout, scarcely averaging herring size, but some of which cut up red, and are of fine quality. Some of its bays contain abundance of beautiful granite sands, much prized for sharpening scythes.

Another old account of the loch is from 1867, written by William Jolly in the *Transactions of the Edinburgh Geological Society*. There, he writes:

In a setting of silver sand, surrounded by naked heights, overshadowed by The Merrick – all treeless waste, Loch Enoch presents a scene of awful grandeur.

In 1884, according to *Maxwell's Guide to the Stewartry of Kirkcudbright*, Loch Enoch was owned by the Earl of Galloway and that trout were plentiful in the loch, weighing on average from four to five pounds.

Loch Enoch drains from the Sluice of Loch Enoch northwards down the wild and tumbling Eglin Lane, through one of the most remote and wild stretches of the hills. Some old maps indicate the upper reaches of the Eglin Land as being the Sluice (or Sluce) Burn. A few streams feed into the Eglin Lane, the second sizeable one on the left bank being the Saugh Burn, which drains from tiny Loch Twachtan. This is a small circular lochan located at the foot of the steep north-eastern cliffs and gairies of the Merrick. The little loch, which is no more than 50 yards in diameter, lies around 1,520 feet above sea level. The waters of Loch Twachtan are dark and sombre, and apart from one area at the foot of the cliff, its shores are difficult to reach, being marshy around most of its circumference. Loch Twachtan has numerous small fish in it, and MacBain, in the early twentieth century, cast a rod there, landing three trout in one single go, one on each fly. The small trout he found were different to the usual, having heads proportionally larger than was normal. On Pont's map the loch is named 'Twaichtan'.

The next watercourse to feed the Elgin Lane is the Black Garpel, a river that is only around one mile in length, but which is braided into various branches as it makes its way through the rough boulder-strewn and peaty moors. The Black Garpel issues from Loch Macaterick, a rather un-shapely loch. The southernmost part of the loch is the biggest basin, and is also the deepest. The southern end is enfolded in the hollow of Macaterick, a hill of 1,618 feet. The surface level is around 940 feet above sea level. Within the loch are numerous islets, little more than lumps of rock sticking through the water, often covered with a peat cap. Most of these islets are tiny – the detailed Ordnance Survey map shows around thirty islets, but there are three which are large and significant enough to have names – the Eagles Isle, Deer Isle and Blaeberry Isle. The Blaeberry Isle is the largest and measures around 250 yards long at its greatest. The island gets its name from the blaeberry plant that grows on it.

A small loch that drains into Loch Macaterick is Loch Fannie, located at the northern end. An elongated loch, it measures around 300 yards in length by around 75 yards wide. Surrounded by forestry, Loch Fannie has no real inflows, and only a small stream flows a few yards from its southern end into Loch Macaterick.

The Eglin Lane flows down to join the Whitespout Lane, the two streams merging to become the Carrick Lane. The Whitespout Lane drains from Loch Riecawr, though on the way down it passes through little Loch Gower, and tumbles over the Whitespout Linn, a tumultuous waterfall. Loch Gower is little more than an enlarged section of the river, a place where it changes direction. The loch is around 350 yards in length from north to south, and 100 yards wide. Part of this loch is fairly shallow, the reeds growing from the bed breaking the surface of the water, but the other half of the loch, on the northern side, is very deep.

According to the *Ordnance Gazetteer* of 1882, Loch Riecawr is a 'troutful lake', its water surface, at that time, being around 960 feet above sea level. The loch's name has been rendered in various forms over the years, from Recar, through Riccar and Ricawr to the present Riecawr. On Ainslie's 1821 map of southern Scotland, it is named 'Loch Star'. Today surrounded by forestry, the loch has been extended by the construction of a dam across the eastern side, raising the level of the water by nine feet. This was constructed as part of the water supply scheme for Ayr. The maximum depth is therefore only 25 feet, the loch being sixteen feet deep at its greatest prior to the construction of the dam. The new augmented works were launched on 23 June 1933, but the outbreak of war meant that the dam did not get completed until 1953. In 1943 the rainfall at Loch Riecawr was measured as 77.85 inches.

Water from Loch Riecawr is tunnelled below the hills of Waterhead and released into Loch Finlas, on the opposite side of the hills. The water was then piped to the Knockjarder Water Filters, between Dalrymple and Ayr, but these were considerably older than the Loch Riecawr scheme (having been established in 1887) and they couldn't cope with the amount of water available.

In the 1990s the Finlas and Riecawr scheme was incorporated into the Loch Bradan scheme, allowing the water to be treated at the new filters at the bottom of Loch Bradan dam.

The fishing in the loch is owned by the Balloch Fishing Club, which has a boat house and boats on the northern shore. Fishing is purely by fly, and there is a large population of wild brown trout in it. Most catches weigh less than a pound, but the odd fish has been landed that weighs over two pounds. However, it is said that the lack of size is made up for in the quality of the taste – rolled in oatmeal and fried in bacon fat make them a gastronomic delight.

Two lochs train into Loch Riecawr – lochs Slochy and Goosie. Of these, Loch Slochy is the least loch-like, for it has almost totally filled up with reeds and silt, so that from a distance it is not apparent that it is a loch at all. When viewed from the heights of Shalloch on Minnoch to the west, it appears more of a large area of reeds, which the burns that drain Shalloch's eastern slopes have to make their way through. Indeed, on present Ordnance Survey maps of 1:50 000 scale the loch is no longer shown with the water symbol, being indicated as a marsh instead.

Loch Goosie, however, is a proper loch. It lies north of the dam across Loch Riecawr's mouth, and the stream from it drains into the dam. It is quite amusing to note that on Armstrong's *Map of Ayrshire*, published in 1775, the loch is named as Loch Goose, and that in representing the lake he has shown the loch as having a shape that from above could almost be represented as a goose shape. The outline of the loch on his map takes the form of a simple looking bird, with a head and beak, but in rendering the lines indicative of water, Armstrong has shaded them to indicate a wing!

Ballochling Loch is a smallish loch, located on the southern slopes of Waterhead and Craigmulloch Hill. On Armstrong's map of 1775 it is named as Balloch Loch. Today, one half of it is surrounded by forestry, whereas the north-western shore is open to the moorland. The loch is fed by a single burn draining from Craigmulloch Hill and the pass to its west, known as Nick of the Loup. Fishing in the loch is private, owned by the Balloch Fishing Club.

Loch Finlas was a natural loch of around one and a half miles in length, formed of two larger basins at each end, linked by an irregular channel. The south-eastern end, from where the Garpel Burn escapes and flows into Loch Doon, had a maximum depth of 26 feet. The north western end, which was fed by a stream from Derclach Loch and other watercourses, was the deepest at forty feet deep. Between the two main pools, prior to the dam being erected, the loch was little more than a rather wide ditch, the water shallow and still. At the eastern end is an islet known as MacDowall's Isle. Earlier maps name this as 'McDill's Isle' and indicate that the larger islet was covered in trees, being beyond the reach of sheep and cattle. Old maps name the loch as 'Finless'.

In 1887 a dam was constructed across the effluent of the loch at a cost of £150,000. A pipe was laid down towards Loch Doon, and then north towards the town of Ayr, providing a source of water. The waters were cleaned at the Knockjarder filters, where they were also joined by waters from the older source for the town – the Carcluie springs on the Carrick Hills.

In 1916 a new dam was constructed across the foot of the loch, the designs being drawn up by John Eaglesham, civil engineer in Ayr, raising the level of the water once more, this time by a further two feet, and increasing the storage capacity. In 1953 a tunnel was constructed beneath the hills, feeding water from Loch Riecawr. James MacBain wrote that water lilies used to thrive on the loch, but that when the dam was constructed and the water level raised he never saw any there again.

In the 1990s the water from Loch Finlas was redirected to the Bradan treatment works. A new pumping station was erected and the water was fed into the Derclach Loch and from there it passes through pipes into the works.

The fishing rights to Loch Finlas and the Derclach Loch are the property of Alastair D. B. Gavin, as part of Craigengillan Estates (Number 1) Company Ltd., but were leased to William Noel Collins and Lucinda Rosemary Collins, along with Finlas Fishing Lodge. They established Finlas Fishing Club Ltd. in 2006, but this company was dissolved in 2013. A roadway leads through the forest to a boat house and jetty at the south-eastern corner of the loch.

The Derclach Loch is separated from Loch Finlas by the shortest of streams, and even prior to the extending of Loch Finlas as a reservoir the stream between the two was short and level. The loch has a maximum depth of twelve feet or so, at the west end, though much of it is around ten feet deep. The Derclach Loch measures around half a mile in length by about one eighth of a mile wide, covering about 38 acres. The water level was 837 feet above sea level.

Loch Muck lies to the east of Loch Doon, a small loch just off the A 713. It measures around 30-40 acres in extent, the deepest part being roughly south of the centre, where the water is 22 feet in depth. The eastern bay, where the Muck Burn leaves the loch, is shallow, with reeds. The waters of the loch have had lime applied to them, to reduce the acidity, and it is stocked with brown trout. The average weight of those landed is from eight to ten ounces, though larger ones can be caught. There is a

4.4 Loch Riecawr dam

boathouse on the southern shore, but bank fishing is more normal. The loch is the property of Eriff Estate, but permission to fish can sometimes be obtained from the proprietor.

There are a couple of small lochs on the moors around Craigengillan estate, south of Dalmellington, known as the Berbeth lochs. The largest of these is Wee Berbeth Loch, which nestles between Shear Hill and Knockmore. It had a small boathouse on its eastern shore. The loch is five acres in extent.

South-west of Wee Berbeth Loch is a small lochan, formed by a dam across the minor stream. It is one and a half acres in extent. Due west of this dam is a third small pool, the source of a stream that flows into the Glessel Burn. This pool does not appear to have had a name, even although it is 1.9 acres in extent.

The Shalloch Burn, which is a tributary of the Dalcairnie Burn, rises in a former loch known as Lochencore. This has gradually filled up with vegetation, leaving only an area of marshland.

On the edge of the area covered by this book is Bogton Loch, a fair sized stretch of water in a marshy meadow. The River Doon enters and leaves the loch. The surface level of the water is around 522 feet and it measures 65.6 acres in extent. The loch is fairly shallow across its whole extent. When it was surveyed in 1903 by E. R. Watson BA, the water was discovered to be only four feet deep at its maximum.

The lochs of the Girvan basin within the Galloway Highlands comprise Loch Bradan and a few smaller lochs. Loch Bradan is by far the largest of these, in fact it is partially man-made, for it presently is held in by two dams, one at the west end and one at the north-east end. Prior to this it comprised of two separate lochs, though there was very little between the two. That to the east, and larger, was Loch Bradan itself, and to the west was the slightly smaller Loch Lure.

Today Loch Bradan is one of the Galloway Highlands's largest lochs, by means of damming. Its name is hard to determine how it came about – *bradan* is Gaelic for salmon, but this seems too simple. On Pont's maps of 1654 he gives the loch two names on two different sheets. On the northern half he calls in Loch Brounhoom, whereas on the southern it is called Loch Brawin hoom, obviously two derivations of the same thing. What these mean is unclear. On a map of 1828, 'compiled from estate plans, etc.' it is named Loch Breelen.

Loch Bradan was originally a natural loch of around one mile in length, through which the Water of Girvan flowed. When it was surveyed by James Murray in 1906 it was still in its natural state, an upland loch. In area it covered around 82 acres, and contained about 16 million cubic feet of water. Within the loch was an islet on which an ancient castle or tower was located, though it was nowhere so fine a structure, nor as historically interesting, as Loch Doon Castle. The depth of the water was slightly more than eight feet deep at its deepest, and in extent it covered less of an area than Loch Finlas. Across the surface of the loch, which was estimated as being around 990 feet above sea level, were many small islets and large boulders which projected above the water surface.

In 1903 Troon Burgh was looking for a larger source of water, for its reservoir at Collennan, which basically held spring water, was becoming far too small for the growing town. Ayr engineer, John Eaglesham, investigated possibilities, and decided that Loch Bradan would provide an excellent source of water. Negotiations to establish a joint water board with other communities failed, so Troon went ahead on its own.

James Watson, a consulting engineer from Bradford, drew up the next set of proposals and a Parliamentary Order was pursued, the Royal Assent being granted on

4.5 Loch Goosie as shown on Armstrong's *Map of Ayrshire*

1 August 1908. By this time it was agreed that the burghs of Prestwick and Ayr could obtain water from the same main, filling their reservoirs at Kerse near Dalrymple and Ladykirk, near Monkton.

From March 1909-10 the new dam was constructed across the mouth of Loch Bradan in order to raise the water level by eight feet. The dam resulted in the waters becoming conjoined to Loch Lure. The engineers responsible for the design of the works were J. & H. V. Eaglesham, a prominent Ayrshire architectural and civil engineering business. The extended loch could store 400,000,000 gallons of fresh water, piped at up to two million gallons per day. The dam was built of masonry, and the surface area of the extended loch was at the time 166 acres in extent. The loch had a catchment area of around 3,560 acres, or around five to six square miles. The works cost £90,000 to complete.

The water supply to Troon was commissioned on 17 October 1910. The pipes led to the Collennan Reservoir, located in the Dundonald Hills above the town, from where old pipes distributed the water to the homes and businesses. Collennan Reservoir had been constructed in 1894-6. The official opening of the water works took place on 18 July 1912 when the valve was opened by the Duke of Portland. To commemorate the event a bronze plaque was unveiled, bearing the inscription:

Troon Water Works Loch Bradan Supply. These works constructed under the Troon (Loch Bradan) Water Order 1908 were opened on 18th July 1912 by His Grace William Arthur, Sixth Duke of Portland KG. John Logan, Provost of Troon. Alexander Muir and William Robertson, bailies. David Wilson, Police Judge. James C. White, John Watt, Andrew Johnstone, Ebenezer Milroy and William Knox, councillors. Robert Young, Town Clerk. H. V. Eaglesham, Ayr, Engineers. Neil McLeod & Sons, Edinburgh, Contractors.

In 1910 Ayr County Council obtained an order which allowed it to obtain water from the Loch Bradan main and distribute it to various other communities in the county. A number of smaller water boards were abolished as a result, and in 1911 the Loch Bradan Special Water District was established. This was responsible for the supply of fresh drinking water to an area of around 110 square miles, supplied through 100 miles of new water mains. The cost of this scheme was £73,663. The formal opening of the new water scheme took place on 11 September 1913 by Richard Oswald of Auchincruive.

The water supplied from Loch Bradan coped with the demand in central Ayrshire for around forty years or so, but after the Second World War it became apparent that it would not be able to keep up with increasing demands. Consulting engineers, Babtie, Shaw and Morton, were brought in to consider the options, and they suggested extending the Loch Bradan scheme.

A new dam was proposed across the glen, enlarging the reservoir considerably, and allowing 20 million gallons to be drawn off each day. Work on this commenced in 1971, a new mass concrete gravity structure being created, 1,420 feet in length. Blocks forty feet wide were constructed independently, being raised in 'lifts' of five feet, and eventually joined together to form the completed dam. The new dam was almost 100 feet in height, raising the waters of the loch by forty feet. Built on greywacke, the dam was completed in 1973. Within it are vertical drains and pressure relief holes, as well as an inspection gallery through the base.

The old plaque was taken from the first dam and built into a stone-built pillar just north of the new dam. Below it a second plaque was added, bearing the inscription:

The plaque above was transferred on 20th December 1972 from the original Bradan dam now submerged in the new reservoir. W. Paterson Esq, JP, Chairman, Ayrshire & Bute Water Board. John Allan Esq, CEng, FICE, FIWE, FIMunE, Engineer, Ayrshire & Bute Water Board.

The new level of the loch would mean that the waters would escape over the watershed at the west end of the loch, so a second dam was constructed there, known as the Lure Dam, being at the western end of the old Loch Lure. This dam was much smaller, but is 35 feet in height and 340 feet in length.

To bring additional water into the reservoir, and increase the catchment area, adits were bored through the hills to bring water from other sources into the loch. A series of dams were constructed across the minor burns in the Balloch Plantation, including the Loch Burn, Black Burn, River Stinchar and other watercourses, the captured water being tunnelled into Loch Bradan.

Downstream from the main Bradan dam a new water treatment works was established, capable of treating 25 million gallons every day. The waters pass through twelve rapid gravity filters and chlorination before joining the water main. The water treatment works was opened in 1977. This was further enhanced and extended in the 1990s in order to improve the water quality. The new works cost around £6 million to complete, and were commissioned in 1995.

At the time of construction it was appreciated that the outflow of water from Loch Bradan was extremely powerful and so it was decided to incorporate a smallish hydro-electric power station in the new scheme. This was built with two turbine generators, creating around 400 kW of electricity.

Fishing on the loch is controlled by the Forestry Commission. The loch is stocked with brown trout and daily permits can be obtained at various local outlets. Some of the loch is controlled by Ayr Angling Club. When caught, the trout usually weigh from eight to twelve ounces, though on occasion some fishermen have landed trout up to three pounds in weight.

Loch Lure was at one time a fair sized loch that lay to the west of Loch Bradan. Prior to the first Bradan dam, the loch was only around one third of a mile in length, by about one seventh of a mile wide at the widest, though the shores comprised of a series of bays. The loch was fairly flat bottomed, and the maximum depth sounded by the Bathymetrical Survey, carried out by James Murray in 1906, was seven feet, the average being four feet. The west end, or head of the loch, was at that time fairly shallow and filled with reeds and other plants. Its water surface was only two feet above that of Loch Bradan, the linking watercourse flowing slowly around numerous islands for around one hundred yards to reach the lower loch.

The little Dhu Loch is located to the north of Loch Bradan, today surrounded by forestry. It is a popular little lochan for fishing, and is reached by a path from the forest road through the Tairlaw Plantation. The loch is about 800 yards in length, and the surface of the water is about 1,130 feet above sea level. No watercourse feeds the loch, but a stream, the Duple Strand, runs from it, heading east and flowing into the Water of Girvan. At one time, according to older maps, this stream was not the only effluent from the loch, there being a burn which flowed south into what was Loch Lure. This is known as the Dhu Strand, but current maps do not show it as rising in the loch. The name Dhu Loch derives from the Gaelic *Dubh Loch*, pronounced the same, which means 'black loch'. The hill to the south-east of the loch is known as Craig Dhu, in Gaelic *Creag Dubh*, the 'black rocks'.

Another popular loch for fishing, and one that is clear of the forest plantations that abound hereabouts, is Loch Brecbowie. It is located in the hill pass known as the

Nick of Brecbowie, and the water surface is around 1,150 feet above sea level. Three small islets are in the loch, which measures around 1,800 yards from north to south, and 1,400 yards from east to west. A large peninsula extends into the loch from the east. The name, Brecbowie, derives from the Gaelic *Breac Buidhe*, which means 'yellow trout'. On the western shore of the loch is an old boathouse. The fishing is administered by the Forestry Commission.

Loch Bradan is fed by the Water of Girvan, a stream that passes through three other lochs before it reaches the large reservoir. The first loch reached upstream from Loch Bradan is Loch Skelloch, a sizeable stretch of water partially surrounded by forests. The loch is longer east to west (at 1,800 yards), than it is from north to south (at 1,000 yards). A popular venue for anglers, being part of the flow of the River Girvan means that there can be sizeable salmon and trout within its waters. On older maps the loch is named as Loch Shalloch, a name that is perhaps more readily explained, there being numerous hills of that name to the south of the loch.

4.6 Loch Bradan and Loch Lure before damming

Upstream once more from Loch Skelloch is the Cornish Loch, held in a fold of the rocky hills, though its shores are quite marshy. The name has nothing to do with men from Cornwall, and is more likely to derive from *Loch Coire an Eas* – loch of the corrie of the waterfall. Older accounts render the name in the more normal Gaelic order as 'Loch Cornish', or 'Loch Cornist', as it appears on Ainslie's map of 1821, and some folk still name it that way. The loch is elongated, about 1,800 yards long by 600 yards wide, covering around fifteen acres, the surface of the loch being calculated to be 1,303.7 feet above sea level. The maximum depth of the loch, however, is only seven feet. The infant Water of Girvan feeds into the loch on the southern shores, and leaves by the north-west corner, tumbling over waterfalls shortly after leaving the calm of the mountain loch. The Cornish Loch is used for fishing by the Balloch Fishing Club, a boat house being located on its shorter western shore, a footpath from the old sporting lodge at Craiglure leading to it. It is said that at the turn of the twentieth century an angler landed one hundred fish in a single day.

The old Ordnance Survey map of 1856 indicates a small building at the western side of the loch, near to the outflowing stream. This is close to where the present boathouse is located, but the map indicates that this was an 'Ice House'. This leaves us with an interesting question – did it mean that ice was gathered from the loch in the winter and stored for use in local houses, a precursor to the refrigerator, or was the house used to store curling stones, which were often referred to as 'ice-stones' in the past?

The final, and highest, loch in the Girvan basin is Loch Girvan Eye. The name is one that is quite romantic, the impression given that the small oval loch is the 'eye' of the infant Girvan, almost as though its tears stream down its face and build up into the sizeable river that meets the sea at the town of Girvan, on Ayrshire's southern coast. The name may have nothing to do with eyes, however, for old account give it a totally different rendition, though it is true to say that it may be but an aural rendition of the name. In the *Statistical Account* of Straiton, written in 1791, it is named as 'Loch Garany'. On Pont's map of 1654 this is spelled Loch Garrony, a name that still appears on a map published in 1851 within Samuel Lewis's *Topographical Dictionary of Scotland*. Indeed, in the early twentieth century, local shepherds still pronounced the name as 'Garrony'. The loch measures around 1,000 yards by 500 yards and is approximately 1,500 feet above sea level.

The shores of Loch Girvan Eye are marshy on most sides, apart from the east, under Craigmasheenie, where there are rocks. The loch is home to trout, and at one time, according to MacBain's *Merrick and the Neighbouring Hills*, an angler once landed 58 fish in a single visit.

The only other lochs that drain into the Girvan within the bounds selected for this book are the small round lochs on the moors between Straiton and Dalmellington. Three of these little lochs drain into the Knockdon Burn, which flows into the Water of Girvan near to Knockdon farm. The largest of the three is the Black Loch, an elliptical stretch of water around 890 feet above sea level. The loch measures 800 by 500 yards, and despite its size was suitable enough for fishing that it had its own boathouse, located on the south-eastern shores.

From the Black Loch a small stream flows south-westwards into a tiny lochan known as the Widow's Loch. Only around 200 yards in diameter, this loch is surrounded by marshy land. Between the two lochs a tiny stream joins the burn, draining from the Little Loch, little more than a large pool in the moss.

Further west is the Baing Loch, about 500 yards in diameter and located in a fold of the low hills which are located in this part of the uplands. The loch is shallow, and marshy around much of its edges. It is 4.9 acres in extent.

One of Galloway's loveliest of lochs, Loch Trool is by no means the largest. It lies, however, in a narrow defile of a valley, where the hills to the north and south of the loch plummet headlong into the glen, the loch meandering through the foot of it. This meandering shape has sometimes been used to explain the name Trool, for it is thought that the name derives from the Gaelic *Loch an t-Sruthail*, which means 'loch of the rinsing', or 'loch shaped like a river'. On Pont's map of 1654 it is named Loch Truiyll.

There are three main basins to Loch Trool, the smallest to the west, north of Caldons, the middle one to the south of Glen Trool Lodge, and the larger, and longer basin, to the east, south of Buchan. The largest basin attains a maximum depth of 55 feet. The Lodge basin reaches 36 feet in depth, the constriction between these two basins only being twelve feet deep. The Caldons basin is only 23 feet deep, the narrow strait, in which is a small islet, being only ten feet deep.

Loch Trool is around 142 acres in extent, and contains around 116 million cubic feet of water. The basin that feeds it is quite extensive, measuring around fourteen square miles. At the mouth of the loch a small weir or sluice was constructed over a century ago to maintain the water at a fairly constant level. It also raised the level of the water by three or four feet. This is around 246 feet above sea level. When the Ordnance Surveyors were compiling the first detailed maps of the country they visited the loch on 26 June 1894 and on that date measured the surface of the loch to be 245.9 feet above sea level.

Within Loch Trool are a few islets, though none is of any extent. At the head of the loch, near to the mouth of the Glenhead Burn, is an elongated islet, comprising fluvial stones and soil. Known as Ringielawn, the island was probably created when the mouth of the burn took a new direction to the north of an older mouth, not unlike a small delta.

Near to the mouth of the Buchan Burn is a small rocky islet known as the Maiden Isle. A third islet, unnamed on maps, is located at the west end of the loch, south of Kenmure Knowe.

The two Glenhead lochs lie above the top of Glen Trool, on the fold of the rocks of Craiglee. The Long Loch is located further west, almost L-shaped, the water surface of which is 977 feet above sea level. This was probably anciently named Loch Amered, for there is a lake of that name on Pont's map of 1654 in this location.

The Round Loch of Glenhead is certainly rounder in shape than the Long Loch, but it is far from a perfect circle, being more like the shape of a figure eight. The water surface is 957 feet above sea level. On Pont's map it is named Loch Kreuy.

Loch Valley lies in a depression above Glen Trool. The name is not thought to derive from the loch of the valley, but from the Gaelic *Loch a' Bhaile*, meaning 'loch of the farm'. On Pont's map of 1654 it is shown as Loch Vealhuy. The surface of the loch is 1,049 feet above sea level. There are four tiny islets within the loch, little more than lumps of rock covered with a thin layer of rough vegetation. As with other lochs in this central part of the highlands, the loch is an irregular shape, occupying various hollows formed by the action of glaciers. That glaciers once gouged out some of the Galloway highlands has been proven by early geologists. William Jolly studied the actions of glaciers on the Galloway hills in the nineteenth century, and described Loch Valley as:

…perhaps the grandest geological sight in the district… I know of no more striking example of a lake whose waters are dammed back by moraine debris than this – none in which the dam has that assertive, artificial look so demonstrative of deposited glacial remains. Seen from the west, the view of the mounds is very remarkable, rising in a beautiful series from a considerable distance down the glen up to the water's edge… Another remarkable moraine is found at the head of Loch Valley [east of Loch Narroch], at the watershed between the Trool and the Dee at Cornarroch Strand. This is deserving of notice, being composed, for the most part, of confused heaps of granite boulders – as huge a barrier accumulation of rocks as we know.

The foot of the loch, which is at the western end, is dammed by a large natural moraine. From here the Gairland Burn drops suddenly down to the glen at the head of Loch Trool. In winter and after heavy rain, this burn is more or less a series of waterfalls.

At one time the sporting tenant in Glen Trool Lodge decided he would erect a timber dam and sluice across the mouth of Loch Valley. Although this only raised the water level by a few feet, the sluice could be opened as required, increasing the flow of water in the Gairland Burn, which he hoped would result in better fishing. However, during some heavy rain the loch was so full that it thrust the weir over, and the dammed waters rushed down the Gairland chute to Loch Trool. Fortunately no-one was injured, and there was no dwelling in the way, for a massive granite boulder was pushed by the driving torrent down the glen to the bottom, where it remains to this day. The story of the boulder was used by S. R. Crockett in his novel *The Raiders*.

A small tributary of Loch Valley runs into the loch at its eastern end. A few hundred yards up this stream is Loch Narroch, a smaller loch that is virtually elliptical in plan, though this is an irregular ellipse. The loch is at basically the same height as

4.7 Loch Bradan from Ballochbeatties

82

Loch Valley, for there is little flow in the small stream. On Pont's map of 1654 it was named Loch Narrach.

Loch Neldricken lies to the west of the Black Gairy of Craignaw, and south of Craig Neldricken. To the west it is bounded by the Rig of Loch Enoch and to the south by lesser eminences, such as Meaul. The name of the loch is thought to come from Craig Neldricken, the hill to the north. According to Johnston, this probably derives from the Gaelic *Creag Neulach Dreachadan*, meaning 'hill of the cloudy shape'. The loch is shown on Pont's map – but thereon it is named as Loch Garrony.

Only minor streams fill the loch, one of which flows down from Loch Arron. The loch drains by way of the Mid Burn down into Loch Valley. Loch Neldricken is divided into three uneven lagoons, the east-most the largest, the middle, or southern one the smallest, and the west-most somewhere in the middle. Between the west/middle lagoon and the east lagoon a long promontory stretches from the northern shores and almost divides the loch into two parts, only fifty yards or so separating the promontory from the other side. The surface of Loch Neldricken lies 1,146 feet above sea level. The Ordnance Survey mapmakers visited the shore of the loch on 4 August 1894 and on that day ascertained the surface of the water to be 1,145.5 feet above sea level.

Loch Neldricken has a fame that spreads beyond its locality, for at the western end of the western lagoon can be found a bay that is known as the Murder Hole. This name appears on Ordnance Survey maps, even although it was made up in the early nineteenth century by the novelist S. R. Crockett, who used it in his story, *The Raiders*. The story of a murder hole in Galloway is one that has existed from long before Crockett's time, being a tale that would be told by father to son to entertain on long winter's nights. The story claims that lone travellers who called at a remote shepherd's cottage in the hills were welcomed in and given a place to rest, only to be murdered during the night, and all their belongings stolen. The bodies were disposed of in the murder hole, a deep hole which meant that the bodies were never recovered.

Whether or not this story of murder was true and that there were numerous murders is not known. The traditional place where the murders took place was elsewhere in the Galloway Highlands, near to a cottage called Craigenrae, or Craigenreoch as it was shown on older maps. Craigenrae is a lonely cottage on the hill road from Newton Stewart to Straiton, and five hundred yards or so to the north east of it was the original Murder Hole, located near to the Water of Minnoch.

The Murder Hole at Loch Neldricken is described by Crockett in his adventure:

> It was a part of this western end of the loch, level as a green where they play bowls, and in daylight of the same smooth colour; but in the midst a black round eye of water, oily and murky, as though it were without a bottom, and the water a little arched in the middle – a most unwholesome place to look upon.

Above Loch Neldricken, and draining into it, is the small Loch Arron, held in a fold of the rocky hills of Craig Neldricken. The loch is approximately 1,456 feet above sea level. Some older accounts name it as Loch Arrow. It is sometimes thought that Loch

4.8 Loch Trool looking towards Glenhead

Arron has no natural outlet, and James MacBain traversed it a few times to try to determine how the waters escaped. He discovered that most of the outflow passed between buried boulders and long grasses, joining a stream that flowed south to Loch Neldricken's Murder Hole. The shores of Loch Arron are surrounded by silver sands, and here and there in the loch surface, large granite boulders rise through the waters.

Moving to the south-western periphery of the Galloway Highlands is another loch. The River Cree at one point widens out slightly into what is termed Loch Cree, or the Loch of Cree. This stretch of water lies between Cordorcan and Drannandow, the river flowing sedately through a very marshy stretch of countryside. To the casual visitor, 'loch' appears a rather strange term for the river here, for it is only yards across. Indeed, Lord Cockburn, the famous circuit judge of the nineteenth century, who recorded in his journals some description of the places he visited, noted that, 'Loch Cree, which I have so often heard complimented, is, as a loch, nonsense. It is no loch. A loch one hundred yards across! It is a widening of the River Cree; the river being only so much worse of the widening.'

However, the Loch of Cree has a historical origin, and up to around 1800 was much larger. Pont's map of 1654 names it as Loch Kree on one page, Loch Cree on another. Sometime at the end of the eighteenth century a rock was cut through to allow the river to flow from it more readily, and as a result the level of the loch was considerably lowered. According to the *Statistical Account* of 1838, 'that cutting gained a quantity of excellent meadow on each side of the water.' The rock was probably blasted at what became known as Cut Island, near to Penninghame House, and the lowering water level left a number of deep pools on either side of the river. A couple of these are known as the Dow Lochs, from the Gaelic *Dubh Loch*, meaning black loch. Other pools are still part of the watercourse of the river. Today, little 'excellent meadow' appears on the sides of the Cree, for much of the land to either side is marshy and un-drained.

There are a couple of small lochs in the basin of the Water of Minnoch, though none is of any significance. The lowest down the valley is the Kirriemore Loch, little more than a kettle-hole lochan. Pont names it as Loch Kerymoir on his map of 1654.

The Balminnoch Loch is a high corrie lochan, located in the corrie of Balminnoch, which lies between the summits of Kirriereoch Hill and Tarfessock. The surface of the loch is around 1,657 feet above sea level. The loch has no stream feeding it, but it has a small burn leaving it – the Cross Burn – which is a tributary of the Kirriemore Burn, itself a tributary of the Minnoch.

The Kirriereoch Loch lies between the Kirriemore Burn and the Water of Minnoch, its effluent draining into the former. A smallish loch, around sixteen acres in extent, it is almost surrounded by forestry. The west shore is free from trees, at least as far as the Minnoch. Most of the shores are of gravel and boulders, though the eastern shore is mainly of peat. The loch attains a depth of up to fifteen feet, its water surface nearly 700 feet above sea level. It has been calculated that the loch contains around five million cubic feet of water. On older maps it is sometimes shown as Loch Kirriereoch.

Fishing in the loch is controlled by the Newton Stewart Angling Association. The club stock the loch with brown trout each year, and average catches are around twelve ounces in weight. Some larger fish are also caught at times. Fishing is carried out from the banks, the western shore, where there are less trees, probably being the best spot.

Loch Middle is a little-known lochan that is almost forgotten in the centre of the Glentrool Forest. It lies at the foot of the west end of Larg Hill, and it is filled by small burns that drain from the lower slopes. Its effluent is the Pulhowan Burn, which joins the River Cree at the Wood of Cree. On Pont's map of 1654 the loch is named Loch Middil.

Clatteringshaws Loch is a totally man-made stretch of water. Prior to the damming of the Black Water of Dee or River Dee, this was a fairly open stretch of countryside, with the Dee passing through a heathery moor. The river separated at one point to create a sizeable island – Craignell Island, but this has long since been lost and forgotten below the extensive waters of the new loch.

The dam across the mouth of the loch is a gravity structure measuring 1,560 feet in length and 78 feet tall at its highest point. Being a gravity dam, the weight of the concrete structure is what holds back the water. The loch is used as part of the Galloway hydro-electric scheme to store water, the level of the loch being drawn down in the summer months, and replenished with the return of the rains in the winter season. The water is tunnelled to Glenlee Power Station. When full, the loch covers almost exactly 1,000 acres.

Fishing in Clatteringshaws Loch is available from the Forestry Commission. The loch is noted for its brown trout, pike and perch, and bank fishing is allowed, the fairly normal size of fish being caught being in the region of ten ounces.

Loch Dee is one of the finest remote lochs of Galloway. The name Dee is one of the oldest place-names in the country, and is thought to derive from the old Celtic word for God – *De*. There are other rivers of the name in Britain, such as in Aberdeenshire and Cheshire, but neither of these rivers has a loch of the name.

Loch Dee is 739 feet above sea level, but it is a remote loch, only in recent years made slightly more accessible by the construction of forest roads. Although a fair size lake as far as extent is concerned, it is not particularly deep. The east end of the loch varies from five feet deep, near the mouth, to twelve feet deep opposite the long promontory that extends into to the loch from the south. The largest basin is that to the west, which was plumbed to a depth of 36 feet.

In 1884 the loch was split between three proprietors – the Earl of Galloway, Captain Maxwell-Heron of Kirroughtree and Mr Drew of Craigencallie. The precise demarcation of the water was needed as it formed an important place for angling, being filled with salmon, trout, pike and eels. Boats were kept on the water for the anglers.

Fishers wishing to angle on the loch today should contact local outlets where permits are available. It is claimed that the loch offers the best trout fishing in the area. Controlled by the Forestry Commission, day tickets for fly fishing can be obtained, the loch being stocked with brown trout. The average size of trout landed is around one pound eight ounces.

Perhaps one of the largest trout caught in the loch was one which weighed in at around ten pounds 4 ounces. It was caught on May Bank Holiday 1993 by Brian Baker using a six pound line on a nine foot fly rod. The trout was passed over to the ranger at Garraries, who sent it on to the Freshwater Fisheries centre at Pitlochry. By sampling scales on the fish it was possible to determine that the trout was eleven years old.

There are three lochs of the Dungeon – the Dry, Round and Long lochs. Although they are generally named as the Lochs of the Dungeon, only two of them on current Ordnance Survey maps have this appellation – Round Loch of the Dungeon and the Long Loch of the Dungeon. In 1654 Timothy Pont indicated that the three lochs were known as the Lochs of the Brishie or 'Lochs of Bryishyis' as he spells it. The lochs drain into the Brishie Burn, itself joining the Cooran Lane and ultimately into the Black Water of Dee.

The Dry Loch is the furthest north of the three lochs, and is in fact in a different water basin from the others, its outflow leading into the Gala Lane and thence to Loch Doon and ultimately to the Firth of Clyde. Today surrounded by land owned by the Forestry Commission, originally the loch was the meeting point of three lairds' lands. Around 1900 there used to be a lady who would make her way to this loch with a collapsible boat on the back of her horse, climbing over the Rhinns of Kells from Fore Bush, in order to fish.

The Round Loch of the Dungeon is fairly descriptive of the wide circular loch that lies at the foot of the Dungeon Hill. Its northern shore is covered in silver sand, and within the loch are numerous rocks and boulders, projecting from the shallow waters. The Round Loch is home to two different varieties of trout, black and yellow species.

A small loch high up on Craignaw drains into the Cooran Lane. The Dow Loch was shown on Pont's map as the Dou Loch, both derivations of the Gaelic *Dubh Loch*, meaning black loch. The Dow Loch of Craignaw is just 75 yards in diameter and is located around 1,630 feet above sea level. Although there is a tiny watercourse leaving the loch, eventually tumbling down the Dow Spout, it is reckoned that no fish can reach the loch by natural means, the waterfall being too much for them. However, MacBain wrote that he had 'reason to believe that two adventurers many years ago deposited some brown trout alive in it, carrying them up from the burn below. Whether the trout are still there, or whether they have added to their number, or what their fate may have been, I am unable to say.' The deposition of trout in the loch sounds like something the keen angler may have tried, experimenting in the extension of fish stocks.

The loch should not be confused with a second Dow Loch, similarly located high on the shoulder of Craiglee, south of Craignaw. This Dow Loch is elongated – 200 yards in length, but its total area is comparable to the Dow Loch of Craignaw. This loch has no stream issuing from it.

Loch Dungeon is one of the more remote Galloway lochs. It is one of three lochs that drain into the Polharrow Burn, and of these it is the largest, extending to around 88 acres. On Timothy Pont's map of 1654 it is shown as Loch of Forrest, this area still being part of Forrest estate. The loch has been dammed in recent years, raising the level of the water by a few feet, but hardly changing the surface extent. The loch is in two main basins, that to the east being the larger, but shallower. Prior to damming, this basin reached to beyond 45 feet in depth. A secondary basin near the centre of the loch was 34 feet deep.

The Point of Ringreoch is a promontory that almost separates the loch into two. The western basin is the deepest, the water dropping to 94 feet deep prior to damming. This part of the loch is located below the steep cliffs of Milldown, and the gradient above water level seems to continue below. The water level at Loch Dungeon was originally 1,002 feet above sea level, but the level of the water could fluctuate by around five feet. When surveyed by the team responsible for the *Bathymetrical Survey of Scotland* in 1903, the waters of the loch was noted as being 'a peculiar leaden or greenish-grey slate colour'.

The smallest of the Forrest lochs, Loch Minnoch is located at the head of the Mid Burn. On some older maps it is shown as Loch Minick. Its water surface is approximately 886 feet above sea level. The loch has been dammed.

Loch Harrow is the northernmost of the original Forrest lochs. Its water surface was 812 feet above sea level, but in recent years its mouth was dammed and the level of the water has been raised. Originally the water had a maximum depth of 29 feet and was 38 acres in extent. Surrounded by forest, the head of the loch is dominated by the steep slopes of Craigbrock, a lower shoulder of Corserine. Prior to the loch being dammed, a boat house was located on the north shore. In 1884 the loch was the property of Mr Maxwell of Glenlee. At one time Loch Harrow was a popular haunt of curlers, its altitude resulting in the ice lasting for longer during the winter months.

The Lumford Burn was trapped behind a dam constructed across the stream, creating a loch 500 yards in length, known as Loch Mannoch. Surrounded by forestry, the loch is fairly shallow. The waters are redirected into Loch Harrow, driving a small hydro-electricity scheme.

There are a few small lochans on the southern fringe of the Galloway Hills. Near to Clatteringshaws is Lilie's Loch, from which the Pulron Burn flows down into the large reservoir. The loch is elliptical in plan, the surface of the water being around 800 feet above sea level. The loch is home to brown trout, and fishing on it can be arranged with the Forestry Commission, permits being available locally. Fly fishing is preferred.

South west of Lilie's Loch is the Black Loch, located in a narrow glen beyond the Grey Mare's Tail on Tonderghie Burn. The loch is also an elongated ellipse in shape, the water surface being around 580 feet above sea level. Fishing by fly for brown trout is available by permit from the Forestry Commission.

Yet another small loch controlled for fishing by the Forestry Commission is the Loch of the Lowes. Fly fishing for brown trout is available by day permit. The loch is curved in shape, with a larger pool at the east end. The surface of the water is around 520 feet above sea level.

5 Lanes and Linns

The watercourses of the Galloway Highlands are numerous and varied. Each river and stream has its own characteristics, and the reader will have their own favourite, that stream that they love to wander by, perhaps fishing from the bank, or just enjoying the scenery and landscape alongside, the water either roaring past, gurgling over stones, or else flowing sedately in deep pools, dependent on where one is.

Commencing in Galloway's highest substantial loch, Loch Enoch, the Eglin Lane flows in a generally northward route towards Loch Doon. The name appears as Eaglin Lane on older Ordnance Survey maps and perhaps derives from *Aigeal an Lain*, the 'flood waters of the abyss'.

The Eglin Lane leaves Loch Enoch at a spot known as the Sluice of Loch Enoch and soon tumbles through some of the wildest countryside the Galloway area has to offer, home to red deer and wild birds. It is soon joined by a few smaller watercourses, adding to its flow, so that soon enough it becomes difficult to cross. From the west the Caldron Burn drains the Howe of the Caldron on the steep side of the Merrick, and the Saugh Burn flows from Loch Twachtan. From the east a small stream tumbles from the bealach between Hoodens Hill and Mullwharchar, an impressive sight after heavy rain. Soon the old cottage of Willie's Sheil is passed, the first remnant of human habitation.

Thus far the Eglin Lane has formed the boundary between Ayrshire and Kirkcudbrightshire. The river slows down a bit hereabouts, as the bottom of the glen is flat but rough. Soon enough, however, is a fairly noticeable waterfall, un-named on the maps. Barely half a mile below the falls the Eglin is joined on the west, or left bank, by the Black Garpel. In the promontory between the two are the remains of old sheepfolds, used by shepherds to gather their flocks.

The Black Garpel drains from Loch Macaterick - as a named watercourse it is only three quarters of a mile in length. Loch Macaterick is fed by the Tunskeen Lane, itself fed by the Castle on Oyne Burn. The latter is named from Castle on Oyne, a low hillock that gets its named from the Gaelic, *Caisteal an Eoin*, 'castle of the birds'.

The Eglin Lane takes in the Black Garpel and flows in a north-by-easterly direction, soon entering the forests and reaching the Whitespout Lane. Here, where it is joined by the Whitespout, it changes its name, the last mile of the river being known as the Carrick Lane, as though the Eglin and Whitespout couldn't agree as to which had precedence, and both gave up their maiden names to take on the name of Carrick.

The Carrick Lane is a fast-flowing stream, dropping amongst the granite rocks and clayey soils before emptying into Loch Doon. At the Carrick Lane Foot, the name of the bay where it joins the loch, is a substantial waterfall, the Carrick Linn. Here the river plunges over a granite cliff into the loch below. When the level of the loch is down, the lane flows for a further few hundred yards before it reaches the loch, but when it is high, the falls more or less plunge into the loch.

The Whitespout Lane is named from the Whitespout Linn, a waterfall halfway along its length. As a river it is rough and wandering, finding a way through wet boglands and boulders, all of its banks afforested. The Whitespout Lane starts where the waters of Loch Riecawr flow into the valley, today the exit being made artificial by the construction of the dam. Above Loch Riecawr, only smaller burns form the headwaters, the Craigencoof Burn, Meowl Strand and the un-named burn past Tunskeen running into Loch Slochy, and thence into Riecawr, the two lochs joined by a stream 700 yards long. The Balloch Lane feeds Loch Riecawr from the north.

A number of old maps and books claim that Loch Enoch has two outlets – the Eglin Lane and the Gala Lane. This is incorrect, for the headwaters of the Gala Lane are separated from the loch by a low rise of around 24 feet. From this pass the Pulskaig Burn falls down a narrow glen between Mullwharchar and the Brishie to join the Gala Lane on the valley bottom. The Gala itself rises in the Dry Loch, flowing northwards towards Loch Doon. Older Ordnance Survey maps indicate the name as Gallow Lane.

There are no sizeable streams joining the Gala Lane before it reaches Loch Doon, only the Pulskaig, Pulbae, Sheil Double Strand and Kirreoch burns important enough to merit names. The latter has a small waterfall on its upper reaches, below Carlin's Cairn, known as the Rowantree Linn.

Loch Doon is fed by a few other watercourses, of which the Garpel Burn is the largest. This flows from Loch Finlas, joining Loch Doon on its western shores, about half-way along its length. The Garpel is only around one mile in length, its volume reduced by the removal of water from its basin by the dam across Loch Finlas. The name Garpel is fairly common in streams, and is thought to mean 'short river', perhaps from the Gaelic *gearr poll*.

The other feeders of Loch Doon are but small streams. The east shores has the fewest – from south to north being the Loch Head Burn, Small Burn, Polrobin Burn, Polmeadow Burn and Eriff Burn. On the western shores, in addition to the Garpel, are the Lambdoughty, Black and Craiglea burns.

The mouth of Loch Doon is where the River Doon starts – a notable river in Ayrshire, for it separates Carrick from Kyle, and one that is celebrated in the works of Robert Burns. As soon as the river is released from the dam across the foot of the loch, it enters one of the natural wonders of the area – Ness Glen.

The Ness Glen, properly Glen Ness, from the Gaelic *Gleann an Eas*, or glen of the waterfall, is a deep chasm through which the River Doon forces a passage. Prior to the creation of the reservoir this was more readily accessible, and it is only in recent years that a new pathway has been created through the gorge. The original path was established by Quintin MacAdam of Craigengillan, sometime in the early nineteenth century, certainly before 1826, when it was described as 'Mr Macadam's new romantic footpath,' from when the walk became a popular location for tourists to visit. Part of the route was cut into the living rock, and an upper loop allowed visitors to meander through the birch and oak woodlands.

One of the retired gamekeepers on Craigengillan estate was employed to act as a guide to the tourists who came to the gorge, and one of his special tricks was to call out to some of the birds which would come and perch on his shoulders. This may have been Hugh Hewitson, who died at Glessel in 1916, aged 71. His gravestone in Dalmellington old kirkyard describes him as 'glenkeeper, Ness Glen'.

Many old guide books celebrated the wonders of the glen, which was likened to gorges in the Nepal Himalaya, if not so deep. Nevertheless, the chasm through which the Doon is forced is one that is unparalleled elsewhere, and certainly is still worth looking at. Writing in the 1880s, George MacMichael in *Notes on the Way through Ayrshire*, described the glen:

> The River Doon, issuing from the north end of Loch Doon, descends at once into the bosom of Glen Ness, an amazingly narrow and deep ravine – a few yards wide, 200 feet deep, and nearly a mile in length. There is a footpath along its bottom, hewn out of the rock, a few feet above the current. The rugged, perpendicular, rocky walls of each side, which are only the length of a fishing rod apart, are beautifully variegated with a rich diffusion of tangled botanic greenery, sprinkled with flower, the slender leafy branches of trees interlacing overhead, away up, up and up among the love-throated birds, to a glimmering streak of sky. It is almost frightful, and exceedingly beautiful.

The path today starts at the southern end of the dam that holds back the waters of Loch Doon. A quick descent from the roadside takes one down to the side of the River Doon, which technically starts here, the upper waters having other names. From the riverside one can look back at the concrete dam that contains the waters of the loch, the arched supports holding aloft the roadway. A number of structures associated with the dam overflow and water release valves are noted, but soon these are left behind and the glen itself begins.

It is not too far before the walker enters the gorge, the cliffs on either side rising considerably from the edge of the river. The waters of the Doon tumble in fall after fall, battering from side to side against the cliff face. The east side of the gorge rises almost vertically, the scrubby trees gripping as best they can to the rocks, only along the top edge the majestic Scots pines adding to the grandeur.

The only major fall in the Doon as it passes through the glen is the Pike Fall, nearer to the top end of the glen, but as the water makes its course through there are numerous other cascades. The Craigs of Ness, as the rocks on the west side of the glen are called, rise up above the pathway, which has had to be built on platforms at various locations, there being no room between the river and the cliff to allow pedestrians to pass through. Indeed, at one point the path has to pass between the cliff and a standing block of natural rock – a sort of Needle's E'e.

Unfortunately, in January 1912 there were major storms in the hills and the pathways in the glen were washed away. From then on it was too dangerous to walk through the ravine, and its majesty was virtually forgotten about, apart from by locals who sometimes risked the passage. In 2004-5 the owner of Craigengillan estate, Mark Gibson, decided that he would like to re-create the pathway, and so arranged for it to be rebuilt. A new suspension footbridge was constructed at the foot of the glen, near to the track from Dalfarson to Glessel, built with steel supports and steel ropes holding up the deck. At one end an ornate wrought iron gate prevents sheep from using the bridge.

A pathway can be retraced back up the west side of the glen, along Blackney Brae, through the woods and back to the dam. Nearer to the northern end of the glen the path reaches a high promontory, whereon grows an ancient oak tree, from where views can be had over the Glessel Burn valley to Craigengillan House, its stable block and tower prominent features.

The Doon is joined by a few minor streams as it passes through the policies of Craigengillan House. On the left appears the Glessel Burn, draining an upland moor around the Wee Hill of Glenmount. In the Glessel Glen, just upstream from the restored cottages, is a small waterfall.

Soon, on the right, arrives the Gaw Glen Burn, draining the moor of Dalfarson Hill on the east. The Doon flows on, a sedate river by now, passing beneath the Stone Bridge, and then a second bridge, over which Craigengillan drive passes, and thence over marshy ground and into the Bogton Loch.

A tributary of the Doon, which joins it at Bogton Loch, is the Dalcairnie Burn. Draining the moor around Shalloch, the stream is not too large, but above Dalcairnie farm it passes through the Dalcairnie Glen, and at Dalcairnie Bridge is the noble falls of Dalcairnie Linn. This cascade was a popular tourist attraction in its time, and it also had an added attraction in that there was a rather popular tale with a moral set in the vicinity, so much so that a monument to the incident was erected at the old Nether Berbeth, due south of the Dalcairnie Bridge.

This memorial still existed in 1902 and commemorated William Stevenson (who lived in the mid eighteenth century) and 'whose hospitality was proverbial', according to John Paterson in *Reminiscences of Dalmellington*. He notes that one instance of his hospitality was taken advantage of, which was recorded on the monument in the following words:

> When William Stevenson, laird, was living here,
> His name and worth the world did revere,
> For he was honest, pious, and sincere;
> He was the widow and the orphan's stay,
> Nor spurned the vagrant from his door away.
> One of that class asked quarters for the night,
> Gave God as Caution that he was upright,
> But yet before the awning of the day

The vagrant stole the bedclothes all away.
Yet, as it were by Heaven's supreme command,
A misty fog did overshade the land,
In which the vagrant wandered all the day,
Back to Berbeth at night was led the way.
'You're welcome here again,' good Stevenson cried,
'For Heaven was both your Caution and your Guide,
And he to whom the Almighty points the way,
He cannot, will not, wander far astray.

The Dalcairnie Linn is about forty feet in height, with one sheer drop of twenty feet, the waters of the Dalcairnie Burn falling from the moors down to the floodplain of the River Doon and moss around the Bogton Loch. Facing north, the cataract looks quite menacing on an overcast day, especially after heavy rain.

5.1 Dalcairnie Linn

The Water of Girvan drains the north-western quadrant of the Galloway uplands, though its basin only occupies a small percentage of the area covered by this book. The Girvan, which may derive from *Gearr Abhainn*, the 'short river', rises on the slopes of Caerloch Dhu, the northern spur of Shalloch on Minnoch. The infant river flows into Loch Girvan Eye, and then down to the Cornish Loch. On leaving the loch it passes over a short waterfall and drops down to Loch Skelloch, and then into Loch Bradan.

Other than the Girvan, Loch Bradan has few major feeders, only the small streams at Ballochbeatties, that draining Loch Brecbowie, and the Dhu Strand. Well, at least that is the only natural feeders, for when the loch was dammed for drinking water purposes, an aqueduct and pipeline were constructed to catch water and divert it into the loch from the headwaters of the River Stinchar.

On leaving the Bradan dam, the Water of Girvan passes down through an attractive valley, partially wooded, and partially grazed by sheep, towards Straiton. Below the Bradan Cottages is a waterfall, and lower down, nearer to Tairlaw farm, is a second, more significant, fall, the Tairlaw Linn. Feeders of the Girvan from Bradan to Tairlaw include the Duple Strand, which drains the Dhu Loch, Fore Burn, Knockdon Burn, Claick Burn, Glenauchie Burn and the Baing Burn. The little Baing Burn, which drops from the upland moors north of Tairlaw, also has a series of cascades in its short length, one of which is known as Drummore Linn. Four hundred yards upstream from this linn was an ancient chapel. Even by the early nineteenth century all evidence of a building here had disappeared, but the tradition of its existence was perpetuated in the name Chapel Burn.

There appear to be two Tairlaw Linns, one on the Girvan proper, the other on the Tairlaw Burn, which feeds it from the south. This Tairlaw Linn is a series of drops where the Tairlaw Burn plummets from its hanging valley, here known as Tairlaw Glen. The cascade is located by the side of the hill road from Straiton to Newton Stewart. The fall was created due to the rocks of the Old Red Sandstone period, here comprising basaltic lavas. The falls have been described as 'the finest single fall in the Galloway Forest Park', according to Louis Stott in *The Waterfalls of Scotland*, especially after heavy rain. The waters of the Tairlaw Burn tumble over the rocks for forty feet, located in a narrow gorge bedecked with birch trees.

A small area of the western highlands is drained by the infant River Stinchar. This great Ayrshire salmon river rises on the northern slopes of Caerloch Dhu. Joined by the aptly named Splinty Burn, it flows past the site of the old Craiglure Lodge and under the hill road at Stinchar Bridge. Just upstream from the bridge are a series of falls, easily reached by forest paths. These falls collectively appear to be known as the Stinchar Falls. Only the uppermost is located within the area covered by this book, one hundred yards upstream from the bridge. The main Stinchar Falls are located downstream from here, the river plummeting over the rocks in four leaps.

The western flank of the Galloway Highlands is drained by the Water of Minnoch and its parent, the River Cree. The Minnoch rises on the slopes of Pinbreck and Eldrick hills and flows under Maggie Osborne's Bridge (named after the last witch to be executed in Ayr). It then takes a generally southern route, through the forests to the Cree at Bargrennan. Near Waterhead on Minnoch it is joined by the Pilnyark Burn, greatly increasing its size. A mile further downstream the Shalloch Burn, Shiel Rig Burn and Knocklach Burn have merged to feed the Minnoch, which it does as the Shalloch Burn.

The next stream to join the Minnoch, which is said to derive from the Gaelic

5.2 Tairlaw Linn

meadhonach, or middle river, is the Pillow Burn. At the confluence the Minnoch leaves Ayrshire and forms the county boundary for about half a mile, until the man-made line on the map leaves the watercourse and strikes west for Loch Moan.

The Water of Minnoch flows on, generally hidden from passers-by due to the forest plantations. The Suie Linn is a rocky fall on the river, where the waters tumble through a gorge. Soon after, the Minnoch is joined by the Kirriemore Burn, draining the corries on the western side of the Merrick and Kirriereoch Hill. The Kirriemore is itself formed by the merger of the Cross Burn, draining the corrie of Balminnoch, with the Kirshinnoch Burn, draining the Kirshinnoch corrie. The name derives from *Coire Shionnaich* – 'corrie of the fox'.

Almost a mile further downstream on the Minnoch, the waters of the Kirkennan Burn join it. This stream drains the western slopes of the Merrick and Benyellary, the lesser streams of the Mullachgeny Burn and Kirn Burn feeding it.

The Water of Minnoch flows on, here and there its bed being smooth and peaty, at other times rocky and tumultuous. Near to Palgowan farm the Loan and Knockcravie burns join in, and further south the Whisky Burn runs in, itself subsuming the Kentie Burn. South again is one of Minnoch's rocky stretches, known as Linncrosh.

The Linn of Glencaird is the next significant fall on the Water of Minnoch. The Black Linn follows, a series of cataracts where the watercourse is forced through a gorge of massive rocks and boulders. The river drops around six feet at this point, plunging into a deep pool, its waters a murky black colour due to the high peat content. Just above the falls is a deep and still pool, known as the Quarry Pool. At Stroan Bridge are falls and rocky gorges readily seen by tourists at the visitor centre, and near to it the Minnoch is joined by the Pulnagashel Burn. These are the Falls of Minnoch, the main cascade being about six feet in height.

Half a mile below Stroan Bridge the Minnoch is joined by the Water of Trool, its basin a most attractive corner of the uplands. The Trool rises at the foot of Loch Trool, a watercourse less than two miles in length. Within that distance it is joined on the north by the Torr Lane, which plummets over the Spout Head waterfall above Stroan House, and on the south by the Caldons, Jenny's and Black burns. The Caldons Burn has a few waterfalls on it, draining as it does the steep northern slopes of Lamachan Hill. Shortly after being joined by the Caldons Burn, the Trool splits, the river forming a series of sizeable islets, known as the Isles of Trool.

Near the foot of the Water of Trool, the river drops over a waterfall below the Black Steps, an ancient crossing point where stepping stones were located. These were positioned at the end of the Black Loup, or Loop. A modern footbridge crosses the river in two stretches, the bridge constructed by the Royal Engineers in 1970.

Loch Trool is fed by four main streams, the Pulharrow Burn on the southern side, the Pulnabrick and Buchan on the north, and the Glenhead Burn at the eastern end.

The Buchan Burn is one of the larger feeders, rising near to Loch Enoch and passing through the hanging valley of Culsharg before dropping in a series of notable falls into Loch Trool. The headwaters of the Buchan are formed by the merging waters

5.3 Grey Man of the Merrick

of the Kirn Burn, Gloon Burn, Eldrick Burn, and Whiteland Burn. In this area, near to the foot of the Redstone Rig, is a rock face that has been named the Grey Man of the Merrick. Where it leaves its hanging valley, the Buchan Burn plunges over a series of cataracts, generally known as the Buchan Falls, or Buchan Linns. The lower falls are to be found just above the Buchan Bridge, three falls where the burn tumbles headlong into deep pools. The first drop is of thirty feet, the second step twenty-five feet, and the third twenty feet. A few hundred yards further upstream is another waterfall, known officially as the Buchan Waterfall.

Straddling the Buchan Burn is an old stone bridge, some of the cascades being visible from the parapet. The bridge was erected by Randolph, Earl of Galloway, in 1851. Inscribed on the stone is a verse from Sir Walter Scott's *Lay of the Last Minstrel*, an accurate description of the wild and romantic countryside:

> Land of brown heath and shaggy wood,
> Land of the mountain and the flood,
> Land of my sires. What mortal hand
> Can e'er untie the filial band
> That knits me to thy rugged strand?

On Timothy Pont's map of the area, published in 1654, the Buchan Falls are still named in a derivation of the Gaelic – 'Eas Buchany', *eas* being Gaelic for waterfall. It is thought that the name derives from *Eas Bothanach*, the 'falls of the bothies'.

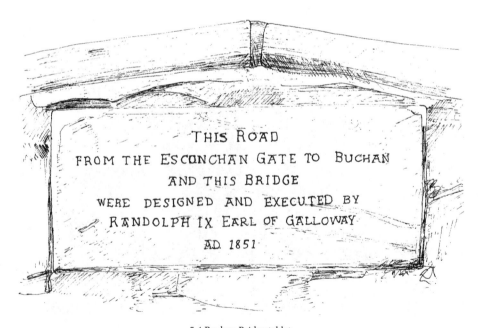

5.4 Buchan Bridge tablet

The Glenhead Burn runs into the loch at its head. Just before it does so, it is joined from the north by the Gairland Burn, dropping swiftly from Loch Valley, itself fed from Loch Neldricken by the Mid Burn. The Gairland forms a magnificent cascade after heavy rain, its waters travelling at speed from the hanging valley in which Loch Valley lies. The Glenhead Burn is also fed by a few other minor streams – the Long Loch Burn and the Round Loch Burn, which flow from the two lochs of that name, the Trostan Burn, and from the south by the Sheil Burn.

Back at Stroan Bridge, the Water of Minnoch starts a meandering course past High Minniwick and Holm farms, through the forest and joins the Cree near to Larg farm. This stretch of the Minnoch has good fishing, and some of the deep pools are significant enough to be named on the maps. These include Potomaras, MacKie's Wiel, Throwfoot, Quaking Ash Wiel and the Cashnabrock Wiel. Wiel is the old Scots word for a deep pool on a river, or whirlpool.

On this stretch of the river can be found the Old Bridge of Minnoch. This crossing is seemingly lost, for it has no roads to either side of it, and therefore doesn't appear to have a reason for being there. Some old accounts claim that it was a Roman bridge, though McCormick calls it the Romany Bridge, but modern archaeologists now date it to the seventeenth or eighteenth century. The bridge has a high circular arch, the deck of the bridge having to climb steeply on both sides. The parapets, if they ever existed, have gone, leaving it a narrow and airy crossing.

5.5 Old Bridge of Minnoch

Streams feeding the Minnoch from the Galloway Highlands side of the river include the Ferrach Burn and Pulniskie Burn, both now draining the extensive forest below Larg Hill.

The south-western limit of this book is formed by the River Cree, which flows from the old Glaik Ford south-easterly to Newton Stewart, and thence into the sea. The river is large and slow, not dropping height by very much, the confluence of the Cree with the Minnoch being less than 100 feet above sea level. The Cree is a notable salmon river, and various pools along its length are named on more detailed maps, such as the Cairdie Wiel, near Larg, and the Cruives of Cree, across the river from St Ninian's Chapel.

The Cree is joined by a number of minor burns dropping from the afforested moors, such as the Tornabens Burn, Lagbaes (or Ballocharus) Burn and the Pulhowan Burn. The Pulhowan Burn drops over a sizeable waterfall before it passes under the road bridge and into the Cree. The falls were originally named the Peakie Noddle, but in recent years have gained the name, Grey Mare's Tail. The falls are fairly significant, tumbling steeply just above the roadside. Surrounded by the broadleaved trees in the Wood of Cree, the falls are most attractive in the autumn, when the leaves turn brown and the berries are red and ripe.

The next sizeable stream to join the Cree is the Cordorcan Burn, which rises on Larg Hill and gathers in the Pinglass, Black and Pulgowan burns before emptying into the Cree. The Cordorcan has a number of significant waterfalls within the last few hundred yards before joining the parent river.

Continuing down the Cree, the main river is fed by smaller streams such as the Washing Burn, Coldstream Burn, and many minor streams before the much larger Penkiln Burn arrives, joining the Cree at Minnigaff kirk, which was constructed on the promontory between the two watercourses.

The Penkiln Burn is a fair sized stream that drains the hillside on the south of Larg, Lamachan and Curleywee. On older maps it is named as the Polkill Water. A few small streams, such as the Pulcree or Glenmalloch Burn, and Glenshalloch Burn, join it from the north. Along the Penkiln is a large pool known as Kevan's Pool, and the lower banks of the river are adorned by the policies of Cumloden House, with the Flower Garden and Walled Garden. Further upstream is the Lady's Linn.

Three large streams form the headwaters of the Penkiln – the Penkiln Burn itself, which drains a glen east of Larg Hill, the Pulnee Burn, which drains the valley between Stronbae and Drigmorn Hill, and the Green Burn, which drains the southern slopes of Drigmorn Hill. The former two have a few waterfalls indicated on the map, the most notable being Hespie's Linn on the Penkiln. The others are unnamed.

The Palnure Burn forms part of the southern limit of the area covered by this book. It flows into the tidal Cree below Newton Stewart and rises near to Brockloch, south-west of Clatteringshaws dam. The headwaters comprise the Black Strand, Tonderghie Burn, Corse Burn, Black Dubs, Kiln Strand and the Grey Mare's Tail Burn. The latter has a series of considerable waterfalls along its course, some of the more significant in the Galloway Highlands.

There are a few cataracts before the burn reaches the Grey Mare's Tail itself, such as the Rough Cleugh. The Grey Mare's Tail is a fall of about fifty feet, plunging headlong into a rocky pool. Below the Grey Mare's Tail the burn drops over the Foot Loup, then the Buck Loup, a fall of thirty feet or so, before passing under the main road and into the Palnure Burn. The Tonderghie Burn also drops over a fall, near to where it passes the Black Loch.

The eastern side of the Galloway Highlands is drained by the River Dee and its tributaries. The Dee rises in Loch Dee, deep in the upland region. The loch is fed by three main streams – the Dargall Lane which flows into the western end of the loch, the Laggan Burn from the south, and the Green Burn at the eastern end. The first and last burns are small watercourses, with little of notice on their length. The Laggan Burn, however, has more to see. It is formed by the confluence of the White and Black Laggan burns. The Black Laggan Burn rises high on the slopes of Millfore, at a spot known as Habbie's Howe. Above the ruins of Black Laggan farm it plunges over two sets of waterfalls.

The White Laggan Burn rises in the pass known as the Loup of Laggan, between Curleywee and Millfore. A lesser stream, with a sizeable waterfall, joins it from Meldens, and the united water flows over the falls known as Laggan Linn. This is a considerable fall of around thirty feet in height. Adjoining White Laggan bothy is a small stream, known as the Well Burn, which has a series of cataracts on it, impressive after heavy rain.

From Loch Dee, the River Dee makes an escape, here a small, but uncrossable, stream, before it is joined by the larger Cooran Lane. The upper reach of the River Dee, as far as Loch Ken, is also known as the Black Water of Dee.

The Cooran Lane is a major tributary on the upper reaches of the Dee. It drains the large middle valley between the Dungeon hills and the Rhinns of Kells, an area of high precipitation. Numerous small streams feed the Cooran Lane, including the March Burn, Hunt Ha' Strand, Saugh Burn, Dungeon Burn, Downies Burn, Green Strand, Brishie Burn, Dow Burn, Black Strand and Cornarroch Strand. The name strand is another of those strange Galloway names for a watercourse, like lane.

The Dow Burn drains from the Dow Loch, high on Snibe Hill, down to the Silver Flow. On its way it drops over the long cliffs of Craignaw, the resultant waterfall known as the Dow Spout, or *dubh sput*, the 'black spout'. When it rains heavily in Galloway, this waterfall become one of the grandest sights to be experienced, the falls dropping over the cliff and cascading over the rocks below.

Below the Loop of Lanebreddon, where the Cooran and Dee join, the Dee is augmented by the Curnelloch Burn, itself having small parent streams known as the Minnaul Burn, Corselusk Strand, Cleugh Burn, Green Burn and Hazelbush Burn. In its lower stretches the Curnelloch Burn divides on a couple of occasions, forming small islets.

The Black Water of Dee gathers other streams on its way to Clatteringshaws Loch. Most of the streams are fairly small, such as the Droughandruie Strand, which tumbles from Cairngarroch, Puldow Strand, Beggar's Lake, Bught Burn, and Small Water

Strand. From the south the Craigencallie Lane is a larger watercourse, draining Glen Owrie. Its headwaters are the Fore Burn, Back Strand and Black Strand. From the north the Garrary Burn is also a larger stream, fed by the Minnigall Lane, and Hog Park Strand.

Today the Black Water of Dee enters Clatteringshaws Loch, but originally this was wide open moorland before the glen was dammed. Streams joining the Dee basin at this point include the Darnaw Burn, Pulran Burn, Pulcagrie Burn, Back Burn, Green Burn, and Corsland Burn, all rather minor streams. The Dee leaves the area covered by this volume when it is released below the Clatteringshaws dam, eventually joining the Solway Firth at Kirkcudbright.

Before the dam was constructed, there was an ancient bridge to be seen across the Dee, on the Old Edinburgh Road. This was Clatteringshaws old bridge, erected in 1703 under the superintendence of the local clergy. Originally the landowner refused to allow a bridge to be constructed, so the local ministers took matters into their own hands and were able to organise its erection. Its remains now lie under water. Below the dam is another old bridge, called the High Bridge of Dee, which dates from 1811, itself superseded by the present road bridge.

The Water of Ken forms the eastern boundary of the Galloway Highlands. As far as this volume is concerned, the Craigshinnie Burn and its confluence in the Ken is the south-eastern limit of the area covered by the book. The Craigshinnie Burn drains the southern slopes of the hill known as Bennan. It leaves its hanging valley and drops to the Ken at Glenlee House. There the burn tumbles over the Buck's Linn first of all, just below the Buck's Linn Bridge, on the minor road towards Clatteringshaws. The next fall is unnamed, but below it the burn passes through Hell's Hole, before entering the pleasure grounds of Glenlee House. A series of paths through the woods here were laid out as part of Glenlee's wider planned landscape.

The Garroch, or Knocksheen Glen, is drained by the Garroch Burn. This rises at Clenrie farm and is joined by small streams such as the Black Burn, before it continues down through one of the more attractive glens in the area. The woods and fields surrounded by stone dikes make a pleasant rural landscape, surrounded by lower hills with rocky outcrops. Near the mouth of the Garroch Burn it is joined by the Dunveoch Burn and Glenlee Burn, the last few hundred yards of the Garroch being named the Coom Burn.

The Water of Ken is a major watercourse through the parishes that make up the Glenkens. This book is more to do with the uplands to the west, so little will be mentioned about the river. The next glen to the north of the Garroch Glen is the Polharrow Glen. The Polharrow Burn starts where the waters of Loch Harrow overflow, now at the dam across the loch. Other streams feeding the Polharrow include the Folk Burn, Lane Mannoch, Lumford Burn, Hawse Burn, Altibrick Strand, Mid Burn, MacAdam's Burn, Craigvey Strand, Gate Craig Strand, and Altiebeastie Burn. Waterfalls can be found on the Hawse Burn, and on the Mid Burn, shortly after it leaves Loch Minnoch.

The Polharrow Burn flows eastwards, gathering waters from the Black Strand, Largvey Burn, Polcardie Burn, Crummy Burn and Rough Strand before passing under the ancient Polharrow Bridge and losing itself in the Water of Ken. Another old bridge is the Knockreoch Bridge, half-way up the glen, giving access to Nether Knockreoch farm. Built of stone, this is a narrow hump-backed crossing. Downstream from this bridge the stream falls over the Waulkers' Linn.

The Polharrow Bridge is now by-passed by the present A 713. The old bridge was originally erected by a local weaver, named Quentin MacLurg. Although he was able to build the ancient arched structure, it is reported that he never earned anything more than four-pence per day. The bridge was later widened but has been abandoned.

North of the Polharrow Glen is the Polmaddy, or Polmaddie Glen. Like the Polharrow, the Polmaddy drains the eastern slopes of the Rhinns of Kells. The Polmaddy rises in the northern corrie of Corserine, heading northwards before turning east. It collects water from the Blaree Burn, Pultarson Burn, Forrest Lane, Braidenoch Lane and Rough Strand before passing it over to the Water of Deugh at Polmaddie and Dundeugh. On the Polmaddy Burn is the Drumness Linn, a small but tumultuous waterfall. Near to Polmaddy village is a footbridge giving access to the ancient settlement. The footbridge crosses a ravine where the water passes amongst the rocks. When the water is low one can look over the parapet of the bridge and see the De'il's Pots and Pans, rounded holes in the rocks scoured out by the action of rotating stones driven by the fast-flowing stream.

5.6 Knockreoch Bridge

103

The Water of Deugh and the Carsphairn Lane demark the eastern extremity of the area covered by this book, both of which are tributaries of the Water of Ken. Near to Carsphairn, on the west side of the Deugh, the Halfmark Burn and Moss Park Strand flow into the Garryhorn Burn, itself fed by the infant Lumps Burn. On the Halfmark Burn is a small waterfall at the head of the gorge known as the Cleugh of Alraith, a rocky chasm hidden with trees.

The Carsphairn Lane is a meandering moorland stream which can sometimes be extensively flooded, especially after heavy rain and when the Drumjohn Power Station is releasing water from Loch Doon into the Galloway hydro-electric power generation scheme. Small streams feeding it from the northern Rhinns are the Polcorroch Burn, Green Burn, Lamloch Burn and Cullendoch Burn. The road into Garryhorn required a new bridge when the hydro-scheme was built; hence the utilitarian reinforced concrete structure dated 1935.

At the north-eastern corner of the area within this book the land is bounded by the Muck Water, a tributary of the Doon. Unlikely as it may seem, it doesn't drain from Loch Muck, but rises to the east, within the Carsphairn Forest. Loch Muck passes its excess water into the Muck Burn, originally a tributary of the Carsphairn Lane, but which has been captured and redirected into Loch Doon.

The Muck Water flows through the narrow defile of Glen Muck and thence through Dalmellington and eventually into the Doon.

Once the early tourist had admired the wonders of the water in the various falls in the area, they gradually began to appreciate the grandeur and ruggedness of the mountains around them. A poem in Malcolm Harper's *Rambles in Galloway*, of 1876, and no doubt written by himself, is typical of this early Victorian sentiment of the ruggedness of the landscape:

> And Buchan's craggy steeps we will climb,
>   Its dungeons of gloom to see,
> And lose ourselves 'mong the gleaming lochs
>   In the course of the Doon and Dee:
> And nature's good and benignant sway
>   Will charm our spirits to rest;
> No worldly cares can vex us here,
>   In our home 'neath the mountain's crest.

6 Wildlife

The Galloway Highlands are home to a variety of wildlife that is quite unique in this part of Scotland. The landscape and natural features are highland in form, and the remoteness of the area has resulted in a number of highland species surviving in these hills, whereas in other parts of the Southern Uplands they have gone.

It is reckoned that there are thirteen birds of prey that frequent the Galloway Highlands, breeding within the open moorland and forests. These are the golden eagle, hen harrier, osprey, red kite, peregrine falcon, sparrowhawk, merlin, kestrel, buzzard, and four varieties of owl – tawny, long-eared, short-eared and barn.

The golden eagle (*Aquila chrysaetos*) was at one time extinct in Galloway, and the magnificent bird absent from the mountains. An old Galloway word for the eagle was *yirn*. The last bird to survive, prior to dying out in 1835, was kept as a semi-tame specimen at Cumloden House, near Minnigaff. We can do no better than relate its tale as recorded by Sir Herbert E. Maxwell, writing in 1892:

> About the year 1835 a pair of eaglets were taken from the eyrie on a precipitous face of Cairnsmore [of Fleet]. One of them died from unskilful treatment; the other was rescued by Mr Stewart of Cairnsmore, and given by him to the Earl of Galloway. It lived for some time at Cumloden; but in a furious gale the wooden shed in which it inhabited was overturned, and the bird escaped. Some months afterwards, a pedlar was traversing the wild road that passes Clatteringshaws from New Galloway to Newton Stewart. It was hard frost at the time. Suddenly he was alarmed by a large bird lighting on the road before him, and, as he thought, threatening to attack him. He killed it was a blow on the head with his stick. It was the tame eagle from Cumloden, which, being hard pressed for food, had come, poor fellow, to beg from the wayfarer. Thus died the last golden eagle bred in the Lowlands of Scotland, for the parent birds never returned to their eyrie.

There is some doubt as to what was the last golden eagle in Galloway, for it is said that the last golden eagle to live at Glenhead in Glen Trool was there until around 1876, when tree felling destroyed much of its natural habitat and food source that it abandoned its ancient eyrie on a rock above Glenhead. S. R. Crockett wrote in *The Leisure Hour* of 1894:

There on the face of a cliff, near Glenhead, is the apparently very accessible eyrie where nested the last of the golden eagles of the southern uplands. Year after year they built up there, protected by the enlightened tenants of Glenhead, who did not grudge a stray lamb, in order that the noble bird might dwell in his ancient fastnesses, and possess his soul – for surely as noble a bird has a soul – in peace…. Generally only one of the young was reared to eaglehood, though sometimes there might be two; but on every occasion the old ones beat off their offspring as soon as they could fly, and compelled them to seek pastures new. Some years ago, however, in the later seventies, the eagles left Glenhead to a more inaccessible rock crevice upon the rocky side of the Back Hill o' Buchan. But not for long, disturbed in his ancient seat, though his friends had done all in their power to protect them, he finally withdrew himself. His mate was shot by some ignorant scoundrel with a gun, somewhere in the neighbourhood of Loch Doon. We have no doubt that the carcase is the proud possession of some noble collector, to whom, as well as the original 'gunning idiot' as a mark of our esteem, we would gladly present, at our own expense, a tight fitting suit of tar and feathers.

The golden eagle appears to have made a return to Galloway in 1906, according to Sir Herbert Maxwell, for he recorded that 'last spring [1906], seventy-one years since the last golden eagles were hatched in Minnigaff, a pair of these noble birds sought out the hereditary haunt of their race and built an eyrie. The female laid but one egg (two is the regulation number), sat upon it for some weeks, but abandoned it, when the egg was found to be addled.'

The golden eagle made a return to southern Scotland in the 1920s, attempting to rear chicks at Mullwharchar, before dying off again, and a further return took place in the 1950s but the eggs failed to hatch. Things improved, and there are now a few breeding pairs in Galloway, indeed, it is reckoned that the arrival of golden eagles into the Lake District came around as a result of young birds heading south to find their own breeding ground. It is also thought that the area required by golden eagles is such that the Galloway hills could only support five or six pairs at most.

Ospreys (*Pandion haliaetus*) were at one time to be found across the Galloway Highlands. Writing in 1884, Captain Clark Kennedy, author of *Robert the Bruce*, and a resident of Knockgray, near Carsphairn, stated that, 'The osprey or "fishing eagle" is also still to be met with, and still, I believe, breeds annually in Ayrshire and Galloway; at all events, it did so since 1871, and is often to be observed by the seashore and sometimes also inland, by the more sequestered of the many mountain lakes.' The bird has returned to the area, but so rare is it that their nesting sites are not publicised.

Ospreys spend their winter in Africa, but fly back to Scotland around April and nest. They breed in areas with lochs and rivers, for their main diet are fish, and the bird can sometimes be seen hovering in the sky, looking down on the water for food. Suddenly, at great speed, the birds lunge down from the sky to catch their prey and carry it off to their nests.

It is known that the osprey frequented the lands around Loch Doon until 1854, there being records of them at that time. A late example of the bird living in Galloway is noted from around 1886, for at that time Edward Hunter Blair shot one on the Blairquhan estate. Within the more remote uplands, it was reported that ospreys nested on rock islets within the Round and Long Lochs of Glenhead up until the 1870s.

After more than a century of there being no ospreys in the highlands, the bird made a spectacular come-back in 2010. People at the foot of Loch Doon, near the dam, noticed a bird arriving on 2 September and swooping down to the loch to grab a fish. A second osprey, its mate, was also spotted, and from that date onward the pair has regularly been seen. They have flown around the loch and across Craigengillan estate to the Bogton Loch, where other fish have been snatched from the water.

The return of the osprey is something that has been promoted for a number of years. The hills and forests have been maintained with a view to creating a habitat more suited to the birds, which are distinguished by their massive five feet wingspan. Forestry Commission worker, Ciril Ostroznik, had been creating nesting platforms in suitable locations as an enticement. One of these sites was constructed near to the dam end of the loch, and Ciril made regular inspections of it. Since the bird's return he noted that on it were various fish bones and scales, as well as the beginnings of a nest being created.

It is hoped that the osprey, if left to fend for itself undisturbed, will start breeding, and also entice other birds to the area. The rare bird would be a great boost to the area's potential for attracting ornithologists.

The red kite (*Milvus milvus*) became extinct in Galloway sometime in the late nineteenth century. A bird of prey, it was seen as being an enemy of the game birds which were then promoted for sport, and gamekeepers were wont to hunt the red kite down. Persecution of the birds started in the sixteenth century, and with the increase in shooting as a sport, the birds were trapped, poisoned or shot to try to get rid of them. Becoming extinct, the birds were never seen in the Galloway highlands. Their last stronghold in Britain was in the Cambrian Mountains of mid-Wales.

In 2001 it was decided to re-introduce the bird to the Galloway hills, and a partnership between the RSPB, Scottish Natural Heritage and the Forestry Commission was set up to oversee this. This was the sixth site in Great Britain where the red kite was re-established. A group of 33 young birds were taken from a different area and were released into the wild from a spot known as the 'secret cages', which is located near to Bennan, above Loch Ken. A further 57 birds were released at a later date. Many of the birds adapted to their new home immediately, finding the terrain ideal for their hunting, and soon they had built up a breeding population. A Red Kite Project Officer was appointed to monitor the birds in the area and where they were observed, assisted by Dumfries & Galloway Raptor Study Group.

To encourage visitors to appreciate what is one of the country's most beautiful birds of prey, a kite trail was created in 2003. This circular route passes through some of the most impressive scenery in the area. The most interesting place on the trail is Bellymack farm, where the feeding station for the birds is located. Each day, at around two o' clock in the afternoon, food is put out for the birds, and this attracts up to sixty birds at one time, all swooping down to pick up the scraps placed on the ground. A nearby hide has been constructed by the RSPB to allow visitors a chance to witness the amazing spectacle from a near distance. The red kites have increased in number over the years since they were reintroduced, and it is reckoned that there are now more than 270 in the local population.

It's not all good news, however, for some of the birds are known to have been poisoned since they were released, perhaps the work of unscrupulous gamekeepers. Most gamekeepers are more willing to help, however, and on some sporting estates the red kite has been encouraged by the provision of food and by watching nesting sites.

In 2010 a report was undertaken to see how the reintroduction of the red kite was having an effect on the local economy. The project was officially started in 2003 and over the following seven or eight years the visitors to the district have increased the economy to the tune of around £20 million. It was calculated that almost £2.6 million was spent by visitors who had come to the area simply to witness the magnificent birds. The project has also supported the equivalent of thirteen full-time jobs per year, with nineteen jobs being supported in 2009.

Another bird that was extinct in the area for many years was the hen harrier (*Circus cyaneus*). These birds were persecuted by gamekeepers as they destroyed the young game-birds. On intensive sporting estates gamekeepers would kill hundreds of them in a single season, such as on the Marquis of Ailsa's estates, when 351 birds were killed from 1850-54. The bird, which has a distinctive grey plumage and yellow legs, was thought to be extinct by 1900.

In 1960 some birds arrived back in the area, finding the forestry cover and lack of grouse moors more conducive to breeding. Soon the bird spread throughout the uplands, but their numbers fluctuated as the trees grew and were cut down. The numbers are now quite considerable.

The buzzard (*Buteo buteo*) became a rare bird of prey in the 1960s, their numbers depleting over the years. Again, with the reduction of sporting estates in the upland area, the bird has returned in greater numbers, preferring the heights of mature trees for their nests. Numbers haven't risen as much as may have been envisaged, for they like to feed on sheep carrion, and again, these numbers have reduced considerably. The buzzard prefers a lower density of trees than the tight conifers preferred by commercial forests, but as conservation becomes more of a priority for the forester, tree cover is being planned to encourage a wider diversity of wildlife. Numbers have increased across the area, and the birds nest in wooded farmland also.

The numbers of peregrine falcon (*Falco perigrinus*) in the area declined considerably after the Second World War. Within the high uplands there were around twenty pairs breeding, but in the decade that followed numbers plummeted. The cause of this was ascribed to pesticides used on racing pigeons, which was one of the principal sources of food for the birds. As a result the thickness of eggs laid by the birds was reduced, resulting in the parent inadvertently cracking them. With the cause identified, certain pesticides were banned, and the decline of the peregrine falcon, which is one of the fastest birds in Britain, was stalled.

Peregrines love to nest on steep rocks, and they often return to the same spot year after year. In some cases, however, they appear to move to other rock ledges for a year, often returning to their original nesting site the following season.

The merlin (*Falco columbarius*), though a close relative of the peregrine, didn't suffer the same drastic fall in numbers. It didn't eat so many pigeons, sticking instead to wild birds. The bird breeds in the uplands, preferring the wild open moorland covered in heather. With the increase in forestry covering thousands of acres of heather moor it was thought that the numbers of merlin would have reduced, but instead it appears to have settled in higher areas. During the winter months it leaves these uplands behind, following the small birds down to the open farmland. The birds often nested on rocky crags and thick heather, but with the arrival of forestry plantations, they have started to nest on large trees on the edge of the forest, scavenging in the adjoining open countryside. Two thirds of their diet comprise of the meadow pipit.

The steep craigs of the mountains and cleughs formed by tumbling streams are the ideal location for the nest of the kestrel (*Falco tinnunculus*). Nesting on crags is not the only place where kestrels go; they are also likely to occupy abandoned nests built by crows and magpies. Kestrels are fairly common, the countryside being ideal for breeding sites, and as the tree cover is reduced in density their hunting ground will increase. Kestrels often eat small rodents, but studies have shown that they will also dine on earthworms, beetles and even larger birds such as pheasant and wood pigeon.

6.1 Kestrel

The sparrowhawk (*Accipiter nisus*) loves the conifer forests created by man, and its population increased when the plantations matured. The numbers of birds were kept low by gamekeepers who regarded them as pests, but in the second half of the twentieth century a national decline of some concern took place. This was found to be due to organochlorine pesticides. Decline in south-west Scotland wasn't as bad as it was in other parts of Britain, but there was some drop off in their numbers. When the pesticide was banned, numbers began to rise again.

6.2 Sparrowhawk

The goshawk (*Acciptiter gentilis*) is closely related to the sparrowhawk, though there are far fewer of these to be found in the mountains. For many years they were extinct in the area, but a few birds kept by falconers escaped and they started to breed. Others were introduced from Finland in the 1970s and have spread in southern Scotland.

The four main species of owl can be spotted in the hills and woods of Galloway. The tawny owl (*Strix aluco*) is the most common, breeding in the woodlands. The long-eared owl (*Asio otus*) is also much at home in the conifer plantations and nesting in abandoned tree nests belonging to birds like crows, magpies, buzzards, etc. Preferring the more open countryside is the short-eared owl (*Asio flammeus*), which hunts across the moors. The barn owl (*Tyto alba*) is the rarest of the owls in Galloway, there being few suitable nesting places for it as the older cottages and sheds that were abandoned crumble further into decay, or are cleared away altogether. Their decline has been stemmed by the introduction of nesting-boxes to replace their more traditional home.

In Galloway the raven (*Corvus corax*) is often called the corbie. According to John MacTaggart, writing in the *Scottish Gallovidian Encyclopedia* in 1824, 'this is one of our most singular birds; he seems to feel more pleasure in flying than any other, and goes through many antics in the air, tumbling himself on his back frequently; he cares nothing about storms, and in fine calm days he will on wing circle often the top of some high hill; his nature, however, is very savage, and when domesticated, as he easily is, he prides himself in doing all the devilry he can.' In recent years the numbers have dropped in the uplands of Galloway, probably due to the decline in sheep numbers, resulting in a loss of carrion.

6.3 Long Eared Owl

Of game birds, the Galloway uplands are home to a variety. The red grouse (*Lagopus lagopus*) is the most common, breeding on the open heather moors or in the newly-planted forests. At one time much of the open moorland was kept as grouse-moors, the gentry or sporting tenants coming to the area to shoot. Numbers fluctuated depending on the weather – bad springs and wet summers were often blamed for falling numbers. As the moors were gradually afforested, their numbers have reduced in Galloway, their place taken by black game, or the black grouse.

The black grouse (*Lyrurus tetrix*) was in danger of extinction in Galloway, but with some careful management of the land its numbers have steadied. Across Britain it is one of the most rapidly declining of birds, but in Galloway it still has a number of breeding areas, especially in the upland regions. In 2010 it was reckoned that there were only 5,000 breeding males in the United Kingdom, a figure that had fallen 10% in ten years. At the time, within the Galloway area, it was reckoned that there were 390 breeding males in 2011, up 160 from the previous year.

A large black bird with a red wattle over the eye, the black grouse is noted for its dawn 'lek', a competition between the males to find the best display site from where they can attract a mate. The sound of the bird bubbling and displaying its plumage is one of Scotland's most impressive displays of nature.

In 2007 £100,000 was spent in trying to regenerate the numbers of the black grouse in the Galloway hills. The habitat where the birds bred was encouraged, and the Forestry Commission removed some areas of woodland to create a more suitable environment. A major forest fire that spread from Loch Doon southward actually was beneficial for the Black Grouse, for many acres of dense trees were destroyed, leaving a more open countryside.

The pheasant (*Phasianus colchicus*) can be found in most of the woodland within the Galloway uplands. A common game bird, they are often bred by gamekeepers on sporting estates and released to allow sport in season. A distinct variety of pheasant, known as the golden pheasant, was introduced to the Newton Stewart area in 1895, and became settled in the Kirroughtree Forest and lower Cree woodlands. As forestry became more common, this game-bird spread, and in the middle of the twentieth century its harsh call could be heard in many woodlands on the southern edge of the area covered by this book. It was assumed that the breed would spread further into the forests, but it appears to have dropped in numbers instead and is rarely seen.

A second pheasant breed was introduced to the Cumloden and Kirroughtree estates – the Lady Amherst Pheasant. These birds seemed to settle and breed for a time, but it is thought that they have now died out.

At one time the ptarmigan (*Lagopus mutus*) was to be found on the high summits

6.4 Ptarmigan

of Galloway, notably on the Merrick range and the Dungeon of Buchan. The bird, which was also known as the mountain partridge, was often referred to locally as the tarmachan, its Gaelic name. The bird was noted in 1684 by Rev Andrew Symson, he wrote that on the tops of the mountains were found 'that fine bird called the mountain Partridge, or, by the commonalty, the Tarmachan, about the size of a red cock, and its flesh much of the same nature; it feeds, as that bird doth, on the seeds of the bull-rush, and makes its protection on the chinks and hollow places of thick stones, from the insults of the eagles, which are in plenty, both the large gray and the black, about that mountain.'

On Armstrong's *New Map of Ayrshire*, published in 1775, there is a note adjacent to Shalloch on Minnoch, reading, 'The Cairn of the Shalloch & the three Hills South of that are exceeding barren & rocky; on them are found the beautiful white Moor Fowl called the Termagant, and no where else South of Stirling.'

Perhaps the last ptarmigan to live in the Galloway Hills existed in the first half of the nineteenth century, for it is said that one of the birds was shot near to the Dungeon around 1820. One account claims that they died out in 1826, known as the 'year of the short corn', a year that was renowned for its lack of precipitation, resulting in considerable drought. Sir Herbert Maxwell remembered being told that 1826 was the last year when ptarmigans were seen in the Galloway Highlands, the information being supplied to him by an aged hill shepherd. The *New Statistical Account* of Kells notes in 1844 that the bird was now extinct.

Attempts to reintroduce the ptarmigan took place in 1843, and again early in the twentieth century, but on both occasions this was unsuccessful, the birds only surviving for a year or thereabouts.

Of other birds that frequent the Galloway Highlands and surrounding countryside, only a quick mention can be made of them. The woodlands and glens are filled with a variety of smaller birds, such as various warblers, which nest in the trees, their spring song a distinctive sound. Tits are mostly represented by six of seven of the breeds available.

The goldcrest (*Regulus regulus*) is known locally as the 'basket-hanger' from its small nest of moss which it builds below high tips of fir trees. This is the smallest bird in Britain, and their green plumage with orange crests can be seen high on the pine trees, leaping from branch to branch.

The dipper (*Cinclus cinclus*) can be spotted flitting around the burns and watercourses, with oystercatchers (*Haematopus ostralgus*) and ringed plovers (*Charadrius hiaticula*) nesting among the stones and rocks. On the hills the dotterel (*Charadrius morinellus*), ring-ousel (*Turdus torquatus*) and golden plover (*Charadrius apricarius*) can be spotted.

With the arrival of large forestry plantations, some birds have returned to the area, or else increased in number considerably. The crossbill (*Loxia curvirosra*) is a case in point. It was reckoned that it died out in the late 1890s but is now breeding in the forests and joined in season by visiting migrants from Scandinavia. The green woodpecker (*Picus viridis*) was unknown in Scotland for many years, usually only resident in England, but it returned to the Galloway forests in 1960 and started breeding.

Birds which have increased in number include the Pied flycatcher (*Ficedula hypoleuca*), its black and white plumage very distinctive, and the bullfinch (*Pyrrhula pyrrhula*), which nests in youngish spruces.

The black-throated diver (*Gavia arctica*) is usually confined to the Scottish Highlands, but in the 1950s appeared in the south, and in the 1960s bred for a time on Loch Bradan, Loch Finlas, and perhaps Loch Dungeon. In the mid-1970s their small numbers disappeared, and it is thought that they no longer breed here, perhaps due to acidification of the lochs.

The nightjar (*Caprimulgus europaeus*) is a summer visitor, but its population in south-west Scotland has been declining for a century. In the 1960s it was still to be found in some locations in southern Ayrshire, but today they are only to be seen on lower moorland, in young forested areas, or in clear-felled woodlands.

The best time to experience the bird, if you are lucky, is on summer evenings. The male 'churrs' can be heard, a sound that old traditions claimed was the spinning wheels of the fairies. The bird had local nick-names, such as the 'moth owl', 'dew-fall hawk' and 'flax-spinning wheel'.

Seagulls often make the upland lochans and islets their breeding ground, and a number of Galloway sites have for centuries been home to them. Before Loch Bradan was extended, the Castle Island was home to many breeding pairs, up to forty at a time. The birds had to find a new nesting site when the water level was raised. A similar tale is told of the breeding spot on the Pickmaw Island in Loch Doon. Located at the head of the loch, this was, during the breeding season, almost covered over with nests of the gulls. When the waters were raised the birds had to find a new breeding ground. It is reckoned that the birds displaced from Loch Bradan went to the Bogton Loch, near Dalmellington, and those of Pickmaw Island to the shores of Ballochling Loch.

6.5 Red Deer stag

Red deer (*Cervus elaphus*) have lived in the Galloway hills for many centuries. They are Scotland's largest native mammal, and the sight of them in herds roaming across the mountains, passing from valley to valley is something that is worth seeing. Stags have large heads of antlers. The deer graze on heather, grass, shrubs, wild flowers and young trees and shoots.

The red deer became extinct in the hills for a time, for according to a tradition recorded by Sir Herbert Maxwell, the last red deer stag was shot in the highlands of Galloway by the minister of Kirkinner church, sometime towards the end of the eighteenth century. The deer seem to have died out in the late eighteenth century, for the account of Kells parish in the *New Statistical Account*, dated 1844, notes that 'deer were occasionally seen, in the remembrance of some old people.'

An old account also claims that in Knockgray Park, to the east of Carsphairn, is a scattered heap of granite boulders with a number of rowan trees growing amongst them. This place is known locally as the 'Deer's Den'. Tradition claims that this is the spot where the last of the 'true wild deer' of the lowlands was killed.

6.6 Roe Deer buck

Red deer were reintroduced sometime in the nineteenth century, perhaps when the Cumloden Deer Park was created, and they have spread throughout the uplands since then. In the 1970s there were around 500 deer roaming the mountains.

It is thought that the Galloway deer interbred with some North American deer of the wapiti strain, which had been brought into the Cumloden Deer Parks. This strain is said to have created bifurcating back tines on their antlers, something not found in other parts of Scotland.

Historically, the red deer of Scotland were hunted by brown bears, lynx and wolves, but when these animals became extinct there was no natural predator to keep their numbers in check. Accordingly, man has had to intervene to control the deer, for should they overgraze then damage can be done to young and not so young trees. In 1965 a Galloway Deer Control Scheme was introduced, which kept numbers to a manageable limit. In a survey of deer numbers within the highlands area, 1,432 red deer were counted.

When the Forestry Commission took over much of the Galloway Highlands it established a Red Deer Range on Brockloch Hill in 1976 to allow the general public the opportunity to see the deer. This range is located mid-way between Talnotry and Clatteringshaws and extends to five hundred acres, comprising Brockloch Hill and The Types. A tall deer fence surrounds the park, and this is home to around sixty deer. The red deer range was the idea of John Davies, the forest conservator, and Peter Kelly, a Forestry Commission wildlife ranger.

A parking area with information boards is located near to Brockloch Bridge on the Queen's Way, and the forest ranger often meets visitors here to take them on tours of the range, allowing the visitor to witness these magnificent animals, with their rich auburn coat and velvet eyes. Depending on the time of year, visitors can experience calves being born from around May until June, or the roaring and rutting stags in autumn, when they are fighting for supremacy.

Visitors on their own can walk up to a hide overlooking the range. The best time to see the deer is in the morning, for they are often down nearer to the hide for shelter. As the day warms up, insects and midges become as much a problem to the deer as they are to humans, and the animals wander further away and higher up, in search of a breeze that blows the insects away. In autumn the rutting season can often be experienced, when the stags bellow and search for a mate. The Forestry Commission often holds special events at this time, allowing the visitor to experience what must be one of nature's most spectacular dramas.

Fallow deer (*Dama dama*) can sometimes be seen in the woodland, for example in Knockman Wood to the south of the highlands. They are distinguished by their spotted hide and are smaller than red deer, but larger than roe deer. The species is thought to have been brought into the country by the Normans and are now more or less regarded as native.

Roe deer (*Capreolus capreolus*) also live and breed in the Galloway forests, but their numbers are kept under control due to the damage that they can do to the young trees. To mark out their territory, the deer often strip the bark from young trees, resulting in its death. The roe deer is the smallest of the deer frequenting the hills.

The deer may have died out totally in the eighteenth and early nineteenth century, but it was reintroduced on the estates of Culzean and Drumlanrig for sport, and it seems to have taken hold and spread across the uplands.

Many wild goats frequent the Galloway Highlands, especially on the wild rock outcrops where they seem to be able to jump and run from boulder to boulder with relative ease. There are numerous goats to be seen in the central range, around Craignaw and Dungeon Hill, but the Forestry Commission has kept a number within an enclosure near to the main road along the southern edge of the Highlands, at Craigdews. Although 'wild' goats, it is reckoned that the animals are descendants of domestic stock which were turned loose when the old crofts and steadings were cleared in the early nineteenth century. It is also claimed that some goats were introduced to the land south of Loch Macaterick in order to frighten the sheep from the land, improving the grazing conditions for deer.

An old account of Galloway's goats was written in 1870 by Captain Colvin Stewart, entitled *The Wild Goats of the Stewartry*. In it he writes:

One gentleman kills as many as 20 goats every year, and in the hills about Newton-Stewart, at least 50 goats are killed every year; a good goat will give about 60 lbs of meat. When a goat is caught and killed in the common hunt, his ear is examined and he is at once sent to the farmer who has fixed his mark upon the beast. This is done with the greatest fidelity; each farmer has his own mark. If a goat is unmarked he becomes the property of whoever catches him.

The Galloway Goat Park was established in 1970. An enclosed section of hill, comprising Craigdews Hill, and extending to around 140 acres, was fenced and 27 goats brought into it. Although the goats are contained, they are able to leave the park if they so wish, for they are very agile animals and can often bound over the fences. The animals are what is called 'hefted' to the goat park, that is, they stay in the area as they are fed regularly by the rangers.

The Forestry Commission feeds the goats, especially during the winter months when natural feeding can be hard to get, and also maintain the numbers in the park area. When the number becomes too large for the goat park itself, the commission tries to give away some goats to other places, but on occasion they have had to cull them.

6.7 Otters

In addition to the Forestry Commission running the park, the Feral Goat Research Group also take a keen interest. This group also monitors the wilder goats that fend for themselves in the central section of mountains.

Badgers (*Meles meles*) can be found in some areas of the Galloway Forest Park, in particular where there are well-drained sandy soils, allowing them to dig dens. They dislike the hard rocky areas and peaty soils.

The otter (*Lutra lutra*) can be found in some locations by the side of rivers and watercourses. They mostly come out at nightfall, and those who would like to see them are advised to sit quietly near woodland streams as the sun sets and the otter starts its evening hunt. The animal does exist in reasonable numbers however.

There are a considerable number of foxes (*Vulpes vulpes*) living within the highlands of Galloway. According to MacBain, the principal colony of foxes at the start of the twentieth century was at the base of the Dungeon Hill. There, where the granite boulders are piled upon each other over many acres, are innumerable gaps and subterranean passages where the fox can make his den. Another location where the fox makes its den is in the large moraine at the foot of Mullwharchar. The hill fox that frequents the highlands is a larger variety than the more common lowland version.

At one time hunting hounds and riders on horseback entered the fastness of the Dungeon of Buchan, in search of the wily fox. It was expected that the quantity of foxes would provide good sport, but the roughness of the terrain and the unsuitable ground for horses meant that this method of hunting was quickly abandoned. The riders couldn't trust their horses to find suitable footings in the ground, the holes and crevices between the boulders resulting in legs disappearing beneath the level of the ground, injuring the horse and throwing the rider from the saddle.

Instead, shepherds and gamekeepers organised a shoot amongst themselves in order to keep the number of foxes at a minimum. The shoot had a purpose, in the killing of vermin, but the event was a social occasion too. Herds and keepers made their way to the foot of Mullwharchar, armed with shotguns and cartridges, dozens of dogs barking around their feet. Walking across the brae-face, the dogs sniffed out the fox's den, sometimes forcing it from its hide. The herds and keepers shot at it with their guns, killing as many as they were able.

Often the keepers would bring their terriers for better flushing, but they had to watch themselves too, for the rough boulders could leave them stuck in narrow defiles between the rocks. Chasing a fox into its den was troublesome for them, for as they ran at speed, the floor of the route could disappear, leaving a vertical shaft into which they fell, wedging themselves between the sharp granite rocks. It was impossible to dig the wedged dog free, and many a hound had to be left to die in agony in the blackness, their barking echoing across the hillside. In the old kirkyard of Minnigaff can be found the gravestone of John MacCallum, 'the old foxhunter who was born and lived and died in Minnigaff parish on the 13th January 1773 aged 75 years.'

A number of wild animals that once lived in the Galloway hills are now extinct within that area. The wolf at one time roamed much of the wild uplands of Scotland, and Galloway was no exception. When the last wolf was killed in this area is unknown.

The wild cat is thought to be extinct in the Galloway hills, having died out around the early decades of the nineteenth century.

The pine marten was extinct in Galloway for over a century or so. The marten is known to have been present in Kirkcudbrightshire in 1796, for it is mentioned in the old *Statistical Account*, but it is reckoned that the animal was extinct in Galloway by 1850. It seems to have lasted longer on the northern side of the hills, for it was reported in Ayrshire later, becoming extinct around 1882.

The pine marten still survived in the highlands of Scotland, as well as in the Lake District of England. Odd sightings of animals which probably strayed from the Lakes were made in various parts of southern Scotland, but it was never proved to have re-established itself in this area.

Workers from the Forestry Commission tried to re-introduce the animals formally in 1980. A total of twelve martens, a mixture of male and female animals, were captured in the forests of Inchnacardoch and Ratagan, in the highlands, and taken to Galloway. Two groups of martens were released on two occasions in 1980 and 1981. One set was released at Backhill of Bush, in the wilder and less-human interfered with part of the forest, the other near to Caldons, in Glen Trool, where human visitor numbers were higher.

From that date onward, sightings of pine martens increased in Galloway and all those notified to the Forestry Commission were plotted on a map. From the results it is reckoned that the Backhill group of animals have either died out, or else moved on to somewhere more appealing to them, perhaps near to Clatteringshaws and Palnure Glen, where some sightings have taken place. The remoteness of the Backhill location may also mean that sightings of the animals there would be much fewer in any case.

The animals released in Glen Trool appear to have migrated further west, into the forests around the lower Minnoch valley, and into the woods alongside the River Cree, adjoining the extensive forests between Glen Trool and Peninghame. Although numbers have not been large, it is reckoned that the reintroduction of the animals has been a success, and that they have now become established in the area.

One of the unexpected bonuses of the reintroduction of the pine marten is the discovery that they seem to help control the grey squirrel. Where the pine marten numbers increased, the numbers of grey squirrels dropped, probably from the fact that the pine marten forages amongst the same habitat.

There are many hares and rabbits occupying the hills. The blue, or mountain hare (*Lepus timidus*) occupies the heather moors that survive in some places. During the

6.8 Hare

summer months these animals are a light brown colour, with a white tail and black tips to their ears. In the winter, to give them camouflage, the hare changes colour to white. Only the black tips of their ears remain the same colour. This change of coat doesn't always depend on the arrival of the snow, for the hare often changes colour without snow, making them more conspicuous on the heather moor.

The red squirrel is still a popular mammal living in the woodlands and forests of Galloway. In recent years it has struggled in other parts of Scotland where the grey squirrel, a non-native cousin, has taken over, spreading squirrel-pox from England. Within the forest park area, rangers and volunteer groups have been actively encouraging the red squirrel by feeding them and improving the habitat where they live by planting suitable seed-bearing trees. Squirrel boxes have also be erected across many woodlands, creating safer places for breeding. A 'Red Squirrels in South Scotland' project was established in 2000 to promote the welfare of red squirrels, and watching for signs of incoming greys.

Many other animals can be found in different habitats around the Galloway hills. Badgers (*Meles meles*) are sometimes seen in the drier parts of the countryside, often where there is sandier soils and where they can build their dens.

According to MacBain, there are two types of rat that live in these hills – the black and grey varieties.

The adder (*Vipera berus*) is the only poisonous snake to be found in the Galloway hills. They can sometimes be seen sunning themselves in the warm weather, often picking gravelly or stony locations to do this, such as the side of forest roads. The largest adders appear to grow to around two feet in length and can be a few inches in circumference at the largest. Traditionally, shepherds and gamekeepers were wont to kill adders, claiming that they ate the young lambs or grouse.

A number of rare butterflies occupy the uplands which can be seen by the keen explorer. The list includes the green hairstreak (*Callophrys rubi*) which frequents the wooded edges of moorland and bogs. Its caterpillar feeds on gorse, blueberry and ling. The purple hairstreak (*Neozephyrus quercus*) is hard to spot as it flies around the canopy of the oak woods alongside the Cree and Trool. The small pearl-bordered fritillary, one of the country's rare fritillaries, can be found in damp woodland clearings and at the edges of bogs.

Dragonflies are popular insects in the Galloway hills, and can be seen hovering above areas of wetland and streams. Some of the dragonflies are quite rare, such as the azure hawker, which can only be found in Scotland. In Galloway there is quite a large presence of them, and they make their homes in areas of marsh, using the pools as breeding grounds. They can most often be seen in the summer months, from mid-May through to early August. Also to be seen are the golden-ringed dragonfly, the largest variety in Britain, which can grow up to four inches in length.

Flowers and plants are not something that one usually associates with the Galloway Highlands. Thick heather, maybe, and spongy green stuff squelching beneath the soles of your boots, or sometimes up around the laces, threatening to run into your socks, are to the naturalist or, more specifically, to the botanist, of considerable interest.

The more interesting plants are perhaps the three small flowers which even James MacBain noted in *The Merrick and the Neighbouring Hills*. He wrote, 'There are three flowering plants growing on the hillside that are likely to attract the notice of the mountaineer interested in such things as he ascends.' These were the tormentil, the eyebright and the blaeberry.

Tormentil is a small plant that has little cross-petalled flowers, glowing bright yellow underfoot. The root of the plant was at one time popularly dug up to provide a red dye that could be used in colouring leather. It grows at altitude.

The eyebright flower stands upright, with spiky purplish-white flowers. Its proper name is euphrasia, but it gets its common name from the fact that it was at one time used as a herbal medicine, treating eyestrain and conjunctivitis, as well as vertigo or as a poultice. It grows as high as the summit of the Merrick.

Blaeberry is a small shrubby plant, which is part of the heather family. Its flowers are rather inconspicuous, being little crimson bells, appearing in May, after new leaf growth. Soon after pollination, berries form, ripening into a dark blue colour just over ⅜ inch in diameter. It is most common on the eastern cliffs and rocky gairies of Craignaw, Mullwharchar and the Dungeon Hill.

The high altitude of the Merrick and Corserine summits make them almost pure highland in their habitat, and some flowers can be found there that are normally only associated with the northern Scottish Highlands, or even Arctic uplands. One of these is *Saxifraga rivularis*, a tiny Alpine plant that grows at altitude adjoining pure mountain springs, hence its name. Having tiny bright green leaves, the plant throws up thin stalks supporting pink-white flowers. It is usually only found above the 2,000 foot contour line, and has been noted on the Merrick and Corserine. Its common name is brook saxifrage.

Bog asphodel can be found above the thousand foot contour line. A relative of the daffodil, it is different in appearance, with a crimson and gold corolla. Despite its name, it doesn't thrive in bogs; instead it prefers the wet peat moss.

The sundew appears in many places across the moors, a unique carnivorous herb, appearing in long-leaved and round-leaved varieties.

For much of the Galloway Highlands, the ground is covered with grass, heather, carex and bog myrtle.

The cliffs of the hills in Galloway were at one time resorted to for the collection of a type of moss that was known locally as 'corklit'. This moss was described by John MacTaggart in his *Scottish Gallovidian Encyclopedia* as 'a whitish kind of fog, used in dying; it is taken from rocks, and feels like cork-wood, hence "cork" the name, and "lit" being a dye.' An older account, by Rev Andrew Symson, notes that, 'In the parish of Monnygaffe there is ane excrescence, which is gotten off the Craigs there, which the countrey people make up into balls …. This they call Cork lit and make use thereof for litting or dying a kind of purple colour.'

The moss is in fact, a lichen, *Lecanora tartarea*, and it grows on the rocky cliffs and screes that deck much of the high mountains. Corklit was in considerable demand for its dyeing qualities, and there was a trade locally in collecting it and selling it on at the markets. The dye produced was at one time in considerable demand for colouring coats worn by soldiers. Locally, there was an old rhyme that was popular amongst the country folk of the district, noting which hills were the best sources for the moss:

> The Slock, Millquharker, and Craignine,
> The Brishie and Craignaw;
> The five best hills for corklit
> John Tamson ever saw.

Who John Tamson was is unknown – he may be the same Jock Tamson used in the Scots phrase, 'We're a' Jock Tamson's bairns', implying that every man is equal. As far as the five hills are concerned, The Slock is the name of the cliff on Hoodens Hill, shown as 'The Wolf Slock' on modern maps, Millquharker is an older spelling of Mullwharchar, Craignine is the rock cliff between the Buchan Hill and the Rig of Loch

Enoch, The Brishie is the name of the narrow ridge projecting north from the Dungeon Hill, and Craignaw is the mountain of that name. All of these mountains and cliffs are composed of granite.

A fairly rare form of fern that is known as the 'filmy-fern' can be spotted on the central Dungeon mountains. Its Latin name is *Hymenophyllum Wilsonii*.

Cowberry, or red whortleberry, is found in the hills. This was the badge of the Clan MacLeod. There are quite extensive patches of cowberry on the hillsides, especially the flanks of the Merrick and Larg Hill. The plant has a complicated system of roots and stems, growing in the thin soils. The plant displays shiny green leaves, small in size, not unlike the box plant. On occasion the plant, which grows in a dwarf form in the highest places, sports red berries.

Much of the Galloway Highlands' periphery and part of its centre is covered in commercial forestry, suggesting to the visitor that the region does not have any great areas of historical or natural woodland. This is not the case, for there are many places where the natural trees of Scotland can be found growing, regenerating themselves over centuries, creating a more gentle and natural landscape.

Some of these historical woodlands are now noted for their natural habitat for wild plants and animals, and make attractive places to visit. The main woodlands include the Wood of Cree, alongside the River Cree in the south western corner of the area. To the south are Knockman Wood and Garlies Wood, extensive woodlands filled with natural specimens. The Glen Trool oak woods are also extensive, occupying land to the west of Loch Trool, alongside the Water of Trool.

As part of the 'Action for Mountain Woodlands', groups of volunteers took part in a survey to identify how extensive the mountain woods were in Galloway, in particular around the Merrick. This upland wood is known also as 'montane scrub' or sometimes as 'treeline woods', being descriptive of the stunted, low-lying and twisted shrubs that grow where the soil is thin and exposure to wind and snow is greatest.

The group walked all over the Merrick to survey the extent of existing woodlands and mountain plants. In some cases this involved abseiling down steep parts of the Black Gairy to identify stunted trees that were growing from fissures in the rocks. As the group surveyed the landscape, they also collected cuttings and seeds from downy willow and juniper which they planted in a nursery in order to create a gene bank for future planting. The group were also excited to discover areas of newly established mountain woodland within the area that had not been noted before, developing from blown seeds, perhaps as a result of less grazing from sheep and deer.

To improve the experience for the visitor, and in order to return part of the hillside to a more natural condition than the stands of commercial conifers, a two and a half acre site adjoining the path to the summit of the Merrick was cleared of spruce and replanted with thousands of trees that had seeded themselves on the Merrick. This planting allows the walker to experience a more natural woodland as they ascend the Merrick, softening the often hard edged line of conifer forests.

The oak (*Quercus petraea*) woodlands of the Wood of Cree, Caldons and Loch Trool form one of the most important woodland habitats in the area. These woodlands are thought to be relics of the ancient sessile oak woodland that covered much of Galloway. The oak takes many years to grow to maturity, and some of the trees in this area could be as old as two centuries. They are home to a variety of birds, insects and lichens. The oak woods alongside the Water of Trool and Loch Trool have been designated as a Site of Special Scientific Interest.

The oaks in the Knockman Wood, north of Minnigaff, were at one time cut down for timber, but new shoots grew up from the boles, and are themselves now quite old, creating a strange-looking grouping of trees, often two or three growing closely together, but in reality a single tree.

Another SSSI established to preserve ancient sessile oaks and other trees is centred on Hannaston Wood, in Glen Garroch, west of Dalry. Here, there is evidence of some ancient trees amongst later examples, which prove to be an ideal location for birds to nest, including pied flycatchers, wood warblers, nuthatches and redstarts.

The Scots pine (*Pinus sylvestris*) is a noble tree that is native to this country, and which can be found in various locations. The older examples are most attractive, often having strange formations – a result of years of battering by the wind and elements, and of the poor nutrients in the soil. In some areas these older trees are the remnants of planted woodlands, for the Scots pine was often planted in upland areas. The trees on the southern side of Loch Trool were probably planted in the 1800s.

The rowan tree (*Sorbus aucuparia*) is a popular native tree to the Galloway uplands, and it grows in many of the boulder fields and cliffs around the mountains. The tree, which can grow quite tall, often throws up numerous branches, and its ash-like leaves indicates its other common name – the mountain ash. There are numerous old-wives tales associated with the rowan, and one of the more popular one was that it was often planted at the front door of a house to keep the witches away. Many folk today still like to plant a rowan tree in their garden, even in urban communities, as it is thought to bring good luck. Its attractiveness is no doubt another reason, for the trunk grows tall, with shiny brown bark, the leaves in spring and summer are bright green, being compound leaves, usually with fifteen leaflets. The tree also flowers, with large heads of small white flowers being replaced by berries. However, in autumn the rowan comes into its own. The berries turn bright orange-red, eagerly eaten by the birds of the district. The leaves turn a golden brown or orange colour, and in low autumnal light these trees can look as though they are on fire.

The birch (*Betula pubescens*) is a common upland tree, some of which can grow at a considerable altitude, where they are more dwarfed in size. Like the rowan, the birch is an attractive tree, its trunk covered with bark that can vary from a creamy white to a treacle-black. The leaves are smallish, and like the rowan in autumn form an attractive golden colour that enhances views of wooded areas.

In some of the lower gorges and glens on the periphery of the Galloway uplands, the hazel tree (*Corylus avellana*) can be found growing. This tree has smallish green leaves and a fairly smooth bark. The tree was often used as a coppice plant, for when it is cut down it sends up new shoots of branches from the bole. For years these new shoots were used for a variety of things, but one of the more common one was in the making of shepherds' crooks and walking sticks. Sticks of up to one inch in diameter were cut from the main tree and dried out before being straightened and used to mount decorative and carved handles made from rams' horns.

The holly tree (*Ilex aquifolium*) can be found growing wild in a number of places in the older woods of the district. In the woods by the side of the Water of Trool some larger holly trees can be found. The tree produces leaves with sharp spikes, which one would assume prevents grazing, but the leaves are still eaten by deer. In the autumn months the trees are noted for their red berries. Only the female holly trees sports berries.

The juniper (*Juniperus communis communis*) tree is another upland plant that tends to be synonymous with open hillsides. Its main habitat is rocky scrubland above 1,000 feet in height, and it grows contentedly up to around 2,000 feet above sea level. In the Galloway Highlands it is more often to be found on south-facing slopes, and one of the largest extents of it can be discovered on the great scree-ridden slopes of Kirriereoch Hill – the Canton Heads. At this location over 250 plants have been listed, thought to be around half the total number of trees that grow within the forest park area. Many of these trees are very old, their size being indicative of this. On Kirriereoch, the plant grows across the ground, some of the older trees being about three feet across, though a few up to twenty feet across have been found. It is sad to report that in recent surveys only one new juniper plant has been found growing, and why this plant is not regenerating in the uplands as quickly as others is unclear.

The aspen tree (*Populus tremula*) is another popular montane tree, growing on the inaccessible rocks and crevices of the mountains.

The downy willow (*Salix lapponum*) is a fairly rare tree that only grows on high mountain countryside, up to an altitude of 2,300 feet. It was thought for many years that there were only three locations south of the Scottish Highlands where this dwarf tree grew – Merrick, White Coomb near Moffat and at Helvellyn in Cumbria. However, recent surveys of the montane trees in Galloway have revealed that it is more popular in this area than was originally thought. Indeed, the Merrick grouping of the tree is one of the largest and healthiest in the country. At least 250 large vigorous plants have been listed, and numerous saplings found growing elsewhere. More exciting, was the discovery of a fourth grouping of the tree outwith the Highlands, on the rocky slopes of Kirriereoch Hill, north of the Merrick.

The creeping willow tree (*Salix repens*) is rarer on these mountains, and no-one was sure whether or not it still survived or not. Early records listed the plant, but it hadn't really been noted for years. However, healthy specimens of it were found on the Merrick, growing strongly on its perfect habitat of rocky cliffs, and it has also been found on islets in upland lochs.

The burnet rose tree (*Rosa Mollis*) can also be found in Galloway's high mountains.

Salmon (*Salmo salar*) are found in the main rivers surrounding the Galloway hills, as well as other watercourses of the uplands. The fish are anadromous, meaning that they are born in the freshwater rivers, migrate to the ocean and then return to the freshwater streams where they were born. This may be two to four years later. The tradition for centuries was that salmon came back to the same location as where they were born, and tracking devices fixed to fish have proved this to be true. The rivers of the area provide excellent salmon fishing from March to October.

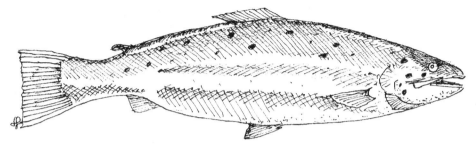

6.9 Salmon

Trout can be found in most of the rivers and lochs of the Galloway Highlands. They are divided into two branches – red and white.

A local resident compiled a book entitled *The Trout and Salmon Handbook*, published in 1989. Robin Ade lives near Carsphairn, and over the years has painted, sketched and drew many salmon and trout, as well as local views. An earlier book, *Fisher in the Hills – a Season in Galloway*, tells of the countryside around Carsphairn, but more generally to the north-east of the village. For lovers of wild fishing, the book has become a classic.

There is a strange situation regarding the trout that swim in the high lochs at the centre of the Highlands, in particular Loch Enoch. These lochs are located in basins of granite, and around the shores of the lochs, and no doubt on the bottom of the lochs themselves, granite sand is found in some abundance. Granite is a particularly hard stone, and the sand is hard and sharp. It is said that the trout and other fish that frequent these lochs have a different shaped tail and ventral fins – the soft tissue being worn away by the friction of the hard granite when they swim through the shallows or at the bottom of the lochs. Loch Enoch trout are said only to have the dorsal fin the correct shape, other fins being deformed.

In the late 1880s there was an attempt at introducing the yellow Loch Leven variety of trout into the lochs and streams of the upper Doon. Huge quantities of fry belonging to the trout, which is regarded as being a superior variety of fish, were transported to the lochs and streams around Loch Riecawr and set in the water. The experiment was not met with great success, for many of the young trout failed to survive in the cooler waters of the Galloway uplands. A number did live, and for some years after a few Loch Leven trout were to be caught in the pools. However, after a time all of these fish died out, and today none can be seen.

The Arctic char (*Salvelinus alpinus*) is a cold-water fish, usually found in northern fresh-water lakes, in places such as Canada, Scandinavia and Russia. In old Scots accounts of the fish they are named charr, with a double R, but there are other names by which they were known in the district – cuddings and red-wames.

There are still a few Arctic char breeding in Loch Doon, one of very few locations in Scotland where this happens. The loch was designated as an SSSI as a result of the fish. The Loch Doon Arctic Char are reckoned to be genetically distinct from other pockets of the fish that survive elsewhere in Britain. The fish have been at risk due to acidification, but sentinel populations of the fish have been established in two other lochs (Loch Talla and Loch Megget) in the Southern Uplands to provide a backup in case the parent stock dies out.

In May 1893 five of the fish in Loch Doon were caught, stuffed and sent to the British Museum by Robert Service.

Arctic char were at one time to be found in Loch Dungeon, for in 1899 M. Moss wrote in the *Dumfries Courier* that, 'Shortly since I had the pleasure of receiving a fine specimen of Char from a friend, who had caught it in Loch Dungeon with a fly when angling for trout. A few are caught each year in this way in the loch named, as well as in Loch Doon.' The last known fish from this loch appears to have been caught in 1952. The fish was also obtained in Loch Grannoch at one time.

In 2012 plans were made to try to save the vendace, a small freshwater fish that died out in Scotland in the 1960s, and which only lived in two lakes in the Lake District. Seventy thousand eggs were gathered from Derwentwater and transferred into Loch Valley in the hope of establishing a new colony of the herring-like fish. The search for a suitable loch to try out the transplant of eggs covered quite a number, and Loch Valley was deemed to be the most suitable. Although it had once suffered from acidity, the water quality had improved. Previous transfer of eggs have had mixed results, with the eggs left in Loch Skeen in the Moffat hills being successful, whereas those placed in Loch Daer Reservoir were not. Historically, the fish only lived in four places within Great Britain – Bassenthwaite Lake and Derwentwater in England and the Castle and Mill lochs near Lochmaben.

7 Archaeology

Much of the Galloway Highlands is too remote and wild for prehistoric man to have found much to keep him here, the terrain being too rough and the land unsuitable for farming. However, around the periphery there are many sites where he has left his mark behind, from tiny microliths to considerable chambered cairns.

The fluctuating level of the water in Loch Doon has proved to be fruitful for the archaeologist. The waters having killed off the vegetation on the shores of the loch has meant that walking along the gravel beaches, when the level of the water is low, has allowed relics and fragments of early man's lifestyle to be discovered. At Loch Head a number of pieces of Mesolithic implements have been discovered, including items made from flint and chert. At Portmark more Mesolithic flint and chert relics were found, including scrapers, blades and microliths.

The Mesolithic period in Scottish history is usually defined as the time from when the glaciers retreated, perhaps around 8,000 BC or later, until the arrival of the Neolithic settler, which was around 3,300 BC. Mesolithic man was the hunter-gatherer, someone who wandered from place to place, never settling, and hunting for food as he went. Obviously these men had their families with them, for Mesolithic people did not remain in one place, and did not farm the lands. Most Mesolithic remains are usually discovered in easily accessed locations, such as along the coastline, but in the Galloway Highlands remains of his passing through have been found in a number of places, in particular around Loch Doon. Indeed, Michael Ansell listed around sixty Mesolithic sites that had been discovered in the Loch Doon vicinity.

The chert implements had probably been made locally, for this stone can be found within the Galloway hills. However, the flint implements must have been brought into the region, there being no flint available. Probably much of the flint found in Galloway had been imported from the flint quarry on the Langdale Pikes in England's Lake District. The stone was used to make scrapers, some of which have been discovered in recent years, as well as to form arrow-heads and other weapons, used in hunting.

There are many sites where concentrations of flint have been found, especially around the shores of Loch Doon. These flint concentrations include various tools and waste materials. Sites where they have been noted are as follows:

NX 479941	At the mouth of the Carrick Lane
NX 482939	On the shore of the loch north of Starr
NX 483937	On the shore of the loch east of Starr
NX 484931	On the shore of the loch north west of Loch Head

The hunter-gatherers may have settled for longer periods as they developed into farmers over the centuries. It is possible that the first permanent occupation of the periphery of the Galloway Highlands took place around 5300 BC. The higher ground, which was drier than the valley bottoms, could be cleared of trees and other vegetation to create areas for grazing sheep and cattle. The settled Stone Age person was termed Neolithic man, and they may have been responsible for constructing the earliest burial cairns in the area. Many of these cairns, however, were also used for burying the dead from the Bronze Age.

There are few relics from the Bronze Age to be found in the Galloway hills. One of the few discoveries was made sometime in the late nineteenth century, when Rev R. MacIntosh, walking on Buchan Hill, which rises steeply to the north of Loch Trool, found a rock on which there were cup and ring markings. This is located quite near to the summit. He reported his findings to the Dumfries Antiquarian Society, but the experts from that organisation were less convinced of their existence, claiming instead that they were only 'the weathered rims of modular pieces of metamorphic shales.'

A second cup and ring marking is found on a natural rock slab on the opposite side of the Buchan Glen from Buchan Hill. Half way up the southern slopes of Benyellary, above the Braes of Mulgarvie, the slab can be discovered on a heather slope. Almost horizontal, the slab measures around seven and a half feet in length by five and a half feet broad. The discovery of the single cup marking, which is surrounded by a ring, was made in 1972 by A. Murray and G. Wood. The ring is 4½ inches in diameter and the cup is around one inch deep. Also on the rock are carved lines, some at angles to each other.

Rev John Henderson Thomson, in *The Martyr Graves of Scotland*, published in 1894, refers to 'the cup and ring markings recently found near [the] summit' of Bennan. This may be an earlier finding of the Braes of Mulgarvie carving, or else another marking, now lost.

During a recent investigation of the archaeological features on the Moor of Barclye, north of Minnigaff, a cup and ring marked rock was found. This is located 440 yards south of the rocking stone of Barclye.

That the Bronze Age people were in Glen Trool is also confirmed with the knowledge that a hoard of Bronze Age implements and ornaments was discovered lower down the valley. At the mouth of a small cave on the rocks of Nig-nag-newan, which is located at the northern end of the Stroan Rig, north-west of Glen Trool Lodge, the implements were found during the First World War. The story of their discovery is one of some humour. Rumours abounded that the Germans had contacts in the area, and that five-gallon and other sized drums of petrol and fuel had been stashed in the hills. Captain Dinwiddie, who was in charge of the soldiers based nearby, was on the Rig of Stroan with his platoon, looking for the fuel cache, and they decided that amongst the rocks was as good a place as any to hide it. The soldiers had been in the area for months, one of their tasks being to keep an eye open for German aeroplanes. As part of the preventative measures employed, they had stretched a rope across the field at Caldons with the intention of preventing enemy aircraft from landing. Should they have tried to land on what was unlikely to be large enough for the task, the rope was attached at one end to a spring gun which, when it fired, would have alerted the locals that such an event had occurred!

What the soldiers searching for fuel found was to be of greater significance, and one that was to interest archaeologists across the country, at the time one of the greatest hoards discovered in Scotland. In the cave a number of artefacts were unearthed, including what was the earliest known bead found in the whole of Britain.

There are hundreds if not thousands of cairns across the Galloway Highlands, some of which can be dated back to the Bronze Age period. Many more are comparatively modern, perhaps erected by hill-walkers over the past century. Some of the old Bronze Age cairns can still be found by the interested reader, starting in a roughly north to south direction, from Dalmellington to Glen Trool and Newton Stewart, then back up the east side of the Galloway Highlands, we will note the numerous ancient cairns to be discovered.

The low hills between Dalmellington and Straiton are home to a number of burial cairns. To the west of Dalmellington, the first hill of any consequence is Auchenroy Hill, which rises to 1,193 feet above sea level. Though low compared with the great mountains to the south, Auchenroy Hill commands an extensive view of the valley of the Doon. The hill has a few different summits, the eastern one being topped by a burial cairn. The cairn measures around 45 feet in diameter but today is only around two feet in height.

South east of Auchenroy Hill, and again occupying a height overlooking the Doon valley, is the Dalcairnie Cairn. This lies 777 feet above sea level on Wee Cairn Hill, really only an eminence above the Dalcairnie Glen. This cairn was 31 paces in diameter in 1895, but it was described as being much-reduced in size and overgrown with grass. More recent measurements put the cairn as being 80 feet in diameter by about three feet at the most in height.

Another cairn is located on Dalnean Hill, west of the Bogton Loch. The locals claimed that this was the grave of some ancient chieftain, which could be true. In any case, it is reckoned that the burial mound is around 4,000 years old. The mound, or barrow, measures around fifty feet in diameter and rises about two feet above the level of the surrounding soil. Dalnean Hill itself is a scheduled Ancient Monument due to its mediaeval dwellings and field boundaries. These can be difficult to pick out by the untrained eye, but in low sun they are more obvious.

The White Laise is a burial cairn located on the moors to the west of Loch Doon, on the slopes of the Big Hill of Glenmount. Old accounts claim that this cairn's name, White Laise, may have been a corruption of White Wraes, or warrior's fort. Measuring sixteen paces or around 44 feet in diameter, it was around six feet high at one end, but it has been much disturbed and the small stones scattered around. A number of smaller cairns to the east of this cairn may also be prehistoric burials.

Above Knockdon, in the Girvan valley, is an ancient cairn, located on a low knoll to the south of a pine plantation. Around 860 feet above sea level, this cairn would have afforded panoramas west down the Water of Girvan and south up the same valley towards Loch Bradan. The cairn measures around twenty feet in diameter by about three feet in height. That prehistoric man lived on these moors is apparent for 400 yards to the north-west are the remains of a circular enclosure.

Near to the track from Knockdon farm up to the cairn and enclosure can be found the remains of five other cairns of unknown provenance. The largest of these measures twenty feet in diameter by around two feet in height. The cairns may have been robbed by early antiquarians, for there are signs that they have been dug into at some time. A similar array of fifteen small cairns can be found on the slopes of the Fence of Knockdon. These are located north of the summit, almost due south of the main Knockdon cairn.

Another burial cairn can be found in the valley of the Water of Girvan, on the opposite side of the river from Knockdon farm itself. This cairn is located at the foot of Clashwinne, and is known as the Knockdon Cairn. According to John Smith's *Prehistoric Man in Ayrshire*, written in 1895, the cairn was fifteen paces in diameter and was three and a half feet high on one side and five feet four inches high on the other. He reckoned that it had been opened up, perhaps by early treasure hunters.

At the Baing Loch, south-east of Straiton, can be found an ancient cairn, located next to a more recent sheepfold. The cairn occupies the top of a low eminence of 897 feet in height, but all around it the hills are taller, meaning that this cairn lacks the prominence that many of the other cairns have. The sheepfold here is known as 'The Loch Rees'. The cairn is a circular chambered cairn, but it has been extensively robbed, no doubt to assist the 'herd in building the sheepfold. The cairn still measures around sixty feet in diameter and rises to a maximum height of six feet. The chamber which existed within it is now represented by two massive side slabs, positioned three feet apart, which protrude through the surface of the mound. Closer inspection also reveals the remnants of a small compartment within the body of the cairn to the north-west.

The wilder moors and forests south of Straiton have fewer antiquities than the moors between Straiton and Dalmellington. However, once we drop down into the valley of the Water of Minnoch then we find burial cairns once more, indicating that prehistoric man also found the upper lands too wild for their liking.

Between Shalloch on Minnoch and Tarfessock farms can be found the remains of another burial cairn. This one is difficult to locate in the forests now, but its remains are protected and a keen map reader and explorer will readily find it. If you can discover it, you will find that the mound measures around 100 feet from one end to the other, and it rises about four feet above the level of the surrounding ground.

One of the main cairns on the west side of the Galloway Highlands is the King's Cairn, which is located in the forest near to Kirriemore. This is an important relic, and is also a chambered cairn. The cairn is relatively well preserved, being positioned on a low mound. Archaeologists describe the cairn as being of the 'Bargrennan' type, which means that there was a passageway into the chamber. The mound of stones has had some robbing over the centuries, but it still remains an impressive sight, rising to almost ten feet in height. At the south-east corner the chamber has been entered, but it is otherwise complete. This has exposed part of a probable passageway. Smaller sized people are able to crawl into the open chamber, but it is recommended that you don't, just in case the overburden of rock suddenly collapses. The upper capstone is cracked, but it is supported by dry-stone walling.

A number of other cairns are located within the vale of Minnoch, but being west of the hill road from Straiton is beyond the boundary selected for this volume. However, keen antiquarians will want to look for the cairns of Cairnfore, Cairn Kinna, Shenchan's Cairn, Cairn Derry, the two White Cairns, and others within the Glentrool Forest. Some of these are also chambered cairns.

On the stretch of countryside alongside the River Cree are a few prehistoric cairns between the river and the heights of Larg Hill. Near to the bridge across the Cree from Clachaneasy another cairn can be found just off a forest track north of the minor road. This cairn occupies a low knoll.

A cairn is located in the forest east of the old Cordorcan farm, by the side of the Cordorcan Burn. The cairn measures around eighty feet in diameter and rises six feet above the level of the surrounding ground. In the centre a depression hints at an early robbing attempt, but no cist or chamber has been exposed.

Less than a mile to the north east is the ancient cairn at Dalvaird, on the other side of the Cordorcan Burn. This cairn appears to be unexcavated, and still measures around 37 feet in diameter and three feet tall. A more recent cairn is perched on the top.

The Moor of Drannandow is home to a considerable number of antiquities, including The Thieves standing stones, stone circles and burial cairns. The Drumfern cairn occupies a rising stretch of moorland.

South of this cairn is another, near to Drumfern stone circle. It is 22 feet in diameter and has a modern cairn on top of it. It doesn't appear to have been excavated. About forty cairns can be seen in the immediate vicinity, some of which are thought to have been little more than clearance cairns, though one is twenty feet in diameter.

Adjacent to Nappers Cottage is a chambered cairn, originally known as the Boss Cairn. At one time this cairn was particularly large, being covered with loose boulders, but it is recorded that most of this stone was taken away in order to build enclosures in the vicinity. When this occurred the stone robbers found a large cavity, or chamber, within, comprising stones too large for them to remove. This was described as being eight feet in length, four feet wide, and three feet high. The cavity is aligned east to west. There are four similar sized cavities on a north-south axis. The stones were described as being very large, laid in regular courses from the base to a fair height, the size diminishing as the height increased. The cairn was excavated in 1922.

South of the Nappers Cottage are two other burial cairns. One is 150 yards south west of the cottage, the other around 500 yards to the south west.

On the Moor of Barclye are a few burial cairns. One of them is located on the improved ground immediately south of the farm. This measures sixty feet in diameter and is just over three feet above the height of the grassland around it. A few stones protruding from the ground are thought to be remains of the cist or chamber that was located within the burial site, but only excavation would reveal more information.

7.1 Nappers Cairn

East of this cairn is the Drumwhirn Cairn, occupying a low knoll 292 feet above sea level. The cairn is twelve feet tall, a massive pile of boulders and stones. Today it is around seventy feet in diameter, although some earlier accounts claim that the cairn was a long cairn, that is, it had a major and minor axis. The cairn is thought to have been constructed in the third or second millennium B.C.

Almost due east one can find the Boreland Cairn, now hidden within the forest west of the Knockman Wood. A chambered cairn, this burial site is located 487 feet above sea level. This cairn is referred to as the 'Grey Cairn' in the *New Statistical Account*, which describes it as being of a similar size and construction to the Boss Cairn at the Nappers cottage. The cairn is described as a 'horned long cairn', which means that it had a shape with projections to either side of the entrance. The cairn is perhaps a 'Clyde' type chambered cairn, measuring eighty feet long by fifty feet wide, though it tapers away from the main entrance. This is located at the south-east end, where larger portal stones mark what would have been the entrance to the chamber. The significance of the cairn was noted in the late nineteenth century, when the landowner refused any more robbing of the mound for stones. Around that time an urn, which had been 'burnt to a jet black', was discovered five feet into the cairn, near to the east end.

Of the Drumlawhinnie Cairn no trace of it can now be found. It was located on the moor at Drumlawhinnie, which was a farmstead north-east of Risk farm, south of the Castle of Old Risk. The cairn is referred to in the *New Statistical Account* of the parish of Minnigaff, written in 1842. In the account it is described as being 891 feet in circumference.

Near to Clatteringshaws Loch can be found the White Cairn, which occupies an elevated moorland site on the Rig of Drumwhar, now afforested. The cairn has been much destroyed over the years, originally by robbing of stones to build sheep-shelters, and more recently parts of the mound were cut into by forestry operations. The cairn is forty feet in diameter and almost three feet in height.

Burial cairns are thinner on the ground in the lower stretches of the Glenkens, but on the moor north of Nether Knockreoch farm, in the Polharrow glen, is a round cairn. Old maps recognised that there was something here, for the six-inch map of 1853 shows a circular feature of stones. More recent investigation has identified this as an ancient burial cairn.

Around Carsphairn there are a fair number of cairns to be found. One has been identified on the low ridge between Bardennoch and Braidenoch hills, south of Carsphairn. Located just below 1,000 feet above sea level, this cairn was discovered during an archaeological survey of the area in 1969. The cairn measures sixty feet in diameter, but much of the material was robbed, perhaps to build the stone dike that crosses it, resulting in the mound now only rising eighteen inches or so above the moor. A couple of larger stones may be the remains of a cist that was within the mound.

Cairn Avel, or Carn Avel as it is sometime called, is a larger cairn, located west of Carnavel farm, across the Water of Deugh from the village of Carsphairn. This is a considerable burial cairn, around fifty feet in diameter and ten in height. The cairn does not appear to have been excavated. Originally the mound was elongated, perhaps as long as 120 feet, but much of one end was robbed to build stone dikes. A number of stones indicate the former shape on the ground, which was probably trapezoidal, but with a squared western end.

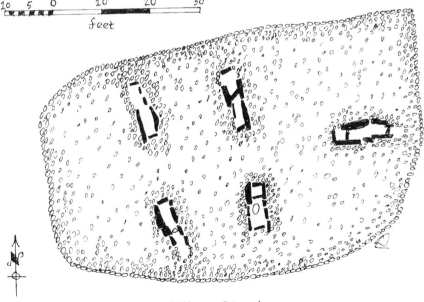

7.2 Nappers Cairn - plan

East of the Carsphairn to Dalmellington road are a number of other burial cairns, some of considerable significance, but outwith the area covered by this book. These include the King's Cairn, a chambered cairn by the side of the Water of Deugh, Lagwine Cairn, near to Carsphairn, and the cairn east of Lamford.

At Holm of Daltallochan farm there are scant remnants of the Cairn of Daltallochan. This is located about 600 yards north by west of the farmhouse, adjoining a small wood next to the main road. The *New Statistical Account*, written in 1844, notes that this was one of the largest cairns in the parish. The stones were removed for building dikes and sheepfolds, and in 1850, when the lower stones were removed, an incised stone was found. This had a Christian cross with a circle etched at the crossing point of the arms.

We return to the side of Loch Doon, and back into Ayrshire, when we reach the Cairnennock Cairn, on the summit of Little Eriff Hill, 1,072 feet above sea level. It is sometimes referred to as the White Cairn of Cairnennock. The cairn was robbed of loose stones in order to build field dikes, and it is said that human remains were discovered at that time. The stone mound we see today is around 65 feet in diameter, rising to around a couple of feet above the level of the moor. A modern cairn has been erected on top of it.

Within the Bellsbank Plantation can be found the Bubbly Cairn, a considerable burial cairn which has been robbed of the loose boulders in order to build the stone dikes hereabouts. At the time the stones were robbed, perhaps in the early nineteenth century, human bones were discovered within. The remains of the cairn, which do not protrude above the level of the surrounding ground, measure around 60 feet in diameter. In the same plantation is another cairn on the summit of Pennyarthur Rigg, 900 feet above sea level. Today this is little more than a shapeless pile of loose stone and earth. It measures forty feet in diameter by around four feet in height.

There are a few standing stones to be found around the edge of the Galloway hills. On the Moor of Drannandow, east of the Wood of Cree, are many antiquities. The most famous are The Thieves, two standing stones that are located on the low eminence known as Blair Hill, six hundred yards north-west of The Nappers Cottage. It is claimed that a number of freebooters, or gangrel thieves, were executed here by the Regent, Earl of Moray, during the reign of King David Bruce. One of these freebooters was Rory Gill.

The stones are located fourteen feet apart, one of them rising to 6 feet 8 inches and the other 7 feet 4 inches. A third stone, 3 feet 9 inches long, sticks up through the turf to the south-east.

At Drumfern, north-east of Drannandow, is an old stone circle. There are still five upright stones forming a ring and a further two lie on the ground. Some boulders have been positioned where an eighth stone no doubt stood. The largest stone is 2 feet 8 inches tall and a similar size across. The ring is about 85 feet in diameter.

Another standing stone that was at one time celebrated in local folklore was the Cairnwhapple Stone, which is now surrounded by forestry at the west end of Loch Bradan, near to the Lure Dam. The stone can be reached through the forest from the track leading to the dam from Tallaminnock. On modern detailed Ordnance Survey maps the stone is not shown as being of antiquity, indicating that current thought is that the stone is merely a natural erratic. However, two centuries ago, on the map within William Aiton's *General View of the Agriculture of the County of Ayr*, the map-maker has indicated 'Cairn Waple a Standing Stone.' Similarly, Andrew and Mostyn John Armstrong, who compiled a map of Ayrshire in 1775, noted 'Cairn Whaple a large Stone'.

At Holm of Daltallochan, near to Carsphairn, a stone circle is located north of the farm. This marked a ritual site, perhaps where the tribe gathered for worship or to perform other religious rites. There are thirteen stones in this setting, which is arranged on an oval plan. Overall, the dimensions of the ellipse are 80 feet by 60 feet. The stones are rather irregular in style, varying in size from two feet across to 7 feet 3 inches in length. Some authorities claim that there is little to indicate that this was, in fact, a stone circle, and that it is little more than a collection of large stones, perhaps natural or else dumped by the farmer when clearing the fields of boulders.

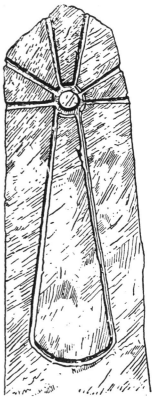

Perhaps of more credible antiquity is a standing stone, located a hundred yards to the east, adjoining a dike north of the farm. This whinstone block rises 3 feet 10 inches above the grass. In plan it is rectangular, 2 feet by 17 inches, its broad face looking to the stone circle.

Not too far away, on the farm of Garryhorn, is the Standing Stone Knowe, located on a peninsula between the Carsphairn Lane, Water of Deugh and the Garryhorn Burn. No standing stone is visible today, but the name probably indicates that something existed there at some point in the past.

7.3 Garryhorn Cross

Prehistoric man often erected huts for themselves and their immediate family to live in. Little remains of these, due to the fragile nature of the timber with which they were built, and the damp atmosphere and weather which has caused them to disintegrate to virtually nothing. Probably the only thing that remains is the outline of hut circles on the ground, sometimes indicated by a series of boulders and stones, which may have formed the base of the wattle and daub walls, or else by the stones that held the fire in its hearth. In some cases, these hut circles were built on sloping hillsides, and early man cut out part of the hillside, building up the soil at the opposite side to form level platforms.

Some indications of these ancient platforms and hut circles can be found in the periphery of the Galloway Highlands. The stones and burnt ashes have in some cases been excavated, revealing the whereabouts of the circles. In many cases, however, only the keen eye of the archaeologist can identify a seemingly random spread of boulders in the long grass and heather as the remains of such a hut.

Sir Walter Scott's friend and supplier of Galloway information, Joseph Train, made reference to some of these ancient hut circle sites in his notes. However, he has not identified the features as being the remnants of primitive homes, and has fallen into the tradition of the country folk of claiming that they were the site of 'Pict kilns'. He writes:

> On the upland farm of Craigencallie, they were, about twenty years ago [1820], very numerous; and on the farm of Risk, there were seven within the compass of an acre. On the Corse of Slaiks [Corse of Slakes – the high road between Creetown and Anwoth], in the parish of Kirkmabreck, they are still more numerous. They are generally about fifteen or sixteen feet in length, and about half that in breadth, forming an elliptic figure resembling a pear. The ridge or side wall is from two to three feet high at the broad end, and at the narrow end, it is nearly level with the surrounding earth at the entrance. The ridge seems to have been formed of earth; but, on removing the surface, it is found to be composed of very small stones, evidently the fragments of blocks broken by ignition.
>
> The kilns are invariably placed on the south side of the hills, on the margin of a brook, or where one has been, with the door or entrance facing the water. The only tradition in the country respecting them is, that they were erected by the Picts for the purpose of brewing ale from heather, which is perhaps not unfeasible, as these ancient inhabitants of the country are said to have been thoroughly acquainted with the chemical process of that operation.

Sir Walter Scott didn't agree with Train's theory – he claimed that they were the remains of kilns where lime was burned. The great bard wrote in a letter from his home at Abbotsford on 20 October 1816, 'The Picts' kiln seems to be a very curious relic of antiquity. Is it not possible it may have been employed for burning lime? We know that these ancient people were traditionally renowned for their skill in architecture. They certainly seem to have been farther advanced in the arts of life than their rival neighbours the Scots, which may have arisen from their inhabiting the lower and more fertile land.' George Chalmers, author of *Caledonia*, also disagreed with the theory, stating that the Picts didn't brew heather ale, but that the Cruithne, a later people who settled in Galloway from Ireland, were responsible.

In the Knockman Wood, north of Minnigaff, old maps make reference to a Pictish underground dwelling. These are better known today as 'souterrains', a term that describes a passageway walled with loose boulders, often covered with flat slabs or timbers and then by earth and turf. These 'earth houses' as they were also known, date from the 1st-2nd centuries AD, being built by the Iron Age people as grain stores. It is thought that they were surmounted by timber houses, and thus were really 'cellars' beneath these. One of them was excavated in 1922.

Whether or not the Knockman chamber was, in fact, a souterrain is debatable, for recent archaeologists have revisited the site and found nothing so elaborate as an underground building. Instead, what they decided the structure must have been was some form of corn-drying kiln.

A number of ancient stone crosses have been found around the Galloway Highlands. One of these was unearthed within a cairn near to Holm of Daltallochan farm, north-west of Carsphairn. The stone was fairly flat, and a Latin cross was incised upon it, the centre of the cross being occupied by a small circular boss, two inches in diameter, so that the three cross bars at the head of the stone look not unlike rays emanating from the sun. The cross measures 2 feet 9 inches in length, by 15 inches across at the arms. The cross was removed from the cairn and kept at Garryhorn for some time, but it was returned to Holm of Daltallochan farm, where it stands near to the farmhouse.

A cross was found near to Bardennoch, south-east of Carsphairn, and was relocated to Dalshangan Lodge, further south down the Glenkens. The cross was originally supposed to have been located near to Cumnock Knowes, just above the Water of Deugh. The stone, which is a thick squarish block of porphyry, stands around 2 feet in height. On one side is carved a cross in relief, the background being chiselled away. Each of the shorter transverse arms is around 5 inches in length, and at the junction is a small circular hole. This stone was later relocated to Broughton House, in Kirkcudbright.

On the slopes of Braidenoch Hill some stone cross slabs still can be seen, perhaps in their original location. These slabs are probably located near to an ancient pilgrim route that appears to have linked Ayrshire with Whithorn, and which crossed the higher ground down through the Glenkens. Another possibility is that they marked the route from Carsphairn to Vaude Abbey in Lincolnshire, for the lands of Carsphairn were in the thirteenth century granted by Thomas Colville of Dalmellington to that abbey.

An old tradition, but one which probably has little historical basis, claims that the cairns with the crosses

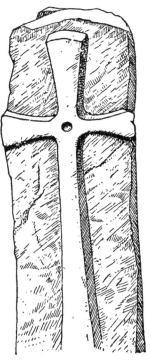

7.4 Dalshangan Cross

found around the Carsphairn area marked the spots where various chieftains were buried, after having fallen in battle here. Similarly, the dead from the opposing side were said to have been buried below the Cairnennock burial cairn, found 1,080 feet above sea level on the flat eminence to the west of Loch Muck, in Dalmellington parish.

A look at some detailed maps of the Galloway Highlands, either old or new, will reveal the existence of a number of 'rocking stones' marked on the maps. Rocking stones were revered in history as being places where huge boulders were perched precariously on top of other stones and should one give them a considerable push, then they would be able to move. Old accounts also use the term 'logan stone' to describe these boulders, a name that is perhaps derived from the local word *log*, meaning to rock, which in turn may be associated with the Danish *logre*, meaning to 'wag the tail'.

Old Ordnance Survey maps often indicate the rocking stones in Gothic script, implying that they were antiquities, perhaps erected by prehistoric man, but recent thought is that they are purely natural, and that the large boulders were left behind when the ice flows which remained in the Galloway Highlands for some time after they had melted around the rest of southern Scotland, eventually melted themselves. Within the confines of the Galloway Highlands, the area covered by this volume, there are six rocking stones that can be identified.

7.5 Rocking Stone, Loch Riecawr

One of the highest rocking stones, and one that the Ordnance map-makers allocated Gothic script to on their older maps, can be found on the Meikle Lump, a shoulder of Meikle Millyea. Located almost 1,900 feet above sea level, this stone is shown as being 'displaced' on the Popular One Inch Map of 1922, meaning that it had lost its equilibrium before that time. In fact, MacKerlie's *History of the Land and their Owners in Galloway*, written in 1877, notes that it was 'now displaced' at that time.

Most rocking stones do not, in fact, rock, and whether they ever did is very much doubtful. Meikle Millyea's stone was referred to in the *Statistical Account* of Kells parish in the 1790s. In it Rev John Gillespie noted that:

> There is a great natural curiosity to be seen on the side of one of these hills. The Rocking Stone, of 8 or 10 tons weight, so nicely balanced on 2 or 3 points or excrescences, that it moves from one to the other, by the pressure of a finger. Captain Grosse, last harvest, sent and took a drawing of it; and some antiquaries think it has been a Druidical place of worship. It should seem that the stone was formed by nature, just as we see it; and lying on a strata of moss, 2 or 3 inches deep, the rains have in time washed away this moss or earth, and left the stone resting on these points.

The *New Statistical Account* of the parish of Kells, in which Meikle Millyea lies, written in 1839, also makes reference to this stone, and notes that 'the rocking stone is no longer an object of attraction. About twenty years ago [i.e. about 1820], it was displaced from its pivot; whether from the effects of lightning or by some mischievous persons, is not known.' In a footnote, the writer states that 'since the above was written, we have been informed that there is another rocking stone, on the same range of hills with the one adverted to as destroyed, equally large and interesting'. What the two stones referred to in the *Account* are not specified, other than that they are in Kells parish. This may be the Rocking Stone that is shown on an old map of Galloway near to Upper Craigenbay, on the north side of Clatteringshaws Loch. The stone is shown just west of the steading, by the side of the Back Burn.

This stone was known as the Laggan Stone, a large granite block weighing approximately ten tons. It measures eight feet nine inches in length and is five feet one inch in circumference. It used to rock on its side.

Another rocking stone is found in the same parish at Darsalloch, on the ridge of Cairnsmore of Dee known as Benbrack. However, that and the one on Meikle Millyea would perhaps be said to exist on separate ranges of hills.

Yet another rocking stone appears on maps at the Garries, the name of the rock cliff above Craigencallie, west of Clatteringshaws Loch. This stone did not have the distinction of being marked in Gothic script on older maps, but it still appears on current two and a half inch maps.

The Rocking Stone located in the forest south west of Caldons, in Glen Trool, was shown on older maps in Gothic script. The stone is found near to the Black Burn, a small tributary of the Water of Trool, about half a mile south west of the martyrs' grave.

On the Moor of Barclye, north of Newton Stewart, can be found another Rocking Stone. Shown on older maps in Gothic font, this stone is located next to a stone dike that crosses the moor, half a mile to the east of the old Barclye farm.

At the side of the Glen of the Bar, just south of the Queen's Way (A 712), a rocking stone appears on old maps of the district. The 1922 Ordnance Survey Popular One Inch map shows it in Gothic script.

The final rocking stone is shown on the maps in the forest south west of Loch Riecawr. This huge boulder is perched on an even larger rock, but is hidden in the forest from the forest road that passes close by. Older maps don't indicate this stone in Gothic script, but it was shown on the map included within William Aiton's *General View of the Agriculture of the County of Ayr*, published in 1811.

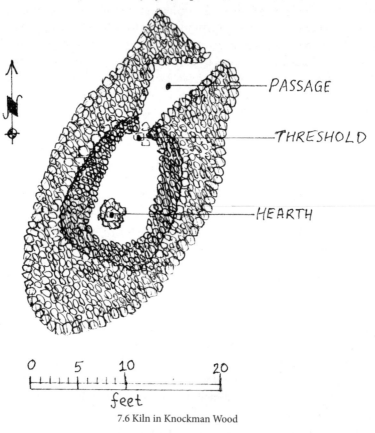

7.6 Kiln in Knockman Wood

Not shown on current maps, but having a tradition of being a rocking stone, was the Logan Stone, which was located on the slopes of the Big Hill of Glenmount, to the west of the north end of Loch Doon. This area has a few other antiquities on it, or at least places that have some sense of antiquity associated with them, such as the Mote Knowe, perhaps a small fort, and the White Laise, a prehistoric burial cairn. The Logan Stone was recorded by John Smith in his *Prehistoric Man in Ayrshire*, published in 1895. He noted that it was a granite boulder that was located on natural greywacke rock, indicating that it was left by the retreating ice flows. Measuring around 4 feet 3 inches long by 4 feet wide and around 3 feet in height, Smith claimed that the stone could easily be moved with the power of a single hand.

There are few hill forts within the Galloway Highlands area, any that do survive being located on the periphery. Two examples can be found on Doonans Hill, south of

Straiton. Not one of the main Galloway hills, The Doonans, as they are also known, are two rounded summits above the Water of Girvan valley. The taller of the two hills is 962 feet above sea level, the other fort being on a hillock to the north east of the higher hill, at around 925 feet above sea level. The larger fort measures 80 feet by 60 feet, with three ramparts. To the east is the probable entrance. The second fort is located 200 yards to the north-east on a lower eminence.

A great antiquity, the De'il's Dike, is something of an enigma. For many years it was believed to be a great rampart that spread across much of Galloway, starting at Loch Ryan and crossing through the high ground of Galloway and southern Ayrshire, before entering Dumfriesshire and terminating again at the Solway, near to Annan. At the latter end of the rampart it was known locally as the 'Britton Wall'. Various accounts of this dike, or rampart, give some indication as to its size, and the general assumption is that the earthwork was 8 feet wide at the base, rising several feet above the ground. The ridge was composed of stones and earth mixed together, resulting in it being severely eroded over the centuries. Most claim that on the northern, or outer, side of the rampart, that there was a ditch, or fosse. One old historian, Dr Hill Burton, gave an account of the dike in which he states that it was 24 feet broad, the rampart being 6 or 7 feet high and 10 or 12 feet thick.

The route of the De'il's (or Devil's) Dike across the Galloway Highlands can no longer be traced with any certainty on the ground. Old maps, however, indicate where it went. The west-most section within the area covered by this book was to be found on the Moor of Drannandow. This was around one and a quarter miles in length, and started at the Washing Burn, near the Cordorcan Burn, and crossed Blair Hill and Nappers before terminating again near to the Threave Cairn, east of Nappers Cottage. A second section, in line with this first stretch, started by the side of the Glenshalloch Burn and crossed the lower slopes of Benera, terminating again near to Pulbae Liggat at the Penkiln Burn.

The following segment of the dike is difficult to identify from the maps, as it is shown as being in line with the Old Edinburgh post road that linked Minnigaff with New Galloway. This part linked the Black Loch, near Craigdews, with the River Dee, passing by Lillie's Loch. This stretch would have been around three miles in length or slightly more.

The next stretch of the dike that has been identified on old maps is that in the lands of Upper Craigenbay, on the opposite side of Clatteringshaws Loch. From near to Upper Craigenbay the dike climbed to the west of Bennan before turning round to join the Lochspraig Burn, a stretch of just over one and a quarter miles. North-west of this point another length of dike, just short of one mile long, could be traced from Craigrine over Drumbuie Hill before stopping at the Garroch Burn, near to Clenrie.

To the north of Clenrie the remains of the dike were identified on the map extending from the Black Burn, over Rough Hill and down the side of a small stream to its confluence with the Crummy Burn. This small watercourse is named the Deil's Dike Burn on more detailed maps. Not shown on maps, the route must have crossed

Broadpark Knowe before appearing again near to the Largvey Burn. The maps show the route dropping through Drumgowan Wood to near the Knockreoch Bridge.

The remains of the dike were next noted to the north-east of Upper Knockreoch, crossing the moor west of Loch Goosie and curving round to the east, before dropping to Polmaddy village. Short stretches of it were noted to either side of the Polmaddy Burn, that on the east heading towards the old cottage of Barlae, now lost in the forest. The route of the dike then leaves the area covered by this book, heading across to Nithsdale, down that valley, then eastwards to Annandale and the Solway.

One of Galloway's antiquarians, Joseph Train (1779-1852), had a deep interest in the dike, and he spent much time trying to clear up the considerable doubt that existed over what the dike was for, or if it really existed in the first place. Train was born at Sorn in Ayrshire but moved to near Castle Douglas, from where he journeyed across Galloway carrying out research. He became a friend and correspondent of Sir Walter Scott, supplying the great novelist with numerous stories and factual details that he investigated from on-site visits that were subsequently incorporated in Scott's works. Train also wrote some books himself, including an account of the Buchanites, a strange religious sect that started in Ayrshire but which established itself at Crocketford in Kirkcudbrightshire, published in 1846.

Train wrote that his 'attention was for several years occasionally occupied in tracing the vast rampart called "The Deil's Dyke" through Galloway and Nithsdale.' This report was subsequently used by William Mackenzie in his *The History of Galloway*, published in 1841:

> From the opposite side of the Loch [Cree], it passes through the Camberwood, and appears again in Cardorkin, in the parish of Minnigaff; thence stretches along the hill of Blair, in the farm of Terregan, and across the moor of Dranandow, between the standing stones called 'the Thieves' and the Nappers. As it passes from Terregan to Dranandow, it runs through a bog, and is only perceptible by the heather growing long and close on the top of it; whereas on each side of it the soil only produces rushes and moss. Near the centre of the bog, I caused the peat to be cleared away close to the dyke, and thereby found the foundation to be several feet below the surface, which appeared to me an indication of its great antiquity.
>
> From the Craw Stane of Dranandow, the dyke passes along the south side of the hill of the Garlick, through the farm of Auchinleck, over the south side of Dregmorn, by the foot of Tonderghie. It crosses the burn of Palnure, and appears again on the south side of Talnotrie. It goes up Craignelder, in the farm of Corwar, passes to Craigencallie, and is very entire in the Garrary, Clanry, Duckieston, Largrave and Knockreach.

George Chalmers, compiler of the three-volume reference work, *Caledonia*, corresponded with Train, writing that, 'there are questions in history as difficult of solution as any of the sciences, such is the "Deil's Dyke". Considering all its circumstances it is extremely difficult to assign it age, its object, or its builders.'

The earliest account of the dike was actually made by Chalmers in his *Caledonia*, published in 1824. He noted that he was indebted for 'a particular account of the remains [to Train], who traced it, and examined the people, who have long resided, in the country, through which it passes.'

More modern thought has suggested that the Deil's Dyke as a linear earthwork does not exist, and that any earthen bank or stone work visible on the ground was in fact the remnant of ancient head-dikes, or march dikes, dating from pre-enclosure times. The dismantling of Train's theory was carried out by A. Graham, who revisited many of the sites indicated on the Ordnance Survey map and discovered that there was either nothing to be seen, or else that the structures were all different, indicating that they were not part of the same great monument. In conclusion he stated that 'the Deil's Dyke, as described by Train, does not, in fact, exist.' Any remains he put down to local functions.

Graham also came up with a theory as to how the idea of a Deil's Dyke came about. Older folk referred to a deil-dike, which he reckoned was an older version of boundary or march dike.

In 1978 the remains of an ancient hut circle or homestead were discovered in the shallow waters of Clatteringshaws Loch. The level of the water was twenty feet lower than usual, and some archaeologists were looking at the shores along the loch side to see if they could find anything of interest. In the bay of the loch where the Corsland Burn enters it, the furthest east part of the reservoir, they found the circular remains of a homestead that was reckoned to date from the Romano-British period. The homestead was excavated prior to the level of the waters rising once more, and within it pieces of charcoal were discovered lying on the cobbled yard. The charcoal was carbon dated and was found to date from around the first or second century A.D.

In addition to the circular stones marking the circumference of the homestead, the archaeologists also found the porch at the door, central hearth, and post holes within, which would have supported the roof. The archaeologists also discovered two coloured Roman glass ring fragments, some stone implements and fragments of burnt bone. Outside the homestead the remains of a stockyard were identified, as well as what was thought to have been a causeway. Near to the homestead Michael Ansell and Jonathan Condry also discovered a Mesolithic flint chipping floor. Among the small artefacts found were blades, cores and microliths.

The Forestry Commission were active with the excavations, and decided to erect a replica of what the hut-circle may have originally looked like near to Clatteringshaws visitor centre. A circular ring of dry-stone walling was constructed, around two feet in height and 25 feet in diameter. An opening was left for an entrance, and to either side of this two 'wings' of stone wall were erected. Lengths of timber were erected over the hut circle, forming a conical roof, covered with smaller timbers and heather thatch and turfs to hold it down.

The Romano-British Homestead, as it was called, became a popular attraction at the visitor centre, located by the side of the path from the centre heading towards the Bruce's Stone on Moss Raploch.

Around the periphery of the Galloway Highlands, in glens that today are seemingly remote and uninhabitable, at one time small communities existed. Known in some circles as 'ferme touns', from the Scots for farm town, these were little settlements of half a dozen or so dwellings, grouped together as though for comfort and protection. Many of these communities have become lost over the centuries, but one that survives in ruins and can readily be visited is Polmaddy.

7.7 Romano-British Homestead, Clatteringshaws

The main road from Dalmellington to Dalry passes by the small village of Dundeugh, itself a small community created to house workers employed by the Forestry Commission. At the Polmaddy Bridge a minor road strikes westwards, passing through the Forestry Commission depot and half a mile into the forest arrives at a small car park. From here a walk through the trees and across a footbridge brings one to Polmaddy, an ancient settlement.

The first ruin one reaches after crossing the bridge is the old inn of Polmaddy, located at that part of the village known as the Nether Ward. This was an important stopping off point on the ancient pack road that made its way through the Glenkens. Traces of this road can be found almost all of the way from Ayr to Dalry, though much of it has become lost over the centuries, becoming either overgrown or planted over with forestry. It was at one time an important pilgrim road, leading towards Whithorn, and it also acted as one of the main droving routes between Ayrshire and Galloway. The route crossed Bardennoch Hill from Carsphairn then gradually descended over Barlae Hill to the great loop of the Polmaddy Burn. At the far end of the meander, where the water level was low and the bottom of the riverbed was composed of shingle, a ford allowed travellers to cross the stream.

The inn was used by travellers on this route, and as well as being able to be put up for the night, travellers were also able to obtain food and drink there. Probably a simple single-storey building of random rubble walls, roofed over with thatch, to the traveller the warm peat fire and the welcome repast would make it a place of comfort. Just beyond the inn can be seen the remains of a circular structure, which was a corn kiln. Corn would have been grown in small fields where the soil was slightly better and when it was harvested the grain would be dried out in these small kilns.

Beyond the line of the old pack road is the rest of the clachan of Polmaddy. There appears to have been around ten or so different houses in the community, though numbers cannot be precisely determined. Some of the buildings that survive in ruins may have been byres, separated from the house, whereas in some cases both house and byre were attached.

Other corn kilns in addition to the one near to the inn existed, perhaps three in number, hinting that they may have been shared by the different farmers. Around the houses and byres were small fields, walled in by stone dikes, forming a random pattern across the low hillside.

One of the old buildings was in fact a mill. This was located at the head of the Polmaddy meander, almost midway between the two stretches of the burn. A dam crossed the burn upstream and a lade directed water down into a mill pond that occupied an area above the mill. Simple sluices could be opened to allow the water to run down towards the mill, the paddle wheel driving the stones which were used to grind the meal. The spent water passed along a second lade and fed back into the Polmaddy Burn.

Above and below the community were some areas of improved ground. This was land that could be ploughed with primitive machinery – perhaps a single bladed plough pulled either by oxen or horses. Below the village the lines of the lazybeds can still be made out on the ground. A second area of formerly ploughed ground is visible above the village, though this is by no means so large. The ground was not so good here, and around its edge are a number of cairns or piles of stones comprising of boulders and rocks lifted from the ground.

The village of Polmaddy was finally abandoned in the early part of the nineteenth century. Ordnance Survey engineers visited when they were compiling their first detailed maps of the district, and they noted at that time, the 1850s, that the community was 'in ruins'. It was perhaps one of the last of these ferme touns to be abandoned, there being traces of others across Galloway and the uplands of Ayrshire. It has also been speculated by Ian Donnachie and Innes MacLeod that the village was probably abandoned shortly after the Napoleonic wars, when agriculture was in a particularly poor state across Scotland.

Some excavations have unearthed mediaeval relics. Near to Starr some pottery dating from the fifteenth century was discovered, including over half of a green-glazed jug. On the opposite side of the loch, at Portmark, more fifteenth century pottery sherds were found.

In 1912 a strange hoard of ancient metal objects was discovered in a peat moss near to Talnotry, in the Palnure Glen. The wife of a cottar who lived at Talnotry was putting peat on the fire when she noticed a metal object fall from it. She thought this strange, as she couldn't understand from where it came, but on further investigation realised that it had been within the peat block itself. The wife then looked at other peats in her stack and discovered a number of other metal objects within them. The next day she and her husband went to the spot where the peats had been dug, and after some investigation discovered many more objects in the moss. The bits and pieces were located at the base of the peat, on the top of the glacial clay. When it was recovered, the hoard comprised of a pair of silver pins with flat circular heads pierced at one side for a chain to be worn between them. There were also a pair of oval loops of silver wire, which terminated in hooks, a plain finger-ring of gold and a globular head of a pin of bronze, decorated with filigree work, a belt tag of silver with a panel of niello-work representing some type of animal, and a lead weight with a brass top, ornamented in detail with an interlaced pattern. There was also a broken cross of thin bronze, three stone spindle-whorls, a circular piece of jet, and a rough, natural agate. A cake of something like beeswax was also found, as well as a few coins of Burgred, King of Mercia (AD 833-874), Northumbrian styeas, one French coin of about the period of Charlemagne and one Cufic coin.

8 Wars of Independence

One of the most popular viewpoints in the Galloway Highlands is that seen from a low rocky eminence above Loch Trool. From that spot one gazes over the loch, lying below and curving around the hillside, to the steep hillside of Mulldonoch beyond. At the foot of this hill is the spot where Robert the Bruce claimed his famous victory over the English in 1307.

The viewpoint from where many gazed in wonder and admiration at the site of Bruce's victory was later to be selected as an ideal spot on which to raise a memorial to the triumph. A massive granite boulder was perched on top of a low cairn comprising of large granite stones. One face of the boulder was polished to allow an inscription to be chiselled into the hard granite:

IN LOYAL REMEMBRANCE
OF
ROBERT THE BRUCE
KING OF SCOTS
WHOSE VICTORY IN THIS
GLEN OVER AN ENGLISH
FORCE IN MARCH 1307
OPENED THE CAMPAIGN OF
INDEPENDENCE WHICH HE
BROUGHT TO A DECISIVE
CLOSE AT BANNOCKBURN
ON 24TH JUNE 1314.

On the back of the boulder the simple inscription, 'Unveiled 5th June 1929', is carved on the rock. On that Wednesday afternoon, which was the 600th anniversary of the death of Robert the Bruce, three hundred spectators came to the rocky knoll to witness the event. Professor (later Sir) Robert Rait CBE LLD (1874–1936), Historiographer Royal for Scotland, inaugurated the memorial. He was introduced by Sir Herbert Maxwell, and the ceremony was conducted by Rev Andrew Hamilton of Bargrennan. Other notables who took part were the Earl of Galloway and Colonel MacKie of Bargally. Lady Jean Dalrymple drew the cords which released the union flag that covered the stone.

The Battle of Glentrool, as it became known, took place sometime around March or April 1307. On that day Bruce and his army of guerrilla fighters had retreated to the head of the glen, where they were unsure what to do next. The Bruce looked at the landscape around him, wild rugged hills with deep chasms, and he reckoned that this could play to his advantage. Near to the head of the loch he spotted a location where the pathway through the glen had to cross a steep section of the hillside. The path surface climbed to around twenty feet above the level of the loch, and above it rose steep cliffs. Bruce thought that this was the very place where he could take on the might of the enemy and be in with a chance of winning.

8.1 Bruce's Stone, Glen Trool

Gathering his men, they headed across to the eastern end of the loch, and began to scale the lower slopes of the White Bennan, a rugged outcrop on the northern slopes of Mulldonoch. During the night, so that they could not be seen, the Scots gathered hundreds of huge boulders and rocks, some of which were loosened from the cliffs that tumble into the loch at this point.

The English soldiers under the command of Sir Aymer de Valence, Earl of Pembroke, had been searching much of Galloway for the Bruce. He had been advised, whilst at Carlisle, that Bruce was in the Galloway Highlands, and he set off with a large army in pursuit. In order to keep their cover as low as possible, they rode across country at night, camping during the day in various spots where they could hide an army. To reduce the size of the force, the English decided to leave their horses at Borgan, near where the Water of Minnoch joins the River Cree, and march into the glen. As they neared Glen Trool, the Bruce was still unaware of their presence. Sir Aymer sent an old woman ahead to try to elicit some information as to the exact spot where the Bruce and his men were in hiding. The woman was poorly dressed, and found it difficult to conceal her true purpose in visiting Bruce. At length, she changed allegiance, and advised Bruce that Aymer and Clifford were in pursuit, and in fact were not far away.

On the following morning some of the Scots forces made their whereabouts known to the English. A few had positioned themselves near to Glenhead, perhaps on the Gairy of Glenhead, as if they planned to attack the English soldiers on the more level land below the cliffs at the head of the loch. The English spotted the Scots, and made their way at haste alongside the Steps of Trool and towards the loch head. They had a group of cavalry, and these were followed by the heavy armed billmen. The flanks of the army were protected by a number of archers. At the Steps, the pathway only allowed an army to pass in single file, and to their left was a sheer drop into the loch.

However, the bulk of the Scots were in hiding on the hillside above, awaiting the English passing below them. The Bruce could see from Glenhead his men on the hillside and, at the requisite time, sent a signal that the situation was perfect. Three blasts from his horn echoed around the glen. The spot where he stood to issue the warning has been known as the King's Stone ever since. At the sound of the horn, Bruce's men hurled the boulders down the hillside. Hundreds, if not thousands, of great rugged rocks bounded uncontrollably from the White Bennan down towards the lochside. The English were in the way of the stones as they fell, and the massive granite rocks were every bit as effective as repeated cannon fire in killing many of the soldiers.

Those soldiers who were not mown down by the stones were attacked by the Scots who lunged down the hillside at them. Drawing out dirks and swords, many more were killed, before at length the Scots withdrew into the mountain fastness of the hills. The English soldiers decided to flee, and many of them who survived ran as far as the River Cree, five miles or more away.

Some headed eastwards, onto the flat ground at the head of the loch, but Bruce's men fell on them and they were slaughtered. All those who were killed in battle were carried to the soft ground at the top of Loch Trool where they were interred. This place has been known as the Soldiers' or Englishman's Holm ever since. Some old books also refer to it as the 'kirkyard meadow', the place where the slain were interred. Nearby is a declivity that is known as the King's Cave. The thin pathway that formed the Steps of Trool was said to have been washed away in a heavy rainstorm sometime in the nineteenth century.

* * *

Robert the Bruce began his campaign in Galloway soon after he had slain John Comyn in Greyfriars' Church in Dumfries. This had taken place on Thursday 10 February 1306. The murder wasn't good for Bruce's cause, so he had to act quickly, and he set about claiming the castles of Galloway where the English forces were based. One of these was Loch Doon, which was taken in order to secure the lands of Galloway. Soon after, on 25 March 1306, he was crowned as king of Scotland at Scone. Edward of

England was quick to react, sending Sir Aymer de Valence to retake the country and kill the Bruce if possible.

At Methven, Bruce was defeated in battle, and he had to go into hiding. Where he went is uncertain, but many historians agree that he probably returned to the fastnesses of Galloway and Carrick, a wild country where he was known and which he knew well. The winter of 1306-7 may have been spent in this part of the country, perhaps some of the time escaping to Ireland to allow things to cool slightly.

After Methven, Bruce and his supporters had to scatter across the country, searching for hideouts where they could avoid the attacking English. Sir Christopher Seton headed for the wilds of Carrick and came to Loch Doon Castle, which was the property of Bruce as Lord of Carrick. The castle was at that time held by the hereditary governor, Sir Gilbert de Carrick.

8.2 Loch Doon Castle from the north, on its original site

Seton was pursued by the English forces, which quickly discovered that he was in hiding within the fastness. They planned to storm the building, and made plans for the attack. Using boats, they made their way across the waters of the loch and surrounded the castle. Within, Seton was hoping that they could defend the building, but Sir Gilbert de Carrick was thinking differently. Carrick was of the opinion that the cause of Bruce was now dead, so he decided to take the side of the English. He offered them entry to the castle, and he arranged for Seton to be held and handed over as a prisoner.

With the castle capitulating, the English were able to take it into their hands without any bloodshed. Seton was locked in fetters and taken by the English to Dumfries, where he was held for a time in Dumfries Castle. Along with two others, he was sentenced to death as a traitor. They were led from the castle to the Gallows Hill, located north-east of the burgh, where they were strung up. Once their bodies were lifeless, their heads were cut off, and these were subsequently displayed on pikes. In later years, when the Bruce had gained the Scottish crown, Christiana Bruce, Seton's widow, decided to erect a chapel on the site of her husband's execution. The charter granting the right to build the chapel was dated 31 November 1323, and the building was endowed by none other than the king himself.

Sir Gilbert de Carrick was luckier. Having lost the castle, the Bruce issued 'Letters of Rancour' against him, but once the Bruce had succeeded in securing Scotland's independence he granted a letter of remission to Carrick, forgiving him for handing over the castle to the English. The remission continued by restoring Carrick to the government of the castle, along with the lands that fell under its jurisdiction.

It was perhaps at this time an attempt at trying to capture the Bruce by Sir Aymer took place in the Galloway Highlands. On that occasion Sir Aymer was making his way to the mountains from Carrick. He had 22 men at arms with him, as well as 800 highlanders. The Bruce was aware of their approach, and he gazed at the marching army from some height near to Loch Enoch. From another side John of Lorne made an approach and the Bruce was forced to retreat. He had only three hundred men with him, insufficient to stand and fight, so to improve their chance of escape, Bruce divided them into three groups, each of which was to take a different exit from the mountains.

John of Lorne had an ace up his sleeve, however. Despite Bruce dividing his men to confuse the enemy as to which group he was with, John of Lorne had a large bloodhound which had previously belonged to Bruce, and which was able to sniff him out. When it was released at the spot where Bruce's army had last been together, the hound yelped and set off in the direction of one of the groups. John of Lorne and his force set off in pursuit, the bloodhound leading the way.

It is thought that Bruce made his way between Craignaw and Dungeon Hill and dropped down into the Silver Flow. The soldiers under Lorne followed, and Bruce noted this. At the side of the flow Bruce told his men to disperse even further, leaving only himself and one attendant, his foster-brother.

However, the scent was still too strong and the bloodhound knew exactly which way Bruce had escaped. Closing in, John of Lorne sent forward five burly highlanders and they were soon able to overtake the king and attack. Three of them fought with Bruce, the other two attacking his attendant. One of the men was slain by the Bruce, causing the other two to recoil for a time. In the interval Bruce was able to kill one of the men who was fighting his foster-brother. The two highlanders had regained their composure and attacked again, but the Bruce was the better swordsman and the pair were slain, as was the man fighting with the attendant.

The fight had exhausted Bruce and his attendant, and they reckoned that they could fight no more. John of Lorne and his men kept on approaching, so Bruce and his aide made an escape as quick as they could. Barbour's *Bruce* notes that:

> The King toward the wod is gane,
> Wery, for-swat, and will of wayn.
> In-till the wod soyn enterit he,
> And held doun toward a vale.

151

> Quhar throu the wod a wattir ran
> Thiddir in gret hy went he than,
> And begauth to rest in hym thair,
> And said he mycht no forthimar.

The 'wattir' was perhaps the Cooran Lane, a deep and slow watercourse that runs alongside the Silver Flow and south towards the River Dee. By walking along the watercourse for some distance the dog was unable to follow their scent. Satisfied that the soldiers were no longer following them, the two men climbed from the water and hid in a wood where they were able to rest.

Some other accounts of the story relate that whilst the king was resting the attendant was able to make his way back upstream and as the soldiers and bloodhound passed his hiding place he was able to kill the dog.

Bruce and his fellow man continued on their way from the hills, trying to find somewhere where they could obtain some food. At one point they met three men who were carrying a wether, or castrated ram. The men also had a number of weapons, making Bruce wary of them. However, as he approached the men saluted. Bruce asked them where they were going, only to be told that they were in the district looking for the king, for they intend to join him in his mission. Bruce replied that if they were willing to follow him, then he would lead them to the king.

The men marched across the moss to a ruinous cottage. It was decided that they should all eat, and so two fires were lit, one at each end of the building. The sheep was divided, and parts of it were cooked on the fire. When they had eaten Bruce expressed a desire to sleep. He told his attendant to stay awake and watch, for they had suspicions that the three men were none other than supporters of the English, out to catch the king in order to claim the reward. As Bruce slept, the attendant became ever drowsier, and soon he too was dead to the world.

The three men, once they realised that the men were sleeping, drew their swords in readiness to kill them. The sound of metal leaving its sheath awoke the king, and he jumped up instantly. Kicking his attendant, they faced the three men, and using all their energy started to fight. The attendant was not so lucky this time, for he was slain with a sword, but the king managed to kill them all, and make his escape.

Left alone, Bruce continued on his way, passing alongside the Black Water of Dee and arrived at Craigencallie, where it had been planned that his men would reassemble. A spot near to the present house is known as Bruce's Wa's, or walls.

An old tradition connects Craigencallie House, which stands at the foot of the steep rocky sides of Cairngarroch, west of Clatteringshaws Loch, with Robert the Bruce. The name Craigencallie is reckoned to derive from the Gaelic *Creag an Cailleach*, sometimes rendered in the old Scots as 'Craig an Cailzie', which means 'rock of the old woman or hag', sometimes referred to as a witch. It is said that the old widow who lived there had three strong sons, and the Bruce wished them to join him in his campaign against the English.

The story relates how the Bruce headed for the fastnesses of the high mountains. He came upon Craigencallie, totally exhausted, and called at the house. He asked the occupier, an old woman, for lodgings, and he was able to spend the night there. The Bruce did not let on who he was, but on the following morning the old woman noticed some items of jewellery that he had were rather fine. Deducing who he was, she asked him if he was indeed her 'Leidge Lord?'

Bruce replied, confirming to her that he was indeed the king, and he asked if she was able to give him something to eat. The lady was sorry to state that all she could offer was some milk and oatmeal, but that she was willing to give this to him. Hungry, the king accepted her hospitality.

Whilst he ate, Bruce asked the woman some questions. 'Have you any sons that could join me on my campaigns?' The woman replied that she had indeed three strong sons, and that they were out on the hill at the time. The sons had been fathered by three different husbands, all of whom had died. Soon the lads returned to Craigencallie, expecting their breakfast, whereupon the old woman explained to them who their visitor was.

The king asked them if they were willing to engage in his service, to which they replied, 'Yes.' He then asked them what weapons they might have, to which they replied that they had nothing but bows and arrows. After breakfast, Bruce asked them to demonstrate their prowess in the use of their bows. The eldest son, named MacKie, placed an arrow on his bow and pulled at the string. High above Craigencallie, on the slopes of Cairngarroch, was the Pin Stone, whereon rested a group of ravens. Soon the arrow was piercing through the sky, and the king was delighted to note that it was able to kill two ravens at once, the arrow passing through both of their necks. He told MacKie, 'I would not wish that you aimed at me!'

The second son, named Murdoch, drew an arrow from his quiver and loaded the bow. His arrow was soon flying through the air and he was able to shoot one of the ravens that had flown from the Pin Stone when the rest of the ravens had been shot. The arrow pierced the body of the raven in the sky and it plummeted to the ground.

The third son, who bore the name MacLurg, also drew an arrow and placed it in his bow. Taking aim, he shot the arrow into the sky, aiming at some ravens that were still flying around. The arrow was close to its target, but unfortunately missed the bird.

The Bruce, however, was impressed with the marksmanship of the three brothers, even MacLurg, and he welcomed them to join him in his campaigns.

Bruce's three hundred men had managed to regroup with him at this time, and they were aware of the approaching English soldiers to the east. The English camped on Moss Raploch, east of the Black Water of Dee. Wondering how he was going to face such a superior force, one of Bruce's men came up with an idea.

The Scots gathered together all the horses from the vicinity that they could, as well as goats from the cottages and hillsides. These animals were all corralled together in a tight enclosure, the soldiers keeping them pushed together. The mix of horses and goats, and their density of numbers, caused them all to bray and bleat, making such a loud noise that it could be heard for miles around. The noise and sight of the animals from a distance made the English think that there was a great army gathered there, so they decided to remain in their camp all night, not daring to approach them.

Early next morning, Robert the Bruce and his small army left their camp near to Craigencallie and made their way along the southern side of the Black Water of Dee. They passed the Half Way Stone, marking the mid-point on their march into battle. Below Craignell, on the flat moor by the side of the river, the two sides met, the Bruce attacking with such a force that the English were taken by surprise. Many of them turned around and fled, but the Bruce's men followed in pursuit and were able to kill a number of soldiers.

8.3 Bruce's Stone, Moss Raploch

The battle is said to have occurred sometime in 1307-8, but exactly when is not known. Today, the site of the battle has been partially obscured by the waters of Clatteringshaws Loch, the large reservoir formed when the Black Water was dammed, but the large boulder known as the King's Stone, or Bruce's Stone, still sits on its original position, now surrounded by forestry.

The detail of the battle of Moss Raploch is not known, other than the Bruce was again victorious. After the battle he is said to have rested by the stone and surveyed the scene before him, reflecting on the victory, whilst his men picked spoils from the slain foe. Not all of the weapons and goods appear to have been taken, for some-time in the mid nineteenth century it is said that a number of broken weapons were unearthed from the peat.

The three Craigencallie sons continued with the Bruce in his battles against the English, eventually succeeding with the victory at Bannockburn in 1314. Robert the Bruce made numerous grants of land to those who had helped him in his campaigns, and the three sons from Craigencallie are said to have been awarded grounds in the area for their help. He asked them what they would like, and they requested the thirty-pound lands of the Hassock and Cumloden. According to tradition, the Murdochs were given the lands of Cumloden, with their castle built at Old Risk.

The MacKies obtained the lands of Larg, the remains of their old tower being located a few hundred yards north of the present Larg farm, east of Newton Stewart.

The MacLurgs were presented with the lands of Machermore, with Machermore Castle standing by the side of the Cree. The farm of Parkmaclurg, located by the side of the tidal River Cree, still bears the family name. All of these lands had formerly formed one large estate that was located between the Palnure Burn and the Penkiln Burn, stretching up towards Loch Dee and the site of the Battle of Moss Raploch.

The three families established by the sons remained in ownership of their estates for some time, but eventually they passed into other hands. The Murdochs remained in possession the longest, only selling their property sometime after the 1745 rebellion when they became bankrupt. Some accounts claim that they were tricked out of their lands by their neighbours, the Stewarts of Garlies. The MacKies were at Larg until the last heiress, Margaret MacKie, married Heron of Heron. The MacLurgs lost their property in the sixteenth century.

The family coats of arms of the three Bruce warriors commemorate their part in the battle for independence. The coat of arms of the MacKies of Larg depict 'argent, two ravens proper with a single arrow through their heads'. The Murdochs of Cumloden have a silver field on which is a fess chequy, azure and argent, or blue and silver. Over this are two ravens, shot through the neck by a single arrow. The Murdoch motto is *Omine Secundo*, meaning 'under favourable auspices'. The MacLurg arms are two ravens pierced through the neck by a single arrow. In the base of the shield is a crescent which indicates a difference. The MacLurg motto is *Omnia pro bono*.

If one visits the old kirkyard of Minnigaff, which is well worth doing in order to see the ruins of the old kirk and the ancient stones located therein, one can see a headstone in memory of a later member of the MacLurg, or MacClurg, family. The stone has a rather fine carving of the family arms upon it, but it has the strange distinction, as far as heraldry is concerned, of showing the two ravens facing to the right, as opposed to the left, as would be more common in heraldry. It has been speculated that the back-to-front arms are a result of the commissioner giving the mason a seal to copy, which of course would give an opposite image once it had been pressed into the wax.

Another tradition associating Bruce with the Galloway Highlands tells how at one time he was in hiding in the fastness. The English soldiers were in the area, trying to track him down, but the Bruce was in disguise, and would have been hard to find. However, the English appear to have been hard on his heels, and he arrived at Polmaddy Mill, which was located at Polmaddy village, near to Dundeugh. The miller's wife recognised the king, and agreed to hide him within the mill. She told him to hide among some sacks of corn that were located behind the 'happer'. The soldiers arrived at the mill, but during their search did not uncover Bruce. Once the soldiers had gone, the Bruce asked the miller's wife what he could do for her. She told him that once he had regained control of the kingdom, if he could grant her the lands of Polmaddy she would be more than happy. Bruce did, of course, go on to regain the crown of Scotland, and he never forgot his promise. Thus, the miller's wife was given the lands she had requested, which remained in her family for many years. To commemorate the grant of land, the miller's wife gathered together all her sons and cousins and they made their way to the summit of the mountain at the western end of their property and there they raised a large stone cairn to commemorate the title. This cairn became known as the Carlin's Cairn, carlin being the old Scots word for an old woman, sometimes used to describe a witch. The cairn was massive, and still to this day marks the summit of the 2,623 feet mountain. The mountain has also taken the name Carlin's Cairn, after the stone mound, though what its original name had been prior to the cairn being erected has long-since been forgotten.

8.4 Murdoch of Cumloden arms

In Barbour's *Bruce*, the story is related of how he came to a goodwife and she took him in. Once she had revealed her love for the king, he revealed himself to her, and she sent her two sons to serve under him:

The king went furth way and angri
Menand his man full tenderly
And held his way all him allane,
And rycht towart the hous is gan
Quhar he set tryst to meit his men.
It wes weill inwyth nycht be then,
He come sone in the hous and fand
The houswyff on the benk sittand
That askit him quhat he was
And quhen he come and quethir he gais.
'A travailland man, dame,' said he,
'That travaillys throu the contre.'
Scho said, 'All that travailland er
For ane his sak ar welcum her.'
The king said, 'Gud dame, quhat is he
That gerris you haiff sik specialte
To men that travaillis?' 'Schyr, perfay,'
Quod the gud-wyff, 'I sall you say,
The King Robert the Bruys is he,
That is rycht lord of this countre.
His fayis now haldis him in thrang,
Bot I think to se or ocht lang
Him lord and king our all the land
That na fayis sall him withstand.'
'Dame, luffis thou him sa weil,' said he.
'Ya, schyr,' said scho, 'sa God me se.'
'Dame,' said he, 'hym her the by,
Fork Ik am he, I say the soithly,
Yha certis, dame.' 'And quhar ar gane
Your men quhen ye ar thus allane?'
'At this tyme, dame, Ik haiff no ma.'
Scho said, 'it may na wys be swa.
Ik haiff twa sonnys wycht and hardy,
Thai sall becum you men in hy.'

Bruce's guerrilla campaign caused considerable trouble to the English who held the countryside. To feed his men, and to prevent the property from falling into English hands, he arranged plundering and destroying raids into the more fertile periphery of the area, such as Dundrennan, where he burnt the granges and destroyed the stores. King Edward had to send additional stores across the Solway Firth to support his men as a result. The land was being 'wasted, destroyed and denuded', according to the Close Rolls of the time, and there was an export ban on crops or cattle being sold from Galloway's ports, the food being needed back in the area.

Old traditions claim that the flat ground below Kirroughtree House Hotel was the scene of a battle in 1308 between the Scots under Robert the Bruce's brother, Edward Bruce, and the English under Sir Dougal MacDowell. It is claimed that 1,400 English soldiers were slain that day, including MacDowell, and that they were buried in mounds, or cairns, that can still be seen today. Thus the cairns that are spread around to the east of Creebridge are said to mark the graves of the dead – High and Low Lessons cairns that lie by the side of New Galloway Road, a third further west near to Holmpark, and three more in the fields near Lessons Park.

8.5 King's Stone, Meaul

There are a few places in the Galloway Highlands area that have the name 'King' associated with them. One of these is the King's Well, located high on Meaul hill. Not too far from the summit, on the eastern slopes, can be found the well, little more than a small spring issuing from the hillside. Adjoining it, however, are three large boulders, each of which is shaped like a chair, with a seat and curved back. The central, larger one, is known as the King's Stone. In front of the chairs is a flat 'table' stone, measuring around three feet by two feet.

On the western side of the highlands, near to Kirriemore farm, is a spot on the Water of Minnoch known as the King's Ford. This may or may not be associated with the Bruce. The ford leads towards the ancient burial cairn known as the King's Cairn, so perhaps is named after some early chieftain. Nevertheless, Andrew McCormick claims the ford is associated with the Bruce and that he was able to throw the hounds that were pursuing him at one time off the scent.

8.6 Seal of King Robert the Bruce

At Forrest Lodge, in the glen of the Polharrow Burn, is a spot known as the King's Holm. This was an area of better quality farmland adjoining the Polharrow Burn, but it is now afforested.

Robert the Bruce was not the only soldier who fought his independence campaign in the hills of Galloway. His predecessor in the struggle, Sir William Wallace, also came here, using the fastness as a hideout at times, and waging his campaign against the English foe.

By the side of the River Cree, just one mile or so from Minnigaff, is an earthwork known as Wallace's Camp. This is locally associated with Sir William Wallace, and its connection is somewhat affirmed by reading Blind Harry's *Wallace*, where he states:

> Now where the Cree rolls down its rapid tide,
> And sees the herds adorn his wealthy side,
> A tow'ring rock uprears its bending brow
> And throws its frowning terror down below;
> Deep in the earth is fix'd its ample bed,
> And mirky night involves its airy head.
> There elder and tough oaks conspire with art,
> To raise on high the rock, a steep fort;
> Where a great gate its brazen arms oppos'd
> And from the visitor's rage, defends th' enclos'd
> Safe in their planky tower, they shelter'd lie,
> And from the oaky wall, the Scottish power defy.
> Wallace behind, and eager to obtain
> The airy fort, he swell'd in ev'ry vein;

And when the night o'erspread the silent ground,
And on black wings dark vapours swim around,
Eager he bids the weary soldiers rise,
And with slow heavings labour up the skies.
Himself and Kierly led the airy sight,
Strain up the steep, and toil with all their might.
The sentinel lay sleeping at the gate,
Doom'd ne'er to wake, unconscious of his fate

Wallace is said to have camped here overnight on his way to Cruggleton Castle.

9 Loch Doon and Other Castles

On the west banks of Loch Doon stand the ruins of a rather strange castle. The road seems to circle the walls, which are built on a low hill, and the visitor has to walk to the far side of the building, on the front away from the loch, to find the entrance. The castle has not always stood here, for it was originally situated on an islet in the middle of the loch until the winter of 1935-6, when it was relocated when the level of the loch was raised by around twenty feet in order to store water for the Galloway hydro-electric power scheme. These plans included the removal of Loch Doon Castle from its island to a new spot on the western shore of the loch, where the castle would be saved and the public would be able to access the ruins readily.

The remains comprise of a wall of enceinte, almost circular in plan, though the walls are angular. There are eleven faces around the courtyard, all irregular in length, being built to follow the shape of the castle island and thus enclosing the largest amount of land possible. The longest wall, the southern, is 59 feet in length, the shortest, the northern, and that in which the gateway is located, is only twenty feet long. The walls vary from nine to seven feet in thickness, and the overall diameter of the castle is about 91 feet from east to west, by about eighty feet north to south.

The masonry in the castle's outer walls is particularly fine. The blocks of stone are regularly shaped, precisely carved to fit together, and dressed smoothly. On seeing the quality of the ashlar work one appreciates just how much effort has gone into building the fortress, especially when one remembers that the castle was originally on its little islet, and that the stones no doubt had to be ferried across the loch to the place where they were built together. The upper masonry is not so well cut, only the corner stones being dressed as smoothly as the lower courses. Around the outside of the castle, the base of the wall is splayed, indicative of a very early age.

The quality of the masonry and the difficulty of getting the large blocks of stone onto the island is something that has been wondered at for centuries. For example, on Armstrong's *Map of Ayrshire*, published in 1775, the map-maker has written, 'This Castle is built on a barren Rock of Island & all of Free Stone, some of them 8 or 10 feet long, a stupendious Fabrick considering the situation.'

According to tradition, the stone used to build the castle came from a quarry located ten or twelve miles down the Doon valley from the castle site, the grey freestone boulders being hauled here by oxen and then transported across the loch in boats. The location of this quarry is no longer known, but it must have been in the vicinity of Dunaskin, between Dalmellington and Patna. There, where the Dunaskin Burn drops from its moorland source, it passes through a deep glen, the rocks of which could have been readily quarried.

The style and quality of the masonry work at Loch Doon has led the great authorities on Scottish castles, David MacGibbon and Thomas Ross, to conclude that it was likely that English masons were responsible for building the castle. They compare the style of stonework with the castles of Bothwell, Lochindorb and Kildrummy, and thus date the castle to before the Bruce's time.

9.1 Loch Doon Castle from west

Externally the castle has only two entrances – the main gateway on the north, which is formed of an Early English pointed archway, and the postern to the east. The main entrance is around nine feet wide and within the arch is a slit in which the portcullis was located. This must have had a portcullis chamber above the gateway, but no relic of this survives. An old tale relates that the portcullis was lying in the waters just off Castle Island, but it could not be saved. There is a story that claims an attempt was made to lift the iron gate on one occasion when the loch was frozen over with thick ice. A hole was broken over the portcullis site, and ropes with hooks were lowered down into the water, fishing for the yett. The iron bars were grappled by the hooks, but when an attempt was made to lift it, the weight of the gate was too much for the ice, and when it began to crack all attempts at rescuing it were abandoned. The tale is probably apocryphal, for no search thereafter could ever locate the gate, and what happened to it is unknown. The Marquis of Ailsa even employed a diver from Ayr harbour to search around the castle island, but he didn't find it, or any other antiquity.

Behind the portcullis the castle at one time had an inner gate which, when it was closed, could be secured by sliding massive timber bars across the entrance. These bars were located in long square holes set into the adjoining walls. The inner archway of the gate is rounded. The level of the gateway is considerably lower than the courtyard of the castle, and it is reckoned that this was to allow small boats to be rowed through the gate and into the safety of the walls.

The postern gateway is much smaller, being only 2 feet 8 inches in width, again comprising of a pointed arch, and within are slots for barring the gate. The level of this gateway is higher than the main entrance, and the smaller entrance may have been used to board larger vessels outside. Another external feature, the purpose for which is no longer known, are two projecting corbels, located around twelve or fifteen feet above the ground level. These are located slightly off-centre on the southern wall, and may have been replicated along the full length of the castle, perhaps carrying a balcony.

In the upper reaches of the castle walls were two windows, but these were not kept when the castle was rebuilt, being from the later reworking of the building. They were located about eighteen feet above ground level, one on the south-east and the other on the south-west corners of the wall of enceinte. Within the ingoing of the south-eastern window a narrow stairway formerly ascended in the thickness of the exterior walls of the castle, no doubt originally giving access to some form of wall-walk that circled the fortress, and also giving access to the portcullis chamber.

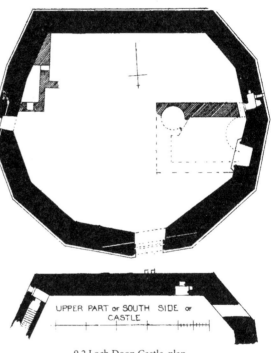

9.2 Loch Doon Castle, plan

Prior to moving the castle stone by stone from the islet to the side of the loch, the fortress was much larger. A look at old pictures and sketches that depict the castle on its original position indicate a substantial tower. This was not as old as the remaining walls, and as it was felt that it would detract from the original thirteenth century remains, it was decided to leave this tower when rebuilding the castle. This keep was reckoned to date from the sixteenth century and stood around four storeys in height. It may have remained in occupation up until the early seventeenth century.

When the water level of Loch Doon is low, the castle island appears from beneath the surface. If you are able to get onto the Castle Island, you may be surprised by just how much of the castle remains in situ, there being a skeleton of the wall of enceinte remaining. The remains of the square tower are also apparent, large slabs of fallen masonry lying at angles on the island. When the castle was being rebuilt on the western shores, only the quality ashlar of much of the building was removed, leaving the rubble cores in the walls behind, thus giving us two castle ruins.

At some period in history, the original castle may have been destroyed, so a later keeper had the new tower erected, but this was not as grand as the original keep. The tower measured 35 feet by 22 feet, and when MacGibbon and Ross visited in the late nineteenth century, the tower walls still rose to a height of around forty feet. In the south-east corner of the tower, built partially within the thickness of the wall, but projecting within the chamber of the tower, was a circular turnpike stairway. According to Robert Burns, who seems to have visited Loch Doon Castle at some point, or at least he gained some detailed information on the castle, this stairway had seventy steps still surviving in the late eighteenth century. He writes, 'Till a recent period, a large portion of this remote insular fortress was entire, and it contained a magnificent staircase of seventy steps. Its dilapidation is chiefly attributable to the bad taste of a late proprietor, who used its stones for the purpose of building a shooting-lodge – a lodge, after all, found too cold to be inhabited.'

That the tower was not the original keep of the castle is evident by the strange way it abuts the exterior wall. The northern wall of the tower came against the wall of enceinte against the large fireplace that survives in the western wall, partially blocking one side of it. The tower was also built of random rubble, erected with loose stones that may have been from the older keep that was destroyed.

In the nineteenth century there appears to have been an attempt at demolishing the castle's southern wall. Someone seems to have removed a number of courses of masonry from the northern walls of the castle, leaving the stones above hanging precariously. Some folk who were desirous of preserving the ruins had built stone props to support the upper walls.

9.3 Loch Doon Castle – entrance from interior

David MacGibbon's sketch of the castle shows the remains of the tower's internal features. From this, and what he writes, we can find that the building was at least four storeys tall, the ground floor, or cellars, being vaulted. On the first and second floors the stair tower gave access to the rooms by means of a small pointed arch doorway, the remains of one being preserved in the present ruins. On the first floor of the tower there was a window opening in the south wall, the internal jambs splayed to spread the light, and a similar window existed on the second floor.

The first floor, which would have formed the main chamber of the tower, was also vaulted. In its south-western corner a small doorway existed, 1 foot 11 inches in width, which led into a former chamber which seems to have been removed at an earlier date. From the passageway a small garderobe was accessible, built within the thickness of the exterior wall. A small window slit, 3 inches wide, lit this chamber, and a chute allowed the waste to fall from the castle to the loch.

9.4 Loch Doon Castle – fireplace

The fireplace on the interior of the wall of enceinte's western side is probably one of the finest architectural details of the castle. The opening of the fireplace is around six or seven feet wide, and carved columns to either side support a massive lintel. The weight of the wall above is relieved by a semi-circular relieving arch of stones built into the wall. The fireplace would have been on the first floor of the original keep, no doubt the great hall of the castle.

A second, but smaller architectural feature is the strange recess in the southern wall. This may have been some form of safe, or strong cupboard, for it has dressed masonry around it, and the top of it comprises a stone archway. A small roll moulding is carved around the stones, indicating that this was a feature that was to be visible in the castle. Within the recess a square compartment is located at the back of the cupboard, and a smaller one to the right-hand side. Again this feature is located on what was the first floor of the castle.

On the eastern side of the castle's courtyard was another building, the footprint of which is preserved in the current ruins. Located next to the postern gateway, the purpose of this building is unknown, but its strange angle does allow a long chamber

165

to be formed with walls erected at a right-angle to the longest wall of the exterior curtain. The little chamber was vaulted, and access to it was by way of a low narrow opening positioned 3 feet above the floor level. Other buildings appear to have existed on the north side of the postern gateway, between it and the main gate, but their shape and use cannot be determined.

The history of the castle is difficult to piece together. It is generally agreed that the building is very ancient, and was probably erected in the thirteenth century. Who built the castle cannot be ascertained, but it is thought to have been the seat of the ancient Lords of Carrick, the Baliol family. Indeed, some old accounts name the castle as 'Baliol' or 'Balloch' castle.

9.5 Loch Doon Castle – postern gateway from interior

The oldest reference to the castle appears to date from 1306, at a time when Robert the Bruce was waging his guerrilla campaign against the English enemy. It is said that some of the soldiers from the castle were able to leave the defence and kill some of the English soldiers on a nearby hill. This hill was known as the Brucean Hill from that time onward, but today it is not known which hill this refers to, and there is no hill of that name indicated on maps.

A tale is told of the castle under siege once more in 1319. How true the account was is debateable, and even the hero appears to have strived for opposing sides, depending on which account one reads. We will tell the pro-Scots account here!

Although the Bruce had won his famous victory at Bannockburn in 1314, the English regularly sent armies foraying into southern Scotland. On this occasion in 1319 the force came as far as Loch Doon, and an attempt was being made to force the occupants of the castle to surrender. The folk in the castle could not leave, for there were too many soldiers around the shores for them to sail across safely, but there again they had quite a stock of food in the building and could wait for a few days before it ran out.

To try to hurry the siege along a bit, the English came up with a plan. They would construct a dam across the mouth of the loch, at the head of the Ness Glen, and raise the waters of the loch by some feet, filling the centre of the castle with water. Accordingly, the soldiers cut down large trees and stretched the trunks across the narrow mouth where the Doon rises. Covering these with large sods, a makeshift dam was quickly constructed.

Back in the castle the occupants wondered why the waters of the loch were rising further up inside the courtyard. As time passed, the water level rose ever more, causing the residents to suffer loss of provisions and nowhere to store other goods. They soon realised what was happening, but they were unsure how to prevent it.

Then one of the castle's men came up with a plan. He would swim in the dead of night down the length of the loch, a full four and a half miles, and using his knife cut the ropes that tied the timbers together. With only this hope of removing the problem of the waters, the rest of the folk agreed.

The man, who was named MacNab, took his short dirk and put it within his bonnet which he placed on his head. At nightfall he slipped out of the castle and into the waters. Slowly he swam through the frozen waters to the north end of the loch. At the dam he removed his knife from his cap and began cutting the ropes of the dam. Silently he worked in the darkness, but the dam was well-made and he found it hard to cut enough ropes to destroy the structure. However, with one final cut the timbers moved, and he knew the dam was about to go.

But go it did – too quickly for poor MacNab. With one part of the dam burst, the force of the waters soon pulled the remainder of the dam with it, and MacNab followed. Hurtling down into the gorge of the Ness Glen, the swollen waters battered his body against rock after rock until at length it left the chasm and reached the plain at the Bogton Loch.

The heroism of MacNab was not to be unrewarded, however, for at the north end of the loch, on the western shores, is an area of ground that is today known as Macnabstone. This is a derivation of MacNab's town, the name of the farm that was granted to his family in appreciation of what he had done to save the castle.

9.6 Loch Doon Castle – aumbry

On the east side of the loch, almost opposite Macnabstone, is a spot known as the Englishman's Stairs, thought to be associated with the same account of the siege of the castle.

The story of MacNab is also related in Barbour's *Bruce*, which sets the story much earlier. In Barbour's account, MacNab was definitely the traitor:

> And worthy Crystoll off Setoun
> Into Loch Doon betresyt was
> Throu a discipill off Judas
> Maknab, a fals tratour that ay
> Wes off his dwelling nycht and day
> Quhom to he maid gud cumpany.

In 1333 Scotland was under the control of Baliol apart from five major castles which held out for King David II. These were Dumbarton, Urquhart, Lochleven, Lochmaben and Kildrummy. In addition to these, it was noted at the time that, 'a stronghold, in Lochdon, on the borders of Carrick, was also retained for David Bruce by John Thomson, a brave soldier of fortune, and probably the same person who, after the fatal battle of Dundalk, led home from Ireland the broken remains of the army of King Edward Bruce.' Thomson and his men may have been ejected from the castle at that time, or else realised that they would be unlikely to hold out in case of attack, and it was most likely them that hid the coin hoard that remained undiscovered until 1966.

It is possible that the occupants of Loch Doon Castle were placed under some form of siege around the year 1335. Little is known about this period in the castle's history, but on 19 April 1966 two Dalmellington men, James Buchanan (then aged seventeen) and George Tulip, were walking along the shores of the loch when they discovered a hoard of ancient coins. Once these had been gathered together and counted, it was discovered that there was a total of 1,887 pennies of various types in this hoard, including coins which were of Scottish, English and continental denomination. The remains of a pottery jug, in which the coins had been hidden, were also found. The coins and jug were analysed carefully by archaeologists and they reckoned that the collection must have been hidden around 1335. The coin hoard was declared treasure trove, and 303 of the silver pennies were presented to the National Museum of Antiquities in Edinburgh by the Queen's and Lord Treasurer's Remembrancer in 1969.

The next major event recorded concerning Loch Doon Castle took place in 1510. At that time there were numerous feuds across Ayrshire and Galloway between some of the major landowning families. These often resulted in bloodshed, families avenging the murders of various members of their own clan. At the time, Loch Doon was in the hands of the Kennedys and it was attacked by William Craufurd, or Crawford, of Leifnoreis Castle, which stood in the parish of Old Cumnock, until it was superseded by Dumfries House.

According to Paterson's *History of Ayrshire*, Loch Doon Castle was destroyed by fire during the reign of James V, which took place from 1514 until 1542. Other Galloway castles, such as Kenmure, were also destroyed at this time, part of the king's policy of reducing the strength of some of his provincial nobles.

The summer of 1823 appears to have been a particularly warm and dry one, resulting in the waters of Loch Doon dropping to a rather low level. Walking along the side of the loch, some fishermen discovered a number of ancient canoes or log-boats half-buried on the shores near to the castle end of the loch. Only three of the canoes were able to be raised, and archaeologists studied them carefully to find out how old they might be. Each of the canoes was formed from a single trunk of an oak tree, the part in which the canoeist sat being hollowed out from the solid trunk. In shape, they were similar to a fishing cobble. One of the canoes measured twenty feet in length. In width the boat was 3 feet 3 inches wide. A second canoe was 16 feet 6 inches in length, the width being 2 feet 10 inches. A third canoe was 22 feet in length by 3 feet 10 inches wide. The largest of the canoes was saved and sent to the Hunterian Museum in Glasgow, where it still remains.

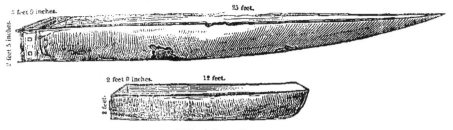

9.7 Loch Doon Canoes

Three more canoes were found in 1831. One of these had a rounded bow and the stern is transom in shape. Over the stern is a projecting shelf. It has been worked out that the canoe was partially formed by cutting into the timber with an axe or adze, perhaps made from metal, but that burning was also used. The log-boats measure about eleven feet in length, almost three feet at the widest and about sixteen inches deep. These canoes were transported on casks to a pool near the foot of the loch, where they were left to allow interested visitors to look at them. They have long-since become lost.

The account of the raising of the canoes makes interesting reading:

> In attempting to pull out the canoes ... which, from their being in nearly a vertical position, were the only ones that could be distinctly seen, or which appeared to offer, at least, the best chance of success, so great a resistance was encountered, that not only the strong ropes and other implements used were frequently broken, but it also seemed probable for some time that the canoes wold be entirely destroyed in the efforts made to move them. It was afterwards discovered that this unexpected resistance was occasioned by a great many other canoes which were lying in all directions above, below, and across those finally got out, but which, from the depth and thickness of the water, and the quantities of large stones, sand, and mud with which they were surrounded, could not be seen, though they were distinctly felt and traced by the feet of the men, who were wading up to their necks amongst them.

Within the canoes were found a few artefacts from an earlier period. One of the canoes contained an ancient battle-axe, now in the Stewartry Museum in Kirkcudbright, as well as the sole and upper part of a lady's shoe. The latter artefact had a complete sole, the upper part being decayed, but was attached to the sole by leather thongs. The relics were given to Joseph Train, the famous antiquarian friend of Sir Walter Scott, and he long preserved them.

Archaeologists have tested the timber of the canoe by radiocarbon-dating and discovered that it probably dates from AD 650. This date could be around three hundred years to either side, but it still confirms that it is a very old canoe.

A second canoe survives in part, also located in the Hunterian Museum. This canoe was thought to be one that was unearthed in 1831. Only the port side of the vessel survives, though part of the transom is still in situ. The canoe measures around

23 feet in length, 3 feet 9 inches across the beam and a maximum of 2 feet 5 inches in depth. The timber used is reckoned to have been oak, and this was covered in a layer of pitch to waterproof it. The other canoes no longer survive.

Some archaeologists have speculated that some of the timbers thought to be other canoes in the water were perhaps part of a crannog, or lake-dwelling, that formerly existed in the loch. Another theory for the large timbers below the surface was that they formed part of an underwater causeway that led to the castle island.

In 1992 some students at the Scottish Institute of Maritime Studies in St Andrews, under the guidance of Damian Goodburn, built a replica of the canoe, in order to discover how it was made and how it performed in water. The canoe was made from a single trunk of a tree in the museum at Anstruther. When it was launched, the canoe looked like a small barge, lying low in the water. A single man could sit comfortably in the canoe and propel it with a paddle. The vessel was tested in the harbour at Anstruther. The replica, once the experiments were completed, was placed on display at the Scottish Fisheries Museum in Anstruther.

In addition to Loch Doon, there are a number of other lochs in south-west Scotland that had a castle on an islet within it. These include Loch Bradan, Lochinvar (north-east of Dalry), Loch Maberry (north-west of Newton Stewart) and Loch Goosey (east of Barrhill). Of these, only Loch Bradan is located within the area covered by this volume.

The magnificent ruin that Loch Doon Castle is, with its quality of masonry and unique shape, has led some antiquarians to investigate Loch Bradan Castle with the same interest. Unfortunately, this castle, if indeed it ever was one, has little of the unique quality or history of Loch Doon Castle, and even today it can no longer be seen, the waters of Loch Bradan having been raised by the massive dam built across its mouth, in order to supply much of Ayrshire with drinking water.

Old maps are vague as to whether there was a castle here or not. Certainly, early Ordnance Survey maps accepted the ruin on the islet as a castle and, prior to the loch being deepened for the second time, indicated the ruin as a castle on their maps. Armstrong's *Map of Ayrshire*, which was published in 1775, does not claim that the ruin was a castle, although its name indicated that it was accepted as such. On the map the cartographer wrote: 'Castle Brady, in an Island, a large Old Ruin.' MacBain reckoned that the ruins were insignificant, and unlikely to be a castle, more possibly a 'cell of some hermit, who, desirous of secluding himself as far as possible from the haunts of men, had the habitation erected.'

What remained latterly of the castle was fragmentary. The Ordnance Survey recorded that only the 'rims' of 'what is said to have been a castle' survived in 1856, when they were surveying the locality for the first detailed maps of Scotland. They found that it had been a smallish square building with walls that were two feet in thickness. These walls were still three feet in height on three sides of the building, but the rest had fallen into ruins. On the same little island on which the castle stood were also the 'rims' of an outhouse, its purpose unknown.

Loch Bradan was first dammed in 1909 and the level of the water raised by eight feet. At the time, the ruins were described as 'now little more to be seen than what is presented by a stone sheep-enclosure'. Indeed, there are many who claim that the castle was nothing of the sort, being more likely to be a place of refuge.

When the first dam was constructed, much of the little castle island was submerged, leaving only some fragmentary ruins sticking above the surface of the water, in particular, one of the gables. Some fishermen, keen that the site of the castle should still be discernible in the grey waters, had erected a cairn around 6 feet in height on top of the walls. However, once the second, larger dam was constructed at Bradan, the old castle totally disappeared beneath the waters, only ever reappearing when the water level in the reservoir is particularly low.

Another significant castle stood at the southern end of the Galloway Highlands. The remains of Garlies Castle are located on the southern slopes of lesser hills that rise up to the mountainous heights of Larg and Lamachan hills. Built on a low knoll, the land drops steeply on the castle's south and south-east side. The oldest part of Garlies Castle may date from the twelfth or thirteenth century, though little stonework of this period survives.

What remains today appears to have been part of a tower house that may have been erected around 1500 for the Stewarts of Garlies. This family owned extensive lands on the south side of the Galloway hills, and they were later to become ennobled with the title Earl of Galloway, which they still hold. The main tower was a structure that measured approximately forty feet by thirty feet, slightly off the square, though most of the walls have tumbled, leaving only sections of the southern wall and the north-western corner to rise to any height, in parts thirty feet high. Having good quality masonry, the bulk of the castle was constructed with locally-sourced freestone, but at the corners massive whinstone blocks have been used. The lime used in the construction of the castle has produced a very hard mortar, and within the mortar can be found burnt shells.

The original entrance to the castle was located on the northern wall, reached from a courtyard. The double doorway, according to MacGibbon and Ross, was 'giblet-checked on the outside, and another within.' This gave access to a passageway 3 feet 6

inches wide through the wall which had slabs over the top of it. At the west end of the passageway a small room off it must have formed a guardroom, a little chamber measuring approximately six feet by four feet. The walls of this room on their upper reaches are cantilevered inwards in stone, to allow the slabs that would have

9.8 Garlies Castle from west

171

been placed over it to span the gap. In the western end of the guardroom is an aumbry, perhaps used to keep keys and padlocks.

If the passageway was followed to the east, this gave access to the foot of a spiral stairway, one that was erected within the thickness of the wall. As with many castles where stairs were included within the wall thickness, this weakened the walls considerably, resulting in the corner falling. From the passageway two doorways led into the ground floor rooms, originally separated by a stone wall. These rooms were vaulted, but their stone roofs have long-since collapsed, or else been robbed for other buildings. At one time the uppermost stones in the vaults were seventeen feet above floor level, indicating that the vaults would probably have had timber decking or mezzanine floors within. The corbel stones that would have supported this floor are still visible. The western vault was probably a store, or strong room, for it was only lit by two narrow slit-windows which still survive on the southern and western walls. A small recess is located in its south-western corner.

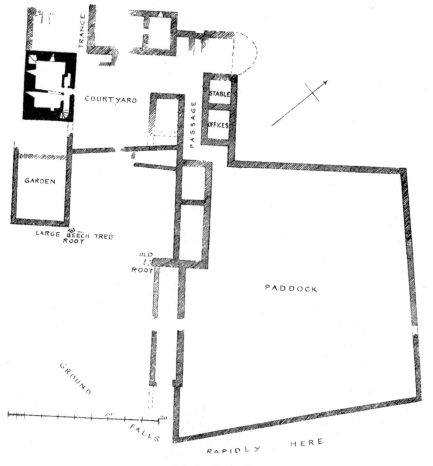

9.9 Garlies Castle, plan

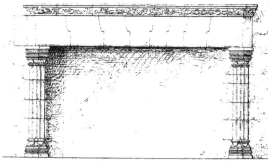

9.10 Garlies Castle – fireplace

The eastern vault was smaller in size, and was lit by a single slit window on the southern side. Within this room, but not in its original position, is a notable fire surround which probably dates from the early sixteenth century, no doubt built at the same time as the rest of the castle. The fireplace has rather distinctive carvings on it – human heads with foliage issuing from them, a hunting scene with stags running across the frieze, and the Stewart arms placed centrally, surrounded by the letters *T T*. The mason work is rather fine, with moulded Gothic side jambs and a heavy lintel comprising a straight arch over the opening. Next to the fireplace is a small aumbry.

As the owners of Garlies Castle expected to deal with troublemakers and lawbreakers, the tower was equipped with a prison. This is found in the south-eastern corner of the tower and was accessed from above.

Garlies Castle was probably abandoned as it proved to be structurally unsound. The northern wall had the staircase and passageways

9.11 Garlies Castle – arms on fireplace

incorporated within it, and this made that side considerably weaker than the rest. When the ruins were cleared, the remaining wall on this side was found to be leaning outward and it is thought that this movement in the building, which no doubt was accompanied by serious cracks in the walls, resulted in the owners moving elsewhere.

Lying to the north and east of the castle was an extensive courtyard, surrounded by other buildings, which were probably stables, offices, workshops, stores, bake-houses and kitchens. Some of the buildings around this courtyard were quite sizeable, but today the walls of most structures are little more than piles of rubble. Adjoining these lesser buildings are walls that probably surrounded a garden and a paddock, the latter reckoned to be around 2,000 square yards in extent.

Sometime in the 1880s the castle was partially excavated, or at least cleared of the rubble that buried much of the structure. Major-General the Hon. Alexander Stewart, third son of the 9th Earl of Galloway, was keen to find out more about the seat of his ancestors, and thus instigated the clear out. Tons of rubble were lifted and removed from the tower, giving a clearer indication of what the building had been like, and during this removal of debris a number of interesting artefacts were found.

An important piece of carved stonework was taken from Garlies Castle and incorporated in Cumloden House, which was a later seat of the Earls of Galloway. Sir

William Stewart, second son of the 7th Earl of Galloway, had Cumloden erected lower down the Penkiln glen sometime around 1825. Little more than a large *cottage orne*, around 1890 the house was extended to include the stone, which was built into the centre gable of the southern front. It comprises an ogee arch over which is carved *ALNS STEVARD MILES FECT.* This translates as 'Alan Stewart, soldier, built this.'

9.12 Garlies Castle – inscription

The Stewart family first obtained Garlies and its associated lands in 1263, when King Alexander III bestowed the barony on Alexander, the fourth hereditary High Steward of Scotland. In 1283 he was succeeded by his second son, John, known as John of Bonkyl, his wife being Margaret, heiress of Sir Alexander Bonkyl of that Ilk. The family received the title Lord Garlies in 1607, and became Earls of Galloway in 1623. When the Galloway earldom was bestowed on the Stewarts, the eldest son and heir to the earldom has held the courtesy title Lord Garlies.

The Castle of Old Risk is located further up the Penkiln glen from Garlies Castle, but on the opposite side of the stream. Far less remains of this building than even Garlies. The building appears to have originally measured around 50 feet by 24 feet in plan, which is in fact a similar area to Garlies Castle. The walls are less well made, however, for they are only around three feet in thickness, and have been constructed from un-mortared masonry. Most of the walls are little more than overgrown rubble piles, though one part of the eastern wall sticks out of the turf to a height of around a few feet. From it we can see that the stonework is roughly coursed, and little dressing has taken place of the stones.

The site is a defensive one, however, for to the south and west of the ruins the building is surrounded by marshland, making any form of attack difficult. The format of the remains makes the building very difficult to date, and there appear to be no real guesses as to when it was erected. Similarly, the castle appears to have been abandoned for many centuries, and there are no tales associated with it.

Ownership of the Castle of Old Risk is believed to have been held by the Murdochs. There is an ancient tale that relates how Robert the Bruce rewarded his staunchest allies in Galloway with various stretches of land, and that the Murdochs received the lands of Old Risk at that time. The Murdochs are thought to have retained the property until the eighteenth century, after which it was acquired by the Stewarts, Earls of Galloway. It was probably around this time that the castle was abandoned completely, though it may have fallen into ruins before this.

10 Covenanters

Across the Galloway Highlands are many places associated with the Covenanters. Around the periphery a number of gravestones recall their sacrifice, such as in Kells, Dalry, Carsphairn and Straiton kirkyards. Even in the countryside locations can be found where the Covenanters were shot and buried, such as at Caldons in Glen Trool and near to the summit of the mountain of Meaul, high in the Rhinns.

The Covenanters were Scots Presbyterians who refused to accept Charles I and II's demands to change their form of worship. Both kings wished to impose Episcopacy on Scotland, against the wishes of most of the country, to bring the Scots form of church government into line with that of England. The kings believed in the Divine Right, that they were the head of the church, and that they could appoint archbishops and bishops to rule the lesser ministers. The Scots Presbyterian form of government was different. Church and state were separate, and all were equal in the eyes of the head of the church – none other than Jesus Christ himself.

The Covenanters gained their name from the fact that they compiled a National Covenant which was drawn up in Edinburgh in 1638 and presented to the king as a form of petition, requesting that they could continue to worship as they had done for years. The king was for none of it, and as the years passed - a full 'fifty years' struggle', as it became known - the Covenanters were repeatedly persecuted, hunted down, and had to endure various degrees of punishment, varying from fines, torture, imprisonment, banishment to execution.

Many ministers refused to conform to the king's demands, and most of those in south west Scotland's parishes left their pulpits and manses rather than accede. One of these was Rev John Semple, minister at Carsphairn. He was one of the protesters in 1657. He was arrested in Edinburgh in 1660 and held in prison for ten months. He was tried before the council but dismissed. He returned to Carsphairn and preached until his death in 1677. In 1727 Patrick Walker compiled *Some Remarkable Passages of the Life and Death of Mr John Semple*. A plaque within the church commemorates him.

John Dempster was one of the unlucky ones, paying for his religious adherences with his life. When this took place is not exactly known, but it is thought to have been in the period from 1684-85 when the persecutions were at their worst – the 'Killing Times'.

Dempster is not one of the more famous martyrs. Indeed, many of the books written on the subject don't mention his name, for no real gravestone exists to mark the spot where he was buried. On the northern slopes of Meaul a low stone marks the spot where he was killed in cold blood, and tradition claims that he was buried where he fell.

John Dempster is known to have been a tailor. His home was at Garryaird, which formerly existed in the parish of Dalry. No farm or cottage of this name exists today, but it was located just over half a mile to the east of Arndarroch farm, which is located near to the southern dam on Kendoon Loch.

Dalry, or St John's Town of Dalry, to give the village its full title, had gained a reputation for being a hotbed of Covenanters, for it was here in 1666 that the ill-fated Pentland Rising had started. Soldiers, who had been sent to track down Covenanter rebels, were about to torture an old man of around eighty years when the locals rose up against them, preventing the persecutors from burning the infirm man with a branding iron, usually used on cattle. The rising ended when the Covenanters, who had marched on Edinburgh, were defeated in battle at Rullion Green, south of the capital.

10.1 John Dempster's Stone, Meaul

Dempster was probably too young to have taken part in the rising, but this is not certain. However, he was a keen enough supporter to join the Covenanters when they fought at Bothwell Bridge. This took place on 22 June 1679. Those who fought at Bothwell had previously taken part in the Covenanter victory over the king's soldiers under John Graham of Claverhouse at the Battle of Drumclog, and no doubt Dempster was active there. Bothwell was a defeat for the Covenanters, and after the atrocities on the field, the authorities began a major clampdown on suspected rebels. Dempster's name was one that had been passed on to the dragoons.

Covenanters who were wanted by the authorities were forced to leave their homes and families, heading to the hills and moors to hide. Those left behind were regularly subjected to parties of dragoons arriving at their homes, just in case their husbands or sons had returned home. Searches were made of rooms and lofts, and hay-sheds often had the haystacks prodded with long pikes, just in case the wife had quickly concealed the 'hill-man' when the soldiers arrived.

John Dempster had to leave home, but lived rough within a mile or so of his house. There was a nearby cave, located by the side of the Black Water, where he spent his time in concealment. At any moment his hiding place could be discovered, but most folk in south west Scotland were either Covenanters or supporters of the movement, so there was little chance of the hideouts being revealed. Dempster was even able to carry on some of his work in tailoring, and there was enough knowledge in the area for the customers to be able to track him down.

On a number of occasions Dempster was almost captured by the soldiers, which would have resulted in certain death, or at best, hauling to Edinburgh for trial and certain banishment to the plantations of America, where he would have been held captive in slavery. However, each time the soldiers were nearby, he was able to make an escape, being knowledgeable of the countryside, and knowing the numerous secret hideouts used by the Covenanters in the Glenkens.

One day Dempster was making his way across country near to the village of Carsphairn. He was on the slopes of Craig of Knockgray, a low but stony hill that rises north-east of Carsphairn. It's not a very big hill as far as Galloway is concerned, but it is a significant eminence above Carsphairn, rising to 1,256 feet above sea level. From its summit cairn a wide panorama can be had of the Galloway Highlands – the northern extent of the Rhinns of Kells and Carsphairn to the west, and the lumbering shoulder of Cairnsmore of Carsphairn to the north-east. To the south a long view is obtained of the Glenkens, and well down through the Stewartry.

Dempster spotted some soldiers making their way across the valley, perhaps heading west from Muirdrochwood, today a farm in the middle of the forests to the east of Kendoon Loch. At the time of the Covenanters this was the home of a known informer by the name of Canning or Cannon, and perhaps the soldiers had received information from him, leading them to the Craig in search of Dempster.

In desperation Dempster made his way westwards, heading for the wilder hills of Galloway at the head of the Garryhorn Burn. He forded the deep Water of Deugh, and ran with sodden clothes westwards, heading for the hills. The evening light was failing, and Dempster was able to dodge back and forth amongst the peat hags and watercourses by the Halfmark Burn. The dragoons followed, but as darkness fell decided to abandon the pursuit. They retired to Garryhorn farm, which sits by the side of the burn of the same name.

10.2 Garryhorn Farm, Carsphairn

Garryhorn today is a sizeable hill farm. At the time of the Covenanters it was probably much the same, though there may have been a ferme-toun, or collection of agricultural labourers' cottages here. The soldiers had laid claim to the farmhouse, and the famous arch-enemy of the Covenanters, Sir Robert Grierson of Lag, had established a small garrison here. Grierson is reviled in Covenanter lore. It was he, so they said, who captured Covenanters and took them back to his family seat, Lag Tower in Nithsdale, where he had them forced into wooden barrels. With the lids nailed in place, Lag hammered spikes into the sides of the barrels, much as a magician would stick pins or swords through his attractive assistant. Lag's trick was no trick – the spikes were real, and when they were in place he rolled the barrel down the side of Lag or Benan Hill, the Covenanter being tortured and hacked to death.

Garryhorn had been commandeered by Lag, and for many years an ancient oak bed was pointed out to interested passers-by as being the very bed in which the friend of the Devil had slept. It was described as being very strong, panelled with boards of black oak, overlapping each other like the slates on a roof. At the foot of it there was a small box which formed the kennel in which Lag kept his dogs. The bed appears to have been broken up prior to 1875 and small pieces of it were taken away by relic hunters. Outside the farmhouse, which has been rebuilt since the years of persecution, the old dog kennels long survived, the very place where the hounds that tracked down John Dempster were kept.

Tired and exhausted, Dempster was forced to spend the night on the hill. He slept rough amongst the rocks of Craighit, a low shoulder of Cairnsgarroch. Worn out and suffering fatigue, Dempster was eventually able to sleep. So well did he sleep that he lay long in the early morning sun.

Suddenly the sound of Lag's hounds disturbed the glen. The barking and howling echoed around the wide valley, the dogs excited and ready for the chase. It was no fox hunt, but a man-hunt, and Dempster was the prey. Quickly bringing himself around, he set off westwards once more, trying to head for the wilds of Loch Doon. The dogs soon picked up the trail, and perhaps one of the soldiers spotted the tailor of Garryaird on the hill above. Dempster ran faster, his adrenalin pumping the blood round his aching veins. He ran across the shoulder of Black Craig to the headwaters of the Garryhorn Burn. The hillside was rough, and running askew across the slopes left his body out of kilter, one leg trying to run at a different level to the other. By the Garryhorn Burn he started uphill, the steep slope seemingly rising steeper and steeper as his energy waned.

The hounds barked and slavered excitedly as they came closer. Dempster had run two miles from Craighit, most of it uphill and across the rough terrain. The dogs had run a mile or so more, but their energy was boundless, and the excitement of nearing the prey seemed to give them more. Hot behind, following the baying and excited barking, were the dragoons, mounted on horseback.

Dempster could run no more. On the ridge-top, between the summits of Bow and Meaul, he collapsed. The dogs circled round him, barking feverishly, awaiting the commands of their masters. When the soldiers arrived they dispensed with any niceties. Dempster was a wanted man. Here he was trying to evade capture, refusing to listen to the demands of the dragoons. It was enough for Lag to order his men to shoot. The body was left on the hillside until some friends felt that it was safe enough for them to bury it. A boulder hewn from the hillside was upended and located at the head of the grave.

The boulder remained the only marker of Dempster's grave for many years. In the summer of 1976 a wooden plaque was screwed to a steel bar and concreted into the ground. It was placed by George Scott and a few members of the Scottish Covenanter Memorials Association. They climbed from Woodhead, one of the party being 77-year old Willie Miller, one of the founder members of the association. In 1986 a new brass plaque was placed in the same place, affixed to a steel frame, also concreted into the ground. On that occasion it was placed by the author and other members of 1st Cumnock Company of the Boys' Brigade.

John Dempster wasn't the only martyr to suffer in the area. A tenant farmer surnamed MacCroy lived quite near to Garryhorn. He was working in the fields one Sunday when he decided to take a rest. It being the Sabbath he began to read from his small pocket Bible, so he lay down in the lea of a stone dike and perused the worn pages. Grierson and his soldiers were passing by when they spotted him. Riding at speed to where MacCroy was studying the scriptures, he was easily captured. Lag inquired what he was reading. 'The Bible', MacCroy responded.

Erected
in Memory of Rodger Dunn
who was born at Benwhat Parish of
Dalmellington 1659. He suffered much
persecution for the cause of Christ and
was killed on the night of Carsphairn
Fair June 1689 on the Farm of Brockloch
Pluck'd from Minerva's breast here am I laid
Which debt to cruel Atropos I've paid
Resting my clayey fabric in the dust
Among the holy ashes of the Just
My soul set sail for the celestial shore
Till the last trump the same with joy restore
also Robert Dunn of Garryhorn died
Oct 6th 1788

10.3 Rodger Dunn's gravestone, Carsphairn kirkyard

'Then your kye will need to find a new herd,' Lag told him, 'for your life is now forfeit as a rebel.' At the time, reading or carrying a Bible in the open fields was deemed as being sufficient evidence to hint that the owner was a Covenanter, perhaps making his way to or from a conventicle service that was being held in the hills. Lag withdrew his pistol from its holster and aimed at MacCroy. The single shot echoed around the valley, and Carsphairn parish gained another martyrs' crown.

The whole of the south-west of Scotland is dotted with martyrs' graves. Numerous memorials and carved stones mark the spots where the dragoons slaughtered the Covenanters. Virtually every kirkyard in the district has at least one martyr's grave, but Carsphairn hasn't. And yet the parish is known for its Covenanting adherences, and many a parishioner suffered the ultimate sacrifice for their beliefs.

Visitors to the kirkyard at Carsphairn can find a few stones of Covenanting interest. Just as one makes their way through the gate in the high stone wall that surrounds the kirk, a low stone is seen to the left. A light sandstone colour, the stone has been broken in two at some time in the past but has been painstakingly repaired by the supporters of the Covenanters. The inscription tells the basic facts of the Covenanter's tale:

Erected
in Memory of Rodger Dunn
who was born at Benwhat, Parish of
Dalmellington, 1659. He suffered much
persecution for the cause of Christ and
was killed on the night of Carsphairn
Fair June 1689 on the Farm of Brockloch.

Pluck'd from Minerva's breast here am I laid
Which debt to cruel Atropos I've paid
Resting my clayey fabric in the dust
Among the holy ashes of the Just
My soul set sail for the celestial shore
Till the last trump the same with joy restore
also Robert Dunn of Garryhorn, died
Octr 6th 1738.

Benwhat is the name of a high moorland hill that rises to the north of Dalmellington. At one time Benwhat, or Benquhat as it is sometimes spelled, was a small farmhouse or croft that lay on the southern slopes of the hill, the site of it probably destroyed when the mining community of Benquhat was established there in the nineteenth century. Today, even the old miners' rows are virtually gone, the encroaching scrub and moss reclaiming for nature man's destruction. Much of the surrounding landscape has also been scrubbed out, open cast coal working destroying all evidence of man's existence on these moors, from the Bronze Age to the present, by the clearing of vast acreages of hillside, the rocks and peat to be thrown back into the massive holes created when the coal has been taken from the ground.

Rodger was a noted Covenanter, who came from Covenanting stock. His father, James Dunn, was a supporter of the movement, and a relative, named David Dun, was to suffer execution in Cumnock, Ayrshire, in 1685. Rodger threw his lot in with the Covenanters, and as such was forced to leave his home high on the moors. Word spread that Rodger was one of the 'hill men' and soon his home was subject to regular searches, in the hope that the dragoons would catch him there. However, he had fled, and found various hideouts across the Galloway hills where he concealed himself.

Rodger suffered a number of near misses. On one occasion he and his two brothers, Andrew and Allan, were attending a conventicle in the parish of Carsphairn. This was taking place at a spot known as Craignew. The dragoons discovered the existence of this service, and made their way there as quick as possible. They were too late to attack the service at it took place, but they started to apprehend folk travelling home. The three Dunn brothers were spotted on the old pack road between Carsphairn and Dalmellington, and the dragoons swooped down onto their prey.

Rodger managed to make an escape, bounding into the wet boggy ground where the horsemen dared not enter. Allan and Andrew Dunn were less lucky and were captured by the soldiers and led back to Carsphairn. What became of them thereafter is not recorded in local history or oral tales. They were probably taken from Carsphairn and transferred on to the main garrison at Dumfries. From there they were no doubt sent abroad to work in the American plantations as slaves, as were thousands of other Covenanters.

From this time onwards Rodger Dunn hid within Dunaskin Glen, which is a narrow rocky defile between Dalmellington and Patna. There, below a waterfall, he had created a hideout where he could dodge the soldiers who were always on the lookout for him. One day he spotted them in the vicinity, but he had no time to escape. Even to try to run away would attract their attentions, and their horses would soon run after him, or at least to within the distance of a single gunshot.

His wits quick about him, he made his way to a soldier and shouted, 'I know who you are looking for.' He then told the dragoons that he had seen Rodger Dunn lower down the glen, at an old cottage which was just visible in the distance. Thanking him for his support, the soldiers galloped off, hoping to find the Covenanter there. Of course, Dunn turned around and fled in the opposite direction.

Following another visit of the dragoons to the home of his father, and where Rodger was at the time, yet another lucky escape was made. He then decided to head south into Galloway, and for a number of years lived in the wilds of Minnigaff parish. Yet again he made a lucky escape, one that required considerable skill and strength.

Dunn was staying at the home of a friend, which was located at the west end of Loch Trool. The cottage was known as Caldons, an old farmstead that has long succumbed to the levelling hand of nature. On Kitchin's map of 1749 it is spelled 'Kildouns'. A later Caldons house occupies a site further to the east. As Dunn and his friends were in the house they were unaware of the arrival of a party of dragoons.

The government soldiers were under the command of Captain Urquhart, whom tradition claims had a premonition of his own death, for in the affray at Caldons both he and another dragoon were killed. Urquhart had been annoyed at the roughness of the route that they had to follow in order to find the Covenanters, and it is said that he swore an oath claiming that he would be avenged upon the hill men. In a dream sometime before he had imagined that he would die with the 'Chaldeans', an ancient Biblical race, but was unable to work out what it meant. However, as he approached the cottage in Glen Trool he was inquisitive enough to ask what it was called. When he was told 'The Caldons', he swore loudly and drew his horse to a halt. As he pondered whether to return or continue, a shot was fired from the cottage and he was killed.

Dunn managed to make his escape from the cottage, and ran through the woods and thick undergrowth in the direction of Loch Trool. As he neared the loch, he plunged headlong into the cold and dark waters. The dragoons were in hot pursuit, pulling ever closer to the Covenanter. As he dived into the water, the dragoons fired shots, but luckily these missed. The soldiers reloaded their muskets and fired yet again, aiming at any dark shadow in the water. Though the force of the musket-balls was deadened when they hit the water's surface, they could still kill or seriously wound.

Dunn swam below the surface of the water as far as he could, heading for a spot where the reeds were thick and long. Still in the water, he was able to surface and grab a quick breath. As soon as he filled his lungs with air he plunged back beneath the murky waters. On his next surfacing he was able to watch the dragoons staring intently into the loch, and quietly he pulled at an old reed. Cutting both ends open, he used it as a small snorkel, allowing him to swim quietly below the surface of the water and off to a spot where he was able to climb back onto the bank and make his escape.

Rodger Dunn suffered from a severe fever after his soaking in the freezing loch. He managed to make his way to a nearby cottage where he was able to remove his clothes and have them dried by the fire. As this was taking place, Dunn was placed in the main bed in the house where he was allowed to sleep. His nurse who looked after him at this time is said to have become his wife a few years later. It took his body some time to recover, but gradually it did, and he survived to the time of the Glorious Revolution, when King William was crowned, and the persecution of the Covenanters was ended. Though persecution ended, Dunn's life was still subject to trouble, for as his gravestone relates, he was mistaken for another and murdered on the night of Carsphairn Fair.

Rodger Dunn had attended the fair to see what goods and cattle were on sale. Carsphairn Fair was one of the highlights of the farmers' social calendar, a day when all manner of cattle, sheep, horses, pigs and chickens changed hands. Stalls were laid out selling household goods, and various items of produce, from cheese to woollens knitted by farmers' wives. People travelled from all around to attend the fair, its location attracting visitors from Ayrshire as well as the lower reaches of Galloway. Music was played by entertainers, and all the fair-goers had a great time –even just to meet up and discuss things with friends you hadn't seen for months made the day worth attending.

At the end of the night Dunn was making his way home. He had just left Carsphairn and was walking along the old pack road that crossed the hill towards Dalmellington. Near to Brockloch, at a spot known as Wee Woodhead, no doubt a long-since demolished cot-house, a stranger came towards him. He pulled out his gun, and from a distance fired a fatal shot that left Dunn dead. As the Rev Dr Robert Simpson wrote in his popular book, *Traditions of the Covenanters*, 'the worthy man, who had so often escaped the sword of the public persecutor, fell by the hand of the private assassin.'

The Covenanters killed at Caldons, where Dunn made his escape by swimming into Loch Trool, were taken from the cottage and buried near to where they fell. Caldons Wood is an ancient broadleaved woodland, now surrounded by the extensive forest of pine. The old trees still grow there, however, and ancient oak, birch, and alder rise majestically in the forest. From the road that leads into Caldons, a path is signposted through the wood to the spot where the Covenanters were martyred.

One doesn't have to walk far through the trees before the stone wall is seen in the distance. A small enclosure, the wall was erected to protect the ancient gravestone that once stood within. However, in 1983, the stone that had stood marking the graves for three hundred years was broken into pieces by vandals who were staying at the campsite. The outcry was immense, and the wanton destruction was reported in the local press. The nationals took it on, and soon newspapers like *The Scotsman* informed the country at large of the vandalism.

A small organisation that had been established by three old ex-Cameronian soldiers in 1966 jumped into action. The Scottish Covenanter Memorials Association exists to protect and maintain the various memorials and gravestones associated with the Covenanters, and an appeal was launched. Donations came from far and wide, and soon enough money was raised in order to have the stone repaired. But things didn't stop there. The funds kept coming, and soon built up to a sum that would allow a new stone to be erected in place of the original. The major contributors were the Galloway Association of Glasgow, the Scottish Covenanter Memorials Association, an ex-Cameronian soldier, J. T. Keighley, the Forestry Commission and public subscriptions.

A white granite gravestone was acquired from Creetown quarry. It was cut to the same size as the original stone, and the mason carved the same inscription into the new memorial. Spelling errors were kept, as was the ungrammatical inscription, the same lines that had told of the martyrdom of the six men three hundred years before:

HERE LYES
JAMES AND ROBERT
DUNS, THOMAS AND
JOHN STEVENSONS,
JAMES McCLIVE,
ANDREU McCALL, WHO
WERE SURPRISED
AT PRAYER IN THIS
HOUSE BY COLNELL
DOUGLAS, LIEVTNANT
LIVINGSTON AND
CORNET
JAMES DOUGLAS AND
BY THEM MOST IMPIOUS
LY AND CRUELLY
MURTHERED FOR THEIR
ADHERENCE TO SCOT
LANDS REFORMATION
COVENANTS NATIONAL
AND SOLEMN LEAGUE
1685

Not only was the same inscription copied letter by letter, the same format of layout was copied. On the stone a number of letters were joined together, an old method that saved the mason from having to carve some strokes more than once. This joining of letters is known as ligatures, and was a form of lettering much used by the old stonemason known as Robert Paterson.

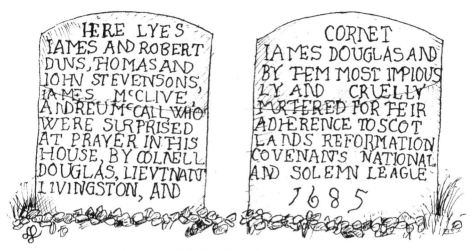

10.4 Caldons Martyrs' gravestone

Readers of Sir Walter Scott's works will know Paterson as 'Old Mortality', the name that Scott gave to him, and which was to be the title of one of his more popular novels, published in 1816. Scott is known to have met Paterson at the kirkyard of Dunnottar, far up the east coast in Kincardineshire. In his story he wrote:

> An old man was seated upon the monument of the slaughtered presbyterians, and busily employed in deepening, with his chisel, the letters of the inscription, which, announcing, in scriptural language, the promised blessings of futurity to be the lot of the slain, anathematized the murderers with corresponding violence. A blue bonnet of unusual dimensions covered the grey hairs of the pious workman. His dress was a large old-fashioned coat, of the coarse cloth called *hoddin-grey*, usually worn by the elder peasants, with waistcoat and breeches of the same; and the whole suit, though still in decent repair, had obviously seen a long train of hard service. Strong clouted shoes, studded with hob-nails, and *gramoches*, or *leggings*, made of thick black cloth, completed his equipment. Beside him, fed among the graves a pony, the companion of his journey, whose extreme whiteness, as well as its projecting bones and hollow eyes, indicated it antiquity.

Paterson was born near Hawick, Roxburghshire, in 1716, at a place known as Burnflat. He moved to Nithsdale, in Dumfriesshire, where he took on the lease of a sandstone quarry at Gatelawbridge, a couple of miles east of Thornhill. The sandstone from Nithsdale is a bright red colour, a stone that is distinctive in its appearance, one that was in demand for carvings and decorative work on buildings.

Paterson became more aware of the story of the Covenanting struggle, and he listened intently to the old folk tell the tales of the persecutions that they had endured. Most of the graves of the Covenanters were unmarked, other than a cairn of stones that may have been raised over them. Paterson resolved to mark the burial places in a more permanent way.

With a slab of stone hewn from his own quarry, he set off to find the graves of the Covenanters. With his pony to carry the weight of the stone, he journeyed to various remote moors and kirkyards where the martyrs lay buried. Tradition claims that the stone at Caldons was the first one that he had erected. This must have been around the year 1750.

10.5 Old Mortality relettering a Covenanter's gravestone

As time passed, Paterson's drive became ever more devout, and he would leave his wife and family for days on end as he journeyed across country, staying at the home of old Covenanters to find out the stories and discover where the blood of the martyrs had been spilled. His wife, Elizabeth Gray, had even to send their son across the south-west of Scotland to try to track down his father, and to plead with him to return home. Paterson did for a time, but was never happier than when he was out on the moors.

At Balmaclellan, a few miles east of New Galloway, Elizabeth Paterson set up a school, trying to earn a living due to the absence of her husband. In later years, when the work of Scott was phenomenally popular across the world, enough funds were raised in order to have a statue of Paterson and his pony erected and these can be seen at the entrance to the kirkyard.

'Old Mortality' died near to Bankend of Caerlaverock, south of Dumfries, and was buried in the kirkyard of Caerlaverock. His grave was unmarked, a sad indictment on the man who had raised dozens of stones over the graves of the martyrs. Sir Walter Scott was keen that Paterson was given the honour that he deserved, but despite numerous inquiries, was unable to discover where he was buried. The 'Wizard of the

North' never did discover where Paterson's remains lay before he too died. It was not for another few years that word reached Edinburgh where the last resting place of Paterson was. Scott's publishers, Adam & Charles Black, knew that Scott had been desirous of marking Paterson's grave with a memorial, and so arranged to have a large headstone erected over the grave. This can still be seen at Bankend, the stone bearing carvings of the mason's tools.

The pieces of the vandalised stone at Caldons, which was important enough in its own right, and doubly so from it having been thought to be the first erected by Old Mortality, were gathered together and sent to Historic Scotland's workshops for repair. They found that the stone had been repaired before, having been broken in two. It was also discovered that the stone used to make the headstone comprised of red sandstone that could easily have been quarried at Gatelawbridge, though it was impossible to confirm that it was. The stone was re-assembled and glued together with bronze pins. It was returned to Galloway, and now can be seen within the museum at Newton Stewart.

The Covenanters shot at Caldons were James Dunn, Robert Dunn, Thomas Stevenson, John Stevenson, James MacClive and Andrew MacCall. The latter two were also referred to as James MacClude and Andrew Macaulay, but the passing of time probably resulted in some error being made in the recording of their names. They, and a number of others who, like Rodger Dunn, escaped the grasp of the dragoons, had gathered in the old cottage of Caldons and were holding a prayer meeting. It was a Sabbath morning, on 23 January 1685. They read the scriptures to each other and sang verses of the psalms. It was a freezing day outside, but with the peat fire blazing red and the comfort of so many in the small room, the men were warm and enjoying themselves.

The soldiers who came to Caldons were Colonel Douglas, Lieutenant Livingston and Cornet James Douglas. Colonel Douglas was actually Lieutenant-General James Douglas, who was the second son of the 2nd Earl of Queensberry and brother of the 1st Duke of Queensberry. He died in 1691.

The soldiers had passed up the valley and entered the narrowing Glen Trool when they probably heard the singing of psalms from the old shepherd's cottage. The Covenanters were found within and, according to Rev Robert Wodrow's account of *The History and Sufferings of the Church of Scotland*, published in two volumes in 1721-22, 'whether the Oath of Abjuration was offered or not my information does not bear; but without any further process they were immediately taken out and shot to death.'

The small gravestone hewn by Old Mortality was in later years surrounded by a stone wall which rises five feet in height, no doubt to protect the venerated spot from sheep and cattle. A small enclosure, ten feet square, the wall was 'erected by the voluntary contributions of a congregation, who waited on the ministrations of the Rev Gavin Rowatt of Whithorn,' Sunday 19 August 1827.

That the Galloway Highlands was an ideal spot for the Covenanter to hide is still noted on maps of the present time. A few place names survive which commemorate the Covenanters who hid in the hills, trying to escape the torture or possible killing at the hands of the dragoons. By the side of a forest road that makes its way up the side of the Curnelloch Burn, about two miles north-west of Craigencallie, stands MacWhann's Stone. Prior to the coming of the forestry and the associated tracks used to haul timber, the stone stood solitary in the open moor, the nearest habitation being Backhill of Garrary, the lone shepherd's cottage that existed half a mile to the north-east.

10.6 Adam MacWhann's gravestone, Kells kirkyard

Adam MacWhann was a resident of the village of New Galloway. What he did for a living is not known, nor is why he was pursued by the soldiers. Perhaps he had been involved in some incident in the area. In any case, he had to leave his home for some time and he hid in the fastness of the Dungeon of Buchan. The large boulder where he often hid was to gain his name. However, the privations of hiding and sleeping rough resulted in him catching a fever. At great risk to himself he decided to return to his cottage which stood near to New Galloway, hoping that the drier and warmer conditions would cure him of his illness. However, word somehow reached the soldiers, who had garrisons in the neighbourhood, and they soon made their way to his cot-house. It was the tenth day of May, 1685, right in the middle of the 'Killing Times', when the persecution of the Covenanters was at its height.

Though MacWhann was ill in his bed and having little energy the soldiers demanded that he got up to face them. He was hauled from his bed and the bed-clothes dragged from him. Weak and coughing roughly, MacWhann was either unable or unwilling to answer the soldiers' questions. With no co-operation forthcoming, the leader, Lieutenant General James Douglas, ordered that he should be arrested and taken into New Galloway. Held a prisoner overnight, he was taken out on the following morning and was shot without any form of trial. His body was later collected by some friends and taken to the old kirkyard of Kells, where he was buried.

The grave of MacWhann, or MacQwhan as it is spelled in the deeply chiselled letters, was later to be marked by a small headstone. This bears a simple account of his suffering:

HERE LYES ADAM MACQWHAN WHO BEING SICK OF A FEVER WAS TAKEN OUT OF HIS BED AND CARRIED TO NEUTOUN OF GALLOWAY AND THE NEXT DAY MOST CRUELLY AND UNJUSTLY SHOT TO DEATH BY THE COMMAND OF LIEVTENANT GENERAL JAMES DOUGLAS, BROTHER TO THE DUKE OF QUEENSBERRY, FOR HIS ADHERENCE TO SCOTLAND'S REFORMATION COVENANTS NATIONAL AND SOLEMN LEAGUE. 1685.

In 1832 a larger memorial was erected to commemorate MacWhann. Rather than just replace the old stone with a new memorial, instead a large granite frame was constructed, and the original small gravestone was incorporated within it. This new memorial was erected following a sermon preached by Rev James Maitland, minister of Kells parish. On it is the additional inscription:

The righteous shall be in everlasting remembrance. Psa. CXII 6. The above stone originally erected to the Memory of Adam MacQwhan was placed in this granite monument AD 1832. Be faithful unto death and I will give thee a crown of life. Rev. II 10. The expense defrayed by the inhabitants of Kells, after a sermon by the Rev. James Maitland, minister of the Parish.

Another place name associated with a Covenanter is Peden's Isle. This is a small islet that is located just off the western shore of Loch Riecawr. It gains its name from the famous Covenanting minister, Rev Alexander Peden, who may have hidden in the area, and perhaps even on the islet itself. Prior to the damming of Loch Riecawr the water level was much lower, and thus the island would have been greater in extent. That Peden the 'Prophet' hid in this district is confirmed by the other hideout, Peden's Hut, shown on the maps above the Water of Girvan, between Loch Skelloch and the Cornish Loch. Peden was never to become a Covenanting martyr, but he was buried in the kirkyard of Auchinleck in Ayrshire. The story does not end there, however, for after three weeks in the grave the dragoons discovered this and disinterred the body. His remains were taken to Cumnock where they had intended hanging the corpse from the gallows tree. The local laird's wife intervened, but the soldiers still buried his body at the foot of the gallows 'out of contempt', according to the old gravestone that was raised on the spot.

Near to the head of Loch Doon, about half a mile south of the site of Loch Head farm, is the Kirk Stone. Today it is very much 'lost' within the thick forestry plantations that clothe the lower slopes of Meaul, but it is possible to follow some rides through the trees and find it. A massive boulder, the Kirk Stone was probably one of the places that was used by the Covenanters to hold their outdoor services, or conventicles as they were known. That the stone was used as a place of worship may have been reflected in its name.

Similarly, by the side of the Penkiln Burn, near to where it reaches the woods around Cumloden House, is a spot known as the Preaching Howe. This is located on the north side of the burn, at the end of the Garlies Wood, an old broadleaved wood. This spot was probably one of the places where the Covenanters held conventicles in the years of struggle, and there is a known reference to there having been such services held near to Garlies Castle, which is just seven hundred yards away.

During the years of persecution, Covenanters held their church services in open-air meetings known as Conventicles. These were held in remote spots, where the authorities were unlikely to find them. One of the more famous conventicle sites in the Galloway Highlands was the Session Stone, which is located near to the Shalloch Burn, east of Shalloch on Minnoch farm. It measures a few feet in extent, lying flat among the long heather and bracken. No doubt when the sheep and cattle grazed these slopes it would have been less difficult to locate than it is today.

Writing in *The Merrick and the Neighbouring Hills*, James MacBain is a little disparaging about the stone, unsure whether there ever was a religious service held there or not. He writes, 'The stone has the reputation of having been the natural pulpit from which some unknown Covenanting preacher addressed his flock, and it is called "The Session Stone." Whether it is a true or a bogus relic the writer is not prepared to say, but its credentials are to some extent vouched for by the many initials of visitors cut into its upper surface. So covered is it with letters that there hardly seems room for another monogram.'

Attendance at conventicles was no easy task, for in addition to having to travel across country to the meetings, as well as risk capture, either at them or afterwards, non-attendance at the Episcopal church would result in a fine. For example, in 1666 the parish of Carsphairn had fines totalling £4,864 17s 4d taken from the parishioners.

A celebrated place associated with the Covenanters can no longer be located on the hill. The Aughty of the Starr was a cave where Covenanters spent some time in hiding. It is believed to have been located somewhere near to Loch Macaterick, west of Loch Doon, and from its remoteness was a spot where the Covenanters could hide in relative safety. Perhaps the Aughty was not a cave at all, more of a man-made shelter that was disguised by covering it with sods and heather, so that from the distance it blended into the background, and to the uninitiated it would appear to have been a subterranean dwelling. In any case, despite its existence having been handed down for years, no one has been able to identify where it was, and certainly nothing is likely to remain of it.

This famous cave was referred to by S. R. Crockett in his works, who also names it as Cove Macaterick. In *The Raiders*, published in 1894, he describes the cave:

'This,' said Silver Sand, 'is the Aughty of the Star. Ye have heard o' it, but few have seen it since the Killing Time. It is the best hiding-place in all broad Scotland.'

I looked about at the famous cave which had sheltered nearly all the wanderers, from Cargill to Renwick – which had been safe haven in many a storm, for which both Clavers and Lag sought in vain. My father told me also how he and Patrick Walker the pedlar (he that scribes the stories of the sufferers and has them printed), went to seek for the Aughty; but, though Patrick Walker had lain in it for four nights in the days of the Highland Host, he could never find it again.

In Crockett's other novel based on the Covenanters, *The Men of the Moss Hags*, published in 1898, the hero hides in a cave in the same vicinity, in that book styled 'Cove Macaterick'.

Another hideout used by a local family of Covenanters was the White Cairn, which lies just to the west of the road from Glentrool village to Bargrennan. From Glentrool a path through the forest leads within a few hundred yards to the cairn, which lies in a clearing. At the time of the Covenant the village was not in existence, of course, and neither was the present forest. Instead we had open moor with the stone cairn rising from the low hill known as the Mark of Glencaird. The laird of Glencaird during the 'Killing Times' was Nathaniel Mackie, who was wanted by the authorities. He and his two sons often resorted to this chambered cairn when in danger, and they were able to hide within the vault, which was described as being eighteen feet in length, five feet broad and four feet deep.

Many of the shepherds and cottars of the Galloway hills were supporters of the Covenanters, and as such would have welcomed those who were in hiding into their homes, these being remote and distant from the garrisons. In Glen Garroch, west of St John's Town of Dalry, is the farm of Largmore, which in Covenanting times was the home of the Gordon family, who were devout people.

Roger Gordon of Largmore died on 2 March 1662 at the age of 72 years. His grandson, John Gordon, was to suffer considerably for the Covenanting cause, and ultimately died of wounds he received at the Battle of Rullion Green. The Pentland Rising started in St John's Town of Dalry, and many local men took part in the march to Edinburgh, where the Covenanters had intended laying their demands before the authorities. However, as they neared the city they became apprehensive of the reception they might receive, and so camped on the outskirts. The soldiers under General Tam Dalzell of the Binns were in pursuit, and the two sides met in battle at a spot known as Rullion Green, on the southern side of the Pentland Hills. Many Covenanters were killed and hundreds were taken prisoner into the capital. Many made a quick exit, amongst them John Gordon, who had received severe wounds with resulting loss of blood. After the battle was over, he had to sleep roughly in the open fields, but he was able to make his way back to Galloway and to his home. The wounds and privations, however, were too much for his body, and he died on 6 January 1667, 38 days after the battle. With John Gordon at the battle was his brother in law, William Gordon of Roberton, but he lost his life in the affray.

The dragoons in Galloway were incensed at the early death of John, for they had intended tracking him down. They had hoped to catch him and send him to the capital in a litter, which was basically a form of stretcher.

Roger Gordon of Largmore, who was probably John's son, was another noted Covenanter. He took part in the Battle of Bothwell Bridge in 1679 but he was able to escape uninjured from the battlefield. Roger Gordon was always being hunted by the dragoons, and there are numerous accounts of him making miraculous escapes from the grasping hands of the soldiers.

One of these took place somewhere 'in a desert place in the neighbourhood of Minnigaff', according to Rev Dr Robert Simpson's *Traditions of the Covenanters*. He was making his way along a ravine towards a conventicle when he was spotted by the soldiers. Gordon and his friends matched the soldiers in number, if not in weapons, and they engaged in conflict. Gordon attacked the leader of the soldiers, a wrestle so fierce that the other men gave up their struggle and began to watch. Gordon managed to wrestle the soldier's sword and break the blade from it. He then struck him on the arm with a club, and the soldier fell to the ground. The Covenanters made an escape and were able to attend the conventicle.

Roger Gordon survived until after the Glorious Revolution of 1689, and settled back into peaceful life in Galloway.

If one takes a wander into the old kirkyard of Kells, located north of New Galloway, an old table-stone marks the grave of some of the Gordon family. It bears the inscription:

HERE LYES THE CORPS OF RO
GER GORDON OF LARGMORE
WHO DIED MARCH 2ND 1662
AGED 72 YEARS AND OF JOHN
GORDON OF LARGMORE HIS
GRANDCHILD WHO DIED JAN
UARY 6 1667 OF HIS WOUNDS
GOT AT PENTLAND IN DEFENS
OF THE COVENANTED REFOR
MATION AND OF MARGRAT
GORDON SPOUSE TO THE SAID
ROGER WHO DYED JULY 18 1667
AND OF JOHN GORDON OF
GARVERIE THER SON WHO
DYED FEBRUARY 24 1670 AG
ED 23 AND OF SAMUEL QUINTI
NE AGNES ANNA ALEXANDE
AND SAMUEL GORDONS THER
GRAND CHILDRING AS ALSO
THE CORPS OF AGNES M^CDUALL
SPOUSE TO JAMES GORDON SON
TO ROGER GORDON OF LARGMO
RE WHO DYED MARCH 25 1725
THE 69 YEAR
OF HER AGE
Also the Corps of
the above James
Gordon who died
the 7th of April
1769 Aged 80 years.

The family arms were carved on the stone, a chevron between three boars' heads. The stone was not erected for some time, however, for Covenanters would not have been allowed burial in the kirkyard, and they were often interred at night, so that the authorities did not find out.

The younger Roger Gordon of Largmore is commemorated on a memorial stone built into the gable of the church. In 1714 he presented a large bell to the church in Kells, as well as a pair of communion cups.

Another incident associated with the Covenanting period took place in Glen Garroch, in fact, at Old Garroch House. At the time the house was used as a base by Grierson of Lag, who had captured William Stevenson of Berbeth and taken him there. His hands and feet were bound with strips of raw hide, there being no rope available, and he was thrown into a locked building overnight. The smell of the hide, however, attracted the attention of rats which nibbled their way through the bands, releasing him. He was then able to burst through the thatched roof and make good his escape.

If one visits Sir Walter Scott's home at Abbotsford, near to Melrose in Roxburghshire, in the collection of artefacts that the great novelist made, one can see a set of 'thumbikins', or thumbscrews. This was a device used to torture Covenanters, and apparently was introduced to Scotland during the 'killing times'. The Covenanter's thumbs were placed through two metal plates, and a thumbscrew was turned, squeezing the metal frame over the digits, compressing the bones until they broke. Often, before this took place, the 'hill-man' had confessed to his support for the Covenant, or divulged the whereabouts of the hiding places of his friends.

The thumbscrews at Abbotsford have a Galloway connection, for they were obtained from the farmer at Buchan by Sir Walter Scott's friend and supplier of information, Joseph Train. How the farmer at Buchan obtained the thumbscrews is not known, but Train noted that they had been 'kept there since the Covenanters were shot at Caldons.'

11 Industrial Archaeology

The wild uplands of the Galloway Highlands are not usually associated with industry, unless it is of the agricultural or forestry kind. And yet, in the past, certain parts of these hills, mainly around the periphery, were centres of industrial production, where folk lived remotely, earning a living mining, smelting, or working in associated trades.

Due west of Carsphairn, in the valley of the Garryhorn Burn, can be seen remains of a sizeable mining community. The Woodhead Lead Mines today form a most interesting industrial archaeology site, one that is spread across the slopes of Garryhorn Rig. Remains of buildings and chimneys are positioned randomly across the hillside, gradually crumbling into the ground once more. In recent years they have become more recognised for their historical and archaeological importance, and as such have become protected.

In 1838 prospectors were in the area and discovered considerable pockets of lead, plus copper, zinc and silver to a smaller degree. The lead had first been noticed by the farmer at Woodhead, who reported it to his landlord, Colonel MacAdam Cathcart (d. 1865). The discovery was acted upon quickly, and the following year new lead mines and associated buildings were established. These veins of ore, or galena, dip towards the north-north-east at around sixty degrees. The veins also contain zinc-blende and chalcopyrite.

Colonel MacAdam Cathcart was a very forward-looking landlord, and he wanted the best conditions that he could for the workers at his new mines. He was very 'hands-on', and took a deep interest in the on-going work at the mines. In his journal he wrote:

Visited the Mine this day, found the water course going on well ... entered into agreements respecting the intending buildings at the Mine after examining the different offers and conferring with the intending contractors on the spot.

Writing in March 1844, Rev David Welsh, minister of Carsphairn and contributor to the *New Statistical Account of Scotland*, was enthusiastic about the new mines and of the possibilities they brought. It is worth quoting him at length:

Nothing has yet been done in the way of purifying the lead. The ore which has been extracted, lies in the state in which it was dug out; but preparations are beginning to be made for washing and purifying it, and it is presumed that no expense will be spared in carrying on the operations on the most approved plans. There is abundance of coal and lime upon the estates of the proprietor on the Ayrshire side, and it is hoped that an exchange favourable to Carsphairn may be made.

Since the preceding pages were written in 1839, Carsphairn has undergone a wonderful change, chiefly on account of the mining operations carried on within the parish. Since the operations commenced, the population has been nearly doubled. In that part of the parish in which lead was discovered, and in the bosom of a remote mountain, where the silence of nature was seldom broken, unless by the barking of the shepherd's dog, or the call of the shepherd, there is now a scene of industry and activity, which requires to be witnessed in order to be understood; and which cannot be contemplated without astonishment.

The proprietor of the mine, the Honourable Colonel MacAdam Cathcart, has spared no expense in obtaining all the necessary apparatus for crushing, washing, and smelting, on the most approved principles. The wheel used for moving the crushing apparatus is about 30 feet in diameter, driven by water obtained from the neighbouring mountains. The smelting furnaces are constructed on the most approved plan; and large houses have been built, and preparations are making in them for separating the silver from the lead. The proprietor has been acting hitherto as if it were his object to exhibit the whole operations in the most perfect manner, rather than to enrich himself. It is to be hoped, however, that the liberal manner in which hitherto he has conducted the whole business, may meet with an ample reward. The Honourable Colonel M. Cathcart retains the mine entirely in his own hands. He has appointed skilful and steady men as overseers; and he takes pleasure in personally superintending the whole.

Everything is done by the proprietor to promote the comfort of the workmen. A large village has already been built upon the side of the hill, additions to which are still making; and from the situation which it occupies, and the cleanliness of its appearance, it presents a picturesque object to the traveller in passing among the wild mountains. The proprietor has likewise evidenced his liberality in his attention to the mental cultivation and moral improvement of the workmen.

Though there are workmen from different quarters, yet greater part are from Leadhills and Wanlockhead,—men who had enjoyed the privilege of excellent libraries, and who regretted their separation from these means of entertainment and improvement. So soon as the Colonel and the Honourable Mrs Macadam Cathcart were made acquainted with their desire of forming a library, they sent a number of books, which laid an excellent foundation for a library, and which, by various means, is rapidly increasing. In addition to this, they have built an excellent school and school-master's house; the school-house is more ample and commodious than any in the district, and they give a liberal salary both to the schoolmaster and female teacher.

The mining operations have changed Carsphairn from being one of the most rural and pastoral parishes in this country, into one of comparative bustle and activity. More money now circulates in one week than was circulated, a few years ago, in the course of the year.

The writer of the *New Statistical Account* makes reference to the number of miners travelling from Wanlockhead and Leadhills in search of work, and this is noted in an account of Leadhills made in 1841. When Joseph Fletcher paid a visit in order to compile evidence for a Royal Commission on Children's Employment he noted that:

At the time of my visit [to Leadhills] there were a number of families remaining in the village, the heads of which, to the number of perhaps 80 had gone to work at the newly opened mine at Carsphairn in Galloway about 60 miles distant, where there is as yet no permanent home for those dependent on them.

However, it was not too long before rows of miners' houses were built. These were strung across the hillside in terraces. At the western end of the community were the Higher Row and Lower Row, but above them were more rows of houses, including the Office Row. North east of the two named rows were further houses, seemingly randomly spread about the complex, as though the miners were given free rein to find

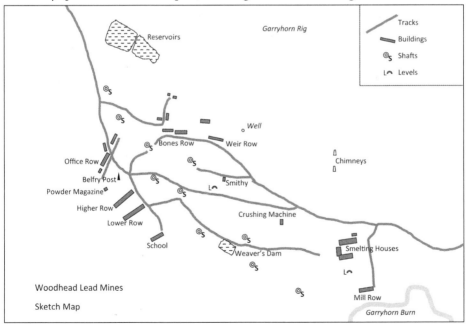

11.1 Sketch Map of Woodhead Lead Mines, c. 1850

suitable ground for building. Some of the rows were named Bone's Row and Weir's Row, probably after some long-term occupants. Mill Row was where the smelters lived. It had five houses within it.

In the 1841 census there were 22 houses occupied, with a population of 200. Ten years later the number of houses had increased to fifty, with the maximum population achieved at Woodhead, 301 persons. All of the houses were single storey and roofed with slates.

As well as miners from Leadhills and Wanlockhead, Colonel MacAdam Cathcart also brought in the experience of miners from Cornwall, many of whom were appointed as overseers.

The manager at the mines for much of the time was Peter Wilson, and he kept a diary from which it is possible to glean some interesting facts. Up to the end of 1852 5,700 tons of lead was produced, providing an income, minus the cost of smelting, of £88,065. Averaging this out over the twelve years previously provides an annual income of around £7,300. There was probably further income, for every ton of lead also produced eighteen ounces of silver, which was sold at a much higher rate. Lead was sold at an average rate of £16 per ton, though the price was sometimes as high as £24 per ton. The cost of smelting was worked out at eleven shillings per ton, including fuel costs.

There were two veins of lead ore worked at Woodhead, named the Woodhead Vein and Garryhorn String. Mine shafts, adits, levels and ventilation shafts were created across the hillside creating a complex series of tunnels and linking shafts. The upper three levels were named the Top Adit, Middle Adit and Deep Adit levels. Below this were two other levels, the 11 Fathoms Level and the 25 Fathoms Level.

The miners required dynamite in order to blast into the rocks, and a powder magazine was located near to the Upper Row. This was a small square building, topped by a hipped roof.

There were at least nine shafts at Woodhead, dropping vertically to seven different levels where the lead was worked. The deepest, which was 312 feet deep, was sunk in 1843. From the shafts the levels spread out into the hillside, where miners worked in cramped conditions, between masses of whinstone. Light was provided by candles, and there are records of two banksmen being given three candles each for twelve hours. The overseer was allocated 5,961 pounds of candles at a cost of £173 17s 3d.

On the surface a crushing plant was established, shown on detailed maps as a 'crushing machine', to break the rocks that were brought to the surface. To drive this plant a large waterwheel was constructed, thirty feet in diameter.

To get sufficient water to drive the crushing wheel and for other purposes three extensive lades were dug out of the hillside. One contoured at around 950 feet above sea level, feeding a rectangular reservoir known as the Weaver's Dam. A second lade was positioned about 750-800 feet above sea level, and contoured from the Garryhorn Burn right into the centre of the community – it was probably this lade that drove the crushing machine's waterwheel. A third lade was located higher up, contouring at approximately 1,000 feet above sea level, diverting water from the Garryhorn Burn and adding to it water from lesser streams. Water was also obtained from the north, the headwaters of the Green Burn being diverted over the shoulder of Garryhorn Rig and into two sizeable reservoirs located in the pass. The lower, and slightly smaller of the two reservoirs, had a sluice which controlled the flow of water from it, and this was directed down a lade towards the smithy and crushing machine.

A washing plant was constructed, where the ore was cleaned. Boys were employed to carry out this task, being paid around one shilling per day. At one point there were twelve lead washers under the age of fourteen years, including six aged ten years. Linking the different plants were small mineral lines, the stone transported along them in bogies. A smithy existed to work metal, and near to it was a wright's workshop.

A smelting plant was built where the lead ore could be placed into furnaces and melted. This was a short distance downhill from the crushing plant, linked to it by a short pathway. Arranged around a courtyard, and only one storey in height, the smelting houses were the largest buildings in the whole works, and two major furnaces had the smoke from them directed through underground flues and up the hillside to two chimneys built above the complex. The lower chimney still stands to a height of around fifty feet. The higher chimney has collapsed and only stands around fifteen feet in height. The slag and impurities were taken off, leaving the natural lead to be poured into ingots. Smelters were paid eighteen shillings per week, and were given a free house and fuel.

Lead from Woodhead was taken by track over the hill towards Lamloch and from there north to Dalmellington, where it was stored for a time in what the locals called the 'Leid Yard'. Continuing on, the lead was taken to the port of Ayr, from where it was shipped south through the North Channel and Irish Sea to Liverpool and even exported to the Netherlands, where the lead was converted into sheets used for roofing and other plumbing purposes.

The same road was also used for hauling coal and limestone from the Ayrshire coalfield to the smelter.

The amount of lead produced at Woodhead varied over the years, but as can be seen from the table, the works produced the greatest quantity within its first five years, after which production diminished.

1840	340 tons	1849	263	1858	63	1867	20
1841	495	1850	290	1859	45	1868	0
1842	905	1851	302	1860	59	1869	30
1843	850	1852	194	1861	61	1870	61
1844	638	1853	93	1862	51	1871	63
1845	416	1854	50	1863	42	1872	34
1846	362	1855	56	1864	41	1873	12
1847	354	1856	85	1865	35		
1848	301	1857	72	1866	29		

The total quantity of lead mined at Woodhead was 6,712 tons.

Woodhead Lead Mines

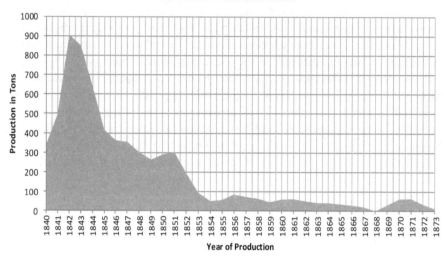

11.2 Graph showing production of lead at Woodhead, 1840-1873

Wages at the mines were paid depending on the output. In January 1839 the Colonel expected to pay the miners around £3 per month, but as the pits deepened the men found it more difficult to keep up with production. Later, miners were paid about eighteen shillings per week, though their labourers only received around twelve to fourteen shillings.

As with all mining operations, there were a number of fatalities. One of these was reported in the *Dumfries Standard* of December 1849:

> On Monday last, a miner named John Bone lost his life through an accident at Woodhead Lead Mine. Deceased had fired a blast, and was proceeding to remove the rubbish, when a large mass of rock, which, unknown to the workman, the gunpowder had detached from its bed, fell upon him. The stone was immediately removed, but so severely had he been crushed that, although little external injury was visible, he survived barely half an hour. With the above exception only one death has occurred at Woodhead Lead Mine for upwards of twelve months. Considering that the present year has been so rife with disease, it is doubtful if any other village in Britain, with a population of from three to four hundred individuals has the same cause of thankfulness to the Giver of health and life.

A second fatality is recorded in 16 January 1852. On that day David Wilson was killed in Harris' Jerry Shaft.

In his circuit tours, Lord Cockburn paid a visit to Woodhead. He noted that, 'it looks like a colony of solitary strangers who were trying to discover subterranean treasures in a remote land.'

11.3 Ruins at Woodhead Lead Mines

In 1843 a new school was erected at Woodhead, located below the Lower Row. This replaced an earlier school, for it is noted in 1841 that John Kidd was employed as a teacher at the village, which had 46 children under the age of 13. The next teacher was Charles Stuart MacLean, who was assisted by his wife, Eliza Finnis. According to the *Dumfries Standard*, 'in the seminary recently opened at the lead-mines, Carsphairn, the Hon Colonel MacAdam Cathcart has there built a most commodious schoolhouse and we congratulate him in the fortunate election which has been made of a teacher who seems in every way fitted from the success which has accompanied his labours during the short period since his appointment to be an unspeakable benefit to the numerous and increasing population of the mines'.

There were 49 pupils at Woodhead school in 1851, aged from five to fourteen. Within the next few years it is thought that the school was closed, for around that time many miners left the works in search of new jobs, the production of lead dropping considerably. The building was later converted into a shooting lodge for the Cathcarts, and remained in use as such for a century thereafter.

The miners at Woodhead wished to establish a church of their own, but Colonel MacAdam Cathcart would not allow them to build one on his property. Most of the miners were English, and they adhered to the Wesleyan Methodist Church. James MacMillan of Lamloch was more sympathetic, and allowed a place of worship to be built there. Until it was erected he allowed the miners to worship in his kitchen. In January 1844 it was decided to build a church, and the miners, along with assistance from the Free Church congregation in Dalmellington, set about constructing it. Lamloch Church was built to the south west of Lamloch House, by the side of the Lamloch Burn, at the nearest point on MacMillan's property to Woodhead village. The miners walked over the hill track, a distance of one and half miles, meaning that worshippers had a round trip of three miles to worship. This was a favourable distance compared with the six mile round trip to the parish church in Carsphairn. However, in 1841 there were eighteen Free Church members at the church who travelled there from Carsphairn. The church was closed in 1876 and the building reverted back to MacMillan.

In addition to the school and church, a library was established at Woodhead to allow the miners to better themselves. Many of the workers had come from Wanlockhead and Leadhills, where there was a strong tradition of using a free or works library, and at Woodhead the Library Society was founded in 1840. In 1849 the library had over eight hundred books on its shelves, including a 'splendidly bound copy of the *Encyclopaedia Britannica*', which Colonel MacAdam Cathcart had presented. 'The library was probably part of the school, and everybody within a ten-mile radius of the mines was allowed to borrow from it so that the fruits of this judicious liberalism are apparent not only in the well-thumbed volumes which may be found in almost every cottage, but in the superior intelligence and orderly habits by which the inhabitants of this district are so honourably distinguished.'

A number of causes, including a slump in demand for lead, resulted in the mines at Woodhead being closed. In February 1852 a number of miners and other workers were given notice to quit, and in 1853 a fair number of residents of the mines emigrated to the United States, in particular to Pennsylvania. Nevertheless, some folk still remained at the houses, and writing in the first edition of *Rambles in Galloway* (1876), Malcolm Harper noted that he saw nearly one hundred workers, 'all busily engaged at work on the surface.' By the time the second edition of the book appeared in 1896, he noted that the mines had been abandoned for several years. In 1861, according to the Census, there were only 88 people living at the mines; by the 1891 Census this had dropped to fourteen people, living in three houses. The houses at the village were gradually abandoned, and the last house to be occupied was in 1954. Sometime between 1917 and 1920 the Ore Supply Ltd company of Newton Stewart did some prospecting at Woodhead, but it is not thought that they carried out any mining.

In the kirk at New Abbey, south west of Dumfries, is a stained glass window in memory of Rev James Stewart Wilson. He was educated at the little school at Woodhead, from where he went to Edinburgh University and studied for the ministry. He was to become the minister at New Abbey.

Another lead mine was located at the south western end of the Galloway Highlands, almost diametrically opposite Woodhead mines. The Wood of Cree Lead Mine was located about three miles from Minnigaff, on the back road from there towards Bargrennan. Near to the foot of the Coldstream Burn, where it joins the River Cree, a lead mine was sunk into the hillside. A larger lead mining concern, the Blackcraig Mining Company and Craigtown Mining Company, had a series of mines in the Bargaly Glen, further down the parish, where most of the miners employed were Welsh, and most were Quakers. A number of these may have come to Wood of Cree for employment.

The mine was probably opened early in the nineteenth century, but it appears to have been closed by 1849, for it is noted as being disused on the Ordnance Survey map of that time. The mine comprised of three shafts sunk into the hillside, joined by three levels.

Today the remains of the mine are difficult to find, but one can still make out the foundations of the old magazine where the miners kept the powder used to blast the rock. Extensive slag heaps surround the mine head, and there can also be found the base of what may have been a water-pressure beam engine.

A later Wood of Cree lead mine was established around 250 yards to the south of the Coldstream Burn. It was first sunk around 1870, there being two levels and a shaft here. The lead ore was also mined by opencast means. It wasn't just lead that was mined at Wood of Cree, for zinc ore was also obtained, in 1918 the mine producing 105 tons of it. The company which operated the mine was known as Ore Supply Ltd, a syndicate of locals which also operated mines at Blackcraig, near to Palnure. The mine was abandoned shortly after the First World War. Today little can be seen to indicate that there was such industry in the area, though the keen industrial archaeologist will be able to discern the foundations of some of the surface buildings and spoil heaps. The old level mouths are also still to be seen, round holes about six feet in diameter.

On the moor above Cordorcan farm, east of the Loch of Cree, was another lead mine, known as the Silver Mine, or sometimes as Silver Rig Mine or Silver Ridge Mine. Located on Silver Rig, just below the Silver Rig Loch, the mine was reached by a path from Cordorcan. Its name has often caused folk to assume that silver was mined there, but the mine was sunk to work lead ore, though silver was a by-product of lead mining.

The mine may have operated in the eighteenth century, but abandoned soon after. It was reopened and is known to have been abandoned in 1836. It was opened for a third time, and in 1850 there were two shafts operating when the Ordnance Survey map-makers passed through. The South of Scotland Mining Company is known to have owned the mine at this time. The 1894 map shows it as disused. At the time of the 1850 map there was no Silver Rig Loch, this being a man-made lake of a later date, the waters of which were diverted to the mine workings.

The mine worked lead to a depth of ninety feet, some of it open cast mining on the surface. The earliest workings are thought to have been the surface workings, the third phase of mining being that which excavated the deepest.

In 1920 it was noted that at the mine 'the ruins of workmen's houses and a water wheel' could still be seen. In fact, the ruins are reasonably well preserved. One can see

11.4 Ruins of chimney, Woodhead Lead Mines

the old water wheel pit, a stone structure measuring 28 feet by 10 feet, into which water from a lade was directed. The wheel probably operated a flat-rod pumping system. Due north of the wheel pit was the main shaft, and west of this was an area where the ore had been worked on the surface. A former mine office is positioned further north, a two-roomed building, probably comprising the main office, with fireplace and windows, adjoining this being a store.

Unlike the mines at Woodhead, there is no evidence of housing for the workers at the Silver Mine, and one can only assume that they were accommodated either in local shepherds' houses and crofts, or else there may have been timber huts, the remains of which are no longer visible.

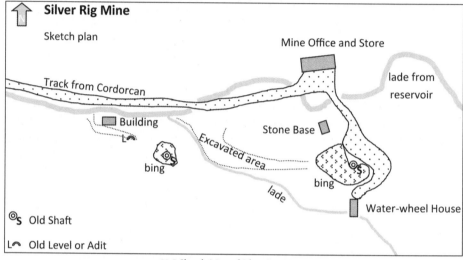

11.5 Sketch Map of Silver Rig Mine

At one time the mining of black lead was carried out in the southern extremities of the Galloway Highlands. At Talnotry, up the Palnure Glen from Minnigaff, investigations in the late nineteenth century discovered an outcrop comprising of two beds of plumbago, or black lead, located near to the Grey Mare's Tail Burn. A shaft was sunk and the plumbago was extracted. The mine was owned by Major Stewart of Cairnsmore. The plumbago was used for pencil lead, and at the time it was discovered was reckoned to be 'the only workable deposit of plumbago in Britain.' Writing in 1876, Malcolm Harper in *Rambles in Galloway*, noted that 'the output promises to be highly remunerative.'

Mining for ironstone, or haematite, has also taken place on a small scale within the Galloway Highlands. High on the slopes of the mountains of Coran of Portmark, Bow and Meaul, are small spoil heaps that look almost natural, so long have the shafts been abandoned. Indeed, just when these mines existed has not been easy to identify – some think they may be as old as the mediaeval period, others that they were test holes made in the early nineteenth century. The *New Statistical Account* of Carsphairn parish, written in 1839, makes reference to iron being discovered on the estate of

Captain Cathcart, and this probably refers to this vein. A series of nine shafts have been sunk into the vein, extending almost two miles in length, running on a north-south axis. The northernmost six shafts are located on the western slopes of Bow and Coran, the southernmost three shafts being located at the head of the glen of the Garryhorn Burn.

It is probably these bores that James MacBain refers to in *The Merrick and the Neighbouring Hills*. He writes that there were two horizontal tunnels driven into the hillside by an iron company. Although they found a deposit of a rich iron ore, the quantity was too small to justify working the vein. The cost of transporting the stone by a new railway to Dalmellington was also prohibitive.

Quarrying was not a major employer in the Galloway hills, but a few smaller quarries have been dug in various locations for different types of stone. In the Cree Wood, by the side of the River Cree, there was an old quarry which was used to excavate slate.

Another couple of slate quarries existed on the southern side of Loch Bradan, on the slopes of Craiglure. One was located near to Craiglure Lodge, the other half a mile to the south. At the latter there stood a small cottage or other building, perhaps the home of the quarryman. The two quarries are shown as disused on the Ordnance Survey map of 1856.

Industry could also be carried out on a small scale in the hills and valleys of the Galloway Highlands. By the side of the River Cree, north of Newton Stewart, is the Wood of Cree, one of the nature reserves maintained by the Royal Society for the Protection of Birds. In the mid nineteenth century, and no doubt for centuries beforehand, the oak woods here were cut down and used for bark-peeling. The bark from the oak trees was used for tanning leather, the tannin or tannic acid being used in the conversion of hide into leather. According to the *New Statistical Account* of Minnigaff parish, written in 1842, the wood had been copsed within the previous few years, the last cutting sold for £6,000.

The granite boss that forms the centre of the Galloway Highlands takes many millions of years to erode down into a sharp sand that is white in colour, but which contains black grains also. This sand can be found in the beds of some streams, but also in bays alongside some of the lochs. The sand was at one time in great demand for the purpose of sharpening scythes, and many loads of it were hauled away over the centuries.

A number of lochs have sandy bays that were used as a source of the sand, but it was always said that the sand from Loch Enoch was the best that could be obtained. This may have been a sales ploy, Loch Enoch being the highest of the larger Galloway lochs, and one of the more remote, thus carrying sand in bags from this loch would have required more effort than any other.

Loch Enoch is a rather magnificent and eerie loch. It has no real shape to it – often it has been described as a ragged butterfly in shape, though this is only apparent to those who can see the shape on a map, or from the heights of the Merrick. The loch has a series of pools, the two roundest being located at the south-east and south-west of the loch, the former almost totally encircled by land. The northern half of the loch has a series of fingers, peninsulas of low-lying moss and rock projecting into the waters between them.

The surface of Loch Enoch is 1,617 feet above sea level, and though the whole extent of the loch is in the Stewartry of Kirkcudbright, the loch has its embouchure at the northern end, at a spot known as Sluice of Loch Enoch, the waters forming the source of the Eglin Lane, one of the principal rivers that flows into Loch Doon. Between the Sluice and the little stream that flows from the Pulskaig pass the shore of the loch is within Ayrshire.

The granitic sand from Loch Enoch is technically disintegrated syenitic granite, and as stated was in demand for sharpening scythes. According to the *Proceedings of the Royal Society of Edinburgh* of 1909-10, the sand from Loch Enoch 'is finer than any other, and is prized above all by shepherds, far and near, for the purpose of sharpening their scythes, although those living in this district frequently use that from the nearest loch for the same purpose.'

Other lochs with granitic sands include Loch Neldricken and Loch Valley. There is a story that a tinker was at Loch Neldricken to collect silver sand but the winter snows engulfed him and he became lost in blizzard. He succumbed to hypothermia and it is said that he was buried near to Loch Neldricken.

I have often wondered how the sand was used for sharpening scythes. I have sharpened a scythe with a stone hone, and could not comprehend how the loose grains of sand could be employed in sharpening a metal blade. The grains were certainly rough enough, and granite is certainly one of the hardest stones, but it was not until I came upon the reference to the sands in the *Proceedings* mentioned above that things became clear:

> To sharpen a scythe, a strip of wood about 18 inches long by 3 inches wide is smothered with butter, which is then sprinkled with sand, and used in a similar way to the ordinary whetsone. Others stick the sand to the wood with glue; the latter, however, has to be purchased, whilst the former is a home product of no monetary value.

We also come across a reference to silver sand in John MacTaggart's *Scottish Gallovidian Encyclopedia*, which was first published in 1824. According to MacTaggart, Loch Skeroch is 'a large, wild, loch, to the north of Galloway, famous for its scythe sand. This is found on the beach of the lake, and is wrought of grey-stones, in the lake by the waters; it is sold in shops during the mowing season, at about twopence the Scotch pint.'

The collecting of silver sand appears to have died out early in the twentieth century. One of the last known men to collect and sell the sand was John Morgan, who travelled across Galloway and Nithsdale with his horse and cart, selling the sand in the villages, along with the wooden strakes used with it. He died at the age of 85 years in the village of Thornhill.

12 Living in the Highlands

Farming in the Galloway Highlands has changed over the years and, as a consequence, the folk who lived in the hill country and around the periphery have had to adapt to this. At one time there were many ferme touns along the edges of the uplands, though these were abandoned in the eighteenth century when the landowners were improving their estates, fencing and enclosing the land and reallocating the properties to new tenants. A 'ferme toun' (or farm town) is the term used to describe groupings of farmhouses where the tenants worked a pattern of fields around them. The old ferme touns were often left to fall into ruin, and in many places the remains of these can still be seen on the ground. Though not of any major archaeological significance, current guidance proposes that they should be preserved, or at least left to decay naturally.

A number of ferme touns can still be visited, and the remains make interesting places to explore. Readily accessible are the settlements that existed at Polmaddy, in the Glenkens, and in the Knockman Wood, north of Minnigaff, where access paths have been created.

The old ferme toun of Polmaddy has already been described in the chapter on Archaeology. Near to Garlies Castle a number of other ferme touns can still be seen, in some cases still having the remains of old corn kilns visible. The ferme touns near Garlies Castle can be seen at Clauchrie, Closy, Knockbracks and Glenmalloch. Around the ruins of the old cottages and byres can be seen the remains of stone dikes which enclosed small irregular fields. Corn kilns were popular among the upland steadings, and a number of these can be discovered among the long grasses and bracken that surround the ruins of many farms. Kilns were used to dry corn before it was milled.

Another grouping of cottages and farmsteads existed at the foot of the Water of Trool, and south past Holm farm. On opposite sides of the Ferrach Burn were Borgan Ferrach and Holm Ferrach, two cottages with second names associating them with the parent farm. Both cottages were abandoned and in ruins by the time of the 1849 Ordnance Survey map, which indicates an old corn kiln at Borgan Ferrach. There are numerous other old ruins in the immediate vicinity, indicating that this may have been a small ferme toun.

Holm farm survives, with a number of acres of better quality ground on the side of the Water of Minnoch. On the other side of the river was Low Minniwick, still occupied until the early twentieth century. High Minniwick is still occupied, and an old corn kiln existed to the west of the steading. North of Holm were Dalane and High Dalane, now gone, and east of High Dalane was Draniemanner. Further east, near to the Rocking Stone below Jenny's Hill, were some other old houses, in ruins by 1849. The names of these are forgotten

In Glen Trool, on the north side of the Water of Trool, were a line of old buildings. Near to the confluence of the two waters, Trool and Minnoch, at Trool Foot, was Fordmouth, which had a corn kiln. At Stroan was an old corn kiln, and Mid Close was a small steading, with the remains of a corn kiln on the hillside above the farm. Near to this was Knockbrae, on the old track heading from Mid Close to Caldons, in ruins by 1849.

To the north of Stroan Bridge, in what are now the extensive plantations of the Glentrool Forest, there were numerous cottages and farm steadings. There may not have been a proper ferme toun as such, but this area was, at one time, populated by a number of country folk, running farms, mills and crofts.

Little remains to hint at the community that once occupied this moorland. However, just upstream from the Linn of Glencaird, on the Water of Minnoch, are the remains of Glencaird Mill, located by the side of the Minnoch, on its western bank. This was abandoned as a mill by the mid-nineteenth century, but the old Ordnance Survey map of the time noted that it had been both a corn and snuff mill.

On the opposite side of the Minnoch, on the lower ground west of Craignacraddoch, were a number of small steadings – Kirriedarroch, Barns and Kirriecastle.

The farmers and cottagers who lived in the ferme touns often lived a life that was more acquaint with the traditions of the district than those in more urban localities. One of the common aspects of country life was the belief in witches and other supernatural spirits.

As with all of Scotland at the time, the threat from witches was something that the kirk authorities had to counter. Old accounts of folklore make reference to the witch of Carsphairn which is supposed to have tried to throw a boulder from a local hill at the church. The stone missed, landing in a nearby field, where it remains to this day. Similar stories are told of stones near church buildings across Scotland, from Craigie in Ayrshire to Cortachy in Angus, but the story at Carsphairn is less likely to be true than the rest for the simple reason that the kirk at Carsphairn is comparatively new, as far as churches are concerned. The parish was only formed in 1636, when part of the parishes of Dalry and Kells were separated and formed into Carsphairn parish.

The main period of witch-hunting took place between 1563 and the early 1700s, but the old traditions and folklore took time to die out, and there were still instances of 'devilrie' occurring right into the first part of the eighteenth century. The old kirk session records of the parish of Minnigaff make reference to a case from 3 June 1702:

> There being a flagrant report yt [that] some persons in this parish in and about the house of Barcly, should have practised that piece of devilrie commonly called turning the riddle, as also it being reported yt ye principal person is one Malley Redmond, an Irish woman, for present nurse in the house of Barcly, to ye young Lady Tonderghee, as also yt Alexander Kelly,

Gilbert Kelly, his son, and Marion Murray, formerly servant in Barcly, now in Holme, were witness yrto, the session appoints ye said Malley, and ye above said witnesses to be cited to ye nixt meeting. [Malley did not appear as summoned, but after some time turned up, whereupon she denied having] practised that piece of devilrie, of turning ye riddle.

The case continued, Malley denying having 'turned the riddle', which was an ancient method of fortune-telling, first mentioned in Virgil's *Eclogues*. However, Malley did admit to have seen this being done by two girls in her father's house back in Ireland. Apparently something had been stolen and the girls had carried out this process in order to find out who the guilty party was. The session interviewed Malley and others at length, in order to find out whether she was guilty. Marion Murray, a lass of eighteen years, was called as a witness and she was:

> ...sworn, purged of malice and partial consel, deponeth, yt she (not having seen any other person doing it before her,) together with ye nurse, held her riddle betwixt ym, having a pair of little schissors fastened into ye rim of the riddle, whereof ye nurse Malley Redmond held one point and she the other, and that the nurse mumbled some words, mentioning Peter and Paul, and that when the nurse said these words, the riddle stirred less or more, and after ye nurse had said the words, she bad ye deponent say them to, and that she accordingly said the same words back again to the nurse, and that the deponent had said to ye nurse Malley, before ever she meddled with it, that if she knew yr was any evil in doing of it she would not meddle with it, and ye nurse replied yr was no evil in it, and further, that to shift the meddling with it, she offered to take ye child from ye lady's armes, but ye young lady put her to it, bidding her go do it. As also, yt further ye said Marion depones, yt ye same day, a little after ye young lady bad her go to ye barn, and yr do it over again with the nurse, which she positively refused; whereupon ye young lady did it herself, with all the circumstances she and the nurse had done it in the chambers before; moreover, that some dayes after, the chamber door being close upon the young lady and her nurse Malley, ye deponent, looking through a hole in ye door, saw ye nurse and ye lady standing, and ye riddle betwixt ym as before, but heard nothing. And further, yt ye lady and her nurse bad her deny these things, but did not bid her swear to it.

For their part in the case, Lady Tonderghee, Mrs Janet Blair and Marion Murray were asked to subscribe to a declaration that was to be read before the congregation at Minnigaff, 'abhorring and renouncing all spelles and charmes usual to wizards; and having been rebuked and exhorted to greater watchfulness for the future they were dismissed.' Malley Redmond appeared before the congregation and was rebuked, after which she was banished from the parish.

Another place where witches are blamed for features on the ground is on the low

Waterside Hill, west of Earlstoun Power Station. There, on the moor south of the summit, can be seen a circular trench cut into the turf. This is known as The Score. According to local tales, there was a man from Dalry who had been drinking rather too much. He was pursued on his horse by some witches, but to protect himself he used the old trick of drawing a circle on the ground around the horse and himself. Witches were unable to cross this. However, his horse had a rather long tail, which at one time hung over the line. A witch was able to grab a hold of it and cut it off, leaving it with a short fringe. According to some, the story influenced Robert Burns when he wrote *Tam o' Shanter*.

The Devil has been implicated for creating a number of difficult to explain features within the Galloway hills. The De'il's Bowling Green on Craignaw has already been mentioned.

When the ferme touns were abandoned, they were replaced by larger farming units, with a shepherd to look after the sheep that were grazed on the hillsides. These clearing out of smaller holdings were the equivalent of the Highland Clearances, but which happened a century before those further north.

Much of the Galloway hills were latterly occupied by sheep farms. Some of these could be of considerable extent, for the land was more or less unsuitable for anything else. According to the *Statistical Account* of the parish of Straiton, there was one sheep farm in the parish which was upwards of 6,000 acres in extent. Although the writer doesn't specify which farm this was, it was probably Starr, one of the largest sheep farms in the south of the country. According to William Crawford, the writer of the *Account*, the farm did not pay the proprietor above £50 of yearly rent, and that was in 1791. The *New Statistical Account* of Minnigaff makes reference to the largest sheep farm in that parish, which was 4,700 acres in extent.

Most of the ground farmed by Starr is tussocky and spattered with large boulders,

12.1 Fore Starr area shown on Armstrong's Map of Ayrshire

most of them left behind by the retreating ice. When the Armstrong's surveyed this area when they were compiling their map of Ayrshire in 1775, they noted 'Exceeding deep Mosses & barren Rocks & not capable of improvement, the whole Farm of the Starr containing upwards of 6,000 Acres, brings a trifling Rent.'

In 1841, when the Census of Scotland was being compiled, the farm of Starr had six residents at it. The farmer was Thomas Paterson, who was 65 years old – though the Census that year rounded ages of adults up or down to the nearest five. He was assisted by three agricultural labourers – James Carson (aged 50), Robert MacMillan (aged 15) and James MacMillan (aged 12). In addition, there were two female servants, Isabella Girrmany (aged 45) and Agnes Limont (aged 15).

Starr was just one of many cottages and farms on the Marquis of Ailsa's estate. In the early part of the twentieth century the cottage was leased (along with Lambdoughty on Doon and Craigmalloch) by John Hutchison of Newarkhill Farm, south of Alloway, Ayr. He placed a shepherd in the cottage, in 1905 this being James MacFadzean, and in 1915 it was Robert MacCutcheon.

The traditional sheep grazed on the Galloway hills was the blackfaced variety. These are a hardy breed, ideally suited to the wild uplands. It is possible that the breed may have originated in the Pennine Hills and arrived in south-western Scotland after cross-border raids made by the Scots from the fourteenth century onward. The blackface sheep were bred for their wool and mutton, as well as lamb. It was reckoned in 1842 that it required four and a half acres per sheep.

One of the main breeders and most successful sheep farmers of the late eighteenth and early nineteenth century was Robert MacMillan (1757-1844), shepherd at Palgowan, on the western side of the Merrick. He spent time selecting the best stock for breeding, and introduced the best rams from other areas of the country. As a result, the Palgowan blackface sheep were among the best in the country at that time.

Robert MacMillan died on 5 January 1844 and was buried in the old kirkyard of Minnigaff. His gravestone tells of the spread of his family, as well as of the number of children who died – typical of the period. His daughter, Mary, died in 1827 aged 26. Elizabeth MacMillan died in 1835 aged 14, and a further four sons and a daughter died young. A son, David, emigrated to Alabama, United States, where he died in 1842 aged 47. Another son, William MacMillan, became the tenant after his father, and died in 1864 aged 66.

The number of sheep across the Galloway Highlands was considerable at one time, and it is reckoned that much of the original denudation of trees in the area was as a result of the sheep eating saplings, so that as the older trees died there were none to replace them. How many sheep there were in the highland area cannot be calculated, but in the 1790s Carsphairn parish was noted as having 30,000 sheep. In Straiton there were 20,000 sheep, in Minnigaff 30,000 sheep, and in Kells 17,400 sheep. Some of these sheep were of course located outwith the Highland area, but it averaged at a density of around two and a half acres per sheep across the four parishes.

Most hill farms had around 2,000 sheep in their flock, which were herded in hirsels. These were groups of sheep which kept together and occupied their own stretch of hillside. Shepherds only kept the hirsel together, directing them back onto the farm land if they strayed, and leading them to better grazing as required.

The steep cliffs on some of the higher mountains of the area could cause some difficulty for the sheep. In some cases the animals would wander along narrow ledges, in search of a juicy bite. However, the ledges became so thin that the sheep couldn't turn around and return. They were also unable to think about walking backward! If the shepherd was not able to rescue them then they could often become stuck, eventually dying of starvation, or of falling to their death if they tried to escape. It was also noted that sometimes the sheep would follow the tracks made by the feral goats which occupied the cliffs, but were less agile than they were, often becoming stuck.

One of the methods used to rescue sheep required three shepherds! A crowbar or metal bar was hammered into a crack in the rock above where the sheep was stuck. A second man operated a rope that was tied onto the bar, and the third tied it to his waist and climbed up to the sheep on the ledge. The rope was then untied from the shepherd's waist and then tied around the sheep's horns. The two men above then dragged the sheep up the cliff-side to safety.

The wild winters of past years often caused difficulty for the sheep, and many could be lost in deep snow drifts. To prevent as many deaths as possible in the winter months 'herds would take their sheep and place them in 'rees', a good old Scots word that describes a circular stone wall wherein they were held. Remains of these old rees can be seen all across the hills of southern Scotland. Shepherds often had different names for the different shelters or enclosures for their sheep, such as fanks, rees, buchts, or stells. Non-farming folk could often mix these names up, and often assumed that they describe the same sort of enclosure, but in fact they were different. According to *The Scottish Gallovidian Encyclopedia*, written in 1823, a ree was:

> ...a round sheep-fold, where sheep are put into on snowy nights, to hinder the snow to ree, or wreath them up; as the wind, by whirling round this circle, lets the snow not wreath in it. *Ree*, is often confounded with *bught*, but a *sheep-ree* and a *sheep-bught*, are different; a *bught* is a little *bight* to catch sheep in, no matter what be its figure.

The quality of build of many of these rees is fantastic, the dry-stone walling being stoutly erected and topped with coping stones on their edges. It was said that a good stone dike had a coping of stones that should be so tightly fitting that a mouse should be able to run along the top of it, no gap being too large to prevent its passage.

One of the main events in the shepherd's calendar was the annual clipping, when the sheep were brought into the folds and their fleeces shorn, ready for sending to market. These clippings could be major events, and early in the nineteenth century James MacNae, a local poet, recounted the events and people present at 'Tairlaw Clipping':

'Twas in the middle of July
When summer days were warm and dry,
Come listen, frien's, and noo I'll try
    To tell o' Tairlaw clipping, O!
The folks they cam' frae far an near –
Fraue Auchincruive and Durisdeer,
And mony mair there did appear –
    That day at Tairlaw clipping, O!

Doon frae the Baing cam' Tam and John,
Anither laddie frae Knockdon,
Glenauchie and his youngest son
    Arrived at Tairlaw clipping, O!
Three frae Linfairn upon the brae,
Frae Craigencallie and Knockskae,
And Sanny frae Dalmorton tae
    Attended Tairlaw clipping, O!

Frae Balloch Beatties ower the hill,
Frae Tairlaw Toll and frae Glengill,
And Genoch men wi' richt guid will
    That day cam' to clipping, O!
Oh, there was mony any able loon
Wi' simmer sun their faces broon,
An' even tae from London toon
    They cam; to Tairlaw clipping, O!

Before they'd start they thocht they'd done,
And a' went to a dinner fine,
It made ye think o' Auld Lang Syne
    When the puddin's we were sipping, O!
Wi' jellies fine and tins o' pears
That made the laddies cock their ears,
And then they sharpened up their shears
    To carry on the clipping, O!

The afternoon was fine and cool,
Each clipper sat astride his stool,
Wi' other three to roll the wool,
    The day of Tairlaw clipping, O!
The Boss he chased ewes oot the rees,
The grippers were as keen as bees,
Some clad in shorts, some dungarees,
    The day o' Tairlaw clipping, O!

213

And some were big and some were small,
And some were short and some were tall,
Some were young and some were aul',
    The day of Tairlaw clipping, O!
A pail of tar held in their fist,
The boys that stampit on the buist,
Among the stools made mony a twist
    The day o' Tairlaw clipping, O!

Back and forward forth they ran,
Then tea arrived for every man,
Wi' baskets fu' cam' Kate and Nan
    An' roon the stools went tripping, O!
Behind them close, cam Mr P.,
For he was pooring oot the tea,
O scenes like these ye seldom see –
    Except you're at a clipping, O!

O everything was up-to-date,
And hardly had the clock struck eight,
When off the stool and through the gate
    The last clipt ewe went whippin' O!
Thus ended up a perfect day,
And everyone was feeling gay,
That night a thousand fleeces lay,
    To close the Tairlaw clipping, O!

Another major event in the shepherds' calendar was the annual games that were held at the House o' Hill Inn, near Bargrennan. This took place at the original inn, which was located on the hill to the east of the present hotel. The games were organised under the patronage of the laird, the Earl of Galloway, who also supplied the food and refreshments. At the games there were road races, where runners stripped to the waist and ran the mile distance in their bare feet. Jumping, putting the stone, and wrestling took place, with 700 folk in attendance to watch. At the end of the day over 100 sat down to dinner. An old account of the games in the *Galloway Advertiser and Wigtownshire Free Press* of 18 May 1849 sets the scene:

> The one to which we allude is held annually at the House o' Hill, where all
> sorts of gymnastic games are practised, and which gives the Minnigaff herds
> an opportunity of communicating to one another....

There are accounts of shepherd's dogs interbreeding with foxes. Writing in 1823, John MacTaggart refers to the offspring as 'tod-tykes', which were 'dogs half foxes, half common dogs.' According to him, 'shepherds *tether* their *het bitches* about fox-haunts, and so this breed of dogs is acquired; they are said to be excellent hunters.'

Some sons of the shepherds in the Galloway hills went on to make their way in the world. One of the most famous, at least in his day, was Alexander Murray, who was to achieve fame as Professor of Oriental Languages at the University of Edinburgh. Today, Murray's name would no doubt be totally forgotten, if it was not for the tall obelisk that rises from the summit of the Big Doon, a conical hill in Palnure Glen. Many travellers on the Queen's Way, as the A 712 is often known, spot the tall obelisk rising above the trees from the hilltop, and some park by the roadside at the Grey Mare's Tail Bridge to make an ascent of the 596 feet tall hill. The climb is not particularly high, being only 250 feet or so, but the prominence of the Big Doon makes the climb worthwhile, and from the summit one can gaze down afforested Bargaly Glen towards

the mouth of the River Cree in Wigtown Bay, or up the Palnure Glen towards New Galloway direction.

The obelisk itself is seventy feet in height, constructed of massive granite blocks, erected in 1835. It was designed by John Parker, an Edinburgh lawyer. When it was officially dedicated around three thousand people turned up on the hillside. For some reason the people at that time reckoned that Murray's name was so well known that it need not be inscribed upon it. Thus it was that until September 1877 the obelisk stood unadorned, but in that year it was decided to add a large polished granite slab with a suitable inscription. This bears the legend:

12.2 Rev Dr Alexander Murray

Alexander Murray DD, Minister of Urr, 1806-13; Professor of Oriental Languages in the University of Edinburgh, 1812-13; born at Dunkitterick, 22 Oct 1775; died at Edinburgh 15 April 1813; reared a shepherd boy on these hillsides; erected by his countrymen in 1835, mainly through the exertions and skill of James Stewart Esq. of Cairnsmore, on whose property it stands.

In the same year the grave of Murray, until that time unmarked, was venerated with the erection of an obelisk of Dalbeattie granite. Murray was buried in the north-west corner of Greyfriars' Church in Edinburgh, where the memorial bears the inscription:

In memory of Alexander Murray DD, born at Dunkitterick in Galloway, 22 October 1775; died 15 April 1813, aged 37 years, and interred here. Minister of Urr 1806-13; Professor of Oriental Languages in the University of Edinburgh, 1812-13. This monument was erected by admirers, chiefly connected with Galloway, to commemorate the genius and fame of 'the shepherd boy' who rose to be the most eminent linguist and Oriental scholar of his day. 1877.

Murray's tale is one of the poor rural Scot who made his way in the wider world with considerable success. Born in 1775, the son of Robert Murray, who was at that time 69 years old, the young Murray worked as a shepherd boy on the local farms, watching the sheep and hill cattle. His patch was the wild open country around Cairnsmore and Loch Grannoch, south of the Queen's Way. Whilst there he was wont to recite ancient ballads and tales in his head, stories that he read about or heard from others. His father spent one penny to purchase a copy of the Shorter Catechism, in editions of which at that time the alphabet and some exercises in monosyllables were included. Yet Robert Murray felt this little book was too valuable for the young lad, and he copied out the letters and words from it onto an old scrap of paper, using a heather stem with a charred end to write with. When the young Murray had mastered the basics, still aged six, his father presented him with the little book, which Murray read with considerable avarice. By the age of eight he had come to the attention of most of the residents of the glen, for he was noted for his magnificent skills of memory, and his avid desire to read everything that he could lay his hands on. This started with a book of psalms, followed by the New Testament and then the full Bible.

The young Alexander's skill was recognised and his parents did what they could to allow him to attend school, though this was only to be for a short time. The cost of his schooling at New Galloway was partially defrayed by his uncle, William Cochrane, and he enrolled in 1784. His teachers were amazed at how quickly he learned, and soon they reckoned that he was intelligent enough to head for greater things. However, the young Murray took ill after six months at school, forcing his return home. He was not to attend again for the next four years.

Alexander Murray did not stop reading and taking in what he read. He worked as a shepherd for the next four years, all the while borrowing texts and books from anyone who would lend them. His intelligence was recognised by some of the locals, and in the winter of 1787-8 he was given the job of teaching some of the children of neighbouring farmers – and he was still only twelve years of age.

Murray was then able to attend the school at Minnigaff for a time, where he excelled at arithmetic. This led him to believe he would make a good merchant's clerk. However, he had demonstrated an affinity for learning languages, and this was soon where his expertise lay. In 1790 he learned French and Latin, in three months picking up what most scholars achieve only after years of study. He started to learn Greek, and he read avidly. During the winter of 1792-3 he worked with Thomas Birkmyre, miller at Minnigaff Mill, teaching his children in the evening. His purpose in taking up this job was so that he could live near to Newton Stewart, in order to attend a school taught by Nathaniel Martin at the Bridgend of Cree.

One of Murray's methods in learning other languages was to obtain a Bible written in that tongue. He knew the Bible inside out, and once he had learned whatever alphabet the language used, he was able to study the Bible closely and from his knowledge of the English version was soon able to learn the language. He thus learned Hebrew, and was making a start at Abyssinian.

Murray tried his hand at writing blank verse, copying the style of *Ossian* and *Paradise Lost*, but he was dissatisfied with his results and he destroyed *Arthur and his Britons*, which he had been writing. He attempted to get the post of teacher at Mochrum School in Wigtownshire, but the minister there reckoned that the heritors wouldn't employ someone so young.

By 1794 word of Murray's intelligence had reached Edinburgh and he was invited there by some clergymen. They found him to be very clever, and they arranged for him to attend the university in the capital. After two years he earned a bursary, enabling him to continue his studies, enhanced by teaching jobs he carried out in the city. He trained for the ministry, but all the while he was an avid collector of information, and studied even more languages, becoming proficient in every European language.

Murray contributed a series of articles to *The Scots' Magazine* as well as the *Edinburgh Review*. Having learned Abyssinian, and variants of the language, he was given the task of superintending the publication of a new edition of James Bruce's *Travels*, staying for some time at the explorer's house of Kinnaird, near Stenhousemuir, where he had full access to his papers. At the same time Murray was able to compile a *Life of James Bruce*, published in 1808.

Rev Alexander Murray, as he had become, was appointed as assistant minister at Urr in Kirkcudbrightshire, succeeding in 1808 on Rev Muirhead's death. Murray served as minister until his early death in 1813.

During Murray's time as minister of Urr a letter was brought back from Abyssinia, written by the Ras of Tigre, addressed to King George III. It had been written in a language called Geez. Murray was regarded as possibly the only person in Britain who could translate the letter, and he did this with ease, letting the king know what it contained.

In 1812, the chair of oriental languages at the University of Edinburgh became vacant and Alexander Murray was successful in gaining the position. His health, which had never been great, suffered from the stress, and he ached too from a pulmonary ailment. This became so severe that he died in bed on 15 April 1813. He was still only 37 years old. He left a son and daughter, and in 1813 a posthumous publication, the *History of European Languages*, was issued. The government awarded his widow a pension of eighty pounds per annum.

The ruins of the humble cottage where Alexander Murray had been brought up were in more recent years stabilised and made accessible to the public. Located due east from his tall monument on the Big Doon, the cottage can be accessed by a footpath over a bridge crossing the Palnure Burn. At the cottage is a large stone inscribed with the words:

Dunkitterick, October 1975. Galloway Association of Glasgow. Bicentenary Memorial.

Life in the remote shepherds' cottages was difficult. There was neither running water nor electricity, and all provisions had to be carried in, often over many miles, from the nearest road-head.

The lonely shepherd's house of Backhill of Bush was at one time one of the remotest cottages in the whole of southern Scotland, and indeed was one of the more remote of any cottage in the country. When it was occupied, which it was up until around 1949, it was six miles from the nearest road-head, meaning that everything needed to live there had to be carried in. A pony was used for hauling some provisions, but it couldn't be used for the whole distance. There are some accounts of the pony being led part-way up the path over the hill. It knew where it was going, and over the years developed the ability to walk to Fore Bush where it was met by the shepherd there. He would take out the shopping list from the panniers, collect the requirements, fill the panniers with the goods required, and then send the pony back in the right direction.

12.3 Backhill of Bush

The shepherd was in the habit of walking to St John's Town of Dalry and there making purchase of his provisions. He then carried them on his back towards Forrest Lodge and the Fore Bush, before climbing the steep eastern slopes of Millfire. At the pass he left the load by a cairn and walked on alone to Backhill. A pony that was kept in a small field was then taken back to the pass, hauling a sledge. Once loaded with the goods for the next few weeks, the pony and sledge were led back down to the cottage. Ponies were also used to flit in the shepherd and his meagre belongings, which seemed to occur every few years or so.

At one time the daughter of the shepherd at Backhill made a journey from the house to New Galloway, where she had an appointment with her dressmaker. She told the dressmaker that she was the first woman she had seen for eight months!

Bereavement could be a difficulty, too. There is a tale told of the death of the shepherd of Backhill of Bush's wife, which must have occurred sometime in the nineteenth century. The funeral cortege was leaving Backhill for the kirkyard at St John's Town of Dalry when they were engulfed in a serious snowstorm. The party tried to keep going, but the snow was getting deeper as time passed, and things were becoming desperate. The route taken had been the high path over Millfire, but the wind was howling across the pass and the coffin was getting ever heavier as the carriers were getting weaker. Eventually it was agreed that they would need to leave the coffin where they had reached and return back down the hill for their own safety. It was three days before the funeral party could return back to Millfire and reclaim the coffin and the shepherd's wife.

It was common in the past for travellers in the middle of the Galloway hills to call at Backhill and be put up by the shepherd and his family. Almost everyone who wrote a book or account of Galloway in the olden days made the journey to Backhill, in order to experience the loneliness of the Dungeon of Buchan, and most stayed the night. Rev Charles Hill Dick, in *Highways and Byways*, published in 1916, noted to the reader, and possible follower in his tracks, 'If, when you reach the Dungeon the shepherd at The Back Hill of The Bush is able to give you lodging, it is an immense advantage.' Similarly, Malcolm Harper, writing in 1876, noted that it was his 'intention, should [he] not be able to proceed further, to make for the Back Hill o' the Bush, and put up for the night.'

No doubt the shepherds at Backhill were welcoming enough to travellers who had made it thus far, for their company and change of conversation would have been something that was desirable and which would break up what would otherwise have been a rather solitary lifestyle. MacBain, writing in 1929, noted that, 'The house is usually in occupation, but the explorer should be warned that it may be tenantless, as I have found it, not having taken the precaution to ascertain that it was shut up. It is the only house in the whole ten miles of valley. If it is a going concern the traveller is sure to meet with a hearty welcome, and to have set before him the best entertainment that can be looked for in so remote a habitation, where provisions have to be carried a distance of six miles over the pathless hills. He will not expect the variety of foods and the service of a city hotel, but if the choicest of scones, pancakes, oatmeal cakes, and ham and eggs will satisfy him, he will have no reason to complain of his fare.'

James MacBain often spent the night of Hogmanay at Backhill. When he finished work during the day he would catch a bus for Castle Douglas and at the point nearest to the cottage, which would have been over eight miles distant, he alighted and walked across the hills to the dwelling. The shepherd would place a lit lamp in the window to help him identify the cottage at night. The New Year was brought in singing the 'auld Scotch sangs' to the sound of fiddle music.

In many cases visitors were rare, however. One woman who lived at the cottage reckoned that she had only three visitors in a number of years. One of these was a passing shepherd, driving sheep across the hills from one farm to another. The other two were engineers employed to measure the elevation of the countryside around for map-making purposes. Another occupant of the cottage noted that their first foot did not arrive until March.

The weather often meant that the occupants of Backhill were snowed in for long periods. On one occasion the shepherd went to Newton Stewart on an errand. He was snowed out and was unable to make his way back for three months. His wife, understandably, wasn't best pleased, and as soon as they could move to a less remote cottage they did.

In 1938 the cottage was occupied by William MacCubbin, and he appears to have welcomed visitors, charging them for overnight accommodation. A letter written by him on 2 July 1938 to a Mr Murray survives:

> Mr Murray
> Dear Sir,
> I received your letter re. your holiday at Back Bush. It will be quite convenient for you to come with your friend. There is good trout fishing here if you care to bring a rod, it is good sport when on holiday.
> The charge here is 5/- per day. It was that before we came, and we have never changed it, and your friend will be charged less seeing he prefers to sleep out.
> Your best way to come would be with the Midland bus which runs between Glasgow and Castle Douglas, and you would need to get off at Roadfoot, about 2 miles before you reach Dalry. You will get the road to Fore Bush there about 4½ miles, and then it is six miles over the hill.
> There is a car at Roadfoot which you could hire if you think it is too far to get here before it is too late.
> Yours faithfully,
> W. MacCubbin

The present building at Backhill is thought to have been erected in the first decade of the nineteenth century, for behind it stood an older building, which in the mid twentieth century still had traces of its old thatched roof. The materials for the new cottage were drawn by horse and cart by a contractor named John Peacock.

Some of the occupants of the cottage can be identified from old accounts of the area. In the 1861 Census there were three residents at Backhill – John McCutcheon was the shepherd, and his wife Agnes lived there also. They had the assistance of one domestic servant, Mary Brown. She was just ten years of age and was living quite distant from her homelands, being born in Inverness-shire.

By 1915 the house was occupied by Albert Forlow, a surname that reminds us of Ralph Forlow, the brave shepherd boy who died tending his sheep during a blizzard.

In the mid-1930s the shepherd was David Thomson, and from 1937 until 1943 it was William MacCubbin. From 1946 until 1949 the shepherd was Alex Renton. The story is told of when David, or Davie Thomson, lived at Backhill. He and his wife, Ina, were given the kitchen table by the shepherd at Black Laggan when he was leaving that cottage. The Thomsons walked the six miles to Black Laggan and then carried the table back with them. They also brought back a small occasional table.

The number of sheep kept on the Backhill ground was considerable. In the 1930s it was reckoned that there were about 550 lambing ewes at one time, meaning that there could be over 1,000 sheep to be looked after once they had lambed.

On older maps, Backhill of Bush is shown as Elderholm, a name that appears to have continued in use until around 1900. Some accounts also name it as Backhill of Burnhead, Burnhead being the neighbouring farm to Fore Bush, on the east side of the Rhinns of Kells. The cottage is named thus in a plan of the estates of the Forbes' of Callendar House, near Falkirk, surveyed in 1800 by John Lauder. William Forbes (1743-1815) of Callendar had in 1783 purchased the estate of Earlstoun from the Gordon family, who had fallen on straitened times. He was married to Jean MacAdam, younger daughter of John MacAdam of Craigengillan, but she died in Madeira around 1800.

Near to Backhill are the ruins of Downies Sheil, located on the other side of the Downies Burn, but further upstream. Downies Sheil appears roofed on the Ordnance map of 1853, but was in ruins by 1894.

There were two other cottages in this remote glen – High and Low Cornarroch. High Cornarroch was located by the side of the Dow Burn, at the side of the Silver Flow. It was in ruins by 1894. Low Cornarroch was located by the side of the Cornarroch Strand, at the foot of the Point of the Snibe. It was in ruins before 1856.

In the valley of the Curnelloch Burn stands the ruins of Backhill of Garrary, located near to the stream. Today the surrounding countryside is afforested, but at one time it was open countryside, grazed by sheep. According to the Ordnance Survey map of 1853 there was no cottage here, the site only occupied by a shepherd's cairn, and on the islet formed by the Curnelloch Burn was an 'old hay ree'. On the opposite side of the burn from the site, Davy's Holm was named, indicating that it had been identified as a better stretch of land than the surrounding countryside.

By 1861, however, Backhill of Garrary must have been built, for the Census lists the cottage in the return for Kells parish. The Ordnance map of 1896, however, names the cottage as Davy's Holm, so the name must have been interchangeable for some time. The Census of 1861 listed the occupants of the cottage, perhaps the first to live there. John Galloway was employed as a shepherd, tending the sheep over a large area. Born in the parish of Barr, Ayrshire, he had married Agnes Logan, born in Minnigaff parish, and at the time of the Census they had five sons from age seven down to 6 months living with them, as well as Robert Murray, a boarder, employed as a shepherd also.

Backhill of Garrary may have replaced another old cottage, known as Dernscloy, which was located west of Mid Garrary, on the lower slopes of Eldrick Hill. Just to the east of this was a collection of buildings, known as Upper Garrary. The Ordnance map of 1849 shows approximately five buildings located here, as does the map of 1896, all in ruins by then. These probably formed an old ferme toun that was abandoned in the early nineteenth century.

Many other remote shepherds' cottages existed in the highlands, but were all gradually abandoned as permanent residences over time. Some of the last shepherds are still recalled. At Black Laggan, MacBain remembers staying with the shepherd on a number of occasions, and comments on how the passing walker was made very welcome there. He writes that:

> ... the respectable tramp will get comfortably put up if he has not been forestalled by an earlier party, and whether or not, he will get food and shelter. It is surprising how many people can be accommodated at a pinch in one of these moorland cottages. The largest of them consists of a but and ben, with very contracted attics. Nevertheless, I have sojourned in one of them when eleven persons, including six visitors, found shelter under its roof, and I was informed by the tenants that on one occasion sixteen persons had perforce to be accommodated for a night at the Black Laggan.

In 1841, according to the Census, Black Laggan (or Lagan as it was spelled, the proper Gaelic version of the name) was home to a family of eight. John Logan (aged 53 at the time) and his wife Mary (aged 50) lived there, John being an agricultural labourer, no doubt a shepherd. They had a family of five children of their own, James (aged 18), William (15), Maryann (10), Jannet (8) and Johnstone (6), as well as William Hewetson (aged 3), all living in the small and remote cottage.

On the opposite side of the glen, White Laggan was still occupied in 1841 – though it seems to have been by a disparate group of four people. These were James Wilson, an agricultural labourer, aged 38. He was assisted by another agricultural labourer, John MacHallum, aged 16, and Jannet Foster, a 19-year old female servant. Also living there was eight-year old Robert Fergusson, described in the Census as an 'indweller'.

The old cottage of Craigfionn stands in ruins by the side of the Whitespout Lane, between lochs Riecawr and Doon. On older maps the name is spelled Craigfain, and MacBain spells it Craigphain, in both cases pronounced in a similar way. The name probably derives from *creag fionn*, Gaelic for the white rock. Today a forest road passes reasonably close, but before the arrival of the trees the cottage was two miles from the road-head at Loch Doon. The cottage was built of large granite boulders, the rounded rocks split to create a face for building. The building measured around 46 feet in length by 21 feet in width, this being divided into two – a house and a small byre adjoining, the latter accessed by its own doorway. The main house had two fireplaces on the ground floor, the remnants of which are visible. The back wall is now fallen to the ground, but it may have had no windows or doors through it. The front had a single door in the middle, with a window to either side. The front of the house faces south-east, almost directly to Carlin's Cairn. On the Ordnance Survey map of 1856 the cottage did not exist, but it was there by 1896, indicating a late nineteenth century date.

When Craigfionn was abandoned is unknown, but the remains of the old garden can still be made out behind the house, and around the building still grow some foxgloves, a cultivated plant that is now growing wild. Near the front of the house grows a stunted apple tree, though whether it ever brought on apples that could be eaten or used in cooking is unknown, the wildness of the weather in this part of the county not being conducive to growing fruit. Certainly, when I visited in mid-August one year, the tiny apples were still not as large as grapes.

About four miles to the south west of Craigfionn were three other shepherds' houses – Tunskeen, Slaethornrig and Cashernaw. These old cottages were still occupied in the mid nineteenth century, for they are shown roofed on the Ordnance Survey maps, and in most cases had hay rees and other indications of occupation around them.

The remote cottage of Tunskeen lies on the moors to the immediate eastern side of Shalloch on Minnoch. Indeed, leaving the cottage it is a steady climb up the steep eastern screes and gairy of the mountain. On older maps, such as Ainslie's map of 1821, it is spelled 'Tonsin'.

The remnants of other old cottages can be found further north – Slaethornrig and Cashernaw. Both these buildings were still inhabited at the start of the twentieth century, but were soon abandoned. Another old dwelling was located a few hundred yards to the south-west, known as Anton's Hut.

Only the scantiest of remains can be seen at Willie's Sheil, a small cottage or sheiling that was located on a fairly level piece of ground by the side of the Eglin Lane. Who Willie was is unknown, but his shieling was in ruins by the time the map-makers of the Ordnance Survey arrived in 1856.

In the southern group of mountains, around Curleywee and Lamachan Hill, are a few old shepherds' cottages now abandoned. Drigmorn was a cottage located in the promontory formed by the Pulnee and Green Burns, within the Penkiln glen. According to the 1841 Census this cottage was occupied by two women, Helen MacJanet, aged 74 and Jane MacJanet, aged 30.

On the east side of Loch Doon were a number of old cottages, at one time occupied by shepherds and small farmers. At the head of the loch was Loch Head, occupied until the latter part of the twentieth century. One of the oldest stones still to be seen in Carsphairn kirkyard commemorates someone named David MacLay, or 'Old Lochhead', who died in 1686. The Forestry Commission has cleared the building away, so that today there is little to indicate that it once existed.

Further north, along the eastern shore, are the ruins of Portmark, located by the water's edge. There has been a cottage here for centuries, in 1749 spelled Partmarl, and in some case spelled Polmark. Adjacent to Portmark is the huge boulder known as the Cat's Stone. Slightly to the north of this is the Port Stone. This may have at one time marked the port where boats were kept to ferry people to Loch Doon Castle.

By some old sheep rees in the forest, there was another cottage known as Polmeadow, located near to the Polmeadow Burn. On Kitchin's map of 1749 it is indicated at 'Powmeddow', perhaps an approximation of how the locals pronounced it. Polmeadow was in ruins when the first Ordnance Survey maps of the area were made in 1850. Slightly to the east were a group of ruins that were obviously even older than Polmeadow.

Another old cottage was Faulds, which stood on the northern slopes of Cullendoch Hill. This was in ruins by 1850.

The old cottage of Little Eriff is located in a low grassy knoll at the north-eastern side of Loch Doon, where a small bay in the loch is located. The older name for this cottage was 'Arrow', a name that is shown on Kitchin's 1749 map. West of Eriff is the Eriff Plantation, within which are the ruins of Muckle Eriff, another ancient cottage long abandoned. Today, Eriff is the name of a cottage located by the side of the Dalmellington to Carsphairn road, at the southern end of Loch Muck. It was erected sometime after 1840 to replace Little Eriff. When Craigengillan was sold in 1999, this part of the estate was retained as a small sporting estate, known as Eriff estate.

The old cottage of Culsharg lies by the side of the Whiteland Burn, a tributary of the Buchan Burn. Today a path from the Bruce's Stone in Glen Trool leads up the side of the Buchan Burn, past the cottage and on to the summit of the Merrick. The cottage has been preserved by the Forestry Commission as a shelter for walkers making their way up or down the mountain.

The cottage was at one time occupied by various families who were employed on the land as shepherds. In the 1841 Census of Scotland the enumerator listed ten people in a single family living there – Robert and Agnes Wilson, both of whom were around forty years of age, and their children, Merron (15) Margret (12), Susan (10) Keatren (8), Jeams (6), John (4), William (2) and Archibald (six months). It is recounted that one of the Wilson mothers carried her child all the way from Culsharg to Minnigaff Manse, where it was baptised, and back home in a single day, a distance of 32 miles.

At Culsharg cottage, by the path that ascends the Merrick, is a cairn. Built into it is an old carved stone, depicting the cottage, and a plaque by the side of the cairn indicates its story. It relates how the boulder stood in the burn that runs past the cottage and was carved around 1870 but was damaged around 1980. To save the stone from further damage it was buried by the river until it was incorporated in the cairn which was built to the memory of Bill MacDonald who loved this area. The cairn was built on 11 June 1983 by a keen hillwalker, Thomas Withers, a member of Annanhill Kilmarnock Hurlford Hillwalking Club.

One of the more remote steadings on the eastern side of the Galloway Highlands was Shiel of Castlemaddie, or Castlemaddy, as the name appears on modern maps. The house stood on the left bank of the Polmaddy Burn, three miles west of the public road. Originally there was no track to the farm, but in recent years a forest road allows more ready access.

The steading has existed since at least the eighteenth century, for another old gravestone in Carsphairn kirkyard commemorates two daughters of Andrew Wight in Shiel of Castlemaddy, one of whom died in 1781 (her name is obliterated on the stone) and Jean, who died in 1792. Before the Wights the farm was occupied by the

12.4 Culsharg

MacTurks, again who are buried in Carsphairn. A stone there commemorates Robert MacTurk and his wife Janet, Robert living at Shiel until he died in 1771 aged 51 years.

The last family to occupy the Shiel was the Wilsons. James Wilson was the shepherd in the latter half of the nineteenth century until he died in 1885 aged fifty. Undeterred, his wife continued to live at the cottage for almost 45 years, dying there in 1929 at the advanced age of 94. The family are buried in Carsphairn kirkyard.

Margaret Wilson had had a difficult life, losing her husband when she was just fifty. The couple had earlier tragedy to bear, for their daughter, Agnes, died in January 1863 aged just three months.

Margaret lived near Newton Stewart when she was young, and on her marriage to James Wilson had to journey across the Galloway Highlands to her new home. The story is recounted in Andrew McCormick's book on *Galloway*:

'My mither and faither were merriet in the hoose o' an aunt at Clachaneasy. They steyed on the waddin' nicht at Culsharg, but as Mr Kennedy was takkin' ower the Shiel stock next mornin' my faither had to mak' an early start to be at the sheep delivery at the Shiel. Sae my mither was left to come later in the day un'er the care o' the best man an' anither shepherd wha baith hailed frae the neighbourhood o' the Shiel. They took her thro' the hills to the Shiel, an' in efter years they used to craw hoo, to test her, they had led her by roun' aboot cuts an' thro' a' kinds o' steep bits across Craignaw, the Dungeon, an' awa alang by Mulwharcher an' the Tauchers, wilder bits I ne'er saw, an' awa oot thro' the quakkin' quas o' the Couran Lane, an' then across to the Shiel thro' a lirk in the Kells range they ca' 'The Thraw Road.' Truly she must have had an exciting and ever memorable honeymoon jaunt. They did it to prove her mettle, and it must have settled her down properly for she remained at the Shiel till she died in her ninety-fourth year.

McCormick also describes the inside of the house at Shiel:

A girdle hung from the ceiling. An old-fashioned swie sustained the pots; the teapot was heated on a ring placed on the hob with glowing peats in the circle. I was shown two small slates which had at one time been part of the roof of the Brucean Castle, Loch Doon. A delft plate had been brought from Glasgow by carrier's cart.

The shepherd at Shiel was paid £17 in cash per annum, and this was to feed a family comprising of nine adults and seven youngsters. There were a few additional benefits, for the shepherd was entitled to two cows, an odd sheep and some oatmeal. That times were hard is exemplified by the neighbouring shepherd, James MacFadzean in Castlemaddy, who gathered every piece of cast wool he could find. His wife spun it into yarn, and he knitted it into various items.

Once a year Rev Thomas Barclay, the Free Kirk minister from Carsphairn, would gather a small congregation and walk over the hill to the Shiel in order to celebrate communion with the family. The party was always welcomed, and the Wilsons put on a spread of food for the visitors, even although it must have been quite a struggle for them financially. After singing a few psalms, breaking bread and drinking wine, the group enjoyed tattie scones, pancakes, and porridge cut in squares from the drawer, covered with thick cream.

Today, Shiel of Castlemaddy is a ruin, but one of the Wilson family was taken back to the old cottage for burial, and their remains lie in the vicinity of where they had lived.

The droving of cattle to market is an occupation that is usually associated with the Highlands of Scotland, and less so in the Southern Uplands and lowland belt. However, the transportation of cattle by walking them across country is something that was at one time common across the Galloway area, and there are some sparse records of this having taken place.

One drove route that is known made its way from the valley of the Girvan Water south-eastwards across the northern end of the Galloway Highlands to the Glenkens. Cattle were thus taken from Ayrshire and transported to the markets of the Borders and into England, without having to travel through many communities. By following such remote routes, drovers could also avoid numerous tolls which would have been exacted had they taken their cattle along the turnpike roads.

The drove route, for there was probably no road as such, made its way up from Straiton and the fertile Ayrshire countryside, through the narrow glen of the Girvan.

The way went past Tairlaw to Knockdon farm, from where a track was visible on the ground, angling along the western slopes of the Fence of Knockdon to the west end of Derclach Loch. The route then made its way across country towards the Nick of the Loup, the name of the mountain pass between Waterhead and Craiglee.

From the Nick of the Loup the drovers directed their cattle south-eastwards, over the rocky terrain to the head of Loch Doon. Passing the Starr and crossing the Gala Lane, the drove route made its way to the low knoll with its cairn known as Dinnins. From there a route was visible on the western slopes of Meaul, making its way askew across the hill-side to the pass between Meaul and the Carlin's Cairn. At the top of the pass, in the saddle between the two mountains are a few small pools where the cattle were able to drink, having made a significant ascent.

12.5 Shiel of Castlemaddy

A quick and steep descent brought the cattle down the east side of the ridge, by the side of the Goat Burn, and into the valley of the Polmaddy Burn. The route took the cattle past Shiel of Castlemaddy and Drumness to the old village of Polmaddy. Cattle could then be directed east across the countryside towards Dumfries. From there cattle were driven to Carlisle and onto the English markets.

At one time the drove route was visible at certain points on the ground, the cattle having worn a pathway across the hills. At places where stone dikes ran across the route there were gates placed in them, gates that to the unknowing individual had no apparent reason for being there.

Further east a drove route or road from New Galloway to Dumfries was officially marked out on the instructions of the Privy Council in 1697, obviously created to fulfil a need. At the time the route selected had been 'the line of passage taken by immense herds of cattle which were continually passing from the green pastures of the Galloway Hills into England – a branch of economy held to be the main support of the inhabitants of the district and the grand source of its rents.'

By 1772, when Thomas Pennant was writing about the area, he recorded that 'the great weekly markets for black cattle are of much advantage to the place [Dumfries] and vast droves from Galloway and the Shire of Air pass through on their way to the Fairs in Norfolk and Suffolk.'

The Galloway Highlands are mostly bereft of public roads, apart from some that make their way up into the more fertile glens. Today, however, modern machinery has allowed the Forestry Commission to bulldoze new tracks through much of the periphery of the highlands, allowing walkers and cyclists a more ready form of access that the former occupants of the shielings and shepherds' houses could only dream of.

The first modern roads were constructed by the turnpike trusts in the second half of the eighteenth century. Acts were passed by parliament that set up the trusts, which created or remade roads across the countryside, and to pay for their upkeep toll houses with gates were established at fairly regular intervals. Toll-keepers were appointed to collect the levies, which, in 1774, varied from eight shillings for a coach drawn by six horses, to sixpence for a wagon drawn by a single horse, depending on which road one travelled. No doubt the Galloway high roads would have been at the cheaper end of the scale. Droves of cattle, sheep or horses also paid a toll, in 1774 five-pence being payable per drove of sheep or lambs.

The road from Maybole to Newton Stewart, often referred to today as the 'Hill Road' was created in 1789, and was operated by the Barr and Straiton turnpike trusts in Ayrshire, and the Balloch Trust in Kirkcudbrightshire. Along the route were a number of toll houses where levies were charged on those travellers and drovers making use of the roadway. On Ainslie's map of southern Scotland, dated 1821, there is a sentence written alongside the roadway, noting that 'By going this Road to Newton Stewart is a Saving of forty Miles.'

Between Straiton and Newton Stewart were five tolls – at the southern end of Straiton itself (near the manse drive), Tairlaw, Rowantree, Suie, Bargrennan and then tolls on the main road from Bargrennan to Newton Stewart.

Tairlaw Toll was located in the Tairlaw Glen, just over one mile south of Tairlaw Bridge, which crosses the Water of Girvan. This was not the original toll site, for the older Tairlaw Toll was positioned one and a half miles further to the south, still near to the Tairlaw Burn. It had been abandoned by 1858.

The Rowantree Toll was celebrated for its remoteness, and its location also meant that there was an inn there for a time, catering for weary travellers. The remains of it lie by the side of the road, just where the Straiton hill road joins the Nick of the Balloch Road. The toll house was abandoned between 1860 and 1895, and MacBain refers to the blackened walls of the toll cottage.

12.6 Map from New Statistical Account (1842) showing Old Edinburgh Road to south and
Pack Road from Carsphairn to Polmaddy to the east.

Suie Toll was located on the east side of the hill road, just south of the Ayrshire-
Kirkcudbrightshire boundary.

Bargrennan Toll was located at the junction of the Hill Road with the road from
Newton Stewart to Girvan. Immediately beside it was Bargrennan School. This toll
gate appears to have replaced an earlier toll, which was named the High Bridge of Cree
Toll Point. This was abandoned by 1848.

Along the northern extremity of the area covered by this book is the Straiton to
Dalmellington road, numbered the B 741. It doesn't appear to have tolls along it.

Along the southern edge of the Galloway Highlands was a roadway that has now become known as the 'Old Edinburgh Road', and is thus named on some maps. From New Galloway this roadway followed a route slightly higher than the present A 712, or Queen's Way, running parallel to the north. As it passed the Craigshinnie road-end, the road crossed the present route and took to the south of it, above Clatteringshaws farm, before dropping to the Black Water of Dee and the Old Bridge of Dee, the site of which is now located beneath the waters of the reservoir. The bridge had gone by 1848, when the Ordnance Survey map of the area was surveyed. The old route reappears on the other side of the loch and climbs slowly towards Lillie's Loch and south-west towards the Black Loch. Near to the latter loch, according to Taylor & Skinner's strip road-maps, published in 1775, there was a 'Precipice called the Sadleleap'.

The Old Edinburgh Road kept to a higher route, behind the present Murray's Monument and above the Black Craigs, arriving at the Loch of the Lowes. It made its way south of the Drumlawhinnie Loch and over Greencairn and Knockawines, passing between Risk and Barncaughlaw farms, before arriving in Minnigaff. Much of this route is still traceable on the ground today, some of it rebuilt as forest roads.

A new route replaced this Old Edinburgh Road, with toll gates at points along it. The road was operated by the New Galloway Trust, and there was a toll house at Talnotry. The toll-keeper in 1841 was James MacGown, who was 62 years of age at the time. The next toll gate was located at Clatteringshaws, the site of which has now gone, but it was a few hundred yards south-west of the visitor centre. The next toll was located beyond New Galloway at the Ken Bridge, adjoining the Spalding Arms Inn, as the Ken Bridge Hotel was then known.

The Old Edinburgh Road along the southern edge of the Highlands is a route suitable for explorers, keen to follow the ancient routes. A similar old route can be followed down the eastern side of the highlands, from Dalmellington to New Galloway. This eastern side is bounded by the road from Dalmellington to New Galloway, now the A 713. This road dates from the late eighteenth century, when it was laid out by the Kirkcudbright turnpike trusts. It replaced an earlier road, one of which certain stretches remain and which make interesting walks.

The stretch from Dalmellington south to Eriff is partially destroyed by forestry workings, but there is a good track up the Gaw Glen and over Little Eriff Hill that eventually drops again to the Muck Burn, near Eriff.

From Eriff south to Drumjohn the old route can be followed on the ground, its line unaffected by forestry planting. At one point it passed an old inn, known as Cadgerhole, the remains of which are located by the side of the Meadhowhead Burn. It passed the original Lamford farm and made its way south to Carsphairn.

South of Carsphairn, the A 713 was preceded by the old pack road that crossed Bardennoch Hill. The route probably left Carsphairn and crossed the Water of Deugh near to Cubbin's Kate Pool onto Carnavel lands, before ascending the northern slopes of Bardennoch Hill. It headed south-eastwards alongside Braidenoch Hill and a spot known as Irongallows before dropping to the ancient village of Polmaddy. On crossing the Polmaddy Burn, the old route ascended the hill and passed over Stroangassel Hill before dropping down again to Carsfad, where the track re-joins the present road.

South of Polharrow Bridge, the old pack road kept to a higher, western route, skirting Barchock Wood and returning to the present road at Craiggubbie, near Earlstoun Power Station. There was an old roadside inn known as Pluckham's Inn, which was located near to Barchock Wood.

The supply of education for the children living in the Galloway uplands has been difficult due to the distance and remoteness of the area. Schools have existed in the upland region in the past, but as depopulation crept up and transport was easier to arrange to nearby villages, all of the remote schools have been closed.

The school at Loch Doon was located at Craigmalloch, near the head of the loch. It was established sometime between 1856, when it was not on the map, and 1896, when it was. In 1905 it was occupied by Mr & Mrs Campbell. In the storms of January 1912 the wall around the school and schoolmaster's house was washed away.

A few other rural schools existed at one time. Rowantree School was located to the south of Rowantree Toll, on the hill road from Newton Stewart to Straiton. It was operated by Barr Parish Council. In 1837 there was no school here, and the *Statistical Account* noted that 'in the winter months, it is common for families to unite together, as convenience permits, and employ a teacher; it is thus chiefly that the children are taught.' The school at the Woodhead Lead Mines has already been mentioned.

On Knocknalling estate there was a small school, established in 1842 as Polharrow School. It was built by the owner of the estate, John Kennedy, who also contributed a small salary of £20 to the teacher. Now roofless, the remains of four windows that lit the single schoolroom can still be seen. A plaque on the gable end of the old building reads: *The Polharrow School, built in remembrance of Marianne Ewart Kennedy who contributed her mite to its support. AD 1842.* Marianne was Kennedy's daughter, but she died before the school was completed.

The Polharrow School at Knocknalling was replaced by a new building, located at Crummypark, in the Polharrow Glen. It was opened in 1891 when Miss Jeannie Brown was employed to teach the infants. In September 1902 His Majesty's Inspectors visited and noted 'the pleasant tone which has in recent years prevailed in this school again calls for remark. Everything is done to make the children's school life interesting to them and they reciprocate the troubles taken with them... Ample attention is paid to recreative and industrial training and this is one of the very few schools in this district in which Nature Study is exactly what it should be.' The roll in 1907 was 20 and in 1911 slates were replaced with paper. In April 1950 the school had one teacher who taught nine children. The school remained in operation until 1951.

The Dee School was opened on 15 December 1896, being located at the end of the hill road from Glenlee to Clatteringshaws, near to Darwood. On its first day fourteen pupils enrolled. Pupils travelled up to five miles to attend, and the inspectors noted in 1900 that 'this small school is in every respect particularly satisfactory... the children are eagerly interested in their work and they are taught with superior skill.' The school only survived for 28 years, its remoteness being something of a problem for teachers, one of whom complained that they were given lodgings three miles distant, to which they had to walk to and fro each day. In 1907 there were only six pupils in attendance, three of which required to walk three miles to reach it. The school was closed in 1924 when a newer school was established at Clatteringshaws, one and a half miles to the west.

The Clatteringshaws School was located adjacent to Clatteringshaws farm, the L-shaped school building being constructed from timber. In 1944 the school had ten pupils, but in June that year the teacher died, resulting in the pupils being transported to Kells School. A new teacher was appointed in November 1945, meaning that the pupils could return, but the school's roll was small and it was closed on 3 February 1947, the building being converted into a small cottage.

Near to Cumloden House, though on the northern side of the Penkiln Burn, was a small school that existed for a period of time in the mid nineteenth century. The building, which survives as a cottage, is located near to the Pulcree Burn, a spot that seems a most unlikely location for a school today. It was established by the Countess of Galloway as a charity school, and it was in operation in 1842, when the *New Statistical Account* was compiled. At that time the school had twenty-five girls in attendance, taught arithmetic, English, and needlework by a female teacher.

The school had been erected around 1836 by Henrietta, Countess of Galloway. She was the wife of Randolph, 9th Earl of Galloway, and both were noted for their good works in the Newton Stewart area. They ran clothing clubs and competitions to find the best-kept cottages. The cost of education was prohibitive for many poorer farmers and shepherds, but the Galloways often paid for them to attend. In Newton Stewart, Lord Galloway erected at his own expense an infant school, where over one hundred pupils were educated. Lady Henrietta established an industrial school for girls.

The names of a couple of teachers at Cumloden School are known, thanks to inscriptions on headstones in Minnigaff kirkyard. If one wanders among the gravestones, a memorial can be found to Jane Ranken, who taught in the school from its erection until 1845. In that year her niece, Wilhelmina Masson, took over the reins. Both teachers were later employed in Lady Galloway's School in Newton Stewart. The stone reads: 'Erected by Wilhelmina Masson in loving memory of her mother, Janet Ranken, relict of Andrew Masson, drawing master, Edinburgh, who died at Newton Stewart, 1st August 1860, aged 76 years. Also of her aunt, Jane Ranken, who was teacher of the Countess of Galloway's Schools at Cumloden and Newton Stewart successively from 1836 till 1864, and who died at Newton Stewart, 1st February 1880 aged 91 years … Also the above Wilhelmina Masson, born at South Bridge, Edinburgh, 18th January 1822, who was teacher of the Countess of Galloway's Schools at Cumloden and Newton Stewart successively from 1845 till 1875, and who died at Newton Stewart, 12 February 1905. The above Andrew Masson, who died at 23 South Bridge, Edinburgh, 14 Nov 1825 aged 42 years, and was interred in Greyfriars Churchyard, Edinburgh.'

The old school at Glenmalloch appears to have been closed soon after the Education Act was passed in 1872, which introduced compulsory education for all children. The cottage was used by the estate for one of its workers, and on the maps of the late nineteenth century it was named Park Lodge. This was soon after (certainly by 1904) changed to Glenmalloch Lodge, the name it retains to this day. The cottage was abandoned as a residence in the 1960s, and it was left to decay. With neither running water nor electricity, it was an unlikely place for someone to live.

But the attractiveness of the building and its historical associations meant that the cottage was too good to let fall into ruins, like the many older buildings on Glenmalloch moors to the north. In 2003, Solway Heritage took an interest in the building and brokered a deal between Cumloden Estate and the Landmark Trust to establish a long lease. The Trust was then able to restore the old school, bringing it back to a wind and watertight condition.

12.7 Glenmalloch Lodge, the former Cumloden School

Today, Glenmalloch Lodge is let as a holiday home for couples, its diminutive size having nothing more than a kitchen, bathroom and bedroom/sitting room within it. Built of whinstone, the school has sandstone quoins and surrounds, a typical Galloway slate roof (with diminishing slates), fretworked barge boards, and a bay window with diamond-paned glazing. At the western end is a massive chimney stalk.

A school formerly existed in Glen Trool, located near to Glen Trool hunting lodge. The school was built by the dowager Countess of Galloway and was named the Eschoncan School after the steep hill that dominates the glen, and towers over the building. The dowager Countess supplied the school for the benefit of the shepherds' children in the district. It existed in 1849 but was closed sometime before the 1890s.

Those children who lived too far from the rural schools still had the chance to receive an education. A school teacher would travel around the more remote farms and shepherds' homes in the mid nineteenth century. It was noted that a group of shepherds contributed towards the cost of a young lad who would travel from house to house, generally staying with each family for a week or fortnight. Other local children would make their way to the cottage, bringing their own food, allowing the cost to be split. It was noted, however, that the shepherds could ill afford to pay the teacher little more than his accommodation and food, so that there was often difficulty in finding one to take on this job.

13 Lairds and Lodges

The Galloway Highlands have been recognised for their sporting potential for centuries. Probably the first real reference to the hills being used for hunting occurs in John Barbour's *Bruce*, Book VII, where it is noted that Robert the Bruce enjoyed shooting deer here:

> In Glentruell a quile he lay,
> And went weill oft to hunt and play,
> For to purchase thame venysoun,
> For than the deir war in sesoun.

At the time, much of the highland part of Galloway had been inherited through marriage by the Comyn family, Alexander Comyn, Earl of Buchan, becoming the owner in 1264 through his wife, Elizabeth de Quincy. It was probably at this time that the name for the upland hunting forest was changed to the Forest of Buchan, the name being transposed from the fertile coastlands of Aberdeenshire and Banffshire.

The next major change in the sporting rights of the hills took place in 1500, when King James IV granted his mistress, Janet Kennedy, the half-sister of the 1st Earl of Cassillis and daughter of John, 2nd Lord Kennedy (d. 1509), the lease of the hunting in the Forest of Buchan. Janet Kennedy appears to have appointed her half-brother as the ranger who looked after the forest, a position that virtually became hereditary. Unlike many hereditary royal positions, this one had no real foundation as such, but it was often said by Kennedy descendants that they held the office of Hereditary Ranger of the Forest of Buchan.

According to Rev Andrew Symson (c.1638-1712):

> Lord Kennedy delighted in the title of 'Ranger of the Forest of Buchan;' and a nobler field for the wild sports of the chiefs of former days could hardly be imagined. Many hunting-lodges were here kept up for his convenience, of which, to this day, there are numerous remains. Of these, his favourite stood under the Dungeon of Buchan, on a pretty green knoll, surrounded by three small lakes; it was called Hunt Hall, and a choice spot it was for a sporting rendezvous. Garrary was another of his haunts, and also Polmaddy, where shepherds still tell that the food for Cassillis's hounds was prepared in former days.

The extent of the forest has been described as comprising a number of large hill farms, namely Buchan, Portmark (on the east shore of Loch Doon), Arrow (or Eriff, at the north-eastern end of Loch Doon), Lamloch (east of Loch Doon, in the parish of Carsphairn), Loch Head (at the head of Loch Doon), Starr (at the head of Loch Doon), Shalloch on Minnoch (in the Minnoch valley), Tarfessock (also in the Minnoch valley), Palgowan (lower down the Minnoch valley), Stroan (at the mouth of Glen Trool), Dungeon o' Buchan (which was probably based on the Hunt Ha' or some other location in that vicinity), Glenhead (at the top of Glen Trool), Garrary (on the north of Clatteringshaws Loch and the Black Water of Dee), Castlemaddy (by the side of the Polmaddy Burn), the Bush (in the Polharrow glen), Cooran Lane (north of Loch Dee and east of Craignaw), Polmaddy (south of Carsphairn) and some others.

Many years ago, prior to the compilation of accurate maps and records, the boundary between the Forest of Buchan and Starr Forest was much less defined than it later became. Lord Ailsa, owner of Starr, and Lord Galloway, owner of Buchan, often disputed as to where the boundary lay, oft-times resorting to litigation. At one of the cases Lord Ailsa brought as his chief witness a weaver from Maybole, who was able to swear on his own life that he stood on Lord Ailsa's ground at a spot Lord Galloway laid claim to. Little did those who were to adjudge the case realise that the weaver had filled his shoes with soil taken from one of Lord Ailsa's farms prior to making his way to the disputed spot!

Sometime in the seventeenth century a new hunting lodge was erected by the Kennedys, about one mile over the border into the Stewartry of Kirkcudbright, in the parish of Kells. The Hunt Ha' (or Hunt Hall) was located in a moorland position at the foot of Meikle Craigtarson, looking south down the Cooran Lane and over the Silver Flow towards the rocky cliffs on the eastern sides of the Dungeon Hill and Craignaw. The little stream that flowed past the new lodge became known as the Hunt Ha' Strand. The Ha' was located 1,060 feet above sea level.

The Kennedys took to hunting in the Forest of Buchan like a deer to the forests, and they contacted a number of friends who had sporting interests to help. Sir Archibald Kennedy of Culzean (d. 1710) wrote to the Earl Marischal in 1695 to ask if he could supply him with hawks to use for hunting, but these did not arrive until the following year. In 1699 Lord Montgomerie, son of the Earl of Eglinton, sent Kennedy a setter that he could use for hunting.

The old Hunt Ha' was abandoned when a new lodge was erected further north, just over one mile to the south of the head of Loch Doon. Known as Fore Starr, this lodge was built around 1765, though whether there is any truth in the tale that the stones used in its construction came from Loch Doon Castle is probably unlikely. However, James MacBain, writing in 1929, stated that 'the ruin is interesting, as having built into its granite walls some sandstone blocks with masons' marks on them. These were presumably brought from the little of such stones at the base of Loch Doon Castle, where there are numerous like stones similarly marked, and they could be got nowhere else.' On my last visit to the ruins, however, I was unable to find any stones bearing such marks.

Armstrong's *Map of Ayrshire* notes that this was 'A Hunting Lodge lately built by the E¹ of Cassillis,' which refers to Sir Thomas Kennedy, 9th Earl of Cassillis (1726-75). The site chosen was a low eminence to the east of Craigmawhannal, 860 feet above sea level, near the Gala Lane, the river that forms the boundary between Ayrshire and the Stewartry of Kirkcudbright. The lodge was a sizeable building complete with bedrooms. From here Lord Cassillis and his brother, Sir David Kennedy, later the 10th Earl of Cassillis (1727-92), could take part in their passion for shooting. When the lodge was abandoned is unknown, but the Ordnance Survey map of 1856 depicts it as in ruins.

The lodge at Fore Starr may have changed hands at one time, for on Ainslie's map of southern Scotland, dated 1821, it is named as 'McWhirter Lodge' – the MacWhirters were at one time owners of Blairquhan Castle.

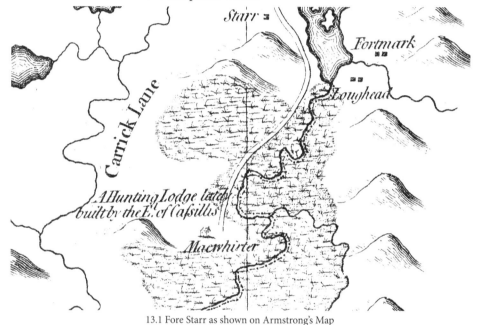

13.1 Fore Starr as shown on Armstrong's Map

Today, Fore Starr stands in solitude on a granite boss, surrounded by open countryside for a few hundred yards and by forest. There appears to have been two parallel buildings at the lodge, with a number of walls around creating enclosures. The large granite boulders used to build the walls are falling to the ground. Many of them have signs of bores used to split the solid granite, creating flat faced blocks suitable for building.

To make fishing on Loch Doon more comfortable, the 9th Lord Cassillis also erected Craigmalloch Lodge near to the head of Loch Doon in 1766, from where he could launch his new fishing boat onto the water and cast for fish.

Ownership of the Galloway Hills has changed over the centuries, and the following pages will give short accounts of each estate or lodge with land extending into the mountainous hinterland.

At the head of Loch Trool is the Buchan, or Buchan Lodge as it is also known. Originally this was an old farmhouse of the seventeenth or eighteenth century, and it was said that the farm extended to 9,999 acres. Thus, locals were often heard to call it the 'Four Nines', though in fact that acreage is said to have been a myth that was perpetuated in story. In 1851-55 the house was completely rebuilt, leaving little of the original cottage. Randolph Stewart, 9th Earl of Galloway, was developing his upland estates as a sporting centre, and Buchan was one of the places that he wished to rebuild. As with most Scottish sporting lodges of the period, neo-Baronial architecture was in vogue, and the Buchan was built in this style. It was felt that it represented the notion of Scotland as a historic and romantic nation, rediscovering its past as a result of the work of Sir Walter Scott. Queen Victoria had also discovered the wonders of the wilds of Scotland, and her erection of Balmoral Castle was to be followed by many of the aristocracy.

The 9th Earl of Galloway was a great lover of mountain sport. His main seat was at Galloway House, but he realised that the high mountains and rugged glens could earn an income greater than what was raised from sheep farming. As a result Buchan was to be the centre of a sporting estate that could be let out to shooting tenants for the season.

The architect chosen to rebuild the Buchan doesn't appear to be known. It was not a large lodge, but it had a distinctive cylindrical double-storey turret forming the entrance doorway, topped with the requisite conical roof. The remainder of the lodge was less baronial in style, only small spirelets being added to the gables. The rest of the building was fairly plain in style, more utilitarian than decorative.

Buchan Lodge was to be the Earl's favourite shooting lodge. He adorned the vicinity, building the Buchan Bridge across the Buchan Burn, which tumbles forcefully through a rock crevice into the loch below. On the parapet of the bridge he had lines from Sir Walter Scott carved on a stone.

The Buchan Lodge was abandoned as a sporting lodge in 1947, and was returned to agricultural use as a sheep farm. Though the ground was sold to the Forestry Commission, the Buchan remained as a farm until 1980, when it no longer proved viable, most of its hill ground being afforested. The lodge was then used as an outdoor centre for a time, but in 1996 it was sold with two acres and became a private residence once more, let out as holiday accommodation.

As part of his scheme to enhance the upland estates, the 9th Earl of Galloway also redesigned Auchinleck, a farm located in the Penkiln Glen, north-east of Minnigaff. This was completed in 1863, in much the same style as Buchan, being a two-storey building erected from whin and sandstone, the cylindrical stair tower being a prominent feature. This is decorated in the baronial style with arrow slits and cannon gargoyles.

The principal lodge for the south-western quadrant of the hills is located on the shores of Loch Trool. There has been a shooting or sporting lodge by the side of the loch for many years. In the seventeenth century, when Andrew Symson compiled his *Description of the Paroch of Minigaff*, the lodge was described thus:

13.2 Auchinleck

The house is surrounded with pretty groves of Scots Pines, black cherries, and other kinds of planting, which make a fine umbello to the house; and from the front, a walk down to the lake, which centers upon a little mote, prettely planted in devices with seats, and a beautifull litle boat, lodg'd there under a shade, for taking pleasure in a fine day upon the water.

The present Glen Trool Lodge was erected around 1860 as a sporting lodge for the 9th Earl of Galloway. It is a storey and a half cottage-style building, constructed from granite. The building is informal in appearance, a selection of gables and dormers facing in all directions, many of the gabled fronts having mullioned bays on the ground floor, each distinguished with their diamond-framed glass. Prior to the present lodge being erected the site was occupied by two shepherd's huts.

At one time the gamekeeper from Glen Trool Lodge was pursuing foxes and managed to track one across the hills to the north. The vixen was followed to its den, and there seven cubs were discovered. The keeper from Glen Trool was in the process of cutting off their heads, for the Earl of Galloway was paying him five shillings for evidence of their deaths. However, he had strayed across the border and was spotted

239

by the gamekeeper from Tunskeen, who came upon him. 'Whaur do I come in?' he asked. The Glen Trool keeper explained that he was due five shillings for each head, but that he was willing to share them. 'No, no,' said Tunskeen, 'I'll tak' the tails. I get five shillings frae the Marquis of Ailsa for each ane!' Thus the two keepers were able to benefit double from the eight foxes.

During the First World War the lodge was requisitioned for the accommodation of troops. At one time the K.O.S.B. were based there, searching for German aeroplane bases.

Although owned by the Earls of Galloway, the sporting rights and tenancy of the lodge was often let out, for example, in 1939 the sporting tenant was the Marquis of Tavistock.

Glen Trool Lodge was later acquired by the Moore family, owner of Littlewoods Football Pools. The family used the lodge for breaks away from the business, and they also allowed many of their employees access to it.

Another property of the Earls of Galloway is Cumloden House, located on the southern edge of the uplands. The house was erected as a summer home for Lieutenant General Hon. Sir William Stewart KCB, KTS (1774-1827), second son of the 7th Earl of Galloway, around 1825. It was extended around 1890.

Stewart signed up to the army at an early age, serving within seventeen campaigns in his lifetime. Amongst these he served in the West Indies, Egypt, and in various countries across Europe. He was in charge of the troops that embarked with Lord Nelson in the expedition to Copenhagen in Denmark. Under the Duke of Wellington, he commanded the second division in the wars in Portugal and Spain. He was to be seriously wounded at Ferrol, the injury being such that he never recovered from it. The House of Commons recorded its thanks to him, but by this time Stewart's health had deteriorated to such an extent that he had to retire from the army.

To keep himself amused, he built Cumloden and decorated the grounds around it. The lands were converted into a sporting estate, with fishing and shooting its main purpose.

Sir William enclosed an extensive area of low hill ground to establish deer parks in 1824. The Cumloden Deer Park and Glenhoise Deer Park were surrounded by tall stone dikes. Cumloden park's dike measured about nine miles in circumference. This enclosed an area of around 1,500 acres, within which were 350 fallow deer as well as 60 red deer. The deer park was reduced in extent prior to 1842, when part of it was fenced off and converted to land on which bullocks were reared, the red deer that were removed being sold to England.

Sir William Stewart died at Cumloden on 7 January 1827 and was buried in the kirkyard of Minnigaff, where a granite memorial was raised over his grave.

The eastern periphery of the hills has a number of smaller estates, with lands extending into the hinterland. Glenlee House is located at the foot of the Craigshinnie Burn, south west of Dalry, on the west side of the Water of Ken. The house, also known as Glenlee Park, was erected in 1823 to replace Old Glenlee, which is located further up the glen. It was designed by Robert Lugar. The estate at one time extended west to include Craigshinnie, Craigenbay, Clatteringshaws, Fintloch, Forrest, Darnaw, Bush and other farms lower down the Glenkens. At one time the property of the Chalmers family, their main seat was Gadgirth House, in the parish of Coylton, Ayrshire. The estate then became the property of another Ayrshire family, that of Miller of Barskimming, one of whom was Lord Glenlee - William Miller (1755-1846). Around 1850 Glenlee was sold to George Johnstone-Maxwell (d. 1858). His eldest son, George, had drowned at Glenlee, so he was succeeded by his second son, Wellwood Johnstone-Maxwell (1829-1866), followed by George Johnstone-Maxwell. Most of this land is now owned by the Forestry Commission, the lower ground the property of Captain Richard Agnew.

Earlstoun Castle lies on the east side of the Water of Ken, but at one time its estate extended far into the Galloway Hills. The estate was owned by the Sinclairs, followed by the Gordons, but in 1799 most of the properties were sold to William Forbes of Callendar House, Falkirk. These were the farms of Garrary, Backhill of Burnhead (or of Bush), Carsfad and Greenloop, Lochspraig, Knocksheen, Dukieston Park, Ringreoch, Clenrie, Drumbuie, Largmore, Over Barskeoch, Stroangassel, Barskeoch, Hannaston, Waterside, Caven and Forehill of Burnhead. The estate has been reduced in size over the years, much of it being acquired by other owners, and subsequently by the Forestry Commission. What remains of Earlstoun estate remains in Forbes ownership.

Another small estate is located in the Garroch Glen, west of St John's Town of Dalry. Garroch estate is based on Garroch House, which was erected on the slopes of Donaldbuie, a rocky hill overlooking the lower stretches of the Water of Ken and Loch Ken. Garroch House was built in the mid-nineteenth century, being described in the *Ordnance Gazetteer* as being 'a modern mansion'. The site was previously occupied by a house named Ballingear.

Garroch House replaced the original Old Garroch, which is located on the other side of Garroch Hill, farther up the Garroch Burn. Old Garroch is a two-storey laird's house of the seventeenth century, perhaps 1633, with a taller double-storey wing of the nineteenth century to one side, and a single-storey extension to the other. Within the grounds of the house is an old grave-slab, its connection with the house unknown, which bears the dates 1633 and 1686, as well as the initials AC. These initials may refer to one of the earliest known owners of Garroch, the Campbell family, the first noted being Finlay Campbell, owner in 1571.

In the nineteenth century, Garroch was owned by William Grierson Yourston. He was instrumental in establishing the Glenkens Society in 1831, made up of landowners and gentry in the district. One of the aims of the society was to give prizes to local schoolchildren for good work.

Ballingear, or Garroch, House has been demolished in recent years, but Garroch estate survives, currently extending to 5,000 acres, covering Garroch, Drumbuie and Clenrie. It is the property of Nicholas Roper Caldbeck.

The estate of Knocknalling lies on the eastern side of the Galloway hills, the mansion house located near the mouth of the Polharrow Glen. The present house is a

13.3 Garroch House

sizeable building, Tudor in style, erected around 1840. The main building has five bays of windows facing south, the house comprising four roofed blocks, the end two projecting in front of the centre block. The entrance porch is on the east side of the house.

Surrounded by woodlands, Knocknalling has a large walled garden to the north. The stable block, immediately behind the house, has two long ranges on either side of a narrow courtyard. That to the north is two storeys in height, the upper windows adorned by pediments over them, probably dating from around 1880. At the east end of the block is a prominent Gothic tower with spire atop. The barn is also a distinctive building, with triangular vents over most of the walls, and small doocot flight-holes in the gables.

The estate was anciently owned by the Kennedy family, a branch of the Kennedys of Ardmillan in Ayrshire. One account claims that the family occupied the lands from at least 1476, whereas another states that they acquired it in 1640. In any case, David Kennedy (1695-1786) was also a merchant in New Galloway. He was succeeded by his son, Robert Kennedy (1730-1779). This Robert, according to his son, 'was a very delicate man and subject to low spirits, which were increased by seeing so large a family dependent upon him, and the very slender means he had for supporting them. This, with a tendency to consumption, soon undermined his health, and he died early [aged 49], leaving us all very young and far distant from the parish school, which was the cause of all our shortcomings in the way of education.' His widow, Margaret Alexander, survived for another 22 years, dying in 1801.

David Kennedy (1764-1836) succeeded, but he and his wife outlived their offspring, and the estate passed to David's younger brother, John Kennedy.

John Kennedy (1769-1855) trained as a carpenter when he was young and moved to Manchester where he joined a business in that trade. His skill was such that he set up on his own, making machinery for the spinning industry, and eventually he acquired property in Lancashire where he established large cotton mills, making his fortune. A plan to establish a large mill at Allangibbon Bridge, near Milton Park, came to nought, however. With a massive increase in his wealth he was able to rebuild Knocknalling into the large country house we see today, the clock tower and spire being a prominent landmark. Kennedy spent much of the summer months at his Scottish estate.

The estate passed to Col. John Murray Kennedy MVO (1841-1928) and on his death he was succeeded by his daughter, Violet Frances Kennedy (d. 1953), who married Archibald James Murray St. Clair, 16th Lord Sinclair (1875-1957). Lord Sinclair moved to Knocknalling, establishing the family there. On his death he was succeeded by Charles Murray Kennedy St Clair CVO, 17th Lord Sinclair (1914-2004). In addition to running the estate, he became Lord Lieutenant of Dumfries and Galloway.

13.4 Forrest Lodge

The estate is currently the property of Matthew Murray Kennedy Sinclair, 18th Lord Sinclair (b. 1968). The estate extends to 5,000 acres or thereabouts, around half of which is east of the Water of Ken.

One large estate that remains in private ownership is Forrest estate. The site of the present Forrest Lodge was originally known as Nether Forrest, for there is another building known as Forrest located further to the north east. The early history of the estate is little known, but in November 1668 it became the property of William Chalmers, a merchant in Ayr, and Agnes MacCubbin, his wife. In the nineteenth century it passed to Samuel Thomson, and in the second half of the nineteenth century it was acquired by Wellwood Johnstone-Maxwell of Glenlee (1829-1866).

In 1910 the present Forrest Lodge was erected at the head of the Polharrow Glen for Sir John Wood MP. He brought the architect G. Ramsay Thomson in to create a modern Scots version of the Arts and Crafts house, with baronial overtones and traditional features. An asymmetrical building, most of the lodge is two storeys in height, though in the main block a third storey is located in the attic. The entrance is located in a projecting semi-circular tower. To the left of this, at the corner of the main block, is a double-storey cylindrical turret, topped with a conical roof. The building was erected from whinstone, edged and corbie-stepped with Creetown granite, the whin harled to hide it. G. Ramsay Thomson was an architect based in Dumfries, who designed some extensions to Dumfries and Galloway Infirmary. The plans for Forrest Lodge were exhibited in 1910 and mention of them was reported in *Building News* that year.

Sir John Wood was born on 8 September 1857 and was educated for the bar. He served as a Conservative Member of Parliament for Stalybridge from 1910 until 1918, and then for Stalybridge and Hyde from 1918 until 1922. In 1918 he was created a baronet. His main seat was Hengrave Hall, Bury St Edmunds. He died on 28 January 1953.

Half of Sir John Wood's estate, comprising the 13,000 acres of Forrest Lodge and its surroundings, was purchased by Thomas Olsen, of Fred. Olsen Ltd. in 1952. The remainder, to the west of the Rhinns of Kells, around Backhill of Bush, was sold to the Forestry Commission. Today Forrest estate extends to over 11,000 acres, now owned by Thomas's son, Fred Olsen. The estate offers deer stalking, fishing, game shooting and clay pigeon shooting. It is now one of very few sporting estates in south-west Scotland that offers red deer stalking.

When a number of forest roads were created in the new plantations around Forrest Lodge, many of these were named after family members, others after long-serving estate workers. Thus we have Professor Hans Heiberg Road, Birger Natvig Road, Robert Watson Road, and roads named after Fred, Kristin and Thomas Olsen.

By the side of the road leading to Forrest Lodge, just over the Forrest Bridge, one comes across a tall kilted highlander, standing on a low cairn. The figure rises between nine and ten feet tall, its height emphasised by the cairn of boulders on which it stands. Closer inspection reveals that the figure, which appears as a colourful statue, is in fact only single-sided and that the back is hollow. This gives away its original purpose, to some extent, for the statue was in fact a figurehead from a ship.

The passenger liner, *Black Watch*, was used by Fred Olsen lines as a cruise ship that travelled between Newcastle and Oslo. Entering into service in 1939, the ship was not to enjoy the trappings of luxury holidays for long, for at the outbreak of war in September 1939 the vessel was laid up in a Norwegian fjord. Germany invaded Norway soon after, and the German Navy commandeered the vessel, using it as a communications centre and supply ship. The *Black Watch* served the German navy for five years, but on 5 May 1945, just two days before the war hostilities were brought to an end, the vessel was bombed and it sank in 150 feet of water at Kilbotn, near Harstad, by the Fleet Air Arm.

The *Black Watch* lay at the bottom of the seabed from then until 1963, when a salvage firm began work on raising the ship, its steel and other components being in demand for scrap. Divers made their way down into the sea and the first item that they raised from the sunken vessel was the figurehead from the bow. The steel statue was cleaned up and sent to Fred Olsen's London offices, where it stood for a number of years. A sister ship, the *Black Prince*, had a very similar tale, and its figurehead was retrieved and sent to Olsen's passenger terminal at Oslo, where it was installed over the entrance.

The London offices of Olsen's shipping company were being rebuilt and the figurehead was no longer deemed to be a suitable item for display there. It was decided that, because of it Scottish connection, the kilted statue should be sent to this quiet Galloway glen, and it was erected there.

Two other items from the *Black Watch* are also preserved in Glen Harrow. On the walls of Forrest Lodge are two elliptical metal plaques, one depicting a soldier lying down playing a recorder, the other showing two kilted soldiers engaged in a highland dance.

Forrest Estate currently extends to around 11,586 acres, much of it planted in trees.

North of the Forrest estate are lands owned by various proprietors, in some cases institutional. Historically, much of the land from Carsphairn to Dalmellington formed part of the extensive lands of Craigengillan, anciently the property of the MacAdam family. The fine country house of Craigengillan, an old Scots mansion surrounded by trees, is located beyond the northern end of Loch Doon, overlooking the River Doon and Ness Glen. The estate associated with it is ancient, records of it being noted as early as 1580.

Craigengillan Estate at one time extended to 30,000 acres, encompassing much of Dalmellington and Carsphairn parishes. The name actually comes from an old building in the latter parish, located by the side of the Polifferie Burn, just before its confluence with the Water of Ken. Northwest of the cottage rises Craigengillan Hill.

The MacAdam family of Craigengillan are an ancient clan, and tradition claims that they were originally a sept of the Clan MacGregor, but when that clan was proscribed the family adopted the name MacAdam, from Adam MacGregor, its first member. Of this family are John Loudon MacAdam (1756-1836), the famous road maker, after whom tarmacadam was named, and the Covenanting martyr, Gilbert MacAdam, whose grave can be found in Kirkmichael kirkyard, Ayrshire. He is also commemorated on the MacAdam burial aisle in Carsphairn kirkyard, where the family arms, three arrows, are carved on stone.

The MacAdams moved from Craigengillan into Lagwyne Castle, near to Carsphairn, but this tower is said to have been burned down in 1756. The head of the family is supposed to have lived in Lady Cathcart's House in Ayr (where John Loudoun MacAdam was born) for a time, prior to a new country house being built at Berbeth, the older name for the house that stood here. This house was renamed Craigengillan, after the family estate, the name Berbeth being retained only for the loch above it. The lands of Berbeth were originally acquired by the MacAdams in 1611.

The oldest part of Craigengillan House may date from the 1760s, when there were considerable improvements being made to the house and estate. This laird's house, built for John MacAdam, is located at the northern end of the main block, and its tall roof has some indications of having been thatched at one time. John MacAdam was a contemporary and early supporter of Robert Burns. The bard wrote a poem to him in thanks, in Nanse Tinnock's Inn, Mauchline:

> Sir, o'er a gill I gat your card,
> I trow it made me proud;
> 'See wha taks notice o' the bard!'
> I lap, an' cry'd fu' loud.
>
> Now deil-ma-care about their jaw,
> The senseless, gawky million!
> I'll cock my nose abune them a',
> I'm roos'd by Craigen-Gillan!

John MacAdam made many improvements to Craigengillan and its extensive estate. He introduced a new method of building stone dikes to the area, one that was to prove to be more robust and longer-lasting than the local Galloway dike used up until that time. It is said that he brought a man from the north, surnamed MacWhinnie, into the area to build these dikes, which were to be to his ideas and instructions. His family lived on Burnton farm thereafter, at a nominal rent, and for some unknown reason changed their surname to MacKenzie, one of whom became a legal practitioner in Edinburgh. According to John Paterson, writing in 1847, 'the Dalmellington dikers, who were taught by MacWhinnie, are still esteemed the best in the country.'

Craigengillan was considerably extended from 1802-5 for Quintin MacAdam, creating the present central block, with its tall, but thin pencil turret on the garden front, big enough inside just for a small closet. Quintin MacAdam was also referred to in Burns' poem to his father as 'young Dunaskin's Laird'.

The house was remodelled around 1827, after the marriage on 18 October that year, of the heiress, Jean or Jane MacAdam, to the Hon. Frederick Cathcart, son of the 1st Earl Cathcart, and the arrival of more serious money. At this time the two prominent wings were added to the front, along with the glazed Tudoresque porch. Jean MacAdam died on 25 April 1878, having outlived her husband, who died on 5 March 1865. He had served as a Colonel in the army, and was created a knight of the Russian Order of St Anne.

Contemporary with the 1802 extensions is the Georgian stable-block, which was added to the south-east of the house, and which, with its clock tower, somewhat overpowers the house. In the courtyard behind are boxes for horses. At the same time the steading of Craigengillan Home Farm was rebuilt, and a gatehouse erected at Dalmellington, at the end of a two-mile-long drive.

The interior of Craigengillan has been restored in recent years. Some of it was the work of the French design firm, Maison Jansen, of Paris, which was commissioned by Charlotte MacAdam around 1905 to soften the design of the morning room and other parts of the house. Charlotte was widowed in 1901.

Craigengillan was not a sporting estate in the true sense, as the mansion was not a sporting lodge, but a country seat for an upland estate. However, much of the land on the estate was moorland, with lochs and rivers suitable for hunting and fishing. The moors were tended for grouse, and gamekeepers were employed to burn the heather, repair the butts, and encourage game birds to breed on the estate. A number of major business and political men came to the estate for fishing and shooting. Among these were Sir William Beardmore, Lord Invernairn, and Lord Halifax.

The MacAdams were socialites in their time, Charlotte MacAdam having numerous important friends and connections, many of whom came to Craigengillan for a few days of peace and quiet. Prince and Princess Rainier of Monaco were regular visitors in the 1930s, and King Gustav and Queen Helena of Sweden are known to have visited on two occasions. The prime ministers, Stanley Baldwin and Neville Chamberlain, have been at Craigengillan.

Craigengillan was broken up as a sizeable estate in 1919. Most of the farms, in addition to Camlarg Shooting Lodge, were placed on the market, totalling 28,177 acres, but the mansion and policies were retained.

The family retained the estate for centuries, though it passed through the female line a couple of times, until in 1999 the last of the family associated with Craigengillan, Alastair Douglas Bulkeley Gavin (b. 1931), sold the mansion and 3,000 acres of land around it. It was purchased by Mark Gibson, who set about restoring the house, which needed considerable work done on the roof and to the interiors. He then began work restoring other parts of the estate, such as some of the old ruined cottages, one of which was re-roofed with reed thatch, an unusual modern example of its use. These cottages are made available for holiday lets. The Georgian Stables, a major feature of Craigengillan, was restored and is once again a thriving stable yard offering riding lessons, hacks and livery, something that Mark Gibson was keen to promote.

In the same way, once the Galloway Forest Park was identified as a Dark Sky Park, he instigated the construction of The Scottish Dark Sky Observatory, a publicly accessible research grade observatory located on a rocky knoll south of the mansion.

Not all of the land was sold to Mark Gibson – parts of Craigengillan estate were retained by the Gavins. This was Beoch farm on Loch Doon and Mossdale in Glen Muck.

The farms of Eriff and Lamford were also part of Craigengillan estate at one time. Today it continues to operate as a small sporting estate, named Eriff Estate. It extends to 1,500 acres, the property of Sandy Moffat.

The north-western extremity of the area covered by this book forms, or formed, part of Blairquhan estate. The estate was for centuries owned by the Kennedy family, though before that was a seat of the MacWhirters. In the early seventeenth century the estate was acquired by the Whitefoord family, chief of the clan Whitefoord. The

Whitefoords suffered financially in the Ayr Bank crash of 1772, and the estate was placed on the market. It was acquired by the Hunter Blair family in 1798, which had made their mark at the same time as the old family of Whitefoord was declining. Sir David Hunter Blair (1779-1857) was a county convenor and served as a Colonel of the Ayrshire Militia during the Napoleonic Wars.

Blairquhan Castle lies by the side of the Water of Girvan, and at one time it was an ancient tower house, typical of the traditional castles of the sixteenth century. With the arrival of the up and coming Hunter Blairs, the old castle was regarded as being too old-fashioned for their liking, and a new building was wanted. A variety of top architects were commissioned to draw up possible plans, and eventually that proposed by the Edinburgh architect William Burn was selected. His plan proposed demolishing the entire old castle and replacing it was a fashionable Tudoresque castle, complete with crenelated parapets, tourelles and chimneys. To the east of the castle a courtyard was created, in which some of the decorative stone from the old tower was incorporated.

13.5 Craigengillan House

The Hunter Blairs took to their extensive estate and shooting was carried out over the low ground around the castle, which was finely wooded, as well as on the lower hills of the Galloway Highlands, such as Craig Hill and Kildoach Hill.

On the summit of Highgate Hill, which overlooks the village of Straiton, stands a massive obelisk. This was erected to commemorate James Hunter Blair, who was killed at the Battle of Inkerman in Crimea. The monument, which was built of white granite blocks, stands 55 feet in height and surmounts a four-step pedestal which is itself five feet tall. On the eastern face of the monument is a slab measuring three feet three inches by two feet four inches on which is the following inscription:

Sacred to the memory of James Hunter Blair, younger of Blairquhan, Lt. Colonel Scots Fusilier Guards & Member of Parliament for this county, who fell in the gallant discharge of his duty on the field of Inkerman, 5th November 1854. Erected by his friends and neighbours, AD 1856.

The hill stands 1,083 feet in height, a lower eminence of the taller Kildoach Hill, though locally the hill is better known as Craigengower, from the rocky cliffs forming the western slopes, from the Gaelic *Creag an Gobhar*, rocks of the goat.

James Hunter Blair was born on 22 March 1817, the eldest son and heir of Sir David Hunter Blair, 3rd Baronet of Dunskey, and his wife, Dorothea MacKenzie of Newhall and Cromarty. He was brought up to join the military, and he served with the Scots Fusilier Guards. In July 1852 he was elected as the Conservative M.P. for Ayrshire. With the outbreak of war against Russia in 1854, Hunter Blair went to Crimea where he served with the Fusilier Guards in the second line of the British Army. He fought at Balaclava as part of the 'Thin Red Line' and then at Little Inkerman. The main Inkerman battle took place on 5 November, and Hunter Blair was one of those who were killed at the charge against the Sandbag Battery. The British fought on, tired and in danger of defeat, until the French and Algerian troops stepped in to back them up. The battle won, the dead on the British side amounted to 597, including 39 officers.

Some of the shooting and fishing on Blairquhan estate was let to others, and a lodge was erected at Balbeg, on the west side of the Water of Girvan. This was built in the nineteenth century but was considerably extended in the twentieth century. In 1908 Major-General Sir Charles Fergusson of Kilkerran, 7th Baronet, commissioned James Purves of Portpatrick to extend the shooting lodge. It was again added to in 1923, by which time the lodge was the property of Sir Gerald Edward Chadwyck-Healey, 2nd Baronet (1873-1955). Although Chadwyck-Healey came from a Surrey family, he was to become a Depute Lieutenant of Ayrshire. Again, Purves of Portpatrick was the architect. The property was acquired by Lady Peto around 1955.

Today, Blairquhan estate covers 2,700 acres, but the castle itself was sold in November 2012 to new owners, Ganten, of Guangdong, south China, which operates it as a wedding venue. The Hunter Blairs retain the remainder of the estate, using Milton as their new seat.

The western side of the Galloway Highlands, including upper Loch Doon, was for centuries the property of the Kennedy family, who became Marquises of Ailsa. They built a number of sporting lodges on this property over the years. The Ailsa estate had various grouse moors, pheasant shoots and fishing stretches in the Galloway Hills, employing keepers at Craiglure, Rowantree and Craigmalloch.

From the car park at Stinchar Falls, on the hill road between Straiton and Newton Stewart, a forest trail wends alongside the infant River Stinchar, passing the falls and heading south through the forest. The path crosses the Stinchar by a footbridge and soon comes to a significant bend in the watercourse. Within this bend is a pile of stones, obviously not natural, containing many hewn blocks. This is all that remains of Craiglure Lodge, a hunting lodge that belonged to the Marquis of Ailsa, whose family seat was Culzean Castle. This was the second Craiglure Lodge to be erected, the older one now submerged in the waters of Loch Bradan.

The original Craiglure Lodge was located by the side of Loch Lure, near to where the little river escaped and dropped into Loch Bradan. Surrounded by a sheltering blanket of pines, the lodge gained its name from the low hill of Craiglure (1,249 feet) which rose to the south-west. The lodge was abandoned when a new lodge was erected further to the south-west.

The new Craiglure Lodge was erected in 1819 for the 12th Earl of Cassillis, later to be raised in the peerage in 1831 as the 1st Marquis of Ailsa. The Earl felt that the new lodge was in a more convenient place, nearer to the rivers and closer to the higher mountains and moors where the deer were to be found. An L-shaped building, the ground floor boasted a 'parlour' that measured seventeen feet by fourteen feet, a kitchen of a similar size, servants quarters and two dog houses. Upstairs were three principal bedrooms, plus two lesser bedrooms and a servants' room. The original drawing of the 'Design for Hunting Lodge to the Right Honble Earl of Cassillis' survives.

Lord Cassillis, though he enjoyed shooting and the hunting life, found Craiglure no longer to be one of his favourite lodges, and began to despair of having erected it. On 12 March 1824 he wrote a letter to Sir James Fergusson of Kilkerran, another Ayrshire landowner:

> You are most exceeding welcome to Fish in any of my Lakes or Rivers you Please, you should try The Doon about Cassillis. My Boys – viz. Kennedys, Bairds and John, had most Capital sport there last year. Killing Four or Five Salmon a day – when you get to the Stinchar Lakes pray make a Home of my Lodge. I have Built a House up there what I don't know now what to do with. I should like to set [let] it and all my rivers for 5 years – more or less – The Weather here is Dreadful. Hail, Snow and Rain alternately.

In 1836 extensions were added to Craiglure, a new keeper's house and coach house being built. Again in 1877 the lodge was refurbished and after the work was completed the building and the sporting rights were let. There was a recession on at the time, and the Ailsa estate was trying to increase its income by letting out such property. In 1877 the first tenant of the refurbished lodge was Henry C. Bucknall, a well-off ship-owner. Whether or not his shipping business suffered from the recession, or whether there was a lack of game and fish at Craiglure, Bucknall only kept the rights for two years, giving them up in 1879. The lodge remained vacant for a year, in 1880 being taken over by Basil Sparrow. He too remained only for a short time, being succeeded in the lease by Arthur Bignold. By 1890 the grouse on the moor were in decline, suffering from disease, and a drop in the rent was needed before a tenant could be found to take on the lease.

The 2nd Marquis of Ailsa was a keen sportsman, and though he preferred to live at the Kennedy seat of The Priory at Reigate in Surrey, he often returned north to

Ayrshire to take part in shooting and fishing. Craiglure was one of the lodges he often frequented on these jaunts, and from there he shot deer on the hills and fished in the lochs and infant rivers. The game book at Culzean notes what was bagged on sojourns to Craiglure, such as on 14 August 1855 when Lord Ailsa shot four grouse, seven black game, a hare and a snipe. On many occasions the laird and the menfolk in the family, as well as guests, spent a week at a time at Craiglure, leaving the womenfolk at Culzean to pursue their own hobbies.

The Ailsa family were suffering financially, and various schemes were proposed to try to save money and reduce the debt burden. A number of residences were sold, and Culzean Castle was kept closed for the summer, it being cheaper to open Craiglure Lodge and the family reside there at that time. During 1903 most of the summer and autumn was spent at Craiglure, much to the annoyance of Lady Ailsa: 'If his Lordship does not see his way to building another lodge as we talked of some time ago, it would be well to make the present one more finished.'

Lady Ailsa must have had some influence over her husband, for alterations and improvements were indeed carried out. By 1907-8 further enhancements were being made to Craiglure Lodge, these being the work of the prominent architect, James Miller (1860-1947). Miller was doing work at Newark Castle for Lord Ailsa at the time, and was asked to make some alterations to the lodge. These were to make it more comfortable for the family, as well as to make it more desirable for letting to sporting tenants. In 1909 a new gas plant was created, allowing the building to be heated using central heating. In the immediate vicinity new stables were also erected.

Financial difficulties and death duties meant that the Ailsa estate had to sell off much of its high ground in the Galloway Highlands, most of this being acquired by the Forestry Commission, which had been set up in 1919 to produce home-grown timber. Craiglure, Rowantree and Craigmalloch were all sold, along with thousands of acres, much of which was subsequently planted in trees. Craiglure Lodge was no longer required by the Commission, and no tenants could be found to take it on. Accordingly, the building gradually suffered from lack of use and was demolished in the mid-1950s.

The final sporting lodge mentioned here is located near the foot of Glen Trool, within a small estate in the Minnoch valley. This was also one of the last country lodges to be erected in the Galloway Highlands. The present Glencaird House was erected in the 1930s, in a traditional manner, a bit of a mish-mash of architectural styles. The architect responsible was Roger Arthur Philip Pinckney (1900-1990), who practised in London. Pinckney's design has a large quarter-circle bay in the re-entrant angle of the L-shaped building. On the face of this bay is a Gibbsian-style doorway. The house is two storeys in height, and its Arts and Crafts style finish is of the highest quality. Some of the elements of the house have perhaps been influenced by Charles Rennie Mackintosh, such as the chimney stack to the right of the doorway.

At first floor level on the entrance front is a stone panel, incorporated into the wall. This contains the date 1694 and is inscribed with initials *I MK, AH* and armorial bearings, all within a circular moulding. On the east front is another ancient panel, perhaps dating from the sixteenth century, complete with armorial bearings and the initials *AH*. These were previously located on the front gables of the earlier lodge, and tradition claims that they were originally located on the house of Eschoncan, located in Glen Trool.

An earlier Glencaird shooting lodge existed, the property of the Murray family for many years. William Murray (1750-1833) was followed by Alexander Murray (1795-1872). In 1872 the occupier was Major J. P. Traherne. The lodge was later acquired by Colonel John MacKie of Bargaly CBE DSO (1857-1934), son of James MacKie of Bargaly, MP for the Stewartry of Kirkcudbright from 1857 until he died on 28 December 1867, aged 46.

John Mackie of Bargaly (1857-1934) carried out considerable improvements both to the house and grounds. Mackie was a keen improver of rough grazing, and he was able to reclaim some of the moor around Glencaird and create better grazing there. He also erected extensive fences, planted shelterbelts and improved the whole aspect of the estate. This took place in the second half of the nineteenth century. Writing in 1876, Malcolm Harper noted that, 'Nowhere in Galloway could those interested in such experiments have a better opportunity of seeing how energy and enterprise, combined with a scientific system of agriculture, may be made to triumph over barren rocks and heath, moss haggs and sloughs of despond, than here.'

A number of smaller shooting lodges have existed in the hills. These tend to be more like shepherd's cottages in appearance, compared with the larger lodge which is more akin to the country house. An example was White Laggan, lying to the south of Loch Dee. It was converted into a shooting lodge in the late nineteenth century.

Although most of the land within the area covered by this book belongs to the Forestry Commission, there are a few areas in private ownership. To the east of Loch Doon the lands of Drumjohn and Blackcraig, most of which is afforested, belongs to the Eagle Star Life Assurance Co. Ltd. and extends to 2,153 acres. To the south of this is Woodhead farm, 1,404 acres of sheep grazing and forestry, owned by the Gordon family. Garryhorn farm extends to 2,000 acres of hill ground, the property of the Cathcart family.

In the Cree valley Drannandow farm extends to 1,548 acres, the property of Dr J. Radcliffe. Apart from smaller properties, such as Holm, and Palgowan, all ground in the south-western corner is under Forestry Commission or Royal Society for the Protection of Birds control.

In the north-west, in addition to Blairquhan estate, are smaller properties such as Craig, Genoch and Largs farms, owned by Andrew Paton & Co., extending to 2,000 acres. Glenauchie in the valley of the Water of Girvan is 1,200 acres, the property of the MacTaggarts. The Kay family run Gass farm, which covers 2,000 acres.

There are also a number of lodges in the Galloway Hills that are owned or leased by sporting clubs and associations. One such is Balloch Lodge, which lies at the head of a watercourse named the Balloch Lane, which flows into Loch Riecawr. The lodge was erected by the Balloch Fishing Club, which was founded in 1892, the fishing rights being leased from the Marquis of Ailsa. The simple exterior belies its Victorian origins. The club now claims to be one of the oldest fishing clubs in continuous existence. The club is limited in its membership, and the waiting list can sometimes be up to fifteen years. Members get the use of the lodge for prescribed periods, and may invite guests to fish with them. From the lodge fishermen would cross the moors to four lochs where they have the rights to fishing – lochs Riecawr, Macaterick, Ballochling and Slochy. Loch Riecawr is the principal loch used by the club, there being a boat house on the northern shores of the loch. This has been rebuilt over the years. At one time boats were also kept on Loch Macaterick and Ballochling Loch, but these have long-since been removed.

The three main lochs offer trout and salmon fishing. Around the year 1885 there were attempts to introduce the yellow Loch Leven variety of trout into these lochs, but this experiment failed, perhaps due to the higher altitude of the lochs (both Riecawr and Macaterick are around 920 feet above sea level), and the high peat content of the water.

Three of the early founders of the club are commemorated by a cairn located on the hillside half way between Balloch Lodge and the boat house on Loch Riecawr. This memorial stands approximately eight feet in height, and has a white granite slab bearing the inscription, made out in lead lettering. It reads:

Erected by Balloch Fishing Club in memory of Claude Hamilton, President 1892-1908,
John Lockhart, Secretary & Treasurer 1901-1918,
Charles D. Inglis, President 1913-1929.

Claude Hamilton (1854-1908) was the first president of the club, and was a very active member. He was well known across Ayrshire and was a noted benefactor – the Claude Hamilton Memorial Hall in Coylton having been erected in 1909 using funds left by him in his will. He was the fourth heir to Sundrum Castle, which he succeeded to in 1898. When he married Miss Evans in 1877 the clock tower at the castle was erected. There is a bronze memorial panel in his memory within Coylton Parish Church, complete with his likeness, the work of Robert Bryden.

John Lockhart (d. 1918) was a sheriff-clerk in Ayr and the founder of Lockharts, a firm of solicitors that still exists in the town. His sons, William and George, were also to become active members of the fishing club.

Charles D. Inglis (1840-1929) was a seed merchant in Ayr, having his own business. He resided in Stair House, an ancient fortified house by the side of the River Ayr, and was buried in Stair kirkyard. His family had been tenants in Stair House for 96 years until 1928. The family had been shooting tenants at Dornal and Glenmuir, east of Cumnock, until these lands were sold to Lord Bute.

A second memorial was erected by the club – a memorial bridge across the Balloch Lane, half-way between the lodge and Loch Riecawr. Although this bridge has since been removed, the memorial plaque is preserved by the club.

One who enjoyed sport in the Galloway hills was W. G. M. Dobie, who wrote a few books on the subject. Born in 1893, William Gardiner Murchie Dobie, to give him his full name, was a solicitor, but spent much of his free time fishing and shooting. He lived at Conheath House, at Glencaple, near Dumfries, and was married to Jane Carter Johnston. In 1927 he wrote a book entitled *Game-bag and Creel*, recounting some of his adventures. In 1938 *Winter and Rough Weather* followed, in which there are accounts of shooting partridges, grouse and deer-stalking. Two more of his books were *Old Time Farming in Dumfriesshire*, published in 1949, and *Lawyers' Leisure*, published in 1963. A number of his articles and poems were published in *Punch, The Field* and *Blackwood's Magazine*. W. G. M. Dobie died on 2 December 1972 at Dumfries and Galloway Royal Infirmary.

The River Cree is recognised as a rather fine salmon river. A number of deep pools can be found along its length, one of which, near to Cunninghame's Ford, was considered to be one of the best in the river. A few pools in the River Cree have been given the name 'wiel', an old Scots term used in Ayrshire and Galloway to signify a deep pool that afforded good fishing. On the Cree is Cairdie Wiel, near to the farm of Larg. The Water of Minnoch, the principal tributary of the Cree, and indeed the larger of the two watercourses where it joins the Cree, has more wiels along its length. These include MacKie's Wiel, near Holm farm, and the Quaking Ash Wiel and Cashnabrock Wiel, both of which lie upstream from Borgan.

Trout can be found in most of the lochs and rivers of the Galloway uplands. In the second half of the nineteenth century Malcolm Harper noted the capture of a 'monster' trout in Loch Dee. This had been landed around the time of his visit, in the 1870s, and the fish weighed no less than 12 pounds. It measured 32 inches in length and at the time the locals reckoned it was the largest that had ever been caught in the loch.

Fishing in Loch Doon has long been a common sport. In the Victorian times, when transport began to be more readily available, anglers were wont to make their way to the district to take part in the pastime. A few hotels in the district offered accommodation to those wishing to stay overnight, among these being the Eglinton Hotel in Dalmellington. The hotel was enlarged before 1889 and James MacDonald, the proprietor, noted in his advertisements that he had eight boats on Loch Doon for the use of tourists and anglers.

A number of anglers established huts for themselves in the lands around Loch Doon. One of these was constructed near to Lambdoughty by Andrew Armour from Kilmarnock. He was the proprietor of a garage in the town and had been asked to build a top for a lorry. It turned out the client couldn't pay for this top, so undaunted Armour transported it to the lochside where he fitted it out as a lodge for his fishing trips. Within were three bunks, a small kitchen area with stove and washing area, and some seats. Windows overlooked the surrounding loch and hills on each side.

Other huts were built elsewhere by the lochside, one at the head of the loch, opposite Loch Head farm, being erected in 1938 as the base for Andrew Gemmell who was a keen hillwalker. A garage proprietor in Dalmellington, Gemmell and his dog roamed the hills of Loch Doon and into the Dungeon, exploring every nook and cranny.

14 Death on the Hills

The extreme weather conditions that can be experienced in the Galloway mountains have sometimes, unfortunately, resulted in the loss of lives. A number of people over the centuries have succumbed to the weather, often overcome by the freezing cold, falling darkness and driving wind and rain. There are a few memorials across the hills marking the spots where some of these unfortunate people died, and many more breathed their last on remote locations that have long-since been forgotten, or else are unmarked.

An old tale recounts how an elderly woman was making her way through the Dungeon of Buchan, from Ayrshire into Galloway, sometime around the start of the nineteenth century. The old woman died on her journey, but no-one was with her, and her body was never found by humans. What time of year she was making her journey cannot be told, and whether or not she died of exhaustion, old age, or was overcome by a snowstorm cannot be determined. In any case, it is related that in 1826 a shepherd from Buchan farm, prior to it being converted into a shooting lodge, was on the hill when he spotted a stot, or young bullock, carrying a bone. The animal was unwilling to let go of this, and the shepherd was convinced that it was a human bone. The shepherd returned to his house and made contact with another shepherd and they both returned to the hill where he saw the stot with the bone. They searched around the hillside and came upon the remains of the old woman's body. Most of it had decayed, leaving only a skeleton lying mutilated on the moss.

Word was sent to George Campbell, farmer in Garrary at the time, and the men returned to the spot, gathered the bones and decently buried them where they were found. A cairn was raised over the grave, marking the spot for many years. It was also said that a shepherd in the area at one time found a piece of the woman's tartan cloak on the moor. Today, the spot has been lost, but it was located somewhere on a level moss, opposite to Dungeon Hill. The account was related in an early nineteenth century book, *Tributes to Scottish Genius*, by John Gordon Barbour of Bogue.

George Campbell was something of a minor poet, and he composed some verses in honour of the woman, whose name never seems to have been found out. He wrote:

> Far, far from haunt of human ken,
>   Where eagles soar around,
> There, fenced by rocks, embanked by moss,
>   Thy lonely grave is found.

From whence or why roamed here thy steps,
        Amid this desert drear?
    Some wild delirium o'er thy brain
        Has made thee wander here.

There is also the tale of another woman who lost her life in the hills. She was making her way through the great valley between the Dungeon and Kells when she lost her way somewhat, and found herself stuck in the Silver Flow. Unable to extricate herself, she remained there all night, suffering from exposure. Not arriving at her destination as expected, a search was made the following morning and she was discovered still trapped in her boggy prison. The rescuers managed to extricate her and carry her to safety, but she died within a few hours of the privations suffered.

Helen's Stone, which can be found in the valley of the Buchan Burn, between Culsharg cottage and Loch Enoch, marks the spot where yet another woman was to die on the hills. Nothing much is known about the situation, or when she died.

Possibly the earliest death on the hills commemorated by a memorial was that of John MacDonald. Who MacDonald was is not really known now, but it is reckoned that he was probably either a tramp or travelling salesman-cum-pedlar. He died near to the Brockloch Bridge, on the roadway between Clatteringshaws and Talnotry. A cylindrical cairn marks the spot, and in its side is a small granite stone bearing the simple inscription:

John MacDonald died here 1878

14.1 John MacDonald's Cairn

Some say that the year on the stone is an error, and that he actually died in 1876, though this has not been proven. The present cairn was erected in July 1983, though a cairn of sorts existed for many years beforehand. When the road was being rebuilt past this spot the old memorial was destroyed and a new cairn was erected. This was built of dry-stanes, in the side of which was a granite stone obtained from Carsluith granite works, on which the inscription was carved. At one time it was knocked down and the inscribed stone was lost. At a later date it was rediscovered and incorporated into the present memorial.

One of the largest memorials to a victim of severe weather is a stone cairn, rising to around twelve feet in height, erected from locally-found whinstone, quartz and granite, surmounted by a roughly hewn block of granite to represent the broken needle. On one side of the cairn is a stone slab bearing a simple inscription:

In memory of David MacMath, gamekeeper, The Mines,
who perished here in a snowstorm. Found 26th Dec. 1925 after a 3 days search.

14.2 David MacMath's Cairn

David MacMath lived in a cottage at the Woodhead Lead Mines, two miles to the west of Carsphairn. He was employed by Major Cathcart, who lived at Ardendee House, near Kirkcudbright, as a gamekeeper on the Garryhorn estate. A few days before Christmas, Dave, as he was known, had taken the bus from Carsphairn to Dalmellington. It had been snowing heavily, and Dave had decided to catch the bus home. The driver was making his way up the narrow defile of Glen Muck when the bus became stuck in a deep drift.

Dave was keen to return home, however, for his eighty-year-old father would be waiting for him. He left the bus driver in Glen Muck and started out walking for home, a distance of around seven miles. A reasonably fit man, Dave was able to stride through the snow storms with ease, making his way up the final stretches of Glen Muck. At the top, near to Loch Muck, the glen opens out, the road arriving on the moors at the top of the valley. Here the winds blew uninterrupted across the open moor, driving the snow against Dave's face. He was beginning to tire, and the cold was beginning to take effect on his body.

Beyond Lamford he dropped down to the Lamloch Bridge, crossing the Carsphairn Lane to the other side. Beyond Lamford he began the ascent over the hill to the mines, where his cottage was located. The snow had covered the track that linked Lamloch and Woodhead mines, and Dave was unable to follow the roadway. He thought he knew the hills here like the back of his hand, for he was back on the estate where he worked, where he reckoned he knew every boulder or bush that occupied the moors. However, the snow had obliterated much of the moor, and he was disorientated by the wind and driving snow, the whiteout meaning that he headed further east.

257

That night Dave's father, also David MacMath, was annoyed to discover that his son had not returned. Thinking that he had been held up by the snows, and perhaps staying overnight at a friend's house, he left things until the following morning. However, when Dave still didn't return home, the alarm was raised. A search took place over the moors between Dalmellington and Carsphairn, the bus driver able to confirm that Dave was last seen by him in Glen Muck. The direct routes were followed, but it wasn't until the search was widened that the body of the gamekeeper was discovered near to a stone dike on the north-eastern slope of Garryhorn Rig. A drainer from the locality was first to find him, and he raised the alarm to the rest, who helped carry the corpse from its moorland deathbed.

Dave was a much-loved man in the Carsphairn area. It was noted that he was not a particularly robust man, but he had a determination to complete things and yet knew when he was beaten. He would never attempt anything if he reckoned that he could not carry it through. However, six weeks prior to his death he had undergone an operation which had left him much weaker than he normally was.

Dave MacMath was buried in the kirkyard at Carsphairn, where a red granite memorial was raised by his father over the grave. He was 42 years of age. His father had previously buried another son, Willie, who had died at the mines in 1891 aged ten, his wife Matilda Gibson who had died in 1904 and another son, John, who died in Glasgow in 1910 aged 40. David MacMath the elder died himself at Auchinleck in Ayrshire in 1928 aged 83.

The locals in the Carsphairn area decided to erect a memorial cairn to mark the spot where Dave MacMath perished. Once it was built, am unveiling ceremony was arranged for Sunday 22 August 1926. Over three hundred people, including most of the residents of Carsphairn, came to the spot on Garryhorn Rig to witness Major Cathcart of Ardendee unveil the plaque. The local poet in Carsphairn, Andrew Hyslop, composed a twenty-six verse poem in honour of MacMath, one verse of which reads:

> Your long, last walk, so full of woe –
> It shall forever haunt my dreams –
> In darkness and in blinding snow,
> O'er rocks and drains and mountain streams.

Ralph Forlow was a young shepherd boy who was to perish in a blizzard in the January of 1954. Walkers making their way from the Polharrow glen, to the east side of the Rhinns of Kells, towards Backhill of Bush by a forest road following the route of the old shepherd's pathway, pass a circular sheep ree in which a small memorial marks the spot where Forlow died. The cairn was built with large boulders cemented together and on a rectangular slab is the following inscription:

> *Erected to the memory of Ralph Forlow, the brave shepherd boy who died in the blizzard of 27th January 1954, aged 17 years.*

Gi'e him his place amang the great,
The men o' war, or kirk, or state,
An' add this message chiselled deep,
'The Guid herd died to save his sheep'.

It was around eight o' clock in the morning of Wednesday 27 January 1954 when Ralph Forlow left Burnhead of Kells farm to do his rounds, looking for sheep that may have got lost or stuck in the snowdrifts that had been formed by the heavy falls that had occurred overnight. The young Ralph, who was only seventeen years of age, lived with David Pringle at Burnhead, which lies just half a mile south-west of Forrest Lodge. He was actually employed by the Department of Agriculture to tend the sheep on the Backhill of Bush hirsel, a lonely and extensive stretch of high ground that is located on the far side of the high Rhinns of Kells. It had snowed almost continuously since the arrival of a fierce snowstorm on the Monday, the falls being around fourteen inches deep. Later in the day the winds had risen, blowing the snow into deep drifts.

It was in such conditions that Ralph left Burnhead and set off for his stretch of countryside in order to help his sheep. By the afternoon, five hours later, when he had not returned, David Pringle began to worry about him. He called on a few friends and they agreed to organise a search party. They scoured much of the hills, but the blizzard conditions worsened and it was getting dark, forcing them back to the lower ground at Burnhead.

The young lad still did not return home, and later that night, after dark, they decided to return to the hills, the wind having settled. More men came to help, and armed with large torches and their sheepdogs, they headed back towards the Rhinns.

The search wasn't going too well, for no sign of Forlow was had. Just after midnight, when they were thinking of calling a halt for the time being, the sound of a barking dog was heard. Instantly they thought it must be Ralph's sheepdog, and they set off to where the sound was coming from. By a sheep ree located by the side of the Altibrick Strand, they found the body of Ralph. He had stopped there from exhaustion and was trying to get some shelter from the biting winds. However, he was so weak and cold that he had died from the severe weather.

14.3 Ralph Forlow's Cairn

The shepherds had no means of carrying the body back down the hillside, so they had to leave it until the following morning. At first light on the Thursday morning they returned, complete with a sledge, and the presence of the local police constable. One of those in the party was Ralph's grandfather. The deep snow and driving winds hampered the rescue, and it took a full day to get the body back down to Burnhead.

Ralph Forlow had been an able and strong shepherd. He had been educated at Wallacehall Academy in Thornhill, Dumfriesshire, where he excelled at athletics. He was a clever student, and a popular member of the Wallacehall Scout Troop. On leaving school he worked as a shepherd, but he had applied for and been accepted for the Royal Air Force. In fact, he was due to leave Burnhead the following week to begin his training.

A fatal accident inquiry took place at Kirkcudbright Sheriff Court, where it was questioned by Sheriff Christie why a seventeen year old boy was deemed suitable to look after such a vast and remote hirsel. Dr Robert Flett of Dalry had examined the body and pronounced the cause of death to be exposure. In 1955, when the lower slopes of the hillsides on Forrest Estate were being planted with trees, it was decided to leave the ground between Loch Dungeon and the North Gairy Top of Corserine unplanted as a memorial to Forlow. In the ree by the side of the burn the cairn was erected in his memory. In more recent years the land around the memorial has been planted with trees, making the spot where the shepherd lad died feeling less remote. In spring, the circular plot of ground within the ree is awash with daffodils.

The four lines of verse on the cairn were written by a local poet, D. Cargen. In 'The Hill Herd' he tells how:

> We learned wi' grief, the ither day,
> Hoo a brave life was ta'en away,
> A young herd-laddie, blithe and braw,
> Perished amang the driftin' snaw.

The lines on the cairn are also repeated on the gravestone to Forlow, which can be found within Kirkinner kirkyard, a few miles south of Wigtown. In front of the four lines the epitaph has a further two:

> On Scotland's page of gilded fame,
> Inscribe the shepherd hero's name.

There were a number of other shepherds who were to suffer an extremely cold death in the snowstorms, not all of whom are commemorate on the hill, where their bodies were later found. One such was John Chalmers, who was a shepherd boy at Loch Head, at the top of Loch Doon. He disappeared in a storm on New Year's Eve in 1817. His father and mother, Thomas Chalmers and his wife Ann (nee MacKie) waited on the storm passing before setting out to search for their son. It was six weeks before his body was found, on 10 February 1818. Aged only 25 years, his corpse was taken to Straiton where it was interred in the kirkyard.

It wasn't just snowstorms that resulted in the death of shepherds. In Glen Garroch a young shepherd lad lived with his father, William Miller, at Drumbuie. A sheep had fallen into the Garroch Burn and was struggling to extricate itself, its wool having become sodden and heavy. Young Miller plunged into the waters to help, but in the ensuing struggle he was drowned.

Another small memorial marks the spot where Agnes Hannah succumbed in severe weather conditions. It is located around two hundred yards off the road, on the southern side of the small forestry plantation near to Stinchar Bridge, not far from the Ayr 22/Newton Stewart 22 milestone. The memorial comprises of little more than a low-built cairn, its angular whin stones concreted together, out of which rises a vertical slab. The inscription tells little of what happened, for in simple capital letters can be read *AGNES HANNAH DIED HERE*. The memorial was erected around 1970 by some Forestry Commission staff to replace an older memorial that had become lost.

Agnes Hannah is believed to have been a mid-wife or nurse who had been at Waterhead on Minnoch to assist in the delivery of a new child. Once the birth was over, and mother and baby were doing well, Agnes decided that she would like to return home. It is also possible that she had heard of another young mother needing her assistance at Tallaminnock. The shepherd and his family tried to prevent her leaving, but she was determined to make her way home, and set off out into the night. However, she had only travelled three miles when she was overcome by a severe blizzard. She tried to force her way onward, but so strong were the winds, and the snow

14.4 Agnes Hannah's Memorial

on the ground and driving snow clouds meant that she was disorientated and wandered off the road, which had become obliterated by the drifting snow. Overcome by exposure and exhaustion, she died on the hills. When this took place has now been forgotten, but it may have been sometime early in the twentieth century.

Some deaths that have taken place within the Galloway Highlands have been as a result of misadventure, as opposed to natural weather conditions. An example of the former is the case of 1813 where a boy who was trying to rob a starling's nest on Loch Doon Castle fell from the walls to his death on the rocks below. The castle was still located on the castle island at that time, and the lad had little chance of getting assistance. The story is reported in the *Dumfries Courier* of 4 June 1813.

A few other deaths have occurred in the hills, none of which have memorials to mark the spots where the bodies were found. Andrew McCormick makes reference to some of these. He mentions a man named Cameron, who was a silver sand and scythe vendor, who died on the brae face of Craig Neldricken. A rough stone is said to mark where his body lies.

McCormick also relates the account of a tramp that was discovered dead, lying at the foot of the Black Gutter on the Merrick. Dan Kennedy paraphrased the shepherd from Kirriereoch who found the body: 'I was horrified to find the dead body of a man spread-eagled, lying face downwards among the boulders. The shoulders were rounded and the body hunched together as if in the act of turning a somersault. By feth! It was an eldritch, hair-raising sight! Judging by the clothes he appeared to be one of those gangrel buddies who sometimes take to the hills for a short cut. Poor fellow! He must have fallen over the precipice in the dark, perhaps while trying to make his way over to Kirriereoch. Be that as it may, whatever happened the body had lain concealed among the rocks for some time for there was little left but the clothes!'

A second 'gangrel bodie' was found near the Point of the Snibe, near Low Cornarroch. Apparently Sean MacLean, who was a shepherd at Buchan Lodge, went to bury the corpse, but forgot his spade, and superstition meant that he couldn't start out again on the same day.

On 14 April 1894 the body of a man was discovered near to Auchinleck in the Penkiln glen. It turned out to be that of Harry Flynn. At the time the tenant in Auchinleck ordered a small headstone to be raised over his grave, but there was a dispute with the mason and it was never erected.

There is a rough upright stone that can be seen by the side of the Muck Water, a few hundred yards downstream from Glenmuck Bridge. It marks the spot where a farmer from near Carsphairn disappeared on the night of 13 December 1869.

Richard Jamieson ran Holm of Daltallochan farm, which lies to the north-west of Carsphairn. He employed a ploughman but his service on the farm was proving to be unsatisfactory and at length Jamieson was forced to dismiss him. He advertised for a replacement, and a man from near Patna in Ayrshire applied. Jamieson travelled across the moor to the head of Glen Muck, down through Dalmellington and on to Patna where he questioned the prospective employee. Once he was finished, he set off on the return journey. He was never to make it.

The last folk to see him alive were his friend, Dr Allan, who lived at Doonbank, and the toll-keeper at the Kirk Bridge, where he passed through at half past seven in the evening. The toll-keeper reported that he was 'unsteady', perhaps hinting that he and the doctor had shared a dram or two.

The next morning, once the family had realised that Jamieson had not returned, a servant was sent off on the same route to see if he could find him. As he crossed the moor and dropped into the head of Glen Muck he found Jamieson's pony and gig, the pony standing in the water unable to pull the gig out. The servant looked around the immediate area, and discovered Jamieson's overcoat in the water a few hundred yards downstream. Without investigating further, he returned with the news.

A search was made for the body, but nothing was found. Rumours in the area began to spread, from tales such as the dismissed ploughman had done away with him, to claims that Jamieson had been drunk and had toppled into the fast-flowing stream. According to the *Kirkcudbright Advertiser* of the time:

> As Mr Jamieson was an extensive sheep farmer and for a great many years held a leading position about Carsphairn and Dalmellington it can easily be conceived that his untimely fate under circumstances calculated to awake suspicion of foul play has spread excitement and inspired rumour far and near throughout the quiet pastoral district where he was so well known and so generally respected.
>
> The prime suspect in all the wild rumours was the ploughman who had been dismissed. He lived in a house belonging to Mr Jamieson for which he owed rent. Both he and his wife were taken to Ayr for intensive questioning, but were released when it was proved that he had been seen by his neighbours and had been heard going to bed on the night in question.
>
> Another cause for suspicion was the pony that had stood all night; its coat was wet in the morning. Perhaps it had been used to convey the body away from the scene of the incident. After all, the people at Dalfarson near the foot of Ness Glen had heard a horse and vehicle being spurred on in the dead of night. Careful investigation showed that the pony's wet coat was not sweat, but simply caused by it standing in the burn all night.
>
> Another mystery remained unsolved. Why was Mr Jamieson's coat found? He could not take it off, since he had injured his collar bone at an earlier time. Perhaps he had been robbed, but at that time no-one could answer that, since his body had not been found.
>
> We hope to hear of his body being found without his watch or any money he carried being disturbed which would so far allay the intense excitement which prevails in the district. It will be observed from our advertising columns that his relations, many of whom are in good positions and by all of whom he was held in sincere regard, have offered a reward of £20 for any information that will account for his fate.

The mystery remained unsolved for a further six months until 22 July 1870 when a number of workers were making hay at Grimmet farm, west of Dalmellington. They were working in the meadow below the farm, alongside the River Doon, into which the Muck Water flows. On a sandbank, left when the level of the river had subsided in the summer, they found Jamieson's body. It was around five miles downstream from where the pony was discovered. On investigation, there were no signs of any robbery or physical violence. In his pocket he still had his pocket book and money, so the procurator declared the cause of death to be accidental.

It was accepted that the death of Jamieson must have been due to an accident. His pony was known to be flighty, and perhaps it had reared up or taken a wild turn as it made its way through Glen Muck. As Jamieson tried to calm it, it may have thrown him from the gig into the swollen Muck, which flows close to the road in the narrow part of the glen.

Although Jamieson was regarded as a pillar of the community, he did have a dark side too! Apparently he got a young girl in the village pregnant. In his will he left thousands to various members of his family. His wife of seven years, and over twenty years his junior, Janet Rowan, continued to farm Holm of Daltallochan for another seven years, before moving into Carsphairn, setting up house in a building her husband had erected, known as Jamieson House. His grave is located in Carsphairn kirkyard, a fairly large enclosure.

15 Air Crashes

The Galloway Highlands has been the location of numerous aeroplane crashes over the years. Almost every hillside in the area can tell of at least one crash on it. In fact, it is reckoned that 35 crashes have occurred within the area covered by the Galloway Forest Park, many of which have occurred on the central massif covered by this book. On a number of hillsides, fragments from these aeroplanes can often still be found, bits of mangled metal protruding from the peat or resting among the stony slopes.

The causes of the crashes have been variously explained, from inexperienced pilots flying over unfamiliar territory, to terrible weather conditions, varying from low mist to thunderstorms. In some cases the granite has been blamed for affecting the instruments on board the flight deck.

Outwith the central core of the uplands covered by this book, Cairnsmore of Fleet seems to have attracted many aeroplanes into its granite hillsides. On the summit, which is 2,331 feet above sea level, a large granite boulder was unveiled in 1980, on which the names of all of those who had been killed in air-crashes on the hill were inscribed. The memorial was the work of the Dumfries and Galloway Aviation Society. The list contains 22 names:

Erected in memory of airmen killed on this hill, Cairnsmore of Fleet. Luftwaffe No. 1 KG4 Soesterburg, Henkel, 8th August 1940, Ltn. A Zeiss, aged 25; Uffz. G F VonTurckheim, aged 31; Uffz. W Hajesch, aged 21; Uffz. W Mechsner, aged 23. No. 10(0) AFU, RAF Dumfries, Anson EG485, 22nd Feb 1944: Plt/Off. J M Gooley RCAF aged 30, W/Off. J J M Ward, aged 23; F/Sgt. M C Simpson RAAF, aged 19. No. 10 AOS, RAF Dumfries, Botha L6539, 2nd March 1942: A/C D J Thom, aged 20. No. 4(0) AFU, RAF West Freugh, Anson N9589, 12th June 1944: Sgt. W A Edwards, aged 23, Sgt. H W G Rennison, aged 31, Sgt. R C Beggs RNZAF, aged 29, F/Sgt. B B Hayton, aged 21, F/Sgt. A W Waughope RAAF, aged 27. No. 1(0) AFU, RAF Wigtown, Anson N5140, 9th July 1944: F/Sgt. R G T Hide, aged 23, Plt/Off. A A Goodill RCAF, aged 26, Sgt. T J Malone, aged 24. No. 9 AGS, RAF Llandrog, Anson DJ126, 22nd Sep. 1942: F/Sgt. B H Vye RCAF, aged 21, Sgt. A W Hawkes, aged 29, L.Ac. G A Horne, aged 20, AC C O M Rawson, aged 20. United States Air Force, 1st Tr. Sqd., 10th TRW, RAW Alconbury, Phantom 680566, 28th Mar 1979: Captain T J Seagren, aged 26, Captain R V Spalding, aged 31.

The boulder was taken from Cairnsmore of Fleet to Dumfries where one side was polished and the inscription added with lead lettering by the monumental sculptor, E. Layden. A Sikorsky helicopter of the USAF, piloted by Captain Frank Grey, then transported the boulder back onto the summit of Cairnsmore. The boulder is six feet long, three and a half feet in height, and varies in thickness from one foot to one and a half feet, due to a taper. The stone was dedicated on 8 August 1980, exactly forty years after the first air crash. The service was held in Old Minnigaff parish church, led by Rev R. M. Farquhar. Unfortunately, the lead lettering in the boulder became susceptible to being removed, so instead a brass plaque with the same inscription was made and affixed to the flat face of the stone in 1989.

15.1 Dragon Fly Memorial, Craignaw

In a stormy August in 1917 a small airship was passing over the mountains in the southern part of the Galloway Highlands. The airship hit the rocks on the face of Larg Hill, the force destroying it. Luckily, none of the crewmen was killed by the impact, though a number received injuries. The winds were so strong that parts of the airship were blown across the slopes and into the next valley, overlooking Glen Trool. James MacBain was in the area soon after the air crash had taken place. Staying with the shepherd at Black Laggan at the time, he decided to ascend Larg Hill to see what he could find. On the hillside he came across a party of sailors gathering the wreckage, which they transported on sledges hauled by horses down the steep slopes and across the moss to Auchinleck farm, the nearest road head in those days.

The first air-crash involving an aeroplane in the Galloway Highlands took place in 1937. The *Dragon Fly* was commissioned by the *Daily Express*, which was owned by Lord Beaverbrook, to survey the proposed air routes that the government intended introducing. In 1935 the government had decided to form a National Policy on Civil Aviation and invited General Sir Henry Maybury to chair a committee to look into this and make its recommendations. When it reported back, the committee proposed what was called a 'junction aerodrome system', where flight paths were arranged on a hub and spoke principal. The hub of the new routes would be centred approximately on Manchester, with spokes radiating from there towards London, Newcastle, Southampton, Glasgow, Bristol and Belfast.

Lord Beaverbrook was a keen aviator and took a deep interest in aviation matters. Indeed, in 1940 he was to be asked by Churchill's government to become the head of the Ministry of Aircraft Production. His son, Max Aitken, would distinguish himself as an ace fighter pilot at the Battle of Britain. Beaverbrook told the Express to run a series of articles on the Maybury proposals, and arranged for the *Dragon Fly* to follow the various spoke routes.

The hill known as Darnaw is not the highest of the Galloway Highlands, but at 1,549 feet is still quite a climb. Most of the slopes are now afforested, making access to the upper reaches problematical. However, one may want to climb to the open summit which is unusual in that it is speckled with a number of mountain lochans. On the north-east face of the hill, overlooking Clatteringshaws Loch, is a cairn of stones, comprising of whin stones cemented together. Within the face of the cairn is a Creetown granite slab with the following inscription picked out in lead lettering:

In memory – Here fell the Daily Express airplane 'Dragon Fly' on February 2nd 1937 with the loss of four brave men. Harold Pemberton, Leslie Jackson, Reginald Wesley, Archibald Philpott.

The cairn overlooks the small hollow in which the aeroplane crashed. For many years fragments from the aircraft's fuselage could be found on the ground.

The *Dragon Fly* was a green five-seater de Havilland aeroplane, registration G-AEHC, owned by the Express group. On the morning of 2 February 1937 it had taken off from Belfast and flew north-eastwards to Glasgow, landing at Renfrew airport. After refuelling, the plane took off once more, bound for Manchester. It buzzed above Nithsdale, heading south east. It then circled and returned up the valley, disappearing over Black Craig in Glen Afton. The next time it was noticed was by a worker at Loch Doon, circling around the hills above the loch. It then turned south and flew over the Galloway Highlands, never to be seen flying again.

Archibald C. Philpott, the aeroplane's radio expert was known in flying circles for his continuous signalling, yet at 11.15 am on Tuesday 2 March 1937 his signals faded and were to disappear completely. Nothing more was heard.

Soon it was realised that something serious was amiss, and a full-scale search for the plane and its crew was organised, the largest ever in Britain at that time. Twelve aeroplanes from the Royal Air Force, along with seven private planes, flew repeatedly over the mountains of Galloway, looking for signs of the craft. In England, the Cumbrian mountains were combed by police and off the coast of the Lake District and south of Galloway, the coastguards of the Isle of Man, Lancashire and Cheshire constantly watched for a sign of the plane – none was found. Much of the search had been focussed on the Cumbrian mountains, for there had been a report of the plane flying over Keswick.

It was three days later before the shepherd of Clatteringshaws-side, Andrew Wilson, was tending his sheep. This took him to near the summit of Darnaw where his dog ran ahead, barking wildly. Andrew went to see what was bothering his dog, and soon spotted the burnt-out wreck, imbedded in the hillside, the tail still standing up pointing to the heavens. His sheep grazed unconcernedly around it.

Andrew Wilson ran back down the hill to raise the alarm. At his farm he jumped onto his bike and cycled the fourteen miles into Newton Stewart, where he passed on the message to the police. Soon a party was formed to climb the hill, comprising of Provost Brown of Kirkcudbright, Chief Constable Donald and Doctor MacTurk of Newton Stewart, along with some others.

At four o'clock the team reached the foot of the hill. The chief constable decided that the bodies should be left until daybreak, as it would be too dangerous to bring them down in the dark.

At dawn on the Friday a party of one hundred began the long trek from Craigencallie. The bodies from the wreckage were carried down on stretchers to an ambulance which transported them to Newton Stewart. There, blinds drawn in the houses, they were placed in coffins and transported onward by rail to London. They were to be commemorated by a special service in the Fleet Street church of St Bride on 9 February at 1.00 pm.

Major Harold J. Pemberton was born in 1890 and received the Distinguished Service Order for swimming a French canal in order to capture a German pill-box. He became a correspondent for the *Daily Express*, specialising in motoring. Leslie Thomas Jackson was a pilot with Personal Airways of Croydon who had been commissioned to make the flight. He was 32 years of age, but had been an experienced pilot with the RAF with over 2,000 hours in the air under his belt. Reginald Charles Wesley was a photographer for the Express and was only 24 years old when the accident occurred. Archibald Philpott was a radio operator and radio expert for the newspaper.

The assistant to the Inspector of Accidents at the Air ministry, Major S. J. V. Fill, stated in his verdict that he thought the pilot was flying in cloud which he broke through and spotted a large stretch of water. Thinking that this was the Solway Firth, and not Clatteringshaws Loch, he dropped height to get his bearings. When he spotted the hill in front of him, he tried to ascend, but ran into the side. Clatteringshaws Loch was, at the time of the accident, a fairly new expanse of water, and as such did not appear on the maps used by the pilot.

The cairn on Darnaw was unveiled on 14 February 1937 by the Lord Lieutenant of the county, the Earl of Galloway. Construction of the cairn had been delayed by heavy snows, but on the day it was unveiled the ceremony was attended by many colleagues of the men, along with various representatives of the county. Present at the ceremony was John MacKie MP. The service was attended by several hundred onlookers and, after the cairn was unveiled and a piper had played 'The Flowers o' the Forest', a De Havilland Hornet Moth belonging to the Border Flying Club passed over, dipping in salute at the group on the bleak hilltop.

Corserine, the highest summit in the Rhinns of Kells, has been the site of at least three air crashes during the Second World War, and for many years debris was strewn across the summit. In fact, on the summit cairn there was a length of metal projecting from it, a relic from an aircraft.

One of the crashes took place on the evening of 9 January 1939. An RAF Avro Anson bomber, L9153, was flying in the vicinity. The navigator radioed Renfrew airport for directions, the plane having become lost. It had taken off from Prestwick with four airmen on board taking part in a night navigation exercise. The control tower at Renfrew replied with instructions, but the contact with the plane was lost.

Avro Ansons were originally civilian aircraft but with the outbreak of war they were adapted to suit military work. Known to their pilots as 'Faithfull Annie's', the planes had a reputation for being noisy, cold and full of draughts. Though solidly built, the planes were comparatively slow, and as such had been liable to attack. The plane had the distinction of being the first in the service of the RAF to have an undercarriage that could be retracted once the plane was in flight.

On the following day a large search party was arranged. Police were mobilised across Nithsdale and the eastern part of the Stewartry. They asked shepherds and other rural residents to help in the search, but the area they had identified as the most likely spot for the bomber to have crashed was wrong, it had in fact crashed onto a shoulder of Corserine.

On 10 January, Billy MacCubbin had risen as usual to take his breakfast and begin his work as a shepherd at Backhill of Bush. On leaving the cottage he spotted smoke on the hill to the north. He made his way there and discovered the shattered remains of the Avro Anson, strewn across the slopes. The fuselage was just a skeleton, with only the tailpiece still complete. The airmen were all dead, their bodies lying across the hillside.

MacCubbin made his way down to Fore Bush to raise the alarm. By chance, the postman was still there with his van, so he was able to take the news to Sergeant Hutchinson at Dalry police station. Soon, a rescue party arrived, and MacCubbin directed them back to the crash site. The rescuers were ill-equipped for the rough terrain and the long trek to the crash-site. They were equipped with a paraffin lamp, basic clothing and little rations. When they reached the site they were exhausted.

What they saw was to be a great surprise. Whilst MacCubbin was away a second aeroplane had crashed nearby. A Tiger Moth (registration number L6932) belonging to No. 12 Elementary and Reserve Flying Training School at Prestwick, had been searching the hills for the wreck of the Anson. When they spotted the charred remains on the hillside they decided to draw closer to observe the remains. The Tiger Moth hit a strange air pocket, causing it to turn upside down and plummet to the ground. Though the plane was wrecked, the pilot and observer survived, receiving only minor injuries. By the time the large ground search-party had arrived the two men had descended to safety.

As night had fallen, the search party left the crash site and moved into Backhill of Bush and its outbuildings. The shepherd's wife, Grace MacCubbin, fed them what she had, and the men crammed into every available space. The autumn night was very cold, but the men were able to get a warm porridge breakfast.

Fed and rested, the men gathered up the bodies and transported them north to the road-head at the top of Loch Doon. A Loch Doon shepherd directed the cortege, which took five hours to travel the four miles. The corpses were then transported to Heathfield mortuary in Ayr.

The four airmen were Flying Officer Ian Douglas Shields, who was the pilot. The wireless operator was Norman Hector Duff. The two trainee navigators were Gordon Eric Betts and Henry Gilbert Stewart Briggs.

A Whitley Mk. V bomber crashed in the Galloway hills on 27 November 1940. The aeroplane belonged to No. 10 Bombing and Gunnery School, Dumfries, and it had taken off from Heathhall, east of the town, on a short flight westwards to West Freugh, near Stranraer. Bearing the registration P5009, the plane was being sent to West Freugh airfield to collect a group of officers who were due to return to Dumfries. The Royal Observer Corps tracked the route of the plane, but its signal disappeared shortly after it flew over St John's Town of Dalry. After that the aeroplane seemed to disappear totally, leaving no trace of its existence, confounding all search parties.

Word of the plane's disappearance spread like wildfire around the Galloway hills, but still no evidence of its wreckage was found. However, it was thought there was a possibility that the aeroplane could have crashed into Loch Enoch, and a shepherd made his way there to have a look. On 11 December, two weeks after the aircraft had disappeared, the shepherd spotted the wreckage in the loch. Below the murky waters he was able to see the circular rings of the badge on the wings.

A party of 35 men and one officer were sent to the remote loch to try to recover the bodies. They were only able to find the corpses of the two pilots – Pilot Officer Leon Szamrajew and Sergeant Jerzy Luszczewski, both of the Polish Air Force. Of Aircraftman Douglas Barnes they found no trace, and it was assumed that he had been trapped in a major section of the fuselage that lay deep in the loch. The craft was never recovered, and the body remains beneath the cold waters. Its site is designated as a war grave.

The bodies of the two Poles were transported down from the loch and taken back to Dumfries. They were buried in a plot within Dumfries's St Andrew's Roman Catholic Cemetery, where a polish military gravestone commemorates them.

A Lockheed Hudson Mark 1, registration number N7235/QX-A, took off from the Royal Air Force's No. 224 Squadron's base at Leuchars Airfield in Fife. Wartime restrictions prevented much knowledge of the flight getting out. However, on board were Wing-Commander Ronald Neville-Clarke DFC, who was at the aeroplane's controls, Flight Lieutenant Edward Ostlere, the 2nd Pilot, Sergeant Alexander Campbell Davidson, wireless operator and air-gunner, Aircraftman First Class John Cordiner and Aircraftman First Class Thomas Edgar Bailiff Price.

The aircraft was being flown from Leuchars to another RAF base, Aldergrove, eighteen miles from Belfast in Northern Ireland. It took off at mid-day on 3 March 1941 and was following a fairly direct route towards Ireland. However, contact with the plane was lost, and it failed to turn up at Aldergrove. The emergency search and rescue teams were scrambled to try to find out where the plane had disappeared, but nothing was found for some time. Eventually the search parties were scaled back.

15.2 Luszczewski & Szamrajew's gravestone, Dumfries

Sometime after the crash had taken place, the wrecked aircraft was found on the hill known as Waterhead, to the south east of Loch Bradan. The bodies were removed for burial. Wing-Commander Neville-Clarke (Service Number 29063) was buried in St Peter's Churchyard, Little Aston. He was 36 years old. Ostlere (Service Number 72064) was buried in the Hayfield Cemetery, Kirkcaldy. Davidson (Service Number 966403) was buried in Carnmoney Cemetery, County Antrim. Cordiner (Service Number 552757) was only seventeen years of age and was interred in the Eastern Necropolis, Dundee. Price (Service Number 942179) was buried at St John's Westgate and Elswick Cemetery, Newcastle.

On 25 October 1941 a Mark IIA Spitfire of the Royal Air Force, registration number P7540, took off from Heathfield Aerodrome, near Ayr, piloted by a young Czech named Flying Officer Frantisek F. Hekl. The plane was part of the RAF's 13 Group, 312 (Czech) Squadron, and the pilot was on a training flight. From Ayr the Spitfire headed south-eastwards, towards the Galloway hills. As it flew, the aeroplane developed engine trouble, and the pilot tried to make an emergency landing. He headed east down the valley of the Garpel Burn towards Loch Doon, but as he banked away from the loch his starboard wing tip touched the water surface causing the aeroplane to crash. The Spitfire sank into the loch and the pilot was killed.

Bob Howitson, who was shooting with his father, cycled to Dalmellington for help. A search organised by the RAF took place over the next six weeks but no sight of the Spitfire or the pilot was made.

Eventually the search was abandoned, and the Spitfire's remains were basically lost, only spoken about as one of the mysteries of the war. However, in 1977 a group of divers from the Dumfries branch of the Scottish Sub Aqua Club decided that they would like to search for it. They were joined on occasion by members from the Northern Federation of British Sub Aqua Clubs. They planned their exploration meticulously, combing the bed of the loch on a regular pattern. The search was hampered by the coldness of the loch, and the dark peaty colour the water took at depth.

Visitors to Loch Doon often saw the divers' small boat out on the loch for the next five years. It was reckoned that the members made a total of 567 separate dives, and that 109 different divers took part. In total 337 hours were spent in the freezing waters. Many thought their search was futile, and that perhaps the plane had sunk into a soft peaty section of the loch bed. However, in 1982 the divers' luck changed, and remains of the plane were found around forty feet under the surface. With growing enthusiasm the search continued, and soon the remains of the fuselage and engine were identified on the loch bed.

Once the plane had been found, the divers had to change their strategy, now working out how to raise the remains from the bed of the loch and transport them away. At length, recovery experts working under license from the RAF were called in and the wreckage was lifted from the loch and brought ashore.

The fuselage was taken to the Dumfries and Galloway Aviation Museum at Heathhall, near Dumfries. After some restoration work, the fuselage and engine were placed on display, where they can still be seen. Of Frantisek Hekl, no sign of his body was found. His name, however, is listed on the memorial at Runnymede.

One of the most unlucky air crashes was that which took place on 2 July 1942. An Avro Anson aircraft (registration number N5297) had taken off from Millom airfield in Cumberland on what was called a 'navex' or navigation exercise. On board were five men, some of them trainees. They belonged to Number 2 (O) AFU. The plane flew over the Galloway Highlands and if only it had been twenty feet higher in the air it would have missed the steep cliff face of Shalloch on Minnoch.

Flying the aeroplane was Flight Sergeant William Thomas Gale, service number R 84287, of the Royal Canadian Air Force. Born on 2 August 1909 at Penetanguishene in Ontario, Canada, he was just 22 years of age. With him was Sergeant John Benson Hall, Wireless Operator and B/A, service number 1354005. He was also 22 years of age and a member of the Royal Air Force Volunteer Reserve. Other members of the RAFVR were Leading Aircraftman James Cameron Campbell, untrained B/A, service number 1346334, aged 30, Leading Aircraftman Joseph Arthur Wild, untrained B/A, service number 1576055, aged 31, and Aircraftman Ernest Everall, wireless operator, service number 1126654, aged 21.

The aircraft left Millom and flew north over Galloway. At eleven o'clock in the morning contact with the plane was lost and the RAF commenced their 'overdue action' procedures. It was suspected that the aeroplane had collided with a hill in low cloud.

The suspicions were right, for search parties discovered the plane on the eastern slopes of Shalloch on Minnoch. The plane had flown straight into the steep rock gairy and a few extra feet higher would have made all the difference. The rescue party found the bodies of the five men and carried them off the hill. Flight Sergeant Gale and Sergeant Hall were both buried in the cemetery above the village of Dunure, on the Ayrshire coast. L/A Campbell was buried in Wellshill Cemetery, Perth, L/A Wild at Burton-on-Trent and A/C Everall was interred at Droylsden Cemetery.

A Liberator aeroplane crashed on the slopes of Drigmorn Hill, part of the greater mountain of Millfore, on 14 September 1942. The aircraft was a Mark 2 version, registration number AL624, of Number 1653 Heavy Conversion Unit of the RAF. The Liberator was stationed at the airfield of RAF Burn in Yorkshire.

15.3 William Gale's gravestone, Dunure

On the day of the crash the crew were joined by three other Liberators, numbers AL597, AL625 and AL635. They were taking part in a navigation exercise.

The Liberator took off from RAF Burn at eleven in the morning. It flew north towards Scotland, and at 12:19 pm the radio operator checked in with the control at Silloth, who asked him to confirm his position. This was to be the last contact with the crew of eight on board.

The weather in Scotland was cloudy – the cover was six tenths of cloud, the base of it being at four hundred feet, whereas over the higher ground the cloud cover was ten-tenths.

Three of the Liberators returned safely to Burn airfield. AL624 failed to return, and the men at the airfield became rather concerned as to its whereabouts. Hopes were that the plane had landed at some other airfield, perhaps due to some difficulty, and they waited with baited breath on a message being sent to let them know. It never came.

The plane was posted missing, and searches were being organised when a shepherd came across the remains on the slopes of Drigmorn Hill, north east of Newton Stewart. Air crash investigators made their way to the site, high up at almost two thousand feet. They reckoned that, as the cloud cover was particularly bad and visibility was at a minimum, the pilot had dropped height slightly. Unfortunately his left-hand wing struck the hillside. The instant drag slewed the whole aircraft around, and the front of it crashed headlong into the rocks. The whole craft then burst into flames, the impact and fire killing all of the eight crewmen on board.

The men killed were Pilot Officer Ivan Harold Betts (aged 31 - Service Number 109064), who was in charge of the aircraft; Sergeant Derek Eaton Warner (aged 20, Service Number 655996), co-pilot; Sergeant John Churley Freestone, observer (Service Number 1311904, aged 29); Sergeant George Douglas Calder (aged 24, Service Number 401366), RAAF, wireless operator and air gunner; Sergeant Geoffrey Crisp Boar, aged 27, Service Number 1310500), wireless operator and air gunner; Sergeant Victor Frederick Talley (Service Number 1320265), air gunner; Sergeant John Edwin Charles Averill Steele-Nicholson (aged 20, Service Number 1591275), air gunner; and Sergeant James Bowrey (aged 22, Service Number 1174321), air gunner.

Of the eight who died on Millfore, five of them were buried in the kirkyard at Kirkinner in Wigtownshire. These were Betts, Freestone, Calder, Steele-Nicholson and Talley. Warner was buried in Camberwell New Cemetery, Boar in Ipswich Old Cemetery, and Bowrey in the Avon View Cemetery, Bristol.

Another Avro Anson crashed on the slopes of Corserine on 23 October 1942. The aeroplane, a Mark 1, registration number DG787, belonged to the Air Navigation and Bombing School. There were four men on board, all of whom were to lose their lives – the pilot, Sergeant Joseph Gerard Millinger; Navigator and Wireless Operator, Sergeant Charles Lunny; and two trainee navigators from the Czechoslovakian air force – Flight Lieutenant Vaclav Jelinek and Sergeant Petr Haas, aged 22, service number 1265369, of the RAF Volunteer Reserve.

The Avro Anson had taken off from Jurby, on the Isle of Man, on a night navigation exercise. It disappeared from radio contact and the control back on the island was seriously concerned. Their worst fears were confirmed when the aeroplane failed to return. Despite letting the authorities across southern Scotland know of the loss of the aircraft, nothing was heard for two days until members of the Home Guard noted the remains. The mountain rescue team based at RAF Wigtown were sent to the site on 26 October and they quickly discovered the remains, strewn in bits across the slopes. The four men were carried back down the hill and taken to the air force base at Wigtown. Jelinek was buried in the kirkyard at Kirkinner, where a small military grave marks where his body lies. Haas was buried at Scottow cemetery, Norfolk.

The proximity of the flight training airfields of West Freugh, Wigtown and Dumfries may have been responsible for the higher density of air-crashes on the

Galloway hills than on other Scottish mountains. Another Avro Anson Mark 1 bomber crashed on the hill near to Craigencallie on 1 September 1943. It was part of No. 1 (Observer) Advanced Flying Unit of the RAF and had taken off from Wigtown airfield. They were taking part in a night navigation exercise when the plane ran into the hillside. Two of the crew were killed, but three were able to walk from the wreckage and survived.

The two killed were Sergeant Sidney Arthur Bussey, the aircraft's wireless operator and air gunner, and Sergeant Jack Arthur Coombes, wireless operator and air gunner. The lucky three were Sergeant Ronald Hunter MacArthur, who was the pilot, Sergeant Manning, navigator, and Sergeant Crosby, wireless operator.

The aeroplane had been flying back to the base at Wigtown but had taken a route rather too far to the north. This had resulted in them striking the hill near to Craigencallie at ten o'clock in the evening. Contact with the plane was lost, and once it had failed to return to Wigtown as expected the alarm was raised. The airmen from Wigtown made their way north to Newton Stewart, gathering at the police station to receive further orders. The search was arranged to start at first light on the morning of 2 September.

The search party combed as many hills north of Newton Stewart as they could, spying out the land with binoculars, looking for signs of wreckage or smoke rising. In the meantime Sergeant Crosby had managed to wriggle from the wreckage. He was suffering from head injuries, and he had a broken bone in his foot. He managed to descend from the hill, and spotting the house of Craigencallie in the distance, went there and raised the alarm.

On the slopes of Shalloch on Minnoch two Hurricanes crashed into the hillside on 13 September 1943. These planes were part of 186 Squadron and were numbered KZ398 and KZ674. The planes were part of a flight of four aeroplanes that had taken off at half past eleven in the morning to take part in low-flying formation exercises. As they were passing over the countryside they entered cloud. The two aeroplanes on the outside rose above the cloud level and were able to fly back to their base. On landing it was noted that the other two planes had not returned and they were posted missing. They were being piloted by Flight Lieutenant Charles Robert Sanders (Royal Air Force Volunteer Reserve - Service Number 64941) and Flying Officer Colin Trevor Hicks (Royal Air Force Volunteer Reserve – Service Number 120121).

Despite the weather remaining poor, a search commenced for the aircraft. Squadron Leader F. E. G. Hayter took off in a Hurricane and flew back to the last place where the aeroplanes had been seen. The cloud was still too thick to allow a view of the hillside. Next day the search resumed, with additional personnel from 1490 Gunnery Flight and a group of men from RAF Turnberry searched on the ground. Despite eleven sorties being made, nothing was found.

On the following day the ground search party came across Hurricane KZ674, which had been flown by Sanders. It was strewn across the slopes of Shalloch on Minnoch. The aircraft had not caught fire, and when Sanders' body was found it was discovered that he had died of a fractured skull. It wasn't until the next day again that the second aircraft was found, about one mile and a quarter away from the first crash site. The plane had struck a soft patch of ground, and most of it had sunk into the moss. Only the tail was left sticking out. Again, the pilot was dead, killed in the impact.

The two airmen were taken from the hill and were subsequently buried in Ayr's Holmston Cemetery. Charles Sanders' funeral was held on 18 September with full service honours. He was 26 years old. Two days later, Colin Hicks funeral took place - his mother and sister able to attend. He was only 22 years of age.

Another aircraft flying from an English base crashed in the Galloway Highlands within a couple of years. On the night of 20-21 January 1944 a de Havilland Mosquito left the airfield at High Ercall in Shropshire on a training night cross-country flight. The plane was a Mosquito N.F. Mark 2, registration number DD 795. The airmen were on a training course, Number 9, at No. 60 OUT. The aircraft left High Ercall and flew north towards Scotland. It was never to be seen flying again.

The search for the missing plane extended over a considerable area; for it wasn't known how far it could have travelled before it came into difficulties. On the day after the plane had disappeared four aeroplanes from No. 60 OYU were sent the same route that the lost plane had taken to try to spot the wreckage. None of them was to see anything.

The Mosquito appears to have flown into the hillside of Corserine in the middle of the night, and the plane burst into flames, which burned brightly but quickly. The fuselage cooled quickly in the January weather, and heavy snow soon covered it over. It was to be over three weeks before the wreckage was found. A team of fifty airmen from Wigtown airfield were sent to the steep corrie of Scar of the Folk on the eastern side of Corserine to recover the bodies of the two airmen on 12 February. The bodies of the two airmen were discovered and carried from the hill. They were Flight Sergeant Kenneth Mitchell, the pilot, and Flight Sergeant John Jeffrey Aylott, navigator.

Another war-time casualty was a Hawker Hurricane, which crashed near to the head of Loch Doon on 18 March 1944. The plane was a Mark IV version, registration number LD564, of No. 439 (Tiger) Squadron of the Royal Canadian Air Force, and was based at Heathfield Airfield, which lay to the north-east of Ayr, just south of the present Prestwick Airport. The plane was being used for training as part of the No. 4 Observer Advanced Flying Unit, and was being transferred from Ayr to RAF Hurn.

On the day that the Hurricane crashed, it was being piloted by Flying Officer Roswell Murray MacTavish, who lived in Vancouver, British Columbia, Canada. He was taking part in a training flight at the time, and contact was lost seven minutes after take-off. The plane had been flying across the hills at an altitude of 3,300 feet, which was sufficiently high to miss all of the hill-tops. However, a number of people in the Loch Doon area heard the plane flying overhead through the clouds. Looking into the mist, they were surprised to spot it plummeting nose-first from the clouds and straight into the moorland, striking it to the south-east of Loch Head farm, at the top of Loch Doon.

When locals managed to make it to the crash site they found that the pilot had been killed instantly. The wreckage was strewn across the moor, to the east of the Loch

Head Burn. Officials from the RAF's No. 5 (Coastal) Operational Training Unit at Turnberry Airfield made their way to the crash site and investigators tried to work out the cause of the crash, but their finds appear to be inconclusive.

Flying Officer Roswell Murray MacTavish (service number J/22385) was only twenty four years of age. He was the son of Wilfrid Lawrence MacTavish and his wife, Edith Jane MacTavish. His remains were collected and buried in Holmston Cemetery in Ayr. The location of the crash has been left open by forestry operations, which now blanket the site. However, walkers who know where to go can find the remains of the Rolls Royce Merlin engine which powered the Hurricane,

FLYING OFFICER
R. M. MACTAVISH
PILOT
ROYAL CANADIAN AIR FORCE
18TH MARCH 1944 AGE 24

A MAN GREATLY BELOVED

15.4 Roswell MacTavish's Military Gravestone, Ayr

and various other pieces of the aeroplane can be found in the surrounding area.

Another air crash from the war years occurred on 21 July 1944. An Avro Anson, registration number MG356, was taking part in a routine navigation exercise over the mountains of Galloway. The plane was based at the Royal Air Force airfield of West Freugh, east of Stranraer, and was part of No. 4 Observer Advanced Flying Unit. On board were Flight Sergeant Raymond John Crotty RAAF, aged 21, who was the pilot; Warrant Officer Peter Smith RAAF, who was 26 years old; Sergeant Darius Bede Northmore RAAF, aged 25; Sergeant (Air Bomber) Bertram Ernest William Becker RAF, who was 24, and Sergeant Edward Hugh Patrick Gresswell RAF Volunteer Reserve, aged 19. The three men from the Royal Australian Air Force were at the base training to take part in the war against Germany.

The Avro Anson left West Freugh and was flying over the Galloway hills. 'Teddy' Gresswell was in the craft working as a wireless operator when tragedy struck. As it flew southwards over the central massif, making its way back to West Freugh, the plane struck the northern slopes of Bennanbrack. This summit reaches 2,247 feet, but is really only a shoulder of the taller Lamachan Hill. The level of cloud was low, and mist hung in all of the glens. When the plane impacted with the hillside it came as a major shock to the crew on board, all of whom were killed instantly.

Investigations into the cause of the accident were inconclusive, but it has been speculated that the altimeter was either faulty or had been set incorrectly, giving the impression that the plane was flying at a greater height than it in fact was. Others claimed that the navigator was new to the area, and that he had made a mistake. The navigator under training was Darius Northmore.

When the plane failed to return a search was instigated to find it, and the remains were discovered soon after. On 22 July the bodies of the airmen were carried from the steep hillside down to Glen Trool. They were taken back to West Freugh and four of them were subsequently buried with military honours at the kirkyard of Stoneykirk, near to Stranraer. There can be seen the graves of Bertram Becker (Service number 1603389), husband of Verna Phyllis Becker, of Portage la Prairie, Manitoba, Canada; Flight Sergeant Raymond Crotty (Service number 410957), son of Cornelius John and Annie Crotty of South Yarra, Victoria, Australia; Peter Smith (Service number 407993) was the son of Albert Henry and Margaret Mary Agnes Smith, of Glen Osmond, South Australia; and Darius Northmore (Service number 432683), son of Thomas and Eleanor Northmore, of Bondi, New South Wales. Sergeant Edward Gresswell's remains were taken back to Paignton, Devon, where they were buried in the cemetery. He was the son of Mr & Mrs E. Gresswell, and had a service number of 1851841.

On the slopes of Bennanbrack remains of the Anson can still be found, including some parts of the landing gear.

The steep flank of Castlemaddy Gairy, which drops from the summit of Carlin's Cairn, was the scene of an air crash on Thursday 10 April 1947. On that day three Dakotas belonging to the Belgian Air Force (169 Wing, 366 Squadron) took off from Evere and headed across the English Channel and over England, heading for the Scottish Aviation workshops at Prestwick in Ayrshire, where two of them were due for maintenance. The plan was for all of the crew to return to Belgium in one of the Dakotas, that registered K-14. On the outward flight, this plane also had a second crew on board, who were due to fly an Airspeed Oxford plane back to Belgium.

The weather was poor, and visibility was virtually nil. Due to the conditions it was decided to abort the flight. One of the Dakotas landed at Silloth, in Cumbria. The other two, however, decided to head on for Prestwick. Only one made it there.

As the planes were heading over the Galloway hills, the Douglas Dakota C-47-B D896 crashed into the eastern side of Carlin's Cairn. The impact was such that the debris of the plane was spread over a large area of the gairy, above the infant Polmaddy Burn. The six men on board were all killed. These were Flt. Lt. Roger Loyen, M. Acr. Andre Dierickx, M. Acr. Michel Cardon, Flt. Lt. Olivier Lejeune, M. Acr. Felix Curtis and M. Acr. Andre Rodrique.

In 2008 it was decided to have a memorial plaque erected in memory of the airmen. Due to the remote location of the crash-site, it was agreed that is should be erected at the aviation museum in Dumfries. Funding was obtained from Comopsair, Dakota and the museum. The plaque was unveiled on 20 August 2009 when a delegation of Belgian airmen came to Dumfries. One of those present was Lt. Gen.

Albert Debeche, who had been the commander of Dakota D413, the one that made Prestwick safely.

Commander Debeche unveiled the large brass plaque within the museum. It reads:

In memory of the crews killed in the accident of the Belgian Air Force (Air Transport) Dakota DC-3 at Carlin's Cairn on 10 April 1947.

It then lists the airmen who lost their lives, and at the bottom are badges representing the sponsors. Above the inscription are the symbol of the Belgian Air Force and a sketch outline of a Dakota.

In the summer of 1951 three men from Brockloch farm were in the fields next to the farm working among the crop of kale. They were the farmer, William R. Campbell, and two farmhands, Joseph Cook and David MacKay, and they were back weeding the crop. It was just after eleven o'clock in the morning and the weather had dried up, there having been some light rain earlier. It was by this time fine and calm.

In the distance they became aware of the sound of droning, coming from an aeroplane. With mild interest, they were happy to straighten their backs from the hard work and look into the sky in order to see it. Away to the north-west, coming from the direction of Loch Doon, they spotted the aeroplane. William Campbell stated, 'I think it's going to crash,' but they continued at their work. However, the sound of the plane made them look back at it once more.

The aeroplane was running at half power, with two of the four engines not working. It took a nose-dive, then flattened out and rolled over twice. William Campbell shouted, 'It's in difficulties and I think it's going to strike the farmhouse.' Fortunately, the plane rose up again and continued down the glen. The plane then righted itself before taking a final nose-dive during which it struck the valley bottom. It was two minutes past eleven.

William Campbell and his labourers ran to the spot where the plane had crashed but there was nothing they could do. He called the emergency services but it was useless. The aeroplane had burst into flames and all the combustible materials were alight, leaving only a charred framework. Of the eleven crew, three bodies were found lying by the side of the wreck, and as the flames subsided the ambulance men could recover the remaining bodies from the fuselage. Their gory remains lay at the roadside awaiting removal – one onlooker fainted.

The aeroplane was a United States Air Force B 49 which had been flying on a training flight from the air base at Mildenhall in Suffolk. The plane was flying as part of a group and it was used as an aerial tanker to refuel other aircraft in mid-flight. The plane which crashed had somehow become detached from the others and as it flew down the glen its fuel pipe trailed across the sky.

The Air Force experts, after studying the remains of the fuselage and wings, proclaimed a verdict that it was probably an oversight on one of the crew's part that had caused the crash. As the plane refuelled the others, the aviation spirit should have been drawn evenly from the two tanks in either wing. However, it is believed that only one tank was emptied, leaving the aircraft in a serious state of imbalance, resulting in the crash. The imbalance caused the plane to 'birl like a leaf', and the pilot had been unable to keep the plane upright.

The bodies of the American airmen were returned to their native country, but often their relatives returned to the remote Scottish glen where the fatal crash on that black Saturday occurred. In 1953 a number of people in the Carsphairn area, with the help of relatives and friends of those who perished, erected a memorial at the spot where they had succumbed. A granite block with leaded lettering was built into the stone dike, around one hundred yards from the main road. It is the second dike south of Brockloch Cottage, near to Brockloch Tower, which didn't exist at the time of the air crash. For many years fragments of the aeroplane were placed in a small stone enclosure in front of the memorial, but as the years passed souvenir hunters have removed many of these.

The memorial was paid for from the proceeds of fundraising dances and raffles held in the area. Prior to the stone being unveiled by Mrs MacMillan of Lamloch House, around four hundred people gathered at Brockloch farm and marched behind a piper to the spot. Originally it had been the intention of the committee to have the slab incorporated in a stone cairn to be built at the roadside, but permission to build this was not forthcoming from the council. The slab reads:

In memory of those who lost their lives in American Air Crash, 7th July 1951.
Capt. T. A. Mertz; 1st Lt. J. A. O'Leary; 1st Lt. C. J. Hayden; 1st Lt. J. W. Keen;
1st Lt. G. M. Foote; S/Sgt W. L. Scott; S/Sgt. N. M. Poppoff; Corp. J. B. Simpson; Corp.
J. P. Finnegan; Corp. R. Y. Russell; Tech/Sgt. H. H. Hill.
Erected by the people of Carsphairn and friends.

The next aeroplane to crash on the Galloway hills was an Auster J/1U Workmaster, which hit the hillside on Dungeon Hill. The aircraft, registration number G-APMJ, belonged to the Cumberland Aviation Services, which was based at Carlisle Airport. The aeroplane was being used by a member of the local flying club at Carlisle to make a journey to Machrihanish on Kintyre. It took off on 18 October 1963 with Charles Brook in the pilot's seat, accompanied by James Graham.

Brook was a fairly inexperienced pilot, with only seventy hours of flying time on his log. He did not hold an instrument rating, and the flying club instructor warned him of the possible weather conditions he might expect. He was told that the flight should be entirely in VFR, or visual flight rules, meaning that he should be able to see where he is going. Should the weather turn poor, he was instructed to either turn back for Carlisle, or else take a longer route around the coast, at lower level.

The men boarded the aeroplane at 9.37 in the morning and took off successfully from Carlisle. The flight should have taken around two hours to complete, and one hour into this the aeroplane was spotted overhead in the Glenkens area, still flying in the correct direction. However, there was a cold front approaching, complete with heavy rain, gusts of wind and poor visibility. The person who observed the plane over Dalry stated that it appeared to be drifting in the strong gusts, but that it was still heading into the Galloway hills.

The next witness spotted the aircraft over Loch Doon, heading approximately south-westwards. This was the wrong direction for the plane to be travelling, and it was heading for the cloud-covered uplands. It wasn't seen again.

When the plane failed to arrive at Machrihanish it was reported missing. A search was made of the Galloway Highlands, looking in the area where it was last seen flying. Wreckage was spotted on the slopes of the Dungeon Hill, in the high pass between it and Craignairny. The two occupants were dead.

The AIB investigation which followed reported that the aircraft was flying with a 'nose up' attitude, and though the engine was producing 'considerable power' the plane was actually descending at the time it struck the granite hillside. It was thought that the descent of the plane was caused by a down draught in the lee of the hill, pulling the aircraft down and onto the cloud-covered rocks.

A small Piper Cherokee PA 28 aircraft took off from Prestwick Airport in Ayrshire on 28 September 1975 on a private flight. Four people were on board, the pilot, two businessmen and a young boy of about sixteen years. They had intended to fly to Blackpool Airport via Arran, perhaps wishing to see the mountainous island from the air. The little Piper, registration number G-BATP, flew from Prestwick over Arran and then circled in the air to cruise down the Ayrshire coast towards England.

Fifty-seven minutes after leaving Prestwick the aeroplane was spotted above Ballantrae, the estimated flying height at that time being fifteen hundred feet. The aeroplane was following the coastline as low cloud and rain obscured the direct route over the Galloway hills. Fifteen minutes later the Piper Cherokee was seen over Dean's Cross in England, five thousand feet up in cloud and heavy rain. When seen there the plane was not flying in the direction of Blackpool, as would have been expected.

For some undetermined reason, the aircraft changed direction and flew north again, back into Scotland. It headed as though returning to Prestwick, directly up the Glenkens, a route it had avoided earlier due to the low clouds. It was still misty and cloudy across Galloway at the time, and at three o' clock in the afternoon three fishermen casting their lines in the Garryhorn Burn heard it overhead. The low cloud obscured any visible signs of it, but they could ascertain that it was flying to the north-west.

At seven minutes past three the fishermen heard a loud crunch and a bang, the sound of metal striking the rocks. The noise of the engine had ceased, and they wondered if that could have been the aeroplane that they had heard earlier. They peered through the clouds, and in a break could see what they reckoned was the wreckage of the aircraft. Two of them rushed to the spot whilst the third ran to Garryhorn farmhouse where the shepherd raised the alarm.

Ayrshire police were the first on the scene, even although it was beyond their jurisdiction. They climbed up into Corrie Bow where the wreckage was strewn across the rocks. Though totally destroyed, the aeroplane had not burst into flames, and three of the passengers were still inside the fuselage. However, the impact had killed them. The fourth body had been thrown clear of the wreckage. One of the policemen on the hillside began to suffer from hypothermia, but this was checked in time.

Investigations into the cause of the crash revealed nothing. The aeroplane, owned by the Air Navigation and Trading Company Ltd., would have missed the mountainside had it been just one hundred feet higher up in the air. No faults were found in any of the instruments or engine, but it was discovered that the flaps were extended at twenty-five degrees, a position normally used in landing the aircraft. Neil Pomfret, the pilot, had a total of 129 hours of flying experience.

The four bodies were returned to England and interred in their respective cemeteries. The businessmen hailed from Preston. A tractor and trailer were taken to the foot of the corrie to bring down the aeroplane wreckage, and as it returned down the glen a door from the aeroplane fell off. For many years thereafter this lay against a stone dike next to the Woodhead lead mines.

The relatives and friends of the men lost in the air crash erected a small plaque in their memory, near to the spot where the disaster took place. On a large round lump of rock, facing up into the corrie, a small stainless steel plaque, measuring 10¼ by 7¼ inches, was affixed. It reads:

In memory of Neil Pomfret, Gerald A. Gibson, Maurice G. King, David Evans, who
died when their aeroplane crashed on this hill, September 28th 1975.
These young men now lie at rest,
In their short life they gave their best,
We who are left remember still,
The friends we lost on this Galloway hill.
Erected by relatives and friends.

In the week before Christmas 1979, the newspapers were filled with the story of an American jet which had crashed in a very remote Scottish hillside. This had taken place on 19 December 1979 when an American crew in a United States Air Force F111E jet crashed into the rocks of Craignaw. The aircraft, registration number 68–0003, belonged to 20 Tactical Fighter Wing of the USAF. The plane had taken off from Upper Heyford in Oxfordshire and was practising bombing at Jurby on the Isle of Man. Once completed, the pilot commenced low-flying training when he misjudged the height of Craignaw and the fighter jet struck the granite cliffs.

There were two crewmen on board the F111 when it impacted on the mountainside – Captain Richard Alfred Hetzner, pilot, and Captain Raymond Charles Spaulding, navigator, were both killed instantly. It was a bright, clear frosty day, so the weather could not be blamed for the crash.

F111 jets were built by General Dynamics and were capable of flying at twice the speed of sound, or Mach 2. The aircraft had swing-wings, which meant that they could retract the wings slightly to allow greater speed. When the plane was taking off, or flying at a slower speed, the wings straightened out, allowing greater lift. The first planes

15.5 F111 Memorial, Craignaw

entered the service of the USAF in 1967. They had two Pratt & Whitney TF30-P-3 engines complete with afterburners, allowing the jet to fly at maximum speeds of 1,452 mph. They could fly at up to 57,000 feet and had a range of 3,632 miles. The aeroplane normally carried one M61A1 gun, plus a mix of up to two dozen conventional weapons, which in some cases could have nuclear warheads.

When the aircraft disappeared from the radar screen a search for it was scrambled. Helicopters combed the area where the signal had last been noted, and it wasn't long before the strewn wreckage was discovered across the granite mountain, near to the Black Gairy, above Loch Neldricken. Many sections of the destroyed plane were taken away by helicopter for investigation into the cause of the crash.

The loss of the F111 resulted in some serious investigation, for it had been the sixth such plane of that type to crash in Great Britain that year. The Cold War of the time had directed the governments of Britain and America to prepare for possible war with Russia, and flying low over the mountains of Scotland was seen as one of the best methods of preparing for flying over the wastes of Russia.

A small cairn with a plaque affixed was erected by some members of Annanhill Kilmarnock Hurlford Hillwalking Club to commemorate the airmen who died in the crash. This was erected on 22 August 1987 by three men, under the guidance of Tommy Withers of Hurlford. A small bronze plaque was affixed to the cairn, reading:

In loving Memory of Capt R A Hetzner 28 USAF, Captain R C Spaulding 30 USAF, F1-11E Crew, Crashed December 19th 79, AKHWC.

Fragments of the F-111 have been collected and laid adjacent to the memorial cairn, whereas other pieces have been sent to the Dumfries and Galloway Aviation Museum, at Heathhall, near Dumfries, which was founded in 1977 at the control tower on a former World War 2 airfield.

16 Hydro Power

The amount of rain and other precipitation that falls on the Galloway Highlands is something that walkers and other visitors have noted with some disgust over the years. The height of the hills, and the fact that they are often the first eminences that the passing clouds reach after gathering evaporated water from 2,000 miles of Atlantic Ocean, means that the rainfall can be quite considerable.

Various readings of the levels of precipitation have been taken across the Galloway Highlands over the years, though the highest rainfall has probably not been measured due to where it falls. At Carsphairn, on the north-eastern periphery of the highest part of the hills, where the village is 574 feet above sea level, at one time the ten year average rainfall was calculated at 61.17 inches. At Kenmure Castle, which lies at the south-eastern extremity of the area covered by this book and which is 150 feet above sea level, the seven year average in the 1830s was 59 inches.

At Shiel of Castlemaddy, also in Carsphairn parish, the rainfall was measured for a five year period and over that time the average annual rainfall was 77.54 inches. Shiel of Castlemaddy lies 850 feet above sea level, in the lee of the mountains of Meaul and Carlin's Cairn.

The volume of rain that falls on the Galloway Highlands means that considerable amounts of water runs off the mountains into the local streams and rivers, before making its way to the sea, either in the Firth of Clyde or the Solway Firth. The quantity of water and the remoteness of the district meant that these rivers were ideal for harnessing in order to generate hydro-electricity. Schemes for damming the rivers to generate power have existed for many years, and it was only on small scales that generators were established, powered by water diverted from streams through them.

The first major project proposed to harness the power of the waters in the Galloway Highlands was the Loch Doon project. This was suggested in 1900, the plans being to dam the mouth of the loch and create a power station at Dalfarson, in the Ness Glen below. The project was proposed by the Marquis of Ailsa, who owned much of Loch Doon and its surroundings, and he employed the consultant, William Robertson Copeland, to investigate the possibilities. He suggested that the level of the loch should be raised by twenty feet, which would submerge 581 acres of land. Almost half of this was already the property of the Marquis. The increased loch would hold 8,543 million gallons of water. Allowing for compensation water that would be piped into the Doon all day every day, evaporation and water lost in floods, it was reckoned that almost 25 billion gallons of water per annum were available for passing through the turbines. This was sufficient to produce two million watts. The electricity generated would have been used in Ayrshire. Progress was slow, and eventually came to a halt with the outbreak of the First World War.

When the war passed and peace resumed, the Loch Doon generating scheme was looked at once more. A scheme of 1921 was considered as a source of electricity to replace the small and inefficient Ayr Power Station. This was to raise the loch by only five feet, but would be sufficient to generate enough power for Ayr, Prestwick, Maybole and surrounding villages. The cost of construction was to be the stumbling block, as the burgh didn't have sufficient funds to compensate landowners, build a power station, pylons and distribution without taking out a considerable loan.

A cheaper option that was still on the table was to use electricity supplied by Kilmarnock generating station. The competition between the burghs was such that Ayr didn't want to lose its independence and control over electricity supply, and Kilmarnock was ready to offer electricity to other towns across the county at favourable rates. The squabble between the two burghs, with Ayr County Council siding with Kilmarnock, meant that the plans had to be considered by a Select Committee of the House of Lords. Although the folk of Ayr were against joining with Kilmarnock, to stick their necks out and push for their hydro scheme meant that they were cutting their own throats, as this would mean an increase in their already comparatively dearer electricity.

The select committee listened to evidence for three days and eventually decided that the scheme would be allowed to proceed, with the proviso that the compensation water released into the River Doon be doubled from that proposed. The proposals were returned to the Commons, and the bill was passed. When it was being taken through the Lords further meetings were taking place in the background, with considerable urgency.

The Kilmarnock and Ayr County representatives proposed to the Ayr representative that Ayr should join them in creating a joint electricity board that could cover the whole county, to everyone's mutual benefit. As the bill was having its third reading negotiations were such that it was agreed to work together, whereupon Kilmarnock withdrew its objections. The bill was passed on 8 December 1923, coming under the control of the joint authority.

All of the squabbling and negotiating came to nought, however, for the plans were never acted upon, despite an extension being obtained.

Around the same time, in Kirkcudbrightshire, a number of folk were interested in establishing an electricity generating scheme also. Around 1922 three notables in the area came together to look at possibilities. These were Colonel William MacLellan, of Merz & MacLellan, Major Wellwood Maxwell, and Captain Scott Elliott. They brought in the firm of Sir Alexander Gibb and Partners to weigh up the options and advise. After looking at the rainfall figures, and heads of water, it was agreed that the River Dee had some potential, but that a number of large reservoirs for storing water would be required. Construction of the dams and loss of land meant that the scheme was too expensive.

In 1926 the Electricity (Supply) Act was passed, establishing the National Grid, which brought about a nationalised industry. This meant that various local schemes could be re-looked at, and it was decided to study the Ayrshire and Kirkcudbrightshire schemes once more, with a view to combining them. The initial proposals of 1927 were tweaked and a 1928 version of proposals was pursued. A total production capacity of 44 MW was available at a cost of £1.7 million. Further changes were made to the plans before the final proposals were placed before parliament for approval. Two of the power stations were changed - one of them being removed from the scheme and the other relocated.

A bill was passed in May 1929 by parliament, allowing the work to progress. There had been opposition from miners, who saw hydro-electricity as a threat to coal-fired power stations, but this was ignored, and the scheme was sold to them as a 'top-up', generating electricity at short notice when peak demand kicked in.

The bill, in its final form, included a number of important clauses, in particular that which stated:

> In the construction of the works all reasonable regard shall be paid to the preservation, as well for the public as for private owners, of the beauty of the scenery of the districts in which the said works are situated. For the purpose of securing the observance of the foregoing provisions and of aiding the Company it shall be lawful for the Secretary of State, after consultation with the Company, to appoint a Committee. The Committee may make to the Company such recommendations as they may think reasonable and proper for the preservation of the beauty of the scenery.

It has been said that the inclusion of the 'amenity' clause in the Galloway bill was instrumental in making the engineers take careful notice of the design of the dams, location of power stations, and camouflage of various works in the whole scheme. As a result, once the new concrete had weathered, the whole scheme blended admirably into the landscape. The 'amenity' clause also influenced later schemes that were constructed elsewhere in Scotland, it being proved possible by the Galloway scheme to construct major civil engineering works in remote landscapes without too much destruction.

As part of the plan to promote art and the preservation of the countryside, the power company commissioned the Kirkcudbright artist, Charles Oppenheimer (1875-1961), to paint landscapes depicting some of the dams as they were being constructed. Among these are 'Galloway Dam – nearing completion', 'Harnessing the Dee', and 'Art in Concrete'.

Not everyone felt that that new dams and associated works blended in with the landscape. Stephen Bone, writing in *Portraits of Mountains*, was of the opinion that 'the landscape has already suffered a lot from the building of dams and power stations ... was it really necessary to build that surge-tower, a cylindrical metal object like a gas-holder, in the most prominent position in the whole glen? And did they have to make such a mess of Loch Doon?'

Similarly, the Galloway writer, W. G. M. Dobie, bemoaned the coming of the construction squad in his poem, 'The Modern Raiders', where he claims the developers will destroy the countryside with their proposals:

> This is our land of Galloway
> Where, in a more heroic day,
> The Bruce contrived to trap and slay
>   An army of invaders:
> Where Patrick Heron, Silver Sand,
> May Maxwell and the smuggler band
> Adventured, - as by Crockett's hand,
>   Is written in 'The Raiders.'
>
> A raider comes to-day who kills
> The glories of our glens and hills
> With unheroic Acts and Bills
>   And 'private legislation':
> The company promoters' pen
> Will dam the Deugh and dam the Ken
> And dam the Dee, - oh, damn the men
>   Who plan such desecration!

The Galloway scheme was drawn up by James Williamson, chief engineer to Alexander Gibb & Partners of Glasgow. He found that the potential in the area was ideal for a 'cascade system' whereby water was passed through a series of power stations over a 35-mile distance. The total fall from Drumjohn valve to the sea at the Solway Firth was only 680 feet, but as the main flow of water passed through four power stations it was an effective scheme.

Negotiations with numerous bodies and landowners in the area were carried out in order to ensure as little opposition to the plans as possible. Some of those affected had strong claims, such as the owners of mills on the rivers, where the water-flow would be reduced considerably, affecting their power source. Some of these were to accept deals whereby the electricity company would replace their old water power generators with new electric engines, the power for which would be supplied at generous rates. Thus the owners of Skeldon Mills and Alloway Mill on the Doon were appeased.

In the Dee and Ken valley there were fewer industrial works reliant on the water as a source of power. One exception was the silk factory at Tongland, but this business fell into administration during negotiations. One objector, the Misses Sinclair of Ashton Villa in Kirkcudbright, were approached and agreed to withdraw their concerns in return for the company installing electricity in their villa, and supplying the power for the remainder of their life gratis, up to a maximum 500 units each year!

The first contracts were signed in January 1931, the barrage at Glenlochar, across the foot of Loch Ken, being constructed. Here, the water was wide and ran over bare rock, meaning that it was comparatively easy to construct a barrage which would raise the level of Loch Ken by four feet. This additional water totalled 320 million cubic feet which was released to top up the supply of water at Tongland power station, further downstream.

16.1 Loch Doon dam from the head of Ness Glen

During the construction of the Galloway hydro scheme, there were around 1,500 men employed by the contractors. One third of this number was needed to dig out the long Glenlee tunnel. At the time of construction unemployment was high, and there were many complaints that local labour, that is Galloway or Ayrshire men, were not being given the chance of a job. It is said that many unemployed men from Glasgow were to head south to Kirkcudbright and Castle Douglas, where they signed on and requested accommodation. This caused aggravation with the locals, especially those of Dalbeattie, where labour in the quarries had been decimated. It is said that the peace in rural Galloway was shattered for five years!

Among the itinerant labourers who came to Galloway were folk like the Irishman, Hashy Dan Gallagher, Stonebreaker Docherty, Slusher Tom, Horse Ryan, and numerous others who earned epithets amongst their comrades. Many of the workers were Irish, and they worked twelve hour shifts. Many of the original workers were elderly, having served on projects in the Highlands before and throughout the First World War. Wages for navvies were one shilling per hour, there was no overtime, and the only day off was Sunday. Crane drivers were paid more, 19 shillings and sixpence a day. That was on a good day, for when it rained, no concrete could be poured, and workers weren't paid when there was no progress. In the winter months, when it snowed, work stopped, and many men didn't get a full week's wages for ages. Digging the tunnels was a different matter, for this was not at the mercy of the weather, but the conditions underground were less pleasant.

Most of those employed in the works were forced to live in labour camps that were established in the Glenkens. Accommodation in these was charged at 22 shillings and sixpence per week, deducted from their wages. The wooden huts could be freezing, even although they were heated by wood-burning stoves. Prior to the huts being erected the workers had to rough it in tents or caravans.

In August 1932 Rev Thomas P. Hitman was appointed as chaplain to the camps, and he held services each Sunday at the camps at Craigenbay, Glenlee, Craigshinnie and Clatteringshaws. To try to make life in the camps more bearable, Rev Hitman also organised a number of events, in particular concerts, where men in the camps could entertain with some of the various talents that they had, or else locals could come along and show off their skills in singing or playing instruments.

As work on the scheme continued, recreation huts were built at Loch Doon, Kendoon, Drumjohn and Earlstoun. At Carsfad dam, the Y.M.C.A. established a large hut which doubled as a recreation centre, with indoor bowls, billiards and other games. It also had a canteen, and was able to provide hot baths for the workers.

The minister was also a regular attendee at the morning first aid meetings and he visited each camp over the week, building up an average travelling distance of 160 miles per week. This was initially done on his bicycle, but soon the presbytery appreciated the nature of his works and bought him a motorbike.

Life in the camps was difficult for some, and attempts were made to make their time there as pleasant as it could be. Locals donated old books, magazines and newspapers and with these small libraries were established in each camp. Radios were acquired from various sources, and billiards and bowls were popular games. The camps even had a small football league of their own, each camp playing the others in addition to some local teams.

At the northern end of the scheme, Loch Doon was negotiated into the plans – the Ayrshire rights to the loch as a source of hydro-power being vested in the new scheme. A gravity dam across the mouth of the loch was constructed from concrete, the roadway being located over it. The dam was 970 feet in length. The new dam raised the level of the loch by 27 feet, holding back 2,900 million cubic feet of water. Much of this was available for electricity generation, though part of it had to be released into the River Doon to allow fishing and salmon breeding to continue.

By raising the level of the loch, a second dam had to be constructed, else the waters would overflow into the Muck Burn and into the Carsphairn Lane. The Muck Burn Dam was 150 feet in length. To add to the waters held by Loch Doon, the Muck Burn itself was diverted and channelled into the loch near to the dam.

Loch Doon was to be the principal reservoir in the scheme, its waters being directed south instead of north. To do this, a large tunnel was dug out beneath Cullendoch Hill, 2,100 yards in length. The tunnel is eight feet in diameter. Water is able to flow through the tunnel from the loch, emerging at a large valve located by the side of the Carsphairn Lane, below the farmstead of Drumjohn.

This tunnel also had the unique property of being able to allow the waters to pass in two directions. In addition to allowing the waters to flow from Loch Doon into the Carsphairn Lane, when the valve at Drumjohn was closed water could be fed into the tunnel and channelled through the hill and back into the loch.

The source of this additional water was the Water of Deugh and the Bow Burn, streams draining the uplands to the east. The Bow Burn flows from Cairnsmore of Carsphairn. Seven hundred yards from its junction with the Water of Deugh, the Bow Burn is dammed and the water is directed by means of an aqueduct along the moor for about one mile to flow into the Water of Deugh, around a mile and a half upstream from its natural confluence. At that point the Deugh is dammed also, a small pool created above the dam. From this pool a tunnel 2,700 yards in length transports the water underneath Lamford Hill to Drumjohn. When the level of Loch Doon is low, and the valve at Drumjohn was closed, the water can be used to help refill the loch.

The initial plan at Loch Doon was for the castle to remain on its islet and be partially submerged – by as much as three-quarters. The electricity company was willing to assist in preserving the castle, by spending £3,000 in repointing and grouting the walls in order to extend the life of the ruin. At first this was accepted by the authorities, but soon word spread that the castle was at risk. Instead, a second option was proposed, relocating the castle stone by stone to the side of the loch. This would have cost £4,000, but the promoters were not keen to follow this through.

At length the campaign to save the castle boiled down to one thing – was saving Loch Doon Castle worth the extra £1,000? It was eventually agreed that it was, and work on relocating the castle commenced. The Marquis of Ailsa granted a plot on the western side of the loch, at Craigmalloch, where the structure could be relocated. The walls were photographed and the stones numbered. All of the main ashlar blocks were transported across the loch on a causeway, and masons rebuilt the castle stone by stone.

No power station was constructed to harness the power of the waters from Loch Doon in its initial stretches. The water from the reservoir flowed into the Carsphairn Lane, and thence the Water of Deugh.

In the vicinity of Dundeugh and Marscalloch, a second reservoir was created. This was Kendoon Loch, formed by constructing two dams, one across the Water of Deugh, the other across the Water of Ken. The dammed waters blended into one loch. The Deugh dam is an arch and gravity structure, 770 feet in length. The Ken dam has a similar construction and measures 820 feet in length. The loch created is a maximum of 80 feet deep.

At the Ken dam on Kendoon Loch, the waters are passed along an aqueduct for half a mile (or 825 yards) to an arch and gravity dam on the Black Water, again capturing more water. From the dam the water is tunnelled for almost one mile before dropping through pipes to Kendoon Power Station, constructed at the junction of the original Deugh and Ken.

Kendoon Power Station was the highest generating station in the whole scheme, and has a catchment area of 150 square miles. It was completed in 1936. The head of water at Kendoon is around 150 feet and this turns two turbines which produce 24,000 kW. The turbines rotate at 250 rpm when fully operational, using 55 cubic metres of water per second. As with all of the turbines and generators used in the scheme, these were manufactured by the English Electric Company.

Almost immediately after the waters that had passed through Kendoon Power Station returned to the Water of Ken, the whole watercourse was captured in a third reservoir, named Carsfad Loch. A curving arch and gravity dam was constructed across the valley above Carsfad, gathering the waters into a new loch. The dam is 545 yards in length. The waters are fed through pipes down into the Carsfad Power Station, constructed in 1936.

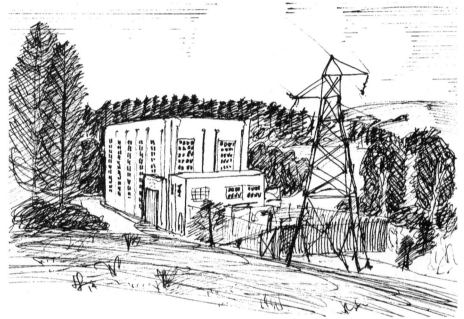

16.2 Carsfad Power Station

Carsfad Power Station has a water head of around 65 feet and draws around 73 cubic metres of water per second. The two turbines produce a total of 12,000 kW. The turbines rotate at 214.3 rpm.

From Carsfad, the Water of Ken flows southwards, being joined by the Polharrow Burn before tumbling impressively over the Earlstoun Linn. Just below this waterfall the waters enter another reservoir that was created as part of the hydro scheme. Near to Milton Park a curved dam was built across the valley, damming the Water of Ken once again. The dam is an arch and gravity structure, 230 yards in length. The new loch was named the Earlstoun Loch, after the old castle and estate that lies on its eastern shores.

The waters from Earlstoun pass along an aqueduct for about 825 yards before being channelled through pipes into Earlstoun Power Station, located by the side of the main road from Carsphairn to New Galloway. The power station was completed in 1936. Again there are two turbines, producing a total of 14,000 kW. The blades rotate at 214.3 rpm, consuming 71 cubic metres of water per second. Like Carsfad, the head is 65 feet.

Below Earlstoun the Water of Ken flows on and enters Loch Ken. Eventually the water flows into Tongland Loch and through the Tongland Power Station before passing into the Solway Firth. At Tongland the power station produces 33,000 kW using three turbines.

A second water basin was captured and the water used for the generation of electricity. The River Dee was dammed near to Clatteringshaws farm and a new large loch was formed, named Clatteringshaws Loch. The dam stretches 500 yards across the valley, holding back 8,000 million gallons of water. At the deepest point the loch is 75 feet deep, though only 40 feet of this can be drawn off to supply the power stations. The highest water level is 585 feet above sea level, the lowest it can draw down to being 545 feet. The gravity dam at Clatteringshaws is perhaps the finest, and largest, in the district, a massive concrete structure built across the valley. The lower sections are tapered to add strength, the upper parts vertical, with a series of archways.

The format of the dam at Clatteringshaws shows Williamson's skill in aesthetics. A simple, 'modernist' design, the dam comprises different elements, repeated elsewhere in the scheme. Part of the dam comprises of arched supports, whereas other parts are tapered concrete gravity dams. The dam has a graceful curve across the valley, the shape having less of an impact than what a straight dam would have had.

When the dam was being built a temporary rail line was laid along the side of the structure, over which steam cranes were able to pass, lifting the large containers of concrete which were poured into the moulds. Some of the cranes were as large as fifteen tons, and these had to be built and dismantled as required. One worker, John Hunter, recalled that he was part of a squad that built the crane in a single day, fired up the steam engine and had it operating by night-time. At the east end of the dam a concrete plant was installed, so that the concrete used was mixed on site, the rock included being quarried on the lower slopes of Clatteringshaws Fell.

Negotiations with the landowner prior to the construction of Clatteringshaws Loch were difficult to start with. The farm of Clatteringshaws had been purchased by the Earl of Mar at Whitsun 1927 for £1,200, mainly for the sporting rights, but also for Bruce's Stone, the king being claimed as an ancestor by the Earl. Agents for the Galloway hydro company were taken aback to discover that the Earl wished £4,500 for the property, and that he was unwilling to break up the farm. Negotiations continued, and the Earl's price gradually reduced. Eventually it was agreed that he would sell the whole farm for £1,900, apart from the Bruce's Stone and the surrounding land over a radius of five yards. This was accepted.

The Earl of Mar, despite his keenness to retain Bruce's Stone, decided soon after to pass it over to the care of the National Trust for Scotland. The stone and its small circle of ground around it, with the right of access over the moor from the main road, were officially accepted by the Trust on 23 April 1932.

On completion, a bronze plaque was erected within a small foursquare stone cairn near to Clatteringshaws farm. This reads:

Clatteringshaws Dam. Constructed by the Galloway Water Power Company 1932-34. Clatteringshaws Dam and the loch occupy ground memorable in Scottish history; close by the dam ran the old Edinburgh road leading to Whithorn (Candida Casa IV-Vth century), the earliest Christian foundation in Scotland. The waters of the loch are gathered from the fastnesses of the Dungeon of Buchan and from the site of that ancient Forest of Buchan where Robert Bruce was hard pressed by his enemies after his return to Scotland from Rathlin in 1307. A victory gained near this place by Robert Bruce or his brother Edward is commemorated by the great boulder known as the King's or Bruce's Stone which stands near the shores of the loch, 700 yards north of Clatteringshaws farm. Mary Queen of Scots passed this way on 13th August 1563. The surrounding wilds were sought as a refuge by the Covenanters during their struggles in the seventeenth century.

16.3 Clatteringshaws Loch dam

The excess water from Clatteringshaws Loch is passed through a tunnel eastwards, below the slopes of Bennan and Glenlee Hill before emerging on the eastern slopes of the latter hill in a series of large steel pipes. The tunnel is eleven feet in diameter and 6,329 yards in length, the final pipe being 8 feet in diameter and 470 feet long. The tunnel flows at a gradient of 1 in 350 from the loch to the adit at Glenlee, then steepens to 1 in 100. The water is piped down the hillside to the Glenlee Power Station, located in the valley of the Glenkens below. The difference in water level from the loch to the generating station is 400 feet or so.

16.4 Glenlee Power Station

The construction of the Glenlee tunnel was regarded as the greatest challenge in the whole scheme. Excavating the solid rock through the hillsides for over three miles was the most expensive single part of the project, costing over ten per cent of the total budget. The tunnel was started on six faces at the same time, in order to ensure that it did not hold up progress on the other works. These were located at either end of the tunnel, plus at two locations en route – from a shaft sunk near to Craigshinnie, and from an adit below Glenlee Hill. The shaft at Craigshinnie was later to be used to add water to the shaft below.

Digging the tunnel was to prove easier than expected, and a rate of 100 feet per week was achieved. The rock was of good quality, meaning that the tunnel was self-supporting when it was excavated, but the plan had always been to line it with concrete. The excess stone from the tunnel was originally drawn out by electric locomotive, but once there was a good supply of air and ventilation, diesel locomotives were used to haul the wagons. The final section of the tunnel was blasted through on 10 December 1933, after which the concreting commenced.

A special gantry, 150 feet in length, was used in the tunnel, the concrete being poured around it. As with most of the dams, the concrete for the tunnel was mixed on site, in this case within the tunnel itself. When the workers were familiar with the method employed, 150 feet could be filled and progressed in one day.

Glenlee Power Station was erected in 1934-5, the building designed by Merz & MacLellan and Sir Alexander Gibb and Partners. The building appears to be built on four floors, but this was a careful design element to the exterior to make it look less massive in the landscape. Finished in white concrete, the simple design was typical of the times, but one which has not dated. The head of water at Glenlee is 375 feet, the largest of any of Galloway's power stations. This largely compensates for the lower consumption rate, for only 25½ cubic metres of water passes through the twin turbines at full load. These turbines rotate at 428.3 rpm, the fastest in Galloway, producing 24,000 kW. The station went into commercial production in March 1935.

When completed, the Galloway hydro-electric scheme was capable of producing 107,000 kW of electricity. Only two of the generating stations were permanently manned – those of Glenlee and Tongland. The stations at Carsfad, Earlstoun and Kendoon were controlled remotely from the control centre at Glenlee.

The reservoirs at Kendoon, Carsfad and Earlstoun are classed as daily storage reservoirs, the water in them only being sufficient for generating power for a period within the day, after which the dam valves need to be closed to allow the reservoirs to refill. Although the hydro stations cannot run all day every day, there being insufficient water, they are ideal, however, to top up electricity demand at peak loads, for they can be switched on and off within minutes. The Glenlee station, for example, can go from generating no power to producing 24,000 kW within five minutes of the demand being made.

The turbo-generators at each power station are all very similar in style. Water is directed in a spiral around a central core, in which vanes are pushed by the water, turning the vertical shaft. This rotates the generator rotor, producing the electricity. The spent water leaves via the outflow pipe.

The electricity generated is an 11,000 volt, three phase supply at a frequency of fifty hertz. At the power station are sub-stations which convert this power to 132,000 volts, which is what is transmitted in the National Grid.

The dams at Loch Doon and Clatteringshaws Loch are used to replenish the reservoirs at Kendoon, Carsfad, Earlstoun and Loch Ken during the summer months, when the precipitation levels are low, and are refilled in the winter months.

In addition to the amenity clause, mentioned earlier, the Galloway bill was instrumental in ensuring that the passage of fish up and down the watercourses was unobstructed. A number of modern designs were included in the creation of fish passes. At Loch Doon the new fish pass is in the form of an octagonal tower in which a continuous spiral of linked pools allows the fish to jump up the cascades from pool to pool, eventually reaching the loch. The lower section comprises more traditional step pools, but the upper part is located within the tower. There, chambers are arranged in a spiral. There is a series of floats in every other chamber which controls valves allowing access to the loch at different water levels. Should the loch drop as far as 676 feet above sea level (its original level), then the pass is switched off and fish are able to enter the loch through the dam's culvert at the original outlet channel.

The Galloway hydro scheme was influential in later, larger schemes that were constructed across the Highlands. One of the amenity committee members was Harold Ogle Tarbolton (d. 1947), an architect who advised the Galloway engineers. He was also responsible for the design of a number of houses erected for electricity board employees. He was responsible in later years for the Loch Sloy scheme, by the side of Loch Lomond (1943-49) and at Tummel, near Pitlochry (1947-51).

The whole Galloway scheme was completed and operational by 1936, the first electricity officially supplied to the grid on 1 April 1935, though the first unofficial supply was produced at midday on Wednesday 6 March 1935. The whole scheme was completed on 27 October 1936 when the second turbine at Carsfad came into service.

When complete, the Galloway hydro scheme employed 78 permanent staff, comprising of six managers and administrative workers, fifty shift workers and 22 maintenance staff.

Unfortunately, Colonel William MacLellan had died in 1934, aged 60, and did not live to see the project come to fruition. He had lived at Orchard Knowes, near Kippford. A plaque was erected in his memory at Tongland Power Station on Friday 11 March 1938, paid for by his friends. Below a bas-relief of his head, it reads:

1874 1934 William MacLellan CBE MIEE of Orchard Knowes, Kirkcudbrightshire,
to whom the conception of this water power scheme was due.
A master of engineering, he devoted his talent to the development of electric power in
many parts of the world. 'Si monvmentm reqviris, circvmspice.'

Five men were to die during the construction of the works. Two of them lost their lives within the Glenlee Tunnel, which was the most dangerous part of the whole scheme. In fact, sixty per cent of the injuries received during construction took place in the tunnel. To commemorate those who lost their lives in the building of the scheme, a small memorial was erected near to Glenlee Power Station.

The most recent addition to the Galloway Hydro Scheme was constructed in 1985. At Drumjohn the waters from Loch Doon were let out from the valve by the side of the Carsphairn Lane, the sight of a massive flow of water being one that passers-by could see regularly. It was realised that this water had immense power itself which could be harnessed, and thus a smaller power station was created at the valve. The first proposal to harness this water was made in 1960, but it wasn't until the price of electricity began to rise that the cost of construction became more feasible.

Work on the new power station started in August 1983 at a cost of £1.25 million. When it was completed in 1984 the new station could generate an average of 1,350 kW, rising to 2.3 MW when the water flow is at its greatest. This brought the total power generated in the Galloway scheme to just over 105 MW.

Not all hydro schemes have been constructed by the electricity generating boards. There are a few small-scale hydro schemes within the area covered by this book as well. One of the larger small-scale schemes was that created on the Forrest Estate. Fred Olsen, the owner, was keen to produce some electricity to power the homes on his estate, as well as putting electricity into the grid as a money-making scheme.

Olsen's scheme cost several million pounds, and he constructed it in various stages. The first stage was the creation of an earth and stone dam across the mouth of Loch Minnoch in 1982, blocking the natural escape of the Mid Burn. The water from the loch was diverted through a 700mm diameter pipeline to a Pelton turbine just over one mile away at Burnhead – the Burnhead A scheme. The head of water is 375 feet, generating 490 kW. The loch, only being fifteen acres in extent, can only store enough water for two and a half days of generation, but water can be added from Loch Dungeon. The annual output over the past few years is around 2.7 million kW hours.

Olsen then moved on to the second phase of his scheme. A concrete dam was constructed across the outlet of Loch Harrow, extending to 250 yards in length. The level of the loch was raised slightly, producing a small head which could be piped down to the new hydro-electricity station constructed at Fore Bush, three quarters of a mile away. This power scheme was switched on in May 1987 by Fred Olsen. The new power generating station was capable of producing 1,900 kW hours per annum, a figure comparable to supplying electricity to 400 homes. The excess electricity not required by the estate was sold to the South of Scotland Electricity Board.

The third phase of the scheme resulted in the creation of a new loch on the estate, known as Loch Mannoch. A dam was constructed across the Lane Mannoch burn and the water diverted through a 24 inch diameter pipe to a 257kW Francis turbine located near the shore of Loch Harrow, giving a head of around 160 feet. The water then passes through the Loch Harrow scheme. The turbine was commissioned in 1988.

Further work took place at Loch Dungeon in 2012-13, increasing the electricity output to 750 kW. A Gilkes twin jet Pelton turbine and a Hitzinger generator were installed at Burnhead, fed from a 30 inch diameter pipeline from Loch Dungeon. The head of water is 480 feet, the water passing through at 130 gallons per second at full power.

The use of natural power to generate electricity persuaded Fred Olsen to invest in green power. In the Polharrow glen, near to Forrest Lodge, can be found a modern timber building known as the Green House. This is occupied by Natural Power Consultants, a business that advises on wave, tidal and wind energy projects. The building, which was designed by Neil Sutherland, was erected in 2000 shortly after the company relocated to the area from Glasgow. The offices won a national award from the Association for the Protection of Rural Scotland for its unique design and innovative green credentials.

Natural Power was founded in 1995 by Stuart Hall. It grew quickly and in 2000 was taken over by Fred Olsen. In 2010 the company employed 68 people at its offices near Forrest Lodge, and by 2013 employed over 250 people worldwide, having established a number of offices abroad.

17 Forestry

The Forestry Commission was founded on 1 September 1919 to provide a source of home-grown timber that could be of use in time of war. The First World War had just ended and it was realised that the country did not have sufficient stocks of its own timber to meet the needs of the population should any further major conflict occur. Thus the government of the day established the Commission, acquiring extensive tracks of upland Britain and cloaking it with coniferous trees.

The principal function of the Commission was to grow a reserve of timber, but as time passed and the possibility of war receded, and the method of fighting altered, this changed to a more commercial basis, and the main function became the growth of timber for profit.

During the years of depression, in the 1920s, another advantage of planting forests was that it created labour in areas of high unemployment. The first forestry plantations in Galloway occurred in what was called Bennan Forest, latterly Cairn Edward Forest, just outwith the area covered by this book. Located along the western shores of Loch Ken, the trees planted were a variety of native and introduced species – Scots Pine, European Larch, Douglas Fir, Norway Spruce and Sitka Spruce.

The first Forestry Commission woodlands in the Galloway Highlands were those planted at Dundeugh, on the eastern edge. Dundeugh farm was acquired and most of the land was planted between the Water of Ken and the Water of Deugh in 1936.

The original method used for planting was purely by hand, the forester cutting a slot in the turf with a spade, into which the sapling was placed. Trees were only planted on dry ground, for it was soon discovered that wet ground resulted in the trees becoming waterlogged and dying.

Around 1928 a new method of planting was introduced from Europe, known as the Belgian system. Drains were cut across wetter soils at 20 to 25 feet intervals, the sods cut from the ground being dumped in lumps around five or six feet apart. Into these sods slits were cut and the young tree planted. As the sod was raised above the surrounding ground, which had the benefit of some drainage, the tree was able to grow more successfully in the drier soil.

The Commission acquired the Glen Trool Forest area at Martinmas 1939. Forty thousand acres of land was obtained on a feuing basis, though Loch Trool and Glen Trool Lodge was not included, as these were leased at the time to the Marquis of Tavistock. Shooting, as well as salmon and trout fishing rights were also excluded. Included within the forestry area were the lands of House o' Hill Hotel, Brigton,

Buchan, Caldons, Cairnderry, Corriefeckloch, Creebank, Dalnaw, Glenhead, Holm of Bargrennan, Kirriereoch, Suie, Palgowan, Minniwick, Kirriemore, Kirriedarroch, Gleckmalloch, Drumjoan, Stroan and Culsharg.

Although the Second World War did not require as much timber as the First War, the need for timber reserves in conflict was reinforced, and further acquisitions of land for planting were made.

The outbreak of war in 1939 put paid to planting in the Galloway Highlands for some years, and it was not until 1947 that the first planting commenced in the Glentrool Forest area. The land around Glencairn and the lower stretches of Glen Trool were planted in 1950, mainly with Sitka Spruce, Norway Spruce and Japanese Larch. In the Glentrool Forest, originally up to 70% of the trees planted were Sitka Spruce, but as with numerous other Forestry Commission, and other forest agency and private landowners' forests, conservationists complained about the blanket forestry with regimented trees of one species.

The arrival of the Forestry Commission was not to everyone's taste. Stephen Bone, writing about Corserine within *Portraits of Mountains*, published in 1950, comments that, 'Soon there may be trees here once more, not the beautiful woodlands of pine and birch that Bruce knew, but dismally commercial plantations of foreign evergreens. Woodlands can be beautiful. The Forestry Commission has shown us that they can also be extremely ugly.'

In 1947 some lands on Garroch estate were acquired, and planting took place in 1949 on the lands around Shiel of Castlemaddy. The old steadings of Castlemaddy and Shiel of Castlemaddy were abandoned as farms, and the planting obliterated the ancient ruined steadings of Halfmark of Castlemaddie (occupied by the MacTurk family in the mid-eighteenth century), Holmhead of Castlemaddie and Northside of Castlemaddie.

New methods of planting had by now been introduced. Large ploughs were pulled by tractors across the ground, cutting deep furrows which became new drainage channels. The upturned soil removed from the furrow was where the young trees were planted, still by hand, the drier soil or peat being ideal for the tree to take a solid hold of the ground.

By the 1950s the need for timber in war abated, for the world had gone nuclear, and the Forestry Commission's role in the country was to be commercial. Timber was to be grown as a crop, preventing the need to import so much from Scandinavia or Canada, so quick growing Sitka Spruce became the main species planted. In the early 1970s the lands of Drumness, Dalshangan and Carminnows in Carsphairn parish were planted.

The initial eagerness to plant hillsides and moors with trees resulted in some plantations that were later regarded as having been a mistake. In a number of cases notable viewpoints along roadsides were obscured when the trees began to grow, leaving the roads to wind through seemingly never-ending tunnels of conifers. As the trees grew and were later thinned, the opportunity was taken to cut down those that obscured vistas of glens and hills.

Similarly, a number of the older plantations had edges that were straight, marching across the hillsides following lines that were probably drawn on maps, rather than adhering to any natural contours and landforms. From a distance, these sudden edges appeared very unnatural. Today, forest edges are more irregular in shape, and where the forest may end at a man-made structure, such as a fence, dike or road, care is taken to ensure that the line of trees is ragged and more complementary to the landscape.

Some of the mistakes of a keenness to plant for financial gain have been learned over the years, and today the Forestry Commission is more in tune with environmental issues. Now, more broadleaf trees are planted where it is suitable for them, and the woodlands to the side of roads and where the public have ready sight of them are more ornamental in style. The hard edges of regimented plantations have been removed by creating sinuous lines, native trees and bushes planted, and deciduous trees encouraged.

As the trees have grown and been harvested, the land is often replanted with a wider variety of species, creating a more variegated forest when seen from a distance, and one that is more conducive to wildlife. More naturally Scottish trees have been planted (though there are only three types of Scots conifer – the Juniper, yew and Scots pine) but these are un-commercial and only planted for their amenity value. The first block of forestry in the area, the Island Block at Dundeugh, was clear-felled for timber in 1981, forty-five years after planting.

By the time of writing, timber production within the Galloway Forest Park has reached figures varying from 700,000 to 750,000 tonnes per annum. This figure is expected to remain fairly static for the next century, as trees cut down will be replanted, ensuring a continuous cycle of production.

The Forestry Commission uses its own nurseries to grow trees from seed. Three nurseries were established in Galloway – at Kirroughtree, Bareagle and Fleet forests. These provided around 15 million young trees each year, many of which were kept in the region, though saplings were sent to other parts of southern Scotland.

The Forestry Commission was divided into two groups in 1996, Forest Enterprise and the Forest Authority. Forest Enterprise, as the name suggests, was charged with making a good return on the money spent on planting trees and acquiring ground. A commercial entity, it was to be treated as a business out to make as much of a profit as possible.

The Forest Authority was given the task of supervising forest plantations, both in commission hands or private. The Authority has to assess the impact of new forests on the visible landscape, on wildlife and how it will affect people. This agency was also given the task of protecting wildlife and conserving ancient woodlands. In 2003 the Forestry Commission was transferred to the control of the Scottish Parliament.

There are a few privately owned forests in the area covered by this book. One of the largest is Forrest Estate, where planting took place from 1953 until 1990. Over that period over 6,600 acres were covered in trees. From 2001-6 the land at Stranfasket was also planted. Thinning commenced on the older plantations in 1969 and the first clear-felling took place in 2000. Around 120 acres are felled each year and subsequently replanted, the forest producing over 20,000 tons of timber per annum.

One of the gravest dangers experienced in the forests is fires. Many of these are probably started accidentally, though few of the culprits expect them to take hold and spread as far as some of them have done in the past. Usually a barbeque, camp fire or stray cigarette end has got out of control, perhaps burning dry grass and ferns before spreading into the trees. A fire in 1926 destroyed around 100 acres of woodland in one of Galloway's first forests, at Bennan on the shores of Loch Ken.

One of the largest early forest fires in the Galloway Highlands area took place in the evening of 8 May 1978. It is thought that a visitor in the forest casually dropped a cigarette and it lay smouldering for a time before the breeze fanned it and started a fire. This blaze grew quickly and soon around 667 acres (227 hectares) of Glentrool Forest, west of Caldons, were burned.

In 2007 a major forest fire occurred to the south of Loch Doon. Some campers had accidentally caused the heathland to ignite, and soon the flames were spreading south at an alarming rate. The forest caught fire and sparks blowing in the wind spread it further, setting other tinder-dry grasslands and trees alight. The fire destroyed around 12,000 acres, some of the damage being as far south as Loch Dee

The Forestry Commission has been given a larger role to play in the encouragement of tourism and recreation in the forests. As a result, the Forestry Commission rangers have been employed to work with tourists, introducing them to the forests, and explaining how the commission works, not only in the growth of timber, but also in the conservation of nature. In the Galloway Forest Park, which extends to 96,600 hectares (or 240,000 acres, or 373 square miles), a number of rangers are employed at various bases.

17.1 Clatteringshaws Visitor Centre

Within the Galloway Forest Park there are three forestry information centres and visitor centres. The principal one is at Clatteringshaws, where the former cottage was converted into a small museum and interpretation centre. In the entrance porch is a stained glass window entitled 'The Hills of Home', depicting a red deer stag at Murray's Monument. Around the deer are numerous other Galloway animals and birds, insects, snakes and fish. Known also as the 'Galloway' window, it was designed by Brian Thomas OBE. The visitor centre was redesigned in 2013, and today the centre offers a small cafe and gift shop. Adjoining it are display areas which highlight some of the wildlife that can be found in the forests, as well as some live creatures, such as frogs.

In the grounds to the north-east of the visitor centre can be found a rebuilt Romano-British homestead. This was based on the foundations of a genuine homestead that was discovered when the level of Clatteringshaws Loch was low. The shape of the low walls were replicated on higher ground, and timber trusses were raised over it and partially covered with bracken and heather thatch, showing what prehistoric man's homes were like.

17.2 Glentrool Forest Visitor Centre

A second visitor centre was established in Glentrool, near to the Bridge of Minnoch. The original building was opened on 30 June 1992 by Councillor Wiliam Service, Chairman of Wigtown District Council. This, too, was subject to an extension in 2011 and renovation in 2013.

303

The Forestry Commission has created a number of walks through the forest in the Galloway Highlands. Many of these are located on the lower ground, often following paths alongside rivers, around lochs, or through woodlands to places of interest. In many cases the paths are either way-marked, so that the tourist can follow the route without the aid of a proper map, or else have made-up surfaces identifying the route.

Some of the oldest forest paths were located in the first areas to be planted, such as the Loch Trool circular trail, the Grey Mare's Tail walk, or the walks at the Stinchar Falls. In recent years, as the forests have grown and matured, further walks have been created, allowing the less energetic walker to follow routes that vary from a few miles to around ten or more. These walks have been established at the main centres of interest, where parking facilities have also been formed.

A walk has been laid out from Loch Doon Castle up the slopes of the Wee Hill of Craigmulloch. Another trail leads from the Stinchar Bridge to Loch Girvan Eye. A selection of walks was formed near to the visitor centres at Clatteringshaws and Glentrool, as well as at Polmaddy village.

Walkers who enjoy long-distance routes will also pass through part of the Galloway Highlands when they follow the Southern Upland Way. This long route, which makes its way across the southern part of the country from Portpatrick in the west to Cockburnspath in the east, passes through part of the Galloway Highlands. The path enters the area covered by this book near Bargrennan. It then crosses the Braes of Barmore to near Brigton, then follows the side of the Water of Minnoch then the Water of Trool and makes its way through the oak woods of Caldons, passing the Covenanters' grave. The Way follows the south side of Loch Trool then strikes east to Loch Dee and follows the forest road to the bridge over the Black Water of Dee. The route then makes its way up through the forests and low hill of Shield Rig to cross to the valley of the Garroch Burn. After the walker has made his way three miles down this glen, he heads over the Water of Ken, leaving the highlands behind at St John's Town of Dalry.

The Forestry Commission has encouraged other pedestrian based sports, such as orienteering and its more modern version, geo-caching. Geo-caching is where an electronic Global Positioning System (or GPS for short) is used to take the walker to a specific point where something has been hidden. By following the signal on the GPS device, the walker tries to locate the hidden point, which often contains a box or other container in which is a small treasure or clue. The geo-caches in the Galloway Forest Park were created by the Forestry Commission in association with the Galloway Mountain Rescue Team. The hidden spots are located in places that vary from low-ground trees to summit cairns. When someone finds the geo-cache, which they will discover where it is by registering with a web-site, they can log back in to that site and upload pictures of them at it, or a log of their visit.

Cycling is another past-time that the Forestry Commission has encouraged on their lands. There are two main types of cyclist catered for, the cross-country touring cyclist, who enjoys linear cycling from place to place, and the mountain biker, who enjoys the excitement of rough routes, challenging terrain, and often races against the clock.

The Forestry Commission has created long-distance cycle routes in various parts of the Galloway Forest. One of the main ones is the Barr to Loch Doon Cycle Route, which enters the Galloway Highlands area near to Stinchar Bridge, having passed through the forests south of the River Stinchar, and makes its way along forest roads from the Lure dam at Loch Bradan, passing Ballochbeatties, and reaching the head of Loch Doon, where it re-joins the public road.

17.3 Carrick Forest Drive sign

Another long-distance route is the National Cycle Network route number 7, which extends from Carlisle to Inverness. It makes its way north from Gatehouse of Fleet, through Newton Stewart and over the hill road to Maybole, before continuing north through Ayrshire. There is a wilder route laid out as well, from Gatehouse to Glen Trool. This passes through the forests east of Cairnsmore of Fleet, and arrives at the Queen's Way (A 712) at Clatteringshaws dam. It then follows the minor road alongside the west of Clatteringshaws Loch to Craigencallie, where it follows the forest road past White Laggan and into Glen Trool, over the pass to the head of Loch Dee. The route then continues along the minor road in Glen Trool to Stroan Bridge, then cuts south past Minniwick to Minnoch Bridge. The minor road along the east side of the River Cree is then followed south-east to Minnigaff and then by way of the old Military Road to Blackcraig and south to Creetown.

At Glen Trool a mountain biking trail has been created, one of the Commission's Seven Stanes routes. This is a series of centres across southern Scotland where mountain biking routes have been established, and at each a large boulder has been set up, carved into something reflecting a local myth or legend. The one at Glen Trool is located east of Glenhead, overlooking Loch Dee, and the stone there takes the form of a giant axe-head.

As part of the forestry operations in Galloway, forest roads have been driven across much of the countryside. In most cases these have been sympathetic to the surrounding countryside, but there are some that perhaps have destroyed the remoteness of a few wilder spots, such as around Loch Dee and right into the Backhill of Bush area. The forest roads are used for hauling felled timber from the forests. However, at other times, indeed for most of the time, the roads are quiet lanes which are closed to traffic, and make ideal routes for walking or cycling, both of which the Commission encourages.

On some occasions, however, the forest roads are used for something more exciting. A number of car rallies have made the Galloway Hills part of their competition, and the wild routes make excellent challenges for the drivers and their co-pilots. Often, in the autumn or late summer, the Scottish Rally comes to Galloway and holds one of its stages in the forests. The Merrick Forest Stages, as it is known, takes routes through the Glentrool Forest, and it has been said that the fourteen-mile route through these woods is one of the finest and most challenging tests in Britain. Indeed, in 2007, the Merrick stage was regarded as the 'best event' in the eight-round competition.

In 2008 the Merrick stage had the honour of starting and finishing in the centre of Newton Stewart, the organisers managing to get the authorities to close off Victoria Street to traffic. The competition attracts lots of visitors, and around eighty competitors and their cars took part in the rally.

18 Conservation

That the Galloway Highlands are worthy of preservation is something that is obvious to most folks. Over the years some official recognition has been passed by the authorities to help preserve the region. A survey by the Wildland Research Institute at the University of Leeds identified the top ten per cent of wildest land in Great Britain, some of which was located in the Galloway Highlands. The remainder of the area covered by this volume was designated as having a 'High' wild land quality index.

In 2012 The Galloway Highlands became the central feature of the Galloway and Southern Ayrshire Biosphere. Biospheres are identified by the United Nations Educational, Scientific and Cultural Organization (UNESCO) for their importance in protecting landscape, wildlife and culture. The Galloway and Southern Ayrshire Biosphere was actually the first to be identified in Scotland, one of 580 worldwide. The highest mountain ranges in the Galloway Hills were identified as the core of the biosphere, comprising the Merrick range, Mullwharchar and Rhinns of Kells, along with the Cairnsmore of Fleet range to the south. This is surrounded by the buffer zone, comprising principally of the Galloway Forest Park. This area is a working landscape which is managed to protect the natural heritage of the area. Activities which are compatible with ecological practices are encouraged. Beyond the buffer area is the transition area, which extends as far north as Ayr and Cumnock, east to Thornhill and Nithsdale, south to the Solway coast from Kirkcudbright to Glenluce and west to Ballantrae and the Carrick coast. The transition area is the part of the biosphere where people live and work together to promote environmental farming and nature-based tourism. The biosphere allows south-west Scotland to be promoted to a wider audience for its natural landscapes and heritage, promoting growth for communities, protecting wildlife and nature.

There are few areas in the Galloway Highlands district which have natural woodlands surviving. One of these is the stretch of woodland alongside the River Cree, where a number of ancient oak woodlands have survived the influence of man.

The Wood of Cree is a nature reserve protected by the Royal Society for the Protection of Birds. It has long been regarded as one of the most ancient forests in Galloway, and is especially noted for its display of bluebells in springtime. It contains the largest ancient oak woodland in the south of Scotland.

The Knockman Wood contains many old trees, though its natural beauty has been compromised to some extent by the planting of regimented conifers. Again this wood is now protected as a nature reserve, in this case by the Cree Valley Community

Woodlands Trust, although the wood remains the property of the Forestry Commission.

Adjoining the Knockman Wood is a smaller wood of ancient oak trees, many of which have been calculated to be in the order of two centuries old. The woodland extends to around 26 hectares, with a further fifteen acres of open ground. Again this woodland is now protected as part of the Cree Valley Community Woodlands Trust, though it still remains the property of Galloway Estates. The Garlies Wood has numerous trees of at least 100 years, and there are a few non-native species growing amongst them, the wood being basically left to grow wild over time. It was part of the Cumloden Deer Parks, which had been established by General Sir William Stewart in 1824.

The Royal Society for the Protection of Birds has acquired various lands within the greater Galloway Highlands area. The farm of Barclye, which lies by the side of the River Cree, just two and a half miles from Newton Stewart, was purchased in 2006 following an appeal to its members. The RSPB had a long-standing interest in Barclye, working with the farmer, Ian Scott, to preserve the remaining oak trees on the farm, and advising on how best to preserve the landscape. After some negotiations the trust purchased the farm, Mr Scott deciding that it was time to retire. Owning the property meant that the RSPB could extend the Wood of Cree reserve.

Extending to 996 acres, Barclye farm rises from the side of the Cree, hereabouts a wide and sedate river, eastwards to the slopes of Glenmalloch Hill and Knockman, reaching the height of around 700 feet above sea level. The lower stretches of the farm, alongside the river, vary in form from wild oak woods, part of the Wood of Cree, wet meadows, and hay meadows. Above the oakwood line the Moor of Barclye is more open, a wide moorland with ferns and wild plants.

As part of the conservation of Barclye, part of the ground was replanted with broadleaved trees, to form a continuous stretch of woodland alongside the River Cree. A quarter of a million trees were planted soon after acquiring the property, and natural regeneration was also encouraged in order to allow the landscape to assume its ancient format. The new trees comprised oak, downy birch, alder, ash and willow, in total covering 670 acres of the property. A few hundred acres of land nearer to the River Cree was left unplanted, for this had been intensively farmed over the years, and the farm would continue to operate.

The woods at Barclye are also noted for their collection of wild flowers, especially the carpets of bluebells that proliferate under the canopy of the trees. Violets and primroses also grow in profusion.

Numerous examples of animals and birds can be seen in the woods, from pied flycatchers, redstarts and wood warblers, all of which breed in the trees, to frogs and toads in the numerous pools and marshlands. Dippers and grey wagtails make their homes by the side of the streams that pass through the woods, which themselves are home to a colony of red squirrels. Dragonflies are a speciality of the reserve, and they can be seen flying around the meadows. One can take a walk to the viewing platform overlooking the River Cree, and in the waters sometimes otters can be spotted, playing in the pools.

The new plantings and regeneration at Barclye is intended to encourage the extension of suitable habitat for the black grouse, one of the rarer birds that can be found in the area. Deer were excluded from the new plantings, and with a lack of grazing, dormant plants and flowers have already started to establish themselves.

Further up the Cree valley, and into the Minnoch valley, stretches of ancient woodland can be found. The Cree Valley Community Woodlands Trust has been actively working with the Forestry Commission in clearing away some of the non-native conifers and replanting the area with native broadleaved trees, adding to the blocks of ancient sessile oaks that still survive. The trust now manages over 3,000 acres of woodland, the largest native woodland regeneration project in Britain managed by a community charity.

The trust relies on volunteers, many coming from as far away as Stranraer, and all work at their own pace, assisting in the preservation of the woodlands. In addition to planting native trees, nesting boxes for birds and bats are made and erected, non-native Sitka seedlings are removed, squirrel dreys are counted and acorns are gathered to be brought on at the arboretum at Daltamie.

Near to the Holm of Bargrennan are some impressive ancient oaks, *Quercus petraea*. Below the taller oak trees in this area, holly is a common tree among the woods. The tree is often browsed by deer, leaving them quite stunted, but further up Glen Trool the bushes are less readily accessible, resulting in them growing bigger. The holly tree, *Ilex aquifolium*, is often noted for its distinctive red berries which are at their best in autumn, but it is only female holly trees that bear them.

The oak woods around Caldons, at the foot of Loch Trool, have been designated a Site of Special Scientific Interest (SSSI) for their sessile oaks. The site also extends along part of the northern side of the loch, specifically below Bruce's Stone and Buchan Lodge. The woods are the remnants of the ancient Galloway broadleaf forests, the bulk of these being cut down for their timber or to open up lands for grazing. The Caldons oaks are home to numerous rare lichens and insects, the latter also resulting in a healthy bird population.

Another ancient woodland is Hannaston Wood, sometimes spelled as Hannayston, which is located in the middle reaches of the Garroch Glen, west of St John's Town of Dalry. Designated an SSSI, the wood contains a fine mix of trees, most of which are deciduous. A considerable number of sessile oak trees grow here, in summer being home to a wide selection of birds. These include Redstarts and Nuthatches, as well as Pied Flycatchers and Wood Warblers.

Ness Glen, at the foot of Loch Doon, is another designated SSSI, especially for its mosses and ferns which grow on the magnificent rock walls of the gorge. Even as early as 1903, when the *Ordnance Gazetteer* was written, this glen was identified as being 'one of the finest examples of a true rock gorge.' In addition to the ferns and mosses, the gorge is home to numerous other examples of wildlife, and walkers through the gorge can expect to find red squirrels, bats, otters and deer, if they are lucky.

Right in the midst of the Galloway Highlands is a vast blanket peat bog known as the Silver Flow, or Silver Flowe, as the name now appears on Ordnance Survey maps.

The bog has been protected as a National Nature Reserve since its designation in 1956. There are seven distinct peat bogs here, lying alongside each other on the floor of the glen.

At one time, certainly before 1850, the Cooran Lane had its flow obstructed by a break out of the peat bog. This occurred between the mouths of the Brishie and Dow burns, near to High Cornarroch. The rising peat bog was so filled with water that it burst the harder soil that dammed it back from the Cooran Lane, allowing the liquid peat to spill into the Cooran. A number of acres of peat flow blocked the river, which had to make a new course around it, further to the west, at the point where the Otter Strand joins it. The Cooran Lane, having circumnavigated the peat flow, was able to re-join the old bed of the river 150 yards downstream. The old course, being the boundary between the parishes of Kells and Minnigaff, was still indicated on maps for many years.

Many of the bogs and flows in the Galloway Forest Park area are being restored to their natural state. Over years of farming in the hills, these bogs were partially drained, in an attempt to improve the grazing for cattle and sheep. Today, however, most of the upland bogs are no longer farmed, and the Forestry Commission has started a programme of blocking the old field drains, making the bog wetter than it has been for centuries, and thus encouraging the return of the natural wildlife.

In the 1980s there was considerable discussion in Galloway about the effects of acid rain on the watercourses and lochs in the area. Acid rain is formed by pollution in the atmosphere being captured in the precipitation which later falls to the earth. In addition, the planting of conifer forests and the quick run-off through drainage channels has also been claimed to affect the acidity levels of the lochs and watercourses.

The acidic nature of the rain is gathered together in the lochs, resulting in the acid content of them rising. This, naturally, is not conducive to the breeding of fish, and as a result the number of young reared in them has plummeted.

Loch Enoch, which was famed for its strange trout where the granite sand and rocks had worn away the lower fins and tails, was said to have become 'dead' early in the twentieth century. Writing in 1916, within *The Highways and Byways of Galloway and Carrick*, Rev C. H. Dick wrote that, 'I know that there were fish here [in Loch Enoch] in 1900; but they are said to have become extinct since then.' He doesn't attribute any reason to the extinction of the fish, but it has since been claimed that it was acid rain that was responsible.

A neutral pH value is 7, and tests at Loch Doon in October 1986 found it to be 6.0, which is on the acidic side. Loch Dungeon was worse, in the same month being 5.4. Loch Grannoch, to the south of the area covered by this book, had an acidic value of 4.3 in December 1984. It is reckoned that fish eggs will not hatch in lochs with a pH of less than 5.0. Each of these lochs was at one time home to the rare fish, Arctic Char, which is thought to have become extinct in them (apart from Loch Doon) due to the acidification of the waters. Lochs Grannoch and Dungeon appear to have lost their Arctic Char population in the 1940s or 1950s, if not before. The acidity level of Loch

Doon means that the fish is at risk there, too, and the loch was designated an SSSI in order to help save it.

One of the greatest threats to the conservation of the Galloway Highlands occurred in the late 1970s. At that time the government was looking for possible sites for dumping high level nuclear waste – the spent rods from nuclear power stations. Granite rocks were identified by the United Kingdom Atomic Energy Authority as being one of the best places for a secure dump to be created, and the central boss of the Galloway hills was chosen as one of the more suitable sites in Great Britain.

The proposal was to create a road into the centre of the hills, carve out a subterranean vault within the slopes of Mullwharchar, and there store nuclear rods for a century or more, until their half-life meant that they were no longer a danger to society. It was bad enough that rods from Chapelhall in Dumfriesshire and Hunterston in Ayrshire would be stored there, but the proposal also envisaged spent rods from around the world being brought to Galloway for storage, an excellent money-spinner for the nuclear authorities.

18.1 Mullwharchar – The Tauchers

The UKAEA wished to carry out some test bores at Mullwharchar, where the rock was to be drilled to a great depth to determine its suitability for storage purposes. This, in itself, was to result in some destruction of the environment, with the creation of new roadways into the heart of the uplands. Locals were up in arms, and various groups were formed to campaign against the scheme. The Scottish Campaign to Resist the Atomic Menace, or SCRAM, was active in opposing the scheme, as was the Campaign Opposing Nuclear Dumping (COND).

The groups started to raise the profile of the threat to the hills, making the public who lived in the district more aware of what was being proposed, and how it might affect them. The radioactive properties of the waste were publicised, as was the fact that this waste would be transported through many local communities to the site. Support for the opposition grew immensely, and soon marches, petitions and other campaigns were underway.

Support came from all over, and fund-raising events were held to raise money to pay for banners, badges and other expenses. The groups campaigned for a public inquiry, and various publicity stunts were organised to gather support. On one occasion, the writer and television presenter, Tom Weir, led the support on a walk to the summit of Mullwharchar, carrying banners.

Nevertheless, the UKAEA applied to Kyle and Carrick District Council, which covered the Mullwharchar area at the time, for planning permission to carry out test bores on the mountain. The council, following a public outcry, turned the application down. The authority then turned to the Secretary of State for Scotland in an appeal. At length a public inquiry was set up, meeting in Ayr on 19 February 1980.

The opponents of the dump managed to call on many friends, and Willie McRae, a solicitor, acted on their behalf at the prime cost of one penny per day. It was noted that the UKAEA had to pay their solicitor £2,000 a day for the same service. A petition containing 100,000 names was compiled and this was sent to the Queen. In 1981 the government gave in, withdrawing all proposals for test-bores.

The unspoilt nature of the Galloway Highlands is evident in many ways. One of the least obvious, at least to locals, is its status as a location where there is little light pollution. Pollution in the form of light, that is from street-lights and other man-made sources, may be relatively, if not totally, harmless, but total darkness is becoming ever more rare, and something that lovers of pure nature want to seek out. In 2009, the lack of man-made light at night-time was noted by the world when a bid was made to the International Dark Sky Association to have the area recognised as the first 'dark sky park' outwith the United States of America. Only three dark sky parks had previously been recognised, in Ohio (Geauga Park), Pennsylvania (Cherry Springs State Park) and Utah (Natural Bridges National Monument).

Keith Muir, who was in charge of the Forestry Commission's environmental and tourism department in the Galloway Forest Park, was promoting the area as a suitable candidate for dark sky recognition. If the area was to become recognised for such a natural darkness, then he reckoned that it could attract many more visitors, resulting in better incomes for locals making a living from tourism. Not only was the darkness an attraction, but also the fact that on cloudless nights, the lack of light from towns and roads would mean that astronomers and others with an interest in looking to the heavens could study the solar system more readily.

As part of the bid to be listed as a dark sky area, a number of light readings were taken over the winter months of 2008-9, and these proved to be low enough to encourage the bid to be made. Light is measured on the Bortle scale, which gives a reading of ten in the city of London, where the density of unnatural light is considerable. The measures carried out in Galloway prior to the bid were found to be around three. On another scale, light/darkness is measured on a scale of zero to 25. In a city during nightfall, the reading would reach around eight, but in Galloway's park the readings were found to be between 21 and 23.6, which is as close to total darkness as it is possible to get.

In order to make sure that the bid wasn't compromised in any way, the team responsible visited farmers and others who had large lights around their properties, to persuade them to shield them from above, so that the light was directed down to where it was needed, and not up into the atmosphere, resulting in it being visible on clear days from miles around. Assistance was obtained from the Wigtownshire Astronomical Society in drawing up the bid and taking readings, as well as from students from the University of Glasgow.

At the annual general meeting of the International Dark Sky Association, held at Phoenix, Arizona, on Saturday 14 November 2009, Galloway was selected as the fourth recognised such park in the world (Exmoor was to be Britain's second park). In order to determine whether the park should qualify for inclusion, readings of the darkness at night were taken on a meter that measured sky quality. The reading taken at Galloway was 23, one of the highest achievable, resulting in it being awarded a gold tier status.

The Galloway Highlands is thus one of Europe's least light-polluted areas, and the weather is also such that it is reckoned that on average the skies are clear enough to allow star-gazing three nights per week. The lack of man-made light also means that in Galloway visitors can experience the 'simmer dim', a phenomenon where there is still some light at midnight, creating a blue sky. By two o' clock in the morning the dawn light starts to appear once more.

With Galloway being recognised as a 'Dark Sky Park', plans were put in place for establishing an observatory near to Craigengillan, at the north end of Loch Doon. As looking south is the best direction for studying the stars, the fact that there are 25 miles of pure darkness due south of Craigengillan made it a suitable location for watching the heavens. At that point there are some lights in Newton Stewart, but beyond that it is almost total darkness for a total of 60 miles to the Isle of Man. Mark Gibson, owner of the estate, invited members of Renfrewshire Astronomical Society to become involved in the creation of the observatory, which was built on the topmost slopes of the Meikle Knowe of Craighead. One of the astronomical society members happened to be an architect, and quickly produced drawings for a double-storey observatory, with a small kitchen and toilet on the ground floor, along with an activity room. In December 2011 the Scottish Dark Sky Observatory had confirmed that it had reached its fund-raising target, and that work on the observatory would start, with completion planned for 2012.

Work commenced in February 2012 and the dome was installed in August the same year. A large steel and concrete pillar, preventing any vibration, was installed through the centre of the building and the large telescope was installed in November 2012. This is located on the first floor, under a dome of sixteen feet diameter. The telescope is a twenty inch corrected Dall Kirkham telescope, which cost £35,000. There is a lesser observatory with a sliding roof, containing a fourteen inch telescope. The whole building cost £700,000 to build. The architectural practice that designed the observatory was G. D. Lodge, based in Glasgow, and the member responsible was Colin Anderson. Patron of the new observatory is Professor John C. Brown of the University of Glasgow, 10th Astronomer Royal for Scotland, Royal Astronomical Society Gold Medallist 2012. The observatory was officially opened on Friday 5 October 2012 by Alec Salmond MSP, First Minister for Scotland.

An observatory already had been established within the Forest Park area, at Glenamour, between Newton Stewart and New Galloway. The observatory was built over the winter of 2006-7 by members of the Wigtownshire Astronomical Society, which had originally been founded in 1998 but which was reconstituted as a charity in 2005. This observatory is located on the opposite side of the A 713 from the area covered in this book. A further observatory can also be found at Craiglemine Cottage, at Glasserton, in Wigtownshire, where the Galloway Astronomy Centre was established. Here visitors can take part in short courses on astronomy or the use of telescopes.

The introduction of Sites of Special Scientific Interest (SSSI) led to the designation of some of the Galloway hills under this title. SSSI's were subject to more protection than other areas due to their various environmental features, including geological and biological reasons. In the first phase of identifying important sites, four upland areas were accepted and subsequently protected – the Merrick environs, Craignaw area and Corserine. In addition, the Silver Flow National Nature Reserve was identified as the fourth SSSI in the central region.

18.2 Craigengillan Observatory

In 1986 the four SSSI's listed were redefined and the area protected was extended by 2,500 acres. The new protected area was designated as the Merrick-Kells SSSI, which is located in two blocks, the larger comprising the Merrick and Craignaw ranges, the smaller covering Corserine and the Rhinns of Kells. The stretch of blanket forestry that separates the two was omitted from the SSSI due to the damage caused by this and lack of significant natural features within it.

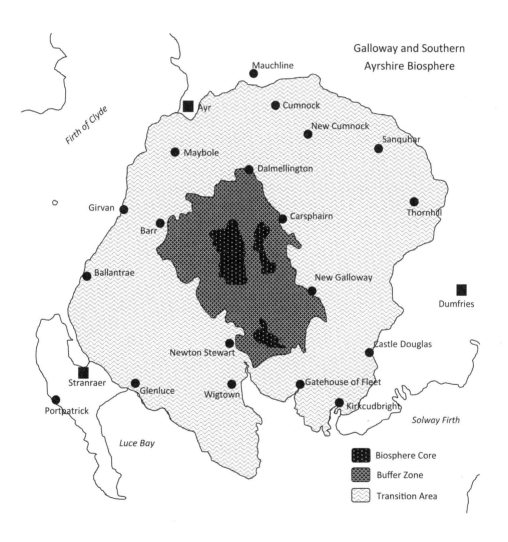

18.3 Map of Galloway and Southern Ayrshire Biosphere

The Merrick Kells SSSI extends to 21,664 acres, the largest area of unplanted upland area in Galloway. In addition to the mountains, the area was deemed of importance for a number of natural features, in particular The Tauchers, one of the finest end-moraine complexes in southern Scotland, which may be important in providing information on climate conditions during the Loch Lomond glacial re-advance. Loch Dungeon area also has the largest collection of fossilised pine remains in south-western Scotland.

In biological terms, the SSSI is important for the blanket bogs, such as the Silver Flow, the southernmost example of oceanic blanket bog in Scotland. Here also can be found a number of animals and plants that are nowhere else to be found south of the Highland Line. A rare hawkweed, known as *Hieracium holosericeum*, can be discovered here, in addition to downy willow, Alpine saw-wort, and the local liverwort, *Pleurozia purpurea*.

The Merrick Kells SSSI was also identified for being the natural habitat to a number of rare insects and invertebrates, including the Blue aeshna dragonfly (*Aeshna caerulea*), *Cubiona norvegica* and *Zora nemoralis* spiders and the *Cyphon kongsbergensis, Enochrus ochropterus* and *Hydroporus longicornis* beetles.

The Merrick Kells SSSI was designated as the core of a new Galloway and Southern Ayrshire Biosphere, which covers 1,100 square miles. The United Nations Educational, Scientific and Cultural Organisation (UNESCO) agreed to the designation of the Biosphere In 2012, the first of the new Biosphere designations in Scotland.

In short, the Galloway Highlands are a magical place!

Bibliography

Books

Ade, Robin, *Fisher in the Hills – a Season in Galloway*, Andre Deutsch, London, 1985.
 The Trout and Salmon Handbook – A Guide to the Wild Fish, Christopher Helm, Bromley, 1989.

Alexander, A. S., *Tramps Across Watersheds*, Robert MacLehose, Glasgow, 1934.
 Across Watersheds, Robert MacLehose, Glasgow, 1939.

Andrew, Kenneth M., & Thrippleton, Alan A., *The Southern Uplands*, Scottish Mountaineering Trust, Edinburgh, 1972.

The Archaeological Sites and Monuments of Scotland, Volume 17 – North Carrick, Royal Commission on the Ancient and Historical Monuments of Scotland, Edinburgh, 1983.

Bell, David E. T., *The Highway Man*, Ayrshire Post, Ayr, 1970.
 The Highway Man Again, Scottish & Universal Newspapers Ltd, Irvine, 1990.

Barbour, John Gordon ('Cincinnatus Caledonius'), *Lights and Shadows of Scottish Character and Scenery*, Archibald Allardice, Edinburgh, 1824.

Brittain, George, *The Galloway Hills: a Walker's Paradise*, Galloway Gazette, Newton Stewart, 1988.

Chalmers, George, *Caledonia*, (3 vols.), T. Cadell & W. Davies, London, 1810-24.

Chambers, Robert, *Domestic Annals of Scotland*, 3 vols, W. & R. Chambers, London, 1858-61.

Clark-Kennedy, Captain Alexander, *Robert the Bruce – a Poem Historical and Romantic*, Kegan Paul Trench, London, 1884.

Connon, Peter, *An Aeronautical History of Cumbria, Dumfries and Galloway*, St Patrick's Press, Penrith, 1984.

Corrie, J. M., *The Droving Days in the South-Western District of Scotland*, J. Maxwell, Dumfries, 1915.

Crockett, S. R., *The Raiders*, T. Fisher Unwin, London, 1894.
 Raiderland: all about Grey Galloway, Hodder & Stoughton, London, 1904.

Deeson, Ralph *The Mystery of the Seven Stanes*, G. Young Ltd, [no location], 2008.

Dick, Rev C. H. Dick, *Highways and Byways in Galloway and Carrick*, Macmillan, London, 1916.

Dobie, W. G. M., *Game-bag and Creel*, W. Green & Son, Edinburgh, 1927.
 Winter and Rough Weather, William Heinemann, London, 1938.
 Old Time Farming in Dumfriesshire, Robert Dinwiddie, Dumfries, 1949.
 Lawyer's Leisure, W. Green & Son, Edinburgh, 1963.

Donnachie, Ian L., *The Industrial Archaeology of Galloway*, David & Charles, Newton Abbot, 1971.

Donnachie, Ian L., & MacLeod, Innes, *Old Galloway*, David & Charles, Newton Abbot, 1974.

Edlin, Herbert L. (editor), *Galloway Forest Park*, H.M.S.O., Edinburgh, 1974.

Faed, James, Jr., *Galloway Water Colours*, A. & C. Black, London, 1919.

Gifford, John, *Dumfries and Galloway: the Buildings of Scotland*, Penguin, London, 1996.

Gow, Bill, *The Swirl of the Pipes*, Strathclyde Regional Council, Glasgow, 1996.

Greig, D. C., *British Regional Geology: The South of Scotland*, H.M.S.O., Edinburgh, 1935.

Grierson, Rev Thomas, *Autumnal Rambles among the Scottish Mountains*, Paton & Ritchie, Edinburgh, 1850.

Haldane, A. R. B., *The Drove Roads of Scotland*, Thomas Nelson & Sons, Edinburgh, 1952.

Harper, Malcolm MacLachlan, *Rambles in Galloway*, Edmonston & Douglas, Edinburgh, 1876.

Hendrie, Rev George S., *The Parish of Dalmellington: Its History, Antiquities and Objects of Interest*, William Murdoch, Dalmellington, 1889.

Henshall, Audrey Shore, *The Chambered Cairns of Scotland (Volume 2)*, Edinburgh University Press, Edinburgh, 1972.

Hill, George, *Tunnel and Dam: the Story of the Galloway Hydros*, South of Scotland Electricity Board, Glasgow, 1984.

Johnston, Rev. James Brown, *Place Names of Scotland*, David Douglas, Edinburgh, 1892.

Kennedy, Dan, *Galloway Memories*, Ayrshire Post, Ayr, 1967.

    Tales of the Galloway Hills, Ayrshire Post, Ayr, 1970.

    Climbing the Galloway Uplands, Ayrshire Post, Ayr, 1972.

Kevan-MacDowall, John, *Carrick Gallovidian*, Homer MacCririck, Ayr, 1947.

Learmonth, William, *Kirkcudbrightshire and Wigtownshire: Cambridge County Geographies*, Cambridge University Press, Cambridge, 1920.

Love, Dane, *Scottish Covenanter Stories*, Neil Wilson, Glasgow, 2000.

    The Covenanter Encyclopaedia, Fort Publishing, Ayr, 2009.

MacArthur, Wilson, *The River Doon*, Cassell, London, 1952.

MacBain, James, *The Merrick and the Neighbouring Hills*, Stephen & Pollock, Ayr, 1929.

McCormick, Andrew, *The Tinkler-Gypsies of Galloway*, J. Maxwell, Dumfries, 1907.

    Words from the Wild-Wood – Sixteen Galloway Tales and Sketches, Fraser, Asher & Co., Glasgow, 1912.

    Galloway: the Spell of its Hills and Glens, John Smith, Glasgow, 1932.

    The Gold Torque – a story of Galloway in Early Christian Times, MacLellan, Glasgow, 1951.

MacCulloch, Andrew, *Galloway: a Land Apart*, Birlinn, Edinburgh, 2000.

MacDowall, William, *History of the Burgh of Dumfries, with notices of Nithsdale, Annandale and the Western Border*, Adam & Charles Black, Edinburgh, 1867.

MacFadzean, Dave, *Tales o' the Back Buss*, G.C. Books, Wigtown, 2004.

MacGibbon, David & Ross, Thomas, *The Castellated and Domestic Architecture of Scotland*, (5 vols), David Douglas, Edinburgh, 1887-92.

MacKenzie, William, *The History of Galloway*, J. Nicholson, Kirkcudbright, 1841.

MacKerlie, Peter Handyside, *History of the Lands and Their Owners in Galloway*, William

Patterson, Edinburgh, 1877.

MacLeod, Innes, *Discovering Galloway*, John Donald, Edinburgh, 1986.

Where the Whaups are Crying – a Dumfries and Galloway Anthology, Birlinn, Edinburgh, 2001.

MacMichael, George, *Notes on the Way through Ayrshire*, Hugh Henry, Ayr, c. 1885.

MacTaggart, John, *Scottish Gallovidian Encyclopedia*, MacTaggart, London, 1824.

Maxwell, J. H., *Maxwell's Guide to the Stewartry of Kirkcudbright*, Kirkcudbrightshire Advertiser, Castle Douglas, 1884.

Maxwell, Sir Herbert, *Studies in the Topography of Galloway*, David Douglas, Edinburgh, 1887.

Meridiana: Noontide Essays, W. Blackwood & Sons, Edinburgh, 1892.

A History of Dumfries and Galloway, W. Blackwood & Sons, Edinburgh, 1896.

Robert the Bruce in Glen Trool, AD 1307, Galloway Gazette, Newton Stewart, 1929.

The Place Names of Galloway – their origin and meaning considered, Jackson, Wyllie & Co., Glasgow, 1930.

Molony, Eileen (editor), *Portraits of Mountains*, Dennis Dobson, London, 1950.

Moore, John (editor), *Gently Flows the Doon*, Dalmellington District Council, Dalmellington, 1972.

Morris, Ronald W. B., *The Prehistoric Rock Art of Galloway and the Isle of Man*, Blandford, Poole, 1979.

Moss, Michael, *The 'Magnificent Castle' of Culzean and the Kennedy Family*, Edinburgh University Press, Edinburgh, 2002.

Murray, Sir John; Pullar, Laurence, & Chumley, James, *The Bathymetrical Survey of the Fresh-Water Lochs of Scotland, 1897-1909*, Challenger Office, Edinburgh, 1910.

New Statistical Account of Scotland – Ayrshire, William Blackwood, Edinburgh, 1842.

New Statistical Account of Scotland – Dumfries, Kirkcudbright & Wigtown, William Blackwood, Edinburgh, 1845.

Paterson, John, *Reminiscences of Dalmellington*, W. Pomphrey, Wishaw, 1902.

Ratcliffe, Derek, *Galloway and the Borders – the New Naturalist*, Collins, London, 2007.

Robertson, John F., *The Story of Galloway*, J. H. Maxwell, Castle Douglas, 1963.

Stott, Louis, *The Waterfalls of Scotland*, Aberdeen University Press, Aberdeen, 1987.

Simpson, Rev Dr Robert, *Traditions of the Covenanters*, Gall & Inglis, Edinburgh, 1850.

Smith, David J., *High Ground Wrecks and Relics*, Midland Counties Publications, Hinckley, 1989.

Smith, John, *Prehistoric Man in Ayrshire*, Elliot Stock, London, 1895.

Starling, Peter D., *Monuments and Moorlands*, Wigtown District Museum Service, Stranraer, c. 1990.

Statistical Account of Scotland, Various Volumes, 1791-99.

Symson, Rev Andrew, *A Large Description of Galloway*, W. & C. Tait, Edinburgh, 1823.

Temperley, Alan, *Tales of Galloway*, Skilton & Shaw, London, 1979.

Third Statistical Account of Scotland – Ayrshire, Oliver & Boyd, Edinburgh, 1951.

Third Statistical Account of Scotland – Stewartry of Kirkcudbright & Wigtownshire, Oliver & Boyd, Edinburgh, 1965.

Thomson, Rev J. H., *The Martyr Graves of Scotland*, Oliphant, Anderson & Ferrier, Edinburgh, 1894.

Wightman, Andy, *Who Owns Scotland*, Canongate, Edinburgh, 2000.
Wodrow, Rev Robert, *History of the Sufferings of the Church of Scotland between 1660 and 1688*, (2 volumes), James Watson, Edinburgh, 1721-1722.

Maps and Plans
Survey and Maps of the Roads of North Britain or Scotland, Taylor & Skinner, London, 1775.
A New Map of Ayrshire, Captain Armstrong & Son, 1775.
Plan of Garrary (Garvorie) & Backhill of Burnhead, property of William Forbes of Callendar surveyed by John Lauder, 1800; National Records of Scotland (NRAS 3626 and 3632).
Map of the Southern Part of Scotland, John Ainslie, Edinburgh, 1821.
Craiglure Lodge, 1819, plan, possibly by James Thomson, RCAHMS.
The Atlas of Scotland, John Thomson, Edinburgh, 1832.

Periodicals
Ayr Advertiser, numerous editions, including the following:
　　26 August 1926 – David MacMath, gamekeeper lost in blizzard.
　　26 February 1931 – Loch Doon School closed.
　　16 January 1941 – Obituary of James MacBain FSA.
Ayrshire Archaeological and Natural History Collections:
　　The Birds of Ayrshire, G. A. Richard, Volume 7, Ayr, 1966.
British Numismatic Journal:
　　The Loch Doon Treasure Trove, 1966, Peter Woodhead, Ian Stewart and George Tatler, Volume 38, 1969, pp 31-49.
Building News:
　　Forrest Lodge, 10 October 1910.
Discovery and Excavation in Scotland:
　　Donald's Isle, Medieval Complex and Mesolithic Materials, Mike Ansell, 1969, p 12.
Dumfries and Galloway Natural History and Antiquarian Society Transactions:
　　The Cairns of Kirkcudbrightshire, F. R. Coles, 2nd Series, Vol. 10, 1895.
　　Lead Mining at Woodhead, Carsphairn, Anna Campbell, Vol. 46, Dumfries, 1969.
　　The Excavation of a Hut Circle at Moss Raploch, Clatteringshaws, J. Condry, and Mike Ansell, Vol. 53, Dumfries, 1978.
　　The Pine Marten – its reintroduction and subsequent history in the Galloway Forest Park, G. Shaw, & J. Livingstone, Vol. 67, Dumfries, 1992.
Freshwater Biological Association - Freshwater Forum:
　　The Status of Arctic Charr (Salvelinus alpinus), in Southern Scotland: a Cause for Concern, Dr Peter S. Maitland, Volume 2, Number 3, 1992.
Glasgow Archaeological Society Bulletin:
　　A Late Single-piece Dug-out Canoe from Loch Doon, Ayrshire, E. W. Mackie, vol. 11, 1984.
　　Excavations at Starr, Loch Doon, 1985, T. L. Affleck, Vol. 22, 1986.
Mining History: the Bulletin of the Peak District Mines Historical Society:
　　The Silver Rig, Pibble and Woodhead Metal Mines, Galloway, Scotland, M. Cressey, J. Pickin, and K. Hicks, Vol. 15, No. 6, Winter 2004.
Nautical Archaeological Society Newsletter:

Reconstruction of the Loch Doon Dug-out No. 1: an Exercise in Experimental Archaeology, Scottish Institute of Maritime Archaeology, Diploma Class 1991-2, Volume 1, 1992.

Proceedings of the Royal Society of Edinburgh:
Vol. XXX, Edinburgh, 1909-10.

Proceedings of the Society of Antiquaries of Scotland:
Account of the Discovery of a Number of Ancient Canoes of Solid Oak, in Loch Doon, a Fresh-water Lake in the County of Ayr, Frederick MacAdam Cathcart, Volume 4, 1857.
Excavations at Minnigaff, Arthur J. H. Edwards, Volume 57, 1922.
Excavation of a Mediaeval Site at Donald's Isle, Loch Doon, Archibald Fairbairn, Volume 71, 1936-7, pp 323-333.
The Deil's Dyke in Galloway, A. Graham, Vol. 83, 1948-9, pp 174-185.

Scottish Local History:
The Woodhead Lead Mines, Anna Campbell, Vol. 31, June 1994, p31.

The Transactions of the Edinburgh Geological Society:
On the Evidence of Glacier Action in Galloway, William Jolly, 1867-8.

Index

Figures in **bold** type indicate illustrations